The Woman from Browhead

'I want none of your charity, Mr Macauley.' She lifted her defiant head and though the soot lay in a fine cloud about it, it in no way detracted from the beauty of her hair. Since her mother had cut it many years ago no scissors had been put near it and it tumbled in a great profusion of rich copper, the curls so tight he wondered how she got a brush through it, falling down her straight back to her buttocks, wild, thick and springing. She pulled her mother's old cloak about her as though it was made of velvet, ermine trimmed, and he felt her courage move him. Her clogs sounded a rebellious clatter on the wooden threshwood as she prepared to close the door but he stood his ground, no sign of the emotion she aroused in him showing in his face, his own proud head somewhat bowed beneath the low door frame. They confronted one another, neither ready to give way.

'And the child?' he asked harshly, angry at something in himself which he did not care to name.

About the author

Audrey Howard was born in Liverpool in 1929 and it is from that once-great seaport that many of the ideas for her books come. Before she began to write she had a variety of jobs, among them hairdresser, model, shop assistant, cleaner and civil servant. In 1981, out of work and living in Australia, she wrote the first of her novels. She was fifty-two. Her fourth novel, *The Juniper Bush*, won the Romantic Novel of the Year Award in 1988. She now lives in her childhood home, St Anne's on Sea, Lancashire.

The Woman from Browhead

Audrey Howard

CORONET BOOKS
Hodder and Stoughton

Copyright © 1994 by Audrey Howard

The right of Audrey Howard to be identified as the Author of
the Work has been asserted by her in accordance with the
Copyright, Designs and Patents Act 1988.

First published in Great Britain in 1994
by Hodder and Stoughton
A division of Hodder Headline PLC
First published in paperback in 1994
by Hodder and Stoughton
A Coronet Paperback

20 19 18 17 16 15 14

A CIP catalogue record for this title is available from
the British Library.

ISBN 0 340 60704 1

Photoset by Rowland Phototypesetting Ltd.,
Bury St Edmunds, Suffolk
Printed and bound in Great Britain by
Mackays of Chatham PLC, Chatham, Kent

Hodder and Stoughton
A division of Hodder Headline PLC
338 Euston Road
London NW1 3BH

For June Hall
who got me started

1

The kitchen at Long Beck Farm trembled into the nervous activity the arrival of Sarah Macauley always produced. Cook, who had been about to sit down in her favourite rocking chair, the one in which no posterior but her own was ever allowed to settle, hastily put away the mug of hot, sweet, strong tea she was sipping appreciatively and with a skilful and fluid movement which belied her years and the 'bad back' she purported to have, dipped a spoon into the enormous 'kail pot' which simmered on the fire, stirring vigorously before lifting it to her lips.

"A smidgin more thyme I think, Dolly, and mind it's no more than a smidgin. Too much can spoil a decent soup."

"Yes, Cook."

"And when you've done that get out the flour and sugar, some butter and eggs. I've a mind to make Master Reed a few biscuits. Lemon, I think, so you can squeeze me a couple while you're at it, and don't throw away the peel. He likes my lemon biscuits, does Master Reed. Oh! there you are, Madam . . ." starting visibly as the grey-clad figure of her mistress appeared at her elbow. "I didn't see you there. I was just about to . . ."

"Yes, Mrs Lewis, I can see exactly what you were doing so don't let me stop you." Mrs Macauley moved towards the fire on which the pan was kept simmering at all times, summer and winter, for there were men, her husband's shepherds and yardmen, who might be in need of a bit of something inside them, especially in the winter. Since this was her kitchen and her soup she took a spoonful and, like Cook, lifted it to her lips. She tasted it thoughtfully and the whole kitchen held its breath. If it was not to her liking she would say so, offending Cook, who was good at her job. If Cook was offended, indeed put out in any way, it would be *they* who would be made to feel her displeasure.

She was a tyrant, was Mrs Macauley who, until her husband had prospered on his farm, had been a true farm-wife, working in her own kitchen with a young maid to fetch and carry and a woman to scrub. She herself had done all the cooking and baking, the making of bread, the pickling and preserving and salting, only allowing – and that thoroughly supervised – the maid to perform the task of making the soap and the candles and any task which, in Sarah Macauley's opinion, any fool could do. Her life had been busy, hard and busy, but she had found it satisfying since she knew nothing else. The day on which her husband told her he was to entertain a wool merchant from Yorkshire had been a shattering one for Sarah since it was the last one in which she was a true farmwife.

"I don't want you fiddling about in the kitchen, my lass. Your place is at the head of the dining table. You're mistress of this house and as such you must help me to entertain this fellow-me-lad and you can't do it chained to the kitchen range. Get yourself a cook and another maid. One that can wait on at table."

"A cook! What do I want with such a thing? I can do my own cooking and I'll have you know there's not a better one in the whole of Bassenthwaite parish." She was scandalised and not only that, affronted, but her husband was adamant. He was moving up in the world and his hill farm, which stretched as far as the eye could see from his farm gate, was growing and thriving. This bit of business with the chap from Yorkshire could lead to even greater things and it would not do to have one's wife mucking about in the kitchen, running backwards and forwards, flushed and perspiring, from there to the table and back again.

It was only a step from employing a cook to having not one kitchenmaid to help her but two, then three. A scullery maid, a dairy maid and the woman whose sole task it was to scrub the kitchen floor, the pantry floor, the dairy, the buttery, the back step, the front step and the long, stone-flagged 'hallan' which led from the front of the house to the back. It had been hard, harder than anyone realised, since she was a woman sparing of words, for Sarah to 'sit about on her behind', a phrase she used only to herself, and it had altered her subtly from a woman who, though sharp-tongued and exacting was always fair, to one who was shrewish, grim, testy, fault finding and not well liked by her servants.

They all waited, Mrs Lewis the cook, her expression one of guarded effrontery, Josie the parlourmaid, Dolly the kitchenmaid and Prudence whose job it was to be everyone's slave. Even the tangle-haired woman on her knees at the bucket by the door leading to the hallan rested back on her heels. There was a child beside her, a young girl with her own bucket and brush. She was no more than ten or eleven years old, scrawny and thin-faced, and she watched, open-mouthed and with keen interest, the very evident contest of wills which was taking place between Mrs Macauley and Cook. Mrs Macauley would have the last word, the girl knew that, for didn't she always, and Cook would be furious, no doubt holding back the left-overs of food, perhaps a mutton chop or a knuckle of bacon, a spoonful of jelly or a broken biscuit which were nothing to her and which, in an off-handed kindly way she would often pass on to herself and her mother. It was a shame for they had lived on nothing but turnip bread for the last week. The juice from the turnip was pressed out, flour and salt added to the mixture and the result baked on the 'bakstone' over the fire. Tasteless and unsatisfying, but it filled an empty stomach and the hard work she and her mother did gave them a sharp appetite. And those tit-bits were a blessing on a tongue which needed something to *taste* now· and again. She'd miss them tonight if Mrs Macauley got the better of Cook, which she was bound to do for this was her kitchen.

It was a big room with tables of yellow-white sycamore which stood up to years of pounding, chopping and scrubbing and from its ceiling hung hams and bunches of herbs, crates of bread, kept there since Sarah Macauley had come as a bride to Long Beck for there had been rats and mice then. Besides the iron pots and pans there was a vast array of highly polished copper utensils. The walls were whitewashed every six months for the climate in the room was always intensely busy, blasted by fires and ovens and rendered moist and murky by steam and smoke. Cook and the kitchenmaids worked flat out from breakfast to supper time. It was a proud boast of Sarah's that everything her family ate was produced in her kitchen and dairy, and even now a leg of pork was being spit-roasted over the open kitchen fire. The farmhouse was old and many of the things in the kitchen had been used by Sarah Macauley's mother-in-law and *hers* before that, dating way back into the last century, but beside the huge open fire which was set in the wall behind strong, horizontal metal bars was an equally huge enclosed range, blackleaded, glowing and dark and cleaned each morning by Prudence.

Set neatly on shelves attached to the spotless walls were trivets and skillets, toasters and grills, tongue presses and beef-warmers. There were jelly moulds of earthenware, copper and glass, for Sarah Macauley prided herself on her good table; copper pans, earthenware bowls and wooden ladles, all playing an essential role in the endless round of preserving, boiling, baking, roasting and toasting, culinary activities which had been carried on for the past thirty-odd years by Sarah herself. The two kitchen dressers of oak were crowded with a blue-and-white china tea set, dozens of cups and saucers, plates, cream jugs and sugar bowls in a delicate willow pattern, and beside them was blue and white dinnerware in the same design. Enormous meat platters, vegetable dishes, soup tureens, dinner plates and ladles. They had been in the Macauley family for fifty years, come from the Staffordshire potters Josiah Spode and Thomas Minton, and it was woe betide any luckless kitchenmaid who touched any part of them unless supervised by her mistress. About the room were several beautifully carved and well-proportioned Windsor chairs, again old, cherished, well polished, but not meant for sitting on, for Sarah Macauley's servants were here to work not loll about, except for the brief period in which they ate their meals.

"Hand me that skimmer, if you please, Dolly," Mrs Macauley said, and the child on her knees held her breath for, on the action of the woman who, if only temporarily, was her mistress since Annie and Lizzie Abbott were 'casuals', depended the left-overs she and her mother would take home with them that night.

The skimmer was slid delicately into the soup. Carefully Mrs Macauley lifted it out again, scrutinising it minutely as though she fully expected a cockroach to raise its ugly head. Cook watched her, her face devoid of all expression, but in her eyes was a gleam which said if looks could kill her mistress would be lying dead at her feet. Cook was a woman in her late fifties, too old to be taken on now in any of the grand houses in which she had once worked and where she had received her training. She was an experienced and imaginative cook and though she was not awfully sure *why* Mrs Macauley seemed to have it in for her, since it was Mrs Macauley who had employed her in the first place, she was well aware that her mistress did her best to find fault.

The skimmer came out clean and fatless. There were tiny, plump onions, shreds of cabbage, slivers of beef, slices of mushroom and carrot in the skimming spoon but nothing else.

Mrs Macauley was clearly annoyed. She would have liked nothing better than to have given Cook the length of her tongue for in that way it would have bolstered her own waning belief in herself and her talents in her kitchen where, since her husband had gone up in the world, it had melted slowly with her self-esteem.

"It'll do," she said ungraciously and was vastly put out when Cook smiled complacently. "Now then, let's see to those biscuits for Master Reed."

"Nay, Mrs Macauley, I'll make them," Cook said ill-advisedly. "You go and sit yourself down and put your feet up."

Sarah was incensed. Put her feet up indeed, and to be told to do it in her own kitchen by a woman who had no right to be there in the first place, in her view.

"That'll be enough from you, Mrs Lewis, and what are these girls doing standing about with their mouths open? Have they no work to do? Really, I've never seen such an idle-handed lot in my life and likely to continue to be so, it seems to me, if I'm not here at their backs. They are in your charge, you know, and I expect you to oversee their work in a more appropriate manner."

She turned away from the thunderous face of Mrs Lewis and right behind her Lizzie Abbott's bucket seemed to leap up and catch her in the shins. She stumbled, the water slopped on the hem of her gown and it was as if a knife had struck her in her side, a knife with a serrated edge which not only sliced into her but turned its blade a time or two for good measure. It was the worst pain Sarah had ever experienced since the first one had struck her over six months ago, and it almost brought her to her knees.

"Get out of my way, woman," she screeched and in her senseless agony she lifted her hand, striking the woman – who was she? – so hard she fell sideways, her arm going up to the elbow in her own bucket. The child who knelt beside her – who was *she*? – went with her and the pair of them sprawled on the wet floor they themselves had just scrubbed. The woman began to cry weakly, the sort of tears Sarah often felt like crying herself, despairing tears, hopeless tears, but the child leaped to her feet and for a minute Sarah thought she was about to strike her, then, after carefully lifting the weeping woman to her feet, where she stood, humble head bowed, the girl ran past Cook and the astonished maids and out through the kitchen door into the yard.

The bright sunlight of the early spring day was in Annie Abbott's eyes as she scrambled over Mrs Macauley's threshwood, and across the cobbles where hens pecked and a rooster strutted. There were a couple of young Border Collie dogs fastened by a chain to the wall, sheepdogs who were not yet fully trained to herding and they stood up, wagging hopeful tails. This was a working farm and up on the fell Alistair Macauley and his shepherds were 'raking in' the heavily pregnant ewes for it would soon be lambing time. But not Alistair Macauley's son. Not his fine, twenty-three-year-old son, Reed Macauley. The young, black mare he rode, dashing, wild and as handsome as himself, skittered madly out of control as Annie came through the kitchen door and, in her haste to get away from her own black rage at what Mrs Macauley had done to her mother, almost went under the horse's hooves. The mare was tall, blotting out the sunlight, crashing her hooves in alarm on the cobbles and rolling her eyes in fury as the child and the hens scattered about her.

Reed Macauley scarcely seemed to notice Annie Abbott. She might have been no more than a wisp of straw which had blown from his father's stable. She was there in his vision but of such little consequence he did not see her. His vivid blue eyes looked directly into hers but his gaze moved on impassively as he guided his restless animal towards the open stable door.

"Albert," he shouted, "rub Victoria down, will you, and give her a handful of oats," then he was gone.

It was their first meeting.

It was October, six months later, when she saw him again, and as at the last time he rode by her with as much interest as he would show a kitten which frolicked in the grass. The track at the back of Browhead led up to Long Beck and he and his mare moved easily along it, his gaze passing over her and her father as if they did not exist. Annie watched him go then bent down, doing her best to lift the swill basket which was filled to its brim with newly picked potatoes, the ones she herself had lifted that morning, and though she heaved and strained until the sweat broke out on her childish brow and ran down her cheeks, she could not move it. She straightened up, rubbed her hands together as she had seen her father do, spat on them then bent down again, gripping the basket at its rim where holes had been left to fit each hand. The basket,

crafted by her own mother for this very purpose, was not
heavy in itself, being made from split hazel rods woven
with white willow, but its contents weighed over twenty
pounds and were too much for a child.

"Will tha' never learn sense, girl? Can tha' not see tha'
load's too big? Tek some out an' put 'em in a pile then
shift what's left down to t' barn. *Then* come back for
t'others. Think girl, think! I don't know why the Good
Lord made women so half-witted. Tryin' to lift a bloody
basket it'd tek me half me time to get off t' ground. Lighten
it, girl, an' look lively."

"Yes, Faither."

"An' tell thi' mother I'm waitin' on me dinner whilst tha's
down there. I've never known a woman so feckless as she
is. Bugger it, it's gone noon an' I'm parched. An' I don't
want no cold tea, neither. A jug of ale'd go down nicely."

"Yes, Faither." Annie had obediently emptied half the
potatoes, piling them neatly on the ground.

"Off tha' go then an' don't tha' drop that swill or I'll 'ave
summat ter say ter thi'. Them potatoes is money an' we've
none o' that ter be chuckin' about an' don't come back
empty-handed. Fetch me some o' that manure in tha'
empty swill."

"Yes, Faither."

The neat rows of healthily blooming plants stretched
out at the backs of the man and child in the walled field
behind the farmhouse, each row exactly twenty-seven
inches from its neighbour, each set, or plant, twelve inches
from the next. They were erect, tall, branching, their tops
crowded in a spreading confusion. The stems had a pink
tinge and the flowers were a lovely red-purple but Joshua
Abbott was not concerned with their appearance, except
in so much as it was a healthy one, only with the smooth,
oval-shaped harvest which grew at their root. He and the
girl had planted them in late March. They had been well
fertilised with the manure from his farmyard, the child's
job again since it was within her capabilities and now they
were to be lifted and those not needed for the family's
winter requirements would go to market.

She was back within five minutes and behind her, carrying a basket which was so heavy it caused her to shuffle lop-sidedly, was Lizzie Abbott. She was obviously pregnant. Though both she and the child who staggered beneath the weight of the swill basket and its stinking, steaming contents were making heavy weather of their loads Joshua Abbott made no effort to help them. He was digging. Glancing round as they approached he threw down his spade, took off his battered and stained felt hat, wiped his sweating face with his forearm, replaced his hat and sat down, his back to the drystone wall which surrounded the field.

"An' about time too," was all he said, his tone peevish.

"I'm sorry, Joshua. I got took badly." Lizzie Abbott put her hand to her distended belly. Her thin, worn face was vastly apologetic just as though she had been caught junketing about the yard with Natty Varty who sometimes gave Joshua a hand at harvest or lambing. "I can't seem ter get over this sickness . . ."

"Aye, well, set basket down, woman." Joshua was not in the least concerned with his wife's pregnancy, nor with the details of its progress, only with its outcome. Married eighteen years and nothing to show for it but this one girl, though by God, he'd done *his* best. A bairn every year he'd given her and a few times she'd gone full term but always it seemed, again as though the blame was hers, contrary madam that she was, bringing forth some sickly infant, three of them boys, who had not lasted a month. One girl! A fine girl, strong and biddable, cheerful too, and if only she'd been a boy which was all he asked for, one boy, Joshua would have been content. It wasn't too much to expect, was it, out of eighteen pregnancies? But no, soon as it was in her belly where surely it was not too difficult to hang on to, *she'd* let it go, time after time, except for the girl. Other men had sons. Look at Jem Mounsey from Upfell Farm. Two daughters certainly but a fine lad going on twelve years now and so big and strapping, like Jem, he could do the work of a grown man. Upfell was small, like his own farm, not in the class of

Alistair Macauley's place up at Long Beck, but between them Jem and Davy Mounsey managed it nicely with no need of paid help like Natty Varty, or at least only in the most dire of emergencies. Of course at ploughing or harvesting, lambing or clipping time, every farmer and his family helped every other. A 'boon' clip, or 'boon' plough-ing, when a day would be set aside and neighbours would come with a plough or a horse or their shears when there were sheep to be sheared and at the end of it there would be a tatie-pot supper, with dancing in the barn, the fiddle played by Dobby Hawkins who was odd-job man at Long Beck. A 'merry-neet' right enough but what had Joshua Abbott to be merry about with no son to take over when he himself was six feet under? If only the girl had . . . well, brightening a little as he studied his wife's thickening figure . . . 'appen it wasn't too late. He was only thirty-nine himself and had many good years in him to pass on to a lad all that he himself had learned from his father.

Browhead farmhouse and its surrounding acres had been in his family for generations, he was not awfully sure how many. Unlike many small farmers who had been forced off the common land with the Enclosure movement, his grandfather, or was it his great-grandfather, had managed by dint of great hardship to himself and his family to buy the land which had been freely held by the Abbotts, or so they had imagined, from time immemorial. Not a great deal by the standards of the wealthy landowners such as the Macauleys but still theirs, and though they had never managed to do more than 'hang on' from harvest to harvest and from lambing to lambing, it was still theirs. Still Abbott land. Joshua Abbott's land and if he could just get himself a son to pass it on to he'd die a happy man.

The girl sat down beside him and Joshua's sheepdog crept up to her, leaning fondly on her shoulder, eyeing the oatcake she had taken from the basket.

"An' don't let me see tha' feedin' that dog."

"No, Faither."

"Ruined he is an' all because of tha' mollycoddlin' ways.

See, woman, tek 'im down wi' thi' an' fasten 'im to t' chain in t' yard. I don't know what comes over the two o' you, pettin' 'im like he was some lap dog. A workin' dog he is an' when he's not workin' he stays in t' yard. Is that clear?"

"Yes, Faither."

"Yes, Joshua."

"Did tha' fetch me ale, woman?"

"Yes, Joshua, 'tis in t' basket."

"Well, then, there's no need for thi' to hang about here, is there. There's bound ter be summat for thi' ter do in tha' kitchen."

"Yes, Joshua," and, obedient as a trained animal, his wife moved off in the direction of the farmhouse which stood slightly lower down the sloping field so that its roof was on a level with where the man and the child laboured.

"Don't forget bloody dog, woman."

His wife turned in a flurry, her face anguished at her own foolishness. What was she thinking of? Day-dreaming, he'd say, though her dreams were not dreams at all but galloping worries on how she was to manage the next four months with the burden she carried . . . oh, please God, don't let me lose this one . . . I must not give way to despair . . . but a boy, a healthy boy so that *he* will leave me alone. So that he will cast off the bitterness and harshness he shows to the girl, smile a little . . . all that work the child does and her not twelve yet . . . all that I do . . .

It was hard to believe that she had once been pretty Lizzie Bowman from Cockermouth since those who had known her then could not remember it and her own child had never seen her other than timid, hard-working, patient, dumb, thin and anxious of face, her skin and hair a uniform greyish-brown. She was thirty-four years old. Her life and that of her daughter was one of unremitting labour from early dawn until they fell into their beds at dark. A hard life which was restricted not just to herself and Annie but was the lot of farm women everywhere in Cumberland. There was the clapbread to be baked, the ale to be brewed, pickling and bottling, baking, cooking and cleaning, rush making, cheese and butter making, the pickling of beef and mutton, the drying of the meat in the smoke of the chimney. There was washday when water must be brought from the spring ready for boiling. There was the vegetable garden, the herb garden and when all that was done there was the spinning of the yarn from the fleece of Joshua Abbott's Herdwick sheep and the weaving of it into the hodden-grey wool from which most of their serviceable clothing was made. She and her daughter milked cows and collected eggs, killed the pig, salted the meat and wrung the necks of chickens. They fed the cattle wintering in the cow shed. In the light of the rush lamps they themselves had made they all three knitted hosiery, fashioned birch-twig besoms and swill baskets to be sold at the next market. They both worked like men at lambing time, cut peat and stacked it for drying, helped at the 'boon clip' and at backend, as winter approached, helped to bring down the flock from the high fells and the moors to the lower 'inlands' which were fenced by dry-stone walls.

Between the three of them, with the occasional help of Natty Varty who hired himself out as casual labour, they ran the farm of Browhead and now, with the growing child within her, already she was beginning to tire before the day was half-way through. She needed to rest, put her feet up now and again with a nice hot cup of tea to steady her but how was she to manage that with the hundred and one jobs that were to be done every day on the farm? You'd think with him being so desperate to have a living son he'd find some way to get her a bit of help but no, she must work just the same, just as hard and just as long and if anything happened to the unborn child it would be her fault.

The dog, she musn't forget the dog, but in her effort to appease her husband, to keep him from venting his spleen on the child, from becoming more irritable than he already was, she lunged awkwardly, tripping on the long skirt of her grey woollen dress. She righted herself but in doing so she knew she was going to step heavily on

Joshua's sturdy potato plants and though it would do them no harm since the potatoes ready for lifting were still deep in the soil, she had a horror of arousing his uncertain temper. The child in her womb fluttered feebly and, unbalanced, with her hand on her belly, she fell heavily. She was up again at once, as light as a feather rises, smiling to let him see there was no harm done, though the awful, familiar sinking in her womb told her it was too late.

"Tha's a clumsy beggar," he said, the ale he was slurping down his long, muscular throat making him good humoured.

"I know, Joshua, that's me. Well, I'll get meself home then," turning, desperate to get to her kitchen, to sit down, to lie down in an effort to hold on to what she carried.

"Tha's goin' wi'out dog now, woman. Bloody hell, it beats me how tha' manages ter get through t'day. Tha's in a maze half the time."

"Tha's right, Joshua." She had the dog now, leading him by the scruff of his neck until she reached the gate which led into the yard, flapping at the anxious animal with her apron until he was through. She chained him to the wall, even managing to tell him to 'be a good boy, then' whilst all the while the liquid flowed down her leg and into her wooden-soled clogs as the child she carried drained away from her on a tide of blood.

"I'm sorry, lass," she said later to her daughter who, being a child brought up on a farm, though she was only eleven years old, knew exactly what had happened to her mother five months ago when she had conceived in the bedroom next to hers, and understood the miscarriage she had just suffered in the very same bed.

"It's all right, Mother. Me an' Faither'll manage," Annie answered stoically.

"But how's tha' to do that, child, wi' me stuck up here in me bed? Tha' can't do milkin' an' butter an' cheese an' tha' faither'll want them ter go ter market at week's end."

"Mrs Mounsey'll help me."

"Aye," sighing weakly. "An' 'appen I'll be up afore long."

And so she was, for Joshua was not a man to sit with his knife and fork in his hands waiting for his supper and the girl was too busy in the fields and the dairy to be of much use in the kitchen. He said nothing, not even in recrimination, when it became apparent he was not to have his son, at least this time, and when in the next eighteen months his wife, despite his nightly assault on her, failed to conceive he began to realise, and to accept that Annie was to be all that he would have. His bitterness was intense and he eyed Jem Mounsey's lad with a jealous loathing he found hard to contain.

It was the day before Annie Abbott's twelfth birthday that he dropped his bombshell, though he gave no reason for his decision since that was not his way. He knew why he was taking this course of action and that was enough.

Annie and her mother, their fingers busy with the rushlights they were making in readiness for the long winter nights ahead, froze in their seats when he spoke, their mouths falling open in astoundment.

"Tha's ter go ter school, girl. Next week. Mornings. Jem Mounsey's lasses go so you might as well an' all."

Annabelle Abbott, Joshua and Lizzie Abbott's fifth child, stood up and the rushes she was coating with mutton fat fell to the floor as Joshua, slinging his hat to his head, set off for The Bull in Gillthrop without another word.

She found her voice at last. "Does he mean it, Mother?"

"Tha' faither never ses owt he don't mean, Annie."

"But . . . *why?*"

Lizzie looked at her daughter, marvelling for the hundredth time on how she and Joshua, despite her own subdued prettiness as a girl, could have between them made a child quite as bright and lovely as Annie. What ancestor had bequeathed to her that look of a thorough-bred, of pedigree that neither the Bowmans of Cockermouth nor the Abbotts of Gillthrop had in their line? Tall she was, already half a head above other girls of her age and though she was far from plump the flesh on her was firm and without blemish apart from the endearing scatter of pale golden freckles across her nose. Lizzie cut her hair regularly since her father said it was unsightly to have it 'all over the bloody place' – his words – but it was thick and springing, a mass of corkscrew curls which stood in a cheerful tangle about her well-shaped head. A bright copper, depending on the light, sometimes russet but, when the sun caught it, so vivid it hurt the eye to behold. It fell about her white neck and ears and over her eyes no matter how often Lizzie hacked it off and she knew it would not be long before Joshua ordered her to bind it up in a length of cloth. There was just so much of it, and then there were her eyes. Deep and enormous, bright with intelligence in her pointed face, almost the same colour as her hair sometimes and at others a pale golden brown which could have been yellow. They were set between lashes which were long and thick, brown at their roots and tipped with gold. Her eyebrows were fine and delicate and her skin was the colour of the buttermilk Lizzie produced in her dairy. She was cheerful, good-humoured and willing, as yet unspoiled by her father's oppression. All flame and brilliance and would it be quenched one day when she was wed to some stolid labouring chap which she knew Joshua hoped to get for her in the absence of a son? Mind, she had a stubborn streak in her which Joshua did his best to curb, succeeding so far, for the child was young, but it could become wilful and when it did what would happen to Lizzie Abbott who would be caught in the middle of it? How would *she* survive?

The girl had begun to twirl, her skirts clinging to her slender legs, her bare feet stamping on the flagged floor of the kitchen. She was going to school, she exulted, she was going to school. For some reason known only to her father she was to be sent to school. She would learn. She would be able to read and write and be somebody for was not an education the key which opened the door to all the dreams she had ever dreamed? She would be a scholar, as good as them up there at Long Beck where her status in life had given Mrs Macauley the right to hit Annie Abbott's mother as though she was nothing but a dog.

Though she could not have said why, nor even tried for she was not quite twelve years old, the picture of the tall and haughty figure of Reed Macauley on his fine black mare moved stealthily across her enchanted, simmering mind.

2

Annie Abbott was not quite fifteen years old when she fell ecstatically in love with the handsome young actor in the travelling company which played at the splendid theatre recently built in Keswick. The year was 1843 and the play was *The Outlaw of Sicily* in which the handsome young actor had the leading role.

On that day Sally and Mim Mounsey were picking blackberries in the lane which led from Browhead to Upfell where their father farmed.

"A nice blackberry 'n' apple tart, that's what tha' lad needs ter pick up 'is appetite," their worried mother had said at breakfast time. "Tha' knows 'ow our Davy do like a blackberry 'n' apple tart an' wi' a dab o' cream from that lot I've just put in t' crock it'll slide down a treat."

Davy Mounsey's strange lack of appetite this last day or two had been a source of mystery to his mother and an irritation to his father who could not abide a 'finicky lad' and especially one who said he 'hurt all over' and could not get out of his bed. A bit flushed he was and not his usual self but it was the Tup Fair at the weekend and how was Jem to get his lambs to Keswick and the tup he meant to hire, back again without the help of his son, he beseeched his wife to tell him?

"'E'll be right as rain by then, you'll see," she answered stoutly, more to reassure herself than Jem. "I'm mekkin' 'im up an infusion of angelica. Sally gathered me some from t' woods, didn't tha' lass, an' wi' a cupful o' that inside 'im 'e'll soon pick up. A rare good tonic is angelica an' it settles the stomach. 'E'll soon 'ave 'is appetite back. 'E needs a bit o' summat tasty inside 'im . . ."

Aggie Mounsey's cure for all ills was a 'bit o' summat tasty' and a good swig of one of her herbal remedies. "That blackberry 'n' apple tart'll do the trick, you just wait an' see if it don't," she added hopefully.

Sally and Mim, quarrelling half-heartedly as they always did, more from habit than ill-feeling, had reached the gate to Browhead having picked indolently for the whole of the October morning at a speed which would have incensed Joshua Abbott. Both big girls, Sally the same age as Annie, Mim a year younger, but in his opinion allowed to do as they liked by the indulgent Jem. As long as they helped their mother when she needed it in the dairy or the kitchen, or in any task she set them such as the blackberry picking, their father didn't concern himself overmuch with how they did it or how long it took providing it suited his Aggie. Good-natured, the lot of them, feckless Joshua would have said, but Upfell farm thrived where Browhead did not so how to explain it? He could not, unless it was his own lack of a son. He did not consider the almost inhuman amount of work his own daughter did each day worth mentioning.

She was trudging up the lane from Hause drawing the sledge which Joshua had made behind her, the harness about her shoulders, the leather straps cutting into her flesh and thrusting forward the young swell of her breasts. She leaned into it, her clogged feet feeling the track for purchase since the load on the sledge was heavy. Her face was dewed with sweat and it soaked the armpits of her shabby grey bodice. Her hair was tied up in a length of cloth, allowed to grow now that it was covered, drawn back severely from her pinched face and braided about her head which the cloth covered. On the sledge were two enormous sacks of milled grain which she had just collected from the miller in Hause.

She stopped when she saw Mim and Sally, her breath scraping from her lungs in great heaving gasps, and drawing off the harness she threw herself down on the grass verge, wiping her face with the sleeve of her bodice.

"Watch out fer me faither, Sal, will tha'? I'll 'ave to 'ave a breather. Them straps are cuttin' inter me summat cruel. Look . . ." She pushed down the neck of her bodice and on her white flesh were two bright red weals from her shoulders to under her armpits and both sisters drew back in horror.

"Eeh Annie, them's nasty. Can tha' faither not fetch grain 'imself. That there load's too 'eavy fer a lass."

"Try tellin' 'im that, Sally. 'Tha's a big girl now, our Annie,' 'e ses ter me, besides, 'e's up rakin' fells for t' sheep an' 'asn't time. Me mother offered ter come wi' me but yer know 'ow it is wi' 'er."

Oh, aye, they all knew how it was with Lizzie Abbott, poor soul. Sad, oppressed Lizzie Abbott who, with her daughter, led the most miserable of lives. A life on the level of an animal, their mother said indignantly though there was nothing *she* could do about it. And like an animal Lizzie bred every year, or had done until three years ago when her overworked body had given up the struggle and simply refused to conceive again. She had strained at every task her husband put her to, overburdened and doing her best to protect her child, taking jobs from her which were beyond the child's strength but now it was the other way around as Annie grew tall, taller than Lizzie and though slender to the point of leanness, strong.

They chatted for a while, the three girls, sitting on the sun-warmed grass verge, idly eating the blackberries Sally and Mim had picked. The sweat dried on Annie's face but it was very noticeable that she was not relaxed, that her head constantly swivelled from side to side, her eyes on the look-out for her father who could, though he never hit her, reduce her to trembling, rebellious fear, calling her a lazy young varmint, his words cold, his jibing voice filled with his contempt, his hard nature venting his spite on her for his lack of a son. She who was a mere girl. She knew he was up on the fell but the habit of a lifetime was so strong in her she could not throw it off but must have eyes in the back of her head on guard for his silent approach.

"We're goin' ter Keswick, me an' Mim, ter see the players. I don't suppose there's any chance tha' can come wi' us?" Sally put a good-hearted hand on Annie's bare brown arm just where it disappeared into her sleeve. The difference, as the sleeve rose a little at Sally's touch, in the skin which had been exposed to the sun and that which had been covered, was startling. A deep honey colour suddenly becoming a pure, alabaster white. Her face was the same, and her throat, but where the open neck of her bodice began it became an almost translucent white. She worked in the open fields or on the fells for much of the day, every day, when she wasn't at school and the constant exposure to sun and wind, to the wild elements which more often than not prevailed in the Lakeland district was, as she remarked mournfully to her mother – for who wanted to look like an old man when you were going on fifteen – making her as weatherbeaten as her father.

Annie laughed shortly. "Don't be daft, Sal. How can I get away from t' farm? Faither knows where I am every minute o' t' day an' night. Besides, even if I could get away, which I can't, where would I get money fer such a thing?"

"It's only threepence ter stand at back, Annie."

"Maybe, but it might as well be three guineas 'cos I 'aven't got it."

"What about tha' mother? 'Asn't she got a bit put by?" as *her* mother had, for the egg and butter money was traditionally the perquisite of the farmwife since she did the work.

"Don't be daft, Sal," Annie said again, but less caustically, with less certainty. There was nothing in the world she would love more than to go to the playhouse with Sally and Mim. To be as carefree, as *free* as they were allowed to be, even if it was only for a few hours. She went nowhere that was not connected with the farm except for the year in which she had been allowed to go to school in the village. She had been twelve then and had known nothing, but in those twelve months she had absorbed more than Sally and Mim had learned in three years. She could read and write and add up and do 'take-aways'. She had learned a smattering of history and geography, for the teacher, finding Annie wanted to learn and was not just passing the time as Sally and Mim and most of her other pupils were doing, had shown an interest in her and had even lent her her own precious books. *Sense and Sensibility* by Miss Jane Austen and Mr Charles Dickens' *Pickwick Papers*. These had given Annie a taste, not, alas, fulfilled, to read more, to see more, to know more and how was she to do that, labouring round her father's farm until she was married when, she presumed, she would do the same round her husband's. William Shakespeare was a great writer of plays, so her teacher at the Dame school had told her and perhaps it might be one of his that was to be shown in Keswick.

"What's on?" she asked abruptly.

"On where?" Mim answered, popping another black-berry in her mouth.

"What play is it?"

"'Tis called *The Outlaw of Sicily*."

"Did a chap by the name of William Shakespeare write it?"

"Nay, don't ask me. Who is 'e, anyway?" Mim was clearly unimpressed, and anyway, did it matter?

"He's a great play writer."

"Well, I don't know if 'e wrote this 'un, but it says on the playbill that there's to be dancin' betwixt each part."

"Dancin' . . ." Oh, how she loved to dance. Not that she'd done much but at the last 'boon clip' she had twirled in the 'Cumberland Square Eight' with Davy Mounsey, to the music of Dobby Hawkins' fiddle and to her astonishment her father had allowed it. The speculative gleam in his eye had gone unnoticed by her as she stamped her foot and threw back her growing hair, again, amazingly, allowed to hang free, though Lizzie Abbott saw it and so did Aggie Mounsey, both aware of its significance.

"What time you goin'?"

"Mid mornin'. Faither'll give us a lift to Keswick but we've to walk back."

"Threepence, you say?"

"Aye." Sally clasped Annie's hand, gazing earnestly into her face, seeing for perhaps the first time what no one had perceived before. Annie had always been scrawny, with her collar-bones looking as though they were about to break out from beneath her delicate white skin. She had thin, square shoulders, an extreme boyish slenderness, brittle and fine-textured, all hollows and angles with a pointed face in which her eyebrows flew rejoicingly up or ruefully down depending on the mood of her father. She had the rich, woodland colouring of a fox, her eyes just as golden and hunted but now, with her expression one of growing excitement, she seemed to light up, come alive, to crackle with anticipation and she was quite incredibly lovely.

"Will tha' come then?" Sally felt her own excitement begin to snap.

"If me mother'll give me threepence. That's if she 'as it, an' that's if Faither's up on t' fell again an' if 'e's to be there all day, an' if . . ."

It seemed Lizzie did have threepence to give her daughter and more besides which of course no one knew about, saved painfully over the years, a farthing here, a farthing there, stolen, Lizzie supposed it was, whenever she could do so undetected, from the egg money, the butter money, money that passed through her hands in the transactions over besoms and swills, most handed over faithfully to Joshua except for what was hidden behind a certain loose stone in the cow shed.

She had been aghast and yet, looking into her daughter's pleading face, a face suddenly lovely and bright with hope, she could not find it in her heart to refuse since the child had nothing in her life but hard work from cock-crow to nightsong. Giving in to the only impulse she had ever known since the one she had succumbed to when she had accepted and married Joshua, she pressed the threepence into her daughter's hand, kissed her cheek and told her to be back before her father returned from Middle Fell. Her face worked painfully as she watched the light, dancing feet of her child, almost fifteen, run down the track towards the farm gate where Jem Mounsey and his girls waited for her. She had on the dress Lizzie herself had been married in, carefully stored in lavender in the press in the bedroom, a light shade of tawny brown which, on Annie, as it had not done on Lizzie, looked exactly right. It was too short and a mite too tight across the breasts, causing a pang of misgiving in Lizzie for, with her glorious hair brushed until it stood out from her head and down her back in a brilliant copper cloud, Annie was enough to catch the eye of any man which worried Lizzie even more. But how could she resist that pleading face, those vivid eyes which, after all, were asking for very little? So innocent. A ride into Keswick with a perfectly respectable family to see the players which evidently Jem and Aggie Mounsey thought fitting for their girls to see.

As Annie turned to wave rapturously, Lizzie's eyes looked up towards Middle Fell and she prayed lustily that Joshua would remain there until nightfall.

They stood at the back of the playhouse, Annie and Sally and Mim, their young minds enchanted, their young eyes bright with the joy of it, for they were no more than children and did not see the tawdry costumes, the artificial deportment and speech of the actors, the triviality of the story. They were transported into fairyland, the land of myth and legend and imagination, and with the rest of the unsophisticated audience they cheered and howled, wept and laughed, loving every minute of it. In the first interval between parts, when Annie felt a tap on her arm, she did not at first recognise the young man beneath the appalling stage make-up as the leading male player she had just seen on the stage. He was quite alarming close to with his drawn-on black moustache, his gypsy ear-rings, his boots and his cutlass and for a moment all three girls shrank back.

"Ladies, forgive me. I had not meant to frighten you,"

he said, smiling his wicked 'outlaw's' smile. His voice was soft, deep and completely irresistible and his chocolate-brown eyes gazed into Annie's. He took her hand and raised it to his lips and the girls, all three, stared at him, hypnotised by his beauty and his charm, like three little rabbits which have suddenly come across an extremely handsome fox.

"I saw you from the stage," he went on, "and could not resist coming down to greet you. I could tell you were enjoying my poor performance and . . . well . . .", his smile deepening to reveal two engaging clefts – in a woman they would have been dimples – at each side of his mouth. "I could never withstand a pretty woman and when there are three of them it seems the challenge is tripled."

The word 'pretty' would have been enough but to be called a 'woman' when one is only fourteen was heady stuff and Sally and Mim began to preen. In sharp contrast Annie's face appeared to pale. She became still and hushed as though in the presence of some being who is truly from another world, a world in which gods lived, for surely this could only be one of those. Her hand had remained in his and her eyes, enormous, clear and incredibly lovely as she fell headlong into the pit of love for the first time, did not even blink. He kissed her fingers again and she could feel his lips burn her flesh and beneath the bodice of her mother's wedding-gown something quivered. It was the most delightful feeling but at the same time it hurt her. She felt a great need to put up her hand and draw this man to . . . to . . . She was not sure what it was she wanted, or what to do about it since, apart from her father, when she was a child, she had been touched by no man.

"The music has begun. Will you not dance?" he asked her softly. Her heart knocked frantically and her mouth was so dry she could not have spoken if her life depended on it but her limbs worked independently of her mind as he led her down towards the stage. Her cheeks burned with a bright flame as, with the practised ease of the accomplished seducer he put his hands gently about her waist and whisked her away in the lively, noisy reel 'The Circassian Circle'. She had seen it performed and had tapped her foot longing to join in on many occasions and she found that her body did the dancing for her while her benumbed mind dwelled in the rapture Anthony Graham had introduced her to.

"Won't you tell me your name?" he whispered in her ear before he returned to the stage for the second part of the play.

"Annie . . ." The first word she had spoken since he had burst into her life like a shooting star across an empty, navy-blue sky.

"Wait for me at the end of the performance, Annie," he pleaded, kissing her fingers again, holding her hand for a moment before he sped away to his role as the Outlaw of Sicily.

"I see you have another little chicken all ready to be plucked," his ageing leading lady said acidly.

"And why not since there's nothing here to excite one's interest."

"They get younger in every town," she replied sneeringly.

"Which is more than can be said of some I could mention."

Sally and Mim were persuaded by Anthony to walk ahead of himself and Annie as the four of them sauntered up Market Place.

"We can't 'ang about, Annie," Sally managed to mutter into the unheeding ear of her friend who was drifting along in the direction of Greta Bridge and the road to Hause on the solicitous arm of The Outlaw of Sicily. He had not stopped to remove his make-up nor change his costume in his eagerness to catch Annie when the performance ended.

"I . . . don't mind if you go on, Sal."

"No, you go on . . . er . . . Sally, is it? I'll see Annie to her door."

Sally eyed him doubtfully. Did he know how far it was

from Keswick to Hause? Did he even know that Annie lived up that way or even where it was and how long it would take him? His queer get-up looked even queerer in the broad light of day. Though she had initially fallen under his fascinating spell, as Annie and Mim had done, she was not quite so bewitched as Annie appeared to be and her reason told her that no man, particularly one as handsome and silver-tongued as Anthony Graham, would walk a girl like Annie a distance of ten miles just for courtesy's sake. He had another performance that evening, he said, and Sally knew he would certainly not be back in Keswick by then, and anyway, Annie was her friend and she couldn't just walk off and leave her with a perfect stranger, could she?

"'Tis five miles or more ter Hause," she said resolutely.

"Five miles!" Anthony came to an abrupt stop, seemingly unaware of the comically disbelieving faces the townsfolk turned in his direction. "I thought you lived in Keswick, Annie." For a moment his face was thunderstruck, then he gently pulled her round to face him, a winsome smile softening what had almost become petulance.

"But you'll come again tomorrow, won't you? There's no afternoon performance so you and I could spend some time together. You could take dinner with me at my lodgings at The Packhorse before I go on in the evening. Please say yes, Annie. I would be devastated if I thought I was never to see you again."

So would she.

"Please, Annie." He whispered her name, softly, lovingly, and in a tone no one, not even her own mother, had ever used. He gazed longingly into her eyes and she thought she would swoon with the sheer joy of it. He held her hands to his chest and she felt the strength, the warmth, the absolute masculinity of him as his heart beat against her hand. Nothing had prepared her for this, this thrill of quivering excitement, this trembling his touch set in motion and which ran deliciously through the whole of her body, right down to her knees. They felt as though they were made of jelly and her face was on fire with it. Her skin prickled and yet at the same time glowed and she could refuse him nothing, her eyes told him.

"Tomorrow at noon," he said encouragingly.

"Yes." Her eyes held stars but it meant nothing to his well-hidden and self-seeking heart.

Sally and Mim hurried, but Annie Abbott floated, light as thistledown along the five miles of lake road from Keswick to Hause, past the darkening mass of Dodd Wood on the right, the quiet beauty of Bassenthwaite Lake on the left. The sun had almost gone from the sky and the shape of Broom Fell across the water was dark and featureless but the glory of it had leaked into the lake itself, turning the flat surface of the water to a burnished golden-orange. The fells on the far side were reflected in it, a perfect mirror-image and a dark trail of cloud, golden-edged, poured across the water and the sky, one silhouette duplicating the other. From over the meadows which lay between the road and the lake, a tiny light burned in the windows of St Bridget's Church, and from those of the farms and scattered houses, looking like golden stars in the deepening darkness.

Annie could not have hurried had she tried. She had just lived through the most exciting experience of her young and drab existence and she still dreamed in it and in the dazzling remembrance of the man who had captured her innocent heart. She would see him tomorrow. She was to 'take dinner' with him at The Packhorse. She hadn't the faintest idea how she was to manage it since her father knew her every movement, or at least he did until today, but she would do it somehow, she told herself airily as she skipped along the last bit of track which led to the farmgate of Browhead.

"Wheer's t'girl?" her father had asked her mother. The men of Lakeland were thrifty, not only with their emotions – of any kind – and with their cash which was more often than not in short supply, but with their words.

"She'll not be far away, Joshua," her mother had faltered placatingly and when Joshua Abbott had demanded to know

exactly where that might be, Lizzie Abbott could not tell
him for after twenty years of marriage to him, twenty
years of servitude and uncommunicative constraint to his
dour and unbending will, indeed ever since she had come
to Browhead as a trembling bride of sixteen, her mental
processes had become severely hampered by her fear of
him.

Her mind had gone dead as Joshua waited for an
answer. Her tongue had stuck to the roof of her mouth
and though he had never struck her or their daughter,
she had cowered away from him as though expecting a
blow.

He was waiting for Annie where the farm track ran
down to the road. He hit her for the first time that
evening.

"Where've tha' bin, girl?" he wanted to know, and who
with? which were the words he most wanted to speak for
since the night of the 'boon clip' when she had danced in
such a lively fashion with Davy Mounsey, his dejected and
faltering hope of a son had risen like air. Not a son, of
course, but the next best thing. His farm and Jem Mounsey's allied in marriage and a man who has land, even if it
comes with a bride attached to it, will look after it. He'd
tie it up, naturally, so that it would still be Abbott's farm,
Abbott's land, with his grandchildren working on it, but
now, in the space of a day, since he had left this morning
feeling more optimistic than he had for years, she had
threatened the tentative dream he had allowed himself and
set it to shaking and crumbling like a weakened drystone
wall. All dressed up in some flibbertigibbet's gown – not
even recognising the dress in which his own wife had married him and in which she had looked as pretty as a hedge
rose – she had been off somewhere on her own and
returned so flushed and brilliant he could only suspect the
worst.

She refused absolutely to tell him since she did not want
to involve her mother who was grovelling by the fireside
like a whipped dog and when Joshua opened the door and
pointed silently out into the yard she had gone, her head

high and defiant, her cheek swollen, the flesh about her
eye already beginning to change colour.

"Tha'll sleep in t' barn tonight, girl," he said to her,
"wheer't th'animals sleep an' in t' mornin' thee an' me'll
'ave summat to say to one another. Think on it an' remember this. No one defies me in me own 'ouse. Now get out
theer an' get some sleep fer there's a field ter be ploughed
tomorrow."

The walk back to Keswick was long and dark and her
clogs blistered her bare feet. She did not weep nor did
she do much thinking except to repeat the words which
had sung in her head ever since Anthony had winked
audaciously at her over the footlights and stolen her
innocently beating heart.

'I love him, I love him, I love him,' the song went and
the rhythm of it moved her tired body along the deserted
road. The night was inky black. She could see nothing,
only her country senses keeping her on the track where
she might have blundered into the dangerous and densely
packed tree trunks of Dodd Wood on her left or down to
the rippling, deep and equally dangerous waters of the
lake on her right. Stones chinked beneath her feet and an
owl hooted close by, the suddenness of it making her heart
leap in alarm. A farm dog, sensing her passing, or perhaps
scenting the fox which was raiding the hen-coop, barked
hysterically, then stopped in mid-voice as though a heavy
hand had persuaded him to do so.

She reached The Packhorse at midnight, just as
Anthony and the troupe of strolling players who were
drinking with him were becoming deep in their cups. They
were singing some bawdy song, crashing their ale pots on
the table and the landlord, whose wife did not care for
such 'goings-on', being accustomed to a less vigorous class
of customer, shepherds and farmers and the like, was
about to remonstrate.

The whole of the bar-parlour fell silent as Annie
hesitated in the doorway. She had the look of a weary
child about her, pale, delicate with great smudges beneath
her wide, frightened eyes. The bruise her father had given

her made her appear even more vulnerable and when
Anthony Graham saw her hovering there his masculine
body surged towards her in ferocious and uncaring need.
He stood up triumphantly, then moved across the room
to take her hands, bringing them to his lips in the gallant
gesture for which her girlish heart had craved on the long
walk from Hause. He turned for a moment to wink at his
friends who whistled and clapped their hands and stamped
their feet in perfect understanding, but Annie was too
tired, too love-struck to know what it meant.

"Come," he whispered smilingly, leading her away from
the noisy group and up the stairs until they reached the
door of the room he shared with three others. Guiding
her through he locked it behind him and within five
minutes, less, Annie's trembling and virginal body was
revealed to his lecherous gaze in all its naked innocence.
He did not speak nor even kiss her. What was there to
say? She was already his with no need of pretty speeches
or persuasion.

It was all over within minutes. She was laid on the bed
with scant interest in her half-hearted protests since she
wanted to tell him how much she loved him; to hear how
much he loved her and desired nothing more than to spend
the rest of his life with her. That was why she had left
Browhead, because of their love but he didn't seem to
want to know. He pulled painfully at her breasts and bit
her belly, leaving teeth marks which would turn black by
morning. He forced her legs open and thrust himself inside
her with such force and rapidity she scarcely knew what
was happening until the pain knifed her between her thighs
and the blood flowed.

He fell asleep on top of her. Her breasts hurt and her
belly was on fire, as was that part of her body that had no
name. The softness and gentleness he had shown her . . .
where had it gone? . . . and where was the man she had
loved so devotedly for the past twelve hours? Was this it?
Was this love? Is this what happened when two people
loved one another? Was it? Mother . . . oh, Mother . . .
where are you? and Lizzie's frightened face slipped behind

her closed eyelids. Is this what she suffers every night of
her life . . . Oh, Mother . . .

Anthony snored beside her where she had heaved him
and outside the door men shouted to be let in but gradually
the noise died away and, being a tired and healthy child,
she slept.

3

The girl on the bed gave one last heave and the child slid out from her as easily as a dab of butter, the woman in attendance was to tell Hesper later that afternoon. It lay peaceably between its mother's thighs with none of the new-born infant's lusty rage at being propelled head first into a world it was not sure it would care for. It was as though it was born with the knowledge of the precarious state of its mother's position in life and the uncertainty of their future together.

"A girl, me duck," Polly Pearsall said cheerfully, "thank the Good Lord, fer there's enough o' the other damned sort in the world already." She expertly cut the cord, tucking everything away neatly, then lifting the baby on to a length of clean linen, bound it up tightly and placed it in the hesitant arms of its mother. "A little beauty an' all. Look at them red curls, just like her Ma's an' wi' nowt of . . ." She stopped speaking, cutting off the words with a sharp, irritated click of her tongue for the less said about him, the child's father, the better. Scoundrel that he was. 'Handsome is as handsome does' was one of the maxims which fell regularly from Polly Pearsall's lips and though he'd been full of charm and a fine-looking chap, what he'd done to this poor child was far from fine. If Polly had had her way he'd have been brought back and put before the magistrate. Made to pay something towards the upkeep of the child just born but he'd be in the next county by now, no doubt of it, and that troupe of strolling players he travelled about with.

She watched as Annie looked into the face of her daughter, waiting for that glow of maternal pride, that bond which is formed between mother and child in the first

moment of their meeting. For that soft-eyed look of
wonder and the awed need to touch the baby's cheek, to
put a tentative finger in the curled shell of the child's hand
which would instinctively grasp it. But it did not happen.
Annie Abbott held her new-born baby in the awkward
crook of her arm, her eyes wary, her expression somewhat alarmed. "What am I supposed to do next?" it
seemed to say. She glanced up apprehensively at Polly
looking exactly like a caller who has had some other
woman's child put unexpectedly into her arms and,
politely, is holding it for the shortest possible time before
returning it thankfully to its rightful owner. Of course the
babe had not been cleaned up yet. Perhaps that was it
though usually, in Polly's experience, a mother will give
even the muckiest of new-borns a cuddle.

"'Ere, give 'er ter me an' I'll bath 'er then you can put
'er to t' breast."

That ought to do it, she told herself. She could remember when her first had folded its pursed lips about her
nipple and even now, twenty years later, the unique joy
she had experienced then was something she would always
remember.

"See, give yerself a wipe round," slapping a bowl of
soapy water and a cloth on to the table by the bed, "an'
I'll send Hesper up ter change bed an' fetch you a cup of
tea. An' there's some soup I made fer the noon trade.
That'll put the heart back in yer, then I'll 'ave ter be gettin'
back downstairs. Seth's bin shoutin' for me, the great
lummox, so I'd best get off. Yer'll be right as rain now,
me duck. Yer've done well an' as far as I can see everything's fine down there," pointing in the general direction
of Annie's belly. "Yer'll be up an' about in a day or two.
Yer young an' strong. An' when yer up to it, later, I'll
fetch them little duds our Maggie wore. Well, they all did,
all my childer and Maggie was last."

All the while she talked Polly was sloshing the quiet
baby about in another bowl of warm water which she had
poured from the big earthenware jug on the dresser. She
doused it vigorously, careful of the top of its head and the

neatly tied up cord on its belly. Again she wrapped it firmly
in the length of cloth, then put it once more in its mother's
arms.

"Give it suck now, child," she said kindly to the equally
quiet girl on the bed. "She'll need feedin', yer know, an'
there's only you can do it."

Annie held the tiny, fiercely wrapped bundle in her arms.
Hesper had been changing the soiled sheets on the bed,
holding the baby, clucking and fond, exclaiming on her
lovely red curls whilst Annie wriggled into an immaculate
nightgown, one which belonged to Polly and which Annie
herself had washed and ironed only yesterday. She had
drunk the tea and obediently spooned the thick vegetable
soup into her surprisingly ravenous mouth before being
handed the child again. Hesper, a bundle of soiled linen
under one arm and the bucket of water in the other, had
gone and Annie was left in the hushed company of the
baby who was hers, hers and Anthony Graham's.

It was a week since he had left, he and the company.
She had been with him for just fourteen months and in
those months she had learned many things, acquiring an
education in a life she had not known existed. She had
gained a knowledge of the world which was to stand her
in good stead in the years to come. The life of the strolling
company had been one of casual drifting from one town to
the next, of bookings which had been cancelled, days of
excitement and others of boredom and uncertainty, thrilling at first to the young girl to whom, in her old life, the
arrival at the door of a pedlar had been one of dazzling
intoxication. She had taken small parts in the production,
those that did not involve speaking and when Anthony, on
a whim, had taught her to speak as the rest did, she had
become understudy to the leading lady. She had passed
out handbills in every town they played. She had, because
she could sew a little, taken care of the company's wardrobe. She had learned how to slip out of town without
paying bills, how to make love to her lover's satisfaction;
how to avoid being made love to by amorous actors and
playgoers alike. How to live well when the takings were

good and how to starve when they were not. She had been a part of them, doing what they did until her increasing girth made it impossible, and last week, as she was doing her best to earn a few pennies, hanging out Polly Pearsall's washing at the far end of the long back garden of the inn, they had all slipped away without her, one by quiet one, leaving their bills unpaid and the landlord, Seth Pearsall, in such a state of menacing rage, Annie had feared for her own safety.

Polly, his cheerful, uncomplaining and phlegmatic wife, had stepped deftly between Annie and her husband's rage, her own hefty proportions complementing his.

"'Tis no good threatening the lass, Seth. She's no money else why should she be workin' fer me, tell me that? This last week while them lot were jabbering their piece on't stage in that there barn, aye, despite size of 'er, she's worked like a good'un from mornin' 'til night so *she* owes us nowt. Yes, I know she were with them but that don't make 'er responsible fer their debts, do it, me duck? So 'tis no good you threatening ter fetch constable. Now, she can go on earnin' 'er keep alongside Hesper in t' kitchen until babby comes an' then . . . well, we'll see. We could do wi' another body ter give a hand, me an' Hesper, so just you calm down an' get back inter t' bar fer there's men wi' their tongues hangin' out fer a pint."

For a week, until she was brought to bed, Annie had filled a pail each morning, scrubbing the floor of the kitchen and the flagged passage which led to the dining room and bar-parlour of the inn. There was mud and grease mixed with straw and even manure stamped into it and though her head swam and the baby inside her kicked and squirmed she did not falter. She washed and ironed and heaved this and that and though Hesper and even Polly Pearsall, who were both good souls, did their best to save her from these heavy tasks, Annie would not hear of it.

"Yer'll 'arm that child, Annie," Polly protested but Annie did not care. The child was not real to her who was merely a child of fifteen herself. What would she do with it when it came? Perhaps it would be born dead which would be a blessing but, of course, it hadn't, and here it was.

She studied the small, round face of her daughter, the fluff on her head which was not red but a pure, golden copper, the shape and colour of her eyes which were open and seemed to be studying *her*. Her skin was like satin, clear, pale, flawless, her mouth pink and pouting and her hands, one of which had escaped Polly's binding and flexed helplessly in the air, were like daisies, perfect in every detail. Carefully Annie unwrapped the binding and the tiny body lay trustingly beneath her gaze. The child's legs jerked and bent and the small, hidden fold of her female gender was revealed. A girl. A female child who would, one day, be subjected to the hurt and fear and humiliation she herself, and her own mother, had suffered. Poor little girl. Poor baby. So quiet, so patient, it seemed to Annie, and she wondered if her own submission to Anthony Graham's mastery of her – since what else had there been for her? – had transmitted itself to the child who was inside her.

Slowly, not at all sure what the correct procedure was but hoping the baby would know, as newly born lambs did, she opened Polly's nightgown and turned the child in the general direction of her breast. At once, but with the utmost delicacy, the small rosebud mouth fastened on Annie's nipple and began to suck. It did not hurt, Annie discovered. In fact it was quite pleasant. Quite companionable really, as though she and the baby were friends and, like friends, one was doing the other a favour. The child's hand rested on her breast and Annie smiled, putting her finger inside the tiny fist. Immediately the child gripped it and it was then that it happened. A great wave of loving tenderness, a great drowning in which she and the child went down together, deep, deep, then floated in perfect harmony to the surface where they lay, fastened together by an invisible, indivisible thread which, she knew, would never be broken.

They were both asleep, she and the child, when, the rush over, Polly put her head round the door several hours later. She smiled. The child was held protectively in the curve of the mother's arm, trusting, well fed, loved, Polly could see that and her smile deepened in satisfaction. That was it then. What had not happened at once had happened now.

"She's all right now," she said to Seth as they tumbled into the great feather bed they shared.

"Why shouldn't she be?" he grumbled, reaching for her comfortable, still enticing breast and giving it a hopeful squeeze.

"She didn't take ter t' little 'un right away, not like I did wi' mine."

"Oh, aye." His hand explored his wife's ample body with greater urgency and Polly let him since, though he was a great daft lummox, she was fond of him and knew exactly how to get what she wanted from him.

"Aye, a grand lass an' a good worker, like I said. We'll keep 'er on, I reckon. Babby'll be no trouble," hitching herself into a position more accommodating for her husband's questing masculinity.

"Righto, Poll. Now then, here's a little mouse lookin' fer a hole."

"'An here's a little 'ole fer 'im to 'ide in," neither of them seeing anything ridiculous in the obviously well-used words.

She was there for six months, sleeping with the child in the furthermost attic of the inn where, Polly hoped, she would not disturb Hesper, the guests, nor herself and Seth who both needed their sleep but the baby, thriving and as pretty as a picture, even Seth agreed, was not the slightest trouble to anyone, least of all her doting mother whose hitherto untapped source of love sprang into full bloom and was lavished unstintingly on her child.

"What you callin' it?" Hesper asked interestedly when Annie was back at the kitchen sink. They worked steadily side by side in the hot kitchen, a good team, Hesper was inclined to think and she said so to Mrs Pearsall, adding that she didn't know how she'd managed before Annie came, her being such a devil for work.

Annie's hands which were busy peeling potatoes with their customary vigour, became still and her eyes turned to the basket where her child's fingers could be seen clutching the air above the rim of the wickerwork. Her feet kicked and her voice murmured some bubbling sound to the smoked hams and dried herbs which hung above her head.

"I hadn't thought," Annie answered slowly.

"She'll 'ave to 'ave a name, duck."

"Yes, I suppose so."

"There's no suppose about it, Annie. *Everyone* 'as to 'ave a name. What were yer Ma called?"

"Lizzie," and for a brief moment, hurriedly put away, her mother's haggard face flowed sorrowfully across Annie's vision. No, not Lizzie, nor Elizabeth which, Annie presumed, was her mother's true name, though she was not sure of it. She did not want her beautiful daughter to bear the name of the woman who would always, in Annie's mind, be connected with degradation and shame, with grief and pain and hopelessness. She could hear her father's voice, when he did not call her 'woman', shouting for 'Lizzie', and that made it even worse.

"No, she ain't a Lizzie," Hesper said equably. "What were yer Granny called?"

Granny? She didn't remember ever having one of those but she did recall her mother telling her that *her* mother, who had come from Scotland, had been named Catriona.

"Catriona."

"Eeh, that's lovely. Catriona. Catriona Abbott. That's nice, that be."

"We need a 'and in bar, Poll," Seth roared one night when, two coaches having come in at the same time, every passenger on board wanting a hot meal or a hot toddy, or both and at once, the place was in uproar. It was February by then, cold and damp and with no hint of spring about it which surely should be just round the corner in this Midland county.

"Well, Hesper can't manage it. She's busy with them

pies an' I'm up to me eyes with the goose. It'll 'ave ter be Annie."

She was an instant success. Her lovely face became flushed and lively and she found her brief training as an actress, and as a 'hander out' of handbills, and the repartee which was part of the job, had bestowed on her a saucy tongue to which the customers responded, demanding more drinks than they would normally have, just to be served by the pretty barmaid. She was quick and light on her feet, watching for Seth's signals on where she was needed and the tips she received which she was ready to hand over to him, were hers to keep, he told her, his huge grin telling her how well she had done.

She brought in custom. She learned to be bold without being vulgar. How to smile and tease without being coarse. How to give the impression that each man was her especial favourite while at the same time allowing no liberties to be taken with her person. Which was fine and perfectly acceptable to Polly until she discovered it was her Seth who was the worst culprit, doing his best to urge the red-faced and vehemently protesting Annie into the larder, his hand already up her skirt.

Polly said nothing then, being a wise woman, merely making an unnecessary clatter to warn them of her approach. She and Seth had a thriving business and she wanted no bad blood between them. He was an old fool, but that was all. A man, like the rest of them, who could not resist a pretty face but she was not about to jeopardise her marriage, her livelihood, her future, over a temporary flush of youthful lust which had come over her Seth.

Catriona Abbott was six months old when Polly Pearsall told Annie, regretfully, that she would have to go. It was June, the day fine and bright, the honeysuckle which climbed up the wall at the side of the inn melting into pink and cream, its sweet fragrance as heady as wine. Yellow irises bloomed in the little stream which warbled through the inn's back garden, threaded with the yellow and orange flowers of mimulus. Linnets were nesting under the eaves and above the sound of the stream their twittering could clearly be heard. The washing Annie was pegging out snapped in the breeze and Annie sniffed at its good clean smell, then sighed in content.

She turned in amazement when Polly spoke at her back. "Leave? But why? What have I done?"

"Nothin', me duck. You've bin a good, 'ard-workin' lass an' it's not your fault you've been blessed wi' that bonny face of yours, nor the shape of yer. I say 'blessed', but perhaps 'cursed' would be a better word. There's Hesper who's as plain as a plank an 'as no trouble gettin' or keepin' a job when she's not 'alf the worker you are. Willin', aye, but she's not got your . . . your way o' doin' things. All of a muddle she be wi'out me ter tell 'er what ter do, but you . . ."

"Then why, Mrs Pearsall, why?" Annie's voice was rich with passion at the injustice of it but deep down where her female instincts matched those of Polly Pearsall, there was a growing understanding.

"I think yer know why, duck." Polly's voice was sad and beneath her steady gaze Annie's face became flooded with colour. She hung her head and tears brimmed to her eyes.

"It wasn't me, Mrs Pearsall. It wasn't my fault. D'you think I want an old man like . . ." like that fat pig who is your husband, the unfinished sentence said, but Polly finished it for her.

"Like my Seth, is that what you were goin' ter say? Well, 'e's not much ter look at, I'll give yer that, but 'e's a good man really an' . . . 'e's mine, Annie. I'm fond of 'im, see, an' 'e is of me . . ."

"Then why doesn't he leave me alone?" Annie's head lifted defiantly and her eyes flashed in golden brilliance. Damnation, but this lass has got troubles ahead of her, Polly had time to think. Wherever she goes it will be the same. Men after her like dogs chasing a bitch on heat and though she doesn't ask for it, not in so many words, the very way she walks, swinging her hips and twitching that little bum of hers, lifting them fine breasts, turning her head to smile, it drives them on until all they can think of is getting their hands on it all. Since the child her figure had ripened. Motherhood – and the good food she ate – had put flesh on her, a rich, creamy flesh and all in the right places, curving her breast and hip but the hard work she did kept her waist small and neat. Her hair grew and flourished, burnished with good health to the deepest copper, unconfined in its glory even when she plaited it where it fell in a swinging rope to her buttocks. She was happy, poor little bugger, and it showed in the vivid and startling loveliness of her eager smile and they were all mesmerised by it. Like my Seth, the old sod.

For a moment her female pride and jealousy for someone younger and prettier than herself took a hold of her and she wanted to smack the silly little cow in the face and tell her to 'hop it' and ply her wares elsewhere but her own sense of fairness returned.

"'E's only a man, Annie, like them all. 'E's right fond o' me an' we rub along right well. So you see, duck, you'll 'ave ter go. An' I'd be obliged if yer'd pack yer things an' leave right now. I don't want yer sayin' owt ter Seth or Hesper. They're both busy so it'd be best. I'll tell 'em you just upped an' took off. Try over Gretton way. There's a lot of inns on that road. 'Tis a busy one an' 'appen you'll get summat. Eeh, Annie, I'm right sorry this 'appened, me duck. I've got proper attached to that babby . . . an' ter you."

She had gone within the hour, speaking to no one, stunned and speechless, her few belongings – Lizzie Abbott's wedding-dress which she kept scrupulously mended and cleaned, and the baby's change of clothing – in a wicker basket Polly gave her. There was food, enough for a couple of days and the few shillings she had earned. It would keep her going until she reached Gretton. Catriona was carried on her hip, held with a length of clean grey cloth tied over Annie's shoulder. She clung there like a small animal, her thumb in her mouth, her enormous golden brown eyes gazing solemnly at Polly who was as close to tears as she had been in years.

It was the same wherever she went and she was never,

in all her travels, to find a place so good nor a woman so kind as Polly Pearsall.

"That babby just won't do, me duck. It'll be a nuisance what with the stink of it . . ."

The *stink* of it, her sweet smelling, dewy fresh little daughter who was bathed every day and changed the very moment she soiled her napkin.

". . . an' then there's the noise. I can't 'ave it near my guests . . ."

The *noise*! That soft gurgling of laughter she and Catriona shared, the nuzzling contented sounds as she settled at Annie's breast.

". . . an' there's no doubt you'd be neglecting yer work runnin' up an' downstairs to it every five minutes, wouldn't yer?"

"No, ma'am, I wouldn't. She's a very good baby, really she is. A quieter baby never breathed. She sleeps a lot and I could feed her when I'm eating my meals. I would never neglect my duties . . ."

"Where did yer learn ter speak like that, me duck? Yer not from these parts, are yer?"

"No, Cumberland."

"Well I never. I'd no idea they spoke so posh up there."

"Would you have a job for me then? Anything . . . scrubbing, bar work . . . ?"

"Well . . ."

"I would work for very little."

"Well . . ."

For the next two years it was the same, working wherever and whenever she could, mostly in the bar-parlours of country inns where folk were kinder than those in the bigger towns. She brought trade with her lovely face and lively tongue but she also brought trouble since there was not a man who drank the pint of ale she put in his hand who did not want her as well, and not a few were willing to fight over it, with each other or with her when she would not allow what they often considered to be part of her duties. Time and again she was asked to move on, she and her child who had learned to be good and quiet in the attic rooms which were allotted them and where Annie was forced to leave her for hours on end. Catriona was to learn that she must wait patiently for her mother's return. That she must not stamp about or shout as other children were allowed to do but must play with the rag dolly Annie had made for her out of scraps of material, sitting quite still in the middle of the straw pallet. She dozed and crawled, then crept on her little faltering legs into a walk and when Annie came up, there she would be, the light from Annie's candle falling on her lovely, blinking eyes, her eager, expectant face, the riot of her soft, bright curls, so like her mother's.

"See what mother's brought for her good girl tonight," Annie would say, popping broken custard tart into her child's mouth, morsels of the daintiest food scraps she could find left over from the dining room and all the while praying that the landlady of the inn at Brigstock or Desborough, at Clipston, Naseby, Rothwell, wherever it was she had tramped to in the hope of finding work, would not blame her for the black eye Jim Sorrell had given to Harry Appleton in the yard as they fought one another ferociously over who had more right to Annie Abbott's favours.

She was in Market Harborough when she saw the newspaper. She had worked for the past week in the kitchen of The Plough in the Market Square, scrubbing, peeling potatoes by the bushel, cleaning vegetables, washing and drying the mountain of dirty crockery and glasses which came from the dining room and bar-parlour by the hour. She wore a bodice and skirt she had bought from a market stall, grey, much mended, too big in order to hide her shapely figure, and round her head she had bound a length of colourless cotton. An enormous apron made of sacking enveloped her from neck to ankle and up in the roof in a space too tiny even to be called an attic, her daughter lay apathetically on a grubby palliasse. She was almost three years old and the life she and Annie had been forced into was slowly reducing her from a placid but bright and contented infant who could, because she slept for a good deal of the day, accept her restricted life, into a dull, spiritless little ghost who scarcely turned her head when Annie crept into the room, the cupboard in which they slept. Annie despaired over her, rocking her in passionately tender arms, whispering into the dazed little face until the child responded, telling her tales about her own childhood which now, in contrast to her daughter's, seemed rosy indeed.

But it could not go on for ever. The little girl was growing, a baby no longer. She needed companionship, the outside world, people, animals, beauty, stimulation. When she had an hour Annie would take her into the market place, telling her what the objects were on the stalls, ordinary, everyday things which were a wonder to the child who stared for hours on end at four blank walls. Annie carried her out of the town and into the countryside which surrounded it, letting her wander in the woodland, watching her absorption with a simple cowslip, a scurrying beetle, the cows in the fields and for a brief moment her child would come alive. They would run, hand in hand, and Annie would shout out loud but Catriona would put her hand to her mouth, her eyes enormous in her pinched face as she looked about her as though, even here, she must make no noise.

The newspaper was the *Lancaster Herald* and was dated several weeks ago, evidently left there by some traveller from the North. It lay discarded beneath a table in the snug bar, the floor of which Annie was about to scrub. It was thick and would make a good pad on which to kneel, she decided and then later, if she could pinch a good candle stub, she would read it in the privacy of her room. Who knew what great events might be taking place in the world of which she was completely ignorant.

Catriona was asleep, her face pale in the flickering light from the candle, her hair in a lifeless tangle on the stained pillow. She had eaten half a pork pie, some cold potato and a spoonful of cabbage, obedient as always, but vague and ready, worryingly so, to go back to the heavy sleep Annie had wakened her from.

Annie watched over her for half an hour, anguished by

the little girl's docility, then, sighing, she picked up the newspaper.

She turned the pages lethargically. What did she care if there was to be a revolution in Paris as seemed likely? Or even if it was happening in the county of Leicestershire from where, no matter how she tried, there was no escaping the drudgery and hopelessness of her life? She was about to throw the newspaper down and climb into the bed with Catriona when her own name sprang out at her from the words which were printed there. The shock of it sluiced over her like a deluge of icy water and she gasped, her breath catching painfully in her throat. Her brain became numb and her hands shook and for several moments she could not focus her eyes nor even keep the newspaper still.

'Annabelle Abbott,' it said, 'late of Browhead Farm, near Hause in the county of Cumberland . . .'

Dear God . . . she couldn't read it . . . the candle-flame flickered so . . . and her hands would not stop their trembling . . . Annabelle Abbott . . . that was her . . . her name and there could be no more than one Annabelle Abbott surely? And if there were, this one lived at Browhead . . . it was her. *It was her!*

At last she reached the end of the words, the words printed in the four-week-old copy of the *Lancaster Herald*, the words which appealed to Annabelle Abbott or anyone who knew of her whereabouts to contact the firm of solicitors, Hancock, Jones and Hancock, in King Street, Lancaster.

4

King Street was a pleasant thoroughfare in the centre of
Lancaster. It led away from the Town Hall which was
large, pillared and handsome and, at this time of the day,
its wide shallow steps were busy with the feet of the
respectable and hard-working citizens who had business
there.

She and Cat had walked from Warrington where her
money for railway fare had run out. They had moved in
an almost straight line going northwards through Wigan
and Preston and Garstang, but happily on more than one
occasion they had been given a lift on the back of a cart,
the farmer taking pity on the weary woman and child and
inviting them to 'hop up' and sit among the crates of
indignant hens and geese, the sacks of corn and potatoes
he was taking to market. Annie had been grateful, smiling
her glowing smile, lifting Cat up where the child would
instantly fall asleep for as long as she was allowed, as she
did herself at times. Weeks they had been on the road
and if they did not get to Lancaster soon, what small
reserve of pennies she had kept for food would be finished
and she would either have to stop somewhere for a few
days to earn a bob or two, or resort to begging.

It was November when they reached the town, a harsh
November day which struck through the increasingly
threadbare fabric of their clothing and Cat shivered as she
and her mother moved along that last mile, the ancient
castle which dominated the town and which had been the
landmark towards which they had been inching for days,
looming high in the November mist. It was a shire house
and county gaol, Annie was told by a tinker who had taken
it upon himself to travel with them the last few miles from

Scotforth, a sprightly Irishman who carried a pack on his back and had a merry twinkle in his eye and who offered to carry Cat as well. Annie could not refuse for Cat was nearing exhaustion and though she was afraid the man might expect some reward, and not of the monetary sort, she allowed it.

On the top of the castle stood a large tower called 'John of Gaunt's Chair' from where, the tinker told them, having been this way before, there was a fine view over the whole of Cumberland and even, on a clear day, across the sea to the Isle of Man. Lancaster was a small but splendid port on the River Lune over which a brand new bridge spanned, with five elegant arches. Market days were Wednesday and Saturday, their informative friend told them cheerfully, handing the dazed child back to her mother, smiling indulgently since he had children of his own, he added, letting her know that though his eyes admired her he had no designs on her person.

It was Wednesday and the streets were busy but, the tinker having given her directions she found her way to King Street easily enough. It was a tree-lined jumble of old houses, one of which had been made over into a doctor's consulting rooms, an architect's office and, on the second floor, the rather grand quarters of Hancock, Jones and Hancock.

The clerk at his high desk in the small front office eyed her and her daughter with the appalled air of a man come face to face with persons of the lower order, those whom, had he been at his own home, he would have ordered to the back door. Annie smiled wryly. Having been on the road for eight weeks she could not blame him since she and Cat were not looking their best. Nevertheless she kept her head high and her expression lofty as she passed him the dog-eared, practically unreadable scrap of newsprint which she had torn from the old edition of the *Lancaster Herald*. He took it between his thumb and forefinger as he might a piece of mouldy and evil-smelling cheese.

"I'm Annabelle Abbott," she said, "and this is my

daughter Catriona. I am here to see either Mr Hancock
or Mr Jones, whoever is available."

"Indeed! and on what business?" ready to show her the
door for her impertinence.

"My own. The newspaper cutting asked for me and I
am here."

"But this is months out of date. I'm not sure . . ."

"I was in Leicestershire."

"Oh . . ." not at all sure why that was significant.

"I walked a good deal of the way so if you will tell Mr
Hancock I am here I would be obliged."

"He is very busy."

"We will wait," and tipping her head regally she guided
Cat towards a chair which was placed against the wall.

It was the same with Mr Hancock, whose expression
of amazement matched that of his clerk. He seemed to
remember something about a farm, he said, when he had
recovered his composure, and the name of Abbott rang a
bell though he could not quite recall . . .

"Why have I been summoned here?" She cut through
his ramblings, his vague fumbling with this paper and that,
his shouted orders to his clerk to fetch the . . . what was
the name again? . . . turning to Annie . . . the box marked
Abbott . . . yes, yes . . . and when her bald question
finally penetrated his tangled mind which, it seemed, had
been thrown into some confusion by her appearance, his
expression was startled.

"Why?" he repeated.

"Yes. What does this mean?" indicating the newspaper
cutting which the clerk had returned to her as though
afraid he might be contaminated by its continued presence
between his fingers.

Mr Hancock had the correct papers before him now
which he studied through the thick-lensed spectacles on
the end of his nose.

"Aah, yes, of course, it's about the farm," eyeing
her abundant hair which, though she had done her best
with it, was cascading in a rippling mass over the weary,
straining cloth of her elderly bodice.

"The . . . the farm? Browhead?"

"Indeed. What else?"

"But . . ."

"Now that your mother and father are dead . . ."

The rest of his words faded away as she entered the dizzy, echoing tunnel which was long and black and shocking and when she came out of it at the other end Mr Hancock was talking of legal matters which, he said, were apparently in order and all that was needed was for her to . . .

"My . . . my parents are *both* dead?"

"Indeed, that is what I said."

"When?"

"Oh, it must be twelve months since . . ."

She scarcely remembered leaving his office, nor the few shillings which Mr Hancock – kindly now – pressed into her hand for her railway fare to Penrith, nor much of the journey either, and it was not until the man spoke to her that she came out of her shocked state.

She was arranging the child's clothing when he first noticed her, twitching its little bonnet more closely about its face, stuffing tendrils of bright copper hair beneath the brim, re-tying the scarf which already fitted snugly about its neck, but doing it so fiercely the child was pulled this way and that like a puppet on strings. She – he had decided the child was female – didn't seem to mind, accustomed to rough handling, he supposed, perhaps knowing no other. She stood patiently, submitting to being turned about for the woman's critical inspection; to a general smoothing down of the drab, ankle-length skirt; to a forceful tug at the equally drab shawl which was crossed over her narrow chest and tied at her back, the last ministration nearly taking her from her small feet. Then, bringing a glowing smile to the child's face, the woman knelt down and planted a hearty kiss on her upturned cheek. The gesture was so spontaneous, so full of irrepressible and loving warmth the man felt his own lips twitch in a smile.

It was a scene with which he was very familiar though

not one he had experienced for twenty years. His own mother had treated him thus before he set off on his short-legged fell pony across his father's land which lay up beyond the splendour of Dash Falls. From there he had dropped down the packhorse route which skirted Lonscale Fell to Latrigg and on to Keswick where he had attended the grammar school.

"Now then, Reed Macauley," she would say in her broad-vowelled but rhythmic Cumberland dialect. She always called him by his full name when she wanted to impress upon him the importance of what she was about to utter. "Now then, Reed Macauley, mind tha' keeps tha' scarf tight round tha' neck. There's a fair bottom wind blowing' down t'valley an' I'll not have thi' tek cold for the want of a bit o' sense."

As if he would, her expression said. Her son! He'd never had a cold in his life, no, nor any of the childish ailments which afflicted other weaker boys, but she had to have her say nevertheless, for it was only in this way that she could demonstrate her deep and abiding love for him. He was the apple of her eye, the darling of her heart, the centre of her universe but if her life had depended on it she could not have told him so. Instead she would fuss about him, her work-worn hands at his neck fixing his scarf to her own satisfaction beneath his chin. His cap would be jammed down on his head until it met his scarf. His durable hodden-grey jacket, the wool from which it was made spun and woven by her from the fleece of his father's own sheep, smoothed down briskly, his buttons checked to make sure they were all done up as she liked them to be.

Her pride in her only son, her only remaining child, was enormous but it was kept well hidden beneath her own snow-white, cruelly starched apron bib where her heart lay. Any physical or emotional manifestation of how she felt about him was beyond her. Die for him she would and right gladly, to save him a moment's hurt, but to kiss him, as the woman had just kissed the small girl, to put her arms about him would have seemed a foolish and wasteful embarrassment to a woman of her practical nature.

So she made sure he was warm, well fed, that his clothes were of matchless quality, laundered and immaculately pressed; mended when he tore them in the endless scuffles lads of his age engaged in. That his boots, the best his father's money could buy, were well polished. In short, that Reed Macauley, her son, wanted for nothing.

The engine of the Lancaster-to-Carlisle train standing at the platform of Penrith station and from which he had just alighted gave a mighty shriek and several horses in the station yard tossed their heads nervously. The noise and the sudden confusion which it caused brought him sharply back from the past and he straightened himself to his full height. He was a tall man, lean of waist and belly and hip but with strong muscled shoulders which filled the roomy, sleeved cloak of navy cashmere he wore. His hair was thick and a rich, dark brown, ready to curl vigorously from beneath the brim of his tall beaver hat. He was amber-skinned and clean-shaven and his eyebrows frowned above eyes which were compelling in their narrowed watchfulness. A vivid blue they were, in which the clear northern light had put the brilliance of a sapphire. They were framed by long black lashes. He could not be considered handsome, though many women thought so, since he was too fierce, his chin too arrogant but there was about him an observant, mocking humour which allowed him to view those of his acquaintance with something less than the serious application they often thought their due. There was in the casual stance of his long, lounging body and the insolent lift of his dark head, a sure belief in his own infallibility and the sense that here was a man who was diverse, complex, a man with many shades and nuances to his nature which no one had ever been allowed to penetrate.

His obvious and complete masculinity did not prevent him from dressing in a way which in another man, particularly one from these parts, might have been considered dandified. The men of the lakelands of Cumberland, his own father among them, wore what their fathers and

grandfathers had always worn. Homespun of hodden-grey
made from the mixed wool of their own sturdy Herdwick
sheep. Serviceable, durable and warm, jackets, breeches,
gaiters and sturdy boots, for the climate of the lakes was
damp and chill for a good part of the year. Not for them
the immaculately tailored dove-grey trousers Reed
Macauley had taken to wearing after the death of his
father, nor the fine worsted, plum-coloured coat, and as
for the cloak which was lined with fur of some sort, well,
what kind of man went in for such fripperies and more to
the point, what would become of him? Certainly not the
taciturn, blunt-spoken, independent men who were Reed
Macauley's neighbours and business associates.

He removed one of his buff-coloured kid gloves and took
out his pocket watch, a magnificent gold hunter, flicking
open the case to check the time before returning it to his
waistcoat pocket. A thick chain hung across his chest and
on the smallest finger of his hand a diamond sparkled. He
took out a cigar case, selected a cigar, lit it and breathed
in the smoke with a lingering pleasure which was almost
sensual.

He had been lounging against the station yard wall waiting for the lad from the inn to bring his horse which had
been stabled there, when the woman and the child had
caught his attention. The clattering of the animal's hooves
on the cobbles, the barking of several dogs which were
bristling and snarling up to one another by the yard gate,
the tuneless whistle of a coachman who waited beside his
mistress's carriage, the nervous whinnying of the greys
which pulled it, all these sounds penetrated Reed
Macauley's state of unfocused abstraction and he shivered
slightly as though the ghost of his mother had touched him
as she moved back into the past.

The groom led the tall black mare towards him somewhat gingerly for she was of a highbred disposition and
had been known to bite at the hand which held the bridle.
A beautiful animal with a coat like satin, rippling as she
stepped daintily across the yard, her head tossing, her
eyes rolling, eager to be away and at the gallop for she

had been stabled at The Fiddler's Arms for three days whilst her master attended to some business in Lancaster. It took all the groom's strength to hold her.

"Theer she be, Mr Macauley, sir, an' a right bugger she were an' all. She's not 'ad much exercise seein' as 'ow theer's none cares to get on 'er back an' theer's none she cares to 'ave on 'er back, neither. Jake led 'er up t'road a piece an' into t' field at back o t' church but a right to-do-ment it were."

Reed Macauley smiled. He threw the butt of the cigar to the ground, stepped on it then took the reins from the lad's very willing hand. He patted the animal's arched and quivering neck, gripping her mane, then smoothed his gloved hand down her nose, blowing into her distended nostrils, his lips close as he murmured something to her deep in his throat.

At once she quietened, standing passively beneath her master's touch, her luminous eyes looking into his, her head beginning to nuzzle affectionately against his shoulder.

Reed's smile deepened, revealing the perfect white teeth his mother had bequeathed to him with her pints of fresh milk, the blue milk cheese known as 'wangy' cheese sliced between thick wedges of home-baked bread which he took to school with him; the fresh vegetables which she had grown in her garden and the fresh herbs she had cooked in her herb pudding. A dish consisting of alpine bisort, nettles, chives, blackcurrant leaves, barley, butter and beaten eggs, made in the spring by most housewives but served once a week on Sarah Macauley's table.

"You have to treat a horse as you would a woman, Sam," he told the groom, who looked startled, since no woman he had approached had tempted him to blow up her nose. "They like to be soothed and petted and have little bits of nonsense whispered in their ear. It's quite amazing what a man may be allowed with the female sex if he treats her kindly and it is the same with a horse I have found." He winked engagingly at Sam who began to grin. "They are strange but delightful creatures and cannot resist flattery, can you, my beauty?" running his hand along the mare's flank, "so you must tell them how splendid they are at least a dozen times a day at the same time stroking them as I am stroking Victoria here. Isn't that so, Victoria?"

The mare actually nodded her head, the groom told Jake later when he was recounting Mr Macauley's amazing words, what he could remember of them since many had been too high-flown for his understanding and just plain bloody daft anyway. Mind you, Mr Macauley's reputation with the ladies was legendary, his exploits in that direction – and the results of them, most with eyes the colour of deepest blue – discussed wherever men gathered as far afield as Borrowdale and Rosthwaite at the southernmost tip of Derwent Water, to the east to Penrith and west to Whitehaven. So perhaps what he advised with the mare, and women, was not as barmy as it sounded. Maybe Sam'd try it next time he coaxed Maggie Blamire out from behind the bar counter of the inn and into the pitchy darkness of the long garden at the back of the privy.

"Try it, Sam," Mr Macauley said as though he had read Sam's mind. "Now then, Victoria, let's be off home. It's a fair ride to Long Beck and I don't fancy the fells after dark."

Placing his foot in the stirrup he leaped lightly into the saddle with the fluid grace of one who has been on horseback from the day he could toddle. He put his heels to the mare's side, guiding her from the yard and out into the busy street of Penrith's centre towards the monument which divided it, noting that the clock on the tower stood at one thirty.

"Hup Victoria," Sam heard him say as the animal broke into a canter.

Victoria! Imagine calling a horse Victoria. It was said in the dales that Reed Macauley had named the foal, given to him by his father in the year their young Queen had come to the throne, after her, which had seemed somewhat disrespectful, even insolent to the intensely public-spirited community of middle-class yeomanry and manufacturers of Bassenthwaite parish, though it had brought a wry smile to the dour men of the fells who, calling no man master, spoke as they pleased and allowed others to do the same.

She was about a mile out of Penrith on the road to Keldhead when he caught up with her, striding gracefully along beside the grass verge, her skirts swinging, her head high, her long back straight and supple, the child almost running beside her. It was just gone two o'clock by then, November, and already the short winter's day was beginning to lose its light. It would be dark within the hour and the road was not lit as those in Penrith were. So where were this young woman and her child headed? He was amazed that they had got as far as they had since last he had seen them in the station yard, particularly the child who could not have been more than three or four years old.

She did not look round as his mare approached at her back. The road was completely deserted since the folk in these parts had more sense than to tramp about, unless it was absolutely necessary, especially on a raw winter's afternoon as nightfall approached. The high banks on either side of the road topped by drystone walls were dank and squelchy with dormant winter vegetation and the remains of last year's leaves. The trees arching darkly across the road were grim and bare against the pale, rain-washed sky and the low sun was no more than a veiled yellow ball setting directly ahead of them. Clouds were moving over the fells from the west and the skies would soon be 'kessened out' as his mother used to say and if he was not mistaken, and as a countryman he seldom was, though it was unusual at this time of the year, it could herald snow. And here was this young woman stepping out with her child as though she, and it, were off on a summer Sunday afternoon stroll, the large wicker basket she carried – her only baggage – holding a picnic perhaps, which they would eat at the end of it! It was none of his business, of course, but could he call himself . . . well, a public-spirited gentleman, which he considered himself to be, if he did not enquire of her intent and destination? She might be a stranger with no knowledge of the district, which was bleak and inhospitable to say the least, or of her own danger in it. The weather could change from minute to minute and though it was clear and fine now within the half-hour she could be striding into the teeth of a howling blizzard. And not only that, there were pedlars and vagrants about, out-of-work colliers and weavers, desperate men who would throw her over the wall and have not only her purse, but her, before she could lift her voice in a shout for help which would, in any case, go unheeded and unheeded.

"I beg your pardon," he said pleasantly, raising his hat as his mare drew abreast of her, for lady or serving wench he was invariably charming to the female sex, which perhaps accounted for his popularity with them.

He was considerably taken aback by his own reaction to her as she turned to stare haughtily up at him. He might have been some common fellow who had insulted her, he had time to think, before his breath caught in his throat and he felt the need to swallow convulsively. She was, without doubt, one of the most extraordinarily lovely women he had ever seen. This was the first time he had actually seen her face, hidden as it had been by the deep brim of her bonnet. Some women are beautiful, as a jewel is beautiful so that a man feels the need to look and look again, to touch, to possess. Others are pretty, as children are pretty, innocent and empty of face since they have experienced nothing, but this woman was lovely, soft and eternally female and yet with an honesty, a humour, a warmth, a strength, a young vitality about her which was, contrarily, mature as though she had known and survived hardships not suffered by many. A woman, and yet still a girl for despite her self-sufficiency, her air of being complete, her hauteur, she could have been no more than eighteen or nineteen.

"Yes?" That was all, asking him to state his business

and be off since what was he to do with them though he noticed she drew the child protectively closer to her skirts.

"I apologise if I startled you," he began, still somewhat taken aback. He frowned, amazed at his own callow need to stare for he had known many lovely women in his thirty years. None like this though, his male senses were whispering and it was true. She had turned away, continuing to stride on, the child trotting beside her as neat and fleet of foot as she, treating him as though he was a beggar who had asked her for a farthing which she was not prepared to give.

He felt the first stirring of anger and his frown deepened. Damn the woman! Let her go her own way. Let her fall by the wayside, be buried in snowdrifts, blunder about in the rolling mists which could come down at a frightening pace; be attacked by tinkers, her skirt thrown over her head to muffle her cries. What was it to him? He had meant to do no more than guide her to the nearest hamlet, perhaps, or advise her to make haste before the storm which was surely coming, devoured her and her child but if she was to take this high-handed tone with him and she no more than a farm girl or maidservant by the look of her, then she could go to the devil and take the child with her.

It was perhaps the child who restrained him and kept at bay the hot flow of temper which was very likely to take him over since from an early age he had felt no need to bridle it.

"Madam, I do not wish to impede you in any way but being familiar with these parts and accustomed to the menace of the changes in the weather, I cannot just ride on and leave you. The nearest village is over two miles away and the landscape is wild . . ."

"Thank you, but we'll be all right." She did not turn her head when she spoke to him and he felt the most foolish urge to make her do so. While there was still light enough in the sky he wanted to look at her again, to study her face, her mouth, the sweetly curving short upper lip, the full lower lip, the square little jaw, and were her eyes brown or hazel? And her hair which was completely covered by the rather ugly bonnet, was it the same bright copper as the child's? God's teeth, what was wrong with him?

He could feel his temper begin to flare even more and a slight wash of colour flowed beneath his smoothly shaved skin. He was not used to being spoken to as though he was some impertinent hobbledehoy she had come across and whom she was summarily dismissing for his audacity in addressing her. He was one of the wealthiest sheep farmers in the district with interests in coal and copper mining; in the newly expanding railways; in the manufacture of woollen goods and other lucrative business concerns in which he had become involved since his father had died. He had a fine, old, recently extended, recently modernised farmhouse set at the foot of Little Calva up and beyond Dash Falls, with gardens about it to display to those who were impressed by such things that he could afford to waste some of his land on frivolities like flower beds and lawns and even a rose arbour. His family had lived at Long Beck since the days before the reign of James I, and the union of England and Scotland. His forefathers had gained privileges, mostly of land, when they had answered the call to arms to defend the borders between the two countries and when the need no longer existed they had clung to their heritage and were allowed to retain their rights. 'Estatesmen' or 'Statemen', they were called, yeoman farmers who emerged as the most powerful social group in Cumberland, and he would not be spoken to by this country girl, for she was no more than that in her clogs and shawl, without proper respect.

"Madam," he remarked coolly, "I wish to do no more than show disquiet for your safety and that of the child but I can see I should not have concerned myself. I will bid you good afternoon."

Raising his hat once more he prepared to move on but suddenly she turned and smiled at him. Not a smile of politeness as one would show a stranger but one of genuine amusement.

"And what danger could I be in along this deserted road, Reed Macauley, tell me that? I've walked on roads such as this a hundred times, aye, and later in the day and come to no harm. Anyway you want to watch that animal of yours. She looks dangerous to me."

She grinned, showing excellent teeth and he had time to notice in the fading afternoon light that her eyes were the colour and had the glowing depths of the topaz his mother had worn on a silver chain about her neck. Transparent and luminous with a strange, almost yellow light in them. They were surrounded by thick brown lashes nearly an inch long which were tipped for half their length with gold.

His mare was beginning to dance sideways, irritated by this unprecedented stop when all she wanted was to wildly gallop her unexerted legs along the road and across the fells to her own stable. Reed spoke sharply to her, holding her tight in by the reins and when he had her under control the woman, without for a moment slowing her pace, had gone on another thirty yards. Swearing under his breath and angry with his own foolish need to find out more about this impudent female who obviously knew him, he jumped lightly to the ground and leading the restive mare, hurried after her.

"You know me?" he questioned as he caught up with her.

"Oh aye. Who doesn't in these parts?"

"You have the advantage of me then," for if he had met her before he certainly would have remembered her.

"Is that so?" and her stride seemed to lengthen so that the child was forced to break into a run to keep up with her.

He frowned. He was not a lover of children since he knew none to love. Though his mother had come from a large family residing in Maryport, and he had many cousins on her side, he himself had been an only child, the last his mother bore, those before him lying in the family plot in the churchyard of St Bridget's by Bassenthwaite Lake. Nevertheless, despite knowing nothing of children it seemed to him that the little girl was being pressed beyond her age and endurance. She made no complaint, merely increasing her speed when the woman did, her small feet almost a blur beneath the dark hem of her rough skirt. Again it was none of his business but still he turned his attention once more to the woman, surprising himself with his own words.

"Perhaps you could slow your step somewhat. That child should surely not be forced to walk so quickly. She can barely keep up with you."

"She's used to it and if she wasn't she'd soon have to learn. I had to."

"Who are you, for God's sake? Can you not even tell me your name since you seem to know mine?"

"Why? You and I won't be moving in the same circles, Reed Macauley. We didn't in the past and I can see no reason why we should in the future." She tossed her bonneted head and a stray curl escaped at the nape of her exposed white neck, the last rays of the weak sun setting it alight with bright copper tints. It was the same colour as the child's.

"Is she yours?" His voice was brusque and she turned to look at him. There was no animosity in her glance, only a cool indifference and once more he felt that disconcerting flush of warm blood run in his veins accompanied by the menace of his own quick temper.

"Yes." Again the proud lift of her head, the indignant flush of rose at her cheek-bone informing him that it was really none of his concern, but for some curious reason he could not let it go.

"And your . . . husband?"

"Aah . . . !" Her breath drifted from between her parted lips and hung in the cold air like smoke before disappearing.

"Does that mean you have none?"

"It does."

The leap of gladness in him was apparent only to himself. "Dead?"

She came to an angry stop in the middle of the road and the child stopped with her, patiently waiting for whatever was to happen next. She showed no strain except in the heaving of her narrow chest which rose and fell rapidly, due no doubt to the pace she had been forced to keep.

The woman spoke coldly. "I cannot imagine why you think you have the right to question me, Reed Macauley, nor to form judgements on . . . my behaviour which it seems to me is none of your business. I am not interfering with you in any way, nor impeding your progress. I would be obliged if you would do the same for me."

He studied her vivid face with increasing interest, wondering for the tenth time in as many minutes who the devil she was. She was dressed poorly. Clean and neat and the obvious tears in her and the child's clothing had been decently mended but the material of her skirt was rough and drab, her bonnet was old and of a style fashionable ten years ago. Her shawl, which was thin and shabby, was faded from much washing and on her feet, and on the child's, were worn, wooden-soled clogs. Had it not been for her exceptional beauty and easy, upright carriage which thrust forward the soft swell of her full breast, no man would have given her a second glance.

And where the devil had she learned to speak so well? There was a clicking vestige of the glottal Cumberland dialect in her voice but it was clear, modulated and articulate. She was no lady but her manner of speaking seemed to indicate that she did not come from the lower classes either.

"Believe me, madam." His own voice was cool and stilted. "I do not presume to judge you." For a moment he was tempted to grin since he was the last person in the world to condemn another's morals but his irritability with this stubborn female, and with his own strange reluctance to leave her here where there was so much to harm her, sent his amusement spinning away. "How could I? I do not know you."

"Precisely, so perhaps it would be as well if you got on that beast of yours since she seems likely to trample us all if you don't, and went on your way. My daughter and I are perfectly well able to look after ourselves."

"I doubt it."

"Well, that remains to be seen."

"Where are you heading?" As he spoke he glanced up at the low grey clouds which were beginning to tumble away to the west over the high peak of Blencathra and the wild fells of Skiddaw Forest. Coming out of Penrith as they had done they were still in the Vale of Eden but up ahead were vistas of wild and rugged splendour, of range after range of mountains, of cascading cataracts and deep, dark-eyed tarns, of wooded dales and windswept moors, of nature's raw and unremitting challenge. Even so, it seemed this woman meant to challenge it with as little concern as though she was to take a walk along the path of his dead mother's rose garden.

"Gillthrop," she answered casually.

"Gillthrop!" He was appalled. "But that's nearly twenty miles. You cannot possibly make that by nightfall."

"I'm aware of that and I don't intend to try." She had begun to stride on as though she hadn't a moment to spare, especially to stand gossiping with the likes of him and again the whip of anger moved in him. His eyes snapped the brilliant blue his mother would have recognised and his voice was steely.

"Are you quite out of your mind?"

"Really, can it be anything to do with you if I was?" She relented a little. "Anyway, Cat and I will find shelter in a barn at Penruddock or some farm along the way. I have money to buy food." She raised her head even higher to indicate that she begged charity from no one, evidently finding great satisfaction in the statement. "We'll start afresh in the morning."

"Even so, it's a long walk for a child."

"She's strong, aren't you, my lamb?" Her eyes were

warm and glowing for a moment as she looked down into those of the child and he noticed with a part of his mind which was not seething with frustration over this bloody woman's stubbornness that they were exactly the same colour as her mother's.

"Besides," she went on, "I shall go by the old pack route round the back of Blencathra and across Mungrisdale Common. I shall follow the track from Skiddaw Forest down to Gillthrop. It is but a stone's throw to . . . where I am going. I shall cut the journey by several miles."

"It's extremely wild up there and . . ."

"Yes, yes, I know, very dangerous. You have told me so before and I cannot help but wonder, Reed Macauley, why you're taking such an unusual interest in me and my child. We are nought to you."

"True, and I can assure you that my concern is no more than any decent man would show for the safety of a lone, defenceless woman and child," but he knew as he spoke the stiff and rather pompous words that it was not true.

"There is no need."

"So you keep telling me."

"Then why don't you ride on?"

"God's teeth, woman, I've a good mind to and leave the pair of you to your own devices. If it were not for the child . . ."

"Why should you bother about her? You and your sort are not in the habit of concerning yourselves with me and mine."

"My sort . . . ?"

"Aye. My mother worked for yours years ago and though she was not deliberately cruel she did not concern herself overmuch with my mother's feelings. And she got her money's worth, and more, from my mother's labours. From dawn to dusk and later she worked in your mother's dairy and kitchen at Long Beck and when she stopped for no more than a minute to rest, being old even then, your mother gave her a right clip round t' lug. Heavy-handed she was . . ."

"You don't have to tell me, madam. I felt it myself a time

or two," and he could not help but smile at the memory as he rubbed his ear.

"'Tis no laughing matter, Reed Macauley. 'Tis one thing to clout a growing boy especially if he's your son and no doubt deserved it but to lift your hand to another woman is not to be tolerated. I'd not have tolerated it . . ."

"No, I can see that."

"And so I'll thank you to get on your way and leave me to get on mine."

"And where is that to be? Does your family live in Gillthrop?"

"Just up along, or at least they did. My mother and father are dead." A spasm of what might have been pain shattered the composure of her face. "I'm going home to . . ."

"Yes?"

She drew a deep breath and in the last fading haze of daylight which was almost gone he saw the flash of bright anger in her eyes and the deep rose of it stain her creamy skin.

"'Tis nowt ter do wi' yoo, Reed Macauley." The dialect of her childhood returned to her tongue in her fury, "so climb up on tha' mare an' get thi' gone. Me an' Cat've walked best part o't'way from Leicestershire ower past few weeks an' we'm still alive an' lively an' all, so don't thi' go tellin' me we need tha' protection."

"Damnation . . ."

"Don't you damnation with me . . ."

"Christ Almighty, could any man do *anything* with you, woman? I've yet to meet a more obstinate, self-willed . . ."

". . . and I a more persistent nuisance . . ."

In his rage which the animal sensed, it took him a good three or four minutes of mad circling to quieten the mare long enough to mount her, and when he had done so the woman was almost out of sight along the dusky road. He put his heels to the animal's side, driving her at once into a wild gallop, her hooves thundering on the road. The woman did not even look round.

He did not know why he said it and she did not know why she answered for they were both in a surprising state of wild anger.

"You never told me your name," he shouted over his shoulder.

"Annie Abbott, not that it's anything to do with you."

5

She and Cat spent the night in a barn, wrapped about in hay and the old blanket the brusque farmer's wife, taking pity on them since the night was cold, had lent them. In the morning she had sold Annie some bread and cheese and, at the last minute, given them both a long draught of warm cow's milk to sustain them. It was almost noon and she was half-way across Mungrisdale Common when she thought about Reed Macauley again. She had known him at once, of course, though he had not recognised her. She had been no more than a child of eleven or twelve and he a grown man of twenty-two or so during that dreadful winter when, besides the work she did at home in her own kitchen, Lizzie Abbott had been forced to labour in that of Mrs Macauley. It had been either that or starve for Joshua Abbott's flock had perished in the scourge of murrain which had attacked his sheep. His crops of oats and barley had failed and they had lived for nearly a month on turnip bread.

Mungrisdale Common was high, over two thousand feet above sea level and the short November day had not improved on the previous one. In the summer the walk from where she had left the road was pleasant and easy, crossing the Glenderamackin River, coming through the bracken of Mousethwaite Combe, going up and up until she and Cat were looking across the rolling upland summit. Bent tufts of cotton grass inhabited in the summer by sheep, and at this time of the year by only the occasional wandering herd of wild fell ponies. She did not know it as well as the fells at the back of her own home, the remote and lonely High Pike, Knott, and the affable and friendly giant of Skiddaw, but the pack routes were clearly marked, for it was not long since they had been used by the men who had walked these mountains. Monks going from grange to grange, drovers plodding behind herds and flocks on their way to market or new grazing. Men with ponies carrying goods to outlying farms and hamlets. They said that if you listened carefully you could still hear the tinkle of the bells which warned of the approach of the pack trains. They had carried salt and wool, hides and charcoal, coal, lead, silver and iron, moving along the complex network of narrow green tracks which lay on the lower slopes or ran between the dales like the veins on a leaf.

But today was not summer and though she knew Cat was almost at the end of her child's endeavour they dare not stop to rest. It was too cold for sitting about. To the right and behind them were the rough crags of Bannerdale and ahead was the climb to the summit of the common but here was peace and tranquillity. The ground, though boggy since it was a watershed and covered by tussocky grass, made for easy walking.

"Come sweetheart, mother will carry you," Annie said to the silent child who was beginning to look strangely pale about the mouth. "Eat this, my lambkin," she added, as she picked her up, thrusting a thick piece of bread and cheese into the little girl's hand, the last of their food. "It will make you feel better."

The child did as she was told, then immediately fell asleep, her head lolling on Annie's shoulder, her white face gaining a little colour as she slept.

Annie strode on, her skirts swinging about her ankles, not at all weighted down by the basket in which everything she and her daughter possessed was carried, nor by the small girl who slept in her arms. Her bonnet had fallen to the small of her back, bouncing as she walked, and her clogged feet made a strange sucking sound each time she lifted them from the squelchy ground but she did not falter.

It was dark and beginning to drizzle when she reached the end of the pack route which ran beside Dale Beck and led down to the farm gate of Browhead Farm. Pitch black dark and had she not known every step of the way, every blade of grass, every rough and broken stone she would have lost herself and Cat a dozen times. She was no longer striding for she had been walking for nearly twelve hours this day and the wicker basket had become heavier with every long, cold mile, as had the child and now, just as she really could go no further, she was home. She was here to claim her inheritance. Browhead.

Her strong, working fingers, on which there was no wedding ring, searched for the enormous iron key where it was always hidden, where the lawyer in Lancaster had told her it would be and for the first time in four years Annie Abbott bent her head and stepped over the threshwood of the farmhouse from which her father had despatched her.

She and her child were asleep in his bed five minutes after she had locked the door behind them.

She awoke to greyness, greyness and a chill so riveting she huddled up against Cat who was still asleep. They were both deep in the – she realised it now, *damp* – feather mattress, only the tips of their noses exposed to the biting cold and they were still fully dressed except for their clogs which she remembered had clattered to the bedroom floor as she and Cat fell into bed. It was the last thing she remembered.

The pale morning light, dim and hazed as it did its best to gain entrance through the small and filthy oak-mullioned windows of her parents' bedroom, revealed the shadowed shapes on the wall of the samplers she and her mother had worked – when had they had the time, she wondered idly? – all four of them beautifully framed by her father.

'Glory be to God' one said and beneath it, 'Elizabeth Bowman is my name' and the year 1810. Another had every letter of the alphabet stitched on it, her own name and the date 1840. The third and fourth, though she could not see the words in the poor light, were embroidered with lines from the twenty-third psalm and the Lord's Prayer. The samplers were worked on plain white linen with hundreds and hundreds of tiny cross stitches in bright thread and she could quite clearly remember how her eyes had ached as she stitched diligently in the light from the rush lamp. To this day she could sew a fine seam and given the materials could have made garments of a good quality and style for herself and Cat.

The carved oak press which her mother had brought from Cockermouth as a bride and in which she kept her clothing stood against the whitewashed wall and still hanging on plain wooden pegs fixed beside the window were a jacket of her father's and her mother's hodden-grey winter cloak. On one side of the bed was a small, gate-legged table, again part of her mother's dower and on it stood a plain earthenware ewer and basin. The floor was bare, the wood of it once so highly polished you could see your face in it. She herself had had the polishing of it.

She wondered what time it was. Well into the morning by the look of the light. She must have slept for over twelve hours but was it to be wondered at, the walking she and Cat had done in the past four weeks? Whenever they could which meant when the distance they must travel was too great for the child to walk – and she could afford the fare, she and Cat had taken the railway train but they must have tramped well over a hundred and fifty miles on their journey from Market Harborough to Lancaster.

And now, here she was, lying in the bed her mother and father had shared for over twenty years and where they had both died within a few days of one another from a virulent fever of the lungs. The lawyer in Lancaster had been none too sure of the details and none too concerned with them either. His duty was done when he handed over to Joshua Abbott's legal heir, this amazingly lovely young woman who stood before him with no sign of nervousness, the deeds to Browhead Farm.

There was no money, unfortunately, the lawyer told her, and, not that he was aware, any livestock, and with his words ringing in her ears, those which told her that in his opinion she would be wise to sell, she had boarded the

Lancaster-to-Carlisle train using the money he had given her to purchase a ticket, getting off at Penrith, and here she was.

Lord, but it was cold and it would not get any warmer lying here next to Cat, tempting though the idea was. A fire first on the hearth of the deep inglenook, that's if there was anything to make it with. Peat was what they had burned four years ago, dug by herself and her mother, and she hoped anxiously that there would be a supply in the barn cut by Lizzie before she died a year last October, ready for the winter ahead. The fire had never, winter or summer, been allowed to go out. Well, it was out now and there was only one person to get it going again.

The floor was so cold it hurt her bare feet and she flinched, drawing in her breath sharply. Tucking the heavy, hand-made quilt more cosily about her daughter who had not yet stirred, she did a hasty little dash across the floor, reaching for the cloak her mother had once worn. She threw it about her shoulders, hunching it more closely to her and from its heavy folds came the smells which had always lingered about her mother and which brought back sharply the patient, pale-faced, anxiously kindly woman who had done her best, Annie could see it now, to take some of the overwhelming load which her father had heaped on her own young shoulders.

"See, let me do that, sweetheart." Annie could still hear the words her mother spoke when Joshua had stumped out of the house. "'Tis more than you can manage, so off you go and play with Sally an' Mim for half an hour. But no more, mind . . ." for if he came back and found his daughter off on some frivolous tack it would be woe betide the pair of them.

Annie lifted the durable wool to her nose and sniffed the mixture of herbs, the smell of hay and buttermilk, fresh bread and clean linen flapping in the wind, of lavender and linseed and all the dozens of aromas linked to the tasks with which her mother had occupied her days and though she had barely – to her shame – given her a thought in the past four years since she had been too busy thinking of her own and Cat's survival, she thought of Lizzie now and wanted to weep.

But there was no time. Not even now. She would weep later when the fire was going and the kitchen was warm enough to fetch Cat down, when there was something cooking in the pot hanging from the randle tree across the fire, even if it was only some 'poddish' for surely there would still be some oats in her mother's oak kist?

Picking up her clogs and taking one last look at Cat she moved down the tight winding staircase to what was known as the 'fire-house' – since this was where the only fire was, a kitchen and living room simply called the 'house'.

The most important feature of any farmhouse is the fireplace for it is around this that the social functions of the farm take place. The hearth of the fireplace occupies most of the stone wall in which it is set, an enormous inglenook above which the chimney hood rises and beneath which, it being the warmest place in the house, the family gather. All cooking and baking is done on the fire or on the 'bakstone' which was built above it, the area to the side illuminated by a small oak-mullioned 'fire-window'. Two more windows were set across the front of the kitchen and in between was the door to what Lizzie had hopefully called the garden.

Annie stood on the bottom step of the staircase and gazed about her. Opposite the fire-window at right angles to the inglenook was a stone partition called the 'heck' and this shielded the inglenook and anyone sitting in it from the draughts which can come, and usually did, through the door which led out into the yard at the side of the farmhouse. Along the heck side of the fireplace was the 'sconce', a fixed wooden bench under which the kindling for the morning's fire was stored and on the opposite side of the fire was a long, elaborately carved settle. To the side of the fire at eye level and set in the wall so that the warmth of the fire kept it dry was a cupboard in which spices and salt were stored. The door of this cupboard was carved with the initials of some long-dead Abbott. FA, it said and was dated 1701.

Nothing had changed. Nothing.

The floor of the kitchen was flagged with slate slabs. Opposite the hearth was placed Lizzie's oak bread cupboard where she had stored the Haver bread she baked. It was carved with the initials of Lizzie's grand-mother who had bequeathed it to her, AB for Annabelle Bowman and the date, 1736. There were two carved oak chairs, similarly decorated and an oak table so big it had obviously been built within the house.

On the hearth was a poker, a copper kettle, a box smoothing iron and iron fire dogs to prevent the fire from falling out and to support the poker and tongs. There was a cooking spit and a dripping pan, toast dogs on an iron tripod with spikes to hold the bread which was to be toasted, an iron frying-pan, a cast-iron kail pot with a lid for boiling meat and all looking exactly as though Lizzie Abbott had put them there before she went to bed in readiness for the next day's work.

Which she probably had, her daughter thought as she stepped slowly down from the stair into the kitchen. She had gone to her bed, probably coughing and feverish with the inflammation of the chest which was, though she had not known it, to kill her. Had anyone nursed her? Or her father? Who had died first? Questions which would be answered soon when she could get out to Upfell, the Mounsey farm, but first she must make the place warm, get some food from somewhere to put inside herself and her child. The room was filthy and draped about it, from the heavy beams, from chair to table, from hearth to heck, were cobwebs, for it was over a year since the farm had been occupied. Every object, every surface, the floor, the table, the low window-sills were thick with dust and the valley's 'bottom wind' had blown a drift of soot down the chimney which had settled wherever the draught, always present, had placed it. It was barely light though her country senses told her that it must be almost midday and when she moved to the window to peer through the veil of dirt which curtained it, a mantle of fine rain moved across her vision screening the fields and even the lake which lay in the front of the farmhouse. She could see nothing beyond the blurred outline of the gigantic hawthorn tree which stood at the right-hand corner of the farmhouse.

She remained at the window for a while and the presence of her mother crept about her again, touching her with that almost shy affection which was all she had ever shown her daughter. Defensive somehow, as though she had expected a rebuff or perhaps her husband's irritation which could not do with any show of what he would have thought of as weakness. What a sad, drab life she had led, her daughter reflected, doing her husband's bidding, working every hour of daylight and then beyond into the dark night with no thought of her own needs, or even if she had the right to any, or her own satisfaction. With no hope of reward, not even that of affection nor gratitude from the man she had married. Her home had been her life. Keeping it neat and clean and the best she could make it and she would turn over in her grave if she could see it now, Annie thought sadly.

Her clear, brown eyes became clouded as she looked back sadly at the hard and empty life her mother had led. And yet had her mother ever done anything to attempt to better it? Had she, in the beginning, when she was young and strong and pretty, perhaps able to cajole a kiss and a smile from her young husband, determined on a place for herself, one of importance in her husband's life, not that of a drudge but as an equal in the equally divided labour they shared? Had she made an effort to achieve for Lizzie Abbott and the family which she presumably hoped to have, some grasp of independence, some comfort, an identity which was hers, a knowledge of who Lizzie Abbott was, not Joshua Abbott's wife, but herself, or had life and Joshua Abbott trodden her down to the browbeaten woman Annie herself had known? Had she done her best to force her will on the harsh reality a daleswoman was destined to know, to twist it until it gave her some measure of peace, content, hope, joy? Perhaps she herself was being unfair. Perhaps there was no way a woman such as her mother could ever gain what surely was due every human being, in some quantity and which Annie Abbott meant to have. Oh yes, make no mistake about it. She had been given this farm, this chance, and she would have all the things her mother had been deprived of. *She* would have these things. She was not awfully sure what these things were but if hard work, tenacity, a resolute will, a powerful determination and a knowledge of her own individuality, her own uniqueness was a gauge to reckon by, then she would succeed. She would not be another Lizzie Abbott. She would not depend on, nor answer to, any man, as her mother had, as she herself had been forced to do when she had run off with Anthony Graham. She would get there by herself. Again she was not awfully certain where *there* was, or how long it would take but she'd reach it somehow. On her own it would be difficult. It would be doubly so with Cat. A child born out of wedlock. A woman with no man's protection. She would be hard-pressed to find a friendly smile, particularly among these taciturn, independent, moral men and women of the dales and fells of Lakeland, not one of whom would give her the time of day when they saw what she had brought back with her from the outside world.

But she had this farm, this land. She had no money, no livestock, nothing but the coppice wood standing beyond the field at the back of the house, but in which surely, with the knowledge her father had ground into her as soon as she could toddle, just as he would a son, she could make a living, something on which to feed her and Cat until she got on her feet? She would dig and plant and sow, weed and hoe and grasp sustenance from the earth as the Abbotts had always done. She would take one day at a time until the winter was over, find work, perhaps, in some other woman's kitchen as her mother had done in hard times. Anything to earn and save some money so that when spring came . . .

Spring! Dear God, here she was, her blood thinning in

her veins, her breath ready to freeze in the air about her, her bare feet shuddering on the icy slate floor, no fire, no food, day-dreaming about spring when the harsh Lakeland winter was still to be got through. She should be looking for kindling to light the fire, for the oats to make clapbread to put in her child's mouth. Oh, please, God . . . just this once . . . Dear God . . . look kindly on me . . . Let there be peat . . . and oats in the kist . . .

It was there, just where her mother had placed it before she went up the stairs to her death. The kindling beneath the sconce, plenty of it, enough to start a fire and out in the barn would be the stacked, dried peat, the tree roots and ash tops her mother would have gathered to put on the slow burning fire. On the little shelf above the fireplace was the flint and striker and next to it in the 'candle-bark' in which they were kept were the rushlights her mother had made during the long winter evenings. When she had 'nothing else to do' since to drag her weary body to bed before she had the permission of her husband would have been unthinkable.

The soot proved tricky. No matter how she brushed it, swept it, wiped it away, it lifted in a drifting cloud to settle on her hair and clothing, getting in her ears and every fold of her fine flesh. It was on her face and hands, she could taste it; she breathed it in with every breath and it made her cough and sneeze, but nevertheless within half an hour she had the beginnings of a fire and a pan of water, fetched hurriedly from the spring beside the house, bubbling gently over it, waiting for something to put in it. But what? The oats in her mother's kist had gone mouldy, she discovered, and were uneatable and besides the salt and the spices there was nothing in the house. No pickled meats in the brine vats, no salted pork. Cat was still sleeping, her face a grey smudge on her grandmother's white pillow, and Annie's only hope was that there might be a carrot or a potato, or a turnip to make turnip bread still left in her mother's vegetable garden. Obviously whoever had locked up the farm for the lawyers had removed all the edible food when they left, the smoked ham and mutton which usually hung under the chimney canopy. If there had been any!

She was just swinging the cloak about her shoulders, ready to brave the elements and see what could be found in the vegetable garden when some fist hammered lustily on the front door.

6

"Dear God in Heaven, what have you been up to? You look like some climbing chimney boy," were his first words and her amazement turned at once to irritation and, surprisingly, momentarily to a deep mortification that he should find her in such a sorry state.

"What do you want, Reed Macauley?"

"Well, first of all I would be obliged if you would stop calling me by my full name. Reed will do, or Mr Macauley. Whichever you feel the most comfortable with. On second thoughts, though, perhaps the latter might be more appropriate since we are barely acquainted." There was a wry gleam in his blue eyes. "And I can't say I care much for your attitude, Annie Abbott . . . there you have me doing it now. I merely happened to be passing on my way to the blacksmith in Hause. Victoria has . . ."

"Victoria?"

"My mare."

"Good God! What a name for a horse."

"So people keep telling me. Or at least they do until I prove to them, usually with my fists, that the name is perfectly proper since I meant it as a respectful gesture to Her Majesty in the year of her coronation, which is when my father gave her to me. Though, to be honest . . ." He grinned and she could feel her own mouth tug, ". . . my sense of humour does not appeal to everyone."

"No, I can see that it wouldn't. Now, if you don't mind I have a lot to do . . ." treating him as though he was an unexpected and unwelcome caller who hoped to take tea with her, he thought irritably, though this time he kept his quick temper in check.

"Yes, I can imagine," he managed to say mildly enough. "A bath would be the first task, I should . . ."

"Mr Macauley, since you prefer to be called that, I have only just this minute got a fire going. My child is . . ."

"Ah, yes, the child. It did occur to me that, being a somewhat . . . er . . . unconventional mother you might not have considered the state in which you would find Browhead, your parents being . . . gone, and the house untenanted as it has been for over a year. I realise it will seriously insult you . . ." again the wry gleam, ". . . being as independent as you are, but . . . yes, yes, it is none of my business you are going to say, I can see it in your expression, but I was presumptuous enough to enquire into your circumstances and as I was on my way down here anyway, I brought something over. It was my cook, you see, a good-hearted woman, so she put one or two things together and I promised her I would bring them over."

Nothing to do with him, of course, he would have her believe. Left to him she and her child could starve to death, or share a bed in the workhouse.

"Not much . . ." he continued airily, ". . . but if you . . . well, the child is bound to be hungry, or so my cook tells me, so, I will be on my way if you have nothing more to say. I am getting confoundedly wet dithering about here on your doorstep."

"Nothing more to say?" she repeated somewhat foolishly.

"Miss Abbott, you strike me as being a woman who always has something to say, more than likely on subjects which don't concern you. I am merely being polite so do not put on that aggrieved air with me and if I were you I should take this basket . . ."

"I want none of your charity, Mr Macauley." She lifted her defiant head and though the soot lay in a fine cloud about it, it in no way detracted from the beauty of her hair. Since her mother had cut it many years ago no scissors had been put near it and it tumbled in a great profusion of rich copper, the curls, so tight he wondered how she got a he said, smiling his wicked 'outlaw's' smile. His voice was soft, deep and completely irresistible and his chocolate-brown eyes gazed into Annie's. He took her hand and raised it to his lips and the girls, all three, stared at him, hypnotised by his beauty and his charm, like three little rabbits which have suddenly come across an extremely handsome fox.

"I saw you from the stage," he went on, "and could not resist coming down to greet you. I could tell you were enjoying my poor performance and . . . well . . .", his smile deepening to reveal two engaging clefts – in a woman they would have been dimples – at each side of his mouth. "I could never withstand a pretty woman and when there are three of them it seems the challenge is tripled."

The word 'pretty' would have been enough but to be called a 'woman' when one is only fourteen was heady stuff and Sally and Mim began to preen. In sharp contrast Annie's face appeared to pale. She became still and hushed as though in the presence of some being who is truly from another world, a world in which gods lived, for surely this could only be one of those. Her hand had remained in his and her eyes, enormous, clear and incredibly lovely as she fell headlong into the pit of love for the first time, did not even blink. He kissed her fingers again and she could feel his lips burn her flesh and beneath the bodice of her mother's wedding-gown something quivered. It was the most delightful feeling but at the same time it hurt her. She felt a great need to put up her hand and draw this man to . . . to . . . She was not sure what it was she wanted, or what to do about it since, apart from her father, when she was a child, she had been touched by no man.

"The music has begun. Will you not dance?" he asked her softly. Her heart knocked frantically and her mouth was so dry she could not have spoken if her life depended on it but her limbs worked independently of her mind as he led her down towards the stage. Her cheeks burned with a bright flame as, with the practised ease of the to be back before her father returned from Middle Fell. Her face worked painfully as she watched the light, dancing feet of her child, almost fifteen, run down the track towards the farm gate where Jem Mounsey and his girls waited for her. She had on the dress Lizzie herself had been married in, carefully stored in lavender in the press in the bedroom, a light shade of tawny brown which, on Annie, as it had not done on Lizzie, looked exactly right. It was too short and a mite too tight across the breasts, causing a pang of misgiving in Lizzie for, with her glorious hair brushed until it stood out from her head and down her back in a brilliant copper cloud, Annie was enough to catch the eye of any man which worried Lizzie even more. But how could she resist that pleading face, those vivid eyes which, after all, were asking for very little? So innocent. A ride into Keswick with a perfectly respectable family to see the players which evidently Jem and Aggie Mounsey thought fitting for their girls to see.

As Annie turned to wave rapturously, Lizzie's eyes looked up towards Middle Fell and she prayed lustily that Joshua would remain there until nightfall.

They stood at the back of the playhouse, Annie and Sally and Mim, their young minds enchanted, their young eyes bright with the joy of it, for they were no more than children and did not see the tawdry costumes, the artificial deportment and speech of the actors, the triviality of the story. They were transported into fairyland, the land of myth and legend and imagination, and with the rest of the unsophisticated audience they cheered and howled, wept and laughed, loving every minute of it. In the first interval between parts, when Annie felt a tap on her arm, she did not at first recognise the young man beneath the appalling stage make-up as the leading male player she had just seen on the stage. He was quite alarming close to with his drawn-on black moustache, his gypsy ear-rings, his boots and his cutlass and for a moment all three girls shrank back.

"Ladies, forgive me. I had not meant to frighten you,"

brush through it, falling down her straight back to her buttocks, wild, thick and springing. As defiant as she was, he thought, marvelling, needing no ribbons or ornaments to enhance its shining loveliness. She pulled her mother's old cloak about her as though it was made of velvet, ermine trimmed, and he felt her courage move him. Her clogs sounded a rebellious clatter on the wooden threshwood as she prepared to close the door but he stood his ground, no sign of the emotion she aroused in him showing in his face, his own proud head somewhat bowed beneath the low door frame. They confronted one another, neither ready to give way.

"And the child?" he asked harshly, angry at something in himself which he did not care to name. A weakness she had awakened in him twice now and which drew down his dark brows in a frown.

She hesitated then for if she was prepared to starve rather than accept Reed Macauley's largesse could she condemn Cat to the same fate? Neither of them had eaten a really decent meal for weeks ever since she had left the bar-parlour of The Plough in Market Harborough. Bread and cheese mostly, which was cheap and filling, a hot potato from a stall, milk, warm and frothy straight from the cow on the farms they had passed.

"I haven't all day to stand here, Miss Abbott, so if you would allow me to bring in this basket I'll be on my way to the blacksmith." She was startled by the asperity in his voice. As far as she knew she had done nothing to deserve it.

He stood to one side revealing a hamper in the yard behind him, a hamper so large he could scarcely lift it. But lift it he did, humping it past her with little ceremony and placing it carelessly on the haphazardly swept oak table from which a cloud of soot rose once more into the air coming to rest on his snowy white, immaculately ironed white frilled shirt cuffs. He brushed at it fastidiously.

Dear Lord, there must be enough in there to feed her and Cat for a month, she thought exultantly, though not a sign of it showed in her face. He might have emptied a cartload of horse manure on her table, by the expression on her face, though she bowed graciously enough.

"It is most kind of your cook, Mr Macauley. Thank her for me, won't you? Cat will be most obliged."

"And not you, Miss Abbott?" he asked ironically.

"Oh, my mother has . . . had a well-stocked vegetable garden. I dare say we would have managed well enough."

"I dare say you would." Again his voice was filled with irony but he managed to smile in her direction. A smile of genuine humour this time, one that said he knew that had she been hollowed out with hunger and ready to faint with it, but with only herself to consider, she would have twitched her skirt aside, tossed her head and told him to go to the devil.

He tipped his tall hat sardonically in her direction. He looked pointedly at her from head to toe, studying her soot-coated hair and face with especial care then he grinned suddenly, surprisingly and turning on his heel left the house, banging the solid door to behind him.

She let out her breath on a long, wondering sigh, then sank slowly into the carved oak chair in which generations of Abbotts had sat, wearing the seat into a shallow depression. Her mother had rested in it, that is if you could call the constant work her busy fingers had occupied themselves with, resting. The sewing and darning, the knitting and rushlight making, always employed at some task, never simply sitting. Doing nothing. Day-dreaming in a square of the rare sunlight which eased its way through the small windows and into the house.

The idea made her smile sadly, then, turning her mind from the preoccupation with her mother which she had seemed prone to since she returned home, she studied the bounty which had just come her way.

Would you believe it, because she couldn't. Mr High and Mighty Macauley hauling the enormous hamper which loomed over her on the table, all the way down the grassy slope which lay beside Dash Beck from his house up at Long Beck and on that skittish animal she had seen him on yesterday. How on earth had he managed it? she marvelled, but then Reed Macauley, from the little she'd seen of him, would not let a small thing like a frisky mare interfere with what he had in his mind to do. And of course his tale about his cook insisting on 'putting one or two things together' just as though she had the running of his house was just pure nonsense. It was her guess that *he* was the master of his own domain and that on some pretext or other he had ordered his footman or his butler or his housekeeper, or whoever it was wealthy gentlemen of his sort employed to see to their needs, to inform Cook that he needed a good, nourishing hamper of food packed. A hamper fit for the needy and poor of which there were a good many, and to have it at the front door within the hour. That would be more his style. A man such as he would feel no need to explain himself to a servant. Why should he? He paid their wages and they were there merely to obey his orders. She could imagine the consternation in the kitchen when the order came, the conjectures on who it was who would receive the hamper of food and no doubt before the day was out it would be known in every village and hamlet between Hause and Keswick and, innocent as the whole thing was, they would, naturally, put two and two together and make it come out five. Her reputation which was already suspect since she had run away from home four years ago, leaving her poor mother and father broken and bereft, would be in tatters even before the folk in the neighbouring farms and villages had clapped eyes on Cat.

Well, it was no good sitting here sighing on the lack of her reputation since it would be gone soon enough as it was. Never look a gift horse in the mouth had been a favourite maxim of Polly Pearsall, and of hers in the past three years and this one was certainly welcome even if it had offended her to accept it, especially from him, though why she should feel that way was not clear to her. The fire was going nicely for, as she had suspected, there was enough peat and wood in the barn to keep a dozen fires burning. Should she go and awaken Cat before she opened the hamper? Make a celebration of it, for the poor lamb

had had little enough in her young life to celebrate. Or
should she take a peek herself? It might contain tea and
there was nothing she would like more in the world at this
moment than to drink a cup of hot sweet tea, not with
milk, of course, since there was no cow in the byre, but
steaming, fragrant tea, in a dainty bone china cup, just like
a lady. To have for a few minutes the illusion of ease and
plenty, of warmth and leisure, as ladies did, before she
tackled the daunting task of putting the house and her life
in order. Her stomach was rumbling and churning in the
most distracting way and yes . . . she felt curiously light-
headed, but then was it any wonder when she remembered
that it was at least twenty-four hours since she had eaten,
and had taken no more than a handful of icy cold water
from the River Caldew as they crossed it yesterday at
noon.

"Mother?" an anxious voice questioned at the foot of
the stairs. Annie turned, her warm smile ready, her arms
held out and, reassured at once, the child ran into them,
her bare feet making no sound on the slate floor.

"I didn't know where I was, Mother," she said in her
childish and yet dreadfully adult way. Contained, as she
herself was contained and Annie wanted to swing her
round and round, make her squeal with delight and the
simple joyous fun of being three years old. "You weren't
there and I didn't know where I was," she went on
solemnly.

There had been so many times in her life when Catriona
Abbott had not known where she was. When she had
awakened in a strange bed, a room she had never seen
before, a view from a window she did not recognise.
Many's the time she had gone to sleep in one place and
woken up in another, her infant days and nights spent
moving along the path on to which her mother's own youthful and innocent indiscretion had forced her. Rooms in
which the only furniture had been a frowsy blanket, a chair
and a bucket. Sometimes in a cellar with others who could
afford no more than a few feet of straw-littered earthen
floor on which to rest. Several times, when her mother had

appeared to be well settled in some low, smoke-blackened, ancient bar-parlour, they had occupied a snug room together, alone and sheltered and allowing themselves – at least Annie did – to think that they had at last found a safe haven, but it had never lasted.

So off they would go again, the regretful words of the landlord, or more likely his wife, ringing in their ears but wherever they went, wherever they 'ended up', never, not once, had Cat Abbott failed to find her mother beside her in the bed they shared. Though she had not known where she was, she had always known who would be beside her.

"We're home, lambkin, that's where we are, and if there is in this basket what I think there is then you and I are going to have our first meal in our own home beside our own fire. What do you think of that, my little love?"

The child looked into her mother's face, her own still serious, then, with a smile brightening across it like the sun shining on the still waters of the lake which she had not yet seen and which lay beyond the door, she turned in her mother's arms, perhaps for the first time in her life with the spontaneous and natural excitement of a child towards the hamper.

"Can we open it, mother, can we?"

They had eaten their fill of the 'one or two things' Reed Macauley's cook had 'put together' for them. Even as she unpacked them, passing each napkin-wrapped packet to the entranced child, the hand of the man who had given it to her was very obvious in the choice of much of the food. A dish of apricot soufflé, evidently meant for dinner guests expected that night and which Reed Macauley's cook would have to re-make. Roast duck, glazed and decorated with slices of orange; an enormous concoction of meringue and chocolate, rich with cream, the sight of which widened Cat's eyes to the size of saucers. Annie could just imagine him stalking through the kitchen where, in all probability, he never set foot from one year's end to the next since what was that part of his house to do with him, as long as it provided him with superbly cooked and imaginatively

planned meals whenever he required them? What would
he care how they came about? 'Send this and this' he would
have said to the flustered and indignant cook, her feelings
on the matter kept hidden from him naturally, pointing to
the delicacies in her pantry, not concerned with her
opinions, her labour. No matter how unsuitable nor how
difficult to replace, if it took his fancy to send it, send it
he would. And when it was learned where it had all gone,
Annie Abbott would be the talk of the valley which would
do her no good. Make all the more difficult the task she
had set herself when she had learned that she was the
owner of a farm and the land which went with it.

Ah, well, that couldn't be changed now. It was no good
worrying over spilled milk, as Polly used to say, and at
least she and Cat would have full bellies for the next few
weeks. There were other things in the hamper, sensible,
durable things which could be stored away for future use,
flour and salt, tea and sugar, oats for clapbread and hasty
pudding, potatoes, carrots, onions, cabbage, a saddle of
dried lamb to make 'crowdy'. A smoked ham, pies of
minced mutton, eggs, butter, cheese, a quart of fresh
milk, a drop of which went into that first cup of tea, alas
not in a bone china teacup but the pewter mug she and
her family before her had used for generations. There
were jars of pickles and preserves and what was evidently
Reed Macauley's cook's home-made jams.

They were children, both of them, laughing with the
hysterical excitement which can soon turn to tears, the
excitement of those who have been set down in wonder-
land and told to take whatever they fancied of the delights
on display. It took all Annie's good sense and restraint,
and the caution she had learned in the past four years, a
caution which urged her to put something away for that
rainy day which was sure to come, to stop herself and Cat
from eating until they were sick.

"No more now, sweetheart. We must put all these
lovely things away in Grandmother's bread cupboard and
then we shall have something to eat tomorrow, and the
next day. You understand that, don't you?" and the child,

accustomed to frugality and the need to think to the future, even at the age of almost three, nodded her head sagely, helping her mother to place their treasures safely away in Grandmother's bread cupboard whilst Annie explained to her about Grandmother and Grandfather who were in Heaven, wherever that might be.

The rain had stopped and a glint of sunshine pushed through the veil of mist which had shrouded the farmhouse though the fells amongst which it was set were still hidden at their topmost peaks. It was cold, raw, with that November dankness which can insinuate itself through layer after layer of clothing, through the very flesh to the bone and even into the veins, making the blood move sluggishly. There was a great fire roaring up the chimney now but Annie felt the need to get out for half an hour, to stand in her own fields and touch the trunks of her own trees. To look about her at the acres of land which was hers. To simply breathe in the damp air which, because it moved across her farm, her land, belonged solely to Annie Abbott. To drink it in and get tipsy on it since its intoxication would be bound to go straight to her head.

"Come on, lovely, let's wrap up warm and walk down the fields a way. Mother wants to show you your new home."

The child, used to instant obedience, stood up at once and allowed her mother to bundle her in her old worn shawl and put on her rough clogs.

"Wait a minute, sweetheart, let's see if Grandmother has any stockings in her chest," and there they were, just as Lizzie Abbott had left them, newly knitted, some of them, carefully darned those that were older, far too big for the child but pulled up her thighs to her drawers they were warm and sturdy inside her footwear. A pair for Annie, the thick, hodden-grey cloak woven from Joshua Abbott's own Herdwick sheep, no bonnet, either of them, and they were ready to step out, hand in hand on to the roughly cobbled path which led through Lizzie's bit of a garden to the rough track going between two fields to the road gate.

Though the farmhouse was small it was sturdily built
with walls three feet thick and a heavy blue slate roof
which had been fashioned to defy the strong winds and
driving rain, the icy cold and measureless snow which
played a large part in the lives of the farmers of Cumberland. A white, roughcast exterior which was an efficient
method of weatherproofing, two cylindrical chimneys, one
at each end of the building for the kitchen and the parlour,
and small, oak-mullioned windows for the farmers were
more concerned with warmth than with a view. There
were four across the front of the farmhouse at ground
level and two above. The porch, designed to keep out
draughts, was low, and let into the floor was an oak
beam four or five inches high known as the 'threshwood',
securing the walls on either side of the door. Nailed
to the side of the threshwood was a horseshoe, said to
keep out unwelcome spirits, and a withered sprig of rowan,
no doubt placed there by Lizzie Abbott twelve months
ago to bring good luck to the house. Much good it had
done her!

The building was extended to the left beyond the dairy,
by the cow house and stable, above which was a loft. A
long, low farmhouse then, set snugly with its back to the
rising fields and wooded ground of the fell. A quiet and
lovely fold of the hills, remote and separate, protected
from the bleak and often wild conditions which prevailed
in this part of the world. To its back and surrounding
it were the majestic heights of Cockup, Broad End and
Skiddaw. In the summer it was a place of smooth, heathery
uplands and low-lying green pastures, wild roses, rasp-
berries ripe in the hedges, purple vetch, small grey farms.
Quiet woods with trees which cast long shadows across
patches of still sunlight. Paths rough with ling and little
golden brown tufts of wood-rush and the spear-like
hog-rush. Deep peaty dykes filled with water over which
larches hung and where grew thrift, heartsease, sandwort
and scented thyme. The waters of the lake cold as ice and
the hot, bleached stones around it, which burned the bare
sole of your foot as you stepped from it. Buttercups in

the meadow, and the wind continually stirring the cotton grass.

But it was the winter which was ahead of them where the same wind could be so strong you could lean on the gusts and not fall over. Flurries of hail whipped like gravel into your face. Great grey curtains of it sweeping violently across the shadowed fell moving the waist-high bracken to a menacing fierceness. The storm-wracked sky from which, without the slightest warning, could come a white vortex of blinding snow to bury the unwary, those who did not heed the fell's warning. Days of hard frost, brilliant sunshine, crackling snow ruts, crusted and deep, heather with icy stalks sparkling and winking. The sky, gold flecked, and whooper swans sailing over the low fields and when the sun disappeared a fine half-moon with a single star above a silent, crisply white world.

A beautiful, treacherous, hard world. Her world and one which she intended to conquer, as her father had never done. And it was to the sloping 'inlands' which lay in front of the house and on which her father's few poor sheep had pastured, and perished, that Annie's eyes were drawn. Down across neatly walled fields to where, beyond hers, sheep were wintering, a slow moving carpet of pale grey against the lush, well-watered green pasture land. Jem Mounsey's flock whose fields lay side by side with hers. Hers which were empty now but one day, she promised herself as she stood at the door, they would be filled again with the flock, her flock which, when she had acquired them, would be brought down from the high fells each winter.

A fell farm has three sections. The high ground across the summits, over two thousand feet up, where the sheep spent the summer; the 'intakes' which are big, grassy slopes fenced by drystone walls and the 'inlands', small, rich enclosures spread about the farmhouse itself where the sheep winter. And one day her sheep would cover this land. One day!

She could see the head of the lake from where she stood. Bassenthwaite, not the most beautiful in this county of beautiful lakes or so she had heard since she had seen only this one and Derwent Water which joined it near Keswick, but to her it was loved almost as much as she loved her child. Instinctively a part of her, as Cat was a part of her. She had known it at all seasons. The angry clouds chasing one another across its surface, the wind patterns ruffling and lifting the waters to dash them against the shore in miniature waves. Veiled in fine curls of mist, flat and mysterious, clear and motionless. Frozen and white and empty of all but sliding ducks and the odd, fearful young lad who had been 'dared' to go out on to its frozen surface. Blue as the skies which were reflected in it, surrounded by leaning slender birches, their leaves shining like golden sovereigns ready to dip into the water which lapped gently, benevolently about their feet, a fine haze of summer midges dancing on its textured expanse.

Already over the fells to the west the dying sun was sinking to its bed, no more than a sliver of it peeping through the high misted summits. Down the valley towards the lake half a dozen wild duck were silently zig-zagging above the water and from down by Chapel Beck several dogs were barking.

Cat had squatted to examine a tiny clump of reindeer moss growing in the shelter of the drystone wall which ran across the front of the house, separating it from the field. She was absorbed with it, studying it with the delight and amazement of a prospector who has discovered a rich vein of gold. Annie watched her, her arms resting on the Cam stone at the top of the wall. She lowered her chin to her arms to stare out across the fields to the lake and when she heard her name called she was disorientated, just as though her mother had suddenly come from the farmhouse doorway, telling her it was time for supper. It took her a long moment to return from that dreaming state into which the familiar and yet new scene had drawn her.

"Annie? Annie Abbott, is it you?" the voice asked hesitantly and when she turned about she did not at first recognise the plump young woman who stood further down the path. She had evidently come up the farm track, the sound of her sturdy clogs muffled by the grass which grew in its unused ruts. The track, which led up from the road, ran at the back of the farmhouse, and then on to farms further up the valley.

"Yes . . . ?" She was as tentative as her visitor. The woman had a look about her that was familiar, bonny and round-cheeked but she was full-bosomed and wide-hipped and much older than Annie, she decided. She had a baby in her arms, as apple-cheeked as herself, and a toddler at her skirt and, Annie noticed, was very evidently near her time with a third.

"'Tis me, Annie . . . Sally," the young woman said, a certain shyness in her, it seemed to Annie, though the Sally she had known had never been shy.

"Sally? Sally Mounsey?" She began to smile, stepping forward in glad recognition.

"Aye, though 'tis Sally Garnett now. Has bin these three years." She preened just as though what she had achieved was worthy of great admiration, a success evidently not granted to the girl who stood before her by the look of her ringless hand. But there was a look about her of being pulled down, of bearing a burden which sat uneasily on her despite her youth since she was the same age as Annie, an expression of weariness and vexation of spirit well known to Annie for had she not seen it in her own dead mother?

"You never married Bert Garnett?" she exclaimed incredulously, then could have bitten her tongue for the glad and welcoming expression on Sally's face at once became truculent.

"Well, at least I got married," she snapped, then just as suddenly the rancour left her and she sighed. Her shoulders sagged and she shifted her burden to her other hip.

"I'm sorry, Annie, I didn't meant to . . . but aye, I did, God help me. An' all I ever get from 'im is childer, 'ard work an' a clout round t' lug every Saturday when he's the ale in 'im. Our Davy died, did tha' know? No, well, you wouldn't, then me faither, so . . . it seemed sensible to marry a lad what knew farmin'. Bert moved in wi' me an' Ma an' Mim. 'E's a hard worker but . . . well . . . I could o' done worse, I reckon."

"Sally . . . oh, Sally, I'm so sorry about Davy, and your father, but all the same it's lovely to see you, and the children, but won't you come in and have a cup of tea. The kettle is on . . ."

"Aye, we saw tha' smoke from t' chimney. That's why I come up. Ma said she'd spotted Mr Macauley come along track on that black devil of 'is. She thought 'e'd bin 'ere, she said. Why don't tha' go up an' find out what's what, she said. I'm not as lish as I was, bein' so near me time, but I come anyway. There's bin rumours . . ."

"Rumours? About what? About me?"

"Aye, that tha' was ter come 'ome. That lawyer chap that'd bin seein' ter tha' faither's place 'ad come round a time or two, lookin' in ter things, 'e said, so we reckoned tha' must be on tha' way, or someone was, an' when I saw tha' smoke . . ."

She faltered then, her eyes going slowly to Cat who had stood up and crept close to her mother's skirts, shy and ready to hide her eyes in the presence of these strangers. Sally had not noticed her but now, as she did, her jaw dropped in slack consternation and her pale blue eyes widened. The likeness between mother and daughter was quite remarkable and when Annie put out her hand, drawing her child closer to her in loving maternal tenderness, the truth was plain.

"This is my daughter, Catriona, Sally. She is almost three years old."

You could see it in Sally's eyes, the slow working out of the dates and the years between. Sally, good-natured and uncritical, generous and warm-hearted could barely add two and two together despite her three years' schooling but she knew what had happened to Annie Abbott for here was the three-year-old proof of it. Perhaps she had been wrong about the ring . . . perhaps . . .

"Your . . . husband?" she gasped painfully, hopefully, since she liked Annie Abbott, always had done and would have been glad to renew their friendship.

"I have none, Sally." Annie Abbott, though she could have done so, would not lie, even for Cat's sake.

"Glory . . . oh, good glory . . ." and without another word Sally, her face as scarlet as the geraniums in her mother's window bottom, turned tail and ran like a monstrous, overburdened cow, dragging her whining toddler so fast down the track behind her, he or she, it was hard to tell its sex, almost lost its balance.

Annie sighed deeply, sadly, then taking Cat's hand in hers led her back into the glowing warmth of her kitchen. At least she had that. A warm kitchen, and Cat. It would have been nice to have a friend though. She'd known this would happen, of course. When they heard. When they heard about Annie Abbott's disgrace, her shame, her dreadful fall from grace which had resulted in the one thing most girls would rather die than suffer, and sometimes did. A bastard child. It would be all over the valley, like the news of the hamper, by morning.

The knock on the door five minutes later took her by surprise, as did Sally Garnett's face when she opened it.

"Bugger 'em," was all she said, thrusting her child in before her as she moved heavily over the threshwood. "I'll 'ave that cup o' tea after all, Annie."

7

The snow came just after Christmas, the first hesitant
flake or two taking Annie by surprise; she could not have
said why, since it was the season for it.

She and Cat were up in the coppice wood at the back
of Browhead. The term 'coppice' meant literally, 'grown
for cutting' and the trees there, oak, ash, birch and sycamore, beech, hazel and alder, evergreen holly, pine and
yew, were the only crop which had never failed Joshua
Abbott. A bad harvest of the oats and barley – known as
'bigg' – which he grew, one which withered in the fields,
caused great hardship since it meant that the food which
would have seen them through the year had to be found
elsewhere. That the fodder for the cattle who were hand
fed in the cow house where they had been brought to
winter was not available. The beasts, of which Joshua
never had more than one, could be fed in an emergency
on bracken cut from the fells, but humans needed more
than bracken. It brought disaster to many a small farmer,
men who had nothing to fall back on as Joshua had in his
coppice wood. One acre of well-grown coppice was
capable of producing 10,000 poles at every cutting. This
was raw material for bark tanneries, swill baskets, grom-
mets, hoops, charcoal and bobbins although naturally,
Joshua was not concerned with all these industries. But
he could sell his poles to those who were and the crop
which was not sold he and Lizzie and Annie had made into
swill baskets and birch-twig besoms – somewhat like a
broom – to be sold at Keswick market.

Bark for the tanneries was cut in early summer when
rising sap in the coppiced oak trees allowed the bark to
be stripped off more easily. Of course this year no bark

had been peeled and it was too late now to do anything about it but next year Annie meant to contact Natty Varty who did casual work for any man who needed an extra hand and would pay him, to fell and peel the bark from the oak. As her father had taught her when she was a girl she meant to turn her hand to making swill baskets and peddle them either from door to door at the outlying and remote farmhouses on the fells, or take them to market.

The actual felling and splitting of the coppice poles was hard and laborious but she was strong and who better than herself knew about hard labour? There were many processes through which the wood must go before she had the materials for the swill baskets which were used in many industries, farming, coal mining, charcoal burning and which went to many parts of the country, even as far as Liverpool where they were in common use on coaling steamers. A good workman could make seven baskets a day but Annie meant to work during the evenings since she would be busy on the actual farm the rest of the time. The farm she intended to build from the ashes of the one her father had worked so desperately to keep going.

And then there were the birch-twig besoms with which Lakeland housewives swept their floors and yards. She and her mother had made hundreds of the things and if they brought in only a few pence, it all helped and she would need every resource she had to begin to build the dream she dreamed of. She had already made two dozen or so, helped by Cat, and the neat bundles were piled in the barn even now, ready for selling at Keswick market.

There was the knitting of hosiery, the weaving of the wool and the spinning of the yarn on the loom and spinning-wheel which her mother kept in the parlour and which Annie had carefully cleaned ready for use. When she had her flock, of course! There were many crafts she could turn her hand to when the spring came but first she must earn some money to get her and Cat through the winter. If she could, she would also put something aside towards replacing the small flock of sheep her father had once owned. She had no idea what had happened to them though

Sally had spoken of debts and a bad summer harvest in the year Joshua and Lizzie had died.

"Me an' Ma came every day ter nurse them, Annie, but by the time we got 'ere tha' faither and mother were off tha' heads an' made no sense. There was no money fer doctor but we did our best. Ma made up one of 'er infusions from the root of Wood avens. 'Tis good fer fever an' colic but it were too late, she reckoned."

Sally had sighed sadly, settling her swollen body as comfortably as she could in Lizzie's chair, sipping reflectively and with great enjoyment the mug of tea Annie had brewed, her feet up to the good hot fire on the hearth.

"Yer Ma went first. Asked fer thi' times, she did. Wanted ter tell thi' summat, she kept sayin', an' Ma said she'd pass a message on, not knowin' when she'd see thi', like, but doin' 'er best ter calm 'er, but she said nowt more. She went quietly, lyin' next to tha' faither. We'd only just lifted 'er out . . . well, with yer faither still alive it didn't seem right ter leave 'er aside 'im . . . when 'e wènt an' all. No more than an hour atween 'em, poor souls. We did it right, Annie. A proper 'bidden' funeral they 'ad an' everyone came, even from Cockermouth where tha' Ma was born. We took it in turns ter' 'laat' with 'em, me Ma an' others from hereabouts, Mrs Gunson and Mrs Strickland an' old Ma Bibby from down Scarness way, 'er bein' a friend of tha' Ma's. They was carried on the 'corpse way', so there'll be no ill omens laid on this 'ouse, Annie. Church bell tolled, nine times fer tha' faither an' six fer tha' Ma an' we 'ad a funeral feast. Ma baked the arvel bread and gave it round. Oh, it were done right, lass, 'ave no fear o' that."

"I must go and thank your mother, and all of them, Sally, and you, of course, for what you did. I didn't know . . ."

Sally sat up cumbersomely and her good-natured face which had became even rosier with the fierce heat of the fire, twisted into a horrified grimace.

"Eeh no, lass, tha' cannot go up ter me Ma's, nor to any of 'em."

"Why not? I am most grateful . . ."

"They'd not 'ave thi' over t' threshwood, none of 'em
would, an' neither would Bert. He reckons 'e's head of
the 'ouse now since me faither died an' he'd 'ave no truck
wi' . . . well not wi' . . ." She indicated with a nod of her
head and a swift glance in her direction, Annie's grave-
faced little daughter who was watching with the greatest
fascination Sally's boy Sammy devour a piece of Reed
Macauley's cook's chocolate meringue, something he had
never before come across and which he plainly found much
to his liking. As he ate his eyes never shifted from what
remained of it and the speed with which he ate it implied
that the sooner he got it down, the sooner he could have
another piece.

"You mean that because I have a child, one born out
of . . ."

"Don't be daft, Annie. Yer know what they're like round
'ere. None of 'em'll 'ave 'owt ter do wi' thi. Did tha' expect
it ter be any different? As soon as it's known tha's back
wi' a . . ."

"A bastard?" Annie's chin rose challengingly.

"Aye . . ." sadly, ". . . an' after tha' ran away like tha'
did, wi' that chap from the travelling show."

"He was ready to punish me, Sally. My father. I don't
know how or what my life would have been like had I
stayed . . ."

"Threw you out, the story went an' served yer right,
they said. Yer'd bin seen in Keswick wi' that actor but I
felt right badly about it. Like it was my fault . . ."

"*Your* fault?"

"Well, if I 'adn't coaxed thi' ter come ter t' play it
wouldn't 'ave 'appened. None of it."

"No, Sally, you musn't blame yourself. I chose to go,
to take the chance, knowing what my father was like, and
so I must bear the consequences."

"What'll tha' do now, Annie?"

"Stay here."

"Nay, will tha' not sell?" Clearly Sally was of the opinion
her friend was off her head for whoever heard of a woman
living alone on a farm? How would she manage without a

man? How would she feed and clothe herself and her child? And more to the point, how could she stay here in this upright and God-fearing community amongst those who would turn their faces from her? Who would have no social communication with her whatsoever. Who would shun her and her child, for what decent man or woman could, without tainting themselves, be concerned with a woman such as Annie Abbott? To accept her would be to condone her behaviour, loose and immoral as it had been, and for all any of them knew, still was. If she could act as she had in the past with one man, or even more, who was to say she could not do it again with another, theirs, in fact, the women would tell themselves, and the men, having daughters of their own to protect, could only look upon her with contempt since to do otherwise might put the idea in their daughters' heads that there was no sin to it.

"No." Annie shook her head resolutely in answer to Sally's question and Sally watched in wondering admiration the play of firelight in Annie's copper curls. They were tight and shining, long tendrils hanging in coils about her slender white neck and falling over her ears. She had bundled it up on top of her head, skewering it with several pins but it was far too heavy and vibrant to remain there, slipping in bright disarray from its fastenings.

With a generosity which held no envy Sally admitted to herself that Annie Abbott had grown into a right comely woman.

"What *will* tha' do, then?"

"Run the farm, Sally. Work. Buy sheep when I have the money. A cow, pigs. A horse. Plough . . . I was hoping the men would oblige with some 'boon-ploughing' when the time came . . ." a custom in which all the men in the community would help one another at ploughing time, ". . . plant oats and bigg on a couple of acres. Get Natty Varty to do some coppicing and in the evening make swills and besoms. Given a chance I can make this farm successful. That's all I need, a chance, or even half a one. Mr Macauley . . . I met him on the road yesterday . . . his mother knew mine . . ." which was half a truth . . .

"brought over this food . . ." indicating the basket,
". . . otherwise we would have gone hungry."

She frowned at Sammy who was reaching with grubby
hands for the chocolate meringue. "That boy of yours,
should he be eating so much rich food?" since he certainly
would not be used to it, her manner said. Besides which,
what was in the basket might have to last her and Cat
through the next few weeks which it wouldn't if he was
allowed to make free with it. She could see that Sally was
one of those good-natured, careless mothers who, as long
as they were not bothering them, gave no concern to the
activities of their offspring.

Sally glanced indifferently at Sammy. "Oh, 'e'll be all
right. Nothin' makes 'im sick."

"Perhaps not, but I'd rather he was sick on someone
else's food, if you don't mind. That's all me and Cat have
until I earn some money."

"Well then, we'd best be off." Sally struggled to get out
of her chair, ready to be offended, but the effort to do
either was too much for her and she sank back, panting
with the effort.

"Give us a 'and, Annie, an' see, Sammy, give over
touchin' that cake. He's never seen 'owt like it," she
explained to Annie apologetically, pushing aside the
smaller child, a little girl she called Janie, and when Annie
had got her to her feet and through the doorway on to the
threshwood, she turned impulsively, putting her hand on
Annie's arm.

"I'll try an' get over ter see thi', Annie, but with me
Ma an' Bert it'll be difficult. Yer know . . ." nodding again
in Cat's direction. The Mounsey farm, Upfell, ran next to
Browhead, the distance between the farmhouses no more
than a mile or so but it seemed to Annie that though the
track was not long it might as well have been a hundred.

"You must do as you see fit, Sally." She lifted her head
proudly, as she had done with Reed Macauley, for she
would have no one, him or Sally, handing out favours to
her, then she relented, for Sally had been good to Lizzie
and Joshua. "Come if you can, Sal. I'd be glad to see

you, and your mother, but don't cause trouble at home,"
meaning with her husband, Bert.

Sally laughed without humour. "If yer thinkin' of Bert,
he don't care what I do as long as 'is dinner's on t' table
when 'e gets in from t' fell an' I'm in 'is bed when 'e goes
up to it."

Annie had not seen Sally since that day. She had seen
nobody. December had come in with a biting furious wind,
unfriendly and finding its way into the house despite the
thickness of the walls, bringing fresh soot down the
chimney and though there was plenty of peat and wood
in the barn she had tried to use it sparingly in order to
make it last thoughout the winter. The house had been
cleaned and polished and scrubbed and aired, even the
tiny windows buffed until they sparkled. Bedding had been
washed and mended and the contents of her mother's
chest searched for suitable garments from which to
remake and replace the clothing she and Cat wore. She
had sewn a new little dress for her daughter from a skirt
of Lizzie's, a dull and washed out grey, vowing as she did
so that one day she would make her one in a bright and
pretty material, but at least she was warm and her appearance was neat and clean.

She had baked clapbread and made a pan of crowdy,
finding the vegetables in what had been her mother's vegetable garden. She had managed to do some digging before
the ground had become too hard but their supplies were
getting low again, the basket of food brought over by Reed
Macauley nearly empty. She needed some money, hard
cash, since it was obvious that those with whom she might
have done a trade, had she had anything to exchange,
would not be willing to oblige her. Some of my oats for a
leg your lamb. A quart of milk for a lump of cheese, or
butter, eggs for a hunk of bacon and though she had been
careful with the food it had been hard at Christmas time
when she had tried to make a little celebration for Cat.
No presents, of course, except for the surprising loop of
bright emerald-green ribbon she had found at the bottom
of her mother's chest wrapped about a shining strand of

copper hair which had matched Cat's and her own. Who had it belonged to? she had wondered before tying the ribbons in her daughter's curls. Someone from her mother's past, or perhaps one of her small brothers and sisters who slept in the churchyard by the lake. It had not occurred to her that the curl had been cut from her mother's own head when she had been pretty, fifteen-year-old Lizzie Bowman.

She had cut a tiny fir seedling from the coppice and decorated it with pine cones and bright red berries and ribbons of paper from about the food in the hamper, fashioned into bows and hearts. Not much, but with a Christmas carol sung as the child drowsed on her knee she felt she had done her best with the first Christmas they had shared in their own home. Next year would be different. This time next year it *would* be different.

No one came near her.

On Boxing Day she and Cat walked down the track to the road which led to the hamlet of Gillthrop where the Highthwaite pack had just set off on the traditional Boxing Day fox hunt, one of the many which took place each winter between November and April. Not a sport as it was known in other parts of the country, but a necessity since the fox was an unrivalled predator in the fields of the local farmers, attacking and taking new-born lambs when they came. The drag for the scent had taken place earlier that day and the hounds were already away, eager to follow the fox over the hostile terrain which, particularly at this time of the year, could strike without warning at a man who did not respect its moods.

A Lakeland village was not the cosy affair of inn, church and pretty cottages grouped about a village green and pond which was known elsewhere but was a line of small buildings in a thin straggle along the rutted road. Women stood in small knots as Annie walked towards them, Cat's hand in hers and as she drew nearer all conversation ceased. Almost as one they folded their arms defensively across their offended bosoms, their attitude proclaiming at once that she was not welcome and that she'd best not try her doxy's tricks here. Shawled heads turned away, eyes sliding to watch her nevertheless.

The hound pack could be heard in full cry, a rushing river of melody fading to a gentle swarming-bee sound as the dogs took flight through the bracken of Orthwaite Bank in the direction of Little Cockup as they trailed the fox. The men had gone, following the excited hounds. Farmers, the whipper-in, the hunstmen in their hodden grey. Sturdy boots and gaiters, snug breeches and woollen jackets and jaunty bowler hats. Some carried fox screws to winkle out the cunning animal should he go to ground in a borran, others had walking sticks and shepherd's crooks for they would cover a good many miles today. There were terriers trained to follow the fox into the borran and flush him out. The thrilling notes of the hunting horn rang out, carried on an echo and for a moment every head turned in the direction of the sound then all the women looked back at Annie Abbott, waiting, silent, accusing, hostile, curious for none had known a bad woman before.

She knew them all. They were decent, hard-working, quick to help one another, loyal and true friends to those who deserved it. Gillthrop was no more than fifteen minutes' walk from Browhead. She had attended the church school with their children and her mother had passed the time of day with the older ones, but none spoke.

"Good morning, Mrs Armstrong," she called out, her stride bold and graceful, not faltering. Her full skirt swung, brushing the tops of her wooden-soled clogs and revealing an inch of the thick woollen stockings her mother, or perhaps it was her father, had knitted. She wore no bonnet and the brilliant sunlight lit her hair to flame. Her back was straight, long and supple and she walked with the ease and elegance of a cat. From the inn yard of The Bull where he had tethered his mare, Reed Macauley drew in his breath admiringly.

Jesus God, but she was a rare one. It took a special kind of courage to do what she was doing. It was easy to carry a sword or a musket into battle, into the heat and fury which was generated when men came up against other men. It was easy to be brave when all about you were being brave with you, but to be one woman, one solitary soldier against so much hostility, called for the sort of valour which had nothing to do with the race of blood which carries a man through an armed conflict.

He had passed at the back of her farmhouse on more than one occasion in the past four weeks as he came down from Long Beck and on to the pack route which led through the fells to Carlisle where he had business interests. He had not called though he had been tempted to do so if only to see how she was managing. Sheer curiosity, he told himself, though why he felt the need to justify himself, even to himself, irritated him. They were neighbours of sorts, weren't they, and any decent neighbour would take the trouble to enquire after the health and condition of another, especially a woman alone who had just come back from what Gillthrop would consider wild adventuring and who would, given the circumstances, be bound to encounter hostility. The hamper had been an impulse. She was nothing to do with him, and, if she was to be given the chance she needed he would serve her best by staying away from her. She was in enough trouble as it was and needed no further gossip about what those in the neighbourhood would see as the questionable visits of a young, unmarried man on a woman of already dubious character. No, best leave her alone to swim, or sink if that was the way of it, in the turbulent waters she herself had stirred up.

But she intrigued him. He thought about her more often than he liked. She was a vastly attractive woman, of course, and promised to be . . . interesting, stimulating, with an air about her of something hidden which could prove diverting to reveal and he was not a man who would take much persuading to reveal it! If he helped her without those of Gillthrop knowing he was helping her, giving her that covert support – of a material sort – to get her through the winter and on to her first step towards independence, which he had a fancy to do, what might she be capable of achieving? She'd not do it on her own, of course. She had nothing, nothing but the farmhouse and the land. No resources, no capital with which to purchase her flock, the livestock she would need, the farming implements, the seed to plant her first crop, nothing but her own strong back and indomitable spirit.

And courage, he told himself. Would you look at her now, striding through the gathering of village women, nodding, smiling, calling her greetings as though she was as welcome as the first daffodils and getting no response whatsoever beyond sour looks and the coldly turned shoulder of every woman in the village. Not showing that she gave a damn either, head held high and a smile on her to melt the coldest heart which meant nothing to these women. Now if they were men! Ah, that would be different for what man could resist that springing step, that neat waist and lilting breast, that glowing, hatless tumble of hair which gave her the appearance of having come directly from some man's bed after an hour or two of delightful love-making.

"Good morning, Miss Abbott," he called out, stepping from behind his mare, hoping perhaps to startle her though why he should want to do so was again an enigma to him but she merely glanced coolly in his direction, nodding politely as she turned into the inn yard. The women in the street watched avidly.

"A fine morning, is it not?" he went on, moving towards her, drawn by some strange and annoying need to have her do more than nod. What? A smile perhaps, one of those he had seen illuminate her great, golden-brown eyes on the day they had met? A curl of her poppy-red lips, lifting at the corners to show her white teeth? Some words to let him know she had not forgotten the hamper since she must know she and the child would not have survived without it.

She did none of these things. The smiles she had showered on the village women were gone and her manner told him, and them, that she was a woman with whom men were not encouraged to dally. She was on some business of her own here and it was nothing to do with anyone but herself and whoever she had come to see.

Without knowing why, not meaning to since it was his intention to go with the pack on the fox hunt over the fells, he followed her inside The Bull, leaning casually, his arms crossed on his chest, against the door frame of the low-ceilinged, oak-panelled bar-parlour of the inn. Though there was a huge log fire burning on the hearth it was gloomy for the windows were small, and an aroma of ale and spirits and tobacco filled his nostrils and caught the back of his throat. It was empty but for an amiable-looking man with wide shoulders and short bandy legs standing in front of the bar. He turned from his lethargic wiping of a glass as Annie entered. At once into his eyes came that foolish, longing-to-handle expression with which Annie was all too familiar but with Reed Macauley at her back and the dreadful apparition of starvation staring into her face she had no choice but to carry on.

"Good day, landlord," she said brightly and smiled.

He smiled back, not yet sure who she was but liking what he saw.

"Good day to you." His glance fell to the child and understanding began to dawn.

"I'm Annie Abbott. I'm looking for work."

Behind her Reed straightened slowly and for a second the man by the bar allowed his eyes to drift in his direction, catching the slight nod which, in these parts, meant a great deal. Among his other business concerns Reed Macauley had substantial sums of money out at interest. And it was not only substantial sums he lent, but small loans to the small man. Perhaps a matter of no more than two guineas but for the period of time that man owed money to Reed Macauley, he was Reed Macauley's man. And the landlord of The Bull, going through a bad spell when the farmers, or the smallholders did, was in debt to the man who now stood in his bar-parlour.

Catching the landlord's shift of inattention Annie turned to look where he did though she was too late to see Reed

Macauley's nod. Her face hardened and her eyes became brilliant with anger.

"Mr Macauley, I would be obliged if you would take yourself off in whatever direction you were heading when I came into the inn yard. Mr . . . er . . . the landlord and I have some business to discuss and I would prefer to do it in private. It is none of your concern."

"Indeed, Miss Abbott, but is this not a public bar and if I want to drink in it then it *is* my concern. Mine and the landlord's."

She was confused for a moment and he grinned, but recovering at once she turned back to the landlord, her glorious head showering small ringleted curls about her forehead. Both men watched her in some fascination. Spying a door behind the bar she indicated to it with her nod of her head.

"Perhaps we could go in there, sir. I have no wish to keep Mr Macauley from his . . . whatever it is he drinks."

"Go ahead, Will. Give me a brandy and I'll just sit here by the fire whilst you and Miss Abbott attend to your business. I am the last person to stand in the way of private enterprise." His grin broadened as he threw his long, immaculately tailored leg in its superbly polished boot over the bench, leaning his elbow on the table.

Annie found it surprisingly easy. She was a very experienced barmaid, she told Will Twentyman. Strong and willing and conscientious. Six hours each evening would be fine though threepence an hour was less than she had earned . . . oh, of course, there would be tips, but by the look of the women in the village their menfolk would not be encouraged to throw their cash in her direction.

"And my supper?"

He shrugged. "There's always food here."

"And . . . my child."

He frowned. He had been given the nod by Mr Macauley to take on the girl, which was no hardship. Good-looking barmaids were always hard to come by since the respectable folk in the parish did not put their pretty daughters to this kind of trade. There was no doubt she would attract custom, not only with her looks but with her reputation. They'd all be here, the men from the village and the hill farms within walking distance to get a look at her, to try it on with her. He would himself if his old woman wasn't looking. Oh, aye, he'd have taken her on without Mr Macauley's say so, that's if his Eliza would let him but he'd not bargained for the nipper as well.

"She would be kept out of the way, Mr Twentyman, I promise. She's used to being quiet and is no bother to anyone."

Aye, he'd not argue with her about that, poor little mite, all big eyes and a solemn expression on her that would have sat well on a judge. Kept out of the way while her mother entertained her 'friends', he'd be bound and what he wouldn't give to be among that number.

"She'll just go to sleep in a corner, Mr Twentyman. You won't even know she's there. I . . . I can't leave her alone at home."

"When can tha' start?"

"Tonight?" She gave him her saucy barmaid's smile.

"Aw reet, but keep tha' bairn out o't way."

"I will, and thank you, Mr Twentyman."

She did not even glance in Reed Macauley's amused direction as she swept regally through the bar and out into the brilliant December sunshine. Her elation showed in the heightened colour of her smooth cheeks and the vivid, transparent depths of her golden eyes.

A week later, with her first week's wage of nine shillings in the tin box beneath the pile of kindling under the sconce, with the few pennies in tips jingling in her pocket, the good, solid meal she and Cat shared every night and the few odds and ends of broken tarts or a mutton chop slipped to her by Will Twentyman, she had taken that first arduous step on the road to success. She was settled. She had a job, money coming in. She was, for the moment, safe. She could, for the moment, allow herself to feel exultant, for despite all her neighbours' cold hostility, their downright longing to see her fall flat on her face, she had shown them all that she did not need them. She had succeeded in hanging on and though she was far, very far, from what she intended, she had for the time being found honest work and had earned her first week's wage.

And when that first snow fell, starting with a sudden flurry of flakes floating in the thin air, she immediately took Cat's hand, banishing all thoughts of gathering birch twigs for the making of the besoms she was accumulating in her barn. She and Cat began to make their frantic way down the track at the back of Browhead towards the farmhouse. She had lived for most of her life in this part of the world and knew well the pitiless cruelty of the blizzards which could attack so quickly. The light was fading rapidly as the slanting snowflakes began to thicken and almost before they had left the comparative shelter of the coppice it had settled thickly on the ground, on their bent heads and bowed shoulders, on their eyebrows and eyelashes so that they were forced to blink rapidly to clear their vision. The cold was devastating and within minutes, though they were no more than a few hundred yards from the farmhouse, they were enclosed in a solid, moving, violent curtain of snow. Had she not known every inch of the way or had they been several hundred yards further from the farm she could not have found it. She was only relieved it was Sunday and the inn closed for the day.

They fell into the kitchen, a great tide of snow accompanying them, laughing and gasping, Cat, who had been ready to be frightened, laughing just as merrily as her mother. The fire was burning brightly. They had rush-lights and warm clothing, a simmering 'tatie-pot' on the fire and when, later, they dozed before their own hearth, warm, well fed, Annie sighed in sheer bliss, and, in perfect imitation of her mother, Cat did the same.

8

She sighed in sheer exasperation the following morning when daylight, what there was of it, revealed the still solidly eddying veil of snow. It had drifted up to the window ledges and covered the drystone wall opposite the farmhouse door and when she opened it a waist-high barrier of frozen, crystallised whiteness rose before her, preventing her from going any further. Not that she needed or wanted to go any further just yet but she was expected at The Bull at six o'clock that evening and she intended to give none of those in the village a chance to mock her female weakness, as they would see it, nor her inability to look after herself and her child. She knew they would be betting with one another on how long it would take her to admit she was beaten; to sell up and move away, take her bastard child and ruined reputation elsewhere and allow them to attend to their moral and, until she came among them, virtuous lives.

It was noon before the snow stopped falling. The beauty of the landscape as she opened the door again took her breath away and for several minutes she and Cat stood in absolute silence, the door latch held in one hand whilst she lifted the other to shade her eyes, for the sheer white brilliance of the immaculate snow was a physical pain. She had forgotten during the four years she had wandered the flat plains of the Midlands, the magnificent and awe-inspiring splendour of the Lakeland which had been, and would be again, her home, particularly after a snowstorm of the proportions of the night before. It sparkled and glittered as though a careless hand had scattered millions of diamonds across the rolling landscape. The sky was the deep blue of a cornflower, cloudless and serene. The trees stood proud, unbowed beneath their burden of snow, a marvel of black and white etched against the silvered lake. It was a mystical land of gentle lowlands and high, sharp-featured peaks, a land unmarked by walls or fences or gates, for they had all vanished in the night storm. It was cold but not the raw biting cold of November. This was sharp, clean, stimulating, making the blood race and tingle. A white, silent cold in a white, silent world where nothing moved and nothing could be heard but the faint bugle call of the whooper swans who came down each year from the north to winter on the lake.

"Well, Cat, my sweet, grand as it is, it's going to create a problem we could well do without."

The child nodded sagely, staring out as anxiously as Annie for even at her tender age she was well aware of the importance of work, of wages, of food to eat and a place to eat it in. She had been her mother's sole companion since she was born and had been suckled to the sound of Annie's voice musing on how to make a penny do the work of two. She had understood nothing at first as she listened to the soft murmur of the words her mother spoke, not to her for she had been an infant at her mother's breast, but to herself. Annie had found that to speak the words out loud, though there was no answer, had given her the feeling she was discussing her problems with someone; that perhaps the solution might be divulged to her, and often it had. With Cat's wide, long-lashed eyes gazing unwinkingly into hers, the child's mouth pursed on the nipple of her full breast, she had talked and talked and gradually, as Cat grew, moving on to a cup, a plate, a spoon, she had begun to understand, to listen as Annie talked to her and if she had no answer, her intense, unchildlike concern was felt by her mother, giving her comfort, and the bond between them was strong and unbreakable.

"We could dig," she offered, her eyes bright, her trust complete in this mother who had never been anything but utterly trustworthy.

"We could, darling," her mother answered doubtfully

for it was a good fifteen minutes' walk to Gillthrop and that was in the best of weather.

"Shall we put our clogs on, mother, and try?" The child's hand slipped confidingly into hers and for a second Annie felt her heart twist painfully inside her. Her daughter was so . . . so lovely, not in the visual sense, though she was that too, but in her sweet child's heart. Wanting to please and console, to help as though she was an adult, to attempt any gargantuan task with her child's strength if it would ease the worry in her mother's heart. To dig a path to The Bull if it should be necessary and would please Annie. She was far too serious for her age since she had never 'played' but her goodness and sweetness shone from her. She was strong, too, and steadfast in her love, and yet these people of the parish of Bassenthwaite wished her nothing but ill. They would shun her and teach their children to shun her and it broke Annie's heart to think about it but there was nothing she could do but go on, work hard, make a place for her and Cat, and hope. That was all she could do. *Hope.*

"Why not? You run upstairs and get mother's cloak and your shawl and scarf. Oh, and the thick stockings from the chest. I wish we had some boots," she added wistfully, "but our clogs will have to do."

The snow had already crusted. Fortunately the big, long-handled shovel Joshua Abbott had used to clear the yard to the side of the house of the manure his animals deposited there, the one with which Annie had been attempting to turn over the hard earth, was still standing just by the side door. First she must get herself out of the house and up on to the level to which the snow had fallen. To cut out steps would be the best, she thought, so that she and Cat could go up them one at a time until they stood, with any luck, at the same height as the window ledges where the snow lay, that's if the snow would hold them.

This proved easy enough and soon she had moved about ten feet from the front door, throwing the snow first to one side and then to the other, forming a narrow, tramped-down path in which the wooden soles of her clogs actually helped. They were sturdy and warm and providing the snow did not seep over the sides, afforded good protection.

At the end of an hour she was hot and panting with exertion and she had almost reached the gate which led out to the farm track and down to the road. To the road to Gillthrop and The Bull. Cat was behind her scooping out snow with the lid of the tin box in which Annie's first week's wages lay, resolutely stamping down the packed whiteness with her little clogged feet. Her cheeks were like poppies and her eyes great golden brown stars and for a moment Annie paused to watch her, comparing her with the inanimate doll she had been three months ago. She had pushed back the scarf Annie had tied about her head and her hair, exactly the same colour and texture as her mother's, fell about her forehead and down her back. Like a rippling sheet of copper it was, catching fire from the sun. The mother and child were singing. An old song Lizzie Abbott had sung to Annie and which she in turn sang to Cat. It was said to be a 'cocking' song before cockfighting was made illegal in 1835. 'The Charcoal Black and Bonnie Grey' it was called, a ballad popular throughout Cumberland and Westmorland, the place names mentioned in it changed to suit the location in which it was sung.

'Come all of you cockers far and near,' it began and they had got as far as the last verse,

'Now the black cock he has lost their brass,
And the Gillthrop lads did swear and curse . . .'
when a deep-throated masculine voice joined in, roaring out the remainder of the song with a dash and musical gusto which, though it silenced them in surprise for a moment, they took up again and finished with him.

'. . . and wished they'd never come that day,
To Bassenthwaite to see the play.'
They looked at one another, she and Reed Macauley, vivid blue eyes locking with golden brown, bewitched by the sensation of pure joy, the feeling of exhilarating pleasure, of sheer, childlike enjoyment of the song they had

shared. It lit up their faces and in that moment, for that moment, broke the fetters which adult human beings bind about themselves and which children have not yet learned. That guarded restraint which is erected to protect dignity and hide from view that innermost vulnerable core of one's self. They looked at one another and, quite simply, fell deep in love and for the space of five seconds their eyes admitted it. She relaxed, ready to sigh over the perfection of it. Soft, her eyes became, and so did his, dazed with awe at this emotion neither had known before and certainly not expected, dazzled with the wonderment and confusion since it had come on them so blindingly, so suddenly, so amazingly. But scarcely before they had acknowledged its sweetness, as though a warning voice had whispered inside them both, at exactly the same time they became business-like, brisk, turning away to fumble with something, she with her spade, he with the sledge he pulled behind him and with the implement he had devised to push away the snow in front of him.

"I knew damn well you'd not stay home like any sensible woman, Annie Abbott." His voice was top heavy with something he did his best to hide from her. "No, not you. Up to our necks in bloody snow and more to come, no doubt . . ." heedless of the sky which showed not a suspect cloud from horizon to horizon, from high peak to high peak, ". . . and where are you and this poor child you drag around with you? Not by your own hearth where a woman with sense would keep herself but out on the damn fell digging like some damn ten-year-old making his first snowman. Could you not for once remain where you are safe from danger? A woman from these parts who is familiar with its weather should know when discretion comes before bravado."

And the strange thing was, though it incensed her beyond measure, she knew exactly why he was speaking to her in such a menacing, furious tone. The snow had stopped falling no more than two hours since and yet here he was dragging a sledge – on which there was yet another hamper – just as though he was a boy about to play the

wild games boys who had nothing better to do often play.
Pretending he was 'passing by' no doubt, on his way to
some important and not to be postponed meeting but in
reality slipping and sliding down the long, snow-drifted
track, hazardous and uncertain at the best of times, as
soon as he could from Long Beck to Browhead to see that
she and Cat were in good condition. This was not the first
time he had come to her rescue and not the first time he
had done his best to give her a hand over the rough path
life had put her on, but it wouldn't do. *It wouldn't do!* He
was Reed Macauley, wealthy farmer and businessman,
son of a prosperous and successful 'statesman' family and
she was Annie Abbott with an illegitimate child and a
derelict farm, and a way to make in the world for both of
them. It would be hard enough to make it without him to
muddy the already unclear waters of her life. To interfere
because he had a fancy, she told herself, to play the gallant
knight to her damsel in distress.

"What's it to you, *Mister* Macauley, *what* I do?" She
had to screech like this. She had to let him see, make him
see that he must leave her alone. She had to fight with
him since it seemed it was the only way to get rid of him.
The last few minutes had frightened her badly. She was
in one of the most desperate situations of her life, ready
to fall over the brink of disaster and into a heaving pit of
despair. She was holding on by a whisker, by the fragile
tips of her fingers and one false move, one tiny movement
that was unbalanced would tip her over into it and she
could not, *could not* afford to – she would not even think
it, let alone *say* the word 'love' – look at any man, not
now, not at this precarious moment in her life and certainly
not one like Reed Macauley. It had been no longer than
the time it takes to blink an eye, that gladness, that meeting, that astonishing meeting of their senses and really,
no harm had been done, not yet, and she must fight to
make sure that that tiny fraction of time in which tenderness, concern and passion had been revealed, was not
repeated. She could only do it with harshness.

"It's none of your damned business, as I've told you

before," she shrieked. "Lord, every time I turn round there you are at my back demanding to know what I'm doing and why. I've only been home a few weeks but already you've had something to say about the state of my looks," – referring to the day he had knocked on her door and found her coated in soot – "the condition of my daughter, my fitness for my work," – which was not strictly true but she did not care in her furious attempt at true rage – "and now my state of mind in trying to get to it. I have a job to do and if I don't get down to it I won't get paid, besides which I'll not have those crows down in the village say that Annie Abbott hasn't the guts to fight her way through a bit of snow to . . ."

"So that's it, is it? You'd chance this child's health so that you can prove to a stupid gaggle of women that . . ."

"Don't you speak to me of my child's health since I'm the one who has worked her fingers down to the bone, and in any way I can, to put good food in her belly and warm . . ."

"In any way you can?" He towered over her, his eyes slitted with his own rage, his mouth suddenly hard and cruel. "Yes, I suppose you would do that since it's an easy way to earn a living, I would say, and you look like the kind of woman who would enjoy her work. Tell me, are you still employed in that profession for if you are I might be persuaded to avail myself of . . ."

He was quick and strong. Had he not been she would have opened his head with the force of the blow she levelled at him. The spade was vicious and her swing true but he caught the handle and twisted it from her and from both the killing fury drained away leaving them trembling and sick.

"I beg your pardon," he said, his voice as cold as the air they breathed. "That was unforgivable. Allow me to help you with your . . . digging," and as though his life depended on it, and perhaps his sanity, he began, turning his back on her and Cat, biting into the snow with the spade, throwing it wildly from him, much further than he need.

She moved away without a word and took Cat's cold hand in hers, hurrying the bewildered little girl back into the farmhouse. She did not look outside again and when, at half past five, she lit a rushlight and prepared herself and Cat for their journey down to Gillthrop there was a clear, well packed path from the sledge which still stood where he had left it, to the first cottage in the village street.

"By gum, lass, we'd not expected thee this night." Mr Twentyman and his Eliza were the only ones in the bar-parlour and though one or two more adventurous men crept in later, stamping their feet and blowing on their hands, those who lived in the village, as Mr Twentyman remarked, there had really been no need for her to have bothered herself. Mind, she'd got gumption had Josh Abbott's girl and if this was an example of what determination could do, she'd go far that one would. He was inclined to like her. A liking which had nothing to do with the way she looked. Not that he wouldn't have said no to a kiss and a cuddle and a little feel of those ripe and lovely breasts but his Eliza had eyes in the back of her head so there was no chance of that, sadly.

And she'd certainly brought in custom, even in the week she worked in the bar, smiling warmly at anyone who addressed her and yet not too familiarly so that none of them could get the idea that what they saw could be theirs. She had added something to the atmosphere which he was at a loss to understand but which nevertheless he was grateful for, though Eliza Twentyman could have told him, had he asked. Annie was polite, pleasant, cheerful, interested in the men who crowded at the bar, getting to know their names, enquiring after their families, sharing a joke but there was an innocence about her which she had never lost despite the life she had led and her own motherhood, and the men liked it, and her.

Their womenfolk did not, and said so, to each other, to their men and to Eliza Twentyman and though she kept it to herself for as long as she could for, like her husband, she had taken to Annie Abbott and the little slip of a thing who was her daughter, she knew the day must come when they could no longer keep her. Eliza had to live with these women who were beginning to cold-shoulder *her*. The folk who lived in the Lakeland communities, often isolated for weeks on end, relied upon one another. They were close-knit, open-handed with those of whom they approved, intensely loyal to one another. Her husband depended on their husbands for his livelihood and though The Bull was the only inn for miles, should they turn against her and her Will they would be hard pressed to survive.

It snowed several times in January, which was the worst snow month, but again Annie Abbott got down from Browhead to Gillthrop. The snow melted partially, thawing down to a manageable level where it was possible to get about more easily. Then it froze, a cruel frost which set the world into a hard, timeless beauty. There were deep, crackling snow ruts, crusted just enough to cover the tussocks of heather on the slopes behind the farmhouse, scintillating in the brilliance of the winter sunshine. The sheep had moved down from the high fells and as they drifted in small groups towards the 'intakes' the ice which had formed on their fleeces tinkled musically. The snow buntings were picking seeds from the bent, a stiff-stemmed, rush-like grass. Grey geese flew south and the crows cruised up and down the rushing streams on the look-out for trout. Foxes, thin, nervous-eyed, starving, crept close to human habitation as they waited for spring and on February 2nd, Will Twentyman reluctantly told Annie that he no longer required her services.

She was devastated. She had worked for five weeks and, with the help of Reed Macauley's second hamper which she had seen as foolish to refuse, particularly as she could not leave it sitting on the sledge on the track up to Dash Beck, she had managed to save £2.14s.0d. but that would not buy her a flock of sheep. She had hoped to save more money from her work as barmaid and when the first market took place in Keswick and she sold the besoms she and Cat had made, the amount realised might buy her half a dozen young ewes. Put to a good ram which

she would hire, they would, by next year, bring her the
start of her flock. She would make swill baskets when
Natty Varty had cut and peeled her poles for her at the
end of April; these also would be sold at the summer
markets.

Now, with a few awkward and apologetic words Will
Twentyman had knocked down her precarious house of
cards and brought her face to face with ruin. She needed
her ewes in the spring. She could not afford to wait until
her besoms or her swills were made and sold at the
summer fairs she meant to tramp. She had a sledge, the
one her father had made years ago. Two, in fact, for
the one Reed Macauley had used to haul down the hamper
still stood in her barn and short of dragging the thing up
to Long Beck, which would cause even more talk, there
it would stay. She needed new clogs for herself and Cat.
She could cobble together clothing for her daughter from
the few bits and pieces left by her mother but something
for herself she could not manage, nor the clogs, not with
the best will in the world. Her own garments, even her
mother's wedding-dress which she still kept in the chest,
were threadbare and falling apart at the seams and the
only clothing in the place of any substance was that once
worn by her father.

"Why, Mr Twentyman?" she asked passionately, in
exactly the same way she had asked Polly Pearsall over
two years ago. "I'm a good worker and have caused you
no trouble" – despite the men who had done their best to
engage her in it. "I've not once let you down even when
the snow was as high as my shoulders."

Will Twentyman watched her mouth form the words
and was fascinated by the sound which came from it.
Where had she learned to speak as she did, almost like a
lady? It was still possible to detect the rhythmic sound of
the Cumberland dialect on her tongue, but she had lost
what some might consider the ugly glottal stop of East
Cumberland. She did not pronounce 'face' as 'fee-ass' or
'butter' as 'boother' and she had taught her child to speak
as she did. And that was one of the reasons, he supposed,

but not the main one, of course, why she was not liked, at least by the women. She was 'different'. She had 'got above herself' and though it fascinated their men-folk, it segregated her from the women of the village as sharply as though she had come from another land and spoke a foreign language.

"What is it, Mr Twentyman? Why am I not allowed to build a life for myself and my child? Why do they hate me so? Oh, yes, I know why it is you are forced to get rid of me. What is it I have done to them that turns them against me to the point where they will not be satisfied until they have driven me from the parish? I've done nothing to hurt them. Nothing to hurt anyone except myself and Cat and I'm doing my best to put that right. I only want to work, that's all. To work as men do . . ."

Aye, that was probably it. As men do, which was not the way of things in these parts . . .

". . . to earn an honest penny, to get back on my feet and be dependent on no one. I don't want to interfere with them or their men . . ." since she was well aware of what the nub of their resentment was, ". . . and I want no one interfering with me. Why are they so . . . so cruel, Mr Twentyman?"

And Will Twentyman had to admit, sadly, that he had no answer. He could only slip an extra sixpence in her hand and some left-over suet pudding his wife had made in readiness for the travellers who would, now that the snows had melted and the turnpikes were clear again, be staying overnight at The Bull.

There was an enormous winter moon, full and mysteriously beautiful hanging in the dark blue velvet sky, its light paling the intense colour about it to a silvery lavender. It illuminated the track up to the farmhouse so that every frost-spiked blade of grass could be seen as though it was noon. The great barrier of High Pike and Knott and Great Calva loomed to her left and before her was the majestic splendour of snow-capped Skiddaw. The path of the moon fell across the silken lake to her right, broad and completely still and from somewhere higher up the intakes a dog fox howled in hungry misery. The sound was taken up by another set of barking, closer and somehow different, a frantic sound in which she could detect fear and she wondered who would have their dogs, and young ones at that by the sound of it, out on a night like this.

"What is it, Mother?" Cat huddled closer to her skirts and clung to her hand as they panted up the steep track towards home, and all the while the frenzied noise of the dogs grew louder.

"It's only a couple of dogs, lambkin. They won't hurt us."

"But why are they barking so much?"

"They've probably scented the fox and are doing their duty protecting the chicken coop."

"Whose coop, Mother?" fearfully, and indeed whose coop could it be since the only dwelling between here and Upfell where the Mounseys lived was her own farm?

They were tied to the latch of her door, two puppies whose breeding, even in the light from the moon, was very evident. Black-and-white Border Collies of the sort used by shepherds and farmers for centuries in the care of their flocks. Silky of coat and lively of eye and so pleased to see Annie and Cat that it was hard to know where one puppy ended and the other began. An incredible squirming tangle of limbs, sharp baby claws and cold noses, long bushy tails whipping against Annie's and Cat's laughing, delighted faces, four bright saucy eyes, ready to love with enormous hearts these two humans who had come to rescue them.

"Where have they come from, Mother, and can we keep them? Please, Mother, see, they are so good . . ." which was not true for the moment they were let inside the house they had knocked over a stool, spilt a jug of milk brought up yesterday from The Bull and had begun to worry between them one of Cat's clogs which she had kicked off as she stepped over the threshwood.

"Sweetheart, they are not ours to keep . . ."

"Then whose are they, Mother? They were tied to our door . . . Oh, Mother, don't send them away. I love them so much and they will be no trouble . . . I will let them share my food . . ." for even in the midst of so much joy the practical matter of food and the money to buy it was not overlooked by the child. "They can sleep in my room and they will be such fun." Cat was down on the slate floor with them now. She lay on her back whilst one pup flopped on her chest and licked her face with the slavish devotion of one who knows exactly which side his bread is buttered whilst the other fondly chewed her bare toes, pricking his ears and casting his bright, intelligent eye in the direction of Annie since it seemed to him she might be the provider of food. He and his companion had already demolished the spilled milk but that did not mean he could not manage any other delicacy which might come his way.

Annie sat down, smiling in a way she had not thought possible an hour ago. She had never seen her grave young daughter laugh, even giggle, as she was doing now. A child she was, a young child playing, giddy with laughter and simple fun, her excited cries filling the room with her joy, her childish normal pleasure. And of course, who would have left the puppies here but Reed Macauley? There was not a soul in this dale or up on the higher fell farms who would give her the time of day, let alone two well-bred dogs such as these. A good sheepdog, well trained to his work, was worth his weight in gold, much prized by the farmers who would part with their wives before their dogs and these two, when she had her flock, would be invaluable to her. They would be loyal and stead-fast, as good as two men, true friends and companions for Cat, and when they were grown would enable her to leave her child alone whilst she herself worked since they would guard anything they thought of as theirs with their lives.

He had done it again. Just as she was at the edge of despair and disaster he had thrown her a lifeline to pull her back from it. She had not seen him since the day he had dug the path through the snow and glad she was of it for it made it easier for her to go on without any . . . complications. Oh, God . . . oh, dear God, let there not be complications, meaning, of course, don't let my weak and foolish woman's heart dictate to my wise and far-seeing mind, for even as she allowed him into her thoughts her pulse started to race in the most alarming way. Her stomach lurched, refusing to be still. Her eyes were full of him again and just because he had brought her two damned puppies, and she couldn't allow it. Dear God, she couldn't allow it. Not now when she had just been fired from her job and somehow must get herself and Cat through the days and nights, weeks, even months before she found another one. The bark peeling could not take place until April. Oak poles must be felled and she must 'speak' for Natty Varty who must be paid for his labour.

She must have work, but where? She could not even knock on some farmwife's kitchen door and ask for it as her mother had done, for unlike her mother whose reputation had been beyond reproach she was known from one end of the parish to the other as a 'fallen woman'.

Then you must look elsewhere, her uncompromising and logical mind coolly told her. You are strong and – so you told Reed Macauley – afraid of no one, of nothing, and certainly not of walking from here to Keswick where you are unknown to find work. There was an inn on every street corner in Keswick. When the snow had gone and it was possible to get there, and without Cat, who could then be left in the company of the two puppies, she could be in Keswick and back again in no time at all. Working her six hours and – if she could get it – at fourpence an hour, with tips and the always acceptable bonus of left-over food she and Cat would hold off that wolf from the door whilst she saved her wage for her ewes. She might pick up some bargains at the Sheep Fair, since she knew a good sheep when she saw it, but she must have them by September and the Annual Tup Fair when the rams were hired out or sold for breeding purposes. Soon the farmers would be bringing their sheep down from the fells for dipping which took place in February, to guard against lice and keds which could badly weaken a strain. The ageless cycle of gathering, lambing, dipping and clipping, of putting the tups to the ewes would begin and she must be ready to place herself in its moving orbit since its pattern must follow the course nature had planned. Each section of that course could take place only at a certain time of the year. Miss one section of it and a whole year would be wasted.

The child squealed with laughter and the puppies yelped with excitement, pulling with their sharp little teeth at the hem of her already frail skirt, digging their claws, uselessly as it happened, into the slate slabs of the floor as they hung on. They could not get a purchase, slipping and sliding with great good humour, growling in mock ferociousness, for the game they played was to their, and the child's liking.

Annie smiled and rose to her feet. She picked up both squirming bundles and deposited them firmly in a high-sided basket from which they could not climb.

"Fetch some of that dry bracken from by the side door, my lamb, and we'll line the basket for them. They can sleep in here tonight."

"And . . . tomorrow, Mother? You're not going to send them back, are you?" Cat's eyes were desperate in their pleading.

"I wouldn't know where to send them, sweetheart, so . . ."

"We can keep them, can we, can we . . ." jumping up and down in a way Annie had never seen her do before.

"We'll see, my darling."

"Please, Mother . . . please?"

"Well . . ."

"Please, Mother, I will look after them and feed them and . . ."

"Clean up after them?" smiling at a suspicious pool by the hearth.

"Oh yes . . . yes . . ."

"And what would you call them, that is if we kept them?" She drew the child to her knee and sat down beside the basket where the pups, like the babies they still were, had fallen instantly asleep.

"Blackie and Bonnie, like the song." Cat did not even have to think.

"But they are both boys."

"I don't care." And after all, Annie thought as her daughter nodded against her shoulder, where else would her lovely child find inspiration for names for her puppies? Annie had not, in her three years, read a story to her, nor even told her one since she had never had time in her desperate fight to simply keep them both alive. 'The Charcoal Black and Bonnie Grey' was the only song her little girl knew.

It was appropriate too, she mused, almost asleep herself in the warmth of the fire. He it was who had sung it with them and brought the dogs to her. Helping her but, she was sure, ready to deny it if she should accuse him of it. Not that they would be likely to meet again, she and Reed Macauley, for neither would wish to be caught in the violence of need which had trapped them for an enchanting moment several weeks ago. They must keep well apart for she knew with every quickened heartbeat and every racing pulse in her woman's body that there would be nothing more wonderful in the world than for it to be possessed by his.

9

The snow had gone from all but the highest peaks. Blackie
and Bonnie had been with them for over seven weeks and
were probably four months old, perhaps a bit more, she
had no way of telling, when she walked to Keswick to look
for work.

It was almost the end of March and in all that time
she had seen only Sally, brave Sally who had defied her
mother and her sister Mim, who were convinced in their
bigoted ignorance that Sally would not only be the talk of
Bassenthwaite parish, consorting with a woman like Annie
Abbott, but would bring home some dreadful disease, the
kind of disease women of her sort were bound to have.
Sally's husband Bert had threatened her with a 'clip round
t' lug' if she as much as looked in Annie's direction, she
told Annie imperturbably, let alone entered her kitchen,
but as she had to pass along the track at the back of
Annie's farm, crossing Annie's land, in fact, which had
been common practice for generations by those who lived
further up the valley, and as Upfell was more than a mile
away and hidden behind a fold in the hill, they'd not know
she'd 'popped in', she said loftily.

She had her new baby under her shawl, another girl
whom she'd called Emma, already shortened to Emm, but
she'd left Sammy and Janie at home with their grandmother
since their Sammy'd be bound to say 'summat' out of turn.

"Come in, oh, come in, Sally." Annie was pathetically
glad to see her, ready to sweep the good-natured girl into
her arms, for she had spoken to no one but Cat since she
had left The Bull.

"Well, I can't stay long. Ma looked at me a mite peculiar
when I said I fancied a walk down to t' smithy. Seth

Armstrong's mendin' some 'arness an' chains fer Bert so I made the excuse that I'd see if they was ready. Save Bert a walk, I said, which sat well wi' 'im, lazy sod. But I wanted ter see 'ow thi' were. We 'eard as 'ow you were workin' at T'Bull. Good fer 'er, I ses ter meself, right pleased tha'd got summat, though Ma an' Mim pulled their faces an' said what were the world comin' to when the likes of Annie Abbott were allowed ter mix wi' decent folk . . . Oh, sorry, Annie, I didn't mean ter . . ."

"I know, Sally, and for pity's sake don't be afraid of offending me. I'm used to them all staring and pointing and whispering behind my back and sometimes they don't even do that but say it out loud as I pass by. The woman from Browhead, they call me . . ."

"Aye, I know, tha's bin the talk o't' valley ever since tha' come home an' now tha's got sack, so Bert tells me. Pleased as punch, he were, just as though tha'd done summat to 'im personal, daft bugger. So what'll tha' do now, lass?" sitting down in the chair before Annie's hearth with a cup of Annie's tea, the last from Reed Macauley's hamper, in her grateful hand. She opened her bodice, more from habit than any need on the part of the infant who was, in fact, fast asleep, threading her distended nipple into its partly open rose-bud mouth and instinctively it began to suck. Cat stared, open-mouthed, distracted from Blackie and Bonnie who had been told to 'sit' and had done so at once. They too, it seemed, were fascinated by the sound the suckling infant made. Into the lady's mouth the tea went, Cat observed, and came out of her fat chest where the baby drank it which clearly was some kind of magic about which she would question her mother at the first opportunity. She and the two dogs surveyed the amazing spectacle with great interest.

Annie was silent, the snuffling sound of the baby, the hissing sigh of the peat fire, the panting of the dogs, both of whom thumped the floor with their tails every time anyone's glance fell on them, whispered about the warm room. It had been miraculously transformed from the hollow, dust-coated barrenness which had been its condition

last November. Everything winked and sparkled, the light
from the fire touching polished surfaces to a glowing
smoothness. The door to the parlour was kept closed since
Annie could not afford to warm two rooms but even though
she and Cat did not use it the parlour was kept achingly
clean and was as tidy as the neat kitchen. In the weeks
since she had lost her job at The Bull she had gone through
the whole farmhouse from the slate roof to the slate floors
of the downstairs rooms. It was a tradition in Lakeland
that spring cleaning must be done by Easter and Annie,
with nothing else to do, had emptied drawers and scrubbed
them, taken out the two beds and brushed and beaten
them. She had boiled all the baking tins, scoured the milking cans and calf buckets with silver sand and scrubbed
the butter boxes until they were as white as the snow
which still capped Skiddaw and Broad End. The dairy itself
and the cow house had been given a coat of the whitewash
she had found in the barn and, having some left over she
had carried outside as much of the furniture as she could
from the kitchen and the parlour, and painted the walls of
those two rooms as well.

All this had taken place, of course, after she had done
what planting she could manage: some bigg, vegetables
and black oat, which would see her and Cat through until
next winter. Her father's barn, untouched since he died
and where over a year ago he had carefully stored them
ready for his planting season, had revealed a sack of seed
potatoes, some gone mouldy but the rest worth a try.
There were corn and parsnip seeds, turnip and carrot,
onion bulbs and all of them had been sown and planted
in neat, well-tended rows as soon as the frozen ground
allowed.

She could do no ploughing, naturally, since her father's
wooden 'stitching' plough needed a horse to pull it, but
she had trimmed her hedges with his bill hook and set his
traps in the hope that, now that spring was almost here
she might catch a fine rabbit to go in the pot with her
vegetables.

She had gone with Cat and the dogs to cut peat on the

fells, pulling it home on the sledge which, as those on the fells knew, was easier to drag about on the grassy slopes than any wheeled cart. The peat had been stacked to dry since what her father had left before he died was almost gone. She had cleaned his tools, sharpening the scythe and the sickle and the shears and even polished the leather horse-collar and harness in readiness for the day when her horse would wear them.

So, she had done what she could. Her house was in order. Her garden tended, her home sweet-smelling and well ordered, welcoming and warm. The sunlight which crept in through the small windows painted a golden haze about the domesticated simplicity of the mothers and their children, and in an old jug, chipped about its rim and therefore useless for its purpose of holding milk, Annie had arranged a great nodding bunch of golden catkins cut from the pussy-willow which grew on the edge of the lake. There was a serenity, an ageless peace in the room, a simple comfort which warmed the senses. In this house generations of Abbotts had been born, had laboured and died, none of them achieving even the status of 'small statesmen'. When other men had prospered they had been dogged by ill-luck, disease, bad harvests, the land which was theirs remaining theirs, but only just. They seemed to crowd at Annie's back, shaking their heads and wringing their hands at her foolhardiness. Sell, they seemed to be telling her. Sell and start a new life where you are unknown but she pushed them away, raising her head to stare about her defiantly as though to scatter them.

"So what'll yer do now, Annie?" Sally asked sympathetically. She pulled her nipple from the baby's mouth, the sound it made like that of a cork from a bottle.

"I'm off to Keswick but don't tell anyone, will you?"

"Eeh no, love, but what are thi' ter do there?"

"Get a job, I hope."

"What sort?"

"Barmaid, what else?" Annie's voice was calm, strong, sure. She was sitting on the sconce and she leaned forward to pull out a stout piece of wood from beneath it, throwing it to the back of the fire. The sudden flaring of the flames heightened the signs of strain on her face which seemed to Sally to be thinner than when they last met, but Annie's eyes were clear and steady.

"I wish there were summat I could do for thi', Annie," Sally sighed, changing the baby to her other enormous breast. The child suckled obligingly, its plump face as ripe and rosy as its mother's.

They chatted for half an hour, of the days when they were children, of their schoolteacher who had smelled of mothballs, of the girls in their class, most of them, like Sally, now young wives and mothers, of Lizzie and Joshua, of Mim who was courting Ben Postlethwaite, a young local farmer with a fair flock of Herdwicks up Binsey way. Mim, because of Annie's close proximity to Upfell, and her and Sally's past connection with her, was terrified that her chances of a good marriage might be dashed, particularly if Sally continued to visit Browhead.

"Silly cow," Sally added mildly as she lumbered to her feet. "Now I'll try and get down again, love, when I can," hitching the sleeping baby beneath her shawl, "but God knows when that'll be. I'll be expected to 'elp wi' dippin' which is any day now. Bert's fetchin' sheep down right now. Natty Varty's bin tekken on ter give a. . . ."

"Natty Varty?"

"Aye, tha' knows Natty. Work fer anyone, 'e will."

"I know. I was hoping to get him to come and cut some of my timber. It'll be ready for peeling and riving by May. How long will he be working for Bert?"

"Nay, don't ask me, chuck. All summer I 'eard tell. We've a fairish-sized flock, tha' knows. Natty's a good worker an' can turn 'is 'and to owt."

Annie groaned. "I know, that's why I wanted him."

"Can thi' not get anyone else?"

"Who? Nobody would work for me, that's if I could pay them which I can't until I get work of my own. Do you know, Sal, I feel as though I'm going round in circles getting absolutely nowhere. I do my best to get over these obstacles which will keep looming up in front of me but

the minute I clamber over one another one appears. I
suppose I'll have to try and cut the timber myself if Natty's
spoken for. I know all the procedures. I learned them from
my father and I have the tools, but he did all the heavy
work. There was a decent stack of birch in the barn which
he must have cut before he died and put there to mature
but most of it's been used by now. Cat and I have made
a fair amount of besoms ready to take to market, and I
want to start on the swill baskets but I can't get going
until the oak's cut. I need to save cash to buy sheep and
I can't get cash until I work. . . ."

"Eeh love, tha's in a right pickle. I only wish I 'ad a few
bob ter lend thi'." Sally's blue eyes clouded solicitously
and she bit her lip as though in anxious contemplation of
her own pitiful resources. Of which she had none.

"I know, Sally, but don't worry. It takes a lot to get
Annie Abbott down and I'll manage this. I've been in
sorrier states, I can tell you."

Sally was torn between an avid eagerness to hear what
sort of 'sorry state' Annie had been in and the certain
knowledge that if she didn't get home soon she'd be 'in·
for it', from her Ma, or her husband, or more than likely
both. The life her friend had known had the fascination of
the mysteriously wicked for her.

It was with great reluctance that she took her leave.

In the end Annie took Cat. She had explained to her
that she would be gone all day; that Cat would be perfectly
safe with the growing dogs to guard her and keep her
company. That she must bolt the door and watch that the
fire did not go out. That there was 'tatie-pot', sadly without
meat, in the oven for her dinner and that Mother would
be home before dark. She knew that Cat was a careful,
sensible child, clear-headed and reliable since she had had
to be all of these things in her short life. She would do
exactly what Annie told her to do and really there was no
need of concern but she was only just three years old last
December and her eyes, though steadfast and trusting,
doing their best to reassure her mother that she would be
as good as gold and as safe as houses, had a small shadow

of uncertainty in them. Blackie and Bonnie stood, one on either side of her, their heads cocked, their ears pricked as though they too understood the seriousness of what must be done and were well prepared for their part in it. Annie had been training them in the field at the front of the farmhouse, doing her best to remember the series of whistles and commands her father had used when he had dogs of his own. A young Border Collie will often have an inborn herding instinct at an early age and both Blackie and Bonnie did their best to 'round up' Cat and bring her back to the safety of the farmhouse door. Annie had already taught them the verbal commands of 'lie down' and 'stay' and they were accustomed to walking on a leash made of rope. She and Cat had spent many patient hours in their training but it was difficult, she told herself wryly, to train a dog to herd sheep, without the sheep!

Still, they were obedient to those commands she had taught them and would obey Cat if the necessity arose. What necessity would that be? she wondered anxiously as she stood in the doorway, three pairs of eyes looking uneasily into hers. The day was fine. Already in the valley 'inlands' the first lambs were clinging to their mother's sides, their heads lost from view beneath her heavy fleece, their tails going mad behind them as they suckled, their plaintive bleat as mother moved to find her own dinner, filling the warming air. The first purple flowers of the self-heal plant, related to the deadnettle family, had appeared on the edge of the rough, tussocky grass at the back of the farmhouse. Blue and white bugle, the red of hedge-wound wort and the creamy pink of wood sage was revealed as the early morning mists rolled away. Annie had found purple mountain saxifrage among the damp rocks when she and Cat had taken the dogs up towards Dead Crags, moving through the heather which was almost ready to burgeon into life. Spring would be here soon. It was all about her, the life, the colour, the readiness to burst forth in its annual exhilaration; the land, the animals it supported, the sustenance which supported

them, and the men who relied on and laboured over it
all.

She stood for several long minutes, biting her lip, then,
"Get your shawl and clogs and the dogs' leashes . . ."
laughing as Cat's face lit up and her eyes blazed in joy.
For five minutes it was bedlam, her own face, still only
that of a girl, as merry and excited as her child's, the dogs
barking and whirling about, knowing of course, that great
things were about to happen.

She took the lake road for though it was longer than
going up and over the top of Skiddaw Forest, dropping
down by Mallen Dodd and into Keswick, it was flat and
easy walking for Cat. They took a short cut through the
inbye fields at the front of Browhead, clambering from one
field to the next over drystone walls and skirting others
which were hedged with hawthorne. In a few weeks the
hedges would be in blossom, a white fragrant border about
each lush stretch of green, but as yet they were straggly
and unkempt, still waiting for their own brief moment of
glory. Annie and Cat, as they stepped out, were flanking
the lower slopes of Ullock Pike, Longside and Dodd with
the breathtaking splendour of Skiddaw rising up on their
left and the still, gentle beauty of Lake Bassenthwaite
falling away to their right. The sky was high, blue, empty,
innocent and though Annie and indeed anyone born in these
parts well knew it could change ferociously within an hour,
today its loveliness cast a magic spell of peace and anticipation on the woman and child. The young dogs were still
unleashed, ready to run wild should they be allowed, for
the smell of sheep was in the air. Their nostrils contained
a memory inherited from countless generations of their
forbears and they were eager to be away to investigate
it. Annie called them to her, looping the rope about their
necks, holding them firmly to her right side since the
last thing she wanted was to send Bert Garnett's flock of
Herdwicks galloping mindlessly about the fields with her
two enthusiastic dogs at their heels.

A man knelt by a drystone wall painstakingly fitting
exactly the right size of stone, first one then another,

trying each piece until he had found what was needed in the repairing of the wall. He stacked them carefully on edge, laying them at the same angle, snug and neat, with nothing to hold them in place, or together, but his own skill. The 'Cap' stones lay in vertical symmetry along the top and he had left a 'hogg-hole' about two feet square at its base to allow yearling sheep to pass through from one field to the next. The hole, when no longer needed would have a slab of stone rolled across it.

He looked up as Annie and Cat approached, ready to nod briefly which was all anyone would get from him even his closest friend, but when he saw who it was his face darkened and he resumed his task without a greeting.

"A lovely day," Annie called, undiminished by his hostility, stepping out along the turnpike road which they had now reached, passing St Bridget's Church by the lake, moving towards the close-knit greenery of Dodd Wood where the ravens were nesting and telling the whole world about it with harsh voices. In a field contained in the narrow strip of fertile land alongside the lake several men were sowing corn seed and in another others were putting in a crop of 'early' potatoes. Wherever there was a farm, sheep, dairy, arable or mixed, the annual task of beginning the year was swinging into its enduring cycle and for a moment or two Annie felt her step falter on the hard, stony path she had set herself. There was so much to do before she even began to think of farming, of actually planting her crops – apart from the pitiful few she had so far managed – of building her flock of sheep and other livestock, pigs and poultry, she intended to have. It was so overwhelmingly daunting in that savage black moment she almost turned back to Browhead where she would gather their few belongings together and use her pitiful savings for a railway ticket to Lancaster.

'Sell it,' she would say to the lawyer, 'and good riddance' but the black moment passed as quickly as it had come. Her natural resilience gathered inside her with a surge which carried her forward excitedly. Glory be, she had been back no more than four months and here she was

ready to give it all up. She had managed to stay alive in
that time, thanks to Reed Macauley, the honest part of
her mind whispered, but she resolutely turned away from
it. She had not touched one penny of the wages she had
earned at The Bull. They, she and Cat, had lived through
the worst of the winter. They had a few vegetables to
look forward to and the good part, the best part, was yet
to come. She had a friend in Sally, she had her child
and a warm place to lay their heads at night. She had a
beginning and she meant to cling to it, to add to it, to
shape it into a bright and wonderful thing.

She began to sing as she stepped out and Cat joined in.
"Come all of you cockers far and near . . ."

The sun burnished the two copper heads to a vivid,
startling warmth and two pairs of golden, transparent eyes
gleamed in exact replica of one another, their joy lovely
to behold. Hands clasped, the woman's long stride
adjusted to the child's, and beside them the young dogs
padded silently, watchfully, for they did not know this part
of the world and their two 'sheep' needed careful guarding.

It was just gone noon when they reached Keswick. It
was market day and crowds swarmed along the length of
Market Place. There were stalls laden with squares of
exquisitely patterned butter, wrapped in muslin and straw,
cheeses, eggs, trussed chickens, the produce of industrious farmwives whose only reward for their labours, in
and out of the farmhouse, was their 'butter money', if they
were allowed to keep it by their thrifty husbands. There
were skinned rabbits, gingerbread and ginger ale, a stall
where baked potatoes were pulled, black and smoking,
from the hot coals. There were pedlars, 'scotchmen' they
were called though they did not hail from over the border,
calling out to passers-by to inspect their printed calico and
cotton cloth, their needles, their sewing thread
and bootlaces with which they tramped the pack routes,
going from farmhouse to farmhouse, from village to
village.

The crowds milled about them, moving on up the street
between the stalls, some stopping to tap their feet and

clap their hands to the rhythmic sound of the organ grinder
and to smile at the antics of his grinning monkey. A cheerful racket which, after the peace and quiet of Browhead
and the surrounding fells, brought excited roses to the
cheeks of Annie and her daughter. They moved along with
the crowds, the dogs keeping close to Annie's skirt, their
eyes darting in some unease in the thicket of moving trousered legs and full swishing skirts of the country folk. Their
noses wrinkled in an effort to identify the mass of smells
which surrounded them and their confusion showed in the
droop of their ears and tails.

She got work in the first inn she tried. Leaving Cat to
one side of the busy, low doorway through which dozens
of men continually moved, the dogs tied to an iron ring in
the wall beside her, meant for the tethering of horses,
Annie walked purposefully across the bar-parlour and
spoke directly to the man she recognised at once as the
landlord.

"I'm looking for work," she said, doing her best to smile
her pert, barmaid's smile.

As in every room she was to enter, whatever its station
in life, conversation dwindled and died to a murmur, the
only men still conversing in normal tones those who had
not yet seen her. She held her head high though her heart
pounded against her ribs. Despite her spirited appearance
she was always apprehensive when confronted by a wall
of male faces, for on every one was that unconscious
predatory look of speculation she knew so well.

"Oh aye, an' what can tha' do?" he asked, looking
about him at the sea of interested faces and winking
suggestively.

"Whatever you like, sir, in your bar, that is."

The crowd were hanging on to every word and this last
caused a great deal of nudging and guffawing but she did
not look round. Her expression was steady, neither one
thing nor the other, neither cringing nor bold and the
landlord relented. This was no raucous pot-house full of
navvies and fist-fighters and where round the back on a
moonless night an illegal cock-fight might be held, which

was why she had chosen it. It was full of men, true. Decent working men, farmers and farm hands, scotch pedlars and such come to market and having a pint of ale whilst they settled a deal, respectable for the most part, but willing, if it could be found, or offered, to have a 'bit of sport' at the expense of a woman who was no better than she should be, a judgement they made on her looks and the job she was seeking.

"You look busy, sir. It seems to me you could do with a bit of help," she said hopefully.

"Does it indeed?" but it was true since the girl he employed already was gathering empty pots and filling them again with the speed and violence which verged on the hysterical. Another woman brought a tray of steaming meat pies through a door behind the bar which evidently led from the kitchen, her face red and sweated, her greasy hair hanging limply from beneath her white frilled cap. The pies were gone in a minute and muttering that she'd fetch another lot she clattered back from where she had come.

With a last desperate image of Cat who stood outside the door of the inn, Annie smiled.

"Tell you what," she said saucily. "I'll give you a hand now if you like. Just for an hour, no wages except one of those pies . . ." which would do for Cat's dinner. ". . . and see what you think. If I don't suit I'll try elsewhere. If I do and we can agree a wage I'll start tomorrow night." It had to be evening employment since, with any luck, she would be too busy working her farm during the day.

Somewhat taken aback, not sure how his customers, who mostly spoke in the Cumberland dialect of these parts, would shape with the way she talked, the landlord hesitated but what had he got to lose? Only one of Aggie Holme's succulent meat pies. And he was run off his feet, as anyone could see.

She smiled and something in him lurched, astonishingly, since in his trade he considered he'd seen everything, none of it moving him to more than mild interest. Her richly burnished hair, which she had deliberately left loose, hung below her waist in a mass of tangled curls, tipping her head to an angle which could only be called haughty. Her pale golden eyes, the brown in them less noticeable in the dim light, narrowed provocatively until the long dark lashes which surrounded them almost meshed together. Her skin, as rich as the cream which floated at the top of the milk, glowed, and her mouth, too wide and full for classical beauty, nevertheless reminded him of the strawberries which had grown in his mother's garden when he was a boy. She was startlingly lovely and there was a gaiety about her which he knew his male customers would like. He was not a man clever with words, or indeed with expressing emotion but by God, this one was . . . bugger him . . . the only word he could think of was . . . *unusual.*

She worked her hour, tirelessly, cheerfully, fending off with laughing good humour the hands which reached for her, the knowing smiles, the winks, the invitations and at the end of it, having agreed on fourpence an hour, he told her she was to start at six the following evening.

She moved on light feet to the door of the inn, waving and smiling at those men who had promised her they would be there the next evening, the tips they had given her amounting to threepence three farthings, jingling in her pocket. Added to what she had brought with her she meant to buy some raw wool from one of the stalls and begin the process of spinning and weaving, ready to knit the stockings she and Cat would need, and to fashion the hodden-grey cloth to replace their sadly lacking wardrobe.

Her daughter was exactly where she had been left and, resting for no more than five minutes whilst Cat shared her pie with Blackie and Bonnie, Annie took her hand and set off along Market Place and towards the road which led out of Keswick.

They had five miles to walk and already the afternoon was beginning to darken. The sun had gone and the dreaded 'messenger clouds' had begun to gather above the rise of Black Combe, foretelling the arrival of rain very soon and they would not be home for at least three hours. She knew she would have to carry her daughter before long for the little girl had already walked five miles and had stood or strolled about the market stalls for most of the afternoon. She was visibly tired though she stepped out bravely in her ill-fitting clogs. She was growing rapidly and before the month was out must have some new ones, was Annie's worried thought.

The sound of horses' hooves on the road behind them was faint at first, growing louder as it gained on them. A wheel squeaked as though in need of a drop of oil and a man's voice 'giddupped' a couple of times to the animal. Annie stood to one side, drawing Cat and the dogs to her for the road was narrow, letting the farm cart pass her but as it drew level the man sitting hunched on the plank of wood which served as a seat, pulled at the reins, changing his 'giddups' to 'whoas'.

It was Bert Garnett. He glanced about him in the gathering gloom as though to make sure there was no one to see him, then turned to look down at her. She could see the whites of his eyes in his weatherbeaten face but no more since the light was going fast. Already the trees in Dodd Wood had run together into an almost solid impermeability, no more than a dark mass against the sky which would soon be of the same density. The height of Skiddaw Forest shaped itself menacingly above the trees and Bert Garnett fastened his eyes on the glorious, forbidden wonder of Annie Abbott. He liked what he saw. He licked his lips.

"I'll give thi' a lift if tha' like, Annie. 'Op up, an' t' nipper. Stick them dogs in t'back."

She could not have been more surprised if the Prince Consort himself had invited her to share his carriage but quickly, before he could change his mind, she 'hopped up', lifting Cat up beside her and dragging the two reluctant dogs by their ropes until they lay in the back of the cart.

"Thanks Bert," she said gratefully, wondering if Sally had mistaken her husband's antipathy towards 'fallen women' though her woman's instinct which had been fine-honed during the last four years, did not believe it.

"'Tis nowt, Annie, only neighbourly," he said, running his smile over her, a smile she knew well, a smile she had seen on many men's faces and though he made no move towards her – well, he wouldn't, would he, not with Cat on her knee and the two young dogs in the back – she was quite sure that, had it been broad daylight, Bert Garnett would not have given her the time of day and she was even more certain that she had just come up against another of those obstacles she had mentioned to this man's wife only the other day.

10

The Merle Collie ran silently at the heels of the black mare, so close it seemed in imminent danger of being struck on its nose as the lethal iron-shod hooves lifted in the gallop. The path on which they travelled was stony and well defined, snaking between the beck on one side and the growing bracken and heathery upland on the other. The horse's coat rippled like black satin across its muscled flanks and straining neck, the sunlight giving it a gloss even the hard work of its groom could not improve on and the two animals, each well bred, moved with that special grace only the thoroughbred can achieve.

The man on the mare's back was of the same breed, sitting so easily and naturally in his saddle he might have been part of the animal, his head high, his back straight and supple, his strong horseman's legs which gripped the mare's side well muscled in the thigh. He was soberly dressed in a dark grey riding coat and breeches. He wore a tall black beaver hat. At his throat was a snowy white cravat, beautifully laundered and impeccably knotted, and in its folds glittered a gold and diamond pin. It seemed to say that though he was a man dressed for the work at hand, whatever that might be in his well-cut, beautifully tailored coat and trousers, he was also a man of wealth and style.

The sound of the horse's hooves on the steep and stony path was barely discernible, obliterated by the roar of the magnificent waterfalls which pounded down the precipitous wooded ravine at the base of the Bakestall plateau from where the mare had just come. Dash Beck, issuing from the vast waste of Skiddaw Forest, leaped exultantly over the lip of the escarpment towards the gentler pastures below, plunging in a series of falls to a mighty torrent of roaring thrashing waters. Whitewater Dash, it was called. A great inferno whose thunder could be heard many miles away down the valley and whose spray shimmered like the diamond at Reed Macauley's neck in a myriad sparkling droplets over horse, rider and dog.

The track became more pronounced as the silent trio dropped down towards the valley, still desolate and lonely but showing signs of the hand of man in the appearance of a well-tended drystone wall running away from the beck and meandering through the bracken until it began to climb up the rolling slope of the opposite fell. There was a farm-house, small and grey, surrounded by a grove of larches, with outbuildings and a yard in which pecked dozens of hens and a showy cock. A couple of dogs barked lustily on the end of chains and a man looked up from some harness he was tinkering with, nodding dourly in Reed Macauley's direction. A cart stood by the gate which led out of the yard and a small boy sat on the plank which served as a seat, flapping imaginary reins and 'gidduping' to an imaginary horse. Fresh white washing strained at the washing line to the side of the house and grey smoke was wisped in torn shreds from the circular chimney. A well-built Lakeland farm, Upfell Farm, belonging to the Mounseys and since he had married Sally Mounsey, Bert Garnett. It was as old as the fells in which it was set, or so it seemed, with its thick walls and heavy roof, its interior like so many Lakeland farms crammed with crooked doors and tilted floors and odd little staircases up and down. There were hundreds of them scattered in sheltered crannies against the fells of Cumberland, the one to which Reed Macauley was drawn but which he had no intention of visiting, none at all, even though he happened to be passing, a mile or so away towards Gillthrop. He could not get her out of his mind – that was his trouble. Three months now since he had last seen her nearly up to her waist in the snow and still, at some part of the day, perhaps for only a flashing second, she came to haunt him. She was always laughing. Though she might be imperious, her head held in that haughty, stiff-necked way she had, her grandness would dissolve into warm and lovely laughter, into the glowing love which she showed her child. Eyes long and brown and clear would narrow and melt with her emotion, her mouth wide and smiling over her perfect teeth, all brilliance and warmth, an enchantment which brought him time and again down the track alongside Dash Beck and on to the lower slopes of Great Cockup where her farm lay.

Each time he went there he would turn about impatiently and gallop off home furious with himself and his own weakness for were not women all the same? This one was no different to any of the pretty and willing females with whom he was acquainted and who were available to any man of wealth. But still he could not rid himself of her. He had been across to the inlands of his farm, the big grassy slopes which were surrounded by drystone walls and where his ewes had been brought to lamb. In winter Reed and all the other sheep farmers brought their flocks down to these safe pastures where if the weather was exceptionally bad – and when was it not, in winter? – they could be given hay to augment their feeding.

He had three shepherds who knew every inch of the terrain but still he felt the need to keep an eye on his flock. It was lambing time – April – and the ewes had been gathered for easier shepherding. The ewes were mated and the lambs of Lakeland were born later in the year than their southern cousins for up in the north where the weather was fickle and menacing, even up to the month of May, new-born lambs would be hard put to survive the fierce late blizzards which were a feature of the district. It had been known for snowstorms to linger well into May and when they were done with there was the hazard of foxes which raided among the newly dropped lambs, of ravens who would tear out their eyes and of eagles who would carry off the newly born in their strong talons. It needed constant vigilance not only on the part of his shepherds, but their sheepdogs who guarded his flocks, one of which ran at his heels today.

Bess was that most unusual of sheepdogs known as a 'Merle'. Most Collies have dark brown eyes but hers were a bright and vivid blue and it had been remarked sourly more than once among his neighbours, many of whom envied him his wealth and position that it was only to be expected that a 'fancy dan' such as he would have a dog whose eyes matched his own. Not for him the usual black and white of the Border Collie but he must have something different and Bess's body colour, though she had the white Collie marking on her face, chest, feet and also her tail tip, was of broken black and grey, giving the impression of torn patches of cloth. The two pups he had given to Annie Abbott were both 'Merles' since Bess was their mother.

He heard her voice as he drew his horse to a walk beside the singing beck and in the most alarming way he felt his heart move lurchingly in his chest. The horse he rode and the dog at his heels both pricked their ears.

"Blackie, Bonnie, come," the voice called, and as he and his animals moved over the small rise which separated the Mounsey farm from hers he saw her. Again his heart bounded and though no blame could be attached to her since she had done nothing to cause it – for could she help her own loveliness? – he felt the angry impatience rise in him. She was dressed in her usual plain hodden-grey skirt, which had once belonged to Lizzie Abbott, though he was not aware of it. Lizzie had been shorter than Annie and the hem of the skirt came barely below her calf, revealing the fragile slenderness of her white ankles and her feet which were pushed into her clogs. The bodice was low at the neck and almost sleeveless and her skin was rich and creamy, as lustrous as a pearl where the sunlight touched it. Her hair had been plaited at the back of her head, one long plait as thick as his own forearm, crisp and glowing a rich copper, swinging down her back to her buttocks where it curled vigorously at its end. She looked glorious, the plainness of her attire, the drabness even, revealing her beauty more than had she worn silk and satin and costly jewels. She lifted her hand to shade her eyes as she watched her dogs progress and her breasts rose in proud fullness, the nipples hard and pointed beneath the thin material of her bodice.

His breath caught in his throat and he felt his manhood stir enquiringly, tight and uncomfortable against his saddle. Jesus Christ . . . Oh, Jesus Christ, but she was the most . . . there was really no word . . . none.

The child was sitting on the wall at the front of the farmhouse, her own bright copper hair catching and reflecting the April sunshine, a halo of burnished curls springing about her small head which turned to look in his direction as he approached.

He had meant – or so he told himself – to ride on by the farmhouse, keeping to the track which ran behind it, but some wayward impulse, some madness – and he knew it was that – had him draw on the reins, bringing his mare to a halt. The collie who ran behind him stopped when he did, standing when he did, though her eyes were bright and watchful and her ears swivelled to listen to the commands the woman gave. They were familiar though of course the dog knew they were not meant for her.

Reed did not get down. He sat and waited for Annie to look in his direction, lounging indolently in his saddle, not at all concerned whether she did or not, his careless posture implied, though in his eyes, should anyone have cared to look, was a prick of light and a narrowed tension which belied his careless demeanour. Both mare and dog waited for a command and when none came the dog lay down, her head on her paws, the very picture of relaxed indifference though her eyes, which swivelled from side to side, gave the lie to her appearance.

Annie Abbott took as much notice of him as she would a passing sheep – less, for if he had been a sheep, she might have wondered whom he belonged to, he thought angrily. She stood, her hands on her hips now, her feet apart, watching the two young dogs as they flew up the field towards her. She let them get within ten yards of her then her voice, crisp and commanding, told them to "Lie

down", which they both did at once. One of them began
to creep on its belly, its eyes on her, its tail moving rapidly
on the tufty grass, loving the 'game' but longing to run to
her and greet her with its joyous affection but her hand
stayed him and her stern eye kept him there until she
spoke the words "Come here" when they both leaped
forward. It took a moment or two of patient handling
since they were young, no more than puppies, but she
had them sitting, one on either side of her, their bright
faces turned up to hers, their bright eyes asking "What
next?"

"Go on then," she said, reaching to pat each fine head,
"Go to Cat," and the pair of them began the frolicking to
which dogs of their age are prone, leaping up at the child
on the wall. Cat jumped down to them, fending off their
loving tongues and exuberant kisses. Laughing and
beseeching them to "Get down, Blackie, get down,
Bonnie," she began to run down the field, the two dogs
at her heels.

The man and woman did not speak. The tension
between them was immediate and both of them were
aware of it. It was ridiculous, of course, since they were
nothing to each other, each was thinking, merely neighbours, and what was in that to cause this tendency to be
short of breath, the reluctance to meet the other's eye,
to shift about in the saddle, to shuffle on the tufty grass,
as she was doing. It was in both their minds confused,
angry, fearful even, and when their eyes met the impact
of it was alarming.

He was already irritated by the way his heart had quickened when he heard her voice, now his alarm, since it was
alarming to be so affected by a woman, when none before
had done no more than stir his loins, made him sharp,
cruel even.

"Those dogs are meant for sheep, not for performing tricks in a field." They were the only words he could
think of to cover his own breathless reaction to her
presence.

"Is that so, Reed Macauley? Well show me some sheep

and I'll set about training the dogs to them. If not, then take them back with you since I know they came from you and if there are limits to be put on what I do with them they're no good to me."

"I did not say they came from me. I know nothing of them but they were obviously bred to be sheepdogs and to have them playing the fool . . ."

"If you did not leave them tied to my door then who did, tell me that? That bitch you have there is very rare and those two are the same colourings. There can't be many Merles in this area."

"I know nothing of that. I am only remarking that it is a complete waste of two good dogs to have them performing tricks and playing with the child as they are doing."

The shrieks of laughter and the excited barking which came from the bottom of the field grew merrier, though the child and the dogs were hidden from view. The grasses were growing tall, studded with bright daisies and cowslips, and beneath the hawthorn tree which stood to the side of the farmhouse wild daffodils swayed and nodded in the light breeze. There was a smell in the air of growing things, of newness and brightness and hope, and of their own volition the eyes of the man and woman met and clung, truth in them, though not acceptance. Her anger grew for it was fed by her fear. Her lip curled, lifting over her teeth as though she would like nothing better than to sink them into some part of him which would hurt, or better yet, maim him.

"Whether they came from you or not, and I can think of no one else in this . . . this God-forsaken place who would part with them, especially to me, they are *mine* now and I shall do with them as I please."

They were not of course, arguing over his dogs but something much deeper and more meaningful.

"That is your privilege, Miss Abbott, naturally since as you say, they are nothing to do with me . . ."

"Then why are you criticising my handling of them? When I have my flock I shall train them properly, of course."

"You are expecting it in the near future, then?"

"What?"

"Your flock."

"Well . . . no, but . . . when I have the money together I mean to . . ."

"The money you earn at the Packhorse, you mean." There was a sneer in his voice though it was put there not by his contempt but by something over which he had no control.

She narrowed her eyes menacingly. Her hands clenched into fists and she took a step towards him. He was still mounted and the wall divided them but she looked ready to leap it and tear at his face.

"It is money honestly earned. I do no more than serve ale and if you are implying that . . . that . . . otherwise . . . then you can get off my land and take not only yourself but those two dogs as well. I want nothing from you, Reed Macauley, nothing, neither your hampers nor your . . . your . . . nothing. Sweet Christ, has nobody in these parts a scrap of decency or humanity in them that they must speak to me, treat me, as though I was dirt beneath their feet, you included, with your filthy mouth? I am doing my best to earn an honest shilling, a start, honestly gained, to the farm my father left me. That's all. I don't ask for their, or your friendship, just the right to get on with my life uninterrupted. Do you think I want to work at the Packhorse where every man in the place thinks he may put his hands on me whenever he has the fancy and that I should not object? Do you think I like to leave my child alone at night with no one to guard her but two half-grown dogs? Do you think I like to walk all those miles in the dark when, as you have pointed out yourself, there are any number of men hanging about ready to do me damage? This world was not made for lone women, did you know that? Of course you didn't, especially one who is as . . . as evil as me . . ."

"No . . . not that . . ."

His voice was soft, gentle. The expression on his face was the same and when he dismounted and, vaulting the wall, moved to stand directly before her, she was so astounded her voice tapered away to silence.

He smiled. "I did not mean to . . . really . . . you are such a firebrand and I am . . . I chose my words unwisely. Dear God, no man could get near you to do you a mischief, Annie Abbott, not with that . . . temper of yours. I meant no offence . . ."

"Yes, you did. You insinuated that I was . . . that men were paying me to . . ." She backed away from him and in her eyes was the dreadful awareness, the sweet knowledge, the glowing warmth of what, as yet, both of them violently denied. It was mirrored in his eyes as he tried to take her hand. He meant her no harm. The gesture was involuntary. A reaching out of his flesh which longed to touch hers but she recoiled from it since she wanted it as much as he did.

"Don't . . . don't, Reed . . ."

"I mean you no harm . . . let me . . ."

"What?" Her voice was suspicious.

"Help you . . ." He shrugged his shoulders, his anger returning, the surprising, terrifying gentleness slipping away for she was looking at him as though he was the same as those men in the snug at the Packhorse. As though he would, if he could, be delighted to lay covetous hands on Annie Abbott, and of course, she was right. Her nearness, the warmth of her breath as it swept his face, the smell of lavender about her, the faint suggestion of sweat on her upper lip, her mouth, parted, sweet, moist, rosy, her breasts rising and falling with emotion, and her eyes, narrowing and darkening in a way he was so familiar with since he had made love to many women and knew the signs of need.

"How can you help me?" she asked, the words meaning nothing, just an answer, vague and automatically given, since neither was aware of anything but the physical beauty of the other, the wave of sensuality in her which was answered in him, the female and male desire which was so very apparent and which was sweeping them both on a course they ardently longed to be on. They wanted to fight it, Annie more than Reed, for had she not more to lose, but his eyes, the most vivid and compelling blue she had ever seen, between their thick black lashes mesmerised her. His lips had parted, softening ready for that first kiss and his hand was half-way to the nape of her neck. She had raised her face, flushed now, eager, her woman's body unwinding joyously its core of desire, ready even before he touched her, for his, since she was no untried girl. It was four years since she had lain with a man, the father of her child, but her body, dormant since then, concerned only with food and shelter for herself and Cat, had not forgotten.

"Hello . . . o . . . o . . ." A man's voice shouted and at once the loveliness was shattered, breaking into a thousand unrepairable pieces, gone, it seemed, and never to be repeated, for she was aware of the danger now, prepared, defended.

She whirled about, her plait flying out and across her shoulder coming to rest on her heaving breast. Within seconds she had put three yards between herself and Reed Macauley and when Bert Garnett's face appeared over the wall there was nothing left of that fragile tender beginning of what might have been between them.

"Oh, Bert, there you are." Her voice and the welcome in it was warmer than it would normally have been for, to tell the truth, Bert Garnett's unannounced and furtive visits to Browhead had become a nuisance to her during the two months since he had given her a lift back from Keswick. But his arrival at that precise moment had saved her from what she realised – now – would have been disaster. She had been ready to fall into Reed Macauley's arms and God alone knew where that would have led. Her bed, she supposed, for she had been fast in an intoxication which had taken her senses, her sense held in some spell he had cast over her, ready to move as she had vowed she never would again, into his, or indeed into any man's arms. Ready to shed her caution and sound common sense, along with her clothing, whilst her body romped, what other word could she use since what else would he want from her, with Reed Macauley's. Thank God, *thank God* for Bert Garnett, her mind was babbling as she scrambled over the wall, revealing even more of her long white legs to which the eyes of both men were drawn.

Reed was, for just a moment, still floundering in the delightful ardour into which Annie's response and sweetness had thrust him. His body was already demanding its masculine victory, glowing with that special male triumph which knows that it is about to conquer and possess. She had been ready, delightfully so, her eyes glazing, her mouth full and swollen and suddenly . . . suddenly it was gone. *She* was gone and looking over the wall was the considerably startled face of . . . what the bloody hell was his name? . . . of the man who owned the next farm up the dale and who obviously knew Annie Abbott well enough to be called by his Christian name. Married, too, Reed was well aware, to the plump daughter of the man who had owned it before he died.

He could feel the blood pump violently in his veins, grabbing at his heart and making it pound in his chest, grabbing at his temples in which a pulse began a rapid tattoo. He saw the flash of her legs . . . Dear Christ . . . and the narrowed speculative prick of male interest in the other man's eyes and for just a second, no more than a fraction of time, he knew he would kill him. Take him by the throat and choke the life out of him, slowly, of course, so that he would suffer, or perhaps he'd beat him with his fists, sinking his hard flesh into the man's stupid face, see the blood spurt and hear the satisfying sound of bone breaking and flesh splitting.

Bert was shifty-eyed and awkward since he had thought Annie to be alone but he had no choice but to say, as casually as he could the words he had come to say.

"I come to tell thi' I'm off to Keswick in t'mornin' an' if tha' wants a ride I'll pick thi' up at bottom."

"That's very kind of you, Bert. I would appreciate it as I shall have Cat with me and it's a long walk. Mr Holme has asked me to work from opening time seeing as it's

Whit Monday. The Hiring Fair will bring in a lot of custom and he will need every pair of hands he can get. He says I can take Cat with me as long as she stays quietly in the kitchen, which of course she will. And I wanted to take in some of my besoms and swill baskets, that's if you have room in the cart. A fortnight ago I spoke to a woman who has a stall there and she said she'd sell them for me, for a small commission, naturally, and I have knitted two dozen pairs of socks from the wool I purchased two months ago and have made arrangements with another stallholder to sell those for me as well. I was wondering how on earth I was to get them all to the market so your offer is a godsend."

She directed a smile so falsely brilliant at Bert Garnett his mouth flew open. He did not see the falseness, only the wide mouth, the perfect teeth, the glittering eyes, the breathless – he did not use the word feverish – way she spoke. He saw Mr Macauley as well, but not being a man of perception or indeed of any deep thought, he observed nothing strange in the wealthy farmer's presence in Annie Abbott's field. Perhaps he wanted to buy her farm since eventually she would have to sell, everyone knew that and he only wished he himself had the ready cash to make her an offer right now. It was a damn good farm lying neat as you please right next to his. A bit neglected but that could soon be put right. Why Reed Macauley should want it was a mystery since he had acres and to spare of his own but that was not Bert Garnett's concern. An insensitive man who saw nothing but what his own eyes looked at, and at the moment that was Annie Abbott's flashing white ankles and glowing brown eyes. A man shrewd and thrifty, his plain craggy features which were framed by a wisping beard, revealing these characteristics. He was known to be level headed in his working life but there were not many men whose clear sight would not be clouded by the spirited loveliness and warmth of Annie Abbott.

Reed Macauley vaulted the wall and reached blindly for the reins of his mare who was cropping placidly at the sweet new grass by Annie's wall. His dog stood up, moving her plumed tail in greeting, then sensing something not quite right in her master, pushed her cold nose into his hand. He touched her head gently and murmured to her and as though the dog had calmed something ferocious in him, he turned to Annie. His eyes were a cold, pale and distant blue and his mouth was hard, cruel.

"I will bid you good day then, Miss Abbott," he said, the words sounding more like an insult than a farewell. "I had not realised you had made such good . . . friends . . . hereabouts. But I wish you well of them." The last word a sneer which, though it meant nothing to Bert Garnett, was clearly a slur on Annie Abbott. She flushed, then turned to Bert, again giving him her glorious smile and, as she had meant it to, bringing bile to Reed Macauley's mouth.

"Oh indeed, Mr Macauley. Bert has been most helpful to me since we renewed our acquaintance a month or two back. We knew one another as children. His wife and I are old friends and our families were . . . were close."

Bert preened and moved nearer to Annie, his shoulder almost touching hers and Reed's hand jerked at the reins of his mount. The mare moved her head fretfully, not accustomed to rough handling, and he turned at once to soothe her and in that moment as he looked away, Annie Abbott's love for him, since what else could it be, she asked herself despairingly, was in her eyes and on her face for anyone, even Bert Garnett to see. He did not see it.

His grace and vigour and style were very evident as Reed mounted his mare. He was a gentleman from good sound stock, going back to the days before the reign of James I, when his forebears had supplied military service and equipment to their King; a man of wealth and position, sitting easily in the saddle, handsome, oh yes he was that, for she loved him now, and unconcerned with lesser men like Bert Garnett and women like herself. The lounging charm he showed suddenly, since what were they to him, his manner said, was light and whimsical and beneath the polish his education had given him whatever he might be feeling was well hidden. *He* was in control, of himself and of the situation and he tipped his hat quite genially to them both.

"I'm glad to hear it, Miss Abbott. And does your wife approve of your . . . er . . . friendship with *her* friend, Mr Garnett?" turning his controlled smile at Bert. "It is always handy to have one's wife's . . . permission, is it not?"

Turning his mare, calling to Bess, though she did not need it, he moved off up the dale in the direction of Long Beck five miles away. Bert Garnett, not at all sure what Reed Macauley had meant, was quite put out by Annie's sudden silence and lack of interest. He had pictured them sitting together on the wall, shoulder to shoulder, him with a tankard of the ale she had brewed recently, in his hand. They would chat and laugh and perhaps, if he could sweet-talk her, or even, being a masculine, firm sort of a chap, persuade her to a cuddle, perhaps a kiss or two and a stroke of her soft breasts which, it seemed to him, she flaunted on his behalf. Nice and polite she'd been to him when, on the quiet, of course, he'd called at her farm on some pretext or other, and always glad of a lift when he went to market. He was very discreet, or at least he had been until today, only slipping down the track to her back door when his wife and his mother and sister-in-law were busy elsewhere, but it seemed to him Annie gave him no reason to believe he was anything but welcome. Lonely she'd be, and glad of a chat with a friendly chap like himself. And she'd be short of summat else, he'd be bound, a lusty woman like her, and him only too glad to supply it. It would give him a great deal of pleasure to dip his hand down the front of her bodice and hold those lovely dumplings cupped in his hand whilst his fingers tweaked her nipples into an even more pointed firmness than they already were. She might even allow him to run his hand up those white legs, along the satin smoothness of her thighs to the joining where the damp, dark, sweet-smelling bush of her womanhood lay and when . . .

His day-dream was cruelly shattered when, with a voice as flat and cool as the lake on a still winter's day, Annie moved imperiously across the bit of garden at the front of the house and went inside. Holding the door she turned for a moment.

"I'll see you tomorrow, Bert," then closed it in his face.

11

The twice-yearly Hiring Fairs held at Whitsuntide and Martinmas were eagerly looked forward to by the folk of Lakeland, for they were regarded as a holiday and a respite from the drudgery of the labours they performed on their farms all the year round. There was no deliverance for them on any other day of the week since even Sunday brought the same round of chores which must be done, but on these two occasions everyone who could be spared had their day out. There were fairs at Cockermouth, Kendal, Penrith, Ulverston, Egremont, Appleby and Ravenglass but no matter where they were held, it was an excuse for revelries. There was even a regatta on Lake Windermere in which schooners took part in sailing events and there were rowing matches, running, leaping and wrestling matches and, as the poster advertised, a variety of other amusements finishing with a ball at the Salutation Inn at Ambleside.

But the serious business of hiring servants and farm hands, those who were not 'stopping on' for another six months and therefore had gathered to find a new place, must first be got through. A straw stuck in a hat or from the corner of the mouth indicated that a labourer was for hire and when the deal was struck between master and man, a handshake was all that was needed to seal the bargain. The hired man or woman received a shilling as 'arles', or earnest money, as a token of their hiring. A man could get between £8 and £10 for his six months with board and lodgings included, and a woman might expect between £6 and £7. No references were asked for or offered, master taking man, and vice versa, on looks alone.

Though Annie had been expecting the increased

excitement and burgeoning crowds of men and women, children, dogs, horses and all the paraphernalia of this lively day, the impact as the cart, with a truculent Bert Garnett at the reins, turned into Market Place, hit her like a blow. Yesterday still clung to her like drifting cobwebs which, no matter how she strived to dislodge them, held her fast, numbing her mind and blunting her senses so that she could hardly think. The worst thing she could ever imagine happening to her, had happened, and she was twined round with her love for Reed Macauley, and would she ever be free of it? Could she function in spite of it? The heaving sea of people crammed between the market stalls only brought her fresh misery for she had to get through today and this evening, smiling and cheerfully fobbing off the often crude jokes and repartee which her customers imagined she was more than willing to enjoy. Grit her teeth and smile, tactfully remove eager hands from the different parts of her body they remorselessly attached themselves to whilst the inner being that was Annie Abbott cringed, rebelling against this humiliation which she was forced to endure. Sometimes looking at the sly admiration and . . . yes, lust, she supposed it to be, in Bert Garnett's pale, washed out eyes, she was tempted to tell him to take himself and his 'helping hand' as he described it, to the devil. She knew what he wanted in repayment for the lifts to Keswick, the vague offers of future 'boon-ploughing' and perhaps other farming activities at which he hinted. Sally didn't know he had been a time or two to Browhead and Annie didn't tell her since one day Bert Garnett might indeed be of some aid to her. She couldn't afford to insult him but she dreaded the time, which was bound to come, when he would get up the courage to tell her what was on his lascivious mind.

"I'll wait for thi' by 't corner," he said shortly. He had scarcely noticed her silence, the pale, lethargic lack of her usually bright spirits. He was too concerned with his own needs and his own offended spirits, for was he not a man of some importance in the parish of Bassenthwaite and did he not deserve more respect than the curt dismissal he had received yesterday from this woman? Laughed and joked with him for two months she had, leading him on, as he saw it, and him helping her out whenever he could – without his wife knowing naturally, for he was not a complete fool – and she'd done no more than shut the bloody door in his face and what had Macauley been doing there, answer him that? Well, child or no child, giving Cat a surly glance, he'd have more than a cool dismissal from Annie Abbott this night.

The market place and all the streets leading off it were jammed from building to building with a wide variety of entertainments. There was wrestling, slack-wire balancing, performing bears and monkeys, sad and hopeless and frightened. There were freaks such as the pig-faced lady and the hairiest man anyone had ever seen, like a monkey himself he was, coming from Morocco wherever that was, and where, the open-mouthed folk of Cumberland decided, all men must be like him, poor sods. Travelling 'doctors' sold elixirs and cures guaranteed to arouse the liver of the most sluggish gentleman; tooth pullers who always placed their booths close to the 'oom-pah-pah' of the customary brass band, since it would not do for the public, those with aching teeth to be got rid of, to hear the cries of distress from those who went before them. There was even a bull-baiting going on further along the passage which ran to the back of The Packhorse, a terrible tearing and rending as the bull, tethered on a short rope to the wall was set upon by dogs. Spectators stood around in their dozens or perched on the roofs of buildings about the passage, while the dogs roved freely round and beneath the exhausted bull, biting and nipping where they could. It was illegal of course, but the local constable, promised a fine cut of the beef when the animal was slaughtered, looked the other way. After all, it was a well-known fact that baiting the bull improved the quality of the meat.

Those who were for hire stood in patient rows, men and women apart, and moving amongst them already, for the best and strongest went first, were the masters, stopping here and there to speak to one or the other.

Annie gave them no more than an indifferent glance before
entering The Packhorse, Cat beside her. She put the child
in a corner of the already overheated kitchen, kissed her
and told her to be a good girl and to do exactly as Mrs
Holme, the landlord's wife, told her, and tying her crisp
white apron about her waist, prepared herself for her long
twelve hours on her feet.

She got through it. She knew she would, of course, for
no matter what the state of her heart, poor weak thing
that it was, her back was strong and tireless. Somehow
she parried the jokes and the teasing and the greedy
hands. She smiled when they demanded it, pocketing their
tips and telling herself that every farthing was putting her
nearer to the end of all this, to the beginning of that good,
hard-working free life she planned for her and Cat. She
had enough already to buy several ewes at seven and
sixpence each, and by October and tup time, she hoped
to have the necessary cash to hire a ram of good quality
to put to them and begin the birth of her flock. She and
Cat were eating well. There was always plenty of left-
overs from the kitchen of the inn. Their vegetables were
doing well, and the herbs she had planted, and she had
even managed, with a little bit of flattery and a great deal
of the smiling and dimpling which men loved, to purchase
a few hens and a cock cheap from a stallholder, which had
happily taken to pecking round her yard and barn. She
worked hard all day, digging and hoeing, tending to her
tiny crop of oats and bigg, praying for good weather, weaving swill baskets and making birch besoms. Her coppice
needed attention. She and Cat went up to the peat moss
to dig for peat, dragging it laboriously downhill on the
sledge to be stacked in the yard. They lived off the land,
except for the milk which Sally surreptitiously left twice a
week for her in a can hidden beneath a tilted piece of slate
in the wall by her gate. The couple of pints not missed by
her mother or her husband since it was Sally's job to milk
the cows. Annie meant to have her own cow one day and
with her spare milk, make butter and cheese to be sold
at the market, but it was enough at the moment that she

was hanging on, getting there by slow painstaking, back-breaking inches. It was all very fragile of course. Just let one tiny thing go wrong and the whole meshed process of her life would topple and fall. An illness, on her part, or Cat's, which would prevent her going to The Packhorse, an accident, her crops to fail, her vegetables to rot, too much rain, too little rain and she would be finished. She needed the gods to continue smiling on her for another six months, just until she had her ewes, her ram, her oats and barley in and safely put away in her mother's oak kist. Please God . . . Oh, please God . . .

The market place was deserted of all but the serious drunkards. There were vague shifting shadows against the walls which Annie knew were the whores who did good business when the inns closed. There was a shouted quarrel at the corner of the square and several men leaned drunkenly against one another as they watched in befuddled interest. She could see Bert's cart and his loose-limbed outline slumped on the seat and from somewhere to her right, where the men and women had stood waiting to be hired that morning – twelve hours ago and, God's teeth, her legs and back ached as though it was twenty-four – there was the sound of someone whimpering. Nothing to do with her, she told herself, hefting the sleeping form of Cat close against her shoulder. It was probably some prostitute who had performed her task and then been diddled by her customer, or a woman grieving the loss of her wages gone on gin, but the sound was haunting, that of someone in deep trouble, or fear.

Dear God, she didn't want to go and find out, really she didn't. She had enough with her own weariness and the need to get her child safe home in her bed and besides which she had nearly three bob jingling in her deep skirt pocket, the tips she had earned on top of her wages which she would get at the week's end. All she wanted was to fall into bed herself and sleep the clock round. She had slipped out for half an hour at supper-time, given permission to go by Mrs Holme, the landlady, who was always pleased with the way Annie Abbott worked, 'going at it' as she liked things to be 'gone at', as she herself went at them, which was like a demon. She worked hard, did Mrs Holme, and she admired it in others and besides being pert and pretty, which drew the customers, Annie was good-natured, hard-working and conscientious.

"O'course, dearie, you slip out for a breath of fresh air and tek littl'un wi' thi'," and Annie had gone to the stall-holder who had sold all her besoms and swills and after giving the woman her commission, had almost another pound, eighteen shillings to be exact, to put beside the tips and the rest of her small savings hidden in the tin box under the sconce in the kitchen. She had not done too well with the stockings since at this time of the year they were not an item women wanted, besides which most knitted their own, but she'd save them until autumn and try again.

A good day, a very good day and the last thing she wanted was to be distracted by some other woman's troubles. Anyway, the noise had stopped now so she'd best get back to Bert who, having seen her come from the inn, was beginning to show signs of impatience as she dilly-dallied by the doorway.

"Now stop that, yer daft little bugger," a man's voice said hoarsely, followed by a thud, then nothing again. Silence. A small sound of something moving just out of range of the light which fell from the doorway of The Packhorse, scuffling perhaps and a grunt or two but nothing more. For some reason though, the hairs on the back of Annie's neck rose and a peculiar dread trickled down her back. It was nothing, she told herself. And if it was, it was nothing to do with her, but some primeval female instinct would not allow her to turn away and walk towards Bert who had now jumped down from his cart and was beckoning to her with every sign of vexed irritability.

She turned away from him slowly, trying to pierce the shadows at the side of the inn, but the darkness was complete. There was an enormous waterbutt put there by some optimistic soul who had hoped, one presumed, to collect rainwater and whether it was full or empty Annie neither knew nor cared as she peeped round its wide girth.

She could see nothing at first, then, as her eyes became used to the deeper darkness there, she became aware of movement, a shifting and twitching which meant nothing to her at that moment. There was someone there, she could make that out. Huddled against the wall and in the corner where the butt touched it, a man and woman wrestling, deep in the throes of fornication, Annie thought disgustedly, the woman's skirt well up about her waist, the man's trousers well down below his knees. There began the most awful guttural panting and the man's white buttocks gleamed in the dark corner, obscene and graceless, but as Annie had already told herself, nothing to do with her. She supposed the whores who plied their trade in the grey areas about the town must ply it somewhere and here was as good a place as any since it was dark and afforded some privacy. But suddenly the words she had heard a moment before came back to her.

"Stop that . . ." a man's voice had said, and "yer daft little bugger . . ." which were not the words a customer says to the one who is supplying him with what he is paying for.

"What's going on here?" she said loudly, commandingly, speaking before she had time to think. It was as though someone else had spoken and not her at all, the words and the way they sounded, giving the impression that she had the whole of Keswick's police force at her back. "Stand up at once," she added, "and let me see the . . ."

"Bugger off," the man snarled over his shoulder and for just that moment as he turned his head, a child's face lifted in terror beneath him, white with deep black hollows where her eyes and mouth were, her hair flung this way and that in snarled tatters across it. She was trying to scream, doing her best to convey to Annie, who stood paralysed with shock, that this was none of her doing, but the man loomed over her again, his bestial greed so great and all consuming he was deaf and blind to anything else. His great back obliterated her again so that all Annie could see were two white legs, thin and splayed, emerging from beneath his great white buttocks, the feet twitching, writhing. One was bare, pathetic in its smallness.

Annie began to scream. At the top of her voice she began to scream and so did Cat for she had been woken from her deep child's sleep to her mother's terror. Annie took no notice. There was another child whose need for protection was greater than Cat's and the only way she could think of to stop what was going on in this brutish corner, was to make a great deal of noise about it. That, and to kick.

The first one aimed with all the force of her sturdy, clogged foot behind it caught him high in the middle of his thick white buttocks but the second, now that she had her aim set square landed low between his buttocks, so low her toe fell firmly on his dangling genitals and with a scream to match her own, he fell flat across the child beneath him.

"Get off her, get off her, you bastard, you low crawling bastard. Get off her or I'll do you so much damage you'll never want a woman again . . . get off her . . . you loathsome . . ."

It was several minutes before Bert could drag her away from the screaming man and several more before she could calm herself to face the weeping, bedraggled young creature who had been his victim and who cowered like some cornered animal, on her knees in the centre of the curious but sympathetic circle of men who had gathered to see what the commotion was about. Several had put out comforting hands to her for though they were men they were not all beasts, but she would not have it, or them, curling up into herself in crazed pain and terror.

Annie shoved Cat into Bert's reluctant arms and slowly, soothingly, letting her soft female voice be heard, she sank to her knees beside the girl.

"It's all right, my lovely . . ." as she would say to Cat when she was hurt. "It's all right now. You're safe now. It's all right. He's gone now. See, stand up with me. I've got you. Put your hand in mine and let me help you up. There. It's all right now, sweetheart. Safe . . . Safe . . .

You're safe with Annie . . ." and gradually, like some small, terrified, trapped young thing which, though it is freed, cannot get up the courage to run away, the girl stood up huddling against Annie, her arms creeping about Annie's waist, her face hidden, shamed and distraught against Annie's shoulder. She allowed her disarranged clothing to be smoothed down. To have her hair brushed back from her shocked white face, all the while clinging to the only safe, female, being in her tumbling universe.

"Where are you from, sweeting? Tell Annie. See, there's no one to hurt you now," for the would-be seducer had stumbled off whilst he had the chance.

"Let me take you to your home. Where do you live? What's your name? Come sweetheart, let me help you . . ." but the girl, deep in shock now, could not or would not answer.

"Well, tha'll have to leave her here, Annie," Bert said rashly since he was eager to be off to indulge in a bit of seduction of his own, and besides, it was gone eleven o'clock and he'd hung about long enough waiting on Annie Abbott. "She'll find her way home soon enough."

"Don't talk daft, Bert." Annie's voice was quite matter of fact. "I can't just leave her here."

"What else can thi' do wi' her, tell me that."

"Take her home with me."

"Nay . . ."

"Don't nay me, Bert Garnett. We don't know where she lives or even her name and until I can get her to talk to me we'll never find out. We can't hang about here waiting, so I'll take her with me, and if she wants to, she can come back with me tomorrow night."

"What if her . . ."

"Stop it, Bert. See, there's a bundle here, probably hers. Pick it up will you and put it in the cart. Cat darling, stop crying and hold mother's hand. No, the girl is not hurt and neither are you so be a good girl . . . yes, sweetheart, I know I frightened you but this girl was even more frightened so I had to help her, didn't I? Good girl, there's my good Cat . . . Now then, let's see if we can get our

new friend to tell us what her name is. What do you think?
Katie, perhaps, or Molly . . ."

Her name was Phoebe, she whispered to Annie when
they were alone in the warm kitchen. Phoebe what? Annie
asked but Phoebe didn't know that since no one in the
place had told her, she said. She'd always been called
Phoebe, just Phoebe. Mrs Pike had left her in the square
because she didn't want her to work at the farm any more
and the man had taken the three pounds Mrs Pike had
given her for her wages and though she'd stood all day
with the other women, no one had hired her and she'd
been so hungry and didn't know where to go or how to
get anything to eat, so when the man said he'd show her,
she'd gone with him and then he'd . . . he'd not given her
anything to eat but had made her give him her wages and
told her she'd to pull her drawers down and when she'd
said no, he'd hit her. See, she had the black eye to prove
it.

The words flowed from her falteringly. She was small
and thin, not very clean and though she could have been
older, Annie guessed she was about twelve or thirteen.

With the intuition which came from her own experiences, not of attempted rape, but of the filth with which
men could coat a woman whom they thought no better
than she should be, fair game in fact, for their insolent
tongues and roving hands, Annie had filled the tub in which
she and Cat bathed, and after putting her small, half-asleep
daughter into their bed, she had coaxed Phoebe to remove
her clothing and step into the warm water. There was
always some heating, or being kept hot, on the slow-
burning peat fire and though Phoebe had hung her head
and crossed her arms across her exposed body, she had
done as she was bid. Annie had bought soap from a pedlar,
parting with some of her precious savings. In the past
Lizzie Abbott had made her own, but having no animals
or animal fat with which to do so, Annie had no choice but
to buy it. It had a smell of lavender about it and taking a
cloth and the soap, she gently bathed the girl, watching
as, in the soft glow from the fire and the rushlight she had

lit, Phoebe relaxed into the warm, cleansing water, the fear and tension gradually slipping from her.

"Would you like me to wash your hair?" Annie asked. Phoebe nodded, bending her head obediently to Annie's hands, and when it was dried, it turned out to be as dark and glossy as the coat on Reed Macauley's mare, hanging straight as a ruler to her waist.

They did not speak a great deal. After the one sudden flow of words from Phoebe, she seemed to have nothing more to say and Annie did not press her. She put her in one of her mother's clean, modest nightgowns, pushed her in with Cat and when she herself fell into bed beside the two of them, they were both sound asleep.

It was as though she had always been there, so easily did Cat, the two dogs and even Annie herself accept her. No more questions were asked and no more information of Phoebe's past life, which Annie could tell had been hard, was proffered. She was strong and, as her fright receded, cheerful and the hardest worker Annie had ever come across. She seemed to know instinctively what needed doing and without being asked, would do it, labouring from the moment her feet hit the floor first thing in the morning, until she tucked them up, last thing at night, in the little truckle bed Annie herself had slept in as a child. The area under the roof had been divided years ago when Lizzie's children had started to come since Joshua had fully expected at least a dozen, and rooms – two, one for the girls, one for the boys, must be provided for them. From the tiny landing led three bare bedrooms, one of them never used except for storing whatever surplus oats or barley Joshua might have, his hopes of sturdy boys to follow him dashed in bitterness and recrimination against the woman who could not give them to him.

So Phoebe was moved on her second night, without a word being spoken by either her or Annie, into Annie's old room and when Annie set off to tramp to Keswick and The Packhorse that night, there was no mention of Phoebe going with her. And there was no question in her mind that, thankfully, she was leaving her child in safe hands.

Later, when Phoebe had become such a part of their life, she was to wonder how she had ever managed without her. Annie had marvelled at her own lack of caution in leaving her precious child with a stranger, a young girl about whom she knew nothing. But it was as though the strong, faithful, loving bond which was to grow between them was forged and tempered on that night Annie took her from beneath the man who had degraded her. He had not – quite – raped her, she told Annie brusquely on the following morning when Cat had run off down the field with Blackie and Bonnie. She said no more than that, shuddering visibly, then, tying up her long hair and binding it with a length of wide cloth, even then as she was always to do for as long as Annie knew her, hiding its beauty from the prying lustful eyes of men, she reached for the wooden bucket, ready to begin a lifetime of devotion and servitude to the woman who had saved her and who was to become the shining light in the world of Phoebe Abbott, as she was to be known.

Bert Garnett was not best pleased several nights later when he slipped round the back of the farm with a leg of pork from a pig his mother-in-law had slaughtered, and with which he had hoped to seduce Annie Abbott, to find the expressionless face of the girl he had imagined long gone, fixing him with a level and unblinking stare from across Annie's table.

"What's *she* doin' here?" he asked truculently.

"She's staying with Cat and me. As our guest," Annie answered tranquilly.

"What the devil does that mean?" Bert was always nonplussed by the way Annie spoke, which was perhaps part of the fascination she had for him. She confused him with the way she put things, not at all like the women of her class in her manners or her appearance.

"She has nowhere to go so she is staying with Cat and me."

"What for?"

"Really Bert, do I have to explain everything I do to you? Surely you must realise that Phoebe . . ."

"Phoebe? What sort of a name's that?"

In his angry displeasure at finding someone in Annie's company when he had expected to have her to himself, and therefore defenceless, Bert was ready to vent his spleen on anything that came to hand, even the girl's name.

"Heavens, Bert Garnett. What on earth's got into you?" though of course she knew. "Phoebe . . . well, I can see no reason why she should not make her home with us, if she cares to . . ." smiling at the sudden radiance which lit Phoebe's plain features. "I am glad of her to see to Cat whilst I am working and though I can pay her no wages, and besides would not dream of considering her a servant, more a friend, she would find no better home than here with Cat and me. You have nowhere else to go, have you, Phoebe?" smiling again at the emphatic shaking of the young girl's head, "so the matter is settled. Don't you think it's a good idea, Bert? It works out well for us all. When I have to be away from the farm, Phoebe will be company for Cat, and she has already proved to be a splendid worker. Will you not try one of those biscuits? They are delicious, made by Phoebe only an hour ago . . . No . . . ?" For at the mention of the girl's name, though he had been about to take one, Bert snatched his hand back from the biscuits as though Annie had told him there was poison baked in them.

He stumped off ten minutes later taking his leg of pork with him and though Annie was glad to see the back of him she had the feeling she had made an enemy.

As though to let Annie know that she would never regret giving her a home, Phoebe stood up and busily cleared away the pewter plates and the tankard from which Bert had drunk his ale. She stored away the biscuits in the oak bread cupboard, already becoming familiar with, and revelling in, the layout of Annie's home and where everything was stored. She wiped the table, moving round the kitchen with her cloth, her eyes darting from surface to surface, as though begging for there to be something across which she could lay it. She fetched in another pail of water and arranged to her liking the kindling beneath the sconce. She rattled the fire dogs and re-arranged the shovel and the poker. The copper kettle was given a brisk polish and the kail pot in which, when better times came, Annie would boil her cuts of meat, a wipe round with her damp cloth.

Annie watched her surreptitiously, saying nothing, her fingers busy with a pair of stockings she was knitting for Cat. She knew Phoebe needed to do what she was doing. The girl had obviously been treated in her short life – wherever that might have been spent, and which one day Phoebe would surely find the peace to tell her about – as no more than a skivvy with nothing to call her own, no one to call her own and the wonder of being allowed to handle these fine things, as she saw them, of being trusted, of being called 'friend', was almost too much for her to encompass. Scrub she would, scour and polish and mop, wash down and wring out, dig and rake and hoe, cut wood and peat and even her own throat if it would please this woman who had given it all to her. If only she would ask Phoebe to *do* something, some Herculean task which was well nigh insurmountable, Phoebe would do it, her expression said, but finally, with a long, complete sigh of pure rapture, she sat down opposite Annie and fell fast asleep.

12

She heard the thunder of his horse's hooves on the stony path for several long minutes before she saw him and when he pulled his mare in and flung himself off her back, Annie could only stare at him in complete and dumbstruck amazement.

She was instructing Phoebe in the correct way to make a swill basket, sitting in a sunny corner of the flower garden her mother had made when she came as a bride to Browhead. Though the garden was wild and overgrown, the stony path crowded with sprawling plants which had not been touched for two summers now, it was pleasant, pretty with the colourful wild flowers Lizzie had transplanted long ago from the fields and hedgerows in the valley bottom about the lake. Thrift was beginning to flourish, its fragrant pink mingling with the snow white of alyssum, and against the wall of the farmhouse where it was sheltered from the worst of the weather was clematis, not yet in bloom, and yellow winter-flowering jasmine. At their back were apple trees in flower, a magical floating cloud of dense blossom from which the trunks of the trees seemed to hang, and early plum trees standing between the rough flower beds and the vegetables which marched in splendid rows at the side of the house. Cabbage and carrots, turnips and potatoes, beetroot and rhubarb and onion. There were daisies pushing their cheerful way through the bit of grass on which she and Cat and Phoebe sprawled. The sun was warm and the dogs panted, their tongues lolling from their open mouths, their eyes bright and watchful guarding this 'flock' of theirs to which, recently, another had been added.

"The timber must be cut between November and May, Phoebe," Annie was saying "and the poles should be straight-grained and free of moss. Now I've peeled and split these and they've been boiled in water for several hours to make them pliable. You understand?"

Phoebe nodded to indicate that she did. She had not yet had a great deal to say for herself but her face was bright with interest.

"Now I've split them again, shaved them and trimmed the wood into these very thin strips. Next year you could do the whole process yourself . . ." Phoebe thrilled to the words 'next year'. It had a lovely sound of permanence about it which was very much to her liking. ". . . but for now we'll just concentrate on the basket. All the strips must be of the same thickness and width and then they are woven into a shallow boat shape. The rim is oval and the strips are nailed to it. See, they're like ribbons . . ." Phoebe nodded, ". . . and look very fine, but when they're woven properly they're so strong the basket will hold water. We can sell them for a shilling each to the coal mines or to the ships in Whitehaven. When we have a horse and cart . . ."

We! Phoebe felt the bursting happiness fill her, every corner of her skinny frame singing with the joy of it. *We! Next year!* It was worth what that stinking old devil had done to her to have landed up here which truly must be heaven, with this lovely lady who truly must be an angel. She would have it done to her all over again if it meant she could stay. He'd not got his 'thingy' inside her, fumbling old bugger that he'd been, but his hands had crawled all over her body, like filthy slugs, invading her private parts and bruising her tender flesh. His mouth had clamped on hers, gagging her, and his tongue had . . . Oh, dear God . . . it made her sick to think of it, her stomach heaving and her skin sweating but she'd have it done to her every day of the week . . . well, perhaps once a week, if she could continue to live with Annie . . . *Annie*. . . she'd been told to call her Annie and the little poppet who was her daughter. Loved them both she did, even the dogs, with all the pent up, dammed up love which no one, in all of her life, had ever asked her for.

She was as astonished as Annie when the chap pounded up on his great horse, astonished and alarmed for he seemed so mad about something, looking as though for two pins he was going to knock Annie for six, which of course, Phoebe wouldn't allow. He'd have to kill her first! The dogs evidently thought so too, barking furiously and standing stiff legged and menacing in the face of his threat to those they had in their care. The man's dog, who was close at his heels, bared her teeth, the warning silent and hazardous.

But Blackie and Bonnie did not back off. They stood their ground, young as they were, and it was not until the man, with a slight movement of his hand, commanded his own animal to lie down, that order was restored. The two young dogs, with the enthusiasm of youth, were still inclined to bristle, but they lay down too, one on either side of Cat, evidently deciding that, being the youngest and smallest, she was the most in need of defending.

Phoebe stood up when Annie did, the strips for the swill baskets scattering about their feet. The man was evidently under the influence of some strong emotion which he was doing his best to submerge and the only way he seemed able to do so, was by hiding it under another, that of anger. He threw himself from his horse, leaving it standing about untethered, its eyes wild and dangerous, or so Phoebe thought, glad it was on the other side of the wall as the man tore his way through the gate, almost taking it from its hinges.

"So it's happened, then," he snarled. "You wouldn't be told, would you? My warnings were completely ignored whilst you flaunted yourself about the parish as though you were invisible and therefore in absolutely no danger from the ruffians who hang about looking for women like you who are foolish enough to think they are immune to such . . ."

"Reed Macauley, would you mind telling me what the

devil you're talking about. And I'd be obliged if you'd not come charging into my . . ."

"I'm talking about you . . . your . . . dammit, Annie Abbott, can you not take more care? Do you have to stride about the countryside after dark . . ."

His face worked strangely and in his eyes was the most dreadful, haunted expression, one which Annie could not decipher. It contained anger, yes, and a curious fear, a dread which was completely foreign to his arrogant nature. There was something deep, something he was trying to hide. A different emotion to the others, soft, vulnerable, protective, *unwelcome*.

She began to understand.

"It's all they can talk about in my kitchens, apparently, and not just in my kitchens, but in everyone else's it seems, the foolish carryings-on of a woman they believe is no better than she should be and therefore, so my housekeeper informed the housekeeper of an acquaintance of mine, who told me, can it be surprising, they are saying when she gets what she asks for. Smirking he was, the man who told me . . . and . . . and . . ."

He stopped and ran his hand across his face, pushing it through his hair, the raw and naked anger in him humiliating him since he did not really understand it. His eyes glared savagely into hers. Annie had the most absurd desire to move towards him and take that hand, to bring it to her lips and brush the back of it tenderly, to comfort him and smile, as she would to a child who has been pushed too far and has lost its temper.

She must have smiled for the snarling blackness of his rage and fear became deeper. He moved closer to her so that they stood face to face.

"It amuses you, does it, madam, to be interfered with by some drunken old sot, or were you yourself so deep in your cups it scarcely registered? Two sodden toss-pots falling down behind a barrel, so I was told and taking pleasure from one another or perhaps he was a customer . . ."

He was not quite quick enough to catch her arm as she

lifted it to strike him, perhaps too incensed, too crazed with his own boiling emotions to see the sudden ferment of hers. The crack of her hand across his face jerked his head to one side and brought all three dogs to their feet, but it also brought him to his senses, and again he controlled his older, more experienced animal with a gesture of his hand. The violence in the air was a palpable thing, affecting not only the animals, but the two incensed humans.

"Down, Blackie, down, Bonnie," Annie managed to shriek flinging out her arms to her own trembling animals.

"Take the dogs inside, Cat, and you, Phoebe, go with her, now, go on."

Cat was crying, great fat tears rolling down her cheeks but she allowed Phoebe to take her into the house, each dog dragged reluctantly by the scruff of the neck over the threshwood and the door closed firmly on the still, cold, silent, menacing figures of the man and woman.

Their eyes were locked, unblinking and without expression. Neither seemed able to look away. They were both breathing deeply as though they had been running and whereas Annie's face was flushed, Reed's was white and drawn except for the imprint of her hand across his cheek.

"What did he do to you?" His voice was harsh and painful.

"Nothing."

"Nothing? Stripped you naked and threw you down behind a barrel, I was told. It's all over the parish and when I came back from Lancaster, it had even reached the inn at Penrith."

"And you believed it?"

"What else was I to do? You . . . take no care. I've been expecting something like this ever since I first saw you last November, striding away towards Blencathra with nearly twenty miles in front of you . . . and . . ."

"It was not I who was . . . and if it was, why should it concern you?"

His voice stopped its desperate tirade, cut off in mid-sentence and his mouth fell open, slack and somewhat foolish.

"What?"

"I was not the one attacked, though I dare say it suited those in the parish who wish it had been to believe it was. I was involved so therefore it must be me, the Jezebel, who got her come-uppance. No more than I deserved for hanging about an ale house late at night. It doesn't matter to them that I have to earn my living . . ."

"Not you?" In his voice was a mixture of gladness and at the same time a ferocious hostility. She was nothing to him; he had told himself so a dozen or more times. *Could* be nothing to him, and yet the anguish which had torn at his heart, moving it frighteningly in his suddenly constricted chest when her name was mentioned, with the implied word of 'rape' affixed to it, not only frightened him, twisting his sound common sense until he was bewildered by it, but ran like explosive fire, angry and uncontrollable in his veins. Why did she not stay at home – safe – where other women stayed? Quiet and self-effacing, making no sound, creating no disturbance, causing no gossip, giving rise to nothing which would reach his ears, therefore allowing him to forget her? To put her out of his life as though she did not exist. Instead she seemed to be always up to something, doing something contrary, displaying her beauty and her careless disregard for those who lusted after it, or despised it and her, so that her name seemed to be on everyone's lips. She should never have come back, they said, flaunting herself and her bastard, or if she had been forced to it, she should have sold the farm and taken herself off into obscurity where no one knew her. Instead she had been seen everywhere decent people went, begging work and showing no sign of contrition, making it quite clear she thought herself as good as anyone and equally clear that she was not only *not* going to be driven away, but was to stay and work the farm her father had left her. A hussy, and worse still, a hussy who showed no remorse and could you wonder that men considered

her fair game? Even the acquaintance who had slyly told
Reed of her brush with the vagrant in Keswick had thought
so and had been visibly astonished when Reed, cutting
through his lustful ramblings on what *he* would like to do
to Annie Abbott should she cross his path, had walked
rudely away.

He drew in his breath and his mouth tightened into a
grim line. His jaw was set dangerously and his eyes were
a pale, flinty blue, but in them was a tiny prick of warmth,
soft and grateful, a thanks of some sort to whoever, whatever it was that had protected her this time. He did not
know it was there but she saw it and her own face became
gentle.

"It was the girl."

"The girl?"

"Phoebe. She has just gone inside with Cat. She
had been at the Hiring Fair, but for some reason no one
took her and she was left to fend for herself. The
man demanded her money and . . . well, you can
guess the rest. I happened to be handy so I stopped
him."

He grinned then. It was like the sun turning the pewter-
grey waters of the lake to burnished gold, light, rippling,
merry. His teeth were a white slash in his brown face and
his eyes became the loveliest, brightest blue. An engaging
grin, infectious, making her own lips curve into a smile for
she knew exactly what was in his mind.

"He won't fancy a woman for a long while," she went
on and her eyes narrowed into gleaming slits of pure,
golden joy.

"I bet he won't."

They began to laugh, the sound lifting on the soft,
rarified air, lilting and filled with such gaiety, the dog at his
feet cocked her head and pricked her ears in mystification.

"You kicked him in the . . . ?"

"I did. He should have trouble walking for a while, I
should think, never mind anything else."

The door opened a crack and the white, anxious, puzzled
face of Phoebe peered through it, her own pale blue eyes

round and uncertain. Annie turned and held out a hand to her and the young girl, with Cat behind her, followed by the dogs, tumbled over the threshwood to stand beside her. The animals, sensing the change of atmosphere, recognising the laughter and easing of tension, wagged their tails, eddying about Reed and his Bess with no sign of their former enmity.

"This is Phoebe. She will stay with us now."

"Will she indeed?" Reed scarcely looked at the plain child, his eyes reluctant to leave the golden burnished loveliness, the radiant smiling good humour of the woman who minutes earlier had struck him in the face. He had no conception of the expression which softened his own, arrogant, compelling features and the line of his well-cut, sensuous mouth. The joy in him was an emotion he had never known before and because of it, he had not yet learned to hide it. For that sweet and special moment, that laughter-filled, bewitched moment, his relief made him careless and he lifted his hand, needing to touch her, to put an enquiring tender finger to her chin or cheek, to tuck behind her ear a wild and curling tendril of her hair. She was looking down at the girl, her own expression gentle and she did not see it, but Phoebe did and the tension, the fear, the wariness she was to know with most men, fell away, for this man would never harm this woman. Phoebe was no more than a young inexperienced girl, but she had been brought up in a harsh world where love, or affection, was scarce and therefore because of its rarity, she was quick to recognise it. It was there, warm, strong, unbreakable, between Annie and her child. A natural love, protective and maternal, but this was different. The same, but not the same. She had never seen it between a man and a woman but, because at that moment he was making no effort to hide it, it was instantly recognisable.

"You seem to attract stray young things to you, Annie Abbott," he said musingly, his eyes twinkling with his rare good humour. "What are you to do with this one?" He winked at Phoebe, who hung her head and drew patterns on the grass with her foot, not awfully sure what to make of it.

"She will be invaluable to me, won't you Phoebe? We'll help one another. She needs a home. I need a . . . friend. I have not many of those and she and Cat will be company for one another when I'm not here. She is already a great help to me, look. I am teaching her to make swill baskets . . ."

"So I see. And do her talents run to fetching me a tankard of ale, that is if your establishment has such a thing? And if you feel the need to pour it over my head, I will quite understand."

They smiled at one another. They knew it would not last, this accord, this lightening and melting of their equally strong and wilful spirits. There was between them an unacknowledged affinity, a magnet which drew them together, whether it be in anger or fascination, a pulling towards each other of their senses which seemed to have the capacity to flare into an instant and flowing pleasure the moment they met. They did not want it, either of them, but a need, a compulsion in him drew an immediate response from her, a female thing which recognised that need and rushed to satisfy it. Her loveliness, her spirit, her defiant rebelliousness towards those who would have sent her packing, her humour, but most of all her vulnerability, called out to the male in him, bringing forth an emotion he had never before known. The need to protect, to cherish, to nourish. All these things lay between them, soft, tender and as yet fragile, but hidden beneath them was a raw and fierce desire to know, in all its glory, the sensual love which can bind together a man and a woman with bonds which are unbreakable. It was in his eyes, narrowed and watchful, even as they smiled, and in the answering curve of her parted lips. It was trembling in the air about them, muted now and subdued in the presence of the child and young girl, but ready to become clamorous and swelling with their ardour should they find themselves alone.

They sat together on the drystone wall whilst he drank

the tankard of ale Phoebe brought him. The sunshine fell warm and benevolent about them. The air was pure and sweet. The wild flowers grew willy-nilly in a great profusion about them, and in every crack and crevice of the wall, filling their nostrils with a heady perfume which can only come with spring. The grass, greening and thickening in the field, was tufted with primroses and cowslips and behind them, standing against the old farmhouse for as long as the building itself, the great hawthorn tree showed the first signs of its golden bronze foliage. Up on the mountain pasture, the ewes and their lambs, returned there after lambing to await 'clipping' in July, called anxiously to one another, and high in Annie's coppice, a cuckoo sang. Larks wheeled in the deep blue of the sky above them, their song vying with that of the cuckoo and Annie and Reed held their breath and their own sharp tongues so as not to disturb this sudden lovely peace which had surprisingly overtaken them.

They talked of this and that. The troubles in Ireland where it was thought rebellion would take place, a disaffection of the people, many of whom lived in misery and privation, predisposing large masses of them to rise up against it. The potato blight of several years ago had been repeated, the crops ruined and the people starving, so could you wonder at the unrest which prevailed there and the influx of the hundreds of thousands of starving Irish beggars who were leaving to escape it, many of them to the north of England.

There was also trouble in France, rebellion again amongst the poor and destitute, where it was said Louis Philippe, King of the French, the 'Citizen King' as he was called, was in danger of losing his head as a Louis before him had done, and last month here in England, Feargus O'Connor, leader of the Chartist movement, had declared his intention of marching across Westminster Bridge at the head of what was to have been a peaceful protest, to lay his beloved Charter at the feet of Parliament. A pilgrimage it was to have been, involving 200,000 men from every part of the country and with so many involved, surely it would be bound to succeed. One man, one vote and a secret ballot was not a lot to ask for, surely, among the six points of the People's Charter?

But it was illegal for more than twenty people at one time to present a petition to the House of Commons. Of the 200,000 who were expected, nowhere near that many turned up for where was an out-of-work weaver or collier to get the fare to travel from Bradford or White-haven to London? There was no march. Those who did get there discovered no grand banners, nor bands to play them in and the confusion was appalling when the barricades erected by the police, expecting violence, were come up against. Special constables guarded every corner. There were many soldiers deployed and when at last those who got through arrived at the House of Commons, it all came to nothing, deflating like a pricked balloon.

"Will they not get what they ask for?" Annie's face was alive with interest and concern, for it seemed to her, had she been a man, one who could find no work and no hope of feeding his children, *she* would have marched on bare and bleeding feet all the way to London to demand it. It also seemed to her that this Chartism had a great deal in its favour if it helped the vast mass of men and women who had no voice anywhere in this great land, to speak up and be heard.

"Not this year they won't, nor next if the men of property have their way."

"Like yourself you mean. You have a vote I presume."

"I have, though the young men who march up and down in military formation do not believe I should, or if I have it, so should they. They will not let it rest, those who call themselves the 'physical force'. They will continue to meet and shout for Justice and Democracy even though they were defeated and sent scurrying home with their tails between their legs last month, and eventually, I suppose, they will get what they ask for. A vote for every man over the age of twenty-one . . ."

"And women?"

"Women? What about women?" He turned to look at her enquiringly, his mind and senses bemused by the way the sunlight tangled in her bright hair, streaking the copper with gold. It curled vigorously about her head, a great chrysanthemum halo which she had attempted to plait but which, with a life of its own, tumbled and twisted across her shoulders and down her back. She had tied a scrap of bright green ribbon about it, dragging it back from her forehead but it only served to enhance the fine, creamy pearl smoothness of her skin, the fierce dip of her golden brown eyebrows and the deep brown concern in her eyes which refused to believe that men should have a vote and women should not.

"What about women! Our brains are as capable as yours of choosing a man, or even a woman . . ." she grinned gleefully, ". . . yes, even a woman to serve us in Parliament. A woman who would know what we need . . ."

He began to smile. A short barking laugh burst from him in sheer and absolute amusement at her effrontery, her wayward and foolish effrontery, since the very idea of a woman having any voice in anything, let alone the running of the country, was so madly absurd that he took her to be joking.

She was not. Her bright face darkened ominously and she jumped down from the wall, her short skirt swinging gracefully about her calves. She reached for the empty tankard which swung idly in his hand and, tossing her wild gypsy hair back from her shoulders she squared up to him somewhat in the manner of a pugilist who has just climbed into the ring.

"What is there to laugh about, Reed Macauley? Why should I not have a vote like you? I am expected, in view of the fact that I have no man to do it for me, to support myself and my child, and I am not the only woman who is forced to it. I have seen them on my travels, wives separated from their husbands by war or other misfortune, deserted when their men go off, as men do, to fight in some God-forsaken place in the Empire. They

have no choice but to work and decide their own lives
and though many of them can't do it and end up on the
Poor Law, many succeed in wresting some sort of
living . . ."

"Don't, Annie, there's no need . . ."

His face, which had been ready to crease into a smile
of disbelief, had become soft, transformed by his amazing
need to help this self-willed woman. The expression on it
was one his own servants, his friends, even his own
mother, would not have recognised. He did not care for
it, this hunger of hers to be independent, to be her own
master, to stand up and take her place among the farmers
of the community as she seemed intent on doing. He had
not been consciously aware of it but he had been waiting,
hoping in his secret heart that she would be overcome by
the sheer enormity of it, unable to manage, forced by
hunger and the need to succour her child, to ask for
help. His help, since no one else concerned themselves
with her except Bert Garnett and Reed was well aware
why *he* hung about Browhead. And Reed would be there
when she did. When she needed him. He got no further
than that. He did not think in terms of what he might gain
from Annie Abbott's delightful dependence on him, but
he was a man, was he not, and would not turn away
from any show of gratitude she might think it politic to
offer.

"Don't struggle like this, Annie. Don't . . . fight so. Can
you not see it will come to nought for they will not let
it. They will do everything in their power to stop you
succeeding, so won't you let me . . . help you . . . ?"

"Help me? How?" She stared suspiciously into his face,
looking for the reason behind his offer but by now his
emotions were well hidden.

"I'm sure there must be something you need, something
I have which . . . Why don't you let me . . . ?" Pamper
you, make life soft and easy, dress you in pretty gowns and
. . . His eyes became unfocused as his dreaming unspoken
thoughts and the images they evoked filled his mind. She
did not like it.

"And what would you expect from me, Reed Macauley?" Her head lifted imperiously and her eyes were a vivid, flashing topaz in her colour-flooded face. "No man gives to a woman without expecting something in return, or so I have found."

"I have not said I want anything." He vaulted from the wall to stand before her and down the field, at the sound of the raised voices, Phoebe and Cat turned to stare, their hands busy with the buttercups and daisies which they were weaving into collars for the two dogs. The dogs stood up uncertainly.

"Can you not accept help without looking behind every offer for an ulterior motive?" he continued, thrusting his hard, uncompromising face into hers.

"No, I can't," and she did not back away. "Experience has taught me . . ."

"Experience! Jesus God, this life you have led has made you suspicious of . . ."

"Everybody, Reed Macauley. Everybody who wears trousers and that includes you. A favour here and a favour there and having accepted them, then I am in your debt and no doubt you would be riding down here on your fine horse to collect your dues . . ."

"Like Bert Garnett, you mean."

"You have a filthy —"

"Dammit, woman, and . . . damn you. You can go to hell on a handcart for all I care, carrying that pride of yours on your shoulders and with your belly flapping against your backbone and your tattered skirt barely covering you . . . Oh, Jesus . . . !"

He turned violently away, unable to face her a moment longer so great was his anger and his . . . what? . . . What was this biting, clawing thing that ate at his guts and hurt him so badly he could not get away quickly enough? Whatever it was he did not like it and, he told himself grimly, he had no intention of suffering it. Not now, nor ever again.

He and his mare thundered up the stony path towards Dash Beck, violent and dangerous, both of them, to any-

one who stood in their way, and at their heels ran the
Merle dog.

Annie stood silently, impassively, or so she led herself
to believe, until all sounds ceased, then, calling to Cat and
Phoebe, moved back to the spilled swill baskets.

13

By September she had saved enough money to buy ten
ewes and hire a ram to service them and at 'backend', the
first Saturday in October, she and Phoebe and Cat set off
to walk to the Keswick Tup Fair. It was tup time, that
strange and mysterious moment in the shepherd's year
when, with the shortening of the days, the ewe and the
ram made it plain they were ready to mate. The lambs
born in the spring were now almost as big as their dams.
They were weaned and ready for sale along with the older
ewes. But it was 'twinters', those of two winters which
Annie was after, for a 'shearling' – of one winter – was
too young to rear a lamb. It was barely dawn, so quiet
she could hear the faint murmuring of the beck running at
the back of the farm. The sun had already touched the
highest peaks and was creeping down the sides of Bakestall and Great Calva turning the gold of the rippling
autumn bracken to a richness and a glory which stopped
the heart with its beauty. Great swathes of heather made
a patchwork of colour, dark and light, as billowing clouds
formed shadows which chased one another up and down
the fells. The wind made patterns on the waters of the
lake and blew the swallows and lapwings helter-skelter
across the patchy blue-and-white sky. It was cold, the chill
of winter which came early to this high and treacherous
part of the world already nipping at flesh which was reluctant to get out of a warm bed to face the cold early
morning.

Annie, in a ferment of barely controlled excitement,
brushed and plaited her hair, roping the plait in a thick
crown about her head. They had all three bathed the night
before. Their neat and much-mended clothing had been

washed and pressed with her mother's old box iron heated on the fire, Phoebe crashing the thing expertly and with that vigour she put into everything she did, up and down the kitchen table until there was not a crease to be seen in any of their poor garments. They would need new for the winter, Annie especially, since nothing of her mother's was fit for anything but cutting up into clothes for Cat. She might fashion a skirt for Phoebe and a bodice or two, salvaging the least worn pieces and carefully re-sewing them to make a whole, but there was nothing from which a gown or even a skirt might be made for herself. She needed to look presentable in her job at the Packhorse for though she had carefully darned and patched the skirt and bodice she now wore, they were becoming dangerously thin. The piece of cloth she had woven from the raw wool she had bought in the spring had been fashioned into a warm winter coat for Cat. Annie had made it long and roomy, lining it with a finer piece and it should last Cat for several years.

She would buy, if she could, some more unwashed wool, perhaps a whole fleece and treat it herself in the way her mother had taught her and from it spin and weave another length of cloth to make into a winter outfit for herself. With new clogs for Cat, and her own and Phoebe's re-soled, they would manage until next spring when *her* lambs were born.

The anticipation of that day made her smile at her own reflection in the old mirror. Her lambs, her flock, and when he saw how well she had done Reed Macauley would be made to eat his words and take back all that humbug he prattled about women being incapable of fending for themselves.

Her hands became still as she allowed herself to ponder on why it should concern Reed Macauley, and indeed why it should matter to her what Reed Macauley was concerned about. She had seen him only in passing as he rode down the track at the back of her farm, nodding briefly in her direction going God knows where since the only roads at the bottom of it led to Cockermouth, Workington or

Carlisle and he would hardly ride that distance on his mare.
Still, it was none of her business what he did and the
rumour which was whispered about the parish, brought to
her by the avid Sally, that he was to marry the daughter
of some rich and influential industrialist from Yorkshire
meant nothing to her. It was time he married, she told
herself carelessly, since a man such as he and of his age
must get himself an heir to inherit his family's wealth and
position. It was his duty to carry on the name and perpetu-
ate a line which had begun in Norman times and had
brought prosperity and prestige to the name of Macauley.
And naturally he could not ally himself or his pedigree with
any but that which would match his. Not gentry, since he
was not that, but good sound yeoman stock which was the
backbone and sinew of England. A common man, a man
of the people, but could such words describe Reed
Macauley who was neither common nor of the masses?
He was a strong man with an unshakeable belief in his
own superiority. A man with a confidence and self-reliance
which knew absolutely that his viewpoint was infallible.
Self-assured, the undisputed master of his own life, he
was not a man who took kindly to opposition. Unique,
unpredictable, uncommon, since he was not merely a
farmer, albeit a prosperous one, as so many statesmen
had become, but since the death of his father he had
entered into the realm of business, his shrewd and imaginative brain guiding him into and through the maze of investments in the many booming industries on offer to men
with cash to spare: the railways, mining, coal and copper,
the trades allied to wool and timber which were prolific in
Cumberland.

But it was not just in his working life that Reed Macauley
stood head and shoulders above his fellows. His nature
was complex and many layered. It demanded satisfaction
in every aspect of his life and where the men of the dales
and fells, those with a guinea or two to spare, were careful
with it, admiring in one another the growing size of their
bank balance, Reed Macauley could see no reason to hoard
his wealth. He surrounded himself with beautiful things,

luxury even, in his home, Annie had heard, and about his person, caring not a fig for what the sensible practical gentlemen of his acquaintance thought of his foolhardiness. Beautiful women, perfumed and bejewelled, had been seen on his arm. Beautiful horses crowded his stable besides his ebony mare. A showy chestnut hunter, a pair of bay carriage horses, a phaeton, a curricle which he drove madly along the winding Bassenthwaite road drawn by a dark brown gelding of a spirited nature. His body was strong, tall, lean and completely masculine and was dressed always in the height of fashion: impeccably tailored coats and breeches, immaculately laundered shirts and cravats and the expensive, beautifully polished boots he favoured.

So, he would marry then, this man who challenged her own independence and confused her mind which needed at this moment to be clear, steady, channelled into only one concern and that was the holding on to what she had gained in the last ten months and the building up of what she intended for the future. She wanted no complications, no distractions, and so, glad that he had the sense to stay away from her since what would Reed Macauley and Annabelle Abbott ever be to one another, she prepared herself for the next step she had planned for, worked towards, dreamed of in the last months of struggle. The starting of the flock. Her oats and barley, the few acres she had planted had been harvested by herself and Phoebe, wielding the scythe her father and his father before him had used, pausing again and again in their labours, to give the blades a new edge with the whetstone. They had gathered ash leaves, storing them in a large kist to feed to her sheep in the coming winter, guarding against the weather which might prevent the animals from foraging on the inlands about the farm. She would hand feed them in the farm yard if necessary for she meant to take no chances with her precious flock.

The bracken, tall and sappy and which, if allowed, spread like wildfire across her precious pasture, had been cut and stored in the barn for it made splendid bedding for stock, should she have any, and who was to tell, if things

continued to go well for her and prices were right, she
might have a cow! They had, all three of them, for Cat
was adept and quick to learn, cut rushes for the making
of rushlights ready for the winter, peeling them and using
the peelings to make besoms, brooms and 'bears', the
crude matting which kept their feet from the cold slate
floor. Her vegetables and fruit had been gathered, some
of them dried, and the rest stored in preparation for the
hungry months ahead. She was ready. Today she was
ready.

They went by the rough track along the Dash Valley
and up beyond Dash Beck and Dash Falls towards the
Great Skiddaw Forest where oak, ash, hazel and larch
stood in silent and regal splendour. They had left behind
the vast withering sea of bracken covering the slopes, the
fronds which had, at the height of the summer, been a
glowing gold, turning as autumn came to a delicate tawny
brown and shading gradually to a subtle lemon hue. The
forest was still canopied with branches full of leaves capturing every shade of autumn colour from the palest brown
to the brightest yellow, with orange and flame and crimson
in between. The leaves were beginning to fall, drifting
lazily, slowly, delicately to the already carpeted forest
floor, caressing their heads and shoulders as they passed
beneath them, and Cat ran on ahead, doing her best to
catch one in her hand, but Phoebe as befitted her new
position as friend and helpmeet of Annie, walked sedately
by her side. Splashes of brilliant red revealed themselves
on rowan trees and on thorn, holly, yew and juniper as
the berries ripened. Annie, on impulse, plucked a sprig of
rowan and tucked it into her own springing curls since it
was known that rowan warded off evil spirits and she
wanted none of those about her today. Good luck was
what she needed and any help in that direction was most
welcome.

The Tup Fair was the climax of the sheep farmers' year
for it was here that the best ewes were matched to the
sturdiest rams. Slight faults in either could be remedied if
the right match was found, for the Herdwick sheep must

be hardy and strong to withstand the rigours of a Lakeland winter. It was a small breed, lithe and agile, with a white grizzled face and long grey wool. It must be able to climb like a goat and leap like a frog. Its mutton was sweet and yet it could live on a handful of briar and shoots and thrive on it. Buried in snow it had been known to survive by chewing its own wool. For centuries it had been on the fells, proving its worth and stamina, its only fault being its real and lasting attachment to its own 'heaf' or pasture, to which it had been known to return when sold miles away.

The market place at Keswick when Annie, Phoebe and Cat turned into it had an air of great excitement about it. Through narrow, stone-walled lanes, great flocks of sheep heaved and cried, and a line of tups stood restlessly under a wall, tossing their fine curling horns which sprang, creamy white, from the base of their heads. They were held in by a hawthorn bush as potential buyers and hirers had a closer look. In every alleyway there were pens jammed from wall to wall with a moving, nervous sea of fleeces, for already the wool clipped in July was beginning to grow again. In the tup ring horny feet pattered on the cobbles and sharp horns clashed and scraped, for the close proximity of so much female flesh was almost too much for the male to withstand. They were ready to break out to get at it, fighting one another to do it. Farmers who had stock for sale were coaxing potential buyers into their own pens and in the circle in which the 'top' sheep were displayed a ram pawed the ground, ready to charge at anything that moved. There was a sheepdog or even two, at the feet of every man, alert, eyes brimming with intelligence, ready, should they be needed, to fetch an escaped hogg – an unsheared lamb – or twinter, or even to tackle a tup.

The only women present were at the market stalls, buying the basic commodities which their husbands' farms did not produce. Decent, well-turned-out women, plain and serviceable, who worked hard in their own homes, dairies and yards but would not dream of presenting

themselves amongst the men with whom their husbands
did business. The area where the tup fair took place was
a strictly masculine preserve and when the strikingly lovely
Annie Abbott stepped out of her place, a woman's place,
and into theirs, every man in the market was instantly
aware of it.

She was dressed in the best of what she had. The grey
woollen skirt she wore in the snug at The Packhorse. A
simple grey bodice and her old shawl and clogs, but the
dull, washed out, much darned outfit made not the slightest
difference to her appearance. Her straight and supple back
swung gracefully; her shoulders moved as she walked and
her long white neck swayed with the glorious weight of
her hair. Her enquiring gaze fell smilingly on each sheep
pen and she nodded graciously at each open-mouthed man
who had them in his charge. A hush seemed to develop,
filled only with the bleating of the sheep and the crack of
the rams horns as, unwatched for a moment, they set
about each other.

Annie moved calmly as though she was in her own
kitchen, one hand holding Cat's, the other firmly pressed
against her pocket where her precious store of money lay.
Phoebe, much recovered from her ordeal and beginning
to unfold into the strength of character and tenacity for
endurance her new security had given her, walked stead-
fastly beside her and, all about them, men, in their best
'setting-off' clothes and carrying their Lakeland 'setting-
off' crooks, stared and began to mutter for though a
woman might do as she pleased on her own acres, none
with a shred of decency would come here where drovers
thronged, drunk already some of them, rough mannered
and foul tongued. Even the poorest woman with a pig or
a goose for sale would do it discreetly away from the sheep
market. And if she had to buy sheep could she not have
found some man to do it for her, some experienced
shepherd, instead of flaunting herself as she was doing in
this strictly man's world. The noise and the stench was
not for women's frail sensibilities and besides, men,
without the presence of women, were inclined to relieve

themselves against any handy wall, as one was doing now. A good 'larruping' was what she needed and there was not a man here who would not be glad to give it to her, and other things besides, some of them more pleasurable.

Annie passed by, hearing nothing, seeing nothing but the sheep, and when she stopped by a pen in which twelve 'twinters' huddled the farmer who was selling them was so transfixed he allowed her to venture inside and even examine a couple more closely, before he found his voice.

"'Ere, what d'yer think yer up to? Your man should be doin' that, lass," he said roughly, but she turned her brilliant gaze on him before drifting out of the pen.

"They're not what I'm looking for," she answered, "but thank you for your time."

It was the same wherever she went. The presence of the quiet child and the equally quiet but perfectly decent young girl who accompanied her, lent her astonishing passage through the market some propriety, for no woman with mischief on her mind would saddle herself with youngsters whilst she was about it. But still they stared and still the stubborn streak which had brought Annie Abbott from a terrified fifteen-year-old abandoned mother-to-be, to a woman with her own farm and a pretty and bright young daughter; to a woman with her life coming together around her; to one with money in her pocket and a dream in her heart which was slowly moving towards fruition, the stubborn streak which would not allow her to falter. She knew the supreme ewes and rams would be spoken for in advance but that did not matter unduly since she could probably not afford the prices asked anyway, but she would have the next best her money could buy. The hire of a ram for the winter was expensive, probably about ten or fifteen shillings since it would have to serve no more than a dozen ewes, which was all she could afford to buy this year, but it would have to suffice. Getting them back to Browhead would also be tricky since they would need to be walked, probably along the lake road which, being walled, would be easier to manage, with only herself, Phoebe and

Cat to control them. The dogs would have to be trained actually with the sheep before they could be trusted to herd them anywhere but in an enclosed field, but first things first, she told herself, her heart pumping with excitement, her eyes burning in her cream flushed face, her head high with justifiable pride.

She found exactly what she wanted about two hours later. The farmer was from Threlkeld way where women knew their place and whose truculent expression boded ill for Annie but she had good money in her pocket and she could see no reason why he should not do business with her. He would, no doubt, assume that any advantage to be had would be his. She had been right round the pens, scrutinising every ewe with an experienced eye, that of her father she supposed, since it was he who had taught her all she knew about sheep and what constituted a good specimen.

"Too slack behind the shoulder," she had remarked cheerfully to one surly fellow, causing his mouth to drop open in consternation.

"Too light in the face for my needs," she smiled at another.

"I'm looking for a better fleece I'm afraid," to a third, and word had got round that the 'hussy' from Browhead knew a thing or two about Herdwicks. The farmer from Threlkeld did not believe it.

"I'm not sure I'm ready to sell yet," he said grimly despite the fact that it was well past noon and his twinters were still mewling and pawing the ground inside his pen.

"Then may I ask what these ewes are doing here?"

"That there's nowt to do wi' thi'." He was aware that those in the vicinity were listening avidly since their ability to see and hear everything that was going on about them was not diminished by their own need to sell their stock. This was a social occasion as well as one in which business was conducted and a man spent almost as much time having a 'gleg' with another whom he had not seen since tup time last year, as he did attending to the sale, or hire,

of his stock. Many of the flocks had been driven from as
far away as the Langdales, the shepherds walking them
over the fells with their dogs at their heels, using the old
pack routes and sheep trods. Some were brought in carts
pulled by enormous plough horses and the drovers were
already beginning to head off towards Bassenthwaite,
Penrith, Rosthwaite, with sheep which had been bought
earlier, their dogs nipping and pushing at their heels, or
flying round to the sides of the restless flock at their
owner's whistle or shouted command.

But the area about Annie Abbott was curiously still.
Several pens away an ancient weatherbeaten shepherd
was counting in the old traditional fashion, the flock he
was to take away. Celtic numerals that had been handed
down from father to son, and thought to be part old Welsh,
part Cornish and part Breton, from all those lands which
were once included in the Celtic fringe, when Cumberland
had been under the rule of the great Celtic Kingdom of
Strathclyde just across the border.

"*Yan, tyan, tethera. . . methara, pimp . . .*" he droned
until he reached eleven when he began again, "*yan-a-dick,
tyan-a-dick . . .*"

Apart from the bleating of the sheep it was the only
sound as the crowd held its breath, waiting on the outcome
of the trading between Annie and the farmer.

"So you are saying these ewes are not for sale then?"

"No, I'm not . . ."

"Then they *are* for sale."

"They might be."

"Well, let me know when you make up your mind and
in the meanwhile I'll go and have a look at some others
that caught my eye earlier."

She nodded pleasantly and prepared to move away. She
had her hand on Phoebe's arm and the trembling in it,
though not evident to anyone else, moved down to
Phoebe's hand and up across her shoulder so that it looked
as though she herself was shivering.

"Please thissen. I'm not sayin' these twinters are for
sale, neither am I sayin' they're not. They might be and

then again they might not. Depends on who's askin' and on t' price I'm offered."

"What are you asking? And for that tup you have in the next pen? I presume he's for sale or hire?"

"Aye, that's right. But it's all good stock and I can't let any of 'em go unless I get right price."

"Sir, unless I know what that price is I cannot do business with you. We are just wasting time here. Time I cannot afford. You are not the only farmer with sheep to sell and so I will just move on."

Annie felt the blood race in her veins, hot and eager and jubilant for this was the moment she had worked towards for the past year. She was about to strike a bargain with this man and it would be in her favour. Shrewd he would be and careful, since most of these independent fell farmers could afford to be no other way. They had their living to make as did any man, but he would be not at all pleased to take his flock back to Threlkeld with him, nor would it suit him to hang on until later in the day when he would be forced to sell at an even lower price to be rid of them.

"Them's fine Herdwicks . . ." he began. "None better in the Keswick plain, nor anywhere else for that matter. Bred from a strong ram what belonged to old Jed Moffatt, him from Rush Farm up near Mungrisdale. Ask anyone . . ."

"I don't need to. I can see what they are, sir, knowing sheep as I do . . ."

"Oh aye, an' how's that then?"

"My father . . ."

"Where did he farm?"

"Browhead, near Gillthrop."

"Josh Abbott."

"Yes."

"I knoo 'im. Lost all un 'is, I 'eard." His unsmiling, unsympathetic mien told her he cared nothing for her father's experience, nor hers, as shepherds, since any man of worth should know how to hold on to what he had and Joshua Abbott had let his slip through his fingers.

Feckless, the farmer from Threlkeld, would have called that, deserving of what he got, which from what he had heard had been as close to a pauper's death as made no difference. And his lass about to do the same no doubt.

Stung by his contempt Annie pulled her shawl more closely about her shoulders and lifted her head in proud defiance. For a moment, the farmer's grudging attention was diverted by the lovely lift of her breast beneath the worn wool and the slipping tendril of bright copper hair which curled about her ear. Her flesh just below that ear was as white as the fleece of his sheep when it had been newly shorn, soft and vulnerable and he was horrified, since he was a man well past such things, to feel a stirring in the pit of his belly, just where the sagging crutch of his breeches divided. It infuriated him further.

"I'm not my father," Annie snapped and so did her eyes, with the bright golden lights of her temper.

"I'm not sayin' tha' are, lass, an' what thi' do wi' tha' cash is none o' my business."

"Quite so, in that case will you please tell me what you want for your twinters and if the price is right perhaps we can agree on a sale."

The farmer smiled, his craggy face splitting open into a hundred seams. The smile revealed his worn and blackened teeth and the pink gaps where a few were missing. He shook his head as though humouring the foolishness of a child who has asked for a completely unsuitable and unobtainable toy and Annie felt the hot joy begin to trickle away. The awful feeling which replaced it, slowly but surely, was a mixture of bewilderment and alarm for she was beginning to get the distinct feeling that this man was playing with her. That he had been playing with her for the past half-hour. Like an angler with a trout on his line, the bait in the trout's mouth, allowing the fish to reel out the line, believing it is going to be free, then drawing it in again before repeating the whole procedure. All about her she could feel the eyes of the other men, the farmers who still had sheep to sell and when she turned for a moment it seemed that everyone in the immediate vicinity was smirking and whispering behind their hands at the joke which was being played on Annie Abbott.

She whirled back to the farmer from Threlkeld.

"What's going on here?" she demanded accusingly.

"Nay lass, what do tha' mean?" and he deliberately winked at someone behind her back. Phoebe's hand had reached out to grasp her arm and beside her even Cat, sensing the strange tension in the air, crept close to her skirt. She didn't really know what she meant, as he smiled into her face, so she could not answer his question. She only knew she had a frozen feeling of dread.

"Will you name your price for these ewes?" she repeated, her voice firm and steady since she wanted no man to see her fear. "I've no time to bandy words with you so I'd be glad to get on. If you're not willing to sell, say so and I can go elsewhere."

"Then I'd do that my lass, if I were you, 'cos I've nothing here to sell to thi', not for any price." His words were soft and quite menacing.

"You have not heard my offer . . ."

"Tha's not enough money in world to buy this lot, girl, not from you at any rate, so you'd best get back to where tha' came from an' tek tha' . . . tha' family with thi'." His eyes fell coldly on Cat, then moved to Phoebe, before returning to Annie. "Tha's no call to come prancin' round here with tha' la-di-da manners and daft ideas of buyin' a flock for the farm tha' father left thi', if it can be called a farm." His mouth which had been smiling, twisted contemptuously, then meaning quite deliberately to offend, he spat on the cobbles at her feet.

"This part of the market is fer men, not women, an' the sooner tha' realise that the sooner tha'll come to tha' senses. These lads hereabout don't like bargaining wi' a woman. There's no need of it since there's plenty o' men to do business with. 'Tis no place for thee, lass, an' my ewes is not for thee so get thi' back home where tha' belong."

"My money's as good as anybody's and if I can pay the price you are asking . . ."

"How about ten guineas each beast then?" He turned to look about him, his face in a grim and mirthless grin of mockery and there were a few guffaws.

"Don't be ridiculous. The whole lot's not worth ten guineas."

"Is that so, then if tha' don't like my price, try elsewhere."

"I will." She turned on her heel, dragging Cat and Phoebe with her, her face as pale as ashes, her eyes like hot coals embedded in them. She allowed no one to see her panic as she moved on to the next pen but even before she had reached the grinning man, who leaned over the fence, he called out to her.

"This lots spoken for, lass," turning to wink at the farmer from Threlkeld, but there was a coldness, a cruelty even behind that wink. She went to them all, even one whose ewes were a sorry looking lot, but everywhere she met the same grim, narrow-eyed resolution which said that women had no place in their men's world and had no business to attempt entry. This part of the market was a strictly male preserve, as indeed was farming, and even wives with husbands who had come to buy from the stalls, never set foot inside it. Messages were carried by small boys from women waiting at the end of the day, to husbands who were dilatory, but it was unthinkable for one, one of decency at least, to move amongst the men who were bargaining here.

They walked the long way home in silence, she and Cat and Phoebe, going up and over the top of Skiddaw by the same route they had so joyfully set out upon that morning. She carried her child when it became evident that Cat, who had been on her feet for over twelve hours, could go no further. And she carried the bitter burden of knowing that the enmity which she had treated so lightly since how could it harm her, was a strong and ugly repression in the hearts of these people. They did not like Annie Abbott. They did not approve of Annie Abbott. She had done what no decent woman would, could do, but she had not been punished for it as harlots should be punished. Far from it, they had seen her survive, thrive even. They took no account, nor did they admire, that it was her own hard labour that had achieved it. So they had turned even more against her. Today had been their way of letting her know, if she didn't already, that she'd get no helping hand from them. They'd have no truck with her, even if they lost money as a consequence.

She glared ahead of her into the falling darkness, her expression as grim as the farmer's from Threlkeld had been.

14

It was the evening of the day Annie Abbott had gone to the tup fair at Keswick. The farmhouse at Long Beck was illuminated in every window, even the bedrooms, with the branches of candelabra Reed Macauley had ordered to be placed there so that not only would his guests be impressed by his own careless disregard for the cost of such things, but also his house and gardens might be clearly visible and easily found as those guests arrived in their carriages. The track up from Gillthrop was, strictly speaking, not suitable for such vehicles, farm carts being the usual transport finding its way up there, but with care and a good coachman, it was possible to manoeuvre up the steep track.

The name farmhouse could really no longer be used to describe Reed Macauley's home. Two hundred years ago there had been four small farmhouses and farmlands belonging to four Macauley brothers but in the generations that followed those four holdings had become one and had gone to Reed Macauley's canny grandfather, Hamish, who had passed it on to Reed's father, Alistair, and so to Reed. There had been, by all accounts, battling Macauleys among Reed's forebears who had not stayed peaceably at home on their farms but had sent their sons to fight against Holland in 1665, against France in 1690 and in Malborough's wars of 1702–1710, two members of the family falling in the Battle of Malplaquet. There was Culloden in 1746, where one had fought for Prince Charlie since their sympathy then had been with their Scottish cousins and another had been in India at the time of the infamous Black Hole of Calcutta, where after being incarcerated in a cell, of the 146 souls put there the night before, only 23 came out alive. War and disease had thinned out the Macauley heirs like young seedlings in a frost until land and farmhouses now all belonged to the one remaining branch of the family.

Beside the farm and its buildings there was ploughland, a peat moss, woodlands, pasture and dozens of small fields surrounding the house. These were the 'banks', steep but low-altitude grazing land close about the farm where Reed's milking cows were kept. The banks were rich and lush and green, studded with animals, knee-deep in clover and buttercups. Enclosed at the time of the 'Enclosure Acts' by sturdy, drystone walls which were kept in fine condition by the 'wallers' Reed employed. There was the moor beyond the banks where his horses, his bullocks, his heifers and 'dry' cows grazed, not enclosed but his just the same. And then there were the fells, high and rolling, where his sheep wandered, watched over by his shepherds and their dogs. Hundreds of acres of rich farmland and all belonging to one man. Since the eighteenth century, farming had slowed down as other industries were born and expanded, and there were fewer farms, but those that remained had become bigger and, of those, Reed Macauley's was the biggest.

The house itself had become, through extensive renovations over the recent years, more of a manor house than a farmhouse. Built in a sheltered fold of the fells, it formed three sides round a square cobbled area which had once been a yard but which was now a standing and turning place for carriages. There were flower beds against the house walls, thick with antirrhinums, dahlia, delphiniums and rock rose. There was, in season, wisteria, fragrant and blue, climbing up the whitewashed walls, and massed rhododendron. Lavender at the right time and lilac, and edging the path was boxed privet, all cared for by a gardener and two boys. The lawns were smooth and green and the trees, centuries-old oak and yew, stood in protective tranquillity about the house.

The house itself looked as though it had not been built by men, but had grown slowly and gracefully, from the

very hills which formed its backdrop. Its mullioned
windows were set deep in its thick walls, not one the same
size as its fellow. The front door was situated not in its
centre, but in one of the angles of its corners, wide and
solid with a fluted porch above. The roof tiles were a
greeny blue, almost grey, and its three enormous sets of
chimneys were cylindrical. Gracious, serene, lovely and
yet strong and protective of those who lived within its
walls, it had been built to withstand any of the malevolent
weather conditions with which the fells and dales of the
lakes were challenged. It was a house which the dour and
taciturn men of the fells eyed suspiciously since they liked
plain, solid, foursquare, no nonsense and in their opinion
Reed Macauley's high-flown ideas of comfort, luxury even,
were pretentious and unnecessary.

It did not prevent them from attending the party at his
home that evening in honour of the young lady to whom he
had recently become betrothed, and her wealthy industrial
family. A good match of course, for would a hard-headed
business man like Reed Macauley have any other, despite
the fact that he had no need, financially speaking, to wed
where money was? From Bradford it was said the family
came, woollen cloth manufacturers, which would do Reed
no harm since it would provide him with a ready-made
outlet for his wool. A shrewd man, was Reed Macauley,
who had always recognised and taken advantage of an
opportunity when he saw it.

They stood, the newly engaged couple, her beautifully
manicured white hand through his arm, just inside the
doorway of what the man who opened the door to them
– could he be a butler? – called, grandiosely, the drawing
room. Parlour, they would have said, since, though they
themselves were not short of a bob or two, that was what
the living rooms in their homes were called. In fact, it was
not long since the living room had been known simply as
the 'house' or the 'down house'.

Reed Macauley greeted them, the 'statesmen' society
of Bassenthwaite parish, with a somewhat ironic smile
about his well-cut mouth. He knew what they were think-

ing, and of course, they were right. Though the girl beside him was devastatingly pretty, with the full-breasted, broad-shouldered figure of an Amazon princess, tall with hair the colour and texture of spun gold, and wide eyes the deep blue of a speedwell, it was not these which had drawn him to her. He would find it no hardship to take her to his bed of course, and was already looking forward to the moment when, after their marriage naturally, he would strip her of her silks and satins and have at his disposal the magnificent whiteness of her young body, but it was her money, her position, or rather that of her father, her absolute qualification to be a perfect hostess at his table and a devoted mother to his children, as she had been trained to be, which had attracted her to him. Esmé Hamilton-Brown, seventeen years old, with a dazzling smile matching the magnificent diamond on her finger, which he had given her on their betrothal. They would be married in the spring, an enormous affair in Bradford, to which the élite of the industrial class would be invited and from where he would bring her back to run his home and bring up the children they would have.

The thought afforded him absolutely no joy and for that fraction of a second when the sterile picture was in his mind, he felt ice-cold waves of despair flood his body and reach his brain. When Ezra Hodgson and his wife Lucy stood before him, Ezra's hand outstretched in congratulations and Lucy's eyes all over Esmé's superb, extremely *décolleté* evening gown of rose-coloured satin, he was momentarily paralysed. He just could not, in that fraction of time, bring himself back to reality, to the reality of who he was and of what was taking place this evening. Instead he felt the impact of two deep, laughing, brown eyes, not a true brown, more golden with luminous lights of mystery in them and a message which, though he did his best, he could not make out. They were fringed with thick brown lashes which meshed as the laughter deepened and in his heart, over which again he had no control, a spasm of real pain shivered and he was desolate. Desolate and lost for

how could he do this . . . with Esmé . . . when she . . .
she . . . ?

". . . and this is the beautiful young lady who is coming
to live among us, is it?" Ezra was saying somewhat
stiltedly since what else *was* he to do when his host, on
whose arm the beautiful young lady hung, was staring at
him, saying nowt mind, with his mouth open and his eyes
glazed.

"It is," Reed said, recovering at once, indeed so completely the strange moment might not have happened.
"Esmé, my dear, may I present Mr and Mrs Ezra Hodgson
from Penrith. Mr Hodgson and I are business associates,
but I hope, friends as well. Ezra, Lucy, this is my future
wife, Miss Esmé Hamilton-Brown. I'm sure Mrs Hodgson
will welcome you most generously, Esmé, into her home
and into society when we are married."

She would, Mrs Hodgson gushed, despite the newly
affianced young lady's rather vacant expression, her
haughty manner and extreme youth. Mrs Hodgson had
girls of her own who were the same age as Esmé Hamilton-
Brown. Indeed she had nurtured hopes of Reed Macauley
for one of them, but the girl smiled, a dazzling display
of pearl-white teeth, so she was evidently good-natured.
Superb they were those teeth, as was she and there was
no doubt she would produce superb children. She would
make a splendid adornment to Reed Macauley's table as,
when they sat down to dine, her creamy breasts proved
when they were half revealed in the candle-light. She was
rich, conventional and none too bright, Lucy decided, saying as much to Beatrice Mossop when the ladies left the
gentlemen to their port and cigars, and what more could
a man like Reed Macauley, who was not one to settle
easily to domesticity, need from a wife? She and Beatrice,
on the pretext of a hem which needed a stitch, had been
directed up Reed's wide staircase to the tranquil, candle-lit
landing off which the doors to half a dozen bedrooms lay.
The door to one was open, revealing what was the retiring
room for the ladies, and in it was Sarah Macauley's old
sewing woman, Dolly, dressed in black but with her snow-

white hair covered in an old-fashioned butterfly cap and
wearing a muslin apron. She was rocking peacefully before
a good fire, a bit of sewing in her hand, her face seamed
and placid. She had been put there by Mrs Stone the
housekeeper, to hand out pins or smelling salts or clean
handkerchiefs to any of the ladies who might need them;
to look after Reed Macauley's guests' wraps and cloaks,
many of which were made from rich velvet, lined with fur.
The other younger maids, of whom Lucy Hodgson knew,
from her own maids, there to be at least five, were too
busy on this important night with their duties of caring for
Mr Macauley's important guests and so Dolly had been
brought out of partial retirement to perform this simple
task.

The big room was bright with firelight and candle-light
in soft shades of cream and rose repeated in the carpet,
the curtains and the bed hangings. There were several
pieces of Reed Macauley's mother's furniture about the
room, in elaborately carved, lovingly polished mahogany,
but the walls were lined with rose-pink silk and everywhere bowls of flowers stood next to silver candlesticks
supporting sweet-smelling candles. It was lovely, so warm
and welcoming that both women gaped, for though their
husbands had wealth, they had not spent it as Reed
Macauley evidently did on luxury such as this. And this was
merely a spare room, so what did those which were occupied by Miss Hamilton-Brown and Mr and Mrs Hamilton-
Brown have in them? The dining room from which they
had just come was low ceilinged since nothing could be
done to alter that, but its dark oak-panelled walls were
relieved with the light from its two windows, which were
shrouded in the costliest pale green velvet. The carpet
was plain, rich and creamy and surely not meant for gentlemen's riding boots, and on the two sideboards were dozens
of bright silver dishes, candelabra and all the appurten-
ances of a rich man of taste and elegance. It was the same
in the drawing room, wide velvet sofas and cabriole-legged
velvet chairs, ormolu-mounted inlaid cabinets stuffed with
fine porcelain and on the walls, heavy gilt-framed pictures

of scantily clad nymphs which those who dined there were not at all sure they cared for. Especially with ladies present.

So this was what Reed Macauley had done to his home during the last months in preparation for his bride, the ladies whispered to one another, neither woman aware that he had not had Esmé Hamilton-Brown in his mind's eye as he did so.

The tall young man moved lightly across the yard at Browhead followed by the two dogs. He was dressed in an ill-fitting pair of breeches and stout gaiters, and on his feet were thick, hand-knitted woollen stockings, pushed into a pair of well-worn wooden-soled clogs. A loose jacket, a woollen waistcoat and a long, also hand-knitted, muffler wrapped warmly about his neck. On his head was a soft felt hat with a bowl-shaped crown and brim, very battered and evidently very old.

The dogs pranced about his long striding legs, young dogs but when he spoke and his hand made some small movement, both instantly went down on their bellies, watching, ears pricked, eyes gleaming with bright interest as he entered the barn. It was several minutes before he emerged and when he did he was pulling the sledge.

"Stay, Blackie, stay, Bonnie," and the dogs obeyed, their eyes never leaving the young man as he eased the sledge back across the yard to the side door of the farmhouse. They did not move until his hand told them they may, then they bounded after him.

"Down." The quiet command was instantly obeyed.

"Good boys, now stay."

The man entered the house and the dogs remained where they were, guarding the empty sledge, sniffing the air with keen noses, alert, bright eyed, quivering with eagerness, but remembering their duty. When the door opened again they turned their heads as one, looking towards it, their plumed tails moving slowly on the ground.

A child came out, a little girl of three or four, carrying an enormous bundle carefully tied about with twine. She

placed it on the sledge. She bent to put a small hand on
the head of one of the dogs and he strained beneath it,
longing to leap up and play but he resisted, contenting
himself with licking the child's hand with his long pink
tongue.

"Good boy, Blackie," the child said, then turned to the
second animal who was doing his best to remain on the
ground where he had been put. He inched forward a fraction and when the girl's hand was within reach licked it
ecstatically.

"Good boy, Bonnie, now stay there, NO, stay, good
boy."

Another figure appeared, this time that of a young girl
of about twelve or thirteen, plain but wholesome, clean
and tidy but shabbily dressed in an assortment of what
seemed to be layers of old bits of clothing. Her dark and
shining hair was strained back from her high forehead and
braided about her head. She carried a pile of swill baskets,
one inside the other, which she placed beside the bundle
the child had already put in the sledge. They both went
back inside the house then returned, carrying more
bundles, more swills and another load of neatly tied besom
twig brushes. The older girl spent several minutes arranging it all to her satisfaction, making sure that nothing would
roll off the cart.

"Yon'll not move now," she said determinedly, evidently
satisfied with her own handiwork. "Them swills is wedged
in against them stockings an' nowt'll shift 'em. I've put the
besoms at bottom so they'll not roll out."

"I hope it doesn't rain," the child said dolefully, her small
face turning up to look with worried concern at the grey
clouds scudding from one high fell to the next, a long,
threatening line of them following one another low across
the sky, with alarming regularity.

"Nay, it'll not do that, chuck. Tha' can hear t'waterfall
up by Dash so it'll not rain, tha' knows that," – which was
true. The sound of falling water or the absence of it was
often a sure indication of whether it would rain or not.
Something to do with the direction of the wind, it was

said, vaguely, by those who lived hereabouts. They only knew their fathers had said the same and their father's father before that. There were many such predictions. The direction in which a cloud moved, the colour of the sky as the sun set, the certain way in which an owl called, or at what time the cock crowed. A cold and windy May heralded a good harvest, a warm Christmas a full churchyard, and if Candlemas day in February was to dawn fine and clear, there would be two winters in one year. And it was found that these old sayings and forecasts and many others, had more than a grain of truth in them.

The little girl brightened. She began to circle the sledge touching a bundle, giving the swills a brisk pat, her small pretty face as intent and serious as though the vehicle was off to the wastes of the Arctic and its safety depended on her vigilance. The older girl watched her, then spontaneously, she knelt and put her arms about her, drawing the child lovingly into a close embrace. Her own face was soft and pale and her blue eyes brimmed, though no tears fell.

"It'll be all right, Cat, honest it will. Us've managed this long, so don't thi' worry."

"But it's such a long way, Phoebe." The child's voice, in sharp contrast to the older girl's, was clear, the words well pronounced, concise with no trace of her northern heritage in them.

"Ah know, lambkin, but tha's not to worry. We've both told thi' that. Dogs are goin' along for protection and they'll not let 'owt 'appen, tha' knows that. Good guard dogs, they be, aren't tha' lads?" turning to put out a hand to the animals. The dogs' ears swivelled and their heads cocked as they did their best to understand what she was saying.

"Come on then, come to me an' Cat," she said, and instantly they leaped up, moving to lean on her and the child, conveying their devoted sympathy in the only way they knew how at this sad time as though they were fully aware of the underlying anxiety.

The child who had burrowed her head in the girl's bony

but comforting shoulder, looked up, brightening once more
as two cold noses nuzzled at her soft cheek.

"That's right. Nothing can happen if Blackie and Bonnie
are there, can it, Phoebe? How long will it be d'you think,
Phoebe?"

"Nay lass, tha knows we've talked about it and it could
be a week or two. But it will be before October's out, tha'
can rest easy on that. Before the snows come but that's
a long walk over to Rosley and back, pulling that thing,
an' all, but as soon as all that stuff's sold and the sheep
bought, they'll be home, tha' knows that. Aye, before the
winter sets in, an' thee and me'll manage. There's things
to be done about the place to keep us busy. An' yer know
we promised we'd keep up wi' our reading an' writing like
yer mam's bin' teaching us, an' then there's the sums. By
heck, we'll be that busy time'll just fly by. Now wipe tha'
face an' smile fer there's enough to be worried about wi'out
tekkin' your tears with . . ."

"Well, that's that," a cheerful voice from the doorway
said. "I think I've got everything. Just put this rug over
the cart, will you, Phoebe, and tie it firmly. You've made
a splendid job of loading up, but it's almost eight o'clock
and I want to be well on my way to Cockermouth by
midday. I can get a good start with this lot and then spend
the night there, that's if I can get someone to take me in
dressed as I am though I think I'll have to find another
way to confine all this."

The young 'man' removed his hat and about his shoulders fell the most amazing and glorious cloak of glowing
copper hair, thick and tight-curled, and both Phoebe and
Cat smiled in delight as the 'young man' revealed himself
to be Annie Abbott.

Phoebe would never forget that day at the Keswick Tup
Fair, nor that night when, with Cat sleeping the sleep of
the truly exhausted, Annie railed about the kitchen at the
fates which had landed her such a savage blow. Hour after
hour the storm of outrage slammed against the whitewashed walls and hour after hour Phoebe listened to it
until, at last, she had had enough and she said so.

She would not allow it, she said, nor the self-pity in which, if not sternly spoken to, Annie was about to wallow. The destructive self-pity which can paralyse and render impotent even the strongest and most self-willed. Phoebe's sympathy had been immediate, and her concern warm hearted since she knew as well as Annie that their future had depended on the small flock of sheep Annie meant to have. They had food, grown by herself and Annie during the summer; they had peat from which to make a fire to warm them; a roof over their head. They were not destitute but she also knew how the thought of that flock of sheep, the beginning of a *proper* farm was the candle-flame of hope which had been lit in Annie's heart twelve months ago. Before Phoebe had come to live at the farm at Browhead.

It was the first home Phoebe had ever known. A foundling from some poorhouse she had been, put to work from the moment she could wield a scrubbing brush in her small, chapped hands, knowing nothing but her bucket and the dozens of pairs of legs, male and female, who had walked by it. Put out to various farming families, she had learned many basic crafts about a kitchen. But girls were hired for their size and strength and though she was willing and worked herself until she could barely stand, she was always 'let go' at the end of six months because she had not the sheer physical strength to perform many of the brutally heavy tasks expected of her about the farm. She worked from five in the morning until ten at night. She could shake mats, scrub flags, fetch water – in a small pail – do a week's wash, light fires, milk cows, blacklead a fireplace, scrub a table until it was white; she could bake and cook a plain meal, but that, apparently, had not been enough and her last employer had taken her into Keswick and, putting her few shillings in her hand, told her to stand in line with the other maid-servants.

She had been shown nothing but indifference, unconcern, an impassive apathy to how she might feel and a total lack of interest in what she thought, or indeed, if she thought at all. She was no more than a pair of chilblained hands which took the bucket, the soap, the brush, a blank face which showed no curiosity since her brain, her mind had never been taught that such an emotion might lead to understanding.

Annie Abbott had revealed a magic, a splendour, a miraculous, exploding world of love, of laughter and beauty to the starved senses of a girl who had been blind and deaf and she had done it with nothing more than what, to Annie and Cat, was a part of their everyday world. The stunted emotion of the child, the young girl, had developed and bloomed, brought about by no more than an affectionate hug, a helping hand, acceptance into a home in which there was love. She had been shown the sweetness and loveliness of a flower, the colour of a sunset, the song of a skylark. The mists hanging low over the still lake, the call of the curlew across Skiddaw Forest, the mingled smells of the valley freshness after rain, the sound of the wind in the pines. All these things and the warmth of love, the power of friendship, the light-hearted merriment of the child and the dogs, the need of Annie and Cat for Phoebe, the security of knowing that this was where she belonged. It had caused a transformation in the young girl, creating in her a resilience and toughness of which she was made aware a dozen times a day. Phoebe would give her life for Annie Abbott and for Cat, and she was not about to let either of them go under, not if she could help it.

Annie wept for the first time in many years.

"Nay lass, cry if tha' must," Phoebe said that night, just as though their roles were reversed. "But don't tha' tell me it's not fair. I'll not 'ave it, so there, an' when tha' comes to thissen, tha'll see the sense of it. Ah knows tha've 'ad a knock an' ah knows it's put us back a bit, but we'll catch up, see if we don't. Thee an' me, between us . . ."

"Phoebe, oh Phoebe . . . you don't understand. They hate me. They want to see me go under with nothing . . ."

"Don't say nothing, tha's got me an' Cat. We . . . we love thee."

"I know that but all the work I've done, the insults and

. . . and contempt I've known . . . a whole year, and now, when I've got the cash, they won't sell me the sheep. It's not fair . . . it's not fair . . ."

"Life's not fair." The girl's voice was soft, sad almost, for who knew better than she how unjust life was to some, how kind to others, but that was something else again and at the moment she was doing her best to lift this beloved friend from the depths of her despair.

It was not like Annie to give way like this and Phoebe knew that when she'd had a good cry and a good shout at the world in general and the farmers who had turned their backs on her in particular, she'd be her old self again, well, almost. A hard and bitter blow had fallen on her and that sort always left its mark, left the victim slightly weakened, but if Phoebe had anything to do with it, Annie'd get what she wanted in the end. Annie had taken it very bad, the refusal of the farmers to sell her their sheep, worse really than Phoebe had expected, for there were other fairs, farther afield, where Annie wasn't known and where sheep might be bought. But Annie had dragged herself about as though she had come to the end of the road and met head-on a wall over which there was no climbing. It was strange really, for on the way home from the fair at Keswick Phoebe had seen the grim clamping of Annie's mouth, the resolute jut to her jaw and the gleam in her eye which meant, as Phoebe well knew by now, that her benefactor and friend had made up her mind to something. Phoebe had gloated as she watched her, knowing that Annie had a plan to put right what had happened that day at the market. They had gone to their beds silently, but, Phoebe had been positive, with hope still about them. It had been several days later when Annie had suddenly broken down and given in to what looked like despair, crying and rocking as though the blow at Keswick had only just fallen.

"Nay," Phoebe said, "it's not like thi' ter give up so easy. I've not known thi' long, but tha've never struck me as bein' someone as'd lay down an' whine just 'cos a few daft buggers . . ."

"Oh Phoebe, I know, I know. Those daft buggers as

you call them are not worth shedding a tear over, but
sometimes something happens, on top of all the other
misfortunes, which just seems to . . . well . . ."

"What sorta things, Annie?"

"Oh, I don't know, things you don't quite expect. They
creep up on you from behind, and even though you're half
expecting them, indeed you know very well they're bound
to happen, they take you by surprise and . . . knock the
breath from you."

Phoebe hadn't the slightest idea what Annie was talking
about and the expression on her plain little face said so.
She was a practical girl who understood the mischievous
tricks life played on you, the calamities which you could
see and feel, just like the one that had befallen them, yes
them, since Annie's troubles were *her* troubles now, but
all this business about things creeping up on you, behind
your back, seemed a bit nonsensical to her. What sort of
things? Did Annie mean like that Bert Garnett who was
always skulking along the path from Upfell Farm and down
to Browhead? Hanging about when his wife and mother-in-
law thought him, she supposed, to be away on farm
business, slipping into Annie's kitchen after dark on some
pretext or other. His eyes were like those of a weasel
fixed on Annie's breasts and he licked his lips as a cat
might, which is about to lap at a saucer of cream. Oh aye,
he was the sort who'd creep up behind your back, he was,
but Phoebe was surprised that it should upset Annie who
was quite capable of giving him a lug round t'earhole if he
so much as laid a finger on her.

They stood at the gate, Cat and Phoebe, waving and
waving to her as she trudged up the lane in the direction
of Gillthrop. The heavy sledge creaked along behind her.
The rope they had hitched to it already bit into her tender
shoulders beneath the old shirt and jacket which had been
her father's. The dogs kept close to her side, looking back
as she did, until they had turned the curve of the lane and
Cat and Phoebe were out of sight.

"Well lads," she said to them, settling her father's hat
more firmly on her head, for it would not do if her hair

fell about her shoulders, "let's get going." She hitched up the trousers making sure the braces on them were secure, for the waist was too big for her. They felt strange, but the freedom in walking was marvellous. No wonder men wore them, denying the privilege to their womenfolk, she thought, as she strode through the village of Gillthrop. Women who stood in their doorways stared at her, aware that they had seen the tall youth somewhere but not awfully sure where it could have been.

She took the road straight ahead to Uldale, squaring her shoulders beneath the chafing rope with which she dragged the sledge, the ache there infinitely less than the one in her heart which had begun when she had heard of Reed Macauley's impending marriage.

15

It was the man from Long Beck, the farm up by Dash Beck, who knocked at the door, and Phoebe opened it knowing they had nothing to fear from him.

"Where is she?" he demanded to know abruptly, almost before the door was ajar, ready to push it wider and stick his foot in it, just as though he expected it to be shut in his face. He peered over Phoebe's shoulder, his frown forbidding but in his eyes was that look Phoebe had seen in them when last he was here.

"The mistress is not 'ere at the moment," she said politely, as Annie had taught her. Phoebe was not to say where she was or how long she would be, Annie had said. On no account was Phoebe to let any caller know that Annie would be away overnight, in fact Phoebe was to act as though Annie was no further away than the coppice wood, or up on the peat moor digging for peat.

"Can I give 'er a message?" Phoebe continued, her face expressionless, empty of all but her need to be courteous but at the same time close the door in the visitor's face since the biting wind was nipping smartly in through the open door.

"Where is she?" the man said again, only his barely controlled awareness of the need for restraint on the doorstep of another's home keeping him from pushing past the stiff figure of the young girl and into Annie's kitchen.

"She's out just now," Phoebe shifted not an inch.

"But where, for God's sake? Is she up on the fell?" he asked, turning to stare up into the high distance of Great Cockup. He shaded his eyes with a gloved hand against the bright, cold autumn sun, then turned again to look down the sloping fields towards the lake as though Annie might suddenly appear. The afternoon sun cast long shadows as it settled behind the stand of trees by the waterside. Tall Scotch pines, dense and darkly green, and all about them and about the lake, on its far side and blazing up the fells to where it met the grey craggy rocks, was the golden glory of the drying bracken. Gold and yellow and orange melting down to the blue and purple waters of the lake where the colours mingled, rippling out from the shore in moving beauty. On the very tops of the tallest fells there was the first faint dusting of winter snow.

"Nay, I couldn't say," Phoebe answered politely, "but she'll not be long."

It was a mistake and as the words left her mouth, Phoebe knew it.

"Then I'll wait," the man said at once and before Phoebe could test her puny strength against his, he had pushed open the door and was inside. The dog at his feet was told brusquely to wait, and the door, taken from Phoebe's hand, was closed upon the animal.

Reed Macauley looked about him, ready for the affronted voice of Annie Abbott to come at him demanding to know what he was doing in her kitchen since he had not believed what the girl had told him. She was in the house somewhere he had decided, keeping her distance, unwilling to confront him, to listen to him, no matter what he had to say to her.

And what *had* he to say to her? he asked himself, as he had done ever since he had ordered his mare to be saddled and had set off in the direction of Browhead. They were nothing to one another, he and Annie Abbott. They had never, in the twelve months he had known her, touched one another, never kissed or clasped hands. They had known no physical contact, had exchanged no promises, no vows, nor even words which might be construed as loving, and yet he loved her. She loved him. He knew it and so did she and he was, in the spring, to marry another woman. So why was he here? To do what? To say what? He did not know, he only knew that the compulsion to come, now that Esmé and her parents had returned to

Yorkshire, going before the winter snows locked them in, had been unassailable. Of course, he had heard of her misadventure in Keswick – who in these parts had not – and he meant to put it right if he could do so without upsetting that proud and rebellious spirit of hers. He'd *give* her the damned sheep if she'd let him, and if not, sell them to her at the lowest price he was able, *if she would let him*. That was the trouble. She was so damned high and mighty, she was likely to take offence and tell him to go to the devil, taking his sheep with him, even if he offered her the pick of his flock. But he couldn't let her go on like this, being humiliated and treated contemptuously by everyone in the district, sneered and jeered at, working her fingers and her proud back right down to the bone in her determination to be successful. Jesus, he had the power, the wealth, the influence to put a stop to it right now for there were not many in the parish of Bassenthwaite who did not owe a favour to Reed Macauley, and it would take but a word from him to set her on her feet and on the path she wanted to go. Of course, if he did that he would also give her the power she needed to snap her fingers at him when all he wanted, all he had ever wanted was to have her dependent on him, soft, loving, submissive, waiting, sighing for Reed Macauley. He wanted to look after her, not give her the means to look after herself. Even if he married . . . *when* he married Esmé, he and Annie could . . . many men had an . . . arrangement to which their wives made no objection. It was, at least amongst the upper classes, quite normal for a man to have a mistress, providing he was discreet and did not fling it in the faces of those with whom he was acquainted. Ezra Hodgson and Ben Pearson both kept a cosy nest with a pretty bird in it, Ezra in Penrith and Ben in Rosthwaite, far enough away not to offend the sensibilities of their wives, but near enough to ride over when they had a fancy for . . . well, what men with good, sensible, but unresponsive wives, needed.

His eyes roamed the room as he waited for her to appear, noticing the shining, fragrant cleanliness of the homely kitchen. So had his mother's looked years ago when he was a boy and the Macauleys, though well set up farmers, had not had the wealth, nor the need for the luxurious living he now enjoyed. His mother had worked in her kitchen, directing her maids in the making of soap and candles, bread and all the good food she had stuffed into his father and himself. A true farmwife, who thought nothing of spinning and weaving the cloth for their clothes, in between her many other household chores. Now, *his* wife had no need to do more than adorn his drawing room when her callers came, sit at his table and make small talk when his guests dined, make herself available in his bed when he needed her, and produce his children which a well-trained nurse and governess, or tutor, would bring up for her. Not for her this gleaming, glowing, well-polished comfort, the good smells of nourishing food which *she* had cooked in her nostrils, and the sight of her children about the kitchen table, busy on their primers, as Annie's child was, dogs sprawled by the fire and . . . dogs . . . where were the dogs? . . . The dogs were not here so where in hell had Annie got to where she needed her dogs with her? She had no sheep so why had she . . . ? Where had she . . . ? Where *was* she . . . ? The two girls round the table . . . reading apparently . . . two places set with plates and cutlery . . . not three . . . two . . . so where the devil . . . ?

"Where is she?" he said for the third time.

She had reached Caldbeck within the week. Though as the crow flies it was no more than ten or so miles from Gillthrop, the roads were winding and tortuous, simply no more than rutted tracks in some parts, high and treacherous, and she had made many detours as she moved from farm to farm, village to village, cottage to cottage, in the selling of her besoms, her swill baskets and her long woollen stockings. Though most of the farm women made their own, her goods had sold well in the villages and the small towns of Uldale and Caldbeck. Women there did not have the materials to make such things themselves, relying on pedlars to bring them to the door or the market stalls at fair time. The stallholders at the fairs in the cycle of trading had bought the goods they sold from the farm women and, of course, wishing to make a profit for their trouble, had put a penny or two on the price, and the tall, good-looking young man with the soft voice was welcome with his cheaper and better-quality goods. She had spent three days in Uldale, moving with her sledge to every house in every narrow street, the dogs one on either side of her. Blackie and Bonnie were uneasy, quick to alarm, should something they did not care for threaten their mistress. They were not accustomed to people, to other dogs, to cats, horses, carts and carriages and every one seemed to them a menace with which they must deal. It took Annie's sharp commands to keep them from lunging at all and sundry. The men who passed her by, though they could not have said why, stared at her, curious and strangely ill at ease with the young man who had the graceful gait of a female which sat awkwardly on his tall, long-legged frame.

She had pulled the sledge, lighter now and easier on her chafed shoulders, through Longlands, Greenhead, Branthwaite and Fellside, going up and up, higher into the rolling peaklands towards Caldbeck Fell, where she could have taken a short cut over the tops had she not wished to go on to Parkend, Whelpo and Caldbeck itself. It was in Caldbeck she knew she would find, as she had done in Uldale, many customers for her wares. She had spent the nights in tiny inns, taking the cheapest room, alone of course, since to sleep in a double or triple, sharing with other men, though cheaper, would have caused no end of trouble; she smiled to herself as the thought came to her.

It was getting colder. The days were shortening and soon the last fortnightly cattle market would be held at Rosley, which was her destination. She had already gone past files of slow-moving cattle, and some sheep, winding their way along the passes and the fellsides, some on their journeys to new pastures and some to the cattle fair.

Whitsuntide was the time of the largest fair at Rosley Hill when travellers with their beasts came from all points of the compass to sell their goods and their animals. Rosley was on the main drove road from Scotland to the north of England and it attracted thousands of men, and women too. Its influence reached across the Solway and into Annan and Dumfries, mile after mile of gentle greenery and lush enclosures which housed the cattle and other animals as they made their way there from the Solway Plain and beyond. To the east of Rosley was the grazing ground of High Hesket, which meant that the market was set in exactly the right place to meet the needs of man and beast. Foot passengers from Carlisle and Penrith as well as Scotland found the going easy. Travelling people such as the young actor who had seduced fourteen-year-old Annie Abbott were drawn there. Pot-selling women came balancing enormous baskets of pots on their heads, the basket resting on a weather-bleached hat braided with ribbon. They wore long gaudy gowns with a blue flannel petticoat showing at the front. They smoked a short pipe for they cared nought for any man's opinion and usually had a horde of youngsters about them who carried baskets on their hips. There were carriers and collectors of news, since it was hard to come by up on the rolling fells of Hesket Forest and Westward. There were men dealing in rags and skins, women who told fortunes, vagrants and Irishmen in increasing numbers who came from Ireland into Whitehaven on coal vessels, making their way to wherever there was a promise of work, and beneath it all was a vague and shifting underworld of organised gangs of thieves and pickpockets, waiting to pounce on the unwary.

But there were none of these about as Annie Abbott approached The Drover's Rest two weeks after she had left Gillthrop. It was too late in the year for the 'fair' people, those who came to beg and entertain at the great Whitsuntide Fair. There were about her the last of the men selling what remained of their cattle and sheep and none took any interest in the tall youth who pulled an old

and empty sledge and at whose heels two silent dogs
trailed. Except one!

He was leaning against the inn wall, a pint pot of ale in
his fist, one heel resting on the stones behind him, one
hand deep in the pocket of his narrow corduroy trousers.
He was tall, young and lean and straight as an arrow. No
bulk about him, but a taut whipcord strength which seemed
to promise toughness. He had brown, curly hair and grey,
cat-like eyes set in a clever face. His mouth had a humorous twist to it, as it dipped into the ale and his grey eyes
were watchful, everywhere at once, keen and alert as
though he was not only guarding his back but planning his
route ahead.

His eyes stopped moving as they came to rest on the
figure of the tall young man and a puzzled, deliberating
expression narrowed them in his brown face. He watched
as the youth moved gracefully across the inn yard, a sledge
at his back, his stride as long as any man's, his shoulders
slightly hunched, his head set somewhat awkwardly on his
shoulders, just as though he was doing his best to hide
something.

But what? He was a perfectly ordinary young man, tall
and slim and very shabby, but then so were many of the
travellers who entered and left the inn. It was a working
man's inn, cheap and clean, where dozens of drovers
stayed as they took their masters' cattle and sheep, to
and from the fair. He studied the young man as he leaned
to put a slim hand on each of the heads of the dogs and
they both lay down next to the exceedingly fragile-looking
sledge. He went inside and the man leaning on the wall
drifted after him. He did not know why.

"Have you a room?" he heard the youth say in a low
voice to the innkeeper.

"We 'ave that, lad, at least a bed if that's any good to
thi'."

"I'd like a room to myself, if you please." The landlord
looked surprised.

"Nay, lad, this is t'last fair an' I'm pulled out wi' drovers.
Tha's lucky to get thi' a bed to thissen, which tha'll have,

I promise thi', but not a room. See, there's only one other in't room an' that's this chap behind thi'. He'll not mind sharing, will tha', sir?"

Charlie Lucas smiled infectiously, raising his pint pot in the direction of the landlord, before turning to look into the softest, most incredibly beautiful pair of brown eyes he had ever seen on any human being, let alone another male, and it was then, as the strange imperceptive feeling of disquiet became stronger, that he began to realise.

"Not at all," he said, looking enquiringly at the youth, waiting politely to see if he was to share his room.

"No, thanks . . . I'll . . . No, thanks . . ."

"There's not a bed to be found in all of Rosley, lad," the innkeeper said somewhat irritably since he'd no time to stand around prattling on about beds with this strange-looking lad, especially one he could rent without trouble, and strange the lad was an' all. He'd better watch himself with some of the men they got around here who, short of a woman, didn't care where they stuck their 'John Willys'. Odd sort of a lad he was, who, had he been a girl, would have looked as pretty as a picture. Perhaps that's why he was so keen to get his own room, having had experiences of a . . . perverted sort before. Still, the other chap seemed harmless enough, the one who'd offered to share, but no, the lad was walking away, shaking his head as though someone had suggested he sleep in a bed with a dozen others and a ewe or two as well.

"No, thank you, it's most kind of you . . ." *Most kind of you!* The landlord wiped his cloth over the bar top, staring in amazement at the young man's back. *Most kind of you!* Whoever he was, he had the manners of a well brought up lass but he'd better watch himself because already several of his customers were nudging one another and staring after him.

Annie could feel the interest in her as she stepped through the doorway and into the sharp autumn sunshine. She would have to be careful what she said, really she would. She quite forgot sometimes that young men, what-ever their station in life, just did not use the same phrases as women, and she had slipped up several times when she had been selling door to door in Uldale and Caldbeck but then it had not mattered unduly since she had been dealing with women who had been inclined to like the politeness of the young man who was peddling his besoms and swills. They had not questioned it when she had smiled and remarked on the weather – when it had turned wet – and on the state of her clogs; the mud which she was traipsing on to their clean doorsteps and how sorry she was about it. How kind they were to offer her a mug of ale, she had said, but thank you, no. She did not wish to appear rude but . . . They had smiled, thinking her quite charming, thinking she was a good-mannered and well-spoken lad to be working as *he* was, but these rough men who lived the lives of nomads and vagrants, some of them, had no such appreciation of pretty manners, and walking was difficult too. It was her habit to straighten her back and shoulders, to walk tall and proud, her head held high, but this action thrust forward her breasts and to hide them she found she must slouch along with her shoulders hunched. The times she had forgotten, striding out eagerly towards her goal, which surely now was in sight, only to remember when some man studied her in puzzlement.

She spoke softly to Blackie and Bonnie as she untied the knotted rope of the sledge, looking up and down the narrow track on which The Drover's Rest stood. She could see at once that there was not another building in the area. The fairground was enormous and empty beyond it. There was a well where water was drawn to water the animals and in the middle of the fairground was a large cow pen in which many animals lowed restively. At the far end of the ground was a public quarry where possibly she might find a ledge with an overhang where she could shelter for the night but all around her was nothing but the vast expanse of Rosley Fairground and the rolling hills of Westward leading to the Solway Plain.

"You'll find nowhere in which to shelter, I'm afraid, not at least where you'll be . . . safe."

The voice was neutral, pleasant, with no accent that

she could place. The words were spoken softly, almost in a whisper and it was obvious that the man who spoke them meant no one to hear but herself.

She turned only her head and that but a fraction. Her jacket collar was up and she had wound round and round her neck one of the long knitted scarves she had fashioned herself last winter. It came up about her chin, almost covering her mouth. Her father's soft felt hat was pulled down to her ears and between the muffler and the hat, her eyes blazed defiantly. Speaking over her shoulder, her own words were as quiet as his.

"What's it to you," she said, "where I sleep?" trying to sound like one man taking umbrage with another.

"Nothing at all . . . lad. Not to me. But it will to you if it's discovered you're not what you seem."

"I don't know what you mean." Disconcertingly, in her panic, her voice rose to its normal pitch and the man at her back smiled.

"I'm sure you do and I'm also sure you have a good reason for your . . . masquerade. Believe me, I mean you no harm but there are dozens who would if they . . . found out you were . . . not as they are. Why don't you go back inside and, before someone else takes it, tell the landlord that you have changed your mind about the bed? That you would be happy to share with Charlie Lucas. Yes, that's me, young . . . sir, Charlie Lucas at your service."

From the corner of her eye Annie saw the impish smile, the slight bow, the raised whimsical eyebrows and, suddenly and for no reason whatsoever, she liked what she saw. Nevertheless she had no intention of allowing anyone, even this rather personable young man, to penetrate her disguise.

Her voice was gruff. "I've no idea what you're up to, mister, and I don't want to. I'd just as soon sleep out of doors with my dogs, than share a room with anyone, if it's all the same to you. As for being safe, I've nothing worth stealing." Her hand, of its own volition, went to the deep pocket of her father's ancient trousers where, sewn into a small bag and attached to the pocket lining was her small hoard of savings. It had come from the sale of her swills and besoms and stockings, and included what she had scraped together over the past year. A tidy sum which was to buy her sheep tomorrow.

The man noticed the movement but he did not let her see it.

"Besides," she went on, tossing her head, unaware that a wispy curl of shining copper had escaped over her left ear, "I have my dogs to protect me," which, if she had thought about it, was a strange thing for a man to say.

"Just as you like then, but before you move off into that crowd of drovers, those who have nowhere to sleep except where, presumably, you mean to lay your head, and who, most of them, are as drunk as lords, I should pull my hat more firmly over my head, or they may take a fancy to see more of that rather lovely curl which is falling round your ear."

Her hand went to her ear involuntarily, frantically pushing at the vagrant tendril, doing her best to get it out of sight, but the more she tried to shove it under her hat, the more it came down.

"Leave it," the man said gently, moving to stand in front of her. "Now do it," and under the pretext of leaning to pat her dogs, they both bent down whilst she adjusted her unruly hair.

"I think you had better take that bed," he said, his voice still gentle.

"I cannot sleep in a room with a . . . a . . . stranger, a man I met no more than ten minutes ago." She spoke through gritted teeth and her voice was normal. The pretence she had kept up for almost two weeks was abandoned.

"I'm not suggesting you do so, though you would be quite safe, I can assure you, if you did. I take no pleasure, believe me, from an unwilling woman." He smiled lazily. "What I do suggest is we go up together as though we *were* to share and then, later, when it is quiet, I will slip out and leave you your privacy."

"How do I know you . . . will keep your word?"

"I have just told you. I like my women to be . . . amenable." Again the grin, sweet and wicked, and Annie could not help but smile back. Though his grey eyes told her he was vastly intrigued by her charade, and was willing to help her in it, and indeed in anything else she might allow, his slanting smile and amiable expression said she had nothing to fear from him. He would take nothing she did not give voluntarily.

She drew a deep breath, again unaware of the lift of her full breasts beneath the roomy jacket.

"Very well . . ."

"Charlie, Charlie Lucas."

"I'm . . . Annie Abbott."

"Miss Abbott." He inclined his head, his eyes twinkling. "But I had better call you . . ."

"What?"

"How about . . . Andrew . . . or Andy?"

"Very well, but I must warn you that if . . ."

"Yes, Andy?" and his smile was so innocent she could not help but smile back.

"I shall take my dogs to the room with me."

"Of course."

"They will not take kindly to anyone interfering with me."

"I can see that," he replied as he fondled the head of the grinning Blackie.

Reed Macauley was in Caldbeck when he found a woman, the wife of the innkeeper of The Flying Fox, who remembered buying half a dozen pairs of thick, beautifully knitted woollen stockings from a slim and handsome young pedlar with two sheepdogs. Oh, days ago now it was, she told him. No, she couldn't rightly remember exactly when, probably a week because her Arthur had worn one pair and they'd been in the wash already on account of him having sweaty feet. Came with standing behind the bar all day, see. His feet swelled something awful, making it worse, so these good woollen stockings would be a boon to him and she only wished she'd got another half a dozen.

Well, so beautifully knitted, and so cheap and the young chap was that polite . . . What? Where was he going? . . . Nay, she didn't know, though she'd seen him moving from cottage to cottage later in the day, pulling that there flimsy old sledge. No, she'd no idea where he'd spent the night. Certainly not at *her* hostelry where a better class of person than pedlars were accommodated. No, he *hadn't* said where he was off to next, sir, and really there was no need to shout. She wasn't deaf and if he was going to be abusive she'd be forced to call her husband. Very well then, she'd ask her husband if *he'd* spoken to the lad if the gentleman insisted, but really, it would do no good to question those in the bar because . . . oh very well, if he insisted she'd make enquiries . . . What? . . . Well . . . as it happened they did have a room for the night seeing as how one of their gentlemen had sent a message to cancel a regular booking . . . a lawyer he was who always came up to Caldbeck every . . . very well, Nancy will show you to your room and your horse will be attended to . . . well, did you see that, Nancy? . . . not so much as a thank you after all she'd told him. I mean to say, she couldn't be expected to know the direction taken by everyone who came to her back door. Could she?

16

Annie fell asleep almost before her head touched the sleazy pillow. She and Charlie had eaten a meal together in a corner of the bar, surprisingly good, consisting of thick wedges of bread in an enormous bowl of rabbit stew, pickles and cheese, again with bread and a tankard of ale apiece. The dogs had dined, lying beneath their feet, on hefty bones on which there was a fair amount of mutton left, and no one took the slightest interest in either her or Charlie Lucas.

They went up to the small attic room, the dogs pattering silently at Annie's back and when Annie sat down on the truckle bed, they lay across her feet and stared, flat-eyed, flat-eared, at the man who closed the door behind him.

"I have to stay until the bar empties, you do understand."

"Yes." Her eyes were on his face, her stiff manner saying that despite her instinct that told her she could believe this engagingly smiling young man when he said he would not harm her, her logical brain said she was quite insane to trust a perfect stranger just because he *seemed* all right.

"I meant what I said."

"Very well, but I would like to . . . to wash and . . ."

"I'll see if I can get you some hot water."

"Won't it cause . . . curiosity when you do? I believe gentlemen of the road don't bother with such things."

He smiled. "I am a gentleman of the road and, on occasion, I like a hot bath."

"Oh, I don't mean to bathe," she said hastily, the idea of removing *any* of her clothing in this room, which, she had already noticed, had no bolt on the door, quite horrific.

"Of course not, but if I was to . . . return to the bar for a last pint of ale you could . . ." he paused delicately, "the dogs would . . ."

The jug of water was hot and though she had no more than a brief wash, hurriedly shrugging herself back into her jacket and waistcoat before Charlie Lucas returned from the bar, she felt a lot cleaner than she had since she left home. She had brushed her hair which had become tangled beneath her hat and was just about to re-plait it when he tapped gently on the door.

"It's me," he murmured, but when she went to the door and opened it, her manner still stiff and constrained, he simply stood in the doorway as though a giant hand held him firmly rooted to the bare, unpolished boards.

"Good God," he whispered. His grey eyes had narrowed to deep grey velvet slits and his lips parted in a half-smile of wonderment. He shook his head. "Good God," he said again, "it's as well none of those men below saw you like that." His eyes moved from the flowing curtain of her hair to the delicate loveliness of the white skin at her bare neck, the soft curve of her mouth, the tilt of her fine eyebrows and the slanting set of her deep, golden eyes. How in hell's name had any chap who had clapped eyes on her, even in her man's clothing and the wide-brimmed soft felt bowler which she had jammed down over the glowing magnificence of her hair, believed that this, this glorious woman, was a *man*? Her jacket and waistcoat were still unbuttoned and the proud jut of her lovely breast strained against the coarse grey woollen shirt she wore. The belt about her tiny waist was drawn tight and her hips flared, womanly and infinitely desirable, beneath it.

"Good God, Annie Abbott," he said softly, "how have you got away with it?"

She stepped back, then swung about, her hair flying round her in a swirl of glowing copper, the light from the candle deepening it into rippling shadows. Grabbing the ribbon from the bed she thrust it under her hair at the back of her neck and with deft, sure fingers, tied it fiercely, straining it from her face. She began to plait it, bringing it over her shoulder and when it was done she wound it round the top of her head and secured it with several pins.

"Don't you get any ideas, Charlie Lucas," she hissed, "or my dogs will tear you to pieces." She picked up the hairbrush which she had thrown on the bed and held it threateningly in front of her, and the dogs, catching her fear, stood up, their hackles rising, their tails stiff and straight. From both throats came a growled warning.

"May I come in for a moment? If anyone was to come along this passage they would find it quite fascinating to see me pleading to enter my own room. Please, Annie . . . Andy, the bar is almost empty and I can slip out in half an hour or so."

"Where will you sleep?"

"Oh, I have found a cosy corner in a shed at the back of the inn. I had a reconnoitre whilst you were washing."

"Very well, but I warn you . . ."

"I know, the dogs will tear me to pieces."

She woke just as daylight crept in through the attic window. The room was dim, shadowed, the sparse furniture, a press for clothes, a chair and dresser, merely darker shapes in the gloom. The dogs slept peacefully beside her and in the other bed, Charlie Lucas slept also, one arm flung out defencelessly, the other under his head. His deep breathing was as peaceful as the dogs. He was fully dressed.

She smiled and stretched, amazed at her own unconcern.

It was whilst they were breaking their fast that it happened.

"Porridge oats," the landlord told them, "an' there's eggs for those who can pay."

"Porridge and eggs, Andy?" Charlie asked, his face innocent and smiling, the night they had just spent in the same room, though it had not been planned since he had meant what he said about the shed, concerning him as little as it seemed it had Annie. She had fallen asleep, exhausted, putting her trust in him, and he would not abuse that trust, he had told himself, despite her desirability and defencelessness. But his own weariness, as he waited for the bar to clear, had been his undoing and when he awoke, she was pulling her hat well down over the top knot of her hair.

"All right?" she had asked, indicating her appearance, making no more of it than that.

"Fine. A real broth of a boy you look."

So now they were tucking into a great bowl of steaming porridge oats whilst she told him how she meant to buy a decent flock of sheep, only small, 'twinters', if she could get them, and the price was right, leaving them here to winter, paying some trustworthy farmer to look after them for her.

"And where will you find such a man?"

"I don't know but I will. I can't drive them home on my own." She spooned the delicious porridge into her mouth, not with the rough eagerness of the men about her, but with the delicacy of the woman he knew her to be, and again he marvelled on how she had got away with it. Now that he knew himself, he was amazed that none of the other men at the inn could tell. Though her hands were brown and rough, they were slim, long-fingered, her wrists, where they poked from the rather short sleeves of the jacket, fine and slender. She wore her muffler again but when she bent her head to spoon the porridge into her mouth, her white neck was partially revealed, as smooth as silk, as white as alabaster. She was lovely, feminine, and the men's clothing only made her more so, at least to him who knew.

Disaster struck as she bent down to take the rope which held Blackie and Bonnie. Blackie stood up at once, catching her unawares and as her head struck the table when she straightened up, her hat was dislodged, falling away and rolling into the centre of the room, just in front of the bar, where it came to rest. Several eyes followed it, then turned to smile at the lad who had lost it. But not only had the hat taken a blow. Pins showered about her and slowly, so slowly – it was as though her womanhood was making a declaration and wished no one in the bar to miss it – her plait unravelled and her glorious hair fell about her like a cloak. The weak sun coming through the window struck it to a living, curling mass which reached to her waist. There was a warm, lively glow to it, which made every man in the room want to bury his face in it. Suddenly she was a woman, glossy, rounded, they could see it now, rosy mouthed and comely.

The silence in the room was unparalleled. From the kitchen at the back of the bar a woman's voice squeaked in tuneless song and there was a great clatter of pans. A boy's voice shouted that he'd fetch some more eggs from the run and the woman stopped her caterwauling to tell him to look lively. In contrast the quiet in the bar was appalling as those who had not seen the hat fall but who had been nudged by those who had, turned to stare in absolute silence at the woman who had miraculously appeared in their midst.

The landlord did not know what to do. He simply stood there, his jaw sagging, his brain paralysed, and when it came to life again, he still did not know what to do. No crime had been committed, as far as he was aware. Was it illegal for a woman to dress as a man? He didn't know. And what about the chap with her? They had spent the night together but again, that was not against the law, was it? Still, he didn't like it and now, as his reasoning and his power of speech returned, he was about to tell her so.

"What's goin' on 'ere?" he asked truculently, and every man's eye, as it had done in Keswick Market, turned to Annie Abbott, and as she had done then, she felt something die of shame inside her. Dear God . . . oh, dear sweet God, was she never to be allowed to draw her life together, to make the most of it, what she had? To better her life, and Cat's? She had been forced to this subterfuge by men such as these who would not countenance doing business with a woman, striking a deal with someone of the opposite sex. They were entrenched in the ways they had always known, the moralistic, male notion that a woman's place was in the kitchen and the marriage bed and by God, that was where she would stay. None of

these men who gaped at her knew Annie Abbott. None of
them knew she had an illegitimate child but still she could
feel their hostility and their salacious thoughts were very
evident in their expressions.

Charlie stood up on the opposite side of the table. He
walked casually across the room, stooping to pick up her
hat, brushing it down with his sleeve and handing it to her
as if it was a task he did every day of the week.

"Put on your hat, my dear, and let us go and look at
those sheep we promised ourselves."

She did as she was told, shoving it on to the back of
her head and from it her hair flowed and rippled down her
back. Her beauty was stunning, unique, indescribable, and
there was not a man there, thunderstruck and silent, who
dared to speak a word in disapproval. Not that she would
have cared if one had. She was looking for no one's
approval any more. Let them think what they liked, the
damn lot of them. She was doing her very best. The best
that Annie Abbott could do, and if it was not to their liking,
or indeed to anyone's liking, then they could go to the
devil. *She* approved of herself. She thought she was pretty
damn smart and that was all that mattered. She'd get
there. She would.

She stood up, her hat set at a devil-may-care angle on
her shining hair. She lifted her chin, shoved her hands
deep in the pockets of her father's baggy old trousers,
thrust foward her breasts and swaggered to the door,
followed by Charlie Lucas. His eyes were narrowed in
smiling admiration.

"Right, Charlie," she said for all to hear, "let's go and
see what's on offer."

Reed could hear them singing before they were in sight.
Two voices, one male and one female and he knew at once
that the female was Annie.

He had spent the night at The Flying Fox in Caldbeck,
setting off at early light on the road which led through
Rotten Row and up the gentle hill, just under a thousand
feet high, which led across Broad Moor to Rosley. He had

been on the road for no more than an hour, the summit of the hill just ahead of him when the words of the song rose in the crisp autumn air and at once the memory of when he had last heard them came to him. She had been singing them then.

"Come all of you Cockers far and near . . ."

He reached the top of the slope as they came towards him.

There were about two dozen ewes, twinters, his experienced eye automatically told him, and one fine ram. Two dogs were working them, Merles, both of them, and though they were young and eager, they were obeying the whistles and commands of the tall young man who strode at their heels. The inborn herding instinct which all good sheepdogs have, showed in the way they kept up with the galloping sheep and, at a word from the youth, shot ahead, one to each flank, to slow the small flock down when it would have gone careering down the rough track.

"Come by, Blackie," and "Away to me, Bonnie," and Blackie kept to the left, Bonnie to the right. "Steady . . . steady," and the two dogs moved the flock along at a reasonable pace.

There was another man who, though he kept up with the flock, gave the appearance of strolling. His hands were in his trouser pockets. His good broadcloth coat was open and pushed back and the wind ruffled his brown curly hair. He and the first youth continued their song, their heads thrown back in unison, their young throats arched, and the empty hills seemed to echo with the sound of their song.

It was Annie who saw him first and at once her throat closed up. The sheep continued to trot towards him and the dogs ran silently from side to side at the back of them. Annie stopped dead on the track and the man with her, who had walked on a couple of steps, turned, surprised.

"What is it, Annie?" Reed heard him say, his voice educated, cultured even, with none of the flat, long-drawn-out vowels of the Northerner. He turned then to stare where Annie did and Charlie Lucas and Reed Macauley looked into one another's faces for the first time.

The sheep had reached Reed's tall mare, parting like the waters of a stream round a rock, and the dogs, with no voice to guide them, continued at a growing speed down the slope. The track to Rotten Row and Caldbeck branched to the left just beyond Reed's mare but, as Annie stood, silently rooted to the bit of stony path on which she had stopped at the sight of him, the sheep overshot it and the dogs followed. They were doing what Annie had trained them to do, herding what was in their care but with no commands from her, the band of animals would soon be out of control.

"You'd best speak to your dogs, Annie Abbott," he said, and though his voice was mild, his eyes were colder than a blue winter sky and there was a thin white line, livid and very noticeable about his mouth.

Still she stood. She had plaited her hair as she and Charlie began the drive down the fell from Rosley, though she had worn it carelessly tied with its ribbon and spilling down her back as she and Charlie had bartered for the sheep she wanted. She had been disagreeably aware that had it not been for Charlie's presence, she would have been as unsuccessful as she had been at Keswick. They did not want to do business with her. Her 'femaleness' got in their way. They could not tear their gaze away from her shining eyes, the soft flush of excitement on her creamy skin, the rippling amazement of her hair across her shoulders and back and the very evident fullness of her breast as she strode, straight-backed, among the pens. How could they make a sale and a profit, if their shrewd minds were plagued with her beauty? And so they would have turned their backs on her as they had at Keswick, but she let Charlie bid for her and it seemed they had no objection to that. He was a man, after all. She showed him the sheep she wanted and, keeping an eye on her as she nodded or shook her head, he bought them for her.

There are crags, bracken and bogs on the fells and the

Herdwicks she chose were the only breed of sheep to do well there. The strain had proved itself for centuries where she came from. They were small, wiry and agile as goats. They had deep, round bodies and rough white faces. They were thick-boned, sweet-fleshed with a massed fleece which was hard to shear, but they could survive in the harshness of Lakeland winters. The ram she had hired had fine curling horns, creamy white in colour, springing from the back of his head, and in May, after he had serviced her flock, she was to return him to his owner at Rosley Whitsuntide Fair.

She found her voice at last, tearing her eyes away from Reed Macauley's terrible anger.

"Come on, Blackie, come on, Bonnie," she called and with a flurry of excited nippings which, with the part of her mind not concerned with Reed Macauley, she made a mental note to train from them, they turned the flock and began to drive them back towards her. It took several long minutes to quieten sheep and dogs alike, but eventually the dogs lay on the grass, their noses on their paws, their eyes first on the flock, then on Annie, the sheep cropping placidly. The ram was already doing his best to mount a willing ewe and again the farmer in her made note of it, thinking hysterically that her flock would have grown by a couple of lambs before she got them back to Browhead.

Charlie moved to stand beside her and though he still lounged in that casual way he had, he was clearly ready to protect her, should it be necessary, from the black-browed horseman who seemed about to spring from his mare and attack her. He said nothing.

"What d'you want, Reed?" she asked quietly enough.

"I came to bring you home." He could barely speak through his gritted teeth.

"Don't be ridiculous." Her voice was low and, it seemed to Charlie, had a deep sadness in it.

"It is you who are ridiculous, Annie. Or rather foolhardy. I don't know who this . . . this . . . gentleman is beside you and I don't care. There will be time for that later. If you would be good enough to climb up behind me, I will take you home where you belong."

She laughed, a short sharp bark and put her hand to her brow as though in deep perplexity. She looked down at her clogged feet which had tramped so far in the last two weeks then up again at him. She saw the terrible fear in his eyes. She saw the wildness, the anger and the love, the deep and tearing love in him for her and her voice was gentle.

"Go home, Reed. I am in no danger. Charlie here . . ." smiling at the man beside her, ". . . is a friend . . ."

"When did you meet?" The words tore out of him, the sound like the ripping of calico.

"When? Why, yesterday. Was it only yesterday, Charlie?" smiling again.

"*Yesterday!* You develop your friendships very easily, Annie Abbott, and very quickly too. This time yesterday you had not met and today you are the best of friends. Is that it?"

"Why . . . yes, that is it, Reed. It just so happens . . ."

"I have no wish to know what happened so if you will bid your friend goodbye, we will be on our way."

"Now look here . . ."

"No! You look here, Annie. I am tired of hearing your name mentioned wherever I go, usually in connection with some damn fool escapade that no sane person, man or woman, would be involved with. You trip lightly here and there, dressed in . . . in . . ." He could barely speak, so great was his emotion, ". . . whatever that outfit you have on is . . . with no thought nor care for your own safety or reputation, men about you like flies to syrup . . . look at you . . . Dear sweet Christ, have you any idea what . . . what men would do to you if they found you alone up here . . ."

"I am not alone . . ."

"You have been. That is if you only made the acquaintance of . . . of this jackanapes yesterday. Or are you being honest with me? Have the two of you been tramping the fells together for the past two weeks? I thought Bert Garnett was your . . ."

"Stop it, Reed . . . stop it!"

". . . but I can see any man will suit . . ."

"I'd be obliged if you'd get down from that horse and apologise to Miss Abbott, and failing that perhaps you would care to remove your coat and insult me instead of a lady who cannot, at least with her fists, defend herself."

Charlie stepped forward, placing himself in front of Annie, gently urging her away, but her two dogs, sensing danger, stood up and at once the flock began to eddy this way and that, one or two heading back up the track in the direction from which they had come. The confusion grew. Blackie was clearly of the opinion that his loyalty lay with his mistress and began to growl threateningly, not quite sure which man should be his target, whilst Bonnie moved to circle the remaining flock, at the same time casting anxious glances at those who had escaped him. He did not know what to do, and he yelped for an order.

"Dear God, will you stop it, both of you, Charlie, please, it's all right. Mr Macauley and I are . . . we know one another and he seems to have the idea that . . . Reed . . . please . . . go home . . . go home to your . . . your fiancée . . . oh, yes . . . I know of her and . . . your . . . What I do is my own affair . . . oh, please . . . dear God! . . . I cannot . . . I cannot bear it . . ." Her eyes were deep and burning in her white face and both Reed and Charlie were frozen by the anguish in her. Charlie, sensing that there was more between these two than he had at first been aware, stood awkwardly to one side. Inside him was a need that grew with every moment since he had met her, to go to her, to put his arms about her, as a friend if that was all she needed, to comfort, protect, shield her from the black and savage anger of the big man on the horse.

Before Charlie could move, Reed leaped from his mare, moving swiftly towards Annie, but she put up both her hands, palms towards him, holding him away from her with the gesture. Her mouth worked and her eyes glared and she shook her head violently.

"No . . . don't come near me. Not now, and not ever. Go home to your bride, to your life and leave me to lead mine. What I do does not concern you and what you do can have no interest to me. I don't know where you got the idea that you have the right to . . . to interfere in what I do. I don't need you, nor your protection . . ."

"You ate my food, took my dogs . . ." His tender concern for her which had replaced his anger, melted away again and he stepped back as though in loathing.

"Take them . . . take them back with you . . ."

"They are of no use to me, Annie Abbott."

"Then go and don't come near my farm again."

"Believe me . . ."

"I wish I could, I wish I could," she moaned.

She turned to Charlie her eyes entreating him to . . . to do what? He did not know but, instinctively he moved to her side and when she turned her face into his shoulder, his arm rose to hold her to him.

Reed Macauley's face closed, tight as a clam, grim and ugly with his hatred of them both. His eyes were terrible, a glazed and icy blue in which there was nothing now of what he felt for Annie Abbott. Only hatred, venom, a cruel and savage wish to hurt in any way he could. To hurt as he was hurting, to tear at flesh and heart and mind, as his flesh and heart and mind tore into agonising shreds.

His breath gasped from between his thinned lips.

"So that is the way of it, is it, Annie Abbott? Not only Bert Garnett and whoever came before him, there is another man with his hand up your skirts now. What they said about you is true then, and I was fool enough to believe that you were . . . innocent. My God, I've wasted my sympathy, I see. They were right and I was wrong. Well, whoever you are . . ." turning his violence on Charlie ". . . I wish you luck of her since you will need it . . ."

He was provoked beyond the state where he knew what he was saying, making no sense, his virulence spilling out of him in a tidal wave and Charlie had a moment's sympathy for him since to love as Reed Macauley loved Annie Abbott was surely not an emotion any man would care to be burdened with. And the trembling violence of the woman in his arms told him she felt the same.

"I should take my leave if I were you," he said calmly to the wildly shaking figure of the man. "Get on your horse and go. There is nothing for you here."

It was as though the quiet words had poured a soporific over Reed Macauley's inflamed brain, soothing, or freezing it, into numbness, so that for the moment the pain went, allowing him to think, to reason. She was standing in the arms of another man so what did that mean? In Yorkshire Esmé Hamilton-Brown wore Reed Macauley's ring, so what did that mean? Only one thing, of course. His brain moved sluggishly along the track and he knew that he must go, go home. Go to his bride-to-be and put her, *her*, this one, out of his mind. "There is nothing for you here," the stranger had said, and it was true. *There never had been*, so . . .

He climbed on to his mare, weary and old, or so he felt and without looking at her, knowing she did not look at him, he put the mare to a quiet canter down the track.

They got back to Browhead three days later. Without the diversions she had made on her journey out to Rosley, to sell her besom brushes, her swills and her stockings, she and Charlie, her small flock, herded more efficiently by Blackie and Bonnie now, moved almost in a straight line from Caldbeck, skirting the high Caldbeck Fells, moving along Parkend Beck, through Longlands and dropping down into Gillthrop on the third day. They had slept in barns, keeping clear of farms, Charlie buying the necessary food from farmers' wives with Annie staying out of sight. They no longer sang. They strode out together side by side, speaking occasionally but only when it was needed. Charlie realised that Annie was in active pain, deeply grieving for Reed Macauley. That her lively and dashing spirit was struggling to survive the slashing words he had aimed, deliberately and accurately, at her heart. She ate when he handed her food. She spoke to her dogs

and watched her flock but the brave excitement had gone
from her and he was saddened by it. She did not question
him, nor ask him where he was going when they reached
Browhead. He was gentle with her and she appeared to
be grateful. He knew nothing of what was waiting for her
at the end of her journey and he did not ask. He watched
her as she slept and when she woke he was on his own
bit of straw in his own corner of the barn.

The people of Gillthrop came out of their cottages to
stare at Annie Abbott as she tramped behind her bleating
flock of ewes and the prancing ram. Her dogs were in full
control and there was no need for her, or the man she
was with, to give them anything but the occasional low
word.

She took off her hat as she strode through the village
and shook out her curtain of hair, allowing it to cascade
down her back. Her legs in her father's breeches were
long and supple and the men and women gawped, open-
mouthed, silent and forbidding. She began to smile then,
turning to Charlie to draw him into some delight she felt.
She took his arm, and taking a cue from her, he strutted
by her side, bowing from left to right as though it was a
royal procession he and Annie were in. This is what it's
about, he remembered thinking. This is what she is doing.
Showing *them* and Reed Macauley that Annie Abbott is a
person worthy of respect and admiration for she is surviving when she should be going under. But why? Why does
she need . . . ?

The answer came running down the track, flying, her
small feet barely touching the ground, her long copper
curls streaming out from her small head, her great golden
eyes snapping in lovely excitement.

"Mother . . . Mother . . ."

"Cat . . . oh, my lovely Cat . . ."

And mother and daughter ran joyfully into each other's
arms.

17

It was Whitsun and the ram Annie had hired was due to
go back to Rosley.

"I'll take it," Charlie offered. He looked round the table
smiling, his eyes moving from Cat to Phoebe and lastly to
Annie, remaining there, as they always did. "I could just
manage a good day out. In fact, why don't we all go?" He
sat back in his chair, grinning engagingly, his eyes gleaming
like those of a schoolboy who has just suggested a wicked
prank. He was twenty-five now, though he had mentioned
it to no one when his birthday came in February, and the
hard work he had done at Browhead had added some
breadth to his shoulders. He still had on the old, threadbare coat he had worn when Annie met him in October
but beneath it was a beautifully knitted long-sleeved jerkin
Annie and Phoebe had created for him between them. A
design of Phoebe's who had knitted the sleeves whilst
Annie had done the back and front. Cat had sewn on
wooden buttons which Annie had found in her mother's
sewing basket.

"Tha' cannot go about wi' nowt' on but that old coat,
Mr Lucas," Phoebe had told him, horrified when he had
attempted to set off up the fell on a day of biting December
wind and a hoar-frost so thick his boots sank in it. Not
that the boots were much better than the coat, good boots
once but now badly scuffed and in need of a cobbler's hand.
"See, ah'll knit thee a waistcoat with sleeves in it. Annie'll
give me a hand, won't tha'? Thou shall have it on by weekend." And he did, along with a muffler, from Cat, and a pair
of the thick woollen stockings Annie and Phoebe knitted
whenever they had a moment to sit down.

The room was cosy and the fire glowed red and orange

in the inglenook. It was May now and the weather, though
warmer, was still cold, but here in the kitchen a small
sanctuary had been created in the vast, windblasted confusion of black rock, gloomy gills, fan-shaped screes and
rippling streams which was Skiddaw in the winter. The
weather was still inclined to be fickle, showing the face of
spring on a soft and lovely morning and by noon, clouds
would be chasing one another across the torn sky with a
wind so strong you could lean on it. Beyond the small,
oak-mullioned windows the grass in the pasture moved in
flattened waves and the sound of the rushing air could be
heard in the branches of the hawthorn tree to the side of
the house.

The two dogs, along with a pretty marmalade kitten
which had been found wandering alone, piteously mewing
behind the farmhouse, lay dozing in a tangled heap in front
of the fire dogs, set to prevent the logs from rolling out
of the slightly raised hearth stone. All three had coats
glossy with health, contrasting sharply not only with one
another, but the scrubbed slate of the flagged floor. The
randle-tree fixed to a beam above the fire supported several pots not quite touching the glowing peat. In one was
the 'poddish' made from oats which they were eating for
breakfast and which was keeping warm for those who
wanted another helping and in the other was 'crowdy' again
made with oatmeal in which beef stock had been mixed.
In the third was Annie's Easter-Ledge Pudding consisting
of young green leaves, not unlike dock leaves, boiled with
barley and mint sorrel, to be served with dried beef. It
was said to have great medicinal powers, especially in the
cooling of the blood.

On the table round which they sat was a platter of
'clapbread', freshly baked that morning. It had been rolled
into a ball in Phoebe's hands, then 'clapped' until it was as
thin as paper, put on an iron plate and set on the fire
until it was baked crisp. They drank tea, hot and sweet,
but without milk since Annie could not yet afford a cow.

She and Charlie sat in two carved oak chairs dated 1742,
come, she supposed, from better days and in which she

could remember her mother and father resting, but Cat and Phoebe sat side by side on a rough wooden bench. The enormous oak table, which had never been moved for the simple reason it was so heavy it could only be lifted by six strong men, was set under the window. A big jar of lavender was placed in the centre of it, filling the room with its fragrant scent. In the window bottom was a vast copper bowl planted with winter hyacinths which were still blooming.

Annie looked doubtfully from Charlie's good-humoured face then out and beyond the window to the field of rippling grasses and the wind-driven silver waters of the lake. The flock with the new lambs had been herded up on to the fell only two days before. The ploughing had been done in March and so there would be a brief respite in the farm work, but the weather was uncertain today and Annie was not sure the walk to Rosley and back was within Cat's strength.

"Oh, Mother, may we?" the child breathed ecstatically, jumping down from the bench and running to lean against her mother's shoulder. "May we? Phoebe says there are all sorts of wonderful things to see at a fair. Clowns and acrobats, and fat ladies and monkeys. And puppets too, aren't there Phoebe?"

She turned her great velvety brown eyes to Phoebe who looked alarmed for she had told the child only of what she herself had spied from the corner of her downcast eyes as she was hurried by her last mistress to the Hiring Fair in Keswick a year ago. She had not meant to fill Cat's head with a longing to see them, only to entertain the little girl as they worked side by side at one of the many tasks they shared. It was not as if she had seen anything properly herself, though, if she were truthful she would dearly love to.

"Nay, lambkin," copying Annie in her use of the endearment for she loved the child as though she was her own. "Ah didn't mean ter say that . . ."

"And merry-go-rounds and . . . and . . ." Without waiting for Phoebe to finish her stumbling sentence, the little girl put her face close up to Annie's, childlike, begging to be allowed this treat which Charlie had suggested.

Charlie smiled disarmingly. "It can do no harm, Annie, and if you are thinking of the distance we could take the sledge with a blanket in it and if Cat here gets tired she could sit on it while I pull her."

"But the weather, Charlie. You know it can be fickle at this time of the year."

"There are shelters, Annie. Every farm has a barn and no farmwife would refuse a child."

"But what of the cost of a night's room?"

"You and Cat and Phoebe could share, and I can sleep wherever I fall. A few pence, that's all."

Cat looked from one face to the other, as the two adults discussed it, her own luminous with her yearning to see the fascinations of which Phoebe had told her. Her hands clung around Annie's neck and her soft young mouth trembled as her breath quickened.

"Oh, Mother, please . . . please . . ."

At last Annie looked down into her daughter's face and her own was soft. She had been nowhere in her life, Catriona Abbott, that could be called 'a treat'. She had trudged at her mother's skirts for more than half of her baby days in weather as inhospitable as any the fells could manifest, if not quite as dangerous. Without complaint she had done it. Not for her the tantrums and whining Annie had seen in other children, like Sally Garnett's boy, for instance, who, on the few occasions he had been in her kitchen, had grizzled and clamoured for his mother's attention the whole time they had been there. Cat had nothing, no toys, none of the 'sweeties', the indulgences other parents gave to their children, and it was only this last year that she had found safe refuge, warmth, security and the growing knowledge that these, surely the right of every child, were to continue. She had known only one thing which had been a continuing, everlasting, element in her young life and that was Annie's love. It was time she had *fun*.

Cat held her breath, her eyes never leaving her

mother's. They were no more than six inches apart, as though the child, with her fixed stare, hoped to hypnotise her mother into acquiescence.

Charlie and Phoebe both sighed in pleasure as Annie nodded her head, but Cat, surprisingly, did not jump for joy or cry out her gladness. She laid her cheek against Annie's breast, burrowing herself into her mother's arms like a young chick, thankfully settling beneath the hen. She was too enraptured to speak, it seemed, her childish heart overcome with this miracle which had been allowed her. Above her head Annie's eyes met Charlie's. She smiled through her tears, her throat too full to speak.

They might have been going to Australia, so great was the planning of this mighty expedition in which, Cat was adamant, even the marmalade kitten was to be included. They must be adequately dressed, of course, with a good supply of warmly knitted stockings and mufflers, and the jerkins, now that Phoebe had the hang of it, she made for them all. Food, stuff that would keep in case there was none to be had on the road, blankets for Cat and 'Dandy' the kitten, and a hurried visit by Phoebe to the cobbler in Hause to get their clogs resoled.

Annie almost changed her mind on the morning they were to go. There was a pattern of clouds, low and light, the higher ones like a sheet, broken, divided, and below them were the rain clouds, ragged, uneasy and dark in the sky. The rain already seemed to hang down, a trailing rain, which did not quite reach the ground but certainly would do so as they moved higher up beyond Gillthrop towards the village of Longlands. They would not touch Uldale, of course, going on the most direct route up to Whelpo, Caldbeck, and on across Broad Moor to Rosley. There would be many travellers en route, for the Whitsun Fair was the biggest cattle market of the year.

But the animals' way – and the unthinking humans' way – even if there are no obstacles, does not go in a straight line. Man and animal will move slowly from one point to another by much the same route, which then becomes a path. Such a path becomes a track if many use it, and so it was with the tracks and sheep trods which criss-crossed the dales and high fells of Lakeland and which they were about to take.

"I don't like the look of the weather, Charlie," Annie said more than half a dozen times between Browhead and Longlands, only to be outnumbered by Charlie, by Phoebe and Cat, none of them knowing the menace of the fells as she did. The 'messenger' clouds which moved ponderously over their heads foretold rain soon, she said, and where were they to shelter out here in the open? It was well known that there were more wet days on the fells than dry ones and with so many people on the roads, coming from every direction towards Rosley Fairground, would there be a place for them to lay their heads?

"Now stop it, Annie. You'll spoil it for Cat. Just see her striding out with Phoebe, the pair of them so filled with glee they might be off to stay the weekend with the Queen and her family. Look at their faces, Annie. Have you ever seen such delight? Phoebe seems no older than Cat in her excitement."

"I know that, Charlie. I'm not disputing it but if it gets any worse up there ahead and we get caught in the open, don't blame me. And this damned tup's not helping, wanting to go every way but the one we want to take. Blackie and Bonnie are doing their best but the thing keeps butting them."

"Let me see if I can bring him into line. He's a rogue but he's certainly given you some fine lambs so you must not malign him or his masculinity will be quite devastated."

Charlie grinned down at her endearingly then, taking her hand, pulled her to him. His grey eyes were warm and filled with his own almost childlike delight with this adventure he had conjured up for them. He would have had to go to Rosley anyway with the ram, but the joy of having Annie with him, almost a renewal of the days they had spent together last autumn, put a glow in them which she did not recognise. He had been so good to her, to them all over the past six months, bringing a merriment into the farmhouse which, though it had always been a snug and contented home, had never known such laughter as Charlie awoke in it.

He produced his own kind of music, teaching Cat and Phoebe how to play on a 'comb and paper', beating the rhythm on two spoons, introducing them to simple tunes and songs which he had known from childhood. The comical, often out-of-tune noises they produced would reduce all four to the kind of laughter they had never before known. A sense of 'silliness' which is infectious and, as Charlie said, as good for you as any medicine the doctor might prescribe. They sang and laughed together whilst Annie and Phoebe knitted and when they were quiet he would read aloud to them from one of the few books it was found he had in the pocket of his broadcloth coat. *Pickwick Papers* by Mr Charles Dickens. *Pride and Prejudice* by Miss Jane Austen and *Masterman Ready* by Captain Frederick Marryat. Only these three, but when one was finished, another would be started and when they all three had been read, he had promised to begin all over again. Their evenings were made lively, for his blithe nature would not allow for dejection or brooding, which he often saw in Annie's face, and of course, he knew why. He had made himself a part of the family, not only in the work he did, but with his humour, his patience, his quicksilver lightheartedness and his ability to turn an ordinary, everyday event into something fascinating and therefore fun.

She had the feeling there was some hidden meaning in what he was saying to her and his eyes still had that wicked gleam in them but she could not help but smile back, allowing him to put a comradely arm about her shoulder as they strode out along the track and across the stone bridge which forded Parkend Beck. Charlie dragged the old sledge which had done such sterling service ever since its first run to Rosley, and perched on the blankets within it was the marmalade kitten, its tail twitching in alarm. Once it had jumped off, stalking behind them haughtily as though the mode of transport was far beneath its feline dignity. But as Charlie said, knowing where its comfort lay and finding it was being left behind, it ran to catch up, jumping back thankfully.

"What a circus we are. We only need a monkey and a parrot and we could have our own side-show at the fair," Charlie joked, his eyes sparkling into hers.

The wind became more biting the higher they got and it was not long before Cat sought the shelter of the sledge and the blankets where, snuggling down with the kitten, they both fell asleep. The fells soared dramatically on either side of them, rising from the narrow green strips of the fertile dales on which, as they marched, they saw falcons spiralling, keeping an airborne eye on the flocks which sought the sweet herbs and grasses growing among the dark rocks. Narrow strips of order and productivity, where rowan-shaded becks ran and whitewashed farms capped with Lakeland slate nestled under craggy buttresses. Men tended sheep on a neighbouring peak, the dogs beside them silent and alert, and Annie breathed a prayer to safeguard her own new-born lambs from the scavengers which preyed on the weak and defenceless.

Despite her misgivings about the weather, though it was cold, the wind, or so it seemed, coming straight from the plains of Siberia, the rain kept off and when night fell the farmwife who opened her door to their knock and whose husband was 'only in't back yard' she said, eyeing them suspiciously, relented when Cat smiled at her, her face beaming in the light which fell on her from the rushlight, the kitten in her arms mewing plaintively.

"Tha' can sleep in' hay barn, Missus," she told Annie, whose strange and masculine garb was not immediately apparent in the light which fell from her doorway. "An' if tha wants some milk for t' bairn, tha's welcome to a pint or two from Buttercup. She's in t' barn now. Tha' *can* milk, I tek it?"

"Oh, yes, and thank you. You are most kind." Annie smiled.

The farmwife, somewhat taken aback by the way her caller spoke, smiled back, despite herself. They seemed a nice enough little family, taking the hired ram back to

Rosley, and it cost her nothing to let them sleep in the barn. They had their own blankets, they told her, *and* food, they said, but they'd be glad of a pan of hot water if she could spare it and very grateful for the milk they were.

"Aye, well then, send tha' husband ower for t' water. Tha'll be snug enough in that hay."

Cat and Phoebe were asleep, curled together with Blackie and Bonnie and the kitten under one of the blankets. They had all washed in the basin of hot water, one after the other, a somewhat sketchy toilet, and Charlie said they would have to put up with him looking like a brigand since there was not enough for a shave. They ate cheese and bread, beef pies Phoebe, who was becoming a very handy cook, had made, pickles and draughts of warm creamy milk from the obliging Buttercup. There was to be no fire, of course. The farmer, on returning from the 'back yard', had been across to make sure about that, telling them so in his blunt, taciturn way. They seemed all right but you never knew with some of these tinkers and vagrants what sort of daft things they got up to. Not that his missus would allow such through the farm gate, never mind in the barn, but the sight of the peacefully sleeping children, the watchful dogs and the quiet husband and wife reassured him.

But it was cold. There were cracks in the door of the ancient stone-built barn and the wind whistled constantly, a low whining which bit at the flesh and tore at the ears, and there was only one blanket left.

"You have it, Annie. I'm as warm as toast in this hay."

"No . . . no, Charlie, I won't have it. We can make a bed of hay and then lie back to back with the blanket over us. It's going to get colder in the night, I can tell, and we must keep warm . . ."

"I *am* warm."

"No, you're not. I can see you shivering from here."

"No, you can't. Look I'll lie down next to the dogs and be as right as rain."

She looked astonished. "For God's sake Charlie. What

do you think I'm going to do to you whilst you're asleep? Seduce you? Don't be a fool. See, we'll lie with the others and you shall lie beside me and the blanket will cover us both."

"I could share with Cat and Phoebe."

"Dear God, man, don't be so ridiculous. Come over here and lie next to me. We shall all keep one another warm. It's the only way, Charlie." She tutted irritably and shook her head. "I don't know why I let the three of you talk me into this. It's far too cold to be sleeping out in the open . . ."

"Hardly in the open, Annie." Charlie shuffled about in the hay next to her, leaving a gap of at least six inches between them.

"Don't argue, Charlie, and for heaven's sake, come a bit closer. Even if you don't feel the cold, I do, and I'd be glad if you would put your back against mine. There . . . that's it, now isn't that better?"

"Indeed . . ." Charlie's voice was strange and muffled but Annie, with his warm back against hers and already half asleep, did not hear it.

The darkness was as thick and as black as pitch when she awoke, and as she opened her eyes to stare into it, she was aware, in that confused moment between sleeping and waking, that something was wrong. The warmth which had enveloped her and soothed her to sleep was no longer there. In its place was a feeling of tension, of great strain, of a presence taut and strung up, with an emotion she did not recognise. An unknown presence which alarmed her. She was aware that Charlie was still there, the warmth of him just out of reach, but from him came a sensation of . . . of . . . of what? What was it? Anger, was that it, or was it pain?

"Charlie, what is it? Is something wrong?" she said softly, not wanting to wake the others. Charlie did not answer. She turned towards him, putting out her hand to touch his shoulder and was shocked to find it rigid, unmoving, almost ready to flinch away she would have thought had the idea not been so ridiculous.

"Charlie? Are you ill?" She sat up and leaned over him, but with an oath he sprang up and without speaking a word, stumbled towards the flimsy barn door. In the corner Buttercup shifted, then lowed softly.

"Charlie? What's the matter?" She was about to stand up and follow him, for surely there was something wrong. Charlie was so good-humoured, smiling and sweet-tempered with never a cross word for anyone. Too light-hearted by far, she sometimes thought. So careless about life and the serious consideration one must take of it, that she was often irritated. So what was troubling him now that he could not even respond to her anxious concern?

"Really, Annie, cannot a gentleman answer a call of nature without explaining what he is about?" His voice from the dark was flippant as he opened the barn door. "Now go back to sleep, there's a good girl, I won't be long."

He was not there when she awoke to the dawn chorus of the birds which nested in the trees about the farmhouse, but when she stumbled to the barn door there he was walking back from the farmhouse with a pail of water.

"Good morning, lazy bones," he said smilingly, none of the tension she had sensed in him during the night apparent now. "I've been up for half an hour. You were sleeping like babes, all of you, even Blackie and Bonnie declining to come with me so I went and begged some water from our benefactor. She even gave me this," and with an endearing grin, he produced an enormous jug brimming with tea.

"Charlie, you angel."

"I know," Charlie's impish smile changed to one of smugness. "That's why she gave it to me, I suppose, because she knew I was not your ordinary sort of a fellow. She could not resist my charm."

"I don't blame her. Now if Buttercup could spare us a drop of milk . . ."

"Just what I was thinking, but as I got the tea, don't you think it's only fair that you should get the milk?"

They were both laughing when Cat and Phoebe peeped

from their nest of hay and blankets. The kitten blinked its
wide eyes and the dogs wagged their tails, and it was as
though the strange moment in the night, if indeed anything
strange *had* happened in the night, might never have
been.

They reached Rosley Hill by mid-afternoon, the great
multitude of those who were on the same road as themselves, and indeed on every road leading to the fairground,
cheerful and excited, most of them, for this was the greatest event in their humdrum year. The actual grounds of
the fair covered forty acres. It would be another fifteen
years before dealers bought their cattle straight from the
byre, but in the meanwhile this was where the drovers
displayed them for sale and not only cattle but sheep and
horses as well.

They could hear the sound of the brass bands as they
approached the fairground, a spirited 'oom-pa-pa' which
lifted the head and squared the shoulders and infected
those who heard it to step out in a grand style, just as
though a procession were under way. The Drover's Rest
was surrounded by a hurrying mass of men, some seeking
a bed for the night, which was, of course, impossible,
others doing a bit of business, shaking hands on a deal, or
shaking their heads in refusal. There were horses tethered
in the inn yard, the stables being as full as the beds. Carts
and carriages vied for position with donkeys, ponies and
any four-legged beast that could carry or pull a load to this
great fair and market. Stalls were set up on the roadside,
those belonging to pedlars and housewives for whom there
was no longer any room in the actual fairground, the housewives selling eggs and gingerbread, the pedlars shouting
of gauze from Italy, ribbons and lace from France, hats
and caps, cloaks, brooms, beehives and baskets. Whips
cut the air as horses were driven along the track with no
concern for those in their path, the quality, who on this
occasion rubbed shoulders with ruffians, jumping out of
their way with the same alacrity.

The fairground was a heaving, seething confusion of
men, women and children, many of the men there to do

business, naturally, but the rest bent on having the best time of their lives. In one corner, a fiddler and a man with a tin whistle played a lilting merry tune and Cat and Phoebe stared spellbound as those who were able danced the 'Cumberland Square Eight', the 'Long Eight', the 'Ninepins Reel' and the 'Circassian Circle'. Country dances which brought forth loud whoops of excited merriment, much twirling and whirling with many a lad glimpsing more than he should of his lass's ankles and sometimes, as she was swept from her feet, her drawers. The tent beside the dancing and which held the circus was so well attended the barker was begging people to be patient since they would all get in eventually and in the meanwhile, why did they not view the 'slack-wire balancing act', 'the pig-faced lady' or 'the hairy man' from Morocco who were absolutely free.

Charlie stopped to watch the Pugilists who were displaying their skills in a ring set up for them, accepting bets from any amateur who fancied his chances against them.

"I could take that chap on," he said to Annie, his eyes bright with that look of anticipation a man assumes at the thought of pitting himself against another. Annie was doing her best to keep her eye on Cat and Phoebe, who were like a couple of sleepwalkers who have wandered into some fairy-tale dream and are mesmerised by it. They moved, hand in hand, their mouths gaping, their eyes wide and marvelling, as they studied the spectacles on every hand, marionettes and musicians, singers, rope dancers, coconut shies and a great sad shambling bear, its muzzled face anguished, as it did its best to dance to the pipe of a gypsy's whistle.

"No, you couldn't Charlie. They're fighting with bare fists," Annie answered tartly.

"But they're betting a guinea, Annie. I've done a bit of bare knuckle fighting in my time. I'm sure I could beat him."

"*You*, Charlie?" Annie eyed Charlie's lean frame disbelievingly.

"Yes, I fought at my own weight of course."

"Well *he's* not your weight, Charlie Lucas. Look at him. He weighs twice as much as you, besides you haven't a guinea to bet with, and if you had, I wouldn't let you."

"That fellow's going to try."

"More fool him, then," and fool he was for the fight was short, crude and bloody, the stalwart young country lad who had climbed into the ring being carried out by his fellows with a face like a piece of raw meat.

The dogs were bewildered and alarmed by the press of people, anxiously doing their best to divide themselves between Cat and Phoebe, who, in their eagerness not to miss a single exhibit, forged ahead of Annie and Charlie who were studying stalls on which there were for sale such marvels as shepherds' bells and leather gaiters, bridles, saddles, whips and padlocks and saws. A travelling salesman, standing on the tailboard of the cart in which his weary horse was still harnessed, begged them to try his 'Balm of Gilead' which would cure them of all that ailed them from warts to the coughing sickness.

A musical farce was being performed by a company of players in another tent. *The Spoiled Child* was its title and Annie was carried back quite ferociously to those precarious months she had spent with . . . with . . . My God, she could not even remember his name, the name of the man who had fathered her lovely child. The thought horrified her for surely she should carry not only his name but the picture of him inside her for ever? But no matter how hard she tried, she could not bring him to mind. Charlie's hand held hers for they were in great danger of being separated as they moved across the track which led from the gate to the camphouse where many of the drovers and dealers had a bed. Behind it was the gigantic grazing ground in which were enclosed the plunging, bellowing cattle and through which ran a stream. Even the valley bottom below the hill was crowded with beasts, the air filled with the grunting and squeaking of pigs, the bleating of sheep, the cries of hawkers, with shouts and oaths and whistles.

Annie was dressed as she had been for the past six or seven months, in the jacket, trousers and gaiters her father had once worn. She had carefully plaited her hair and Charlie had helped her to stuff it beneath her hat which was then jammed down on her head almost to her ears. She could barely see from beneath its brim, but it at least hid much of her female features. If anyone thought it strange, or even noticed in the vast crowd, that two men, herself and Charlie, held hands, there was too much commotion to dwell on it. The ram had been returned to the farmer who had hired it to them. Charlie pulled the sledge at his heels and in its nest of blankets the kitten cowered, its mews of astonishment unheard in the hubbub. Annie was creased and crumpled from sleeping in her clothes, as was Charlie, but he looked decidedly worse for wear than she did, since he had almost two days' stubble on his chin. He never wore a hat as he did not own one and his hair hung over his collar and ears in a wild, uncombed tangle. They looked slightly disreputable, she was well aware, but what did that matter since there was no one she cared about here to see it.

"Phoebe, Cat, don't get too far ahead," Annie called out, her voice lost in the strident tumult. They did not hear it but the man coming towards her did and when he stopped dead where he stood, the beautifully dressed young lady on his arm almost fell over. Charlie had not noticed them, walking on ahead of Annie, their hands still clasped and for a moment the two couples, Charlie Lucas and Annie Abbott, Reed Macauley and his beautiful young wife, became entangled in wild, appalling confusion.

No one spoke. Charlie's eyes ran swiftly over the couple, particularly the man, and his hand tightened on Annie's, drawing her protectively to him. Reed Macauley instinctively steadied his wife, who was looking quite astonished that two such ruffians should have been allowed to impede the way of a lady like herself and her husband, who, or so she thought, should have had them instantly arrested. Such *strange* young men too. One attractive in a rough sort of way, the other . . . well . . . how could you describe him? She certainly could not, averting her eyes, for they seemed to he *holding hands*.

"Reed," she squeaked, as her husband of three months turned violently and began to run with her across the uneven ground towards their carriage, and when she was able to see the look on his face, it so frightened her she was glad to cower back in her seat and head off towards Carlisle and the luxurious hotel in which they were staying.

18

The weather broke as Annie had foretold it would as they made their way back across Broad Moor and down the track which would lead them to Caldbeck. Across the fells a procession of dark clouds whipped, angry and boiling, moving on at first, one after the other from the North towards Skiddaw. But just as though there was no more space to accommodate them beyond the heights of Caldbeck Fells they piled up on one another, low and glowering. A torrent of rain fell suddenly, shaking loose from the greyness and moving in a heavy curtain through which it was barely possible to see. It fell relentlessly, drifting in a cold, steady stream before them, and the noise it made was a constant, rhythmic thrumming against the grey rocks and sodden ground. Great blinding sheets, lifting and shifting, parting now and then to reveal the rough tussocky grass, the water-logged track which was dangerous with stretches of slippery stones.

Annie had removed her hat as they left Rosley since its weight on her head was more than she could bear, she muttered, tossing it into the sledge beside the startled kitten. Charlie watched her anxiously as they slithered down the track and though it took all of his strength and attention to keep the sledge upright, he could not help but be fascinated by the way the rain fell on her bare head. As it touched the darkened russet of her hair, a mass of tiny curls sprang upon her forehead. Droplets of moisture slipped to the end of each wet tendril, falling on to her brow. They touched the arch of her eyebrow, running smoothly to hang upon the ends of her lashes. She blinked to clear them and they dropped to her cheeks and ran to her parted lips where she licked them away, her pink

tongue moving in an unknowingly sensual gesture which
lit a small but growing flame in the pit of Charlie's belly.

She was not aware of it, of course, nor of the rain, the
cold and searching wind which accompanied it; the violent
lightning flashes splitting the dark clouds on the high peaks,
nor the thunder which roared and cracked amongst the
crags. She was not aware of her child who had been
huddled by Charlie and Phoebe beneath the rapidly soaking
blankets beside the kitten, nor of Charlie and Phoebe
themselves. Her pace lengthened and quickened as she
endeavoured to get away from the pain which the sight of
Reed Macauley and his new young wife had gouged into
her, and Charlie Lucas's heart despaired for her, and for
himself.

She had been quite devastated by the encounter, her
face ashen, her eyes wide and senseless as though she
had seen some ghastly apparition which had taken her
mind. He had felt the tremble in her hand at first, a quivering of her fingers as they clung to his, then, as the spasm
took her, moving to her arm, her shoulder, her neck, her
whole body, until even her teeth chattered and she shook
as though she had been attacked by the ague.

"Take me away, Charlie," she had managed to say
between her clenched teeth, her hands, both of them now,
clinging to him as though his lean, strong frame, his male
strength, his caring, cheerful endurance was all she had
to keep her upright.

"Hang on to me, sweeting." She did not question his
immediate understanding. Why should she? She knew
nothing of his true feelings, only seeing the smile he
smiled, the device that he used to hide what was inside
him. A complex man who protected his heart and emotions
beneath the layers of flippant geniality he had wrapped
about himself ever since he had met Annie Abbott.

They reached the farm where they had stayed the night
before but it was still daylight and the farmwife, at first
surprised but not displeased to see them for they had been
no trouble, got a good look at Annie and the men's clothing
she wore. Her eyes, flinty as the rock which rose behind

the farm, moved from Annie's white demented face and her tangled hair which was plastered to her skull and down her back, to the jacket she wore and the long shape of her trousered legs. The jacket was open for what did Annie Abbott care about anything at that precise and agonising moment, and the rain had sculpted her shirt to her breasts, the nipples of which stood out like cherries.

"May we shelter in your barn again, madam?" Charlie said in his scrupulously polite and engaging way, doing his best to signal to Annie to close her jacket. Indeed he had tried to persuade her to wait at the gate, knowing full well what the reaction of the farmwife would be. "My wife and . . . and child are so very wet and the weather shows no sign of abating, does it? We would not trouble you . . ."

"Indeed, tha' won't 'cos tha's not stoppin' an' if tha's husband to . . . to . . . that . . . woman tha' should be ashamed to let her be seen by decent folk dressed like that."

"Madam, really, does it matter? The child is soaked to the skin . . ."

"That's nowt ter do wi me."

"But you allowed us to stay here last night and we are the same family . . ."

"Nay, tha's not. Ah thought tha' was a respectable family, tekkin' t'tup back to t' fair, but ah can see ah was wrong. Ah want no . . . vagabonds in my barn so tha'd best be on tha' way."

"We are not vagabonds, madam. Annie . . . my wife . . . and myself have a farm near Gillthrop . . ."

"Then tha'd best be on tha way to it for tha've a long walk."

"Please, madam . . ."

The farmwife did not like to be called 'madam', nor did she like to be hoodwinked, which she considered she had been. The woman on her doorstep who looked as though she'd seen an apparition, was a different one to the pleasantly smiling person of the night before. She had no right to be bothering honest, virtuous folk with her flagrant disregard of the proper way for a woman to dress, and

she'd have no truck with her, nor any of them. She kept
her eyes firmly from the bedraggled figure of the child,
who was doing her best to shelter from the downpour
beneath the blanket on the cart, lest she weaken.

"Be off," she said, "or ah'll call my husband."

They went, moving slowly along the farm track until
they got to the gate, turning left towards Caldbeck and
the long, wet road to home. At every farm they tried up
to and beyond Caldbeck, they got the same answer from
the stiffly disapproving women who came to the door,
eyeing the strange figure of Charlie's 'wife' and it was not
until, nearly dark, they came to a derelict hut, used for
what purpose Charlie could not imagine, in a dip beside
the track, that they found some kind of shelter. The wind
still howled in their faces and the rain pelted down in a
heavy swaying veil and when they got inside they were
so wet they might have all been hauled from a nearby tarn.
No one spoke. Charlie handed out what was left of their
food, even the ravenous and pathetically unkempt kitten
condescending to a morsel of Phoebe's two-day-old beef
pie. Annie refused everything, even the rain water the
others drank, then lay down where she was told on a
scrap of relatively dry ground, Phoebe and Charlie on the
outside, the silent child and her equally silent mother in
the middle. Phoebe knew, of course, what had happened
without being told for she had seen the retreating back of
Reed Macauley and the young lady he dragged on his arm.
She had not questioned Charlie's abrupt statement that
they were to return home at once though Cat had cried
broken-heartedly. She could not understand why this
miraculous outing should be curtailed when it had scarcely
begun, she wept, though not in those exact words, and
for the first time in her young life she turned on her mother
and beat at Annie's trouser leg in angry disappointment.
She might have been no more than a troublesome fly for
all the notice Annie took of her.

The fire was out when they got home and it was an
hour before any warmth crept into the cold kitchen from
the one Charlie kindled.

"Take them both upstairs, Phoebe," he said to the young serving girl, who was half dead with cold herself, but the only one on whom he could rely. "Strip them both and rub them down then put them in dry clothes and bring them here to the fire. I'm sorry Phoebe, to put this on your shoulders but . . . well, I cannot do it, for obvious reasons, so I will see to the fire. Wrap them both up well in blankets or anything else you can lay your hands on and then do the same for yourself. The fire will be going by then."

"What about thissen, Mr Lucas?" Phoebe answered through teeth which were held rigidly in her locked jaw.

"I'll be all right, lass, I'm used to it. Now off you go. See poppet . . ." to the dreadfully quiet child, ". . . go with Phoebe." He sighed, "I think you'll have to carry her, Phoebe." He turned to Annie: "Annie . . . darling . . ." – the endearment slipped out unnoticed, certainly by Annie – ". . . go with Phoebe . . ." and when Annie simply stood there, dazed and mindless with cold and despair, "You go up Phoebe . . . I'll bring her". And somehow, together, Phoebe and Charlie pulled the little family together, got them warm, including themselves, wrapped about in quilts and blankets before the steadily leaping fire on which Charlie had heaped half a dozen stout logs. Tea was made, and porridge, though again Annie refused both. The dogs steamed at their feet and the kitten lay on the hearth almost in the heart of the fire, licking himself angrily, his haughty expression saying quite plainly that he would never forgive them, any of them, for what he had suffered.

Annie sat where they had put her on the settle beside the fire. The quilt Phoebe had draped about her slipped from her shoulders revealing the long flannel nightgown that had been her mother's. Modest it was, high necked and long sleeved, but Lizzie Abbott had been shorter than her daughter and Annie's bare feet and ankles stuck out from beneath the hem, white and fragile, strangely defenceless. She had gained some colour. It touched her cheeks, high on the bone, and her eyes which stared into the fire were brighter though still unseeing.

"I'll tek little 'un up, Mr Lucas," Phoebe said quietly, "and I reckon her an' me'll share a bed tonight. I want to keep me eye on her though I don't think she's tekken much 'arm. She et that porridge . . ." She eyed Annie anxiously but Charlie put out his hand to touch her arm affectionately. He was in Joshua's nightshirt, and had a coarse grey blanket which had once served Joshua's horse, about his shoulders. His feet were bare, like Annie's, and they tingled painfully as the warmth returned.

"I'll get her up, Phoebe. You're exhausted so off you go. Can you manage Cat? Right then sleep well, and Phoebe, thank you."

"Ah need no thanks, Mr Lucas. And Annie . . . well, she's not . . . she's down now but she'll be right as ninepence when . . . well . . . tomorrow, or the next day. She's 'ad a shock so . . ."

"I realise that, Phoebe, but you know she'll be all right with me."

Phoebe did. She had no idea what Mr Lucas had in mind for Annie but whatever it was she prayed it would bring her from the shocked desolation, the desert of emptiness into which the sight of Reed Macauley and his beautiful young wife had toppled her. A lovely man was Mr Lucas and if he . . . meant to . . . be *with* Annie, well, Phoebe went no further than that for it was none of her business. Only if it hurt Annie did it become Phoebe's business, and Mr Lucas wouldn't harm a hair on Annie's head.

Charlie took Annie's unresponsive hand between his own. They were sitting side by side on the settle. The animals had fallen into the deep contented sleep which comes with full bellies, warmth and shelter, and he wished it could be as simple as that for Annie Abbott. At that moment he hated Reed Macauley with every fierce and furious beat of his heart. He could feel the loathing creep insidiously through his veins, heating his blood to boiling point, and all he wanted was to rampage up to Long Beck, take the man by the throat and squeeze it until the breath in his body was stopped forever. God, if he could only crash his fists into that bastard's arrogant face, feel the flesh break and the blood flow, but what good would that do the empty-faced, empty-eyed woman who grieved for him?

"Come Annie, let's get you to bed."

She stood up and the quilt about her fell to the floor. Her lovely breasts stood taut and proud beneath the thin stuff of the nightdress and Charlie groaned in real pain. Her hand was warm in his, hot even, and dry, and from her he could feel a wave of warmth emanate. She looked at him listlessly though her bright eyes did not really see him and with a sigh which was heated with the vapour from her body, she fell against him.

"Oh, Annie, Annie, what has that bastard done to you?" he murmured into her hair as he lifted her into his arms and carried her to her bed.

He and Phoebe nursed her for a week before she recognised them. Between them they tended to her every need, neither feeling embarrassment as together they stripped her soiled nightgowns from her, bathed her naked body and put her in another. She was burning and freezing in turn, her hands to her head as it was wrenched in two, she muttered deliriously, by an iron claw. There was a knife in her chest she said, looking from one to the other accusingly, not seeing them at all.

"She's strong, Phoebe, so don't alarm yourself." It was not Phoebe Charlie was reassuring, but himself. "She'll come out of this, you'll see. By morning she'll be sitting up and shouting for her 'poddish'."

"Aye, that's right, Mr Lucas," but Phoebe was watching in horror the smooth roundness of Annie's cheeks as they melted and sank into the bare bones of her face. The fierce, dry heat of her seemed to be swallowing her before their very eyes and though they did their best they could not make her drink.

"Sweeting . . . Annie . . . oh, my dearest heart . . ." he murmured to her when they were alone, for Phoebe was needed elsewhere, attending to Cat who fretted to be with her mother. She was a rock to whom they all clung, himself included, as she quietly went about the business of cooking hot nourishing meals for them, and washing the piles of soiled linen from Annie and her bed, of caring for the animals and the newly planted vegetables, of doing the cleaning and mending and making sure that the home Annie had given her ran as smoothly as she knew Annie would have liked. There was only one relief in their routine, which moved from sick room to kitchen to the needs of the farm, and that was that the lambing was over and the ploughing done. The planting of oats and barley could wait a day or two until he could get to it, Charlie told Phoebe, as they covered the fretfully tossing body of Annie for the hundredth time.

They took it in turns to sit with her, dozing fitfully in the chair beside the bed, but when Phoebe, on the third night, fell asleep with Cat on her bed, sliding into a state which was almost that of unconsciousness, Charlie did not waken her. She was barely beyond childhood herself. She had borne stoically the hard task of looking after them all, of nursing Annie whilst he himself had an hour's sleep, of even, he had noticed from Annie's bedroom window, hoeing the vegetables when she had a spare moment. Now she was done in and could she be blamed?

Annie moaned and tossed, fever glazing her eyes, her lungs wheezing agonisingly in her rapidly rising and falling chest and for the first time Charlie faced the appalling fact that she might not survive. She was thin, her body bare bones and hollows for he had seen it, looking at it not with a lover's eye but with the detached concern almost of a doctor. He had seen men like this on the long marches he had made beside them in the cause of Chartism, through wet and cold nights, men with fever, with the coughing sickness and many had slipped silently away before the cause they espoused could come to fruition.

He loved Annie Abbott and had done for over six months now. She was an extension of his own body and spirit. Part of himself which no one knew of and now she lay wasting away before his eyes and he could do nothing about it. The full horror of losing her, though he knew he did not have her, was more than his anguished heart could stand and he leaned over her, putting his face in the curve of her neck beneath her chin. His lips touched the hot flesh of her throat and he murmured her name.

She seemed to quieten, sighing as she turned towards him.

"Reed . . ."

Dear Christ! *Reed!*

Again she said that hated name and her arm fumbled beneath the bedclothes which he had just tucked about her, as though searching for something.

"Annie . . . I'm here . . . I'm here, my darling." Lifting her head gently, he put his arm beneath it, drawing her close to him and though she still fretted and mumbled, her hot and feverish body seemed to strain towards him.

"Reed . . ."

He wanted to weep. He could not contemplate the world without her bright defiant spirit, her lovely glowing smile which lit her eyes to golden glory, her unshakeable belief that she would win through, her dauntless heart, brave and strong, and yet was he to nurse her back to health only to see her forever yearn for that blackguard up at Long Beck? And if he did . . . Oh, Christ . . . *if* he did? What was he thinking about, lying here next to the woman he loved, deliberating on what was to happen if she survived. She *must* survive no matter what she did in the future. The flame of her must not be allowed to go out, not if he could help to keep it flickering.

Again he lifted her head, replacing it on the pillow, moving away from the bed for a moment or two, and at once she twisted and turned, her breath rasping like a rusty saw through the clogged filth in her chest. When he had removed his outer clothing he climbed into the bed and took her in his arms, holding her burning body close to his.

"I'm here, sweetheart, I'm here," he murmured, his hands caressing her shoulders and back, stroking her tangled hair away from her face, his kisses sweet on her chin, the arch of her brow, her parched lips.

"Reed . . . aah . . . Reed." She turned to him, her

fever-racked body not knowing, her senseless mind deep in the loveliness of Reed Macauley's arms.

He awoke to a great drenching sweat which poured from Annie's body, soaking himself, her nightdress, the bedclothes. She was asleep, a quiet natural sleep which seemed to him to have a healing about it. He held her for a few more minutes, savouring the sweetness of her arm across him, her cheek on his chest, the tumbled mass of her hair in a drift across his face, then quietly lest she wake, he moved from the bed and it was as though his heart tore from his body, the pain of it so unbearable he bent his head, steadying himself for a moment on the back of the chair. She was better, sweating still, but peaceful, her mind and body soothed to that condition by her dream of Reed Macauley.

He dressed quickly, not taking his eyes from her sleeping face, then knelt beside her to study her, for he knew he would not share Annie Abbott's bed again.

It was another three days before she was completely herself again, weak as a new-born kitten and skinny as a post, she said ruefully, but yes, she thought she might eat a mouthful of 'poddish' and if her body remembered the night she had spent with Reed Macauley, her mind told her it was dreams and that Charlie and Phoebe had nursed her back to health.

Charlie watched her from the chair where he sat, one leg thrown carelessly over the arm of it, his usual expression of easy-going smiling insouciance on his thin face. Annie Abbott was not the only one to lose weight that week. The days moved on and she was improved, continuing to do so rapidly, the day at Rosley Hill not mentioned and if sometimes there was a pensive sadness in her eyes and a strain about her soft mouth, she did not allow it to interfere with the plans she had for her farm which she discussed with her good friend Charlie Lucas and the dreams she had for her daughter which she also shared with her good and dearest friend, Charlie Lucas.

"She's four now, Charlie, in December, which God

forgive me, I let slip by me as though it did not matter. That child has had nothing."

"She's had you, Annie."

Annie turned to smile at him, her hand reaching out to take his. Charlie was always saying things like that. He was such a blessing to her with his mischievous good humour and wit, his wicked, often ribald sense of fun, his easy, shared companionship. He took nothing seriously except the work he did on the farm and even that was done as though he found it all extremely amusing, something which suited him at the moment to perform. He would smile endearingly and raise self-mocking eyebrows before taking himself off to weed the acre of oats and barley he and Phoebe had sown at the end of May, whilst she herself recovered from the illness.

"Well, I'd best be off to pretend I'm a farmer," he would say, his step jaunty, his hands in his pockets, a whistle on his lips as though for two pins he would throw himself down on the grass and read his book, and yet she knew he did the work of two men though he tried to give the impression he was doing none. She knew very little about him for whenever she tried to question him on his past, he always laughed and said he had known a misspent youth and a wild young manhood.

"My family despaired of me. I broke every young lady's heart in the neighbourhood and my mother was forever in tears for I showed no inclination to settle down to marry one of them."

"And where was this, Charlie? Which part of the country do you come from? Certainly not Cumberland."

"Oh, further south than that. You will not know it."

"I have been as far as Leicestershire so I'm not exactly untravelled," for by now Charlie had heard of *her* past since she felt no need to keep it from him.

"My word, *Leicestershire!* You *have* seen the world have you not, Annie Abbott," he teased her.

"Never mind me, tell me what you have done since you grew to manhood. I know you had a university education but what did you do after that?"

"Oh, I moved about here and there," he said airily.

"Here and there, *where* and doing *what*? Don't try to play the mystery man with me, Charlie Lucas."

"That is exactly what I am and mean to stay. A mystery man. Don't you think it makes me more exciting? Look at Phoebe's face. You can see she is wondering what I've been up to and am I a wanted man. Isn't that so, Phoebe?"

"Nay, not me, Mr Lucas. I mind me own business I do, an' I tell no one mine," which was endearing really for what had Phoebe to tell, or hide?

"Quite right, Phoebe, that's what I always say."

And by means of teasing, making jokes about his reckless past, changing the subject cunningly so that one minute they were discussing him and then something else entirely, they knew barely more about him than on the day he had entered their lives.

"So what am I to do about Cat, Charlie?"

"You want her to go to school?"

"I do, but how will she fare in the village, even if they would take her? It is only a dame school which cost my father a penny or two a week."

"You certainly benefited from the experience."

"But Cat is far cleverer than I ever was, Charlie. All I learned there was to read and write and sing hymns."

"Is there not a 'monitorial system' in the North? In Almondbury, which is close to where I come from, there was a reverend gentleman, a curate and headmaster of the Grammar School there, who opened up his school for use as a Sunday School. Above its doors were inscribed the words of George III: 'May every child in my Kingdom be able to read the Bible,' it said but the Reverend Walter Smith did much more than that. In ten years fifty-one boys and thirty-five girls, each paying threepence a week, were taught by two teachers, but then those who were taught became 'monitors' teaching others. That is the 'monitorial system'."

"It sounds a wonderful idea, I would give anything to send Cat to a grammar school where she would learn more than reading and how to add one and one. Already she knows a little Latin and French that you taught her but a girl has not the chance a boy has."

"I will willingly teach her all I know, Annie, but is there not a grammar school, perhaps in Keswick or Carlisle, which will admit free pupils of poor means, girls as well as boys?"

"I don't know, Charlie, perhaps." Of course there *was* a grammar school in Keswick for had not Reed Macauley been educated there? Had she not seen him on his new, highstepping, black mare when she was no more than five or six years old and he perhaps sixteen? Lordly, he had been, riding easily in his saddle, arrogant even then as he galloped past her father's old horse and cart, those that had gone in the year the murrain wiped out Joshua Abbott's flock. She had been perched in the back of the cart, wedged against the evil-smelling fleeces Joshua Abbott had hoped – vainly – to sell at the market, a small silent girl whom her father had done his best to turn into a boy. The haughty youth had not even seen her, only coated her with dust, as his young mare, a recent present from his father, stirred up the dry track with its wildly galloping hooves.

It all came back to *him*. Every thought, however diverse, came back to him. To Reed Macauley. Every conversation, now matter how far removed, seemed to lead her in the direction of the pain he had wrought in her and though she knew she must bear it, sometimes it could not be borne. He was married now. She had seen him with his wife on his arm and though, naturally, she had been well aware that there could be nothing between her and Reed Macauley, in hearts that love there is always nurtured that tiny, unseen, unrecognised really, seed of hope.

"What is it, Annie?" They were sitting on the drystone wall at the front of the farmhouse. It was a June evening, Midsummer's Day and Annie was completely recovered from the illness which had laid her so low. The wall on which they sat was a riot of wild flowers which had seeded in every crack and cranny. The vibrant blue of speedwell, sea lavender, and a patchwork of pink and white where lady's smock had taken over. Up the wall of the farmhouse behind them was a demented blossoming of sweet rose briars, pink and profuse and scenting the evening air with their aroma. Daisies grew thickly at their feet, with buttercups and clover and down in the pasture Phoebe and Cat called to the dogs whilst the marmalade kitten, much grown now, stalked behind, its tail in the air, pretending a great indifference.

Charlie put his arm about her and drew her head down to his shoulder. She could smell the tang of the sharp soap he used, bought at the market from a housewife who made her own. It had a lemony fragrance and mixed with it was the good smell of earth and new grass. She did not answer his question and he did not repeat it, for of course, he knew what ailed her. He knew of her love for Reed Macauley and he would not press her. Charlie, dear Charlie, on whom she relied so much. What would she do without him? She leaned on him, depended on him, cared for him and about him. He was her friend and dear companion. He made her laugh and taught her patience.

Charlie. What would she do without him?

19

There had been great excitement in the parish of Bassenthwaite when Reed Macauley brought his bride home from the honeymoon they had spent in Italy. Italy, of all places, which no one in the parish, nor indeed in Cumberland, had ever been to, but trust Reed Macauley to do things in style. Though it had taken place in Bradford, where his bride came from, the wedding was said to have been a very grand affair, since the bride's father was one of the wealthiest men in the county of Yorkshire. Wool, of course, and all that went with it, which was enough to buy his daughter a wedding gift of the most magnificent diamonds anyone in the parish had ever seen. Not that her husband couldn't afford to do the same since he was not short of a bob or two himself and, naturally, with the dowry that came with her, he had made himself even wealthier.

They had been married in February and when they returned to Long Beck in May, just before Whitsuntide, it was soon whispered, as these things were, in such a close-knit community, that young Mrs Macauley was not yet pregnant. Disappointing for Reed Macauley who'd be looking for a son within the year, but there was time yet. Mrs Macauley was a fine young woman, tall, deep bosomed, broad shouldered, full hipped, the sort of woman made to bear children they would have said, and Reed Macauley would be doing his best, since he was that sort of a man anyway, the ladies whispered amongst themselves. Not coarse, nor even earthy, but very masculine in his ways.

All of Bassenthwaite parish and beyond, those of the upper and wealthy classes, landowners, manufacturing gentlemen, men whose money came from mining, were invited to the first dinner party the Macauleys gave. Mrs Macauley proved to be a splendid hostess. It seemed she had taken to running her husband's home with an efficiency which was a credit to her mother's training.

A placid, even docile, young woman was Mrs Reed Macauley. One with whom Reed Macauley would have no trouble and when the subject of Mrs Lewis was brought up by the new bride to her husband, no one could have been more surprised than he was himself.

Mrs Lewis had been cook to Reed Macauley for many years and he had been perfectly satisfied with what she had sent to his table. But it seemed that Mrs Reed Macauley was not, she told her husband, one morning at breakfast. Mrs Lewis and Reed Macauley's housekeeper, Mrs Stone, had run his home between them, uninterfered with, ever since his mother died, for though their master was exacting, demanding the best, it seemed that what they did was perfectly acceptable to him. Not to *Mrs* Macauley, who needed, she told Mr Macauley innocently, of all things, a French chef who could prepare the epicurean bonne-bouche she had, in her father's house, been used to.

"I am not at all satisfied with the standard of Mrs Lewis's cooking, Reed, and I'm afraid she will have to go. Mother, who has been in London, has interviewed one or two likely persons for me, persons with style and experience in the kind of cooking I want. French chefs since the people I mean to invite for weekend parties are used to certain standards, and I'm afraid Mrs Lewis has proved she cannot provide them."

"I beg your pardon," Reed Macauley lowered his newspaper slowly and the breakfast room became hushed.

"We have been home a month now, Reed, and though what she sends to the table is . . . adequate, she cannot manage many of the dishes I have asked her to prepare. Mrs Stone is also really in need of pensioning off to some cottage which I am sure you could provide, since she is past doing what I require of her, and of course, we must have a proper butler. That man who comes in when we have guests is all very well . . ."

The three housemaids who stood about the room, known as Peg, Jenny and Josie, before the coming of their new mistress, but now called Askew, Hall and Baxter, at least by her, since it seemed she was not in the habit of calling her servants by their Christian names, did their best to blend into the wallpaper, their eyes like saucers in their rosy country faces.

Reed regarded the smooth and equally rosy face of his wife, wondering wearily for the hundredth time in the last four months how he was to season himself to the realisation that this artless, innocent, young woman was to be his companion for the rest of their lives together. That from now until one of them died she would sit opposite him at the breakfast and dining table; that she had, as it seemed she was now intent on doing, the right to fire or hire his servants as she pleased. She was not silly, nor even empty-headed. She had been brought up to be the wife a man like himself needed. Not clever, for if she had shown signs of it, it would certainly have been erased from her childish mind years ago. She had been moulded from birth for her place in life: to extend a wide-eyed, unquestioning docility to her husband, as she had to her father. Embroidery, a few scales on the piano, French verbs and a prayer or two in English. That was all she knew. To sing and smile and take part in the small-talk thought suitable for a lady, and the understanding that man was the master and she his weak and female shadow. She could deal with servants, run her home with the efficiency a man of shrewd business sense would not despise, but she had no thought in her head which was not put there by her husband. Except in her own domain, which was her husband's home.

She was smiling at him in perfect innocence, anticipating no argument, merely showing him the courtesy of telling him what she intended doing in the running of their home, which was, after all, her job. To make it as comfortable as she could for him, for their children when they came, and for their guests, who would, since he was a man of business, and she a woman with friends, be many.

He sighed, doing his best to be patient since none of this was her fault, this disaster he had brought upon himself. He waved his hand at the maids, indicating that they should leave the room, praying that they would not go blabbing to Mrs Lewis and Mrs Stone, and that if they did, which seemed likely, he could smooth it over without undermining his wife's new authority.

"Esmé, Mrs Stone has been in this house ever since my mother died and Mrs Lewis before that. My father employed them to look after us and when he went I saw no reason for change. Mrs Lewis is a splendid cook and Mrs Stone, though I dare say she has had her own way and has become used to it, will quickly adapt to what you need of her. They are neither of them old enough to be pensioned off. Mrs Lewis is not yet fifty and Mrs Stone only a few years older. That is not ancient, you know."

It was to eighteen-year-old Esmé Macauley, but she waited politely for her husband to finish what he had to say before starting, sweetly, to explain.

"I agree that Mrs Lewis is splendid, Reed, as you say, but only with the provincial dishes she is used to preparing. She cannot manage French cuisine. You will, I'm sure, want the gentlemen with whom you do business and who will be dining with us, to have the very best you can give them, and I, as your wife, can only supply it if I have the proper servants. I intend to begin house parties as soon as I have the staff since my friends from Yorkshire, from Cheshire and Leicestershire, where I have often hunted and been their guest, will wish to be mine. And now that the weather is warmer, I thought it would be charming to have champagne picnics, like we did at home. I shall need another carriage or two to carry the ladies who do not ride and then, at the proper time, a harvest ball, perhaps with a marquee on the lawn for the tenants . . ."

"Tenants?"

"Why, yes, that is what my friend Lady Harrison of Edenthwaite does every year. Her husband's estate . . ."

"This is not an estate, Esmé. This is a working farm."

"Oh surely more than that."

"Shepherds, I employ. Men in the yard and the fields. A gardener or two, stable lads. There are no tenants, only those who live in cottages on my land."

"Very well, no marquee for the tenants, but a ball nevertheless and a hunt ball at . . ."

"We have no ballroom Esmé. This is a farmhouse."

"But the salon is large."

"Salon?" since he was not aware he had one.

"The drawing room then. The carpets could be removed and chairs set about . . ."

Her voice tripped on, light and silvery, and for several minutes he let it flow over him. She was so very pretty. She wore a simple morning gown of sprigged cream muslin, the neck high and frilled, the sleeves long and tight fitting. About her eighteen-inch waist was a broad sash of cream silk tied at the back in a bow. The bodice of the gown was tight, showing off her magnificent breasts, and the shoulders were sloping. Her hair was immaculately arranged with a centre parting and cream velvet ribbons threaded the side curls in a golden cloud over her ears. Her cornflower-blue eyes were wide and clear with nothing in them but her desire to please and her complete ignorance of what was in her husband's mind. She looked utterly enchanting, composed and unruffled, at eight o'clock in the morning, turned out by the lady's maid she had brought with her to a faultless perfection which, though it spoke of hours of effort, had, he knew, taken no more than the half-hour in which he himself had bathed, shaved and dressed. There was not a sign of the night before in which he had made love to her with the despairing strength of a man who fears he is losing his mind and who is convinced that only by plunging his male body into female flesh, can he save his sanity. She had made no objection. She had made no response. He had turned her, tossed her, this

way and that, studying the young magnificence of her
nakedness from every angle, in every position his imaginative mind could devise. For hours on end he had caressed
her, doing his best to take into his mouth, into his own
body, the most intimate parts of hers, going into her again
and again, since if he could get her with child, at least
some good might come of the charade they played out.
He had exhausted himself, falling asleep with his face
pressed into her flat, empty belly. He felt bruised, weary,
drained this morning and she looked as though she had
never known a man's hand in her life. Perhaps that was
because, in a way, she had not. Like a doll she had been.
Acquiescent, submissive, dutiful, *doing* nothing. There,
beneath his hands, his lips, his worrying teeth, his body,
but not . . . not with him. Not as . . . as *she* would have
been.

At once Annie Abbott's vibrant laughing face swam into
his vision and the room, the bright sunshine which
streamed through the window, his wife's smooth face, his
wife's tinkling voice all dissolved and vanished. Eyes, deep
and golden brown as the waters in the high tarn and just
as gleaming. Eyes which had melted to a rich warm chocolate on that day, long ago now when she had almost,
almost moved into his arms. The day he had heard she
had been interfered with and he had gone rampaging down
to Browhead, only to find it had been that wisp of a child
she had taken in. She had hit him, he remembered, though
he could not bring to mind why, then, later, when he had
drunk the tankard of ale she had given him by way of
apology, if Annie Abbott could be said to apologise to
anyone, there had been sweetness for a while, a hint of
what might have been between Annie Abbott and Reed
Macauley. Then they had argued again and he had ridden
off in high dudgeon, his temper a furnace within him at
her defiant stubbornness.

As he had the last time, the day on Rosley Fairground,
the last day. The day he had seen her with her hand in
that of another man's. The day she had looked into his
eyes and held the man's hand and . . . he had run . . .

Reed Macauley had run away from her . . . It had been an agony, a pain so great even now it festered and bit deep inside him and would not let him rest. Dear sweet God, if he could only escape it, and rest. She was as ingrained in him as though she was a living part of his body. As much his flesh, his muscles, the arteries which pumped his blood, his mind which dwelled on her every hour of the day, the heart which beat and beat and grieved for her. All these elements were contained in Reed Macauley and so was she, a living extension of himself, which could no longer be complete since she was missing from his life and always would be. For weeks he had hated her. Through the winter when tales of her doings had come to him he had hated her so much the bile had come to his mouth and choked him. She was just as they said she was, brazen and unblushing, indecent in her shamelessness, a woman of easy virtue, who would use any man to achieve her own ends. They said all these things of her and he agreed, and yet, deep in his heart, which knew Annie Abbott for what she truly was, a small voice to which he refused to listen whispered that if she was all these things, why had she not used Reed Macauley? Surely, of all the men in the parish of Bassenthwaite, he was the one who could have given her the most. She had known she could have it. She had only to put out a hand to him and comfort, security, love, could all have been hers without doing a hand's turn to achieve it. A house somewhere, for herself and her child, money, jewels, clothes, his protection. Anything she wanted, needed and yet she chose to work herself and that girl she took in, into the ground to keep her independence. Putting herself in danger, dressing like a man, tramping the fells alone but for her dogs, in her eternal search for what she was after.

His wife's voice interrupted his painful thoughts and, though they were painful, they were also precious and guarded and he wanted to strike out at Esmé for ripping them apart.

". . . so I will summon Mrs Lewis first and give her a

month's notice. I think that is fair, don't you? I shall of course give her a glowing reference since she . . ."

"And where in hell's name do you think she is to go at her age? After all these years of devoted service, where is she to go, Esmé? A woman of forty-five thrown out in the street just because she can't manage bloody French cuisine . . . ?"

"Reed . . . oh, please, Reed," Esmé's face crumpled in distress but Reed Macauley did not see it, or if he did, he did not care. His mind was battered with pictures of a woman, any woman really, who is forced by circumstances to struggle in this cruel, man's world, to survive on her own. To stoop to tasks which were beyond her, physically and emotionally. Humiliated and cast out to fend for herself after all these years. He could not, would not stand for it, no, not if he had to ride over there and . . . and . . .

Jesus . . . Jesus God! it was *Mrs Lewis* who was being discussed here . . . not . . . not *her*. And he would not allow it. She had no right to even think of dismissing her, not Mrs Lewis, even if Esmé was mistress of this house now . . . Dear sweet God . . . let there be a child soon . . . a son . . . or a daughter . . . anything to ease the ache in him which wouldn't let up, anything to put Annie Abbott out of his mind, his heart, his *life*, or he would go mad with it. She was destroying him, his torment . . . his love.

"Mrs Lewis stays, Esmé." His voice was cold, implacable and his young wife shrank back in her chair as he stood up. He saw it and was sorry, but there was nothing he could say to reassure her. Not now . . . not just now when he needed to get away.

"She is . . . a member of the family . . . no, no, not related . . ." he added irritably as his wife's astonished face could plainly be seen to be dwelling on the horror of having a common cook's blood mixing in the veins of her children, when they came. "And I don't want to hear another word on it. Those with whom I'm acquainted and who have been dining here for years seem to have taken no harm from Mrs Lewis's cooking, indeed they have often praised it. Your friends I'm afraid must learn to do the same. Of course, if their fine sensibilities cannot overcome it, then they are at liberty to stay away."

Ignoring the fat child's tears which had begun to form in his wife's beautiful eyes, he strode from the room, banging the door behind him.

The long moving ribbon of sheep wound slowly down the track towards the lower pastures, a jostling, steaming throng of animals which now and then jumped as though in joyful anticipation of what was to come. The air was filled with their bleating and baaing and their hooves made a sharp clatter on the rough stones, before they reached the more profuse grass of the inlands. Two dogs worked them, as silent as shadows, moving in a sweeping blur from side to side, keeping them together, chivvying down those which were reluctant to go. At their back were Annie Abbott and Cat.

Blackie and Bonnie were experienced sheepdogs now, running as 'doubles', obeying Annie's orders with no more than a high whistle and a short command. They had gathered her ewes and the twenty or so lambs which they had dropped in May, and others besides, since any man's flock may roam freely on the high fells and sheep know no enemies amongst their own, mixing with one another as they cropped. Despite this there were not many strays. A Herdwick will stick to its own 'heaf', the pasture where it is weaned. It has in it an incredible homing instinct which fortunately had not been too deep in the ones Annie had bought at Rosley, since it had been known for a sheep sold miles away, if it is able, to return to its own 'heaf'. Annie's had not done so. There would be a 'meet' in November at a local hostelry where shepherds would gather, not only to celebrate the end of a successful farming year but where all strays, or neighbouring sheep had to be displayed by noon of the day decided, and all sheep whose marks were not in the 'Shepherd's Guide' started some twenty years ago were to be drawn into a fold apart from the others to be inspected by all at the meeting. Those who infringed on this rule were fined sixpence each. Every sheep and lamb, as it was born, was branded with the owner's 'smit' on the fleece, and all of Annie's new flock now had her 'lug' mark on their ear. Those she found without her mark among the sheep she had gathered must be taken to the meet and how the farmers in the parish who had managed over the past year to treat her as though she and her flock, indeed her farm, did not exist, would cope with that, she could not imagine. Nor did she care. She had bought her flock. She had mated each ewe with the eager ram which had been driven back to Rosley in the spring. At lambing time the four of them, Charlie and herself, Cat and Phoebe, and the two dogs had gone, day after long wet day, searching out the new lambs which stood, small and white and defenceless against the dark contrast of their mother's bulk. The dogs even at such a young age, knew instinctively that gentleness was needed, driving the ewe and her staggering lamb, sometimes two, towards Annie, where with a deft twist of her crook, she caught the ewe, checking her udders for milk supply, since the lamb's survival depended on its mother's ability to feed it. The lamb was marked with exactly the same colour and spot as its dam.

When each lamb was thriving and trotting sturdily beside its mother, they were moved from the lambing field where Annie and Charlie had put them earlier, on to adjacent land, so that gradually, as a lamb was born and checked each day, all of her flock were driven up on to the more exposed pasture. At that time of the year, as the winter snows melted, the streams were swollen and dangerous, and she had lost several babies whose first staggering steps proved to be their last. Carrion crow and foxes were a hazard but from her twenty ewes she had bred seventeen lambs including four sets of twins.

Today the air was clear and warm but wisps of mist hung over the ends of the fells. Birds were pouring out their song from throats in which the splendour of summer was scarcely contained. A plover called to its mate, and a curlew glided across the valley, its warbling note ending as it touched the ground. The sun was out, her flock's fleece was dry and ready for clipping and she felt the peace, the content, the pleasure settle in her. All around her was her land, not a great deal but enough to form the small farm she had dreamed of. Her sheep streamed out before her and when they were sheared she and Charlie were to take the fleeces to market to sell. She would keep the ewe lambs for breeding and sell the others at the lamb fair at Penrith. Hire a tup to service her ewes and so another cycle in the year would begin.

"Come bye, Blackie," she called. "Away to me, Bonnie, steady, steady . . ."

There would be no 'boon' clipping at Browhead for who amongst her neighbours would lend *her* a hand? She must do it all herself since neither Charlie nor Phoebe had the necessary skill which she had learned when her father considered her strong enough.

Charlie would drag the sheep to her, and when it was clipped, Phoebe would salve the shorn animal which involved the application to the skin of a mixture of tar and grease. The salve smelled abominable but it would not only encourage the lamb's next fleece, making it stronger and thicker, but would protect it against parasite. Charlie had promised Phoebe he would fashion a harness of sorts to attach to a ring in the wall so that each beast could be kept still while she did it.

"Ah'll be as reet as nine pence, Mr Lucas, don't tha fret," she had told him stoutly. Phoebe never called Charlie anything but Mr Lucas, no matter how many times he begged her. Cat called him Charlie as naturally as she called Annie 'Mother', but Phoebe had seen right away that Mr Lucas was a gentleman and as such must be shown proper respect. She liked him well enough, for who could dislike such a good-natured, amiable chap? Do anything for anyone, would Mr Lucas, especially Annie. He worked hard, though he was not much good with his hands, try as he might. Willing, oh yes, but give him a hammer and he hit his thumb, an axe or saw and he cut himself, or dropped the log he was chopping on his foot. He had helped Annie to cut the oats and bigg and rye and when they had dried, he would take them to be ground by the local miller. He had cleaned and oiled Joshua Abbott's old plough and in the spring had supplied the 'horse power', laughing as he did about absolutely everything, pulling it whilst Annie guided it along the furrows. The hay was next and how Mr Lucas would fare with that there scythe didn't bear thinking about, but he had done his best. He couldn't help it if his skill lay in other directions, could he? Read anything he could get his hands on he did, always writing something he was, or talking his head off about politics, but what they would have done without him, Phoebe couldn't imagine.

She and Charlie were waiting beside the gate leading into the big field in front of the farm, both ready to give a helping hand to Blackie and Bonnie as they herded the flock through. A catching pen had been set up so that when the sheep flowed between the gateposts they were immediately enclosed in a small area which was easily accessible to Charlie as he reached in for the animal which was to be clipped. To the side of the farmhouse, just beyond the gate, was the cobbled yard and it was here that Annie had set up the special two-tiered stool which was used for clipping. She sat on the highest tier and the sheep was tipped on to its back on the lower, its head between her knees. Beside the stool were her father's shears, freshly cleaned and sharpened.

The spring, as though at last the gods were inclined to smile on Annie Abbott, had been a good one, dry and sunny. The blue sky arched away above their heads and high at its zenith a sky lark sang its heart out. The dogs, their work done for the moment, lay panting in the shade by the kitchen step, their tongues lolling from their open mouths. There were midges dancing in the warm air and in the meadow, buttercups and daisies and clover made a patchwork of delicate colour in the green of the grass.

The sheep bleated anxiously and Annie could feel the

steady rhythm of her heart quicken. The results of a year's, no more than that, eighteen months', arduous back-breaking labour was about to be realised. Her fleeces would be sold, and the male lambs, and she would have ready cash again to expand her flock. To grow! Oh, Lord, keep my hand steady, she prayed, and my back strong, since it all depends on me. And let me remember how to do it!

"Righto, Charlie," she called, to the man at the gate, no sign of the tension in her. "Bring the first."

The struggling sheep was hauled, hooves scraping, towards her, whilst Charlie sweated and swore. The ewe's bleats added to the growing hubbub as her frantic lamb tried its best to go with her. The sheep stank as Charlie manhandled it on to the lower step of the stool, struggling to get back to its lamb, and for a moment, Annie felt a weakness in her arms and back. She could not do it, dear God, the thing was so enormous. Its fleece was thick, brown, tangled . . . filthy with . . . then her father's voice muttered irritably in her ear, telling her not to be such a great gowk! and to get on with it, girl, and her hand reached for the shears.

She did eight sheep that day. Sweat poured from her so that she looked as though she had been dipped in water. Phoebe squeaked a lot since she had had nothing to do with sheep before, and even swore as Charlie did, but each shorn ewe was efficiently salved against the dread scourge of scab with rancid butter and tar, each taking her an hour to do, and the fleece was rolled neatly into its bundle before mother and lamb were re-united. Many of the lambs were confused for they did not recognise the snow-white apparition, which, once a browny grey, their mother had now become. The bright blue 'smit' mark stood out on her newly shorn back. Each ewe called for her lamb, and when found, udders which had filled in the separation were quickly emptied.

The next day it was the same, and the next, and up beside the beck where he sat quietly on his coal-black mare, his patient dog beside him, the man heard her laugh of jubilation, her shout of triumph which echoed about the fell. He watched her as the man with her put his arms about her and when they capered round the yard in a rough semblance of a polka, he lowered his chin to his chest, turned the mare and began to make his slow way towards his empty home.

20

Charlie Lucas was a Chartist who, in April 1848, had done his best to march with Feargus O'Connor to hand the Chartist petition to Parliament demanding that every man should have a vote, and that in a secret ballot, which was the essence of their People's Charter.

The petition was not successful. It had been presented by men who believed in peaceful persuasion and when that failed, those who were inclined to think that 'physical force' spoke with a voice more likely to be heard, marched with their pikes, their green rosettes and banners through Halifax and Bradford, through Nottingham and Manchester and other northern towns. A Chartist mob with sticks and stones fighting against the drawn cutlasses of squadrons of dragoons. One of that 'mob' was Charlie who, having found that peaceful means had not achieved the justice and equality for all men he believed they should have, had decided to fling in his hand with the more violent sort, though he was not a violent man.

Arrests were made, Chartist leaders who had led the riots. The Irish Chartist, John Mitchel was sentenced to transportation on a convict ship to Australia. Three hundred others were sent for trial and it was generally agreed that those still at large should lie low for a while. Charlie had fled even further north, moving from town to town, working at anything he could find; many tasks of a menial nature not suited to his qualifications since, as the son of a lawyer, he was an educated man. He walked for weeks, months, sleeping rough through the summer of 1848, the flame of him growing dimmer, leaving only a footloose, weary man, who, though he evaded arrest, no longer had the fire and idealism of his beliefs to keep him going.

He had been idling about Rosley, undecided which way to go with winter coming on, north or south, east or west, what did it matter? It was then that Annie Abbott, in her threadbare, overlarge men's clothing had come striding up the track, her two dogs beside her, her fragile, lop-sided sledge behind. He had at that moment, no inclination to do anything positive, like getting on his way, wherever that might be, so he had watched her, not aware that the youth he studied was in fact female, his curiosity caught nevertheless. He had followed her into The Drover's Rest, simply because there had been nothing else to do. His grand and noble ideas had come to nought. He had dedicated himself for years to the Charter which had come to nought. He was needed by no one, until he met Annie.

On this day in October, he had been at Browhead a year and in a small way, Annie was prospering. Her lambs had been sold at Penrith and up on the fell the ewes were waiting to be covered by the fine hired tup who was butting his head in frustration in the field before the farm. In November he would be allowed to mate, but not before since Annie did not want her lambs to be dropped until April or May when the worst of the winter would be over.

The potato crop was in, the potatoes stored in clamps, long heaps in the barn covered with straw, soil and hedge-trimmings. The hay was cut, and built up into an enormous haystack, a gigantic task which had been almost beyond the three of them and next year Annie was talking of hiring some of the Irish vagrants who tramped with their families from Whitehaven having come on the coal boats in search of work. Vegetables were stored ready for the winter. Sieves had been cut and each evening the four of them had fashioned the rushlights which would illuminate the long dark nights ahead of them. Peat had been brought in and was stacked and drying in the empty cow byre attached to the house. Annie's own ewes having proved good breeders, instead of slaughtering a couple for meat, she had parted with some of her precious cash and bought two sheep at Penrith market and these had been killed and some of the mutton pickled in brine in the huge vats in the kitchen, the rest smoked above the fire in the ingle-nook. Charlie and Annie had felled timber last winter, the straight-grained poles which, as Annie had showed him, must be peeled, split into pieces and boiled in water to make them pliable. They were then further split with the 'lat-axe' and shaved and trimmed on Joshua Abbott's 'swillers-horse'. All was now ready for the winter months ahead when the swill baskets and besom-twig brooms, the materials for which were stored in the barn, would be fashioned ready for market in the spring. Which market Annie had not yet decided, she said, but Charlie knew she had some idea brewing in her clever head. She had kept a fleece from one of her ewes and would card and spin and weave in the winter months, making the hodden grey which would become garments of clothing for her and Cat and Phoebe. She was settling, thriving, coming through, *winning*!

The sky was a low, leaden canopy of grey clouds draped from fell to fell as Charlie trudged down the track towards the village of Hause on the edge of which stood the mill. Behind him he pulled the sledge which, though still in the state it had been when he had first seen Annie Abbott, over twelve months ago now, had been used for carrying everything from potatoes and peat, from fresh-cut sieves to a tired child, and now the oats and bigg he was taking to be milled. The runners had come off a time or two causing some consternation and great hilarity when one slid all the way down Middle Fell, scattering sheep in every direction, until it splashed into the beck. He had followed it, gathering speed as it did, and finishing up beside it in the sweet tasting, icy water.

He sighed as the memories of the past year came flood-ing through his mind. Good, sweet memories which were filled with Annie, with laughter and tears and worry, with peace and fulfilment. Annie's lovely face strained so often into deep hollows of weariness as she took on tasks which were beyond her, but which were performed just the same. Annie's face laughing, bright and glorious as it had been on the day the runner came off the sledge and her tears, channelling through the birth blood which had smeared her cheeks as she had fought to save a lamb's life. Peace he had seen in her eyes as they had sat together in the dusk on the drystone wall before the farmhouse, and fulfilment as her complete flock of twenty ewes and their offspring moved placidly from one sweet tussock of grass to another. He had known her every mood, the brave goodness of her, the spirited temper, the merry humour, the bright resolve that said she would never be beaten. She was proud, defiant and independent. She was strong and beautiful and she was in love with Reed Macauley who had married some heiress from Bradford.

So what was to happen to Charlie Lucas who loved Annie Abbott? he asked himself, his eyes cast down to the rough ground before him. His good leather boots in which, with the Chartists, he had tramped the long miles from Manchester to London, moved one beside the other in his line of vision and he noted with a part of his mind which dwelled on practicalities that if he didn't get them repaired soon, they would be beyond it and he would have to take to wearing the wooden-soled clogs Annie, Cat and Phoebe wore. Not that there was any shame in that. They were warm and serviceable but somehow it seemed to him that clogs would be a symbol of his complete isolation from the class into which he had been born and the life he had known as a child and youth. A reforming family, his had been, despite their rank, taking him to reform meetings, where he had learned about Luddism and Chartism and the injustice of man against man. His father, a good man, a lawyer who had acted on behalf of many radical men on trial for their beliefs, had become bankrupt in the process, worn out from protecting other men from starvation, rarely charging for his own services, dying, as had his wife, Charlie's mother, in genteel poverty in West Yorkshire.

So Charlie had gone on the tramp, enduring what his fellow men, those with nothing, endured, moving up and down the country, speaking at Chartist meetings, passionate and ready to do whatever was asked of him in the fight for freedom and equality. It had been important to him. There had been nothing else and no one else. He had known many young women, liked them, some of them even loved a little, but lightly, good humouredly, with none of the strength and passion with which he loved Annie. He wanted Annie very badly, and how was he to continue to live beside her, with nothing more than the friendship which was all she had to give him? He slept in the snug loft above the dairy and cow byre and between his bed and Annie's was a wall a foot thick but it might as well have been thirty, or a veil of flimsy gauze, it would not have mattered, since Annie was not for him. Her demeanour told him so. She was open, generous with her friendship, her affection even, which he had seen grow as the months went by but he wanted more than that. Much more. He wanted her not only in his heart where she already was, but in his bed. He wanted her for wife and mother, to him and to their children, and her nearness, the soft curving flesh of her breasts and waist and hip, the fine delicacy of her white wrist, the sweetness of the flesh beneath her chin, her fragrance and warmth as she moved about his nights and days, were killing him as slowly and irrevocably as were the years. He had nothing to offer but himself, and his labour, and his love. She had her land, her farm, her flock. She had her child and a good friend in Phoebe and though she was not accepted into the community which lived in the Vale of Borrowdale, Bassenthwaite and Keswick, surely that would come when they realised, the people in that community, her worth. She had no need of Charlie Lucas. She would argue of course, since she could not see into his heart and would be distressed when he told her he must go. She knew nothing of his Chartist background, but if she did she would not understand, since the Chartist movement was dead so what was there for him to do, she would ask and he must think of some reason to satisfy her.

He turned at the foot of the track where it led out on

to the Hause road, looking up at the high fells where he had lived these last twelve months. He could see Annie and Phoebe scything the last of the bracken with long graceful strokes. When it was cut, which must be done each backend to prevent it encroaching on pasture land, it would be used as bedding for any animals which were brought inside for the winter. As yet of course, Annie had none, but still the bracken must be cleared. They were late with the end-of-autumn task, but the previous weeks had been frantic with all the work which must be completed by only three adults before the snows began.

The two women were tiny figures amongst the reds and browns and yellows of the vast sea of withering bracken, the fronds of which had turned over the last weeks from a delicate tawny brown to a subtle lemon hue. In the coppice beyond, oak and ash, hazel and larch stood regally with branches capturing every shade of colour from the palest brown to the brightest yellow. The leaves were falling rapidly but here and there were brilliant splashes of red on rowan, thorn, holly, yew and juniper as their berries clustered. He would miss it. Annie . . .

The giant water wheel which moved the rollers inside the mill was tumbling round at great speed since there was never any shortage of water in these parts to turn it. The mill was quiet but for the noise the wheels made when he poked his head inside the door, the enormous stone discs which ground the corn, the barley and the oats, moving ponderously one on top of the other as they did their work. A fine mist filled the air from the grain which was fed through the hole in the middle of the wheels and particles lay an inch thick on every surface. Two plump cats were curled together on the window-sill, their size proof of their labours as catchers of the rats and mice which fought for a living here. There were several sacks stacked against the wall, filled with threshed and dried oats waiting to be ground, but little else and Charlie congratulated himself on coming as early as he had. It seemed that Annie's grain would not have to wait and neither would he. If he left the sacks they should be ready by morning.

"Hello," he shouted. "Are you there?"

"Aye" a voice floated from somewhere above him, coming down the narrow stone steps. "Ah'll be down in a minute. Ah've just to . . ." the words lost in a jumble as the owner of the voice evidently stuck his head into some task pertinent to milling.

"Nah then, what can ah do for thee?" he was saying as he lumbered down the steps. A big fellow used to manhandling up and down them, the enormous sacks of grain brought to him.

Charlie smiled pleasantly showing his good teeth in a face which the weathers had painted a rich amber. His brown curls, long and uncut these past months, since Annie had been too tired of an evening to be barber – and could he bear her lovely touch? his heart had asked, glad of the excuse – lay over his brow and the collar of his shabby broadcloth coat.

"I would be glad of my oats ground, sir, and by tomorrow morning if I may. I seem to have come at a good time since you appear to have a lull at the moment." It had seemed impolite to imply that the miller had no work, as though the folks hereabout did not care to use him.

The miller's face had become quite expressionless, the comradely smile of welcome he reserved for his customers sliding away to nothing. He stood, already tall, towering above Charlie on the next to bottom step, both hands on his hips, his eyes cool as he looked down at him.

"Nay, can't be done," he dared Charlie to argue.

Charlie did. "And why is that?" He looked about him, delicacy gone. "You don't seem very busy."

"Can't be done, not today." The miller's bottom lip protruded truculently.

"Then tomorrow will do. I'll call back at . . ."

"Ah'm too busy. Stuff coming in this afternoon."

"I see. Then I will have to wait my turn. When *can* you do it?"

"Ah couldn't say."

"But surely you must know when you . . ."

"Nay, ah'm up to me eyes in it for weeks now. You'd best find someone else to tekk it."

"But you had no such problems last year when I brought my oats to you. Last November when . . ."

"Ah didn't know who tha' was then."

"And what has that to do with it? You are a miller who, presumably, is desirous of earning a living. I am a man with grain to grind. Why should who I am prevent us from striking a bargain?"

"Ah've had me say. Ah can't do tha' grain so tha'd best tekk it elsewhere."

"You are the only miller in these parts."

"Aye, ah know."

"Look here, this is bloody ridiculous. I have grain to be ground here and . . ."

"Bugger off. Ah'll ground no grain for thi' or for that hussy up Browhead. She'm not fit to be called owt else, trampin' about in her faither's clothes like she does. Ah knew Joshua Abbott an' poor sod'd be turnin' in his grave if he knew, an' if tha' wants a thumpin' then tha' shall 'ave it if tha' raises tha' fists ter me. Ah've nowt against you since I reckon any chap'd be glad ter get inter Annie Abbott's drawers, meself included, given a chance, so tha' can't be blamed if . . ."

Despite his size it took him all of five minutes to fling the tall, much lighter figure of Charlie out into the road. His own fists were grazed where his knuckles had connected with Charlie's nose, his eye and chin, and surprisingly he had a shiner of his own where the lad, give him his due, had landed him one.

Though he did his best to clean himself up in the beck which tumbled beside the mill, Charlie's face was a mass of contusions as he dragged his burden and his aching self back up the hill to Browhead. From higher up the fell, Annie had seen him return, waving her arm in greeting then, realising that he could not possibly have got the grain milled in the hour he had been gone, she dropped her scythe and began to run, her long legs still clad as they had been for the past year in her father's trousers, eating up the shorn stretch of bracken, the long dip of the 'inland' pasture and leaping the drystone wall as easily as any steeple chaser.

"Dear God . . . Charlie . . . dear God . . ." Her face turned white and inside her chest her heart crashed against her rib-cage in terror. Surely someone must have tried to kill him, but through the blood which refused to stop flowing from a burst lip and the agony of his eye which was already closed, he tried to smile.

"It's all right Annie. I'm not hurt."

"*Not hurt*, my God, who did this to you?" She moved towards him bringing with her the fragrance of the lavender she scattered in the chest where her clothes were kept, the smell of the bracken and the fresh, wild aroma of the Lakeland fell in which she laboured. It was her own particular fragrance, sweet and pure, and his love for her gushed through him, drowning his senses. She put her hands about his face, cupping it to hold him still and he froze in a paralysis of need which her nearness awoke in him. Her face was close to his, her eyes warm, concerned, probing and her breath was sweet.

"I got in a bit of a . . . fight," he managed to say endearingly, trying once more to smile.

"*A bit of a fight!* My God, what hit you? You won't be able to see in the morning . . ."

"I can't see now . . ." he mumbled, wishing she would go on holding him. Wishing she would put her arms about him, hold his weary, aching head to her breast and comfort him as she did Cat . . . No, not as she did Cat, but as she would a *man*. Phoebe had joined them by now and Cat had come out of the kitchen where she was at her lessons, those Annie insisted on, and they clustered about him in concern, none of them noticing at that moment the untouched sacks of grain on the old sledge.

She bathed his face and Phoebe made him tea, though quite honestly he could have done with a stiff brandy to put out the still smouldering fire of rage which had been lit in him by the miller's words. He would not tell her, of course, what the man had said. Let her think they had

fought because the miller had refused to grind her oats
and bigg. That he himself had been so incensed he had
taken a swing at the man. He would not dirty her by
repeating the man's words. But she knew, of course.

Phoebe had gone to her bed, not much behind Cat who
now had her own small room between Annie's and
Phoebe's. She and Cat were both tired for besides her
school work, Cat collected the eggs and fed the hens which
moved freely about the yard, saw to both the dogs' evening
meal, brought in peat and kindling and any other light task
which was within her grasp. She was nearly five years old
now, growing tall and strong, her young character forming
already into an image of her mother's. She was a beauty,
with a sweetness in her which Charlie loved for it was so
like Annie's. Not a sugary sweetness, but one which was
mixed with spice and fire making it all the more palatable.

"He said something about me, didn't he? About you and
me?" Annie leaned back in her mother's small rocking
chair, her long legs crossed at the ankle, her feet bare
and slender to the crackling fire. She had been carding the
wool from her own fleece, a task which he knew gave her
immense satisfaction, and the hand carder, used by her
mother and her mother's mother still lay on the table.
Carding involves tufts of the washed wool from the fleece
being set between the wire points on the carder and
'combed' which action disentangles the fibres, loosening
them ready for spinning. Next to the carder were the
long combed fibres which Annie was still in the process of
smoothing.

"I beg your pardon," he mumbled.

"You heard me, Charlie. Don't deny it. Nothing else
would have made you set about a chap as big as Jack
Bibby. He said something you didn't like and it involved
you and me living here, unchaperoned . . ." She gave a
snort of unamused laughter, ". . . since we can't count
Phoebe. Oh, don't worry Charlie, I'm not daft. Do you
think I don't know what they are *all* saying? I've seen the
looks they give me when I happen to come across a
shepherd on the fell, or Mrs Mounsey or Mim go past the

back of the farm. Even Sally has stopped coming since . . ."

"Since I arrived. That's only because . . ."

"It's because that husband of hers has threatened her with the biggest hiding of her life if she does. They think the worst, Charlie, I'm afraid. Our reputation is ruined, yours and mine." She laughed lightly but there was deep in her voice a strange note which seemed to say it was hard being an outcast. No matter what she did, nor how innocently, they wouldn't have it. They thought the worst of her so really, what was the point of dwelling on it? She and Charlie were friends, dear friends, who supported one another as friends did. He had come into her life just when she needed one, and she had done the same for him. She gave him a home and one day, when she could afford it, she hoped to give him a wage, a decent wage, which was what he deserved.

"My reputation doesn't matter since . . ." He had been about to say since I will be going soon anyway, but the expression of vulnerability on her face, a young look of being lost for the moment, stopped him. He could not strike her with the blow which he knew would hurt her badly, just when she was suffering another. Somehow she must get her grain milled and the question was where, for there was not another miller in the parish of Bassenthwaite. But when that was done, he must go. He would tell her when all her labour was done. When she was settled for the winter, her crops in, her animals safe, her oats and bigg ground, and stored in the kist in the corner of the kitchen.

He watched her, her face pale and drawn, her weary body slumped. She was chewing her bottom lip, staring into the glowing peat fire as she worried on the question of how she was to get her grain ground and his battered face, though no emotion showed through the dried blood and bruising, was soft with his love for her.

It was noon the next day when Jack Bibby thumped on the door of the kitchen. Annie was up on the fell, scything the last of the bracken, Phoebe with her, only Charlie,

Cat and the two dogs at home. He had sworn he was able to go, and had twitched the scythe from Phoebe's hand saying she should stay at home and make him a bilberry pie from the last of the fruit they had picked from the great swathe which grew at the summit of Bakestall.

"All right then, Mr Lucas," Phoebe had said tartly. "Let's see tha' swing that scythe," and when he did the pain which had nagged him all night, flared hideously through his chest, making him gasp.

"Off with your shirt, Charlie," Annie had ordered, gasping herself as did Phoebe, at the great purple and black bruise which coloured his white skin just below his left breast.

"Oh, Charlie," was all she said, sadly, her fingers touching lightly the skin of his chest and shoulders and despite the agony he was in, he felt a stirring in the pit of his belly and the thrusting of his penis as his desire awoke.

"It's nothing really," stepping hurriedly away from her, but of course they must bind it up, they said, and did, and he must rest for a while since a rib might be cracked. So he and Cat were alone when the miller called.

Charlie stared in astonishment, his one good eye looking into Jack Bibby's one good eye. Behind the miller was a strong cart pulled by a sturdy fell pony and perhaps it was then that Charlie got the idea though it was not a conscious thought at the time.

"Ah've come for t' grain," the man said shortly.

Charlie gaped and behind him Cat held Blackie and Bonnie by their scruffs to let them know that neither they, she, nor Charlie were threatened.

"Is it handy?" the man went on, his manner truculent, his gaze shifty. Still Charlie could not speak. They both bore the scars of yesterday's fight and yet here was the miller, just as though it had not happened, enquiring for the grain which yesterday he had refused to grind.

"I don't believe this," Charlie said, his battered face a picture of bewilderment.

"'Appen tha' don't but I've no time to be standing here

whilst tha' think about it. Do tha' want tha' grain milling or not?"

The man was evidently under some strain and in his one good eye was a gleam which said he would dearly love to close Charlie's other eye but nevertheless he stood his ground.

"What the bloody hell's going on?" Charlie begged to know, wanting to laugh really, for the whole thing was so ridiculous, but not daring to, not only because of the pain in his chest which hurt each time he drew breath, but because he didn't want to turn the miller against him yet again. The man was looking over Charlie's shoulder at Cat who smiled and dropped a curtsey. For a moment his face softened and he almost smiled back then he turned to Charlie.

"Does tha want it doin' or not? Ah found that . . . well, ah've got an hour or two ter spare so ah thought . . ." he shifted uncomfortably from one big foot to the other, "well . . . mek tha' mind up."

"For God's sake man, of course we want it doing. Look, I can't lift it, not after our little contretemps yesterday." He grinned painfully and the miller wondered what the hell he was talking about but he nodded and, after Charlie showed him where the heavy sacks were, lifted them easily on to his cart and drove off.

"Ah'll have 'em back first thing tomorrow. Will that do thi?" he called over his shoulder.

"Of course, splendid and thanks."

Charlie was still grinning as he closed the door. He looked at Cat and she looked at him and though it sliced through him like a hot knife, he began to laugh.

"Now what in God's name was all that about?" he asked her, scratching his head.

"I don't know, Charlie. He must have changed his mind."

"I suppose he must, but I wish he had done it before he set into me."

The miller drove the cart along the two miles of road between the gate of Browhead Farm and Hause. He had gone no more than a mile when a man on a tall, high bred, black mare which was cropping the grass verge beside the road, held up his hand for him to stop. A Merle collie eyed him suspiciously. The miller scowled, but drew on the reins.

"Everything all right, Bibby?" the man asked quietly.

"Aye, 'tis in the back."

"And you'll have it ground by tomorrow?"

The miller sighed. "If you say so, sir."

"I do say so, Bibby, and I'm much obliged to you."

The miller sighed again.

"Aye, well . . . I'd best get on."

"Of course, and, Bibby, I won't forget this."

"No sir, neither will I."

21

The blizzard struck at the dales and fells of Lakeland early that winter, coming with very little warning at the end of November. January was the usual month in which the big snow was expected, only a light dusting on the peaks appearing before Christmas. In December, the frost would sting hard, every blade of grass and frond of bracken decorated with a hoary fringe. The sun would shine, turning the white peaks to a delicate rose, and the sheep would move down to where the herbage survived, with slivers of ice jangling on their thick grey fleece. Snow buntings, harbinger of bad weather to come, picked seeds from the bents, and grey geese flew in formation, heading south.

But in November the wind began to blow, thin and bitter. The hedges were black and the winter trees cowered beneath the growing force of tumultuous air. The peaks turned grey under the long snow-clouds and darkness fell before three o'clock in the afternoon. A steady flurry of powdery snow danced wildly in the turmoil of the elements, violent eddies sweeping across the fells, then it became calmer and the snow began to fall thickly, steadily, a white and impenetrable curtain through which nothing could be seen. The sheep, instinct telling them what to do, found places against rocks and walls where there was shelter, settling down to wait, and farmers did the same, knowing there was nothing else they could do. To go out in it, even to check on their precious flock, was madness. Men had been known to simply vanish in the white and eerily silent world, their bodies not found until weeks later when the thaw came. In the night, the wind returned, driving the snow directly into the face of Browhead Farm.

Morning light revealed a world in which nothing could be heard except the call of the ravens high on the peaks, nor seen but great drifts of snow across the farmyard, field, dales and fell, undulating deserts in which not even a gatepost was revealed. The grey crags stood up sharply in the white world, emerging from the snow high up the fells, beginning to turn pink as the rising sun fell on them. Trees were recognisable only by the shape of them, snow laden and top heavy. It had not yet crusted and when Charlie ventured forth on to it from the back door, which, being sheltered from the full force of the storm, could be safely opened, he fell right through it up to his waist.

"I'll have to make a path up to the barn or those hens will set up a racket to wake the dead if they're not fed," he shouted, and at once Cat and Phoebe were eager to help him, though Annie's first thought was to get up to the 'intakes' to check on her flock. Thirty-two ewes now and the ram who had been put out to service them only two weeks ago. Had they survived or were they buried in drifts which, until the snow crusted, could not be checked? The dogs would find them wherever they were and even if they were not found at once, a sheep can live in a drift for up to two weeks. The warmth and the fat of its own body would keep it alive but she could not help but worry. She was surviving by a hair's-breadth, treading delicately and it needed only one small setback, just one strand of the fine network of her life to snap and the whole structure would unravel.

"Don't even think of it," Charlie's quiet voice told her, reading her mind. She had not been aware that he was there as she stood, her eyes shaded by her raised hand, staring up into the blinding whiteness beneath which her hopes and dreams were buried. For good, or only until the snows allowed her up there, her mind agonised? She turned and smiled, though, tucking her hand in the crook of his arm.

"I wouldn't be allowed, even if I was daft enough to try, would I? The three of you would set up such a cater-wauling I would be completely overruled." She cast another anxious look at Middle Fell where she had last seen her tiny flock, then hugging his arm to her, pulled him towards the sloping drift in which Cat and Phoebe were floundering.

"Come on, then, let's have some fun. We can do nothing outside once the hens are fed and the eggs collected, so let's make a snowman." She bent and scooped a handful of snow, making it into a ball, then threw it at Phoebe who turned, surprised. For a moment she looked bewildered, not knowing even yet how to play, then her own face split into a young grin of joy and she did the same, aiming at Annie who began to shriek, the sound echoing across the valley. At once they were all at it, throwing snowballs, shouting with laughter, the dogs barking and chasing the snowballs which, when they landed, they could not find. Scarlet cheeks and brilliantly vivid eyes, smiling mouths and fast beating hearts, hands and feet tingling as the blood flowed and when the game was over, the paths dug, the hens fed, the companionable comfort and warmth of the kitchen, hands cupped round pewter beakers filled with thick vegetable 'crowdy'.

The dogs found every ewe the following week when the thaw set in. Not one lost and Annie was exultant as they were brought down to the safer inlands, the grassy pastures set directly about the farmhouse where, when the blizzards came again, as they were bound to do, they could be hand fed on the hay cut in the autumn, or even on ash leaves or holly, should it be necessary.

There was a second blizzard in January, worse even than the first, and then another so that the drifts were as high as the eaves of the farmhouse, every window and the door at the front completely blocked. There was the sound of wild geese honking, a great skein moving across the brilliantly blue sky in a huge formation, the leader a little way ahead. Crows picked at the frozen streams for signs of food and ravens searched vainly for twigs since it was coming up to nesting time. Hungry foxes barked across the frozen wastes in desperate need of sustenance. The bitter cold continued, a great frost by day and night, and the snow was crisp and beautiful and could be walked on with ease and safety. Becks and tarns were still frozen over and the lovely tinkling sound which was a constant song in the ears of those who lived beside them, was stilled, a strange silence which was quite unnerving. The crags were covered by shimmering icicles, field gates, if they could have been reached, were frozen and sealed. Bassenthwaite Lake was solid to a depth so great and so thick, people could walk their horses across it and when the wind shifted the fine powdery snow from its surface, it was like mist about those who skated there, twirling across its surface like birds on the wing. Ponies pulling sledges could be seen crossing the vast expanse of snow about it and in Annie's 'inlands' her ewes were heavy with their unborn lambs. From the farmyard where Annie paused to stare in silent wonder the fells stood up proudly, great sleeping monsters of white and blue. In the late afternoon, angry sunsets touched the snow about the farm and glowed across the dark frozen waters of the lake below.

The first intimation of the thaw in March came from the ewes themselves as they lifted their heads and sniffed the air. There was the sound of water tumbling down the beck's rocky course, sky clouds to the west, and lower down the fells, a thin yellow vegetation showed itself. Annie saw storm-cocks perched on a tree, singing of the coming of spring and heard the sweet sharp music of a dipper, perched on a boulder near the waterfall at Dash Falls. The snow melted from around the plants in the farmhouse garden and suddenly there were snowdrops, 'the fair maids of February', revealed a month late.

Easter came and went but those at Browhead were unaware of it, cut off as they were from all contact with those about them. Annie would not have cared had she known since her lambs would be here soon.

"I'm walking up to have a look, Charlie," she said. "D'you want to come? It's a grand day for it." She sniffed the air as her sheep had done, the pungent smell of the new fern and heather already beginning to sprout, a delight to her.

The dogs watched her intently, waiting for the command which meant she would take them with her.

"No, I'll . . . I've things to do." Charlie did not look up from the sledge which, its runners discarded temporarily, he was attempting to patch together.

"What things?"

"Well, this for a start. You really could do with a small cart, you know, and a horse to pull it."

"When I have the money Charlie, in the meanwhile the sledge will have to do."

"And what about the ploughing? It will have to be done any day now . . ."

"Charlie dear, we managed last year and we will again."

"With me pulling the plough you mean."

"Which you did last year with no problem. Look Charlie, don't be down in the dumps. Come with me and we'll look for that fell pony you've been talking about."

She squatted down beside him, trying to win a smile from him. He had been out of sorts lately, she was inclined to think, not exactly short with her and Cat and Phoebe, but sparse with words, ready to spend time in his own room above the cow byre instead of in the warm kitchen with them. The winter had been long and trying. Four people forced by the weather to spend day after day in one another's company and though they had made enough swill baskets, besoms, woollen stockings and lengths of hodden grey wool to open a shop, or so Charlie said, busy from morning to night, it had not been easy for him, she supposed, stuck in the company of three females and two dogs. He did all that was needed out of doors, feeding the hens, collecting the eggs, bringing in peat and wood for the fire which was never allowed to go out, fetching water, checking the ewes who were still on the 'inlands', but he was restless, seeking his own company rather than theirs. When he did sit down in the kitchen, he took on the job of schoolteacher, continuing with the lessons he taught Cat, the Latin and French, showing her how to write in the beautiful copperplate he himself used. She was bright, quick, and was far beyond anything Phoebe had learned, or even what Annie could teach her. She read the Bible fluently, could add up and subtract as quickly as Annie, and the question of where she should go to school must soon be addressed. But for now Annie must get her lamb- ing over, her fields ploughed, her vegetables and crops planted and all the other dozens of jobs which she and Charlie shared. And the idea Charlie had discussed with her was a splendid one and that was to catch and break a wild fell pony, not only to pull a cart when she could afford one, but to draw the plough. She meant to buy a cow and a pig if the ewes did well . . . Oh, God, let the ewes do well . . . please . . .

"You go on, Annie, I'm busy." Charlie's voice was short and he stood up, moving away from her. She straightened slowly, brushing her hands down the legs of her father's trousers. She had an idea about these too, if things went right . . . if . . . if . . .

"What's the matter, Charlie? You seem . . ."

"Nothing, really. There's nothing," but it appeared to her that he was angry about something.

"Of course there is. Won't you tell me? Is it your ribs?"

"No, they're fine now. Mended weeks ago."

"Then what . . . ?"

"Oh, for God's sake, Annie, can you not see I'm busy?" and he strode away in the direction of the barn, the long muffler Cat had knitted for him streaming out at his back.

"Very well then. If you feel like that, I'll go alone."

She went directly up the track behind the house in the direction of Middle Fell and Great Cockup, her crook in her hand and the dogs at her heels. Her sheep were on the higher intake land below the snowline and when Blackie and Bonnie brought them to her it took her no more than two hours to examine each one. They were all fat and healthy and she smiled in satisfaction. A lamb from each would double her flock, please God. Nearly seventy sheep she would have, if her luck held, and with the money she saved and would get from the lambs she sold, she could have that cow and the pig. Her own milk. Her own butter and, when the time was right, bacon.

Her elation carried her on and up moving through the bracken and sprouting heather towards the white-streaked Brockle Crag which was really no more than an untidy fall of rocks. There was a sheep trod leading up beyond it. A wreath of wet mist as white as the insides of a sheep's fleece rolled off the summit of Skiddaw, but she went on. The dogs, knowing they were no longer working, frolicked in and out of the growing vegetation, scenting rabbits, chasing one another, acting the fool since they were still young.

"You'd best call off your dogs, for mine is too old to fight."

His voice came at her from nowhere as she day-dreamed. She had been watching the steep track on which she was climbing, her mind dwelling pleasurably on the spring and summer to come. Blackie and Bonnie had gone on ahead, bounding away towards a group of tall grey-pitted crags and as she approached them, both dogs were standing, muzzles raised, ears flat, eyes fixed on a dog which was doing the same.

Beyond them was Reed Macauley.

It was a year since she had seen him and the shock of it struck her a blow which made her gasp and almost bent her double. Her peaceful heart exploded within her, galloping wildly to a beat which threatened to choke her and she felt the blood drain away from her brain, making her feel faint. She stood rigid and paralysed, her hands which she had brought in reflex up to her midriff, clasped tight together to prevent them shaking. Her mouth dried and she could not have spoken if her life depended on it.

They looked at one another across the hours, the days, the weeks and months which separated them, to the few precious times they had met. The day on the road from Penrith. The first day as she strode out towards Browhead and her inheritance. The time he had brought her the hamper and again on Boxing Day as she had gone to find work in Gillthrop. He had dug her out when it snowed and brought her Blackie and Bonnie, denying it as though she

had insulted him. The day she had been training them and
he had come . . . It was as though it was yesterday when
they had sat together on the drystone wall whilst he drank
her ale. Their love had shone clear and unsullied between
them then as it did now, and slowly her hands unclenched
and fell to her side.

He was dressed in black, nothing about him of contrast
except the snowy waterfall of his cravat. A great riding
cloak covered him from shoulder to ankle thrown back to
reveal the fine broadcloth of his jacket, his waistcoat and
breeches and the glowing black polish to his boots. His
hair was shaggy, not recently cut, falling over his scowling
forehead and the fierce, angry dip of his eyebrows. But
in his eyes was the soft blue of his love for her. His frown
might speak of disapproval but his eyes did not. There
were deep, forbidding lines from his nose to his mouth
and across his forehead but his lips parted, not knowing
whether to smile as he wanted to, or fold into grimness
as he felt they should.

"What are you doing here?" were the first words she
threw at him.

"The same as you, I suppose." His face had closed
somewhat but there was a look of vulnerability about it
which sat strangely on its strength.

"I am checking my sheep."

"As I am."

"I see none."

"And where are yours?"

"Back there . . ." indicating with her hand though her
eyes never left his.

"I see, well, you'd best call off your dogs," beginning
to smile at last, stepping forward, an action to which
Blackie took exception, bristling and baring his teeth.

"Make them behave, Annie," he said patiently and she
called them to her, patting their heads. They dropped on
to their bellies, as Bess did.

"I see I have no need to worry over your safety then,"
roughly.

"I did not know you felt . . . worry."

"Don't, Annie. You know exactly how I feel. Do you want me to say the words . . ."

"No . . . it would be better if we both went back to . . ."

"Better? Yes of course, and back to . . . the people who concern us. My wife and your . . . whatever he is to you. Why do you not marry him? Annie?" His voice had become harsh. "Surely it would make things more . . . comfortable for you. Must you always fly in the face of . . ."

"Marry him?" She let out a short laugh. "Marry who? You don't mean Charlie, do you . . . ?"

"Charlie? Is that his name, and who else would I mean? The man who . . . shares your . . . lives with you at . . ."

He swallowed painfully and the sinews in his neck stood out. The colour beneath his skin flared, then receded, and he clamped his jaw together, his eyes flat now and lifeless.

"Marry Charlie? Why on earth would I want to do that? He and I are friends. Good friends, as Phoebe is." She was clearly so astonished Reed could feel the loosening of the painful constriction around his heart, allowing it to expand, to draw in deep breaths of joy, though of course it made no difference to their situation. None. And yet his gladness could not be contained. He lifted his head, arching his throat, his eyes on the pale blue bowl of the sky above them and the ferocious scowling threat in his face melted away as he lowered his head again to look at her.

"He is not your . . . lover?" His mouth could scarcely form the last word.

"Charlie? Of course he is not."

"Then . . . why does he stay?"

"I told you, we are friends. He needs a home. I need someone to help with the farm. That is all."

He took another step towards her, then caught her waist and pulled her into his arms.

"Annie, my dearest love." His voice shook. "Oh, my darling, I love you, I love you, I thought . . . I thought he . . ."

"Don't . . . don't . . ." She was sharp and awkward,

bitter because this man who could have spoken to her
months ago, when they were both free, was saying the
words she had whispered to herself on so many sleepless
nights. Into the silence of her pillow she had whispered
them, to him who could not hear them and now, when it
was too late, they were in the air about them, soft and
true, she knew that, but no longer allowed.

"Annie . . ."

"Please . . . please, Reed, don't make me . . ."

At once his arms fell away from her and she almost fell.

"You're free to do as you like, my darling, but by Christ,
I cannot bear to lose you again. I've been in hell these last
months, thinking of you with that . . . that man. When I
saw you at Rosley Hill . . . he held your hand . . .
I wanted to knock him to the ground . . . in front of my
wife. I . . . I thought you were lovers . . ."

"Which if we were had nothing to do with you."

"I know." He bent his head in anguish. "I have no right
to feel as I did, as I do, but a man does not choose . . .
where he loves. I married when . . . I shouldn't. You were
. . . with him, I thought so what did it matter? The arrangements had been made. I wanted a son . . . children and
even in that . . ." He trembled visibly since it was well
known in the parish that despite almost a year of marriage
Reed Macauley could not seem to get his wife with child.

"Please, Reed, don't . . . don't tell me of . . . I don't
want to know. I cannot bear to think of it. To see you
. . . with her . . ."

Somehow they had moved toward the rocks, seeking
shelter perhaps from the keen wind which blew up on the
heights, or was it a place to hide, to remain unseen by
those shepherds who roamed the fells in the care of their
flocks. They leaned face to face against the mossy grey
stone and when he took her hand and kissed it, then,
turning it over, put his lips to her wrist, her pulse leaped
to meet them. He wrapped his arms about her again,
holding her gently, lightly, as her body knew it had always
needed, wanted to be held, and she turned her face into
his shoulder.

"I love you, Annie Abbott. Whether you love me or not, and you do not deny it. I love you. It is my curse to love you, my cross to want you and I shall carry it always. I am married and should certainly not be here with you, nor should I love you but I do. Everything brings me back to you. Everywhere I go I see you . . . oh yes, you have not known . . . striding about in that ridiculous outfit . . ."

"I have no other." Her voice was muffled. Her hands were clasped tightly at his back and she could feel the wonder of it, of this day, reach inside her, soothing the wounds, already healing them, those which her life had inflicted on her.

"You will of course, not allow me to buy you one."

"No."

"I thought not."

They were silent then, their bodies for the moment perfectly content to simply lean against one another, two strong people, who despite their separate strength, gained and grew together. But they were man and woman, their bodies long denied this which they had hungered for, and presently they both lifted their heads and looked for a moment into one another's eyes. Moving slowly, they drifted into their first kiss. Delicately, both of them, laying their lips against one another, closed at first, then parting gently until they were breathing into one another's mouths. Moving their heads, their lips clung and trembled and as urgency overtook them, began to suck and bite. Their tongues met and his arms pulled her closer to him. With one hand he threw back his cloak, then undid the buttons, first on his jacket and waistcoat and then hers, pulling her closer to him so that between them was only his shirt and hers. Drawing the cloak about them both, he held her in its shelter as their kisses deepened and warmed.

"Dear Christ," he gasped at last, "don't do this if you don't mean it. This is no dalliance, Annie. I want you, I want your body, but I want *you*, Annie Abbott. Jesus, I don't know how . . ."

"Reed . . . perhaps we should part now . . ." but her lips covered his neck, his smooth cheeks, his eyes, with kisses.

"Never . . . Oh, God, I cannot bear to let you go . . ."

"You must . . . soon . . . Charlie will be looking for . . ."

He pushed her away from him harshly, holding her wrists with hands which hurt and his face snapped with menace.

"Don't . . . don't mention that bastard's name in my presence. If you had not been with him that day . . . the first time when you came back from Rosley . . ."

"What?" She threw back her head angrily and her hair fell about her in living beauty. "You would not have married? Is that what you are saying?"

His eyes burned into hers, hot and hating, then suddenly they lost their madness. His chin sank to his chest. She freed her wrists, putting out her hands to smooth back his hair. Beloved hair, beloved man . . .

"Don't, Annie . . . don't let's quarrel." His voice could barely be heard. He put his face in the hollow of her shoulder resting his lips on the soft skin of her throat and she smoothed the hair at his neck. Their arms were about one another again and for several minutes they said nothing. Their ardent bodies had quietened and carefully she put a hand to his cheek. She laid her mouth on his, kissing him as gently as she would her sleeping daughter, her lips lingering there to retain the feel of his and the clean, sharp tang of his masculine flesh. To carry it home with her, to keep and hold and cherish for she might never see him again.

"I love you, Annie," he said quietly.

"I know. I love you, Reed."

"Thank you . . . for that. When will I see you again?"

"I don't know."

"But I will?"

"Yes."

She felt him relax against her, for the moment satisfied, and wondered how long that would last. He was a man used to his own way, to having what he wanted. He wanted her, but would he be content to meet her up here on the wild fells where no one could see, or would he feel the need, and the right, once he had taken her body, which he would of course, to put her somewhere safe and secret, where no one else could have her? Would he turn sour if she would not allow him to take her away from Browhead, to set her up in a house somewhere, handy of course, and in some style, so that he could visit her whenever he felt the need? Or would he be prepared to let her keep her independence, and her farm, and her way of life as Reed Macauley would continue to do? To be free and unfettered and snapping her fingers at convention, or would he, which was more likely, want *all* of her at *his* beck and call? And what about her body, which wanted his as much as his wanted hers? What of the child it might produce? Would she, because of her female fertility, be forced to live in that secret house of his, rearing her secret child, for though she had already had one, which was illegitimate, it had not been Reed Macauley's and so no slur could be attached to his name, as it had to Annie Abbott's. If it should get about the parish, even a whisper of it, that Annie Abbott was in trouble again, and the fault lay with Reed Macauley, though men might smile and nudge one another, since a man is allowed his little distractions, the women certainly would not. His wife would not. His wife who would, no doubt, one day bear him a child of her own, a legitimate child.

It was no more than a minute or so but in that time these thoughts circled frighteningly inside her head, making her dizzy, for how was she to refuse him what they both wanted, and how was she to acquiesce when the simple honest truth was that so long as they remained in one another's lives, there was no peace for either of them? She loved him. She had admitted that to herself a long time ago, admitted it, accepted it and, believing that they could be nothing to one another, had locked him, and her love, safely away in the tender recess of her heart where he would always be.

Now he was in her arms, his body quickening against
hers, his mouth moving warmly, demandingly against her
throat, his lips dipping down into the neck of her shirt
where the top button was undone. His breathing had
become more ragged as he pulled her closer into his arms.
His head rose and his mouth closed over hers and her
hands flew to his hair to pull him and his questing lips
deeply into hers.

"Dear God . . . I love you . . . want you . . . need to
take you here, now, before you change your mind and
go . . ."

"No, not here . . ." but her hands clutched at him
and the anguished thoughts of moments ago were flung
carelessly away for how could they matter when his
rough hands were invading her clothing, cupping her bare
breasts, pressing her hard nipples into his palms. He was
not gentle as he nailed her to the stone behind her, his
need to possess her, somehow, in any way he could, to
make her his, to put his mark on her, tipping them both
over the edge of sanity. He loved her so, had suffered in
his love for her, for so long that he must assuage it *now*
and hang the consequences. Their lips clung together
whilst their hands were busy with buttons and belts,
neither of them prepared for the ferocity of love and
passion, of tenderness and need which vibrated from his
body to hers, from hers to his. Folly, oh yes, but such
sweet folly, as her breasts were sweet in his hands
and hers found the silken smooth mat of his body hair
which ran down his flat stomach to where his penis jutted
arrogantly, demandingly . . .

"These bloody trousers . . ." she heard him mutter and
as the ice-cold roughness of the stone at her back struck
her violently exposed buttocks, her reason returned,
the sense and sanity and balance which, except for a
moment when she was fourteen years old, had never left
her.

"NO . . . no . . ." The cry which tore from her throat
soared high into the air above the crags and at once all
three dogs were on their feet. Blackie and Bonnie who

had been dozing, at the same time keeping one eye on the strange animal and the other on the man who was with their mistress, growled deep in their throats, sensing the danger but not awfully sure from which direction it was to come. They began to advance on Reed who had straightened slowly as Annie struggled against him and when he turned away to lean his back on the grey rock, they confronted him threateningly, waiting for a word from Annie.

She had turned her back on him, re-arranging her clothing, sweeping back her hair and thrusting it in a tangled mass beneath the old hat of her father's which she had found hanging on a nail in the barn.

"Lie down Blackie, Bonnie . . ." and they did so. Bess looked questioningly at Reed, then seeing nothing to threaten him, lay down beside them.

"You don't trust me." The words which he flung at her were bitter.

"I trust you to do what you think is right." Hers were low.

"What does that mean, for God's sake?"

She hesitated before she spoke, not looking at him.

"I know you love me. I have always known. I love you. I have always known that too. I have wanted . . . this . . . I still want it . . . but not like this. Held against a wall like a . . ."

"I did not mean to offend you with my . . . lust." He was stiff, vibrant with anger and frustrated need.

"Reed . . . try to understand. Give me time."

"To do what?"

"To . . . to think what this is to mean to us."

"I know what it means to me, Annie. I want you. I want you to be mine. To belong to me. I did not mean to happen . . . what almost happened here . . . but when you . . . allowed it . . ."

"I want it too, Reed." Her cry of love was urgent and her dogs stood up again. The sky had clouded over, brought low with the rain which threatened. The wind had freshened, sighing over the stiff grass, bending it, ruffling the coats of the dogs. She shivered and with a low groan he pulled her to him again, sheltering her in his arms, warming her chilled body with his own.

"My love, my love, what are we to do?"

22

In May, Margaret Mounsey, known to her family from
being a baby as Mim, married Ben Postlethwaite and went
to live with him and his widowed mother on their farm
up Binsey way. A week later, her own mother, Agnes
Mounsey, who had, from being a young girl, worked as
hard as any woman in the parish of Bassenthwaite,
dropped dead on her own kitchen floor, the scrubbing
brush and bucket in her hand with which she had been
about to 'go over it' crashing down beside her. Even at
the last she carried the implements of her labour with her
and her tearful daughter, Sally Garnett had the idea that
they should go in the coffin with her, to which her truculent
husband replied 'that any more daft remarks like that and
he'd give her a clip round't lug.'

When Annie hesitantly knocked on the door of Upfell
Farm it was Bert who answered it. She had told no one
she was going, not even Phoebe and certainly not Charlie,
who was quartering and splitting oak logs in readiness for
the first step in swill making. They would both have been
horrified had they known, wanting to come with her, convinced that she would be abused, spat upon maybe, but
definitely humiliated in some way, for Bert Garnett made
no secret of the fact that he thought Annie Abbott should
be whipped out of the parish at a cart tail, especially since
she had taken up with that fancy man. Over-protective
both Charlie and Phoebe were since they well knew that
she was thought of as a pariah in the district and was
received by no one. She was still dressed in her father's
clothes for it was all she had though in her chest at home
she had a guinea saved with which, when her lambs were
sold at backend and she felt that tiny bit closer to 'safety',

she meant to purchase a length or two of good, *coloured*,
woollen cloth. A rich green, or a tawny amber, perhaps a
deep sapphire blue. There was a piece of hodden grey
cloth she herself had woven resting in the press next to
her savings and before winter she meant to make it up
into a well-fitting pair of breeches and a jacket, warm and
practical. But the bright woollen gown was one of the
dreams she held to her amongst the many she had. In
the meanwhile she continued to wear the increasingly
threadbare trousers, shirt and jacket which had been
Joshua Abbott's.

It was Charlie who told her of Aggie Mounsey's death.
They had seen the wedding party the week before going
past at the back of Browhead. A true Cumberland wedding
where each of the men rode to church on his horse or
pony but when the ceremony was over, raced back to
Upfell with a girl, a guest of the bride's, up behind him.
It was said that the young lady who rode with the winner
would be a bride herself by the year's end. There was a
great to-do, guests coming and going, most in the last
stages of inebriation, great gales of lunatic laughter far into
the night, for Aggie Mounsey wanted her girl to go off in
great style. A splendid feast, singing and dancing, the party
not dispersing until Mim and Ben Postlethwaite, for that
one night, were in Aggie's bed. All the guests saw them
there, of course, with a great deal of coarse ribaldry,
standing round the bed until she had 'thrown her stocking'.
She would keep her back to them casting the stocking
over her left shoulder and the girl who caught it would be
the next bride. It was not quite clear whether she would
beat to the altar the one who had come home first on the
sweating pony!

The man clattering by the back of the farmhouse the
following week on his lanky raw-boned horse, who was
the undertaker for the district, though he did not approve
of Annie Abbott, nor of the chap who lived with her, could
not help but shout out the electrifying news that, a week
after her daughter's wedding, Aggie Mounsey would be
coming this way in her coffin.

Bert Garnett, one hand on the door latch, the other in his pocket, his mouth falling open in astonishment, looked Annie up and down, from the rich fall of her tumbled hair which was not covered, to her slim trousered legs and wooden-soled clogs. His eyes were like small rats, running across her breasts and waist and hips, narrowing to a lascivious gleam as they came to rest on the former. His loose wet lips parted in a nasty smile and he licked them coarsely, suggestively.

"What does tha' want 'ere, Annie Abbott?" he said loudly as though to let those somewhere in the depths of the farmhouse know of his displeasure, but he continued to smile and run his eyes over her body like a farmer at the market considering a cow he might decide to buy.

Annie gritted her teeth and held the hot, flowing tide of her temper in check. Though she had little time for Bert Garnett, despite the lifts he had given her into Keswick, she remembered what Sally had said when Annie had returned to Browhead, about how she and her mother had nursed Lizzie and Joshua when they were dying. They had done everything she herself should have done, had she been there, making sure her parents' passing was peaceful, that they were not alone and when they had gone, giving them a decent funeral. They had sat with the corpses until the 'coffining'. The coffins themselves had been carried on the 'corpse road', down past Hause and along the track to St Bridget's by the lake, but it had been the woman now dead who had seen to it all and Annie could not forget that. She might be rebuffed, probably would, by those married women who would already be 'laating' or sitting round Aggie Mounsey's body, but she could not do anything else but offer the Mounsey family, particularly Sally, whatever help or comfort she might need of Annie Abbott.

"Can I see Sally, Bert?" Annie kept her voice low, courteous.

"What for?" Bert grinned, knowing that no one but Annie saw the expression on his face. He was tickled pink that his mother-in-law was gone for though Mim Mounsey,

Mim Postlethwaite now, had a small share in the farm, most of it was his, well his and Sally's, but *she* was nowt 'a pound and would do just what he told her to do. And he enjoyed the feeling of power he now had in what Aggie Mounsey had always considered to be *her* farmhouse, and in the knowedge that he could keep Annie Abbott cooling her heels on *his* doorstep. He could do as he pleased. Ask her in or tell her to go to hell, if he had a mind.

The thought made him magnanimous. He turned shouting over his shoulder.

"Sal, there's someone here to see thi'."

"Who is it, Bert?"

"Come to t' door, an' see, tha' daft cow, but before tha' does, fetch me a jug of ale."

It was several minutes before Sally's face appeared in the doorway, pale and tear-streaked, her jutting belly testifying once again to Bert's 'manhood'. Annie had heard, through the half-open doorway, through which she could see nothing but a portion of Aggie Mounsey's well-scrubbed kitchen flags, Bert's indelicate fumbling with his wife's person and the several loose-lipped kisses he had bestowed on her. She knew perfectly well it was done for her benefit and Sally's whispered embarrassment as she somewhat timidly protested since Bert did not take kindly to rebuff, was clearly heard. The flesh round Sally's mouth and chin was red and chafed for Bert wore a scratchy, three-day stubble on his chin. Sally was already in the deepest black of mourning, the dress she had on, the one her mother had worn since the day her husband, Jack Mounsey, had died. Fortunately Aggie's girth had been wider than her daughter's, but still it strained dangerously across Sally's distended stomach.

"Annie," Sally's uncertain face lit up for a moment and she was ready to reach out and draw her into the kitchen. Then her hand fell back to fiddle with her apron and she looked over her shoulder to where Bert was evidently still quaffing his ale.

"It's all right Sally, I didn't come to . . . well, I only wanted to say how sorry I was to hear about your mother.

You and she were kind to mine and my father, and if there's anything I can do for you . . ."

Before his wife could answer, the cheery voice of Bert Garnett spoke from his comfortable chair by the fire. "There's nowt this family want from thou, Annie Abbott."

"I'm offering nothing to you, Bert Garnett, only Sally," Annie shouted. She put out her hand and took Sally's. "Are the women here laating?"

"Aye, they come up from t' village this morning." Sally's woe-begone face worked convulsively and sad tears slid down her plump cheeks for how was she to stand living alone with *him* now that her Mam was gone?

"Don't cry, Sally. You still have Mim," for who knew better than Annie the nature of Bert Garnett. Though he had made no move on her when he had sat beside her on the cart, during the long ride from Keswick to Hause, nor on the occasions he had 'called in' at Browhead, she had known that eventually he would. It was in his gleaming, greedy eyes and falsely smiling mouth, and though it was very evident that Sally suffered his nightly fumblings, he would not be averse to the same with Annie Abbott, his attitude had plainly said.

"Aye, but she's up near Binsey."

"I'm only a step away, Sal. You're welcome any time, night or day." This last in a whisper.

"Eeh, that's lovely of tha', Annie, but . . . well, that chap that's with tha'. Bert'd give me what for if I was to . . ."

"I know, but the offer is always there. If ever you can get away . . ." meaning perhaps when Bert went to market ". . . come and have a cup of tea. Bring the children . . ."

"There'll be five of un next month." But Sally's eyes had brightened at the thought of Annie 'only a step away', a glowing light in the long dark tunnel which yawned before her without her strong, outspoken and resolute Mam to stand between her and her bad-tempered husband.

"I can see that." Annie's eyes went to Sally's waistline, narrowing in that gleaming golden smile which had so fascinated Sally when they had been re-united two and a half years ago. "Now don't forget."

"I won't Annie . . ."

"What the bloody 'ell are the two of thi' whispering about?" Bert jerked the door open, almost pulling his enormously pregnant wife off her feet. As the door widened the room was revealed. At the table sat four children. Annie recognised Sammy who would be nearly five now, she thought, and Janie who had been twelve months old when last Annie had seen her. There was another little girl who must be the new baby Sally had been expecting then, Emma, Annie seemed to remember, a toddler her-self now, and another boy strapped in a chair, who could be no more than nine or ten months old. Dear God . . . poor, poor Sally. In her bad moments, Annie often thought there was no woman who had more to bear than herself, but surely nothing could be worse than having to suffer the nightly advances of Bert Garnett.

"Nothing, Bert. Annie was just sayin' how sorry she . . ."

"Well, she's said it so let's shut bloody door," which he did.

Annie and Reed had met three times since their dramatic reunion on the boulder-strewn slope of Broad End. Each time it had not been planned, as the first meeting had not been planned and each time they had moved, thankfully, into one another's arms as though the action, the clinging, the closeness, the simple joining and twining of their bodies against one another, gave them both air to breathe, sweet water to drink, food to eat, sun on their sun-starved faces, life. They did not make love. They had done nothing from which they could not, with honour, both withdraw. They were content, it seemed, after the wild passion of their first meeting, merely to be together, neither wishing to disturb the sudden sweet harmony which flowed between them. She was happy, blindly, rapturously happy, blissful in the sweet, secret knowledge that perhaps today, or tomorrow, when she went with her dogs and her shepherd's crook to check on her growing lambs, she might see him. And for now, that was enough. Each time they met they made no plans to meet again. They would sit together in the sunshine, Reed's back resting against a rock, hers against his chest, his arms about her, his cheek against her wind-blown hair. They talked, she could not remember afterwards what about. His lips would capture hers, but with a loving patience which confounded her, soft, gentle, so tender, so . . . so moderate, she was aware that Reed Macauley was, for the first time in his life, humbled by an emotion stronger than his own demanding need. That his love was true and selfless. He was an individualist, an opportunist, self-indulgent and arrogant, but what he felt for her had softened him and his fear of losing her had awakened a quality in him which, perhaps again for the first time, had him putting another before himself. Maybe it would not last for he was a man, and his masculine sexual curiosity, his desire, could sweep away this gentleness in the necessity of satisfying his own male loins.

"Do you need anything? Anything at all?" he asked her, begging her to want some tremendous, difficult to come by thing that would stretch him to the utmost to get for her.

"No, nothing. I am managing very well. My lambs are thriving . . ."

"I know, I've seen them." He smiled into her hair.

"Are you spying on me?" She turned to look up at him, her lips beneath his, and when he took them, she sighed into his mouth with the sheer joy of it.

"Keeping an eye on you," he said when he could. "You won't let me do anything else for you, or give you anything, not even some trumpery bit of jewellery, so I do what I can by making sure your sheep are as fit as mine. They are grazing together on the same fell after all."

"Thank you."

"Dear God, if there was only something I could do to make your life easier."

"There is."

At once he turned her in his arms, straining into her face in his passion to give her the moon, the stars, his own heart plucked out of his breast, any of these easy things but not the one thing he wanted to present her with, his name.

"What? Say it, anything."

"My daughter."

"Yes . . . ?" He leaned back, disappointed, for what was Cat Abbott to him and what could he give to her that would satisfy *his* obsession with this woman.

"I want her to go to school."

"Well, that's easy enough. There is one in Gillthrop."

"No, she is clever. Charlie has taught her . . ."

"Goddammit woman, don't talk to me of that man. Have you no heart that you must mention him in my presence?" He stood up, thrusting her from him and his dog and hers stood up with him. All three animals were still uneasy with one another and it took very little to unsettle them. They sensed the tension and anger in him and Blackie raised his muzzle warningly.

"And you can tell that bloody dog of yours to back off or I'll take my whip to him."

"You'll do no such thing, Reed Macauley. They don't like your attitude any more than I do. I'm sorry if it upsets you when I speak of Charlie but I thought, unlike the rest of this damned community, that you understood my relationship with him. I have told you before that he and Phoebe are my only friends, except perhaps for Sally Garnett. There is nothing . . . *nothing* between us. Do you think I would be up here with you if there was? I met him at Rosley when I went to buy sheep since no one at the Keswick market would sell me any. I needed a ram and he helped me. The men there are as pig-headed as those around here and when it was discovered I was female despite my 'disguise' . . ." indicating her masculine clothing, "they wouldn't sell to me either. Charlie did it for me, and helped me to bring the tup and the ewes home. And that is all."

"*All!*" He stamped up and down, his boots crushing the tussocky grass and a clump of celandine which grew there. The wind lifted his tumbled hair from his frowning forehead and he brushed it back impatiently. His eyebrows scowled ferociously over his piercing blue eyes and it was obvious that peace had gone leaving jealousy, and his own anger at suffering it.

"Dammit, Annie. You make light of this ridiculous 'get-up' you wear but can you blame men who only *deal* with other men, when they mistrust it, and you? They don't know what to make of it, or you. They are used to their women in decent skirts and bonnets, keeping their place in the home as they have done for centuries. Then you come along, so obviously female despite this . . . this bloody outfit you wear, and they are distracted from the purpose of their transaction which is to make a profit. Not only are they insulted by what they see as your immodesty, they are seriously affronted by their own need to stare at your . . . attractions. Which, by the way brings me to the subject of how they *discovered* you were a woman and not a man! Oh, yes . . ."

"It was my hair, dammit. What do you think I did? Exposed my . . . my body to them? My blasted hat fell off . . ."

"Fell off! *Fell off!* Or did you take if off to show Charlie . . ."

"What the devil are you insinuating, Reed Macauley? Are you saying . . . ?"

"Dear sweet Christ, I don't know *what* I'm saying, woman." Again he twisted and turned in his savage distress. "I only know I cannot bear to think of you living under the same roof with him, with . . . *any man*. . . no matter how innocent. *Yes! . . . Yes! . . .*" He held up his hands in acquiescence. ". . . I know it is innocent since I know you well enough by now to understand you would dishonour neither yourself, nor me, nor him. I know you love me, Annie Abbott, I can see it in your eyes. Even now, though your face is furious and you're ready to black my eye for my impudence. Forgive me . . . I cannot help the way I am, Annie . . . my Annie . . . don't let's quarrel . . ."

"You began it by inferring that Charlie and I were more to each other than friends." She slapped away his placatory hand but he grasped her forearm and pulled her roughly to him.

"Only because I'm so jealous, dammit. I want you . . ."

"You could have had me. We were both of us free."

"Aah . . . don't . . ." He bowed his head in sudden desperation and his hands fell to his side. His stance was one of such hopelessness that at once she put her arms about him, dragging him to her in an agony of remorse.

"Reed . . ."

"I know . . ." His words were muffled in her hair. His arms rose again and held her to him. "I know . . . Christ . . . do you think I have not regretted it a hundred times since. I thought . . . you were with him . . . they said you were . . . he was living at the farm . . ."

"He needed work. I needed help . . . that's all."

"He is . . ."

"*That is all*, Reed."

"I should have married you when I had the chance but . . ."

". . . But I was . . . who I am." Her words were soft and they said she did not reproach him.

"Do you think that would have mattered? As my wife you would have been accepted no matter what you had done." His voice was arrogant and sure. Was he not Reed Macauley? One of the Macauleys who were 'statesmen', men of standing and wealth in these parts. There would not have been a hostess in the parish who would have shut her door in *his* wife's face, or if she had, her husband might have found himself in a poor way of business. So many owed him something, money, a favour, a bit of business put their way, and it would not pay them to insult him or his wife. Under his shelter and protection Annie Abbott would have been treated as a young queen.

"Perhaps."

"There is no perhaps about it. They would not have dared . . ."

"Does it matter now, my darling? Really, does it matter? It is too late. You are committed elsewhere and I can see no . . . future for us . . ."

"Don't say that." He clasped her to him in an agony of despair pressing her face into the hollow of his neck beneath his straining jaw line. "Don't . . . don't . . ."

"How can I help it, Reed? I've . . . been so . . . happy . . . meeting you again up here. It was so . . . unexpected. I did not allow myself to think about what was to happen tomorrow, or next week. It was enough to just be with you, to touch you and hear you speak. I blinded myself to everything else and turned a deaf ear to the voice of reason which whispered that this was madness . . ."

"If you are trying to say we should not meet again I won't allow it. I will not. We can make some . . ." He paused suddenly as though aware that he must tread carefully with his next words.

She lifted her head and looked up into his strong but vulnerable face. He was unsteady with the tumult which was beginning to overwhelm him. The angle of his hard, fighting jaw jutted ominously and the taut muscles in his throat worked. The flesh of his face was tanned and smooth, but there were tell-tale lines about his eyes and mouth which she had not noticed before.

"Listen to me," he growled, his truculent jaw threatening anyone who stood between himself and what he wanted. "It's time we talked, *really* talked about the future. We *do* have one you know, whatever you might say. I need you. I need you in my life. I want to make a commitment to you . . ."

"How can that be, Reed?"

"It could be arranged, if you'd agree."

"To what?"

"Well . . . a house somewhere. You and your daughter. She could go to school as you want her to. You would, both of you, be secure. I would look after you and there would be no need for you to slave on that blasted farm.

You could sell it. Keep the money, as your own . . ."

"Thank you." Her tone was formal.

". . . invest it so that you would be independent . . ." though he would not like that, of course since Annie Abbott's total dependence on him was what he was after.

"Thank you, Reed, but I cannot accept your offer." Her voice was cool and she moved backwards, putting space and air and a certain constraint between them. He loved her. He was suffering because of it and though the day was mild, she felt him shiver beneath the good broadcloth of his jacket. He turned away from her jerkily, his face tight, moving to stand on a flat grey rock, his hands clenched in the pockets of his jacket, his eyes on the lake below. The surface of the water changed constantly, becoming ruffled where the breeze touched it. The sun stretched a path of gilt across it on which, as the water moved, an explosion of diamonds scattered and burst. He saw none of it. Its beauty and the beauty of the hazed peaks which stretched on and on into infinity, meant nothing as Reed Macauley, loving truly for the first time, struggled with the realisation that this was one woman he could not have. She could sense the tension in him even with a dozen feet between them, the tight-clenched pain and the absolute determination to overcome it, and her.

"Christ, this is bloody ridiculous. You say there is nothing . . . there is no other man in your life and yet you won't allow me into it. I cannot bear to see the way you are treated by the people in the area, nor the struggle you are having to make . . . to turn Browhead into a decent farm. Look at you . . ." He turned violently, his face black and snarling, the menace in him dangerous, his hand raised as though ready to strike her. He passed it across his face. "Look at you dressed like some confounded vagrant, your hands worse than a labourer's and your face as brown as a gypsy. And there's no need for it, Annie. I can look after you. After *both* of you, even that skivvy you took in. You'll want for nothing – servants, a carriage, fine clothes and jewellery. A house wherever you like . . ."

"Where, I suppose, you will visit me whenever it is convenient?"

"Confound it Annie, I can do no more. It would be a good life for you and the child. You could be the widow of . . ."

"I would be a whore. Your whore."

"Don't! Don't say that. I love you . . ."

". . . and if you stopped loving me? If it should become tedious to get on your horse and travel the ten, fifteen miles, or perhaps more, I would need to hide myself to keep your reputation untarnished, would you say 'Oh, to hell with it, I'll go another day!' Whilst I and any children we may have as a result of this 'arrangement' will sit and wait patiently until . . ."

"*No*, no, never. You mean more to me than . . ."

"I would be no more to you than a mistress. Loved perhaps but condemned to a life of secrecy and deceit."

"Dammit to hell, Annie."

"No Reed, *no*! I can't do it. I just cannot do it. Already I am an outcast in this parish, but despite that I am gaining a measure of success. My flock is growing . . ."

"Less than a hundred sheep." His voice was contemptuous, made so by his bitter disappointed love.

"Don't sneer at me or my efforts, Reed." She was doing her best to keep her temper, but her eyes which had shown concern for his pain, had begun to glow hotly. "I've worked hard . . ."

"There is no need for it, Annie." His voice was pleading.

"Yes, there is. I want to do this, Reed. I *must* do it. I . . . I love you . . ."

"Then let me . . ."

"I love you and had you . . . well, if things had been different, I would have gladly shared your life though how the good folk of Bassenthwaite would have taken to . . ."

"For Christ's sake, Annie, don't turn me away. Don't turn the idea down without thinking about it. What about Penrith? No one knows you there." His voice was boyish, shaking in his eagerness, and he grasped her hands, holding them between his own, then bringing them tenderly to his mouth where he covered them with kisses whilst his vivid blue eyes held hers, the love in them as soft and tender as those of a mother gazing at an adored child. He was not a man to beg. His nature was to take whatever he wanted and if he could not take it then he was prepared to pay for it, at *his price*, naturally. His nature challenged hers, willing her to give in and yet he was making a decent offer to curb that arrogance in himself that demanded his own way in all things.

"Take me seriously, my darling, for I don't give up easily. If you don't like the idea of Penrith then we could go north, or south. You see I am saying 'we'. We would go together, travel as man and wife. Make a home together. I would come back to Long Beck just as often, and for as long as it was needed, to keep the gossips away from . . . from my wife. I could run my business from wherever we went. And the farm. A factor and half a dozen good shepherds. Bloody hell, woman, do you not see what I am willing to give up for you?"

There was a long moment of strangled silence, then, with a familiar, defensive growl, he took her by the forearms and shook her.

"Godammit, Annie. Tell me you agree. I'm . . . I cannot stand this need I have of you. Say you'll come, say it . . . say it . . ." and he shook her more violently.

"I cannot." Her voice was soft.

"You can, you *will*."

"No, Reed. I cannot."

"Why, for Christ's sake, why?"

"I don't know."

"That's no bloody answer."

"It's the only one I can give you now."

He threw her from him, his violence so close to the surface it was in danger of breaking through and attacking her. Blackie and Bonnie were ready to fling themselves on him, their muzzles raised warningly, and his old dog placed herself between them and her master.

"Then there's no more to be said."

"No."

"I shan't give up."

Why was she so pleased to hear him say that, she wondered desolately as she watched him click his fingers to his dog and move stiffly in the direction of his mare. She wouldn't change her mind! Ever. What she had feared at their first meeting a few weeks ago had happened. He had not been satisfied with what they now had. He wanted more, as *she* wanted more so was it to be wondered at? She loved him so much, so much she wanted nothing more than to call his name, to open her arms and hold them out to him. To go with him wherever he wanted to take her, but she couldn't. She didn't really know why since she already had a reputation as a harlot so why not husband stealer, or even worse, but she couldn't.

He mounted his mare and inside her, just beneath her left breast the pain was unbearable where her heart broke. He did not look back at her as he spoke.

"I'll make arrangements for the child," he said, then with a soft murmur to his dog, put his heels to the mare's side and threw them both down a length of scree with an abandon so wild and dangerous the animal whinnied in fear.

Annie sank to her knees and bowed her head.

23

Why did her body ache as though she had been stricken with some dreadful debilitating illness or as if she had been given a sound beating with a cudgel, her dazed mind wondered as she staggered down the steep hill at the back of Browhead. She seemed to hurt all over, even to the roots of her hair, which was ridiculous really, since it was her heart and soul and mind which had been badly damaged this day. It was hard to put one foot in front of the other and twice she fell as she descended Broad End. The water in Barkbeth Gill was icy cold as it crept over her clogs, when she missed her footing crossing it, and though it was high summer she shivered, the spasms rippling across her skin in cold feathers.

There was no sign of Charlie in the old shed where once her father had worked on his 'swiller's horse'. Lengths of straight-grained knot-free oak saplings leaned neatly against the wall and dozens of logs had already been quartered with the lat-axe prior to placing them in the cast-iron boiler where they would stew overnight. The three of them, Phoebe, herself and Charlie had already fashioned several dozen swills and Annie meant to make the journey to the coastal town of Whitehaven soon to sell them, for the baskets were used in the coaling of ships. Thirty pounds of coal each one could hold, hauled on the backs of the crew, basket by basket until the coal hold was full. In the lull between planting, lambing and harvest, and the sheep fairs where she hoped to sell her unwanted male lambs, they could make many more baskets, selling them wherever there was a need. She was also toying with the idea of producing charcoal from the juniper trees in her coppice wood since she could not afford to waste the utilisation of any crop which might make her money. The gunpowder manufacturers of Westmorland and Cumberland would buy the charcoal from her, for it was a major ingredient in the making of explosives. Not that she had ever done any charcoal burning, nor even seen the process, but she could learn, she told herself, since she intended to leave no stone unturned, no avenue unexplored in her aim to make Browhead into a successful, profit-making farm.

Phoebe was at the table, a fine mist of flour dancing and drifting in the shaft of sunlight which came through the window and fell across her. She was kneading dough, her big-knuckled hands folding it over and over on itself, then pushing her clenched fist into its centre. She had watched Mrs Holme at The Packhorse in Keswick one market-day morning whilst she waited for Annie and Mr Lucas who were moving from stall to stall buying provisions. Mrs Holme was a good-natured woman and on seeing Phoebe's interest as she peeped through the inn's kitchen window, had called to her cheerfully to 'come inside'.

"Tha's Annie Abbott's girl aren't tha?" she had asked, bearing no ill-will it seemed towards Annie who had left The Packhorse rather suddenly a couple of years ago.

Phoebe admitted that she was and within minutes had mastered the art of breadmaking and memorised the ingredients with which it was made. Though she had found it a terrible strain, and indeed had hardly done so, to learn and retain the letters of the alphabet, Mrs Holme had only to tell her once what went into this or that dish and it was in her head for ever with no need to even write it down. She had been given a brief sketch of several of Mrs Holme's favourite recipes which Phoebe had tried out on her 'family', finding to her own amazement and their delight, that she had the makings of a decent cook. A talent for serving up the best oatcakes Annie said she had ever eaten. Her porridge was the creamiest and her tatie-pot, the tastiest, and though, as she well knew, she had no gift with words or letters or numbers as Cat did, and no interest if she was honest, she loved the creating of some splendid dish, many out of her own imaginative brain, with which to please Annie, Mr Lucas and Cat.

"Tha' can tekk them clogs off for I've just scrubbed them there flags, Annie Abbott," she said tartly as Annie came through the door, her eyes flickering from the dough to Annie's feet and back again. "An' them dogs can stop outside an' all." This was Phoebe's domain in the 'fire-house' as the kitchen was still often called. She had taken over not only the kitchen but the whole farmhouse to Annie's relief, scrubbing and dusting and polishing, throwing open windows and filling the place with wild flowers and her own, home-made pot-pourri, derived from the dried petals of roses and lavender and larkspur. She burnished the copper bowls and pans to a fine glow with wood ash, fed the basket of kittens which miraculously had been found one morning, mewing and suckling around the complacently purring Dandy, who had turned out to be female after all, and whenever the weather was clear there would be a line of sparklingly white bedding and undergarments pegged out on her line across the yard. She had a passion for cleanliness, not only about the farmhouse but in herself, washing, starching and ironing the aprons once worn by Lizzie Abbott and had even taken to wearing the frilled cap women of Lizzie's generation had worn. It covered her dark glossy hair completely and Annie had pondered on whether it was an unconscious defence against the eyes of men, of *man* who had once tried to misuse her. Her hair was her one claim to beauty.

"Nay, what's to do?" Phoebe said on seeing Annie's face. She reached for the cloth to wipe her hands for even in the direst emergency, her mind worked to the pattern of cleanliness she had set herself. "What's happened to thi'?"

"Nothing, Phoebe, I'm just tired."

"Give over. Ah've seen thi' tired when tha've clipped a dozen sheep, an' tha' didn't look as bad as tha' does now. Have tha' seen a ghost?"

"Perhaps I have. A ghost of what might have been." Annie's voice was low but she did her best to smile. The effort was agony but how could she tell this innocent, inexperienced girl of the torment of love, of bitter despairing love that reached, in one moment, the pinnacle of rapture only to be dashed on the hard, damaging crag of despair in the next.

"Nay, I don't know what tha's talking about, love."

"No, I don't suppose you do, Phoebe, and what's more, neither do I."

"But where've tha' bin?" Phoebe sat down on the settle next to Annie and leaned forward to peer anxiously into her face. "Ah thought tha' was off up Broad End to tekk a look at lambs."

"Yes, but . . . I saw more than the lambs, Phoebe. I saw my own future, and I didn't like it."

"Nay, tha've lost me, Annie. What future's that then?" Phoebe screwed up her plain little face in an effort to understand. Her own future was so bright and rosy. She asked nothing more than to be allowed to stay here in this lovely kitchen and serve her family, Annie, Cat and Mr Lucas in exactly the way she had been doing for the past two years. She often thought she had died and gone to Heaven, really she did, remembering her life as it had been with the old missus, worked her poor fingers to the bone she had, which she didn't mind in the least since she didn't exactly sit about on her bum all day long here at Browhead. But at Browhead she was needed, respected for what she did and . . . aye she would say it . . . she was loved. She and Cat thought the world of one another and as for Annie, well there was no one in the world like Annie, for she'd given life to Phoebe, and a fond affection which wrapped about her like a warm blanket in the winter.

"It's hard to explain, Phoebe," she said now, her eyes faraway and hazed, her poor face all screwed up as though something bad hurt her somewhere. Just like it had on the day that chap . . . what was his name . . . him from Long Beck . . . had sat on the wall with her and drunk a jug of ale. They'd quarrelled. Phoebe had heard them and then he'd gone clattering off on that there horse of his and Annie had . . . had . . . And what about the time when

Annie had gone to Rosley? Before Mr Lucas had come. That there chap had ridden off with a face like thunder when Phoebe had told him where Annie was and since Mr Lucas had moved in he'd never been near. Phoebe had loved no man, and never would. No man had loved Phoebe, and never would. Phoebe was convinced of that. Just as some women are made for loving and having babies, others were not and Phoebe knew she was one of the latter. Not that she hadn't the capacity for loving in her, oh no, for didn't she love her 'family', but not for a man. But she knew it when she saw it and Annie loved him from up Long Beck and she reckoned, though it was said he was married now, that he loved Annie.

"What's to do, Annie?" she asked softly, hesitantly for she was not one to poke her nose into other people's business, even in that of her beloved friend.

"Nothing new, Phoebe. Just some bad dreams come to haunt me again."

"What have tha' done today, love? Did tha' meet anyone up Broad End?" It was said diffidently. "Tell me if you have a mind to but I'll not be offended if you don't. I'm here should you need me." Her face was awkwardly soft and her hand touched Annie's with a feather of tenderness.

"Oh, Phoebe . . . what am I to do?"

"About . . . him? It's . . . him from Long Beck isn't it?"

"Yes, him from Long Beck. Reed Macauley, a married man with whom I've been foolish enough to fall in love."

Phoebe sighed in deep, deep sympathy, her pale blue eyes fixed on Annie with the soulful look of a devoted dog. Without being aware of it since she was still somewhat constrained in the giving and receiving of demonstrations of affection, she clasped Annie's slim hands between her own. They were big-boned, wide, made for hard work, but gentle and soothing just the same.

"I thought it were him. I've seen the way tha' looks at one another an' he were like a man demented when tha' went off to Rosley Hill that time. But what's happened today? He's not hurt thi' has he?" At once Phoebe was like a mother hen whose chick has been threatened, her

ruffled feathers wild and furious, her beak ready to peck
out the eyes of the predator. If Reed Macauley had hurt
Annie Abbott, which, to Phoebe, meant what that randy
sod had almost done to her in Keswick, and would have
done but for Annie, then he'd Phoebe to reckon with.
She'd take her kitchen knife, the one she had sharpened
only that morning and cut off that foolish but dangerous
bit of flesh which dangled between his legs and stuff it in
his mouth, so she would.

"No, he's not hurt me, Phoebe, not physically, but he's
not done my heart much good."

"How's that, then, Annie?"

"He really does love me, you know." For a moment her
face was transformed to an unearthly rapturous beauty.
Her skin flushed to rose and her eyes were great drowning
brown pools in which liquid gold ran, then it all flowed
away, leaving her white and drained. "But he wants to
change me. Turn me into a doll for him to play with whenever he has a fancy for it. Do you know what I'm saying,
Phoebe?"

"Well . . ."

"To put me in a doll's house. Dress me in silken gowns
and expensive jewels and when he has the time, he'll come
calling . . ." Her voice faded away on the last word and
her clouded eyes closed and from between the lids fat
tears oozed, hanging for a moment on her lashes before
sliding across her cheeks.

"Eeh, love, don't . . . don't . . ." Phoebe could not bear
it. She just could not bear to see the pain Annie was
suffering and in an uncharacteristic gesture, she swept her
into her own strong arms, pulling her close, doing her best
to get Annie's head to her own shoulder which was difficult
since Annie was almost a foot taller than herself.

"Don't cry lass, don't cry. See, tha's none of 'em worth
it, none of 'em."

"I know that, Phoebe, sweet Jesus, don't I know that.
My father was a sanctimonious old bugger who worked
me like a horse. Cat's father wanted nothing from me but
to get into my drawers, and when he did, and made me

pregnant, ran off and left me to cope as best I could.
Fifteen I was . . . Dear God! Then there's Bert Garnett
who . . . well, never mind, we all know what he's after
don't we . . . ?"

"Oh, aye. Eyes like slugs all over thi' . . ."

". . . and the only one who has a scrap of decency in
him is Charlie . . ." She spoke in a soft, broken murmur,
the steady rhythm of her weeping punctuated by her
desolate words. Phoebe rocked her and shushed her and
patted her shoulder, even wiped her nose on the scrap
of scrupulously clean linen she kept in her pocket for just
such a purpose.

She wept for ten minutes but the paroxysm of grief
gradually died to a muted and occasional sniffle and at last
she was quiet. She still lay in the comforting circle of
Phoebe's arms, her eyes on the flickering flames of the
fire in the inglenook. She sighed then and sat up, tossing
back the tangled brush of her hair, turning to smile at
Phoebe.

"There, it's done with. I'm all right now."

"Ah know that, Annie. There's nowt much can break
thee."

"Nor you, dear Phoebe."

"True, now what about a nice cup of tea."

They were sitting companionably side by side, sipping
their tea, when Cat came in. The dogs got up to welcome
her, swirling about her skirts, nudging her for attention
and in her basket Dandy purred her satisfaction as her
kittens, three marmalade and two tortoiseshell like the
tom from Upfell who had sired them, climbed all over her
ready to leave the basket now in their inquisitive search
for adventure.

"Where have you been, sweeting?" Annie asked her as
the child sat down beside her, nestling within her mother's
cradling arm. Annie was still deep in the desolation her
encounter with, and rejection of Reed had forced her into,
and her question was absent-minded. The apathy which
nature provides to protect against deep hurt was bound
about her, giving her time to start the healing process, or

if not that, then the strength to take up the burden life had decided her back was broad enough to bear. She loved Reed Macauley. That was a reality, a truth, that she had carried in her heart for a long time. He could never be hers. That was another reality, another truth that had to be borne. Nothing had changed from the uncertainty of what it had always been where Reed was concerned, but given time, the hard work and determined resolve towards the future which had borne her up in the past, she would survive it. There was a great emptiness inside her. She felt like squatting down on the floor, as an animal that is hurt does and putting her hands about her ears so that she might not hear her own cries of pain, but she would pull herself through this, as she had always done.

She held her child closer and put her cheek on her windblown tumble of bright copper curls. Cat smelled of heather as though she had used the springing, colourful plant for a pillow and probably had for she would often take one of Charlie's books up on to the fell and with only the dogs for company, read in the clear sunlight or while away the hours in dreams. She was getting on for six years old, slim and tall for her age, a quiet child who, probably because of her early years, was shy and liked nothing better than her own company, though she and Charlie were good friends.

"Have you been along by the gill?" Annie asked when Cat did not answer, for the bank which ran beside the tumbling waters was a favourite spot of the child's.

"Mm, we were reading."

"You and Charlie?"

"Yes." Cat did not waste words.

"And where did Charlie get to?"

"He said he would try for Yorkshire first and then if there was nothing there he'd go to London."

Annie smiled despite her grief. Charlie was a great one for jokes, for teasing, for dreams and fantasies. He filled Cat's head with them, telling her far more about himself than he ever told Phoebe or herself and was still, despite all this time, an enigma, a merry, absurdly endearing man

with an air of mystery about him which she knew many
women would find attractive.

"Really, and did he say how he would get there?"

"He said he was to walk, mother, that's if his old boots
would allow it." The child gazed solemnly up at her
mother, then sighed deeply. "I shall miss him."

Very carefully Annie sat up, disentangling herself from
Phoebe who had not yet been stricken with the curious
feeling of dread which had laid itself on Annie, a dread so
heavy it was like a suit of armour on her already weary
body. She withdrew her arms gradually from about Cat
and looked deeply into her face. Cat's gaze did not waver.
There was a tremble in her soft lips and the golden brown
depths of her eyes were troubled but she did not look
away. Phoebe, sensing something now, leaned forward.

"What is it?" she asked doubtfully.

Annie did not answer. She spoke instead to Cat.

"What exactly did Charlie say, sweetheart?"

"He said he would try for Yorkshire first . . ." the child
repeated patiently, ". . . but . . ."

"Yes, yes . . . but . . . what did he mean? Was it something you were reading together, or a story he was telling
you?"

Her heart thudded painfully out of control and she did
not know why for it was absolutely ridiculous to think
that Charlie, dear, dear Charlie, would . . . Oh, sweet
Jesus . . .

"No, Mother, he said it was time to leave now. He was
needed elsewhere and I was to tell you . . ."

"No . . . Dear God . . . no, not Charlie . . . please God
. . . not Charlie . . . I cannot manage it without
Charlie . . ."

"Mother . . ." The child drew away, frightened.

"Annie . . ." Phoebe put out a restraining hand for
surely Annie was about to do herself a mischief.

"How could he . . . it's a joke, isn't it? He's hiding in
the yard, isn't he? I'll give him his old boots, the rascal.
I'll kill him for teasing me like this . . . really I will . . ."
and she sprang up leaving Cat and Phoebe to huddle

together on the settle while the dogs, aware that some drama was being enacted, wagged their tails placatingly, ready to take the blame as long as Annie would pat their heads to reassure them.

"Charlie . . . come on in, you devil." She ran into the yard, her head turning frantically from side to side. She raced over to the wall and stared across the fields to the lake, shading her eyes for a sight of his jaunty figure. Where was he? Where had he hidden himself? In the barn, or the cow shed? Perhaps the dairy which, without a cow to produce the milk, was still not in use. Oh, dear Lord, let him suddenly jump out at her . . . please Lord. She would scream and curse and probably strike him for frightening her so but . . . she needed him. She loved Reed Macauley, but her greatest need was for Charlie Lucas, who, she knew now, had been the hand to guide her, the arm to cling to, the rock to steady her . . . Charlie . . .

"He left you this letter, Mother." Cat's voice was timid at her back but Annie did not turn. She stood in the middle of the yard and from somewhere in her head, she heard Charlie's flippant laughter, his cheerful whistle, the sound of his voice singing 'The Cocking Song' from way up on the fell, and her world tumbled down about her ears.

She did not read it until Phoebe and a tearful Cat had gone to bed.

"My love," it said. "I can call you that now I am no longer with you. That is what you are, you see. My love, my dearest love, mine, in my heart, but not mine, for I know yours beats faster, not for me, but for Reed Macauley. I have watched you turn your head to stare over the fell which divides Browhead and Long Beck and felt your pain and longing and my own has been, at times, a burden too great to bear. I love you, Annabelle Abbott, but I simply can no longer live beside you knowing the strength of your love for him. It's too much to ask of any man. I have stayed as long as I could, as long as you needed me. You are on your feet now . . ."

"No, no, I'm not, Charlie . . . I need you with me . . ."

she whispered and the words had nothing to do with Charlie's work on the farm.

". . . your flock is healthy and your crops. You have a guinea or two put by . . ."

". . . and you have nothing. You have taken nothing that rightly belonged to you, not a penny . . ." She rocked in an agony of remorse, her tears soaking the notepaper, blinding her eyes so that she could barely see to read.

". . . and can hire a man to help you at 'backend'. What a charming way with words you people of the lakes have. 'Backend' and that is what it is to me. An ending, my darling Annie. I shall never forget. I shall never forget you, Charlie."

Phoebe crept down an hour later. Annie sat where she had left her. The letter was in her left hand and her right rested on the head of Bonnie which was in her lap. Blackie's muzzle rested across her bare feet, keeping a vigil with her as she stared, dry-eyed now, into the future which would be bleak and empty without Charlie Lucas in it.

"Phoebe . . ."

"Aye, love, I'm here."

"What am I to do without him?" and Phoebe was not awfully certain of who Annie meant. Reed Macauley or Charlie Lucas?

Annie walked to Keswick the next day and when she found no trace of Charlie there, set off along the road which ran alongside the great heights of Helvellyn by the lake of Thirlmere, down to Grasmere and Ambleside and Windermere. She stopped every man and woman she met asking them if they had seen Charlie Lucas, describing him and causing a great deal of consternation among the women since they had thought her to be a young man until she spoke. There was also a great deal of ribald comment among the men, though her white, strained face and deep staring eyes soon silenced them all. She took the dogs and her shepherd's crook and on her back was the bag of food Phoebe had packed for her but she did not eat what was in it, merely carried it because it did not occur to her to put it down. She slept wherever she happened to be, her dogs close by her, but only for an hour or two before getting to her feet and moving on.

Three days later she was just leaving Windermere, a stunned and stumbling figure, dazed to the point where she could not decide which road to take since her choice was Kendal or Newby Bridge and Charlie might have gone by either. He was a man, strong and was more than twelve hours ahead of her. Perhaps he had taken the road to Penrith and south from there to Yorkshire. She just didn't know but she must press on and find him, she must . . .

"Annie." She heard her name through the fog of her own exhaustion and lack of food. There was a hotel to her left and with a portion of her mind which was still capable of thought she noticed it had the strange name of 'Elleray'. There was a great deal of activity in the yard. A coach was about to set out, its destination Carlisle, its roof piled high with boxes and portmanteaux, the horses which pulled it striking fretful hooves on the cobbles as they waited for the off. Ostlers and hotel servants shouted at one another and passengers who were about to embark on the long journey fussed and fumed as they changed their minds a dozen times over what they should take inside with them. There were dog-carts and riding horses, the hotel and the yard overflowing with men who seemed intent on fighting one another to get either in or out.

"Annie," the voice was sharp and she turned about, disorientated by the clamour. The horseman who had called her name dismounted, throwing the reins to a passing ostler who, knowing a man of authority when he saw one, caught them obediently.

"I've come to take you home, Annie," the horseman said, moving to bar her path. "Come, let me lift you up on my mare's back and . . ."

"No, no, really. I cannot. I must find Charlie." A spasm crossed the horseman's face but he did not falter.

"No, my darling, he has gone."

"No, no, he has not. He will be on the road ahead of me and I shall catch him up shortly."

"No, Annie, he was seen boarding the train at Penrith three days ago."

"He had no money for train fare."

"It seems he sold . . . a watch, Annie." Reed Macauley's voice was very patient, very gentle and for the first time Annie was suddenly aware of who he was.

"Reed . . . ?"

"Yes, my love, I am here." He put out a hand and the people passing by were astonished to see the tall, well set-up gentleman smooth back the curling tendrils of hair which fell about the forehead of the shabbily dressed youth. "It's time to go home now. Your maid and daughter were worried about you, so I . . ."

"How did you know?" She was beginning to see two of him now. Two Reed Macauleys who fused together before drifting apart again. Both had concerned faces and a pair of blue eyes brilliant with what she could have sworn were tears but of course Reed Macauley would never weep. Why should he?

"She came to my house yesterday."

"Phoebe?"

"Is that her name? She would speak to no one but me, she told them, and would not be moved until I came. A strong-willed lass and devoted to you. She said you would probably turn her out for interfering but nevertheless she could not let you tramp the length of the country looking for Charlie Lucas."

"You knew him?"

"No. *About* him. I made it my business to . . ." but the rest of the words went roaring away into a pale grey, fast moving shaft which gathered speed and became darker and darker until she fell into the blackness.

24

The face of the man at the door was familiar but for several moments Annie could not put a name to it. He was small and wiry, as lean as a greyhound but there was a look about him which spoke of strength and endurance despite his lack of bulk. His skin was heavily seamed and in each seam was a fine line of grey as though the soap and water he sketched over it, were thrown so hastily they did no more than whisk across the surface. He wore an old-fashioned soft-brimmed hat slung on his grizzled curls, a wide-cut shirt, breeches fastened beneath his knees, stockings with gaiters over them and a waistcoat so ancient its colour was unrecognisable. He carried a labourer's sleeveless smock made from sacking.

"Tha' wants a man," he said briefly, his expression taciturn, his speech the same.

"I beg your pardon." Annie eyed him from head to foot, not sure whether to laugh or slam the door in his face but his eyes were stern, steady, with an expression in them which was completely without humour.

"Does tha' want a man or not?"

"I can't say that I do," she answered and it was then that the man's name came to her. It was seven years or more since she had seen him and then it had been with the eyes of a child, a young girl who had looked at anyone over the age of twenty with the belief that they already had one foot in the grave. All the men of her acquaintance including her father had grey hair and weatherbeaten wrinkled faces. Some had bent backs and bowed legs for the loads they carried would have burdened a horse. This man had moved on the fringes of her child's world, an unseen part of the scenery, like the tree at the side of the house or the dog which had moved at her father's heels. He had had no home as far as she was aware, no family nor friends, moving from farm to farm, a man able to set his hand to any task, coppicing, shepherding, mending the drystone walls in which not a dab of cement was added, planting, ploughing and clipping sheep, his own master and man, for as long as any one could remember. Grey but unbent, born to toil on other men's land, industrious, a man who would labour until he fell dead at some other man's plough, free, stubbornly independent and working for reasons best known to himself, for Bert Garnett.

"Why, it's Natty Varty," she smiled, the lovely glowing smile which no man could resist, but Natty did. A look of deep disapproval set his lips in a rigid line and his eyebrows moved fiercely over his eyes like two small animals.

"Aye." He stood his ground, saying nothing more. He had said all that was necessary, his attitude told her, and the next move was up to her. She'd best make up her mind what it was to be, though, for he'd no time to be hanging about waiting on the word of a lass who was no better than she should be, or so he'd heard.

"Well . . . what can I do for you, Natty?" she asked politely, still ready to smile, opening her door a little more so that if he was of a mind to, he could come inside, or not, as he pleased.

"Nay, lass, tha' can do nowt' fer me. It's more what I can do for thi'."

"For me, Natty? In what way?"

"Does tha' want a man ter work for thi', or not? Speak up an let's get it settled."

"Work for me?" Her mouth fell open in bewilderment. "Why should you work for me? And who told you to come here? I've not advertised for a labourer."

"'Appen not, but I was told tha' needed one just the same."

"But you work for Bert Garnett, Natty. You have done for as long as I've been back so why should you . . ."

"Before I tek up wi' thi' let's get summat straight. I'm Mr Varty to thi', an ah'll work where ah like. An' it weren't

Bert Garnett who hired me but Aggie Mounsey an' she be dead. So if ah've a fancy to 'ave a change, that's my business. Ah was told tha' needed someone to help wi' tha' lambs, so I upped it an' come along."

Though the words were spoken with a firm resolution which defied her to argue with him – and why should she – his grim manner and plain expressionless face told a different tale. This was not to his liking, Annie could see that. It was almost time to take the sheep to market for the buying and selling of stock, a busy time on any sheep farm and good men like Natty Varty were worth their weight in gold. There was not a man at the Tup Fair who would argue with him, even if he did work for Annie Abbott. Her passage would be smoothed enormously with Natty Varty by her side and the stock she meant to buy with her small store of coins would be readily available to her. Her flock would need salving and marking, and in a few weeks the oats and barley harvested and threshed in mid-summer would be prepared for taking to the mill to be ground. Already the trees needed for the making of her swill baskets were ready for felling, a task to be carried out approximately between October and April or May. And she had still not been able to get to Whitehaven to sell the swills she and Charlie and Phoebe had already fashioned. They were piled neatly in the dairy but they could not be stored there indefinitely since, with the milk she would get from the cow she intended to buy before winter, she meant to make butter and cheese. A stall, she and Phoebe had talked it over. They would rent a stall at the fortnightly market and with Phoebe, starched and neat and eminently respectable behind it, she could sell Annie's produce which included the eggs her hens laid, butter, cheese, chickens, perhaps a swill or two and a besom brush, and steadily they would build up Annie's tiny profit. And the cow, which would be quartered for the winter in the cow shed, would need to be hand fed on the bracken which would be cut and brought down from the fell. There was some hay, of course, but that might not last the winter, particularly if it was a hard one and the sheep were brought down to the intake land. They would need hand feeding . . . Dear God, the list was endless and without Charlie . . .

"I do need a man, Mr Varty, but I can't pay much."

"I'm not asking for much."

"Name a figure."

He did and it was so ridiculously low she gasped.

"You can't live on that, Nat . . . Mr Varty."

"I'll decide that. Can tha' give me a bed an' me grub?"

There was Charlie's room above the dairy, snug and achingly tidy since he had left and Phoebe had ferociously 'bottomed' it. Bare whitewashed walls, bare scrubbed floor, a narrow bed and a press in which nothing of Charlie's had ever been stored, since he had owned only what he stood up in. His broadcloth coat rested there in the summer with his knitted jerkin and scarf and a book or two. All gone along with the engaging good humour, the impish lazy smile, the wickedly wry tongue of the man who had come into her life with the casual manner of someone who had not a serious thought in his head, not a serious bone in his body. He had worked beside her in sleet and snow and rain and storm and made light of it, giving the impression that nothing much mattered in life besides an absurd talent for laughing at it. A gift for avoiding anything which smacked of stuffiness or monotony, nevertheless, without appearing to move at any faster pace than an indolent saunter, he had done the work of three men. Without appearing to speak in any way that was not droll and teasing, he had guided her wisely, invigorated her when she was drained and weary, gladdened her heart when it was sad, encouraged and inspired her and she could not envisage a future without him in it. It was two months since he had gone and in that time there had been no word of him, no letter, nothing, and if Reed Macauley knew of his whereabouts, he was not telling Annie Abbott.

He had brought her home that day, sleeping in the crook of his arm as she lolled before him on his black mare. On that long road from Windermere up through Ambleside and Grasmere and on to Keswick where the good folk milling about Moot Hall and the market place fell silent, gaping at the sight of Reed Macauley with his arms about Annie Abbott. As bold as brass he was, raising his hat to those with whom he was acquainted, smiling round the expensive cigar he had clamped between his good white teeth, just as though there was nothing unusual in his behaviour. As though he and Annie Abbott were accustomed to riding together on his mare Victoria, and perhaps they were, for anything could be believed of that strumpet. Those appalling clothes she wore and would you look at her hair, her long thick plait all undone and a living mantle of russet falling across Reed Macauley's arm and half-way down the mare's belly. Sound asleep in the middle of the day and what could they deduce from that except to wonder how she had got in such a state? And him with a young wife of no more than a year at home. No children and could one wonder at it if he was . . . cavorting about the parish with Annie Abbott.

The valley had rocked with it, adding fresh fuel to the fire in the middle of which they would have liked to burn Annie Abbott, for surely that was what she was, a witch! Annie had woken in her own bed the next day with no recollection of how she had got there and certainly none of the ride through Keswick and if the men and women she met on her occasional walk along the lake road, and in Hause, Gillthrop or Keswick averted their offended eyes when she strode by, what difference did it make to her since they had done so for the past three years? She missed Charlie. That was the foremost ache in her burdened heart and if the village women hissed at her as she went through, she scarcely noticed.

She had not seen Reed Macauley since.

Now, two months later, here was Natty Varty offering his invaluable services to Annie Abbott and she was immediately suspicious.

'Mr Varty, there is nothing I would like more than to employ you, but I cannot understand why you are asking me to. What was suddenly . . ."

"Look lass, doest tha' want me to work fer thi' or not?

Just say yes or no. That's all that's needed. Tha' knows ah'm a good worker . . ."

"Oh, indeed, Mr Varty, but I really find it hard to believe that you should, for no apparent reason, take it into your head that you want to work for me. Won't you come inside and we can . . ."

"Bloody 'ell . . . beggin yer pardon . . ." since for some reason it suddenly did not seem right to swear in the face of this polite and lovely woman, even if she did wear trousers and a shirt. His eyes touched briefly on the thrust of her breasts then looked hastily away. "Ah said ah'd get this argument when . . ." He stopped suddenly, realising he had said too much, his discomfiture showing in the way his angry old mouth worked and it was then Annie began to know.

"Someone has sent you, haven't they? Someone has asked you to come and offer yourself . . ."

"Nay, lass, tha's talkin' daft. Natty Varty pleases hissen where he works."

"Really, then tell me this. Why are you offering yourself at half the going price a labourer would get? £8 for half a year you could demand so who is paying you the other half?"

Natty's eyes were flat and expressionless but he did not look away. His mouth was clamped in a thin white line of contempt and something else which Annie did her best to decipher. He was standing his ground, staring at her as though he would like nothing better than to spit at her feet, but something held him there on her doorstep and she had no idea of what it could be. Reed Macauley had sent him, of that she was sure, but not even Reed could make Natty Varty work where he didn't want to. So what hold did he have on this old man, as he had on many men in the district, that he could force him to go where he did not want to go? Suddenly she made up her mind. She lifted her head haughtily as she spoke.

"Very well, *Natty*, I will employ you. You will sleep over the cow shed and Phoebe will bring your meals to you there. But there is one thing. I am to be addressed as

Miss Abbott. I give the orders and you take them and I shall pay you, *I shall pay you* the full rate. You can tell the person who sent you that you do not need his bribe, if that is what he has offered you and if I hear that you have disobeyed me then I shall fire you immediately. Is that clear? Have you your own dog? Ah, yes, I see you have," eyeing the quiet Border collie which lay with its nose just beneath the closed farm gate, "then I'll be obliged if you would keep it away from mine. Now perhaps you could start by bringing my sheep down to the 'inlands' so that they will be ready for market next week. Good morning to you, Natty. If you require anything, speak to Phoebe."

Reed Macauley rode openly across the lower slopes of Cockup Fell and down the track from Dash Beck to Browhead the following day. It was almost October and a day of damp, drifting rain, light as mist but coming to rest just as wetly on collars and cuffs from where it crept insidiously inside clothing. It dripped down boots to soak into stockings and collected on the brim of hats from where it ran in a steady trickle to cling to flesh which shivered at the touch of the oncoming winter. Slender birches drooped sadly as though they too knew well what was ahead and larches, hung about gracefully with a tapestry foliage, trembled in the shifting rain. The rowans were heavy with berries. Down by the lake at the foot of Annie's farm, trees hung over the water, clinging to the sketchiest of foothold.

Beside the mare ran Reed's old dog, stopping now and again to lift her muzzle, sniffing the air with the practised ease of an animal well used to Lakeland conditions. The heather through which horse, rider and dog moved was a mass of tiny purple flowers, giving the appearance from far off, of a solid purple carpet.

"She's in t' dairy," a startled Phoebe told him and though he knew Annie must have heard the clatter of his mare's hooves on the rocky track and cobbled yard, she did not appear.

She had her back to him, her hands busy as she stacked a pile of swills, tying them neatly into a compact bundle.

Just outside the door of the dairy, standing in the rain, was the sledge, the one which had seen such service over the past years and on it, again tied neatly in two tight-fitting rows, were more swills.

"I take it you're tramping off somewhere with that sledge I see outside," were the first furious words he spoke.

She did not turn. "Yes, I'm hoping to sell them at Whitehaven." Her voice was low.

He jerked about violently, the determination he had steeled upon himself to remain calm no matter what passed between them, exploding at once in his fear for her. "Bloody hell, woman! Whitehaven? Do you know how far that is . . . !"

"Yes . . ."

". . . and you intend walking over twenty miles there and the same back dragging that damned sledge . . ."

"Yes . . ."

". . . and October no more than a week or so off . . ."

"Leave me alone, Reed. Let me get on with my life."

". . . and God knows who tramping from the ships which dock there. Irishmen on the look-out for work or anything else they can find along the way which could include you. Do you realise . . . ?"

"Yes . . ."

". . . that any one of them could . . ."

". . . Yes . . . So you have said a number of times."

"Jesus Christ, Annie, don't do this to me. Don't put yourself in danger. Let me help you. I'll find someone to buy your bloody baskets."

"Like you found Natty Varty?"

Her voice was quiet and her head was bent low as she gripped the edge of the stone slab on which, in better times, bowls of milk were left to stand for 'three meals' before the cream was carefully removed. The knuckles of her hands were white with the fierceness of her grip.

"You know I only did it to help you. That's all I want to do, is help you. To make your life easier. I can't bear to see you working yourself into the bloody ground, getting thinner every time I see you. That fellow helped you and though it tore me apart to know he was living under your roof I told myself that he was at least taking some of the load off your back. Now he's gone . . ."

"Because of you."

"Because of me?" The bewilderment in his voice was genuine and at last she turned to look at him. She wore an apron of her mother's, an enormous thing which covered her from neck to knee. One worn for dairy work where cleanliness was essential, laundered and ironed by Phoebe to a crisp and pristine whiteness. Her hair was neatly plaited, wound about her head like a weighty crown, tipping it back so that she gave the appearance of a proud young queen. She was pale, no colour in her face but in contrast, her eyes were a deep and glowing tawny brown. Warm, filled with that velvet textured softness which betrayed the depth of her love for him. It couldn't be hidden, had she wanted to hide it. Everything he did was with her welfare in mind. From that first day when he had carted down that enormous hamper to this last when he had sent – somehow – Natty Varty to labour for her, he had done his best, what she would allow, to make her life easier and if sometimes it had further damaged her reputation he had done it with the best intentions. She was aware that the last time, after what Phoebe had told her about it and the ride through Keswick, he had irretrievably damaged his own.

But he must be made to see that it would not do. He must be made to see that he could not keep on rescuing her from the results of her own mistakes. That, and the truth must be faced by him. She did not need him now. She was glad of Natty Varty and grateful that Reed had somehow made him leave Bert Garnett and come to her, but she would manage on her own from now on. She had a tiny cache of savings, pennies put by, one by laborious one, since she had sold her first lambs, her besoms and swills, and she meant to see it grow again with this year's profits. She and Phoebe and Cat lived off the land, except for the milk which, when her husband looked the other way, Sally Garnett left hidden by the farm gate of Upfell Farm. Annie stocked up on tea and flour when she was in Keswick but apart from that they were self-sufficient. They ate mutton, dried over the fire, from the sheep she and Charlie had killed, and they managed. She did not need Reed Macauley.

Only with her body, her anguished heart cried. Only with her woman's body which even now surged joyously beneath her enormous apron, beneath her father's shirt and baggy, much patched breeches, towards Reed Macauley. Her heart hammered until she was sure he could see the movement of it beneath the bib of the apron. The glow in the pit of her belly spread a filament of need up towards her breasts and her nipples instantly hardened. Her breath was trapped in her throat and she parted her lips to allow it to escape and inside her she felt the whimpers begin, whimpers which would become a moan if she could not get a firm grip on herself.

She saw the answering need in him. He groaned in despair, moving almost reluctantly towards her. They met in the centre of the dairy and when their arms rose to one another, holding, holding on desperately, clinging lest they fall, she could hear the tremble in his voice as he spoke into her hair.

"Sweet Jesus . . . Sweet Christ. What are we to do? I love you . . . starve for you . . . think of you all the time. I can't work . . . sleep . . . my mind is full of you. I'm dazed with it . . . with the pain . . . I'm not a man for fanciful things . . . I want a woman I take her . . . but you are buried so deep in me I can see nobody, nothing . . . your face . . ."

He was hurting her, crushing her, the bones in her back and her ribs, his own body a taut, shuddering length of bone and muscle. She lifted her head from his chest where his heart was pounding so hard it deafened her and his lips flattened against hers with such force she felt her teeth break the skin inside her mouth. His gentled then, parting hers, so sweet and soft she knew that this time . . . this was the time . . . here, here in the dairy, wherever he could lay her . . . on the stone bench . . . the floor . . . she would allow him to take her . . . *allow*. . . she would *glory* in it . . .

"Where does tha' want to put them besoms?" The voice which came at them through the bright and rapturous aureole of their love was grim and in it, even those few words, was the realisation that had told its owner exactly why he had been fetched here by Reed Macauley. So that was the way the wind blew, was it, and though it was nowt to do with him what folk did, that didn't mean to say that he had to like it, nor would he put up with it. Reed Macauley had promised him a cottage right up on the edge of the fell, away from other folk, where Natty could live out his days as he pleased. Work a bit, he would, when he felt like it, or stop in his own place, when he felt like it. His dog beside him, a few hens, do a bit of rabbiting, fishing, for though Natty would admit it to no one the truth was he was nearer eighty than seventy and he couldn't quite do the things he had been doing since he was a lad. Stop with *her* for a bit, Mr Macauley had said, and when he wanted it there would be the cottage waiting for him up beyond Tarn Nevin. But he'd be buggered if he'd be used as a convenience whilst these two fornicated under his bloody nose.

They whirled to face him, both for a moment looking foolish, guilty, flushed with something Natty had long forgotten. Her eyes were the loveliest, deepest brown, like the ale he drank at The Bull in Gillthrop which was a strange thing to come into his mind, but Natty liked his ale and admired its colour.

"An' I'll be off now so tha' can get back to tha' fun an' . . ."

He saw Reed Macauley's face turn the colour of the beetroot he himself had only the day before yesterday been digging up a mile away at Upfell and Reed Macauley's roar of rage could be heard on the same farm, Natty was sure. And he would have knocked Natty to the ground, Natty was sure of that too, if she hadn't put a hand on his arm. At once, mysteriously, since Reed Macauley was known for a man of violence if crossed, he became quiet.

"What d'you mean, Natty? You'll be off where?"

"Back where I come from." His contemptuous eyes, his curling lip told her exactly what he thought of a woman like her but she did not falter or look ashamed.

"To Upfell?"

"Aye," and he shouldered the axe he carried with which he had been about to go up to the coppice to do a bit of felling.

"Why?"

"Ah work for decent folk, allus have done," and all the while Reed Macauley stood patiently by and Natty was astonished that this woman, with a light touch on his arm, could keep him from hurling Natty Varty to the ground and stamping on him for his effrontery.

"You must do as you think best, Mr Varty, of course, but I would be most obliged if you could find it within your power to stay with me for a while. I need you, you see."

"Ah knows that, lass, but ah don't need thee, or him an' his cottage," which was not true of course, and as though to emphasise it, the 'rheumatics' with which he was increasingly plagued, tweaked at his shoulder painfully.

"I see, so that's what was promised you?" and still Reed Macauley stood like he was some grey dove perched on her hand.

"Aye, but I reckon ah've bin tricked an' ah don't like that."

"In what way have you been tricked?"

"Well . . ." Well he couldn't say really, if he was honest, especially with them great big brown eyes of hers looking at him as though what he had to say was of the greatest concern to her, and suddenly, he knew it was. She *was* concerned. It really mattered to her that Natty Varty was an honest man, with ethics which said he'd have no truck with a chap who carried on an adulterous relationship with a woman . . . well . . . like her. He'd known her all her life, ever since Joshua Abbott had lost that last lad of his and he'd realised, Joshua that is, that this little lass was all that he was going to have. No wonder she dressed herself in her father's clothes since the old man had used her like a lad since she was five or six. Worked her hard he had, but she'd always been sweet-tempered. Joshua'd not broken her, and what he'd taught her had stood her in good stead, but when Natty looked back to that day when it got round the valley that Josh Abbott's lass had gone off with some chap from a travelling company, he distinctly remembered thinking at the time, "and is it any wonder?"

Now she was back, looking at him with the desperate entreaty he had once seen in the eyes of a young doe he had cornered up on Great Calva. There had been a fawn at her back, no more than a couple of hours old, and she wouldn't leave it, but her eyes, almost human, had looked like this woman's did! It was then, for the first time in his life, he changed his mind.

"Won't you reconsider, Mr Varty? Mr Macauley and I . . ."

"Nay . . ." His anger flared. ". . . I want to know nowt about that. 'Tis nowt to do with me so . . ."

"I was only going to say that . . ."

"Ah don't want ter know what tha' was going ter say so if tha'll tell me where tha' wants these besoms put I'll be off up to't coppice to see what wants felling."

"Of course, Mr Varty. Leave the besoms by the sledge and I'll pack them later. I'm to be off to Whitehaven."

"Aye, so I heard. Ah'll come with thi'. There's a tobacconist over there that sells tobacco I like . . ."

"Oh no, Mr Varty, I can get it for you."

"No, tha' can't. Tha'd only get wrong sort. Women knows nowt about tobacco."

"That's true, Mr Varty."

"An' tha' can call me Natty, Annie."

They both had a strong tendency towards hysteria, Annie and Reed, a great bubbling laughter which welled up inside them so that they turned to one another, clinging together, not in passion, but with the merriment, the foolish absurdity which comes when a great strain has ended. They were not laughing at Natty, though his paradoxical change of direction, the sudden reversal of his antipathy towards her was comical in the extreme. It was his last words that amused Annie and it was relief that made Reed lean against her whilst great gales of laughter shook them both.

"I don't know how I kept my hands from the old fool."

"No, he's not that, Reed, but what was it do you think, that made him change his mind?"

He put her from him. Not far, no more than six inches but enough to look down into her shining eyes.

"Don't you know?" The turmoil of their bodies had subsided now and there was peace and a quality of honesty between them. "Don't you know what you have? You are beautiful Annie Abbott, but rarer than that is your absolute unawareness of your beauty. And not only your face is beautiful but so is your heart and soul. It shines through and when men look at it, men who recognise it, as I do, as Charlie Lucas did . . . oh yes, my darling, I realise now why he left . . . and as even an old man like Natty Varty does, there is nothing we would not do for you. Dear God, if only you would let me do it. Which brings me to the purpose of my visit. Do you still want that girl of yours to go to school? Ah, I see you do, well you can give me a glass of ale and sit beside me on the wall while we discuss it."

25

The day before they were to set off for Whitehaven, the last day in September it was, Sally Garnett came running down the track from Upfell, her youngest in her arms, her face crimson, her pale brown hair in a tangle about her head and her plump figure, never given a chance to right itself between pregnancies, wobbling all over the place like a sackful of blown up balloons.

"I can't stop, I've left Sammy in charge of little 'uns but he's only five himself and Alfie's a real handful. This is Aggie, I called her after me mam."

"Come in, Sally, oh, do come in and have some tea. Phoebe's in the dairy. We have a cow now, you know, and she says the place needs a good scrubbing out every day, just as though she hasn't done it once already today, and Cat's at school . . . Oh, yes, didn't you know? Oh, please come in and drink a cup of tea with me and let me tell you all about it. Here, let me take Aggie while you get your breath," and though the baby stank like a ferret, making Annie turn her head and think sadly of Aggie Mounsey and her passion for cleanliness, she took her from Sally's arms and tried to propel Sally into Phoebe's shining kitchen.

"Oh no, I dassunt, Annie. He'd kill me. He'd kill me if he knew I was even speaking to yer. He's in a fearful temper . . ." and now, as Annie got a good look at her, she could see what Bert's fearful temper had done to his wife's eye. It was set in a deep purple socket and her cheek-bone seemed to stand out in a peak from the rest of her face.

"Sally, come in. He's obviously away from Upfell or you wouldn't be here . . ."

"Aye, market in Keswick . . ." Sally was getting her breath back now and she eyed the interior of the kitchen and the offer of a drink of tea with some longing.

"Well then, he won't be back before dark . . ."

"Ah knows that, but ah dassunt, Annie." Sally's terror of Bert's fearful temper evidently could not be convinced that even the distance between Browhead and Keswick Market would hide her from his wrath. "Ah've just come to tell thi' that he's livid about Natty Varty. Oh, Annie, I'm that frightened he'll do summat bad to thee, or to tha' farm or even that lass of yourn. He don't care how he goes about it, but he's right set on doing thi' a mischief. That's how I got this," fingering her swollen face. "I said no more than pr'aps he'd best be careful an' he landed me one that . . . well, tha' can see for thissen. He reckons tha' coaxed Natty away wi' . . . well, I'm too ashamed to tell thee what he said, an' Natty an' all . . . an old man! Bert . . . well, he knows about thee and him from up Long Beck. I'm sorry, lass . . ." putting a contrite hand on Annie's arm, watching as the soft creamy blush and the bright glow brought about by her own arrival at Browhead slipped away from her friend's face. "He says that any man what . . . Oh, Annie, lass, he reckons tha'll lie down for any man, an' it were then when he said that, that I spoke up and he clouted me."

"Oh Sally, I'm so sorry, for you and for myself. Dear God, I've been with one man in my life, no more, and then I was a child, fourteen, ignorant, in love or so I thought. He said we were to be married . . . and for that one mistake I am to suffer this. Seven years, Sally and still they turn on me . . ."

"Aye, love, ah know. Everyone's talking about yer an' that's all they'll do, but not Bert. He'll hurt thi', Annie. Can thi' not ask . . . ?" she tossed her head awkwardly in the direction of Long Beck and Reed Macauley. "Will he not protect thi'?"

"Sally, there is *nothing* between me and Reed Macauley, nothing." Annie's words came through gritted teeth.

"He'd like there to be though, wouldn't he, lass?" Sally spoke with a sad wisdom and Annie sighed.

"Oh yes, Sal, he'd like there to be."

"Buggers, the lot of 'em."

"Oh, Sally, why won't they let me get on . . . ?"

"I don't know lass, but I'd best get back. God knows what them lot's up to. But tha'll be careful, won't tha'. Watch out for Bert."

"I'm to go to Whitehaven tomorrow with Natty."

"Eeeh, whatever for?"

"To sell my swills to the coaling ships. There's a good market there. I've sold them here and there, one or two at a time, but I reckon I could get rid of the lot in one go."

"An' tha's leaving thi' lass on er own with only that girl with her?"

Annie's face lit up for a moment.

"No, that's what I wanted to tell you. Cat's gone over to . . ."

"Tha'd best tell em to lock t' door."

"Bert wouldn't hurt Phoebe, Sally. He's no quarrel with her and Cat's gone to . . ."

But Sally was sidling away, unconcerned now with anything but her agitated need to get back to Upfell and her children. She had tied Alfie and Emma to the legs of the heavy kitchen table but she wouldn't put it past her Sammy to have released them, and God only knew what devilment or danger the four of them had got up to. Dear Lord, but she missed her mam. She wouldn't have this shiner if her mam had still been alive. He wouldn't have dared lift a finger to her, not with Aggie Mounsey at his back, the rotten sod, but he'd been that incensed when Natty Varty had left, not saying where he was off to since Natty Varty was not one for blurting his business to anyone. Natty had not been settled ever since her mam died, Sally knew that. And when Bert had found out where Natty had gone, well, she and the children had cowered in the barn for more than two hours until he'd slammed out of the kitchen and set off in the direction of The Bull. He'd abused her

something awful when he got back, no doubt putting
her in the family way again, and that was when he blacked
her eye. Oh, God . . . Mam . . .

Annie and Natty were gone five days. They had walked
the shortest route, dragging the sledge round the top of
Bassenthwaite lake and up and over the top of High Side,
bypassing Cockermouth, crossing the river Cocker and
spending the night at the Beehive Inn below Deanscales.
On across Dean Moor and High Moor in an almost direct
line until they reached Whitehaven. They were lucky.
There were many coaling ships and tramp steamers tied
up in the harbour and by the end of the third day they had
sold all their swills, though short of going from door to
door, the besoms, in any number were not wanted. Annie
was uneasy. Sally had put a worm of disquiet in her mind
and the whole time she and Natty were away, she had the
strongest compulsion to do everything on the run, longing
to tell customers to hurry and make their minds up as they
dickered between this swill or that or should it be three
or half a dozen? One man on the harbour had wanted to
discuss a bit of business, saying he would take as many
of Annie's swills as she could get across to him. His ship
called at Liverpool, Belfast, Greenock and many other
ports where the colliers docked, and he was sure he could
sell them for her if they could agree on a price, he said.
There was no disparagement in his eyes or voice, or in
those of his crew, at the sight of her strange rig-out, for
these were men who had been to the far-flung outposts
of the British Empire in their time, and though they eyed
her long trousered legs and soft bowler hat somewhat
curiously they were accustomed to seeing stranger sights
than her. She was a bonny lass or would be underneath
those baggy jacket and trousers and the unflattering man's
hat she wore, but that was nothing to do with them.
Besides, the old man she had with her was sharp-eyed
and sharp-tongued and gave the impression he'd take his
sturdy shepherd's crook to any man who looked sideways
at him, or her.

She and Natty had got on quite well together, she had

decided. It seemed he had taught himself to read when he had worked on the estate of some wealthy landowner just on the border between Cumberland and Scotland, in his youth. There had been broadsheets left about in the kitchen and being a resolute lad with little to say to his fellows, he had puzzled it out until he could decipher the squiggles on the paper. The *Glasgow Herald* had been his master's particular favourite, costing the exorbitant sum of fourpence halfpenny, and the young man Natty had grown into had become used to that one newspaper, looking out for copies wherever he went. He read everything printed in it from advertisements of cottages to let or for sale, the doings of the County Sessions, the finance accounts of the treasury, reports from the House of Lords, notices to shippers and passengers on sailing vessels and even an account of Her Majesty's Drawing Room held at St James's Palace. But anything of a political nature was bread and butter to him and he liked to discourse on it to anyone sensible enough to listen. Not many were, not of his acquaintance, but he found a ready listener in Annie Abbott.

"That were a right sad do about Peel," he said shortly, right out of the blue on their first morning together. They were passing through the wooded area just north of Bassenthwaite Lake. The sun had ventured forth in a last effort to prolong the autumn but it was cold, sharp with the feeling of the winter to come. The oaks and alders, the willows weeping into the water were fast losing their leaves and the woodland floor was rich with a spongy layer in every shade from the palest cream to the darkest red, through which tiny saplings were reaching up to the light, thick as spring snowdrops. There was a cascade of silvered water running down the beck into the lake and propping up a drystone wall over which Natty clambered as spry as a boy was a huge and noble old yew tree. Natty's dog pattered at his heels. He had no name. His eyes never left Natty and it needed only a movement of Natty's hand or the click of his fingers, perhaps just a turn of his head and the dog knew exactly what was required of him. Annie had left Blackie and Bonnie for company with Phoebe.

"Oh?" she answered delicately. She had heard of Peel but she had no access to newspapers and the only people she met or spoke to were not of a mind to discuss current affairs with her.

"Aye, I reckon country'll be worse off without him." He took his pipe from his mouth, turning to look at her and seeing that she had nothing to say on the matter, clamped it between his teeth again.

"Did tha' not know he were gone?" His tone was biting as though to say what could you expect of a woman.

"Gone?"

"Aye, dead. His 'orse threw him an' he died a few days later."

"Poor man."

"Aye, poor man indeed. An honest an' true man I reckon he were. An' I reckon it were due to 'im that this country's had peace for t' last two years. Revolution everywhere, but not here. Oh, no." He shook his head wisely and his dog watched anxiously lest there were some message for him in the movement. "You'll 'ave eard of t' 'Peelers'. Well, it were 'im who founded the Metropolitan Police. Prime Minister, he were for a while in '34 and again in '41. An' it were 'im who repealed the Corn Laws which put food in a lot o' folks' mouths, I can tell thi'."

"Do you know, Mr Varty, I had not even heard of it. Do tell me more."

By the end of the journey Annie had been informed on many matters which concerned the welfare of the people, ranging from Chartism, which Natty heartily endorsed, to his opinion of the Prince Consort, whom Natty had not cared for at first, him being a foreigner, but who was proving an able sort of chap. Well, look at this Great Exhibition he was planning.

"An exhibition, Mr Varty?"

"Aye, up in London next year . . ."

He was deep in the throes of Lord Palmerston's foreign policy, as they drew near Browhead, particularly with reference to Greece and the attack on the property of a British subject who lived in Athens and who was demanding compensation. It appeared that Lord Palmerston supported him and . . .

Annie's instincts, which had been troubling her ever since they had left Browhead, sensed that something was wrong as she and Natty, still in full spate, came over the crest of the hill and crossed Chapel Beck. Though there was nothing obviously wrong – smoke came from the chimney and the hens pecked and squawked in the yard – there was an air of something out of kilter about the farm. A feeling of unbalance, of discord.

She began to run, her old hat flying off and spinning away as she did so.

Bert Garnett glowered round the tap room of The Bull, his figure somewhat indistinct in the smoke from the dozens of long-stemmed pipes which were being puffed by most of its customers. His hard brown fist was clamped about a pint pot of ale, the fifth he had drunk since he had entered the inn, not more than an hour ago. He didn't so much drink the ale as tip the pot up and pour the liquid down his throat in one great draught, hardly pausing to swallow, then thumped it on the bar, calling to Will Twentyman to fill it up again. The violence of his thoughts was kept to himself but they were very evidently of an explosive nature, as demonstrated by the way he crashed the pot to the counter. There was an empty circle about him for there was not a man there who cared to even sit next to him let alone enquire what ailed him. They knew, of course, for it had got about the valley like wildfire that Natty Varty, much in demand at the busy times of the year, had left Upfell and gone to that lass of Joshua Abbott's. Working for her he was now, leaving Bert in the lurch and Bert was not at all pleased about it, as anyone in the bar could see.

Bert smashed his pot on the counter for the sixth time and the room fell silent for a moment. Will Twentyman was a mild-mannered man but he did like a quiet house. Men didn't come here to fight. They were honest,

hard-working labourers and farmers and shepherds who
liked a nice peaceful pint before they ambled off to their
beds and the warm back of the missus, and how long would
it be before Will spoke up?

"Summat wrong, Bert?" he asked good-naturedly
enough.

"There's nowt wrong, Will Twentyman, except wi' my
pot which is empty."

"Right Bert, but watch what tha' doin't wi' it, will tha'?"
said Will as he placed the sixth foaming pint in front of his
truculent customer.

After the downing of his tenth pint, Bert staggered out
of The Bull without a good night to anyone. The night was
dark, a great mass of clouds as malevolent as Bert himself
pressing down on the towering fells and hiding any vestige
of light from moon or stars. But Bert needed no light to
guide him between the high stone walls of the road down
from Gillthrop, fording the beck and along the track which
led at the back of Browhead towards Upfell. He'd done it
a hundred or more times since he'd married Sally, though
Ma Mounsey had not been pleased about it, old cow.

He could feel the dam of bitterness surge inside him as
he stopped to glare at the back of Annie Abbott's farm.
Bitch, bloody interfering bitch, taking the only decent
labourer to be had in the district, stealing him from Bert
with them tarty ways of hers, lying down, taking off her
drawers, even for an old chap like Natty. But when a
full-blooded chap like himself had let it be known to her
that he'd be willing to accommodate her she'd turned her
bloody nose up as though he was something one of his
own cows had deposited and which she'd nearly stepped
in. She did it for everyone but him, opened her legs and
showed off that sweet bit of fluff which Bert Garnett would
dearly love to get his hands on and his prick in. High and
bloody mighty Macauley was sniffing round and probably
getting his in an' all like the rest of them, and yet Bert
Garnett wasn't given even a smile or a wink let alone a
feel of her. Bitch, cow, whore . . . and not only that, she
had taken the one good man everyone in the area would

give their eye-teeth to have working for them. And she was doing well, it was said, that flock of hers sold and new stock added and even a bloody cow and a pig in her yard. Oats and barley in her barn ready to be milled and a store of vegetables enough to feed the Queen's army. Gone to bloody Whitehaven she had, her and Natty, to sell her swills and there was his Sal sitting on her fat arse all day with nothing to do but stuff her face and could *she* make a swill? Could she hell! She could do nowt except produce bairns one after the other whilst that bitch in her snug farmhouse . . . By God . . . !

The dam burst and any hold Bert Garnett might have had on good sense and sanity was swept away on the roaring tide of his obsessed rage. Reaching for a rock from the track, he moved round from the back of the farmhouse to the front, picking his way as quietly as a mouse, his feet finding, as though by instinct, the soft thick grass at the side of the track. There was no light showing anywhere since it was past nine o' clock but in the fire window beside the inglenook a faint golden orange showed where the fire, tamped down for the night, glowed warmly. He heard the two dogs begin to growl warningly from inside the house and he grinned as he threw the rock. Their growl became a frantic barking as the glass in the small mullioned window shattered and in a moment or two a light flickered in an upstairs window. It wavered behind the curtains and he waited. It appeared again moments later, moving behind the kitchen curtain as whoever held it came downstairs and the dogs continued to howl and bark but he did not move away. He stood in the shadows of the tree at the side of the house and again he watched and waited. He was not sure what for nor did he care much. He was enjoying himself. He was doing something to scare that bitch, even if she wasn't there. She'd know when she got home, that you didn't cross a man like Bert Garnett, and if you did, you only did it once.

To his amazed delight, the door opened. He'd not expected that. Another couple of rocks would have done him. Perhaps one through each window for good measure,

but the sight of the open doorway and the figure who stood
there holding a bloody candle and shouting 'Who's there?'
for Christ's sake, well, it was too good a chance to
miss . . .

Wait a minute though, he didn't want to get his hands
mangled or his throat taken out by one of them dogs, did
he? Caution was needed here until he found out what was
what. He'd no idea what he meant to do, but by God, he
was enjoying this and he'd no intention of moving on home
until he'd wrung every drop of pleasure and satisfaction
from it.

The dogs, which he had expected to rush out into the
dark did not appear. He'd been prepared to leap over the
wall and leg it up to Upfell or even up the bloody tree but
the daft cow in the doorway swung her bloody candle
shouting 'Who's there?' and it began to dawn on him that
the dogs weren't *coming* out, that . . . that she must have
tied them up . . . Jesus . . . she'd tied them up . . . !

It took him two strides to reach the doorway, pushing
Phoebe aside and sweeping back the door until it nearly
came off its hinges and in the corner where Bonnie and
Blackie were tied to the fixed settle their barking was high
and frantic with hysteria.

"What do you think you're doing, Bert Garnett?"
Phoebe said, her eyes livid in her outraged face. She was
not afraid, not then. She had seen who it was, when she'd
peeped from her bedroom window and she could see he
was drunk, the daft sod and Annie'd give him what for
when she saw that broken window. Good job she'd tied
the dogs up before she'd opened the door or they'd have
gone for him.

In answer to her outraged question Bert didn't really
know what he was doing. He bore Annie Abbott a deep
grudge and wanted nothing more than to vent his animosity
and resentment on her for her treatment of him. Chucking
the rock had been an impulse and if Phoebe hadn't opened
the door that was probably all the damage that would have
been done. But the sight of Phoebe's spotless kitchen,
the reflection of fire and candle-light glowing in the deep

rich polish of the oak table and the kist, the gleaming whitewashed walls touched to gold, the copper bowls filled with branches of autumnal leaves, the lovely fragrance of Phoebe's pot-pourri, and fainter, but just as pleasing, the bread she had baked that morning, all in such direct contrast to his own slovenly hearth where his wife seemed to live in stinking chaos since the death of her mother, brought the blood of madness to his head. He knew Phoebe was on her own. It was all over the parish where Annie's brat had gone, and who was paying for *that*, they were asking themselves, and Sally had let slip that Annie was over Whitehaven way selling her swills. Bugger the woman. She seemed to be doing better even than Bert Garnett, and living in a comfortable style if this kitchen was anything to go by. By heck, it wasn't to be borne the way some folk got on, especially them that didn't deserve it. As cosy a kitchen as he'd ever seen but by God he'd soon fix that, see if he didn't.

"Shut tha' bloody gob, woman." His voice was high and incensed at the injustice of it all, and *hers* as she shrieked at him, was grating on his nerves.

"Get out of my kitchen, tha' great daft loon," she was saying, her white nightdress flapping round her skinny ankles. Her hair, dark, long, straight as a ruler and heavy, with a shine on it in which the candle-light was tangled, fell across her shoulders and back. She confronted him, her white face glaring through it and when he struck her backhanded, she was knocked, sprawling, several feet across her own shining flags. She lay on her back, winded, dizzy, for the blow had landed at the side of her head. The room was swaying as she tried to stand but she saw his boot coming towards her. She did her best to avoid it but despite her efforts to protect herself, it struck her just below her ribs. The pain rocked her back, but again she tried to get up, which was a mistake for Bert Garnett's clenched fist caught her cheek-bone. The flesh split open and the blood poured from it and when he hit her again, and then again, his fist slipped in it. She had the good sense to stay down then, watching through the curtain of her blood-soaked hair as he systematically went about the business of destroying Annie Abbott's home.

She was sitting on the settle, the only seat remaining since the dogs had been tied to it, when Annie burst in through the front door. For an horrific moment, Annie wondered who she was, for the person by the fire was unrecognisable. She had Phoebe's figure, her snow-white apron with the pretty butterfly cap on her well-brushed and neatly arranged hair, but the face beneath it was swollen, the skin scraped away, the eyes, both of them no more than puffy slits set in a deep purple bruise. There was a scabby cut down one cheek and her lips were split open like rotten plums. Sweet Jesus . . . Who? . . . What? . . . She'd known . . . somehow she had known . . . all the while she was in Whitehaven . . . she'd known . . .

"Phoebe?" She could not help the questioning note in her voice. The dogs after the first nervous inclination to bark, ran forward swirling about Annie's legs for a moment before returning to crouch defensively at Phoebe's knee as though to say this time . . . *this time*, they would be ready. Not even Annie to whom they were devoted, would be allowed near her, but Phoebe touched their heads briefly before turning to stare back into the fire.

"Oh, God, Phoebe . . . sweetheart . . . who did this to you?" But of course she knew. Who else hated Annie Abbott enough to do this to the only friend Annie had? In Annie's absence he had come to the farm and beaten Phoebe's face to pulp, smashing it with his fists. She became aware then of the damage that had been done to the room. It was neat, clean, tidy but on the whitewashed walls something – what was it, for Christ's sake? – had been smeared and where there had been bowls of flowers there was nothing. The rug was gone and many of the utensils with which Phoebe had prepared and cooked their meals, and other meagre comforts she and Phoebe had made in the long winter nights. Cushions, a hodden grey shawl, even the samplers which had been brought down from the bedroom to decorate the kitchen walls. The curtains were missing and the room, though clean, was bare, as barren as it had been on the day Annie came home. Only the heavy oak table, the kist and the settle remaining and through her rage she wanted to weep. Not only for the Phoebe who had taken the beating meant for Annie, but for the Phoebe who had painstakingly, *agonisingly*, by the look of her, put back together what was left, tidied and cleaned, even herself, where any other woman would have run screaming into the night looking for help. She had picked herself up and bathed herself, tidied herself and then started on the room, but then, where would she go for help? Who besides Sally would give Phoebe the time of day, let alone a helping hand when she needed it? She was Annie Abbott's friend, wasn't she?

The figure on the settle stirred and began to mumble through her torn lips, but it was several minutes before Annie could decipher what she said.

"Take your time, darling." She had sat down beside her and gently taken her hand. From the doorway Natty watched quietly, saying nothing but knowing, as she did, who had done this. "It was Bert Garnett, wasn't it? How did he get in? Surely the dogs . . . what happened? . . . No, take your time, your poor, poor face . . . Oh, Phoebe . . . don't fret, we'll make him pay. Natty will fetch the constable . . . we'll see that he's put away . . ."

"No . . ."

"What . . ."

"Not him . . ."

Annie bent her head, for surely her ears were mistaken. Phoebe seemed to be telling her that it was not Bert Garnett who had attacked her, wrecked every room in the farmhouse – for Annie had seen Natty run up the stairs and come down again shaking his head – which was ridiculous, for who else . . . who . . . ?

"Phoebe darling, look at me . . . I know, I'm sorry, love . . . it is just . . . it must be agony to move" – and yet she had cleaned the whole place . . . "but we must know the truth. If Bert Garnett did this . . ."

"No . . . stranger . . ."

"A *stranger*? A stranger came in here, just off the fell

and ransacked the place? You let someone in that you didn't know . . . ?" Annie shook her head in disbelief but Phoebe remained passive, turning her face away to stare through the slits of puffed flesh into the fire and nothing that Annie or even Natty could say would make her change her story.

"No," she mumbled through her painfully cut lips. The man had not hurt her in the way bad men hurt a defenceless woman. He had smashed his way in . . .

"But the door was not broken, Phoebe."

. . . and hit her when she had protested . . .

"There's nothing stolen, Phoebe, so why should he . . . ?" for everything that was missing was found, battered, torn, wrecked almost beyond repairing but safe in the barn where Phoebe had painstakingly put it.

. . . No, she didn't know who it was . . . no, it was not Bert Garnett and no matter what Annie said or did, Phoebe would not change her story and at Upfell Farm Bert Garnett smiled to himself.

26

The school in which Catriona Abbott was enrolled, though
her mother had not been inside it, naturally, was devoted
to the nourishment and education of the minds of those
girls and young ladies whose parents wished them to be
proficient in more than how to sew a sampler, speak a
word or two of French, paint a watercolour or strike a
chord on the piano. Its enlightened headteacher and the
owner of the school, Miss Amy Mossop, was the daughter
of a clergyman, now dead. He had given his only child a
sound grounding in Greek, French, Latin, the arts, geography, history, literature and mathematics, all the subjects
he himself had been taught as a boy and, having no son,
only this one clever girl child, to whom to pass on his
knowledge, he had done so along with a house set in three
acres of garden in Grasmere and a small annual income.
By then Miss Mossop was a spinster of some twenty-eight
years, plain, sensible and not at all prepared to sit on her
hands for the rest of her life. She did not care for the idea
of marriage, had the possibility been open to her, and her
hundred pounds a year was barely enough for herself to
live on, let alone keep the large old house and the servants
needed to maintain it and the gardens.

It became the 'Mossop Academy for Young Ladies' in
1839, though many of the neighbouring gentry and those
able to afford the fees asked themselves why they should
trust their girls to Amy Mossop? It was, they found after
all, easier than going to the trouble of finding a governess.
It was also very convenient to board a sometimes . . .
well . . . an awkward child knowing she would be brought
up exactly as she would at home. The dormitories were
bright and cheerful, the dining hall well appointed and the

gardens, where girls were encouraged to grow their own flowers, were private and safe.

Catriona Abbott was one of those 'awkward' children, intelligent, there was no doubt of that, but very shy, simply dressed in the plainest of hodden grey when she arrived in the carriage of Mr Reed Macauley who told Miss Mossop that the child's mother, who was a distant relative of his, wished her daughter to be educated to the highest standard. Her mother was unable to bring her, he informed Miss Mossop crisply, due to family circumstances, but she wished the child to be sent home every Friday afternoon. His carriage would fetch her, weather permitting, returning her at eight thirty sharp each Monday morning. The uniform of the school, ah yes, he agreed with Miss Mossop that young ladies should dress identically and he would see to it this very week.

Naturally, she did not voice her suspicions but Miss Mossop took it that Catriona Abbott, though she looked nothing like him, was Mr Macauley's daughter, the outcome of some misalliance outside marriage, she supposed. It did not concern her. Catriona was not the first, nor would be the last little indiscretion of the gentry, even the aristocracy, who found their way to her tolerant and fair-minded gates.

Annie had insisted that she provide her child's outfit for the school. Reed had told her about the scholarship which was to be awarded to a promising scholar, in this case her own Cat, marvelling that her child was so clever that Miss Mossop had chosen to give it to her. It included her tuition and board from Monday to Friday, Reed had told her straight-faced, but not her clothes which he would be willing to pay for but she would not hear of it.

The length of hodden-grey wool, the one she had woven and put by to make a new outfit for herself for the coming winter, had provided Cat's well-fitting, well-made dress and jacket. The egg and butter money, her new black boots. Phoebe had knitted her stockings and the crisp white cotton lace-trimmed drawers, petticoat and chemise had come from Lizzy Abbott's beautiful bedsheet, the one her mother had made with her own hands including the lace. They had wept, she and Phoebe with their arms about one another when Reed had taken Cat away, his carriage standing for all the world to see on the road at the bottom of the track which led up to Browhead. Like a little princess, she had looked, although try as they might, they could not contrive a bonnet for her, smiling, flushed, excited at the thought of going to a real school. At the last moment she had run back to hide her face in Annie's waist, clutching at her with frightened arms. She was not too sure she wanted to go off with Mr Macauley who was very stern and how was she to bear losing Blackie and Bonnie and Dandy and the flock of kittens which pranced about the yard? She had never been parted from her mother and Browhead was the only home she had known.

Annie had knelt to look into her face, unaware of the man who stood to watch them, his heart wrenched and torn with his love for her, that love written plain on his face and in the deep blue sadness of his eyes. He was doing this for her, the only thing she would allow him to do and even now she thought it was all free. If she could have taken Cat to Miss Mossop's school herself, she would have done so, but how could she shame her child by going to this wonderful place, where Cat was to learn all that she had never learned, looking like a vagrant, clean and darned and patched, but a vagrant none the less. But Reed would take her and his carriage would call for her each weekend and so she would swallow her pride and her deep aversion to accepting Reed's help on this one thing for the sake of her child.

"Darling, this is to be a great day for you and me, you know that, don't you?" she whispered into Cat's weeping face. "You are a brave and clever girl, lambkin, and such bravery and cleverness cannot be wasted. Think of what you will be able to tell Phoebe and me, to teach us when you come home at the weekend, and then there is the farm. When it is as big as Mr Macauley's it will need a clever, well-educated brain to look after it and that is what

you will have. And you will be home on Friday. We will
have a little party to celebrate. Would you like that, sweetheart?" and Reed Macauley had to turn away from the
glowing maternal loveliness in Annie Abbott's face. God
help him if she found out it was himself who was paying
the fees and for the uniform which Cat would wear for five
days of the week. She was so proud that she, Annie Abbott
was doing this for her daughter with help from no one.
That she and Cat between them, since it was Cat's cleverness that won the scholarship, had clawed their way up
from their precarious beginnings to become a woman with
a small but increasingly successful farm, and a child with
a promising academic future ahead of her. He could not
take it away from her, her belief that it was all hers and
Cat's doing. It could prove to be tricky, making sure that
Annie Abbott's daughter had everything that every other
pupil in the school had without arousing Annie's suspicions,
but he just hoped her lack of knowledge about an establishment such as Miss Mossop's would allow her to believe
that it was all free.

The first weekend she came home, her legs flailing like
small windmills up the track from the road and from where
Reed Macauley's carriage was just drawing away, Annie
was half-way down to meet her, her face alight with her
radiant smile, her arms opened wide to catch her. The
child flew into them and they strained together for a
rapturous moment then Annie whirled her round and
round, both of them laughing and half crying at the same
time. About them circled the barking ecstatic dogs and,
sidling indolently behind, backside swaying, tail up and
curling gracefully from side to side, came Dandy. The
kittens from Dandy's third – or was it fourth – litter
scrambled and danced at her rear and for five excited
minutes there was happy pandemonium.

"Darling, darling . . . we've missed you so . . ."

"I know, Mother . . . but the school is . . ."

"What . . . What . . . ?"

"Oh, it's splendid, Mother. Already I have learned
something called 'geometry' and Miss Mossop was most

gratified, that's what she said, to know that I already had some Greek and Latin, so I explained about Charlie and she said he must be a clever gentleman and I said that he had gone to Yorkshire . . ."

"Oh, sweetheart . . ." but by now Cat was rolling on the rough grass with the animals, all vying with one another to be first at her.

"Cat . . ."

"Blackie . . . Bonnie . . . Oh, Dandy. I've only been gone a week . . ."

"Cat . . ."

". . . and just wait until I show you what I painted for Phoebe . . ."

". . . Cat . . ."

"I knew she would like it because she loves flowers so."

"Cat, darling . . ."

"Where is she, Mother? . . . Where is Pheobe? I must show her . . ."

"Cat, come here to Mother, lambkin."

"But I must show Phoebe . . ."

"I know, sweetheart, but . . . well . . ."

"What is it, Mother? Where's Phoebe?"

"She's at home, darling . . ."

"Well then . . ." and the child turned, ready to scamper up the rocky track to where she knew Phoebe would be waiting, probably with one of Cat's favourites like Fig Sue or blackcurrant tart. In fact she was surprised that Phoebe wasn't here with mother and Blackie and Bonnie and Dandy, with Cat's family, for that was what they were, all those who lived under Browhead's roof.

"Cat, come here."

"Mother, I must . . ."

"CAT, come to Mother, darling. Before we go up to the house I must tell you that Phoebe is not very well."

The child stood instantly still and the satchel she held, a present from Mr Macauley, which she meant to show, in all its glory to Mother and Phoebe and of course, the animals, fell limply at the end of her arm, dragging on the grass. Blackie sniffed at it, interestedly, and so did Bonnie, absorbing its curious scent.

"Not well, Mother? What's wrong with her?"

"She . . . had a fall, lambkin, and hurt her face and . . ." How to describe to a child of almost six the strange and silent state of a young woman, for that was what Phoebe was now, who a week ago had been their cheerful, outspoken, faithful, hard-working Phoebe. Phoebe, whose face had lit up like the sun coming over the top of Great Calva whenever Annie or Cat came into the room. Phoebe, who now, when she was not scrubbing dementedly at the walls, or bare floor of the farmhouse, sat staring into the fire in the inglenook. Her face was less swollen but it was black and purple, green and yellow with the fading bruises. Scabs had formed where her flesh had split on her cheek and lips but it was not these that worried Annie but her deep and unnatural silence, her absolute refusal to talk about the event of a few days ago, and her absolute denial that the man who had attacked her and devastated their home was Bert Garnett. Natty had set to and with his usual dexterity had repaired chairs and kitchen utensils, even replacing the samplers in their frames and hanging them on the wall. He had gathered a great bunch of grasses and fading ling, placing them awkwardly in the battered copper bowl Phoebe had loved, so that their home had begun to look as it had before it had been treated with such violence. Bed linen which had been torn and sullied with the nasty waste of the attacker's body had been washed and could be repaired and the oatmeal and barley spilled from the kist in which they were stored had been gathered up and replaced. The child would not notice now any great difference in her home, only in Phoebe.

"She's not been at all well since she . . . she fell and hurt her face, so I want you to be especially gentle with her. Her poor face it is . . . well . . . it is dreadfully bruised, sweetheart and cut, so . . . you are a good, kind girl and I know you will not mean to upset her so . . . don't let her know you are . . ."

"I will show her the picture I painted for her, Mother."

"Of course, darling, that will make her feel better. She will be so pleased and happy to see you. I'm sure she will begin to mend at once."

The little girl was hesitant at first, not at all accustomed to seeing Phoebe sitting down, doing nothing but stare at the crackling logs in the fire. She moved across the kitchen to place herself in Phoebe's direct line of vision since it seemed Phoebe was not going to turn her head to look at her and her eyes widened as she looked at Phoebe's ravaged face.

"Phoebe, it's me, Cat," she said, then, hesitation gone, she clambered on to Phoebe's lap and hugged her carefully, gently, before placing a butterfly kiss on Phoebe's bruised cheek. "There," she said cheerfully. "All better now," just as Phoebe and Annie had said a hundred times to her, and Phoebe stirred and without conscious thought her arms went round the child.

"Oh, Phoebe, I've missed you so much, really I have, but I've so much to tell you and show you. I've painted the loveliest picture for you. They're chrys . . . chrys the mums . . . well, Miss Mossop has them in her study . . . yes, a study, it's called, and she sits there at a big desk and she said I could paint them. I told her about you and me being friends and she said *of course* I could bring my paints . . ."

Her voice went on and on, describing the wonders, the marvels which had been revealed to her during the past few days. Her eyes never left Phoebe's face, but they did not see Phoebe's scars, only the shining expression of love and amazed interest which had come to Phoebe's eyes. She would repeat it all again and again for her mother, for Blackie and Bonnie and Dandy, but it was as though at this precise moment, she knew with that curious wisdom which is bestowed on the very young, that *this* was for Phoebe since Phoebe had need of it.

". . . the food is not as nice as yours, Phoebe, so I'm looking forward to a blackcurrant tart . . ."

"and tha' shall 'ave it for tha' tea, sweeting, as soon as I've heated the oven . . ."

". . . and I tore the lace on my new drawers when Alice . . . she's my new friend . . ."

". . . Alice . . . that's a pretty name and I'll mend that tear as soon as ah've a minute . . ."

". . . so I'll get my satchel . . . yes, isn't it *lovely*. . . Mr Macauley said I should need it . . ."

". . . by heck, that's grand . . . grand . . . and kind of Mr Macauley . . ."

". . . isn't it, but wait until you've seen your painting. Mr Macauley said he would frame it for you . . . there . . . now what d'you think, Phoebe, aren't the colours lovely . . ."

"Eeh, lovey . . . lovey . . ."

"Now you mustn't cry, Phoebe . . . your face is not so bad . . ."

"Eeh . . . lovey . . . lovey . . . Phoebe's missed thi' . . ."

"I know . . ."

". . . and I've never had such a lovely picture, an' all me own, an' all . . ."

Beside the doorway Annie turned away. She lifted her forearm and leaned it on the wall. Placing her face in it she wept the tears of gladness, for Cat's return, for Phoebe's return and for the deep enduring love Reed Macauley gave her.

The little church of St Bridget's which stood in splendid isolation on the shores of Lake Bassenthwaite was generally full each Sunday but on the one following Cat Abbott's return from her grand school at Grasmere, every pew was jammed to capacity and several of its parishioners were forced to stand at the back. The church was very old, no one was sure just how old, since it was rebuilt in the reign of King Richard I. The register was begun in the sixteenth century and the font bowl was dated back to 1300 and in it, thirty-three years ago, Reed Macauley had been christened. There were many graves in the churchyard bearing the name of Macauley, including those of Reed Macauley's mother and father, and several containing his infant brothers and sisters.

The church was reached by a long track leading from the road between Hause and Keswick, down which, to reach St Bridget's, those with no carriage must tramp in all weathers, but today it was sunny and crisp, November, the sky the loveliest winter blue with not a cloud in sight. There was a stretch of woodland between the road and the church but round the actual building and the walled churchyard was a lush green pasture on which sheep grazed, and beyond it was the lake, its gently ruffled surface silver and the palest grey blue. Beyond the lake rose the browning fells, on and on into the distance as far as the eye could see.

Reed Macauley sat straightbacked beside his lovely young bride. Eighteen months they had been married and still no children and not likely to be if the rumours which were whispered in every drawing room and on every street corner in Keswick were true. And Mrs Macauley so elegant and fine looking, a perfect lady in her dove-grey velvet two-piece outfit, the skirt so wide after the narrow angle of the last decade, those who were already seated were quite amazed that the church aisle could take it. Her jacket bodice was shaped to her tiny waist and flared out below it with a basque extended over her hips. It was close-fitting to her long white neck and edged with a small white lace collar. The buttons which ran from neck to waist were of mother-of-pearl. Her bonnet, also of dove-grey velvet, was tiny, slipping far back on her proudly held head to reveal the astonishing golden glint of her hair. She wore pearls in her ears, neat white gloves and extremely high-heeled dove-grey kid boots. She looked quite magnificent, aloof, unconcerned with anything other than the long and tedious sermon to which she listened intently, her cloudy blue eyes never wavering from the rector's face.

Her husband was also splendidly dressed, like her in grey, but his was a charcoal grey, immaculate and expensive with a watered silk lavender waistcoat beneath his

coat. A swallow-tailed coat from which a snowy white
stock cascaded. His trousers were tight, well fitted, showing off his splendid calf and strapped under his instep. He
carried a tall grey top hat. His face was grim, looking
neither to left nor right as he had followed his wife's wide
skirt up the central aisle but during the parson's sermon
had there been anyone – bar the parson – in front to see,
they might have noticed he closed his eyes several times
and his face clamped itself into what might have been pain.

"We shall go to church this morning, Reed," Esmé
Macauley had announced after breakfast. "Do not think I
intend to skulk at home, hiding my face as though I had
something of which to be ashamed during this . . . difficult
time. I can do nothing to stop you acting as you are doing,
causing gossip of the most unsavoury sort, but I can show
society that I have nothing to hide."

"You *have* nothing to hide, Esmé, and I have done
nothing of which I am ashamed."

"Really, then may I ask you why you are taking so much
interest in the daughter of a woman who, or so I have
been told, has a reputation for being . . ."

"Yes, Esmé?" Reed's voice was dangerously quiet.

"She is not married, Reed, and has a daughter. Surely
that is all that need be said."

Esmé Macauley was not quite twenty years old. She
had been ready to love her handsome husband though she
had scarcely known him on the day they were married.
He was wealthy and influential, not quite of the gentry,
but then neither was she for her father's father had been
a weaver and her father was of that new class, the *millo-
cracy*, those coming to power and wealth in this new industrial age. She had been gently reared and her governess
had instilled in her all that a lady should know. It was, she
had hinted, quite acceptable for a man to have a mistress
providing he was discreet and if she was honest, Esmé
had not concerned herself when it came to her notice that
Reed was no exception. She had not cared for his rough
embrace and the indignities to which he subjected her, but
she wanted a child so she must, to get one, perform her

wifely duties, she had thought. There was no child and it mystified and distressed her, though she spoke of it to no one and certainly not to her husband. So what was she to make of his interest in the bastard called Catriona Abbott?

She had asked him since she did not want her own position in society to be jeopardised. She tried to be reasonable, calm, remembering the teachings of her governess that a lady never, *never* showed emotion, but she had her household to consider, her friends, most of whom came from Yorkshire, Cheshire, Leicestershire since she found the wives and daughters of the local society somewhat parochial.

"I have no interest in her other than to give her a decent education."

"But why? Why should you concern yourself with this child in particular, who is, after all, from the lower orders?"

Reed clamped his teeth about the fragrant cigar he was smoking and on his face came that scowling expression she had come to know so well and which, in the past, before she had learned to control herself, had made her cry. His eyebrows dipped ferociously over his eyes which had in them the blue chill which made his wife shiver, for she was an affectionate, placid girl who had known, and needed, nothing but kindness. She wanted Reed to be as her father had been. *Exactly.* Indulgent, fond, generous, not this truculent, grim-mouthed, pugnaciously jawed stranger who was always polite, who shared her bed most nights, at least for half an hour, and who often looked through her as though she were made of glass.

"This child from the 'lower orders', as you so quaintly put it, is bright, exceedingly so. She even knows a little Greek and Latin. Can you imagine that . . . ?" smiling in a way Esmé had never seen.

Esmé couldn't, since she herself scarcely knew how to add one figure to another and as for languages or dates of battles, they would just not stay inside her head, no matter how hard Miss Humphries, her governess, had tried to put them there.

". . . she can read the Bible from cover to cover and

speaks some French and is proficient in mathematics and
she is no more than five or six years old."

"But who has taught her? Not her mother, surely."

"Some chap who . . . lived with them." His face closed
up tight as a clam but his wife failed to notice.

"The mother's lover?"

Reed struck the mantle shelf so hard with the flat of his
hand several ornaments which stood on it jumped half an
inch into the air, and so did Esmé.

"No, he was not, dammit." He glared at her so fiercely
she shrank away from him but nevertheless she would not
give up.

"How do you know that, Reed?"

"Because I do, confound it. She is not a liar and when
she told me that they were not lovers I believed her."

He had told her all she wanted to know. She was not
clever, not it seemed like the woman's child was clever,
but it did not take a great intellect to see the anger, the
longing, the frustration which ravaged her husband, though
once again his face had become smooth, closed up, his
eyes expressionless.

"You and she discussed it then?" She lifted her lovely
head and her upbringing and the practical Yorkshire
common sense she had inherited from her father was
evident in her smooth young face. She had to be a fool
not to understand and inexperienced though she was,
Esmé was no fool.

"For God's sake, Esmé, what sort of a question is that?"

"A simple one, I would have thought. You and she have
talked of the child and her education, it seems, and from
what you tell me, of other things, I am . . . I think I
am entitled, as your wife, to know what she means to
you?"

"She is . . . a neighbouring farmer . . . she fell on hard
times and . . ."

"You helped her out."

Reed's face took on the menacing hue and expression
those with whom he did business would have recognised.
He was not a man to be questioned on his actions,

whatever they might be, and he was certainly not going to explain to this child, even if she was his wife, the undercurrents which eddied about his relationship with Cat Abbott's mother. He had known from the first that his carriage at the gate of Browhead, with Cat Abbott in it as they drove on the road to Grasmere, and as it drove back, his coachman at the reins, again with Cat Abbott in it, would not pass by unnoticed. His name had been linked in a vague, unformed way with Annie Abbott's for some time, but the presence of Charlie Lucas had silenced the whispers. Now they were becoming a full-throated roar and he found that he did not care any more. He was sorry if they should hurt his wife since she was no more than a child herself. A child to whom he had done a great mischief, but his obsession with Annie Abbott was running out of control and he could not seem to harness it. He wanted to cosset her, hold her, protect her, wrap her in luxury and hide her deep and safe in the love which filled his heart, but she wouldn't let him and so he must do it through the child.

"This has nothing to do with our marriage, Esmé . . ."

"It has if you are to . . . to flaunt yourself with . . ."

His roar could be heard in the kitchens and the servants froze in terror. The little skivvy who was carrying a stack of pans she had just scoured, squeaked and dropped them with a deafening clatter and the butler Esmé Macauley had employed a year ago tut-tutted angrily.

"That is enough, Esmé. I will not be told how to conduct my life. Not by you, nor anyone. You are my wife and will remain so for as long as I live, but what I do outside this house is my own concern. You have my name and my protection. No one will ever harm you or insult you, in my presence or out of it." He twisted the massive gold and onyx ring he wore on the little finger of his left hand, then turned and walked toward the window, putting as much distance as he could between himself and his pretty young wife in case his snarling anger should become unleashed. He took another cigar from the gold case in his pocket, then returned to the fire to light it, inhaling deeply before he leaned down towards her. She shrank away.

His lips hardly moved as he spoke and his eyes were slivers of blue ice between his thickly lashed lids. He was in command of himself now after that curious defence-lessness.

"But you will obey me, my girl, and you will do it with that certain style you have which marks you for a lady. You will do as you have done for the past eighteen months. What you have done well. You will look after my house and my guests. Nothing will change. I will not change it. I will go to church with you. I will be here at our table and in your bed since I want a child. I don't know why we have not had one for you must admit I do my best to oblige. I am well aware that you find the . . . procedure distasteful and when you conceive I shall bother you no longer."

Her face became crimson at his coarse reference to what went on in their bed, then it drained away to leave her white and trembling, for she was afraid of this violence in her husband, wondering frantically on the emotion which had caused it.

"There is nothing more to say. Whatever you may hear about . . . the child you are to disregard it. Contrary to popular belief she is not mine and I will not have her discussed, *or* her mother in my house. Is that clear? Very well, put on your hat and we will go to church."

"Yes, Reed," she said, and went to fetch her bonnet.

27

They did not see Cat from the beginning of January when the snow began until the end of February when it thawed. They saw no one, spending the winter months cut off from the rest of the world by the deep snow. She and Natty had, at the first onset of the bad weather, brought down the flock to the intakes so that if it became necessary they could be hand fed with the hay cut from the meadow grass in the summer. The cow, christened 'Clover' by Cat was housed in the cow shed, cared for by Natty in the nature of feeding, watering, mucking out and bedding. Phoebe milked her daily, and she was justifiably proud of her dairy work. The actual dairy was intensely cold, set on the north-facing wall of the farmhouse as it was, even at the height of the summer. There was a boiler, a stone floor with a slight slope for drainage, and the walls were lined with a great many stone shelves. It was all spotlessly clean, the pails and crocks scoured meticulously for it would not do to find one of Clover's hairs in the butter or for the cheese to become too soft. There were no second chances in a dairy.

"That butter's a long time comin'" was a timeless lament from Phoebe, just as though she was heartily sick of the task and for two pins would give it all up, but Annie knew she relished it, tickled to death with the produce of her own labour. The upright butter churn in which a long 'plunger' was 'dashed' up and down was in use twice a week. There was a box churn which was for when only a small quantity of butter was to be made, and when the churned butter was ready Phoebe 'worked' it with her own cold, bare hands to remove the excess buttermilk. She had cream setting dishes made of the wood from the sycamore tree, a butter board, a hand-carved butter stamp, a butter barrel, again made of sycamore which did not taint the flavour of the milk, and in which the butter was stored. She heated her cheese-making milk in a copper cheese kettle before adding the rennet and after the numerous and complex processes through which it went, the cheese was put in the 'press' where it would remain for weeks or sometimes months before it was ripe for eating. Phoebe chafed at the bad weather which kept them from the market place in Keswick. The eggs which were not eaten by herself, Natty and Annie were pickled in vinegar and pepper. The butter and cheese was wrapped in a constantly changed wet cloth kept in hay and ice, brought from wherever it formed, and stored in the barn to keep it fresh. On the first day they were able to get to the market place, drawing the produce on the sledge, Phoebe was overwhelmed by the profit that was made. "Sixpence three farthings for each pound of cheese an' all from nowt really," she said, discounting her hard labour and refusing absolutely to accept the few pence Annie would have given her to spend.

"Nay, lass, buy summat for't bairn. 'Appen she'll be 'ome at weekend," and she was, receiving a rapturous welcome from everyone, even Natty who poked a finger in her cheek and told her she looked 'right sprightly'.

During the winter months Annie worked on her diary, not as one might suppose a record of her social activities but of her farm, and the past three years she had spent on it. Begun at Charlie's suggestion, week by week she had put down each meticulous detail of every moment of her busy day, from early sowing and planting, weeding, hoeing, feeding the land to the day it was all harvested, stored, threshed, milled and the land ploughed ready for the cycle to begin again. Each animal she possessed, marked with her own mark, was recorded and its progress noted, ewes, lambs, hoggs, gimmers, twinters and the wethers, the castrated males she was fattening for sale. When she had bought them, and from whom, and the quality and price she got for her fleeces. All the hundreds of details of which her farming year was made up. Her tiny profits after she had deducted what she was forced to buy in the way of provisions, those they could not themselves grow or produce.

She and Natty spent hard days, sometimes until dark, prodding long sticks into snow drifts the height of the stone walls they faced, their dogs helping them, looking for the 'daft buggers', as Natty called them, sheep which continued to wander off up on to high ground. They were all found, with the sharp nose of Natty's dog who was more experienced than Blackie and Bonnie, digging furiously until the wanderer was released from a snowy grave.

As they worked they could see far below, the stone of the farmhouse standing grey against the surrounding whiteness. A wisp of smoke curled from the chimney and inside Annie knew Phoebe would have a hot and nourishing meal waiting for them, 'neaps and tatties' or 'crowdy'. It was still on this day but the skies were heavy with fresh snow waiting to fling itself down on those who were careless in their regard for the weather signs. They had fed the ewes with their daily ration of a pound of hay, those that had been 'tupped' in November and were already heavy with their lambs.

Natty worked alone when he repaired the gaps in the drystone walls on her 'inlands'. It was a never-ending task. Deep snow drifts piled against the walls and alternating frost and thaw inevitably caused gaps. The gap must be pulled right down to the base and rebuilt. The job, long and exhausting, could only be done when spare time was available. Natty tidied the barn and the cow shed and spread the fields, when the snow allowed it, with manure. To earn a bob or two and at the right time of the year, it was his custom to help the keeper of a local landowner's estate by acting as a 'beater' during the grouse-shooting season, and, for a lark, and to see if she could do it without being spotted, Annie joined him. She was inevitably noticed since she was by now a familiar figure in her threadbare jacket and breeches, her gaiters and wooden-soled clogs. She wore her heavy woollen jerkin beneath the jacket and a long muffler wound about her neck. Her soft felt hat, the brim turned down, was pulled well over her forehead but when the keeper, a man called Abel Greenwood bade her a dour "Morning, lass", she was quite astonished, not that she should have been recognised but that she should have been spoken to. More amazing still was the nod Jackie Ingham, a neighbouring cottager, aimed in her direction and the gruff "tekk the drag, lass" from another, Willy North. As she said later to an equally astonished Phoebe, you could have knocked her down with a feather. "Are they beginning to accept me, Phoebe, at last?" she asked.

"'Appen the men, chuck, but it'll tekk time wit wimmin."

Sometimes Annie felt that Phoebe was the older of the two of them. She was cheerful again now, her old self after the beating from the 'stranger' but she had an old head on young shoulders, careful and prudent without Annie's inclination towards humour. She took her position as 'housekeeper' very seriously. She was neat and exacting, brusque with Natty if he should bring muck in on to her clean kitchen floor. Big-hearted and generous, she was nevertheless always conscious of the precarious state of their world and was never careless or carefree in the way she approached each day.

At the end of March, a Friday, the burning of the heather began. There was a light wind blowing, the heather was tinder-dry, the air crisp and clean and below where Annie and Natty stood they could see more than one dale spread out before them. The heather was to be burned in strips so that the sheep and grouse who were to benefit from it could pass easily through it, seeking out the various stages of regrowth which were the reason for burning it. The breeze must be at a man's back. A handful of bracken was set alight, transferred to the dry heather and from there carried along the desired line.

Phoebe was 'pegging out' a line of snow-white, billowing undergarments, those which her lambkin had worn and brought home from school. Though the day was nearly over there was a good 'drying wind' and an hour or two would see this little lot ready for ironing. The child had begged to go up and find her mother, wanting her to see her painting but Phoebe had said no, wait in the yard, she'd not be long and here, eat this oatcake she'd made while she waited. Her satchel was still on the step and guarding it were Blackie and Bonnie for they were not allowed on the fell when the burning was in process. Natty's dog, in canine years as old as her master, had found a sliver of sun in which she dozed but suddenly, though nothing untoward had happened, at least that Phoebe had noticed, all three sprang to their feet, their hackles rising and to her horror, Blackie and Bonnie lifted their heads and howled.

Dear sweet Lord! The clothes peg she held in her mouth fell to the ground and instinctively she looked around for the child.

"Cat, where is't tha', come to Phoebe, lambkin," for whatever it was that had set the dogs to making such a din it must surely be frightful, and might it not be threatening the child?

"Cat . . . where is't tha', Cat?" she quavered but she was not there and Blackie and Bonnie were acting in the strangest way, crouched and quivering, their tails between their legs, their ears flat on their heads as they both stared up towards the line of fire on the fell.

"Tha' should've asked Jackie Ingham and Willy North to give us a hand, lass," Natty said as he struck the tinder.

"We can manage, Natty. I'll beat at this flank and you keep to the other. It's not a long line and we can easily hold it in check between us. I can't afford any more wages, you know that. Not after paying you," for she had kept her promise, giving him the full labourer's wage of £8 a half year plus his food and room over the loft.

The burning went well. The flames advanced in a long, sizzling, crackling, smoking line, leaving behind a charred dark blue mass of pungent-smelling ash. The lusty growth in front of the line of fire contrasted sharply with the charred remains it left at the back, where next year the new green shoots would show. The rotational burning of the heather was to help both sheep and grouse but it must be done before the bird nesting season began. If the spring was wet, chances to burn were few and Annie pressed ahead, allowing the line to get longer and longer, the distance between herself and Natty growing until there was a great swathe of fire in the middle which was unsupervised.

Neither of them, frantically beating to control their end of the line of leaping flames saw the small figure of Cat Abbott, nor heard her excited child's voice as she called to her mother, for the noise the flames made was loud and angry. She ran towards them up the slope, the breeze blowing into her laughing face, exactly in the centre of the line of fire which was galloping in her direction, greedily devouring everything in its dry path. She wore her hodden-grey dress and jacket, the outfit already becoming too short for her. In her hand she carried a sheet of paper, upon which was a painting of Blackie, Bonnie and Dandy and which she had finished during the past week. She had a talent for it, Miss Mossop had told Annie in one of her polite reports and she hoped Mrs Abbott would not mind if it was encouraged.

Cat Abbott stopped when she saw the line of flames leaping towards her, paralysed by the sight and the speed with which it approached. The laughing anticipation with which she had run to meet her mother was quenched in total, panic-stricken terror. Her clever brain which at the age of six and a half could cope easily with the mathematical problems Miss Mossop set her, became blank, senseless, without thought or reason as the fire flew across the dry heather towards her.

It was her mother's agonised scream and the hoarse shout which tore from Natty Varty's throat which moved her, turned her, set her little legs to running away from the conflagration but it was too late by then. She tripped at the last moment, her face pressed into the heather as the flames swept over her.

*   *   *

Phoebe's hand went to her mouth as the most appalling sense of dread trickled icily through her veins. When the screams began, high and demented, leaping from fell to fell and rock to rock, echoing and echoing so that women in their farm kitchens cowered and covered their ears, Phoebe began to run, the three dogs close at her heels. She was already weeping, the breath rasping painfully in her chest as her legs propelled her across the beck behind the farmhouse and up the grassy slope of the intakes and beyond to where the heather began. She could see the line of fire, badly out of control, coming towards her, but guided by the instincts of the dogs she veered off, following them round it and across the smoking, pungent-smelling carpet of burnt heather. For some reason Natty Varty was running like a hare, *away* from her, going across and up the slope of Cockup in the direction of Dash Beck but it was not to him her eyes were drawn but to the kneeling, rocking, moaning figure of Annie Abbott who cradled something in her arms. Phoebe could not immediately recognise it but when she did her cries echoed Annie's, causing the women who had come to their kitchen doors to stare, eyes shielded, up the hill, to cower back again inside, drawing their children with them. One was Sally Garnett.

It was Reed Macauley who took charge, brought from Long Beck by the grey-faced trembling old man who had once been the phlegmatic and unruffled Natty Varty. He could not speak at first, so deep was the shock he was in and Reed had to shake him roughly to bring him from the appalled and appalling state into which the sight of Cat Abbott and her deranged mother had sent him. It was Reed Macauley who had sent him to Browhead in the first place but it was Annie Abbott who kept him there. He had developed to his own astonishment, a growing admiration for the woman who employed him. For her steadfast refusal to be browbeaten, for her spirit which snapped its fingers at those who tried it, for her courage and faith and hope, her humour and loyalty and her tenacious determination and belief that she and her family, which it seemed included not just Phoebe but himself, would find success. She was so proud of her child, and rightly so. She worked the work of ten men, she was beautiful and, he had discovered, she was honourable.

There were men, those who worked for Reed Macauley and who had followed him, for surely something of a shocking nature had occurred. Natty Varty had been incoherent but when they saw what it was they covered their eyes and their mouths with shaking hands and one, Jake Singleton, who was Mr Macauley's yardman with a snug little cottage at the back of the farm with a wife in it, sent for her and any other woman who would help, for surely Mr Macauley would need it.

Reed brought them down from the hill, Annie and Cat and Phoebe. Annie was so deep in shock as she stumbled after Reed Macauley she was no trouble to anyone. The women took her and her child and Mr Macauley stood in the farmyard his arms still curved in the gentle cradle in which he had carried down the burned body of Catriona Abbott. Tears streamed across his blanched face and his lean figure trembled as Natty's had done but when his men, awkward with sympathy would have drawn him towards his home since there was nothing else he could do here, was there? he turned on them snarling.

"Leave me be, you fools. For the love of God, don't touch me or I swear I'll kill the first man who does. I must stay here. She might need me."

It was then he noticed Phoebe. The women, Maggie Singleton, Jake's wife, Nell Tyson and Lily Gill, whose husbands all worked for him in his yard and stable and on the fells herding his flocks, had disappeared into the farmhouse, but nobody seemed to consider the strange and silent behaviour of the young woman who worked for Annie Abbott. She was not *family*, merely a servant at Browhead and so worthy of no particular attention, they had assumed, but Reed knew better.

She was pegging out the small undergarments she had boiled and scrubbed and rinsed only an hour ago. The dogs, bewildered and frightened by the death and chaos which had entered their lives, slunk about her as though the normality of her task reassured them and hovering at her back was Natty Varty as though he felt the same.

Reed moved slowly towards her, his body bent and ancient in his furious grief. His face was still wet with tears, the furrows deep in it and his mouth worked painfully as though he could not come to terms with this frightful and surely mortally wounding blow which had come to strike his love.

"Phoebe," he said gently, "will you come inside?"

"Nay, ah've things of t' child's ter see to."

"But surely one of the women will . . . see . . . here is someone." For running headlong down the path was Sally Garnett, her plump figure all over the place, her hair streaming out behind her with the force of her speed. "She will help you . . ."

"Nay, ah must see to it. Cat'll need them . . ."

"Phoebe," his voice was anguished. "Leave them . . . please."

"Ah've work to do 'ere, Mr Macauley and I'll thank thee to let me ger on wi' it."

He took her arm, or tried to but she shook him off, turning on him like a spitting cat but still he tried to draw her away.

"Leave me be. Cat'll need . . ."

"*No she won't*, Phoebe. Cat . . . is gone. She doesn't need . . ."

"So she's to be put in her coffin in them . . . in them things she 'as on then? Well, I'll not let my lambkin go off to Heaven in stinking clothes . . . all . . . black . . . an' . . . No! . . . let me be, Mr Macauley. I want this lot dry an' ironed before dark so that . . . so that . . . oh, sweet, sweet Jesus, so that she is . . . tidy an' clean. Now, get out of me way fer ah've things ter do. . . ."

It was traditional to 'bid' two people from each farm in the area in which a funeral was to take place but no such custom was carried out for the funeral of Annie Abbott's child. The small coffin was watched constantly until the day of the funeral by the women of Reed Macauley's household, taking it in turns with Sally Garnett, who, with a fierce bravery furnaced by her sympathy for Annie Abbott had defied her husband's rage and left her four children – she was still nursing Aggie – and him to fend for themselves. Phoebe had dressed Cat in her sweet-smelling, freshly ironed undergarments and with only her unmarked face showing above the white, lace-trimmed cover which lay over her, the child seemed to sleep. Phoebe had baked the 'arvel bread' which would be served to the men and women who would walk the 'corpse way' with the coffin. She had put herself and the silently distant figure of Annie Abbott into the black dresses Mr Macauley had produced from somewhere, Annie making no demur, as she made none about anything but her absolute refusal to leave her child's side where she stayed for two days and nights. She had not shed a tear since they had brought her down from the fell. Her eyes burned fanatically in their sockets and when anyone spoke to her she turned them on the speaker with what seemed to be hatred. She addressed not a word to anyone, not even Mr Macauley who was there day and night, going home only to bathe and shave and change his shirt. There was hatred in her, bitter and venomous and it could be felt in the farmhouse, in the air they breathed and the food Phoebe cooked and which they ate. She hated. She hated the gods or God who had done this to her. She hated the world which had forced her into the life she had led. She hated the men and women who peopled it, even those who now helped her. Where was Cat?

They took her to the church of St Bridget's by the lake, over the corpse way, for any departure from the recognised route would have been regarded as an ill omen. In certain parts of the district it was necessary to remove fencing so that a funeral procession might pass along the traditional route and all along the way there were 'resting stones' so that those carrying the coffin, often containing a large corpse, might rest the coffin and themselves. No such rests were required for Cat Abbott. Reed Macauley was one of the bearers. Jake Singleton was the other and behind him walked Annie Abbott and her maidservant Phoebe, side by side but not touching. Natty was there and Sally and several members of Reed's household. Will Twentyman came with Eliza for they remembered Annie Abbott's cheerful, willing labour in The Bull three years ago and the placidly silent child who was being buried today. There was a quiet woman dressed all in black who turned out to be Miss Mossop. No one else. Not a woman nor a man from Gillthrop or Hause for it was their belief that the sins of the fathers were visited on the sons, and surely mothers and daughters came into the same category.

They all went back to their homes after the funeral, leaving Annie and Phoebe beside the grave, with Natty a respectful distance behind, and lying quietly at his back were his dog, Blackie and Bonnie. Reed stood at the church gate, waiting, waiting for her to speak, to turn to him, to acknowledge his presence which, as yet, she had not done since Cat died, but when she and Phoebe went by him, neither looked in his direction. He might not have existed.

"Let me know if anything is needed, Natty," he said as the old man made to follow them. "Anything, no matter what it is. If she needs me . . . speaks of me at all . . ." since he was beyond caring now about anything but the withdrawn, hating grief which corroded inside Annie Abbott. The neighbourhood was agog with speculation, gossiping about him and the woman from Browhead, for surely his behaviour over the death of her daughter, his constant presence in the farmhouse, his purchase of mourning dresses and the bonnets – which *she* had not worn, it was said, though the maid had perched one on her dark head – his attendance as pall-bearer, meant that he was deeply involved with Annie Abbott. It had been enough when he sent the child to school and paid for her tuition but since then he had not been over the fell to Browhead himself, sending his carriage and coachman each week, when the weather allowed, to take and bring back Annie Abbott's daughter from Grasmere. The gossip had foundered and the speculation died down since it had nothing to feed on, but now, with the death of her daughter, tragic as it was, the conjecture had sprung up again. They felt so sorry for his wife, poor thing, sitting there all alone in her drawing room whilst her husband, not to mention half her women servants, spent days and nights under Annie Abbott's impure roof.

Reed Macauley shrugged his shoulders and ignored them. Not that anyone had the nerve to speak directly to him, or even, in his presence, make an out-of-place remark. They would not dare, for his temper was uncertain at the best of times. He seemed not to care at all that his reputation was finally and irrevocably in tatters.

Not a man, or woman, in the district would have found fault with him, nor thought it out of place if he had carried on an illicit affair with the 'woman from Browhead' as she was increasingly called, providing he had been discreet about it. But he had not. He had made it very obvious where his affections and loyalty lay. He had flown in the face of convention, flaunting his misdemeanours and they did not care for it.

Reed Macauley no longer even noticed their averted faces. He would stay away from her, for a while, he told himself as he watched her walk gracefully away from him as he had watched her on that first day, over three years ago at Penrith, but not because of them and what they said about him and Annie behind his back, but to give her time to steady herself. To do her grieving, come out of the shocked state into which Cat's death had impelled her; to recover a little, to accept. Natty would watch out for her and Maggie Singleton, who had turned out to be a dependable woman. Report on her progress, her health, her farm, her household. If help was needed, with her flock, her crops, he would provide it. She would want for nothing he could give her. He would wait, he loved her and his love made him patient, a characteristic he had never before known.

He turned then, striding off towards the lower slope of Ullock Pike and Longside Edge. He would walk back to

Long Beck – he would not say 'home' since his home was where Annie Abbott was – climbing over Bassenthwaite Common and Broad End and down past Dead Crags to White Water Dash waterfall. Long Beck was just beyond it. Long Beck and Esmé.

28

Edmund Hamilton-Brown did not like to see his little girl in tears. He never had done and if there was anything he could do to prevent tears from sliding down her cheeks in that heart-rending way they had he would do it. From being an astonishingly beautiful baby, pink and white, silver gold and blue, he had adored her. She was the most treasured of his possessions, and he owned a great many of those. He had been reluctant to part with her at the age of seventeen, even into the wealthy, important and competent hands of Reed Macauley. Of course, girls were married in his society from the age of sixteen, transferred from one man's care to another, always advantageously, and he knew Esmé must do the same, but it had been the most difficult thing he had had to do in his life. She was his only living child, and she, and the fortune she would inherit when he had gone, must be put in the charge of a man who could look after both, but his house would be empty without her. Her childish, lilting laughter, her bobbing ringleted embrace, her kisses when she badly wanted something she thought he might consider foolish, the way she had of snuggling on his knee and telling him of what she had done whilst he had been at the mill, her fragrance, her schoolgirl giggles in a corner with her friends, her flounces of satin, her extravagance, her innocence, her loveliness. She was the light of his life, though his gruff Yorkshire heart would not have admitted it had he been put to the torture. He had given her, from the moment she could talk, everything she had ever asked for, delighting in her delight, besotted and extravagantly indulgent. She was a lady, in his eyes, from being a small girl, surveying the world with a cool, charming stare, her cloudy blue eyes, which were sometimes, depending on the light, a clear turquoise, delighting in what her Papa made it for her. She knew she was beautiful and saw no reason to learn her letters and add up a sum or two for her Papa's household made a fuss of her whatever she did, and he was inclined to agree for what did a *lady* need of these things? She would marry well, present him with grandchildren, preferably boys who would go into his mills, and his old age would be pleasantly spent introducing them into the world of yardage and quality, of profit and loss, of expansion and gain.

He had been considerably put out when she had confided to him that his dinner guest from way up in the wilds of Cumberland, a man with whom he had done business on several occasions since the quality of his fleeces had been of the best, had taken her fancy, and could Papa please get him for her? Not in those words, of course, since Esmé was gently reared, a well brought up young lady with no knowledge of the world, of men or of business and was not even aware that Cumberland was a great deal further away from Bradford than Shipley, or even Halifax. He was not at all prepared to let her go so far away though he did not say so, putting forward the charms of this young man and that, sons of nearby business associates and personal friends, but it had not done at all. She had cried, great fat crystal tears which had wrenched at his heart. Mr Macauley's affections might be engaged elsewhere, he had said desperately, and her tears had flowed the harder.

When, with what he thought was great tact and delicacy, he had approached Reed Macauley, amazingly the man had been willing, saying that he had been looking for a young, well brought up wife, and, it seemed his Esmé was exactly what he wanted.

He himself had wept in the privacy of his room when Esmé drove off in the carriage with her new husband, waving and smiling, exquisite in her happiness and he had turned away from the harrowing pictures of what Reed Macauley would do to her that night. Instead he began to look ahead to those grandchildren he would have and the visits they and their mother would pay him. Long loving visits when the house would be filled again with her high excited laughter, the pretty parcels she would have brought in from the carriage, parties, dances, dinner guests. It would all come alive again. The nursery would be filled again. With the advent of the railways, all the way from Carlisle right down into Yorkshire, Cumberland was not so far away, was it? he asked his passive wife, who counted for nothing in his life except for the bounteous gift she had given him in his Esmé. Isabel Crowther was twenty when they married and himself thirty-five and Esmé had been the last fruit of his loins, born when he was forty-six years old. There were half a dozen before Esmé lying in the graveyard. So far none of his dreams had materialised. Two years his Esmé and Reed Macauley had been wed and her still not a mother. It was hard to understand for what he had seen of Reed Macauley he would have said he was a lusty man, not a man to waste time in the getting of a family, though the image this conjured up was not one he dwelled on. Esmé's tear-soaked letter came as a bombshell in the middle of the silent breakfast he shared with his wife of thirty years. His roar of rage rattled the coffee-cups and shook the chandeliers and in her chair at the foot of the table Isabel dropped her spoon into the bowl of creamy porridge she ate each morning. It splattered up and over the bodice of her dark brown morning dress but it went unnoticed as she gaped in terrified amazement at her snarling husband. The maidservants – Edmund did not care for butlers and footmen and such fiddle faddle, the only men he employed working in the yard, the garden and the stables – cowered back against the sideboard, clutching coffee-pots and cream jugs to their palpitating breasts.

"The bloody bastard's fornicating with another woman," he roared. "No wonder he's not got my Esmé in the family way. Playing a game away from home, the talk of the bloody parish, she says . . ." brandishing the letter as though he would dearly like to smash the fist which held it into Reed Macauley's face ". . . some damned farm woman he's taken up with and he's round there from morn-ing till night . . . an' through the night an' all, I'll be bound. Well, we'll see about that. There's no sod going to play fast and loose with my Esmé's affections, I can tell you that, woman . . ." just as though the whole thing was the fault of the open-mouthed, white-faced trembling figure who sat at the foot of his table. *His* Esmé, not hers, as she had always been. The two maid-servants, now that they realised that the savage anger of their master was aimed, not at them, but at Miss Esmé's husband, or so it seemed, relaxed their hold on one another and exchanged a glance for this promised to bring a frisson of excitement into the long tedium of their hard-working day. Wait until they got back to the kitchen, the exchanged glance seemed to say. Wouldn't they have something to tell the others? They simultaneously edged a little closer so that they would not miss anything.

Suddenly aware of them, for even in the midst of the direst emergency Edmund Hamilton-Brown was careful of his mouth, he turned on them so that they again reared back.

"And you two can clear off. I'll ring the bell when I need you."

There was nothing for it but to leave the breakfast room but they had the meat of it, hadn't they, and the rest would soon be revealed, one way or the other. Scandal always was.

"What are you . . . to do, Edmund?" his wife quavered. Edmund leaped to his feet, his wrath too much to contain sitting down. He strode to the window, flinging aside the heavy velvet curtains which were fashionable but which kept out most of the daylight. The fringed bobbled tie-backs bounced with his ferocity and his wife winced. He turned again, his wildness flaring about him, his blue eyes withering her, his mouth twitching, the saliva almost running down his chin.

"I'll tell you what I'm going to do. I'll tell you what I'm going to do, woman. I'm going up to bloody Cumberland

and I'm going to sort this lot out. No one, *no one's* going to make a fool of my Esmé. No one's going to make my girl cry, or if he does he'll live to regret it. I'm not without some influence and in my years of doing business I've come across some gentlemen who owe me a favour or two. They'll make Reed bloody Macauley toe the line I can tell you. I should have known. The high-faluting, ladi-dah boyo with his fancy duds and fancy ways," his voice became vicious, "but he'll rue the day he made my Esmé shed tears, that he will. Now then, set them girls to packing my bags and send that stable lad to the station to find out the time of the next train to Carlisle or Penrith, or wherever the nearest railway station is to bloody Long Beck. I've a bit of business to attend to at the mill but I'll be back in an hour. Is the carriage at the door? Good, then jump to it, woman. I've not got all bloody day."

Reed had kept his promise. He had not been over to Browhead but each day he made enquiries of Maggie Singleton, who had, questioning her closely on Miss Abbott's health and state of mind. Was she eating, sleeping, working on the farm, or up on the fell? Maggie was to collect the eggs, and the butter and cheese that maid-servant of Miss Abbott's made and see that they got to market. How? How did he know? There was a pony and trap in the stables. Could she drive one? She could. Good, and if she hadn't the time, or Miss Abbott needed her, surely there must be some farmwife with whom Maggie was acquainted who could take them, and of course, she would be paid for her efforts. She was to keep him informed. Take any profits made down to Miss Abbott's farm, talk to Natty Varty and Jake could go with her and any help Natty needed at Browhead, Jake was to supply it. Now was there anything else, he asked the astonished young wife of Jake Singleton? Anything Maggie herself could think of to make Miss Abbott's grief less . . . well . . . easier to bear? He was putting Miss Abbott's welfare in *her* hands since, as yet, Maggie had no children, she and Jake having been wed no more than six months. Jake was Reed Macauley's yardman and Maggie worked in the dairy but they were to consider themselves, for the moment, as working for Miss Abbott, was that clear? Just until Miss Abbott recovered from the dreadful death of her child.

Maggie Singleton came from Sharrow Bay on the far side of Lake Ullswater and Annie Abbott's reputation was unknown over there. She had heard tales, since she had come to live at Long Beck, of her strangeness and the odd way she dressed, but she had never seen her, and her true 'wickedness', the gossip and speculation about her relationship with Mr Macauley, were none of Maggie's concern. She was unbiased and unprejudiced and Reed could not have chosen a more kindly, tolerant young woman to keep an eye on the woman he loved. She saw Miss Abbott twice a week. Once when she slipped into the Browhead kitchen to collect the stuff for market from Phoebe, and again when she took her the money they had earned. She did not speak to Miss Abbott. The silently staring, white-faced, dead-eyed woman who sat all in black on the sconce aroused a fierce compassion in her but they were strangers to one another and she could not intrude into the grief-wracked world in which Miss Abbott dwelled.

She did not say this to Mr Macauley, poor man. He was not himself at all these days, almost as bad as Miss Abbott, she would have said, moving about the farmhouse without his usual crackling vigour, his fierce, dauntless energy which defied any man to keep up with him. From six in the morning, she had heard, up on the fells, or rummaging about the farm making sure every man who worked for him was *doing* it, ten to the dozen. Off on his wild black mare to Keswick or Penrith or Carlisle and even, Jake told her, travelling down to London on the railway train. Tireless, bloody-minded, but ready to dirty his hands, not like some, a real man and would you look at him now, drifting about the place as though he had no idea how to fill his day, only brightening when she herself approached him.

"How is she? Did you see her?" he would ask, no matter who was with him, even Mrs Macauley, who had gone as white as the driven snow at his words. She had run into the house, she had, her skirts in her hands, and Maggie had felt sorry for her, as well as him.

"She's calm, sir," was all Maggie could say, for what else *was* there to say? She's off her head with grief? She's in another world? She never speaks and only eats when Phoebe makes her open her mouth and sticks food inside?

"Calm? What the bloody hell does that mean?"

"She's grieving, sir, and still not herself, but from what I hear she's a strong woman and will recover."

"Aye . . ." he said, ready to turn away. He swung back violently at her next words:

"And she's young, sir. She's plenty of time to have another child."

"Another child! What are you blathering on about, woman? She's not even married." His face had lost its usual healthy colour during the past few traumatic weeks and now it became even more drained. His eyes were haunted but the menace in them was lethal. Nevertheless Maggie stood her ground. She had been asked to keep an eye on Annie Abbott and report back to Mr Macauley. Give her opinion on her condition and that was what she was doing.

"That could be remedied, sir."

"Remedied! What the hell does that mean?" he said for the second time.

"She's a beautiful woman, sir, with a farm which is beginning to prosper . . ."

"Prosper, prosper! A beautiful woman. Jesus Christ. She's just lost her child and here you are with her waltzing up the aisle on the arm of some fortune hunter and ready to give birth within the year. Are you mad . . . ?"

But it was not Maggie Singleton who was mad. She realised she had gone too far. She had been trying to comfort, to give him hope, though really, need she have bothered? He wanted to hear that Miss Abbott was recovering, but at the mention of the possibility that she could return to what Maggie thought of as a normal life for a woman, a house, a husband, children, he had been ready to turn on her and knock her to the ground. It was a strange job she had been given and one she did not relish. She felt a great and overwhelming pity for Miss Abbott. Though she herself had no child as yet, she was a woman, and already within her grew the seed her husband had implanted in her three months ago so she could guess, to a small degree because of it, what Miss Abbott was suffering. But what she did not care for was the way in which the other servants, knowing where she went, questioned her about Miss Abbott's home, her demeanour, just as though the poor woman was a . . . well, a loose woman and was available to every man who had a bob in his pocket. Poor woman. Gripped fast in the inflexible blackness of her mourning and them in the kitchen at Long Beck were only interested in the colour of her petticoats and the width of her bed. Prying and poking into what did not concern them. Lily and Nell, the two women who had 'laated' with Maggie before the child was buried, were more sympathetic. They had seen Annie Abbott's grief, her devastation. They had done their pitying best to contain it, but the others were 'nowt a pound' as far as Maggie was concerned.

There was a carriage, a hired hack, coming up the track towards the front of the house and Reed Macauley turned away from the troubled figure of Maggie Singleton to stare without much interest at its progress. Its wheels bounced crazily between the ruts, it was going with such speed, and when it came to an abrupt stop, the door to it was flung open with such force it hit the window of the carriage with a crash which lifted a flock of crows from the nearby trees. A man sprang to the gravelled driveway. Not a young man but expensively turned out in an impeccably cut black broadcloth frock-coat with waistcoat and trousers of the same material, the latter not quite as tight-fitting as was thought fashionable, for the man was portly. He carried a long, double-breasted chesterfield overcoat and on his head was a tall, silk top hat.

For a moment Reed was astounded. What the devil was Esmé's father doing here? In the years since he and Esmé had become engaged to be married, and since their marriage, Edmund Hamilton-Brown had been to Long Beck only once and that was on the occasion of the party to celebrate their engagement. It had been Edmund Hamilton-Brown's suggestion that it be held at Long Beck and at the time Reed had been well aware that it had been no more than an excuse for the man to inspect the house and the surroundings where his daughter would live, the servants who would wait on her, and Reed's friends and acquaintances with whom she would socialise. He had made it his business to poke here and there in every room that was available to him, noting the contents and their value, checking the service she would receive since it must be efficient, and looking over Reed's guests to ensure they were fit to sit in his daughter's drawing room. Had he found any deficiency in either the house, the service, or the people with whom she would come into contact he would, no doubt, have rectified it. Since then the only visiting done had been on Esmé's part when she returned to Bradford, and by Reed himself as business called him to that part of the world where he sold his wool.

"Edmund, this is a surprise," he called out as he moved from the side garden where he had been talking to Maggie Singleton, his hand outstretched, for despite his own misery, the civilities must be carried out, particularly to one's father-in-law.

At that moment, before Reed could reach him, the door to the house flew open, Edmund turned in its direction, dropped his overcoat to the ground and with an incoherent cry, opened his arms wide to receive his weeping daughter.

"Papa . . . oh, Papa . . . thank heavens you have come," she cried into his broad shoulder. He held her close and patted her back whilst he shushed her comfortingly, and all the while he turned an expression on Reed

Macauley which would have badly alarmed a lesser man. His face was broad and fleshy, highly coloured, for though his doctor advised against it, he drank a great deal of port and brandy and was rarely without an expensive cigar clamped between his teeth.

It was his grandfather who had begun it, the business which had made Edmund wealthy. He had been a merchant who had gone with his string of packhorses wherever there was decent wool to be had, bringing it back to independent men to be spun and woven. But as the industrial revolution, as it was to be called, had intensified he had, from the profit he made, built his own mill in which weavers and spinners, as their trade declined, worked for him. One mill, then two, as his son grew to manhood. A carding and combing mill, then another as Edmund Hamilton-Brown himself took over and though he had never known want, since he and his father before him had called themselves rich, he was, as Yorkshire men had the reputation of being, a careful man except where his daughter and *himself* were concerned. The best of everything for Esmé and Edmund Hamilton-Brown, and his appearance testified to it.

"To what do we owe the honour of this visit, Edmund?" Reed managed to say, doing his best to be polite though did he give a hang *why* the old man was here? he asked himself wearily. He had been badly shaken by Maggie Singleton's careless inference to the probability of marriage for Annie Abbott and to her bearing another child. He had wanted to hit her and tell her to shut her vile mouth. Annie belonged to him. Not bodily, not yet, but surely when she had recovered somewhat from this mortal blow which had been struck her, she would agree to let him look after her, to settle her and Phoebe in some luxurious place away from all these bad memories, to give her the soft and special things she deserved so that she could live a life of ease and never again worry her head about money. *He* would do that for her. He would love her, care for her, protect her from all hurt and if there was any child to be given, *he* would be the one to give it to her.

"Never mind that, Macauley," his father-in-law was saying, jolting him out of the pleasant dream of the future
which was the only thing that mattered to him now. He
cared nought for his farm, for his businesses, his investments in copper, in iron, in the railways and many other
concerns, those which had made him a wealthy man. He
would do again, of course, when he and Annie were
together and Annie was tucked up safe and snug, but all
he could think of just now was the slow worry which
invaded him night and day, and the impatience he must
curb until it was all over. His wife's tears concerned him
not in the least. She was always weeping over something
these days, moping about the house, refusing to go out
or entertain, which he was glad about since the idea of
engaging in small-talk at the dinner table was abhorrent
to him. But it would all die down, the gossip and speculation, when Annie moved out of the district. He was a
man. The men who did business with him would think
him a lucky dog and wish him well of his liaison with the
Browhead woman, and the women would do as they were
told. As his would when he had found out what her father
wanted and sent him on his way. Reed Macauley might
be low, not quite himself lately, but he was master of his
own home, and his own life.

"Let's get inside, my lass," Edmund said gently, his
arms still about the heaving shoulders of Reed Macauley's
wife. "See, you go and wash your face and have a rest.
You and I'll have a nice chat later. I've things to say to
your . . . . husband but it'll not take long."

"Won't you have some coffee, Papa, or a . . ."

"Nay lass, off you go. I'll have something when you
come down."

He kissed her fondly then watched her as she drifted
up the stairs, a tired little girl whose world, which had
been so safe and happy, which *he* had made safe and happy,
was tumbling about her innocent head.

"Right then, lad," he snarled at Reed when she had
disappeared, "you and me have something to talk about,
I think. Tell that chappie who brought me from Penrith he

can get off now and have one of your servants fetch my coat in. I dropped it by the coach. And I'll have a brandy and some sandwiches. I'm taking the three thirty train back to Lancaster and I reckon you can find someone to take me to the railway station."

"Certainly." Reed's voice had become chilled. He was not used to being given orders, nor to being spoken to as though he was a schoolboy who had misbehaved. He was beginning to get an inkling of the reason for his father-in-law's visit and though he was not overly concerned he did not greatly care for the idea of being given a talk on discretion by his wife's father. Still, best get it over and send the silly old fool on his way. He had guided Edmund Hamilton-Brown into his study, indicating brusquely that he should seat himself by the cheerful fire which burned in the grate. He pulled the bell rope and when the butler came, gave the necessary orders, then lighting a cigar he went to stand by the window, looking out across the vista of his garden and beyond to the slopes of his inland fields. They were white with his ewes which were waiting to lamb, a constantly drifting scatter, forming and re-forming into tiny groups which cropped peacefully on the lush green grass the snows of the winter had nourished.

"You know why I'm here." Edmund had found it difficult to control himself whilst his daughter moved slowly up the stairs, whilst his son-in-law nodded courteously and the butler and parlourmaid set out the decanter and glasses, the delicious sandwiches which had so quickly appeared, and the servants had barely left the room before he began. He held the brandy glass in a trembling hand and he looked ready to throw it at Reed rather than drink what it contained.

"I can guess." Reed did not turn round. His voice was indifferent.

"Is that all you have to say then?"

"What do you want me to say?"

"You have the bloody gall to . . . to carry on a filthy affair with some trollop of the district . . ."

"Be careful what you say, Hamilton-Brown." Hamilton-Brown took no notice.

". . . carrying whatever diseases she might herself have to my daughter for I don't reckon you'll have stopped paying her the attention a man pays his wife. But as if that wasn't disgusting enough, you flaunt it about the bloody district as though it concerned no one . . ."

"It doesn't."

"Is that so? Well, you're wrong, you bastard. It concerns my girl and what concerns her concerns *me*. I'll not have it, d'you hear. I'll not have her name dragged all over Cumberland and probably Yorkshire too, since news travels fast, and I'll not have her made unhappy. I've never cared to see her weep and she's weeping now and that's your fault. It's got to stop. She's your wife and I'll have her treated with some respect . . ."

"Oh, for God's sake, man, who do you think I am? Some sixteen-year-old boy who has been trifling with the under parlourmaid . . ."

"You'd get a thrashing from me if you were. That's what you need, a thrashing . . ."

"And you will give it to me?" Reed's voice was weary as he turned towards his father-in-law.

"No, not me, Macauley, but I know several men who would be only too glad to oblige."

"A threat, then." He smiled and Edmund Hamilton-Brown felt the hot blood of rage move in his veins.

"Aye, a threat. If I get another of these letters from my girl about how unhappy you're making her, or soaked with her tears as the last one was, I swear I'll make you so unhappy yourself you'll be glad to stay close to your home and your wife where you belong. Not only glad but unable to do anything else. Do I make myself clear?"

"Do you mean to say you think you can make me . . . do as you say by telling me one of your bully boys will give me a thrashing if I don't?" Reed's voice was incredulous.

"It would be more than a thrashing, lad, but you'd still be able to perform your . . . marital duties . . ."

"You stupid old man."

"Not really. I'm a wealthy man and so are you so there is little I can do to you in that direction. I realise my limitations as far as bringing you to heel where business is concerned. Besides, I want my girl to continue to live in her husband's house in the comfort she has been used to but there are other ways to make you . . . see the light, shall we say."

"Say it by all means, you interfering swine, but if you think that the threat of receiving a beating at the hands of some thug – "

"Not even if the one to be beaten was not yourself but someone you . . . might care for?"

The air in the room seemed to hang, lifeless, still, unmoving and for a moment Reed Macauley was the same, his face quite blank, his eyes staring at Edmund Hamilton-Brown with complete incomprehension, then, as realisation came, his mouth opened wide in a lethal roar of rage and his eyes narrowed to menacing gleaming slits.

"By God, you bastard. I'll kill you, d'you hear me, I'll kill you with my own bare hands if one hair of her head is harmed. D'you think I give a damn about your precious 'girl'?" His mouth twisted contemptuously and Edmund Hamilton-Brown felt his own hatred twist in his guts at the sound of it. "She's worth a hundred of your daughter, a thousand, and if she'd let me I'd bring her here and send 'my wife' back to her Papa. Oh, yes, you'd better believe it. If she'd have me I'd go and live with her at her farm and leave your precious Esmé, and all this, but she won't. She's the bravest, most honourable woman I know and I love her more than my own life. She loves me too, you bastard, though I don't suppose you know anything about that since all you seem to have experienced is the rather sickening emotion you feel for that poor child upstairs. Yes, *child*! She cannot even conceive like a *woman*. Dear God . . . Oh sweet Jesus . . . how dare you come here with your sanctimonious mouthings . . . like them all . . . they do the same, while she . . . she suffers . . . grieves.

There's not one man or woman who is worth . . . Oh God, what's the use. Get out of my house, and if you want to, take your daughter with you because she's no use to me and, perhaps more importantly, I'm no use to her. I love elsewhere, you see, and I always will."

29

"It were Bert Garnett what thrashed me."

They were sitting, one on either side of the inglenook, Annie straightbacked and blank-faced on the settle, Phoebe in the rocker which Natty had repaired. Natty crouched by the window. He was making a new crook, carving the head of it into some design which he favoured, and his craggy face was twisted into an expression of great concentration. At his feet lay the three dogs, their muzzles on their paws, their ears pricked for the slightest sound, their bright eyes moving from one human face to another. Blackie got up for the second time in ten minutes and went to sniff at the bottom of the door which led outside and Natty stopped to watch him. The dog would just not settle, not since the bairn had gone, restless and constantly searching for her. Bonnie watched him, his eyes so doleful they seemed to say he missed her too, and the cat jumped up on Phoebe's knee, settling passively under her comforting hand. The feeling of unutterable sadness was thick in the room and it was perhaps this, this air of finality, of ending, of hopelessness which had prevailed for the past six weeks that made Phoebe break the vow she had given to Bert Garnett on the night he had beaten her and violated their home. Besides, it made no difference now, did it? His threat to kill her lambkin if she told anyone was no longer a threat, was it? What could he do to harm any of them here in this dreary room? and it might just bring Annie from the long and black apathy in which she crouched day after day, night after night, week after week. It would destroy her soon if she did not break free of it. They had their lives to lead, that was self-evident, but it seemed that Annie had been reduced to the level where

she endured hers without living it. She had drawn away
from the realities of sowing and planting, of lambing time
which was upon them, and had it not been for the help Mr
Macauley sent down, Natty would have been hard pressed
to manage. Phoebe would have gone out with him, into
the fields and up on the intake lands, but she was afraid
to leave Annie alone for long. She worked in the dairy and
about the farmyard with the hens and the pig. She moved
up to the meadow with her churn and milking stool to see
to 'Clover'. Again Mr Macauley helped out, ensuring that
the butter and cheese and eggs went to market, with that
girl he sent down, and the few shillings they earned were
put in her hand by the same girl who walked across the
fell with it.

Sally Garnett came regularly, her Aggie at her
enormous breast, the rest of her brood trailing behind her
in a long quarrelsome line, braving Bert's displeasure and
sporting the evidence of it about her sad, good-natured
face. She had been pregnant again but had miscarried –
thankfully, she said to Phoebe who knew nothing of such
things, her tired body unable, for the sixth time in as
many years, to carry its burden. She drank Annie's tea,
constantly flying out to the yard to prevent Sammy from
chasing the hens, the pig, the offended Dandy, his brothers
and sisters, separating Jamie and Emma who, having their
father's belligerent, crafty nature, fought with one another
unmercifully. She addressed kind, embarrassed words to
Annie who nodded politely then, without a word, would
walk out of the room and through the yard and the noisy
children, going up and over the slope of the hill in the
direction of the burned heather where her child had died.

"Ah'll 'ave to go after 'er, Sally," Phoebe had said,
suddenly frantic, leaving the open-mouthed Sally to fend
for herself.

The dogs were up on the fells with Natty, checking on
the ewes whose lambs would be dropping any day. When
Phoebe caught up with Annie she was standing, tall, thin,
gaunt in her black dress in which, for the first time, the
folk about the parish of Bassenthwaite approved of her,

her eyes with that awful inward-looking expression which frightened Phoebe. She herself was deep in sorrow, badly damaged by her grieving for the child she had loved, but she was appalled by the suffering of that child's mother. Annie's despair was savage at times. She turned on them, on Natty and Phoebe, when they spoke of some ordinary thing about the farm, her eyes hollow, living, breathing, but dead inside. Though it was spring now and the snows had gone, the year had plunged into a cold, wet drizzle of rain which swept across the fells and lingered in the dales whilst all the living creatures huddled beneath tree and wall and hedge to escape its misery. It was as though the world about her mourned with Annie, keeping out of sight, birds and sheep, rabbits and all the small, wild creatures which normally squeaked and rustled in the undergrowth as she passed by.

She took to walking the fells wearing the long hooded cloak which had been her mother's, going up behind the farmhouse, turning on Phoebe with a tinge of madness in her hot-glowing eyes, sending her back, glaring, teeth bared, saying she would be alone and if Phoebe followed she would hurt her badly. She walked and climbed long, solitary miles, without, it seemed, the least purpose, or even direction, exhausting herself, punishing herself for surely Cat's horrible death must be the fault of wicked Annie Abbott? She was never alone, though she did not see Reed Macauley as he protected her, warned by a message from Phoebe, through Natty, and when she came home, her cloak so heavy with rain water she could barely stand, she would let Phoebe put her to bed where she slept like one dead.

She turned her head now to look at Phoebe and for the first time since Cat's death there was a light of reality, of sense and understanding in her eyes. Natty held his breath. They'd known, of course they had, but now it seemed Phoebe was to confirm it. He waited to see what Annie would do.

"What?"

"He made me promise ah'd not tell."

"I don't . . . understand."

It was the first interest she had shown in anything for six weeks.

"'e said e'd . . . 'urt Cat if ah was to say owt."

"Hurt. . . ."

"Aye, but now . . . well . . ."

There was a deep and terrible silence, so deep and terrible the dogs at once began to turn restlessly, sensing something they did not like, and Blackie whimpered. Natty stood up and very carefully leaned the half-finished crook against the table. It was dark beyond the window and the wind flung a handful of rain against it and blew a drift of smoke down the blackened chimney. The fire danced a merry jig, bright, cheerful and uncaring of the human conflict which was contained within the walls it warmed, and over it, hanging from the randle crook which was attached to the fire crane, the iron kail-pot bubbled with its burden of stew which was to be their dinner. On the square iron bakstone a row of oatcakes, baked earlier by Phoebe, were being kept warm. She would spread them with butter and some of the blackberry-and-apple jam she had made last backend, hoping to tempt Annie's laggard appetite.

"You are telling me that it really *was* Bert Garnett who . . . beat you? That he threatened my child . . . that you kept quiet . . . ?"

"I were afraid, lass, of what he would do to Cat."

"You need not have bothered, it seems."

"Annie . . . don't."

"She is dead anyway."

"Aye."

"And he goes scot free?"

"It weren't him what . . . killed 'er."

"I know that, Phoebe, but by God, he shall be punished just the same. If I'd a gun I'd shoot him but I haven't so . . . so . . ." She stood up slowly. Her face was thoughtful and she plucked at her lip. Her eyes were alive and burning in her white face and in them was her hatred, not only of life and the fate which had stolen the only thing of value she had, her child, but of Bert Garnett who had threatened her. He would pay for what he had done to Phoebe and for the damage to their home. She felt alive, powerful, rejoicing in the hot blood which ran through her veins where, for the past six weeks sluggish ice water had flowed. She had a purpose, a reason to breathe and she gloried in it.

Wrenching open the kitchen door before Phoebe and Natty could collect their thoughts, let alone arrange them into stopping her, she ran out into the dark. The rain flew in, patterning the stone floor and the dogs milled about apprehensively. She was across the yard before Natty and Phoebe were across the threshwood and when she came out of the cow shed she carried the horsewhip her father had used to flick in the air over the back of the horse he had once owned to pull his plough.

The wind blew more fiercely, lashing the tree at the side of the farmhouse, and the air began to shriek with its strength. Annie was wet through in a minute and in the yard she stood, teeth bared, madness in her, fighting at her pain with anything she had to hand. At last, *at last* she had something to *do*, something which would shut out that whispering voice inside her head which asked her over and over again where Cat was and how had Annie Abbott lost her? The future was too awful to contemplate now. There was no hope, no relief, no comfort, not even from Reed whose silent presence she had been aware of on the periphery of her demented mind all the while they . . . tended to Cat. But she wanted none of him, nor his love. She wanted the lashing rain and wind to drench her soul and her crippled spirit and at the end of it she wanted to wrap her father's whip about the body of Bert Garnett, to slice into his flesh, as her pain sliced into hers. For what he had done to Phoebe. For what he had threatened to do to Cat.

"Oh, Jesus . . . oh, sweet Jesus . . ." Phoebe babbled. "What have I done? Stop her, Natty . . . stop her . . ." but Annie would not be stopped by such an insignificant little man as Natty Varty. Strong as he was, she was stronger in her insane rage. Contemptuously she threw him aside, and Phoebe too, striding off along the track which led to Upfell. It was dark and the rain made the path slippery but she went on, the whip trailing behind her, and behind it stumbled Natty whilst in the yard Phoebe wept, sinking to her knees defeated, to the muddy cobbles. Even the gentle hand which lifted her did not startle her, nor did she seem surprised to see him there, for had he not always been there when he was most needed?

"Which way?" he asked.

"Upfell. She's going to kill Bert Garnett, I know she is."

She was in the Upfell kitchen when he got there. Natty was at her back doing his best to stop her but the old man stepped aside unhesitatingly to let the newcomer reach her. Bert Garnett had a stripe of running blood across his face where the whip had caught him and in front of him, where he had pulled her, was his terrified wife, her bodice open, the baby pressed against her huge, pendulous breast.

"Get out of my way, Sally," Annie was saying, for even in her demented state something stopped her from aiming the devastating lash at the woman and child.

"Annie . . . for God's sake . . . stop it . . ."

"Get out of my house, tha' bitch . . . Ah'll have thi' in gaol for this . . . see what tha's done to me face. Tha're mad, they said tha' was off tha' head an . . ."

"Annie . . . please, Annie, the bairns . . ." for in the corner of the squalid kitchen the four children huddled and wept.

The man put his hands on Annie's shoulders, strong, soothing, gentle, and his voice settled over her, as familiar as the sound of the beck above the farm, warm with his love. She knew at once who he was and the whip which was flicking like a snake about the floor, looking for an opening with which to get at Bert Garnett, dropped slowly, limply.

She turned then and looked into his face.

"Charlie . . . oh, Charlie is it really you?" She was dazed and beginning to tremble.

"Aye, I've come to bring you home, darling. You've been a long time gone and they miss you."

His arms were there to hold her as she fell into them. Neither saw the expression on Bert Garnett's face as they left, nor heard the low, vicious words he spoke, only his wife, and she didn't count.

"I read of it in the *Carlisle Patriot*, the day before yesterday. I came at once. It was an old newspaper, one the landlady where I lodge was going to use for kindling for my fire. I might have missed it . . ." He bent his head, his chin on his chest, as he remembered the wild shock and grief as the name Abbott had sprung out at him. He had read the account of Cat's death with disbelief, not willing to trust the newspaper, for how could the bright and lovely child of Annie Abbott be dead, but he said nothing of this to the woman who leaned in his arms on the settle. She had wept wild, passionate, relieving tears she had not been able to shed before, and he had wept with her. They held on to one another, sharing, drowning, together in their sorrow for the child who had been Catriona Abbott. Annie was like a wildly shaking vine, clinging to the support of a strong and steadfast tree. One which would never allow her to fall but would be there always with its roots sturdily buried in the solid earth. Charlie Lucas who smiled and teased his way through life like a whimsical summer breeze, like a drifting summer cloud, held her strongly, sustained her tenderly and would continue to do so for as long as she needed him. She talked to him as she had talked to no one, not even Phoebe, of that day. Of her guilt and conviction that she was to blame. She should have listened to Natty, made the line of fire shorter, more controllable. Hired more men to help them but in her obsession with money, with the need to save it, to put it back into the farm, to be successful, to show *them* that the woman from Browhead could be as good a farmer as any in the dales, she had sacrificed her child. Her own pride had caused Cat's death . . .

"No, no, darling, it was an accident. You can't blame

yourself. All these years I've seen you work yourself into
the ground. From the moment the dawn came you were
on your feet, working on the farm until the light failed and
then, when other women were off to their bed, you would
take up your spinning, or weaving, making swills or rushlights and you did it not just for your own pride, as you
call it, but to make a life for Cat, for Phoebe, for yourself.
And if you were proud of what you achieved, what of it?
You had reason to be proud. Look what your labour has
provided. Look how far you have come. You have a working, profitable farm, small but making its way, paying for
itself, feeding four mouths . . ."

"*Four* mouths, Charlie . . ."

"Sweet Jesus, how could I . . ."

"It's . . . all right, Charlie. I do it myself. I see her
everywhere. Wait for her as though she is just . . . beyond
the door and will come through it in a minute. Four of
us . . ."

"There will be four again, if you will allow it."

"You mean . . . ?"

"I am home, Annie."

"For good?"

"Yes . . ."

She began to mend from that moment. Would she ever
be completely whole again? That was for time to reveal,
but though Charlie had not yet regained that wry, lively
way he had with him, that self-mocking humour which was
so endearing, it seemed his presence gave them all, Natty,
Phoebe, Annie, those who had *seen* what Charlie Lucas
had not, a strange peace. They talked, the three of them,
far into the night, while in the background, whittling on
his shepherd's crook, Natty listened, saying nothing,
wondering how Mr Macauley would take the return of this
chap into the life of the woman he had, so to speak, put
into Natty's care. It was almost a year, it seemed from
what they said, since Charlie Lucas had gone.

"Did you not go to Yorkshire then, Charlie?" Annie
asked him, the bright interest in her eyes a relief to Natty,
who had begun to believe they would never see the return

of the Annie Abbott beside whom he had worked since Charlie Lucas left.

"No, I stood on the station at Penrith and decided to toss a coin, north or south but Yorkshire is a long way and the fare to Carlisle was all I could manage . . ."

"You sold your watch."

"How did you know that?"

"I was told by . . . a friend." Her eyes became shuttered. So, it was still Reed Macauley then, Charlie's loving heart anguished, for who else would know such a thing, but then had he expected anything different? When Annie Abbott gave her love it was not given lightly, nor withdrawn easily, if at all.

"Well, I went to Carlisle and fell in with some old Chartist friends who had begun a small newspaper, one the working men, those who could read, might afford. They had gone up there to . . . avoid the law years ago. As I had when I met you."

"You were a Chartist?"

"Oh yes, and in my heart I still am. I was always one for the underdog, Annie, having been one myself on so many occasions." He grinned impishly and Annie took his hand between hers.

"Oh, Charlie," she said seriously, "I do love you."

"I know, sweetheart, and I love you, and Phoebe, and . . . I loved Cat, you know that."

"I know you did. She went to school, Charlie, did you know that? She was so clever."

". . . to school, a *real* school . . . ?"

"Yes, she was given a scholarship. Miss Mossop who was the headteacher and the owner of the school, awarded it to a girl who could not ordinarily afford her fees and Cat was chosen." Her face glowed with loving pride, though her eyes brimmed with tears.

"I knew she had it in her. She was bright beyond her years. Did Miss Mossop see her work then? How did she get to hear of Cat? Was there a judge who . . . ?"

Annie leaned back on the settle reflectively and Natty's hands stilled.

"Why, I don't know. I don't know how . . . it was . . ."

At once, his mind, quicker than Annie's who was still not completely out of the numbed state into which Cat's death had thrust her, studied the question of the scholarship which had been awarded without the work of its recipient having been glanced at, coming, of course and at once, to the truth. Not that he would tell Annie since to take away her pride in her daughter's abilities, real as they had been, was beyond his love.

"They would have seen it when she went to be interviewed," he said quickly.

"There was no interview."

"Then . . ."

"Yes, Charlie, then *how* was it revealed to Miss Mossop that there was a clever child near Gillthrop who would benefit from her teaching? Only one man . . ."

"Nevertheless, she *did* win it, Annie."

"If it existed."

"Then who . . ."

"He paid her fees, Charlie. He must have done."

There was a long awkward silence. Into the room came the tall and thrusting presence of Reed Macauley and for the first time Annie allowed it, re-living that moment when he had told her Cat was to go to school. He had lied to her, knowing she would refuse charity. He had tricked her so lovingly. Given her what she most wanted for her child, but allowing her to believe for her wretched pride's sake that he did nothing beyond ferry Cat backwards and forwards to Grasmere. And how happy Cat had been. She had thrived in those few months, leaving behind the silent, withdrawn child her life had made of her, becoming lively, vivid, fulfilled, as she soaked up the knowledge Miss Mossop poured into her receptive brain. He had given her that. He had given it to Annie, and to Cat, without looking for gratitude or reward. It had not lasted long, but Cat's short life had been enriched by it, and Annie Abbott would never forget it, or him.

She continued to wear the black dress but beneath it she had on her father's trousers and when she strode off up the fells to look at her ewes and their lambs, she tucked up her skirt into the belt, as she had seen gypsy women do, giving herself the freedom she had known for years. When she came down again, or when she and Phoebe went to the market in Keswick, her modest skirt swirled about her clogs and though she did not wear a bonnet, her hair was pulled back fiercely from her face, braided, then coiled tightly about her proudly held head. She had an air of decency about her, of respectability, and it was seen that one or two men nodded amiably to her as she went by. Her farm was thriving. She had over a hundred sheep, counting her ewes and the lambs they had dropped at the beginning of the month. A cow, a pig, hens, acres of land under cultivation and *two* men working for her.

When at the end of May it became known that Reed Macauley's wife had left him and gone home to Yorkshire with her father, the whole of the parish of Bassenthwaite rocked with it, wondering, as it held its collective breath, what was to happen now.

They had not long to wait.

He was at her door a couple of weeks later.

"She has gone," were the first words he spoke to her. She stood, her hand on the latch, her face white and thin above the dense black of her dress, but more beautiful than ever. Her drawn back hair allowed the fine bones of her face to show, the delicacy of her arched brows, the faint suggestion of hollows in her cheeks, the deep, glowing depth of her golden brown eyes. About her broad white brow tendrils of copper escaped the severity of her hair style and over her ears longer wisps fell and curled. She was not yet twenty-three years old and he loved her so much, it was all he could do not to pull her over the doorstep and into his arms.

"I've been to London to see a lawyer about a divorce. An Act of Parliament, it'll take, and plenty of money but I will have it no matter how long it takes and if it costs me every penny I own. Two bloody weeks I've been there but I came directly from Penrith. Will you marry me?"

Behind her she heard the indrawn hiss of Phoebe's

breath. They were eating their evening meal, the four of them sitting about the sturdy oak table beneath the kitchen window. The dying day cast a washed and muted light about the room which was restful, cosy with the crackle of the fire, comfortable and easy with the presence of the dozing animals and the four people who understood one another so well. Even Natty who had been Annie's friend, since that was what he was now, for only a year, was as much a part of her daily life and her affections as though she had known him a lifetime. All four had frozen in dread when Reed Macauley's mare clattered into the yard, and all four had different reasons for it. Charlie's was one of a man who sees his woman threatened, Phoebe's that of a woman who sees the composure of a dearly loved friend, one who is still frail, ready to be smashed to pieces, and Natty's, who knew exactly what lengths Reed Macauley would go to to get what he wanted, was fear, not only for Annie, but for the man at the table who was ready to stand in his way. Annie's fear was not of what Reed might do, but that she would not be able to resist.

"I'll go," she had said, standing up slowly. With the return of her senses, and her reason, had come a return of her love for the man whose thunderous knock at her door had the dogs barking in furious unison. A hurting love which had been buried deep beneath the agony of her loss. A love which she could not deal with in her damaged state so she had hidden it, but now it was back and she could not help the bright glow of gladness, the tricky leap of joy inside her as she looked, her love in her eyes, into those of Reed Macauley.

"Will you, my darling?" His voice was tender, his eyes as soft a blue as she had ever seen them and she swayed towards him, unable to stop herself. "It could be years but in the meanwhile . . ."

"In the meanwhile she's to become your doxy, is that it?"

The latch was taken from her hand as the door swung open and behind her the tall figure of Charlie loomed. He put his hands possessively on her shoulders, drawing her back against him and the physical snarling menace of Reed Macauley who did not care to see another man's hands on *his* woman, never far below the surface, surged and escaped, trampling on the aching tenderness which had bathed Annie Abbott in its glow. His eyes, which had smiled so softly into hers, suddenly held a terrible blankness but the scorching heat of his jealous rage lapped against her and she put out her hands as though to prevent him from coming nearer.

"What the bloody hell are you doing here?" His voice was harsh and he struck at his own booted leg with his riding whip, evidently wanting nothing more than to lay it across Charlie's face.

"I might ask you the same."

"That is between me and Annie. Now let go of her before I do you some damage."

"I will when she tells me to."

"Tell him, Annie."

"Reed . . ."

"*Tell him*, Annie. Come here to me and tell this . . . bastard who you belong to." His black snapping anger would be let loose in a moment and it threatened those who lived beneath her roof, he was telling her. His face was as white as bleached bone but high on each cheek a flush of scarlet had appeared. His eyes were pale blue murderous slits in the slowly deepening gloom.

"Tell him, Annie, or I swear he will suffer . . ."

"Stop it, Reed . . . *Charlie*, for God's sake, stop it. Have I not had enough . . ." She wrenched herself away from Charlie who trembled visibly in the grip of his own rage and tormented longing.

"You see, *Charlie*," Reed said, his mouth cold and hard and contemptuous, "it is not you she belongs to, whatever you might think, or hope, but me. I thought we had seen the last of you, but I was mistaken. No matter, you can go to the devil or stay and run her farm if she cares to employ you. She will not be here. She is coming to live at Long Beck with me. As soon as it can be arranged we will be married . . ."

"Reed . . ."

"Don't worry, my dearest love, you have nothing else to concern yourself with. Just climb up on the mare behind me and I shall take you home. You need bring nothing . . ."

"Reed." Her voice was very quiet. "Go home, Reed."

"Annie . . ."

"No, go home, Reed, to *your* home. Yours and your wife's. I know she has . . . gone away . . . but she will be back. She is your wife and always will be . . . *no* . . ." as he would have pulled her to him.

"No . . . don't . . . hurt me any more, Reed, please. I can take no more. This is my home. These are my people . . ."

"Annie . . ." His voice was anguished. The lethal anger was gone, and the arrogance, as his love, the strong unselfish love which had developed in him over the slow years since he met her, smoothed it all away, exposing his fear. He could not bear to lose her and he knew if he forced her, pushed her too far beyond her small reserve of strength, he would. To keep her, he must let her go, for now.

"Annie . . ." One last desperate entreaty.

"No, Reed."

"You heard her, Macauley, so get on your horse . . ."

"*Charlie*, stop it . . . leave me alone."

"I won't give up, Annie." Reed's voice was quiet, but strong. "I will have that divorce and when I do . . ."

"I know."

"Will you wait for me, my darling?"

"Go home, Reed . . ." and this time he did.

30

The herd of ponies browsed peacefully, cropping the short tussocky grass with strong, yellowed teeth. Their ears swivelled constantly as they listened for signs of danger, and their tails flicked in graceful, unhurried movements up and across their rumps, disturbing the flies and midges which pestered them. They were not tall, standing no more than fourteen hands, but sturdy, well proportioned and muscular. Their heads were small, as were their pricked ears. Their eyes were lively and prominent, their tails long and full and their coats varied from bay to brown, black and grey.

Any horse, whatever its breed, has such a strong sense of smell it is said that a stallion can detect a mare who is on heat from a distance of half a mile away. The wind, blowing from west to east, carried away from the ponies the scent of the two men and one woman who were creeping up on them from the east, and they continued to tear at the grass, rummaging peacefully amongst the heather shoots which grew above a thousand feet on Ullock Pike.

"Theer's a herd o' ponies up the top o' t' ridge on Ullock," Natty had declared at breakfast that morning. "An' theer's a grand 'un among them an' all. Two, two an' a half years, I'd say. Just right ter train fer t' plough. When 'tis broke, o' course." His tone was laconic and he stuffed his pipe which he had removed to speak, a long speech for him, back in his mouth.

"Can we do it, d'you think?" Annie breathed, her pale face colouring a little with excitement.

"Oh, aye, straight up th'Edge. It be but a short walk an' as long as wind's blowin' towards us . . ."

"No, I meant can we break a wild fell pony to pull a plough?"

"I told you we could years ago. D'you remember the one Jack Bibby had to draw his cart from the mill?" Charlie watched the lovely flush of rose to her cheeks, rejoicing in the improvement in her during the past weeks. It was August, five months since Cat's death, and though she still grieved, deeply and silently within herself, she was beginning to take an interest in her farm again. Not just the forced interest that is needed to fill the enormous hole left by the loss of a loved one, but a genuine concern for the well-being of what she had already gained in the years behind her.

Charlie had taken over Cat's room, sleeping in the narrow truckle bed in which Annie's daughter had slept and about the walls were the simple paintings Cat had done in the six months she had been a pupil at Miss Mossop's school. Flowers, trees, birds, a sleeping basket of kittens, all very crudely done but showing the promise Miss Mossop had hoped to foster. There was a rag doll, made for her years ago by her mother, a hairbrush on the dresser which had once belonged to Lizzie Abbott, her unknown grandmother, and in a drawer her tiny store of treasures. The books he himself had given her, a fir cone she had thought pretty, her beloved satchel, a dried wild flower pressed between two sheets of paper and placed between her freshly laundered undergarments which Phoebe washed and ironed almost every week since she did not want them to become stale, she said. It was her small, loving memorial to the child she had come to think of as her own.

Charlie would lie on the bed at night, the window wide, the stars burning a myriad holes in the blackness of the night sky and sometimes, muffled and barely discernible to anyone who was not listening for it, there would be the sound of desolate weeping but he did not go to her. He was afraid. Afraid to damage the fine thread of understanding which was growing between them and had been ever since Reed Macauley had made his devastating and foolish

statement that he was to get a divorce and marry Annie
Abbott. It was as though, knowing finally that there could
never be more between herself and Reed than the involve-
ment of a man and his mistress, however loving; that his
desperate throw of the dice had made it plain to her how
impossible anything else was, she faced the certainty of
Charlie Lucas's love for her, and that a life with him would
be worthwhile. Would be strong and honest and made up
of a great deal which was valuable. Nothing was said but
in small ways they were growing closer, more intimate.
They did not touch except in the most casual, ordinary
way. In the way she and Natty sat shoulder to shoulder
on a wall, or she and Phoebe would link arms as they
walked up the field, but it meant more between himself
and Annie. She *knew* now how he felt about her. She
knew what he wanted and made no objection to it and,
recognising her honesty, he was aware that had she not
wanted it, or him, she would have said so at once. He
would wait. He loved her and would wait. He wanted her
so badly. To know that she was no more than a couple of
feet away from him was a constant gnawing agony to his
male sexuality. Her long slender body lying in its sheath
of modest nightgown which *his* masculine body badly
needed to take from her; which his masculine eyes longed
to look at, to study, to marvel at and love. His hands were
desperate to touch and hold the naked thrusting curve of
her breasts, to smooth and caress her long back, her
sweetly turned waist and hips, the softly rounded satin of
her belly, his fingers to investigate the moist and hidden
sweetness at the meeting of her thighs. He had not been
celibate in the months he had been away from her, burying
his aching loins in other women's bodies but not once, as
he pierced them, had he thought of anyone but Annie as
he did so.

The pit of his belly flared now as she leaned back in her
chair and put her hands behind her head, her mind dwelling
thoughtfully on how they were to capture and break one
of the fell ponies Natty had described. She and Natty had
meant to spend the day 'riving' the pieces of wood into

strips for her swill baskets. When the steaming pieces had
been removed from the boiler where they had 'stewed'
overnight, each one must be held between the knees to
be split, and so she had donned her trousers and shirt that
morning so as to be more comfortable. The weight she
had lost had been regained and as she raised her arms the
buttons on the collarless shirt strained and gaps appeared
between them. She wore nothing but a thin cotton chemise
beneath it but it was cut low, the two top buttons undone
and the soft white skin of her upper breasts was clearly
visible to Charlie as he sat beside her. He could see the
rosy aureole beneath the fabric of the chemise, as big as
guinea pieces and in their centre the pink buds of her
nipples, small and pointed. She leaned further back and as
he watched her the chemise dropped further and almost
the whole of her breasts and both nipples became free
beneath the shirt. They were magnificent, dark and yet
rosy, surrounded by the creamy white satin of her skin.
The shadowy valley between was deep and lovely, the
flesh warm and full. He could not look away. His own flesh
strained painfully against the crotch of his breeches and
his heart hammered in his chest. His mouth became dry
and with a muttered excuse he stood up and stumbled
from the room into the warm, summer sunshine.

He stood for ten minutes, fastened by his pain, not just
the physical pain of a man roused and refused an outlet
for that arousal but the need, the strong emotional need
of a man who loves honestly, truly, and is denied a means
to show it. It was so unbelievably beautiful on this empty
shore of the lake. There were fields between it and Browhead, and trees, but he could see the ripples on the water,
shading as the breeze moved it, into patches of gold which
eddied to silver. The patches grew and merged until half
the lake was gold, the other half silver, two separate enti-
ties divided by a path of both colours where the sun shone
across it, surrounded by a necklace of trees of every shade
of green amongst which, on the other side of the lake, a
small white farmhouse sheltered. There were celandines
growing from the rocks on the water's edge, rough, grey

rock patterned with the green of moss. Charlie loved it, loved her. They were intertwined, the beloved woman, the beautiful lake, and he knew he would never leave either, not while he lived.

They walked the wide shoulder of rough fell which turned south and climbed as a narrowing ridge to the dark and symmetrical peak of Ullock Pike before they saw the ponies. Annie strode beside him, coatless, for the day was warm and he was breathlessly aware again of her glorious breasts as they bounced, joyfully unconstrained with nothing between them and Charlie's eyes and hands but the thin stuff of her chemise and the worn fabric of her father's shirt. He could still see the outline of her nipples and he was forced to drop behind, conscious that the exquisite folly of looking at her, at her body, must in some way be curtailed.

They passed through The Watches, a strange huddle of upstanding rocks growing from the grass which were believed to be a Druids' Circle though Charlie said he was of the opinion that the formation was natural. His voice, as he spoke, sounded high and strained but Natty and Annie did not seem to notice. The ponies were above them, just before what was known as The Edge began and at once Natty signalled for them to drop down on their bellies.

"Wait here," he whispered, slithering off on some errand of his own and, shoulders touching, so close he had only to turn his head to look into her face, they lay side by side, hidden in the fragrant depths of the summer weather.

He turned his head. Her cheek was pressed flat to the earth and her brown, excited eyes smiled into his. He smiled back, the warm strength of his love for her stripping away inhibition, restraint, sense. He moved a fraction closer and with great delicacy laid his lips to hers. For a moment, an appalling moment he thought she was going to flinch away, then she relaxed. Neither of them closed their eyes. Pale grey looked into golden brown, truth between them since he knew she did not love him as he

loved her and what did it matter? he asked himself for her
mouth softened and opened for him and it was sweet and
willing.

"My love . . . my love . . ." His breath, fresh and pure,
brushed her chin and her cheek, then his mouth moved
to her throat and she let him, arching her neck, lifting her
chin so that his lips might move more freely towards the
open neck of her shirt.

"I love you so much."

"I know, Charlie."

"My love . . ." and his mouth found hers again so that
when Natty crept back they were unaware of it until he
touched Annie's shoulder. They did not jump apart guiltily
but turned their heads to smile at him and in Natty's eyes
was a deep, glad understanding. She would be all right
now.

"Theer's a fine little bay, theer, can tha' see 'im,
Charlie?" His whisper was close to Charlie's ear and reluc-
tantly Charlie took away the arm he had placed across
Annie's shoulders.

"Yes, but how are we to get him away from the herd?"

"Nay lad, ah've catched many a youngster such as 'im
in me day. Let's see if ah remember 'ow. Ah want thee
an' Annie ter creep round t'other side of 'em so that they
get wind o' thi'. Shout as loud as thi' can. They'll run this
way and ah'll be ready fer 'un." He patted the length of
rope he had wound about his waist.

There were sixteen of them. A mature stallion, seven
mares and their foals. It was surprising to see a young
male amongst the herd since a stallion will drive away any
usurper when he is about eighteen months old, but the
colt grazed peaceably enough though it was noticed it kept
well away from the 'leader'. Several of the foals were lying
down in the sunshine.

It was like a child's game and both Charlie and Annie
were giggling like children as they slithered through the
heather, stopping frequently to lift their heads to see
where the ponies were. Once he stopped her with his
hand on her arm and when she turned questioningly, he

kissed her again, more deeply. It was as though he was reminding her, placing his mark on her, telling her that the previous exchange had been serious despite the lightness of their embrace. She made no objection again, lifting her face to him willingly, smilingly.

When they stood up and shouted the herd at once took flight, the foals, perhaps only months old, scrambling to their feet and following their mothers without a moment's hesitation, fast, automatic, a fundamental reaction which had been bred in them when predators such as wolves had threatened their ancestors. In the panic which ensued the ponies could barely see where they were going, and when Natty stood up directly in their path, the whistling song of his rope settled over the bay's head. It went unnoticed by the stallion, and certainly by the mares who had one ear on the disturbance and one on their own foal.

Annie looked as she had done before Cat's death. Her eyes were a brilliantly deep golden brown, clear and sharp with her joyous laughter. The colour ran gloriously beneath her skin and her mouth was wide in a great cry of excitement. She jumped up and down and clapped her hands when she saw that Natty had the bay, looking so like her own daughter in her delight, Charlie felt he could weep. For sweet, lovely Cat who was gone and for Annie who, at last, was coming alive again.

It took a long time to fetch the colt in. He squealed and stamped and kicked, his eyes rolling and wild with terror and rage, his hooves lethal as they struck out at Natty who held the rope and at Charlie who tried to throw an arm about his neck.

"Let 'im go, tha' daft bugger," Natty shouted. "Let 'im wear 'imself out fer a bit. Bye, but 'e's in a right royal temper, that 'e is."

They called him 'Royal' and those first few weeks with him were hard and sometimes dangerous, but he was basically sweet tempered and, giving in to the inevitable, gradually became tame, domesticated, not only willing to put up with the hard work and strange things which were expected of him, but becoming interested in these curious but kind creatures who had taken him from his freedom. He was accustomed slowly to what was needed from him, accepting Natty, Annie or Charlie as his leaders and companions, as he would other horses. Natty did the training, of course, for neither Annie nor Charlie had known horses. Royal became playful, almost a family pet, walking towards them with ears pricked, a 'long' nose, a jaunty prancing step and high tail, ready for fun since he was only young and Annie learned to ride him bare-backed since there was no such thing as a saddle at Browhead. It seemed to amuse him, to please him and she loved him as she loved Blackie and Bonnie.

On the day they caught him Natty and Phoebe had gone to their beds early as though by mutual consent, though nothing was said, and Charlie and Annie sat on by the fire. They could hear Royal's 'caterwauling', as Natty had put it, out in the pasture where, in case he should try and jump the drystone wall, Natty had tethered him. He sounded sad and dejected as he called to the herd but gradually his lonely whinnies died away and the dogs, whose ears had pricked in bewilderment at this strange sound, settled to doze in that half-wakeful, half-dozing state they fall into. It had turned cold and Charlie threw a couple of short logs on the fire, the flames leaping in a lively scatter of sparks up the chimney. Normally at this time of night as they made their way to bed the fire would be covered by the 'curfew', a low metal dome which kept it burning slowly, and the glowing embers would, the next morning, then have life breathed back into them with the bellows. But both Charlie and Annie knew that something must be said about what had taken place on Ullock Pike. Charlie with eagerness since he was certain that the time had come for him to stake his claim to the woman he loved. In Annie there was a tinge of dread mixed with a strange resignation since she loved Charlie and could not imagine life without him.

He lounged opposite her on the settle, his long legs stretched out before him crossed at the ankle, his hands thrust deep in his trouser pockets. He had removed his boots and his stockinged feet were close to the fire. His eyes were on her and when she looked up at him he smiled, sat up and leaned forward.

"May I kiss you again?" he asked softly, whimsically.

"You needed no permission this morning." Her own tone was light.

"I am an impetuous devil at times," but though the words were humorous the expression in his eyes was very serious.

"I noticed."

"You did not object?"

"No."

"Then . . . may I?"

She leaned towards him, lifting her mouth and he took her lips with the sweet delicacy which is the mark of the true lover. When they drew apart his eyes were steady, candid, filled with the deep and endless love which was hers for the taking. It was all there, everything she needed, just as he was always there when she needed him. He was so fine, Charlie, so fine and good. Trustworthy, making light of everything from the twelve, fourteen, sixteen hours' work he often did each day, to the poor state of his old boots, but trustworthy, honest. A man of his word. A gentleman, not just by birth, which he was, but in his very nature. He made her laugh with his droll humour but he was a man, not a milksop, and could curse with the fluency of a soldier. He was her true friend but she knew he wanted more and if she turned him away could he be expected to stay and continue as if this morning had not happened? Her heart ached with the thought of losing his friendship, the deep, satisfying companionship and support which had always been there when she needed it. He had gone away once because of her love for Reed Macauley. Would he do so again for there was no doubt in her mind, no swerving from the truth in her heart which was that she loved Reed and would do so until the day she died. Should she tell Charlie this? There should be truth and trust between friends, as there was between herself and Phoebe, but would the same apply to the man who sat opposite her? There was a great deal of difference in Charlie's masculine love to the female affection she and Phoebe shared.

"I love you, Annabelle Abbott. Will you marry me?"

"Oh, Charlie . . . !" She was taken aback. Though she had expected something, a declaration of his love, something, it had not been an offer of marriage and for one awful moment she was terror-stricken. Not marriage, no . . . not marriage for it was so *final*, so irrevocable. Reed was married but he had said . . . a divorce . . . *no, don't be foolish*. . . and if she married Charlie . . . *she would be tied*, this dreadful voice said and then if Reed got a . . . could be made free to marry her . . . *No! . . . No! . . .* it's not possible . . . *folly. . . madness. . .* and yet something inside her struggled desperately to avoid the commitment Charlie was asking her to make. But think of the peace, another voice said, the comfort, the protection, the end to the perpetual storm of Reed's love, his demanding love which, if she did not marry Charlie, and end it, would go on and on until she succumbed to it, and him.

"I had not thought of marriage, Charlie," she said slowly. Her thoughts, so many and varied, so harrowing and conflicting had taken but a few seconds and he seemed to assume her hesitation to be no more than any woman's at the offer of marriage and yet a woman who loves, in the way a woman *truly* loves a man, will not hesitate.

"I have thought of nothing else, my darling. I love you . . . so much, there are no words to describe it." He smiled, a smile of such blinding sweetness, understanding and love she felt the warmth of it, the glowing tender warmth wrap about her, hold her in safe arms, as *his* would be, but again she hesitated.

"I said once that I loved you, Charlie, do you remember?"

"Yes, but you meant . . . as a friend. I *can* tell the difference, my love, but it seems I do not care. I want you to come to me and . . . I nearly said 'to be mine' but I don't believe that one human being can possess another . . ."

How wrong you are, dear Charlie . . .

". . . I want you to love me in any way you can. Love is such a worthwhile emotion and should not be despised if it is . . . not quite what one hopes for, but if you will marry me there is no doubt in my mind, none, that what we will have will be a worthwhile thing, Annie. Don't waste it, my lovely girl, don't waste us."

"Charlie, sweet, darling, Charlie . . ."

An appalled expression flooded his eyes. "Christ, you're going to say 'no', aren't you?" He made a small, painful sound in his throat and turned away from her to hide his fear. Bonnie, sensing the distress in him got up and came to his knee and Charlie placed a trembling hand on the animal's head. His pale, cat-like eyes were almost black in the dim light as the pupils widened and darkened.

"Charlie, I'm not ready yet, to say yes or no." You lie, the cool voice within her said. If Reed Macauley, free of all encumbrances, stood before you with an offer of marriage you would snap it up so eagerly you would take his hand off at the wrist to get at it. And yet it was true, what she had said to Charlie. She was still not the Annie Abbott she had been once. She was not in a fit state to make any decision and to take Charlie's love and twist it for her own convenience was not only unfair but cruel. The temptation was great. To thankfully fall into his arms. Let him take her to bed, now, tonight, so that in the morning she would, despite what he said, *belong* to him. There would be no looking back to Reed Macauley, nor looking forward to the foolish promise he had made. It would be irreversible, no going back or changing her mind, no more decisions to be made. She and Charlie, the farm, perhaps children . . . oh, yes, another child, a daughter . . . like Cat, but not Cat for she would have Charlie's blood in her, a son . . . a boy to inherit the farm. She would be Mrs Charles Lucas, respectable, no longer Annie Abbott, the woman from Browhead. The farm would grow and prosper. Her future, with Charlie to stand beside her, work beside her, would be secure, hard, for certain, but secure in Charlie's love. She was well aware that in the last few months she had

let her weakened state lean on Charlie, had allowed him
to anticipate perhaps, more than she intended. They had
shared secret smiles, a subtle changing in their relationship, a small degree of intimacy which had suggested,
hinted at, a growth of it in the future.

He turned back to her, his hands reaching for hers and
he did his best to smile.

"Annie . . ." He looked down at their twined fingers
and his throat worked painfully. She wanted to soothe him,
comfort him, run her fingers through his brown thatch
of curls and smooth them from his forehead. Her loving
friendship surged through her on a great tide and she
almost said it. Almost said 'yes'. She wanted to lift the
misery which had come upon him, which *she* had caused.
Take him in her arms and tell him she would be his wife
and anything else he wanted until their wedding day, but
it was not *love* that made her want to do it, but compassion.
How could she hurt him when he had given her so much?
Her sanity. A reason to live.

"Annie," he began again. "I have hoped, these last
weeks. . . ."

"I know, Charlie, and perhaps . . ."

At once he looked up at her, hopeful, ready to smile if
she would.

"Perhaps . . . Annie?"

"When I'm . . . oh Charlie, you know how much . . ."

"Yes? How much you love me? You must not say it if
you don't mean it."

"I *do* mean it."

"A man and a woman love in a special way, Annie.
Good Christ, you know that." His voice was passionate,
". . . and that is what I want from you but if you can't give
me that, then by God, I'll take anything you *can* give
me. Bloody hell, I'm not proud, Annie, I'm a man who
loves . . ."

"I know, Charlie, but . . ."

"Let it . . . lie for now, Annie. Don't say no. Think
about it. Dammit, I shouldn't be pushing you, not now
when you are still mourning . . ."

"I'm . . . I still seem to be incapable of decisions, Charlie. My mind is stunned . . . sometimes, and it . . . hurts . . . I hurt so much without her."

"Ssh . . . ssh . . . my love . . ." and without conscious thought, without the sexual ardour which had so unmanned him that morning he drew her from her chair and on to the settle beside him. His arms were round her tightly and hers crept about his neck. Her wet face pressed into the hollow beneath his chin as the devastation of her grief overwhelmed her and he rocked her back and forth. The thick plait of her hair became untwisted and it fell in a rippling, dishevelled tide about her face and shoulders, falling down her back to her waist and across her breast. His hands gripped it and his arms crushed her shivering body to him, his love, strong and incontestable, holding her secure in her grief.

"Oh, Charlie, what would I do without you?"

"There is no need to wonder, sweetheart, for I have no intention of going anywhere."

"Charlie, I lo . . ."

"No . . . no, don't say it. Not now. Not until you mean it in the way I want you to mean it. But . . . Annie . . . don't take away my hope. You know you and I could live a good life together. To be friends, to trust one another as you and I do is a fine start. The best. The rest will come, my darling. I won't rush you, though being a man of normal needs I want nothing more than to pick you up and take you to bed . . ."

"That would be . . ."

"Please . . . don't say it, whatever it is. I cannot find it in me, tempting as it is, to take advantage of your . . . vulnerability." He laughed softly. "If anyone had told me, years ago, when I was a hot-blooded youth, that I would say such a thing to a woman I would have thought them mad."

She had quietened now, lying calmly in his arms, her head on his shoulder, and he spoke into her tumbled hair. His lips touched her brow, moving softly to the smooth white flesh, pleasant but undemanding.

"But I was not in love then, Annie, and, being a male, a willing female, no matter her weakened state nor what had caused it, was fair game. I am a different man now. You have made me so. Now then . . ." he became brisk, "it's time we were in our beds . . . yes, I can even say that, Annie Abbott, though I warn you that I mean to get you into mine one day."

They were both smiling as he put the 'curfew' on the fire. She turned on the bottom stair to watch him as he opened the door to let out the dogs for the last time and unbidden, Reed Macauley's words, so like Charlie's in their content, came back to her.

"I won't give up, Annie," he had said. As Charlie had just said and though she continued to smile her heart was heavy and painful, torn as it was between two men's love.

31

Annie was high on the fell. It was October and time for 'raking' in the gimmer ewes for breeding, and swirling before her in a constantly shifting pattern were her flock. As Blackie moved away from them, coming to crouch beside her, they formed into a long grey ribbon, one behind the other, moving purposefully down towards the intakes. They went at a steady pace with no need of a push and Blackie watched them, looking out for any rebel which might be diverted by a sweeter patch of heather. The lambs were as big as their dams now, fine and sturdy. They were weaned, completely self-sufficient, and when Annie had selected those she was to keep for breeding purposes, the rest would go to the lamb fair. The Keswick Tup Fair would take place next week on the first Saturday in October and it was there she would sell her surplus stock and hire a ram for the season.

It was the real start of the sheep farmer's year. The libido of the tups, which included the one she meant to hire next week, was at this time in the calendar mysteriously ready to be linked to any ewe which they could heave themselves on to, and every ewe must have her chance. If she was not mated she could not carry a lamb through the winter months and there would be no profit in that for Annie Abbott.

Far below, almost out of sight, Charlie, with Bonnie a minute speck of darker colour beside him, was herding part of her flock into the walled inland pastures where they would fatten up for a week in readiness for the backend fair and, away to her left beyond Broad End and completely hidden from her, Natty was raking another dozen or so who had wandered that way. They were still on their own 'heaf' but in that mindless way a sheep has, a few had gone one way and a few the other. He had his dog with him, ready to take them down with the rest, and occasionally Annie could hear the faint but piercing whistle which Natty used to give it orders.

"Steady, Blackie," she murmured as the dog, one foot raised, looked up at her questioningly, waiting for her command to take the sheep down. He knew as well as she did where they were going and how to get them there and even, she often thought, why they were going. Almost four years now since Reed had left him and Bonnie tied to her door and in that time they had proved to be friend and protector and as good as any sheepdog she had ever known. A sheep will soon learn to outwit man but will seldom challenge the prowess of a well trained dog, and all the dogs asked in return for their labour and faithfulness was a good meal once a day, a decent bed and a little kindness.

"Off you go then," she told him and he went, streaking down the stripped grass, following at a distance the line of sheep, taking them towards Charlie down almost at the level of the lake and the safety of the pastureland.

Annie stood, one foot resting on the grey, moss-studded rock, her knee bent, her arms folded across it as she looked out over the loveliness of the autumn lake and its surroundings. It was late afternoon. The great sheet of water was stretched at the feet of the majestic giant, the affable and friendly Skiddaw. Dark cloud shadows crawled across the water and the quiet woods dozed about it in the last bit of sunshine. The trees cast long-fingered shade and higher up the fell the land was a riot of colour, the dying bracken fronds and red-berried rowan trees, the whiteness of the bents and the faded green of the grasses. The deciduous trees each carried an umbrella of multi-coloured leaves, robins sang, and the air was so clear Annie could hear the clatter of blackbirds in the hedgerows which lay along the lake road. The mountains all about her were going to sleep as night approached, giants crowding the sky from lilac to deepest purple before they began to fade into evening blue.

The scream of a hawk brought her from her deep reverie, echoing across the fell and bringing to absolute stillness the multitude of small creatures who lived there. She turned, lifting her hand to shade her eyes, searching the deep and darkening bowl of the heavens for the hawk's presence, and as she did so her heart gave a great and sickening leap in her breast. Standing at her back and leaning on an enormous rock as tall as himself was Bert Garnett. He had his arms crossed on his chest in a pose of casual indifference. He even smoked a pipe, looking for all the world like some weatherbeaten shepherd who stops for a smoke as he watches his flock. He was looking at her and when her gaze met his, he nodded pleasantly, then with great deliberation took the pipe from his mouth and placed it carefully on a small rock beside him before walking across the grass towards her.

She took a step backwards and almost fell as her heel caught the rock on which she had recently rested.

"Watch tha' step, Annie," he said pleasantly. "We wouldn't want thi' ter fall an' hurt thissen, would we?"

She became perfectly still, like the creatures in the undergrowth had as the hawk passed over, but her voice when she spoke was calm, cold and expressionless.

"What do you want?" she asked him, her anger icy inside her, and her pain, for in some way, though her logical mind knew it was not so, Cat's death seemed to be linked in a grotesque way to this man. She supposed it was because he had threatened Cat and now Cat was dead. Was it her turn now? Was it her turn to be abused as he had abused Phoebe? Or was it just coincidence that he should be up here when she was alone? She didn't think so.

Her alarm, which had been brought on by the sudden shock of finding him at her back and which had ebbed away when she saw who it was, began to surge again, for the expression on his face was not agreeable. Smiling, oh, yes, but overlying the smile was a patina of venom which boded ill for the one at whom it was directed. Herself. Clearly in her mind's eye she could see Phoebe's face,

that battered, split, scraped mass of raw flesh in which
Phoebe's eyes had been embedded, pale and unseeing in
her pain and shame. Phoebe had done her best to stand
up to this man but she had been no more than a thread of
a girl, tossed to one side by his cruel hands. She had
protested and, Annie supposed, threatened him with the
law but he had merely turned Phoebe's threat on her,
frightening *her* into silence with the weapon of intimidation,
of damage to the child Phoebe had loved. To Cat.

To Cat. Her darling Cat who was gone now and who
could no longer be hurt. Not by Bert Garnett. Not by
anyone. Annie had meant to punish him, not only for beating Phoebe but for using Cat to blackmail her into silence,
to lash him with her father's whip but Charlie had pre-
vented it, taking her in his arms and guiding her from the
kitchen at Upfell, her mind dazed and stricken with her
hating grief.

The scene played itself out again. Sally with the baby
at her breast. The children seething in terrified confusion
in the corner, blood, a stripe of it across Bert's face, Sally's
screams, the children crying. They had come away, she
and Charlie, and her mind had shut itself down, enclosing
in a small portion of itself the words which had spewed
from Bert's mouth and the vicious loathing in his eyes.
That part of it had been buried, forgotten, and if she had
been questioned on it she would have been forced to admit
that she had no recollection of it.

But now, as Bert smiled, revealing the broken state of
his teeth, it was as though a curtain had been lifted, a
window opened to allow her to see the picture of his face
as it had been then. To hear the sound of his voice as it
had been then, and the words he had spoken. Wild, violent
enmity, a deadly virulence which had pledged retribution,
a hatred so thick and threatening it promised to search
her out to the ends of the earth and beyond. He would
make her pay for this, he had screamed, she remembered
it now, and for all the insults she had slung at him, at his
pride, at his manhood. Her haughty contempt for Bert
Garnett would not be forgotten, his foul tongue had told

her, though she had not listened then. She had not seen him since.

"Ah said me time'd come, didn't ah, lass?" His smile deepened, becoming even more genial but at the back of his eyes some nasty thing stirred, telling her quite plainly that he was neither amused, nor genial.

"I haven't the faintest idea what you are talking about, Bert Garnett, and I'd be obliged if you'd get out of my way," for somehow, in a cunning manoeuvre he had cornered her in the angle between the two tall rocks.

"Ah haven't the faintest idea what tha's talkin' about, Bert Garnett," he mimicked, then, making her jump violently, he put out his hands and grabbed at her. At the last moment, as she cowered away, he drew back, playing with her as a cat plays with a mouse, laughing.

"Get out of my way, Bert. If you lay one hand on me I swear I'll scream so loud I'll bring every man on the fell running up here."

"Ah mean ter lay more'n a hand on thi', Annie Abbott. 'Tis time ah 'ad my share of what tha' pass out willy-nilly. Tha' seems ter be willin' ter open tha' legs fer any man what 'as a fancy fer it but when it comes ter poor old Bert what's done more fer thi' than most round 'ere, well 'tis 'Ta-ra, Bert, see thi' termorrer,' an't bloody door shut in me face. Ah were the only one what spoke kindly ter thi' when tha' first come. Fetchin' yer ter market, tekkin' tha' swills an' besoms in me cart but was ah thanked fer it? No, not poor old Bert Garnett. All I got were a slash across t' face wi' tha' faither's 'orse-whip."

Bert's smile twisted suddenly, allowing to the surface the malice which had festered in him, smoulderingly at first, when he had been thwarted in his desire for Annie Abbott's favours, then in an eruption of hatred which had been dangerous, when she had snapped the whip about his face and body. He had seen her come and go, up the sheep trods to examine her lambs and ewes, riding her pony sometimes, working the fields about her farmhouse, striding out along the lake road or over the top of Skiddaw to the market in Keswick but always one of her household

had been with her. She had finally discarded the black
dress of mourning and wore instead a new outfit she and
Phoebe had made between them. A well-fitting pair of
breeches of the hodden-grey wool so popular in the district, which tapered to her ankle, flaring slightly above the
knees in the fashion of riding breeches. A full-sleeved
man's white cambric shirt over which she wore a sleeveless woollen waistcoat. Her jacket was loose and easy,
comfortable for the many jobs she did about the farm and
on her feet, a sure sign of the small prosperity she was
enjoying, were a pair of stout walking boots. Her hair was
braided and at its end was an enormous bunch of bright
green ribbons, her only concession to her own femininity.

"Ah've waited fer thi', Annie. Day an' bloody night ah've
waited fer thi' an' now 'tis my turn."

"Don't be ridiculous, man. You must be insane to
imagine I would have anything to do with you."

"Yer were glad enough ter 'ave summat ter do wi'm me
when ah took thi' ter market . . ."

"I was . . . yes . . . I was grateful but . . ."

"Well then, 'ow about tha' showin' me 'ow grateful?
Let's settle oursen down on this bit o' grass . . ."

"Don't be ridiculous," she said again. "Even if we had
remained . . . friends, and it is doubtful we were ever
that, after what you did to Phoebe you should have been
put in gaol. You damn nearly killed her . . ."

"Nay, a bit of a slap were all she got an' so will you if
yer don't shurrup. Let's give over this bletherin' an' get
down ter some . . ."

"Oh, get out of my way." Her voice was filled with her
contempt. She could feel the violence of her own rage
begin to course through her own veins, the small flare of
unease his words and manner had lit in her quenched by
the memory of Phoebe and the pitiful state this man had
reduced her to.

"Go on, get away from me. You make me feel sick, you
little weasel. Can you not pick on someone your own size
to bully? Poor Sally gets a regular beating from you and
how she stands you in her bed is a wonder to me. And

not satisfied with knocking your wife about you had to take your fists to Phoebe. Now it seems it's to be my turn, you little rat."

Taking him by surprise with the suddenness of her movement, she shoved him hard, and he was so unprepared he retreated before her, going backwards down the trod where sheep had worn the grass down to the hard earth. He put up an arm to defend himself, mesmerised in that moment by her towering rage, by her wild and passionate beauty, as he had always been mesmerised by it. She pushed him again, spitting abuse, words she had heard in the yards of the inns in which she had worked, listening to herself in amazement, beginning to wonder if she was going mad, her heart banging and enormous in the small cavity of her chest. Like a drum it was, her pulse racing as common sense was driven from her by her hating rage.

"You touch me and I'll kill you, Bert Garnett," she shrieked. She felt ten feet tall, twice as big as he was. He slipped and sat down heavily and it was then that she should have taken her opportunity and raced off down the slope but he was up again in a second, still moving backwards away from her flailing fists and the knee she was doing her best to drive into his groin.

But he was beginning to regain his equilibrium now, dodging her blows, reaching out his own hands and when he saw his chance, grabbing her by one wrist. She tried to wrench it free, her eyes a pale savage amber in her livid face, her other fist striking him high on the side of his head but to no avail.

"Let . . . me . . . go . . . you bastard," she panted. "You put one hand on me and I'll scream . . ."

"Aye, so tha' said, Annie. Well, scream away 'cos there's no one ter hear thi' except bloody sheep an' rabbits. That sod Natty Varty's down Browhead by now an' tha' fancy man's on th'inlands. Theer's only thee an' me, lass, an' that's 'ow it should be so why don't tha' settle thissen down an' stop fightin'. We could 'ave a right good time. There's plenty ter go round, ah'd say. Him what lives wi' thi', *an'* Mr Reed Macauley, so ah 'eard, an' even owd Natty, I shouldn't wonder. Ah bet 'e's not bin missed out so 'ow about a kiss first afore we . . ."

"Let . . . go . . . of . . . my . . . arm . . ." She hissed the words through teeth which were clenched tight in revulsion but Bert had both her wrists in his hands now and though she kicked out at him with her newly booted feet the lunge she made was her undoing. She lost her balance, falling heavily on to her back and at once he was on top of her. He was big and strong and dangerous in his lust and hatred for Annie Abbott. What he wanted was here, squirming delightfully under his man's body, her every movement arousing his already aroused body to further menace. He bunched his muscular shoulders, forcing her hands high above her head, holding them both in one large fist whilst the other reached greedily for the neck of her fine cambric shirt. He knelt over her so that his knees were on either side of her writhing body and though she continued to kick her legs only threshed the air behind his back and her heels drummed ineffectually on the hard ground.

Oh God! . . . oh, dear God! . . . it was happening, just like Reed had always said it would. Even on the very first day they had met he had warned her of tinkers, travelling men who would toss her on her back, fling her skirts over her head and take what they wanted as casually as a dog mounts a bitch. But he had not thought to warn her against Bert Garnett.

His hand pulled at the fabric of her shirt. He had no time for buttons, tearing savagely at her, his filthy nails raking her skin, drawing four lines of blood from her throat to her breasts, the beast surging in him as for a moment his mouth found hers. She turned her head away in horror and his lips moved like two wet slugs across her cheek. But whilst he kissed her he could not see what his savage hand had uncovered so he leaned back for a clearer look, putting his weight squarely across her heaving thighs.

He began to grunt rhythmically, his body pounding at hers though as yet their flesh was not joined, nor even touched. His pleasure filled him and he erupted swiftly and brutally at the centre of his own body as he climaxed. At once he fell forward, his panting breath hoarse and animal-like against Annie's averted cheek and for several moments he lay, winded, replete, but by no means finished with her. Not by a long chalk. He was temporarily satisfied but he meant to do it again and again, and *inside* her. Inside her wherever he could stick it and when it was over she could crawl back down the track and blab all she wanted to that sod she lived with because Bert Garnett would be at home by then, safe in the bosom of his family where a family man would naturally be. Her word against his, that was what it would be and who would believe a woman with *her* reputation against a man, a respectably married man such as himself?

He sat back on his haunches and with great deliberation and with one hand, undid his trousers, bringing out his limp penis. Already it was becoming engorged again and he smiled as he stroked it for a moment before transferring his attention to her bared breasts. He took them one at a time into his hand. They were full and pink-nippled and he wished he had a third hand since he was forced to hold *hers* above her head which left him with only one to fondle her. Trouble was he couldn't get to that tantalising goal between her legs for the silly cow had on those daft bloody trousers. If she'd worn a skirt it would have been an easy enough job to shove it over her head. Keep her quiet an' all. 'Course, he could clip her round t' mouth, that'd do it . . .

She fought him like a tigress, doing her best to get her knee up to where it would hurt him the most, but it was *his* knee which was between *her* legs now, forcing them apart. His face loomed over hers then his mouth was at her breast . . . biting . . . Dear God . . . she was weakening . . . she could feel the waves of nausea as he relentlessly moved his mouth down her body to where the fastening at the waist of her breeches lay.

A knife of terror stabbed her again and again since he had only to cuff her across the head, stun her and in her senseless state strip her of her clothing and she would be completely defenceless. It was only her breeches and the awkwardness of getting them off that was stopping him from brutally raping her. She had only one chance. Throwing back her head so that her throat arched agonisingly, she began to scream.

Bert Garnett was displeased. He looked up, his mouth, on which there was Annie Abbott's blood, snarling like that of a crazed beast. Her voice echoed from crag to grey crag, sounding exactly like the cry of the hawk as it dives for the kill and down on the inlands Natty Varty's dog raised its head. Charlie was further down the pasture with Blackie and Bonnie. They were holding the flock for him as he opened the gate and beside them the noise of Chapel Beck as it roared over the stones in its bed, distorted the sound.

Natty Varty's dog rose to its feet and looked questioningly at its master.

"T'were only that 'awk, dog. Lie down."

But the dog turned, looking up the fell this time. Natty watched him, puzzled, for the dog was a part of himself, an extension of his own mind and body having no thought nor sense in its head but what was put there by Natty. It gave a short 'yip' and Natty's puzzlement turned to amazement. The dog *never* barked, never, and certainly his behaviour was strange. An old dog, was the dog who had no name and certainly no concerns but its devotion to Natty, its liking for the fire now that they lived this soft life with Annie Abbott, and a bit of good grub. Not flighty as Annie's young dogs could be and definitely not given to fanciful shenanigans as it was doing now.

"What's up?" he asked it, moving towards the gate which led from the inlands to the yard, but before he could open it to let the elderly animal through, it leaped, *leaped* the wall and began to run, a streak of blurred black and white, up the field at the back of the farm, again jumping the wall and on to the open fell. It disappeared then into the browning bracken and no matter how Natty whistled, the sound piercing and shrill and clearly discernible to his old dog, it had gone as completely as if the ground had opened up and swallowed it.

"Well, I'll be buggered," Natty said, scratching his head and staring up into the heights of Ullock Pike.

"What is it, Natty?" Charlie asked from behind him and then, as though they too had lost their wits, Blackie and Bonnie lifted their fine heads, sniffed the air and without a sound, their ears flat, their bodies the same, their bellies almost touching the ground, they followed Natty's dog up the field.

"Nay . . . 'appen theer's a lamb . . . ?"

"A lamb . . . ?"

"We could've missed it. 'Appen it's trapped."

"Annie wouldn't have sent Blackie down without checking."

"Annie . . ."

They looked at one another and then without a word both men surged forward, even the old man going like the wind, springing over the wall as nimbly as his dog, following Charlie who was fifty or more years younger than he was and so could be expected to get going faster than himself.

The dog, Natty's dog, raised its voice as Charlie reached The Watches, the spill of stones which was the beginning of the Edge. It sounded frantic and though already his lungs were on fire as his breath laboured in them, Charlie forced out a hoarse cry.

"Where are you, Annie . . . for God's sake . . . where . . . ?"

The dog continued to howl high up on the fell where the heather began and in a moment the sound was taken up by two more canine voices.

"Oh, Jesus . . . oh, Jesus . . . oh, Jesus . . ." Charlie kept repeating though every breath he took and every word he spoke was agony to him. His long legs crashed through the bracken, leaping every obstacle in his path, and his coat flew out behind him like bats' wings. Sweat poured from him coming from every pore in his body, bathing him in the cold slick of fear.

"Annie . . ." His voice rose to a scream as high and agonised as hers had been, the one he thought to be that of the hawk – yes, he remembered it now – and the noise the dogs made grew louder and louder though he thought he could detect a lessening in their frenzy. Jesus . . . oh sweet Jesus . . . let her be safe . . . unharmed . . . and a hundred yards behind him, his back to the breathtaking beauty of the lake and the patchwork quilt of fertile grassland which ran beside it, Natty felt the pain claw at him in the centre of his chest, exploding and extending in its fury down his left arm. It hooked him into an arch, throwing back his head, then just as violently doubling him over forwards but still he kept going.

The dogs stopped howling and the sudden silence seemed to Charlie to be as menacing as the noise.

"Annie . . ."

She was sitting, her back to the grey-pitted stone, her knees drawn up to her chest, her head bowed over her folded arms. About her, huddling close in protective formation were the three dogs. Voiceless they were now, quivering with some fierce emotion, some dangerous, barely controlled menace and for a second, as Charlie came over the rise before they recognised him, all three were up again ready to tear him to pieces.

"Annie . . . God in Heaven . . . Annie . . ." He could barely speak and his chest rose and fell in agony.

She did not look at him, keeping her face buried in her arms but as he flung himself down beside her she put out a trembling hand to him. He took it between his own, his head bent in an effort to look into her face but she seemed calm, unharmed, her hair dishevelled certainly, the heavy plait unravelled but then that was not out of character for Annie. Then why had the dogs set up such a caterwauling? They had known that something was wrong, Natty's dog at first, and then Blackie and Bonnie, their fine instincts in tune with that sixth sense which knows of disaster before man.

"Annie? Darling, what is it? Look at me. What happened? The dogs took off . . ."

She began to shake then, no more than a slight trembling in her neck and shoulders which moved her head on her folded arms, but it spread slowly and steadily down to her hands which, one held by Charlie, the other clasped about her knees, quivered and jerked dementedly. It grew worse, more violent, racing through her body and into her bent legs. Her teeth chattered and she began to moan in her throat, deep, appalling, agonised.

"Annie . . . Dear Christ . . . what happened to you?"

Charlie put his arms about her drawing her to him in a passion of love but she began to struggle, pulling away from him frenziedly, fighting him, striking out at him, deep in the grip of some emotion which seemed to him to be one of loathing.

"No . . . no . . . don't . . . please . . ." she shrieked, and though Blackie and Bonnie both rose to their feet, circling the struggling couple anxiously, Natty's dog slipped quietly away, moving off down the path along which he had come.

"Annie . . . sweetheart, it's me."

"I know, Charlie, I know . . . but please . . . let me go . . ."

Still she kept her face averted, her great heavy mass of hair falling about her in a protecting curtain but through it, now, he could see white flesh, deep claw marks, BLOOD . . . Jesus . . . blood . . . a leopard . . . wolves . . . ! His appalled mind, though it knew very well that there was no such thing up here, grappled with images of Annie in the clutches . . . or the claws . . . fangs . . . of some wild creature . . .

"Darling . . ." Putting the pictures from his mind he allowed her to pull away from him though his every male instinct shouted out to hold her close, to comfort, to protect. "Tell me what happened, Annie. Where are you hurt? Let me look . . ."

"No . . ." Her voice rose in a great cry and Blackie whimpered before coming to lean against her in sympathy. She allowed it, sinking her face into his silky fur, holding him about his neck and beginning to weep. Great wrenching cries which threatened to choke her but the dog stood rock still, his eyes sad and loving.

"Will you not come home then, Annie? Phoebe will . . ."

"Oh yes, Phoebe . . . please Charlie, get me to Phoebe." She did not turn to him but her voice changed, becoming more composed as though the thought of Phoebe strengthened her.

"Let me help you up, my lovely girl."

"No . . . no, please Charlie, I can manage."

"But . . ."

"Don't touch me, Charlie. Let me . . . please . . . take me home."

She walked, or rather stumbled ahead of him, clutching her body in her folded arms, her hair swinging about her, hiding her face and the bloody tracks across her breast.

About half-way down the Edge they came to where Natty Varty lay dead, his faithful dog crouched beside him and her cries which had swept the fells in March for her child, rose again in a growing, maddened crescendo.

32

The constable looked sternly from the man who stalked dangerously about the warm kitchen of the farmhouse to the woman sitting quietly in the chair by the fire and the expression of distaste on his face deepened. He stood with his hand on the latch of the door as though he was ready to be off. He was a member of the brand new police force which had been raised following the County Police Act of 1839 and though even now, twelve years after the Act was passed, there were still counties without a professional police force, Cumberland was not one of them. He had come from Keswick on his sturdy bay to investigate the ridiculous charge brought by Miss Annabelle Abbott of Browhead Farm that she had been 'set upon' – the constable's words, not hers – by Mr Bertram Garnett of Upfell Farm and wished him to be arrested and taken to the County gaol to await trial. She had been alone on Ullock Pike at the time, she said, bringing down her sheep ready for the Keswick Tup Fair and it was there that the crime against her person had been committed.

Eyeing her trousers, the man's grey woollen shirt and the waistcoat she wore over it, the constable had been hard pressed not to answer to the effect that could any man be blamed for thinking that *Miss* Abbott was not the sort of female to whom respect should be shown, or indeed, if it had happened, though she had not mentioned the word, that *rape* could be done to a woman of her character!

Mr Garnett certainly did not seem to think so when the constable, apologetically, had approached him an hour or so earlier.

"Bugger me, constable, d'yer mean ter say that trollop's

accusin' me of interferin' wi' 'er?" Bert's expression was bewildered, innocent, ready to be offended for really, should a man be accused of such gross indecency – or that was how it would be described if levelled at a *decent* woman – in front of his own wife and children? Grouped about the table they were, the children's faces given a wipe over with a sleazy cloth for the occasion, their mouths agape, their eyes round and wondering, his wife's swollen belly a handy place to perch the youngest. A respectable man with a respectable wife and what, he asked, with outrage in his voice, would he need, or want, with Annie Abbott? Mind you, she was free with her favours. Ask any man around these parts, having had an illegitimate child before she was sixteen. Take that fellow she lived with. Why didn't she marry him? Bert wanted to know and then there was him up at Long Beck. A married man with a wife any chap'd be glad to have beside him but *his* carryings on with the slut from Browhead had caused his wife's father to take her away before her health suffered. No better than a prostitute was Annie Abbott and it was well known you couldn't rape a prostitute, now could you, and as for himself, well, giving his enormous wife an affectionate squeeze, surely the constable could see that Bert Garnett had all he needed in his own cosy kitchen at Upfell.

The constable, embarrassed beyond measure, could only agree before getting on his bay and riding back to Browhead.

"Mr Garnett denies everything, Miss . . . er . . . Abbott, an' with no one ter bear out yer allegation, no witnesses, ah mean, then there's nothin' the law can do. Tha' needs a witness, yer see . . ."

"Miss Abbott has marks on her body which she has shown to Phoebe here."

"Aye, so yer said, but if she was attacked by a man, an' who's ter say it were a man, that doesn't mean it were Bert Garnett what done it."

"Miss Abbott swears it was Bert Garnett. Is that not enough? And the wounds to her body surely bear out . . . ?"

"Ah suppose tha've seen these wounds then, Mr . . . er . . . ?" The constable's tone was insulting.

"Lucas." Charlie *was* insulted and his white face said so.

"Mr Lucas."

"No, I have not see them, naturally, but as I have just said, Miss Abbott's companion has. Tell the constable, Phoebe."

Phoebe shrank back on the settle, the forbidding regard of the constable unnerving her. She was a servant, a foundling brought up to believe that authority was all powerful and to have seen what she had on Annie's breasts and belly was hard enough without having to describe it to this man in uniform. Charlie was nodding at her encouragingly, but when she turned to Annie, her expression desperate, asking did she really want it exposed – even in words – for all the world to ogle, Annie merely continued to stare, hands clasped in her lap, into the smouldering peat fire. And could you blame her, Phoebe agonised, for not taking a great deal of interest in the constable after what she had suffered, not only this year, at the hands of men, but going back to her childhood when her father had treated her no better than a labouring beast in the field. There was that bugger who had seduced her and left her with a child and even that small and precious gift had been ripped away from her in the cruellest way when Cat died. She had been humiliated, shamed, spat upon, reviled and yet she had held her head high, held her tongue still and got on with her life, but still they would not let her be. The men! The men who lusted after her. Not all, of course, for the goodness of Charlie Lucas's love shone from him every time he looked at her, which was most of the time, and Natty Varty's devotion had been strong, impeccable, unassailable. Poor old Natty who lay on the table in the parlour, washed, tidy, peaceful in the deep sleep of death, waiting for someone to put him in a coffin and carry him along the corpse way to St Bridget's by the lake.

And who was that to be? Phoebe wondered painfully for not one man had come forward to help, not even those from up Long Beck. Not even Mr Macauley himself.

"Speak up, Phoebe," Charlie said gently, "tell the constable about Annie's injuries," coming to squat before her, taking her hands in his but she hung her head for how could she shame Annie by describing to this stern and hostile man what was on her body? How could she say the words, the intimate words she had spoken to no one in her life, not even another woman? It was impossible, really it was, and the worst thing about it – well, not *the* worst for that was surely what had been done to Annie – was that when the trial was held, as Charlie was determined it would be, she would have to stand up in court and say it, not to one man but a dozen. The jury in fact, and how was she, a simple country girl who could barely read, cope with that?

"Charlie, leave her alone. Don't waste your breath, or the constable's time since it will come to nothing. I only agreed to it so that . . . well, you know why."

And of course he did. Phoebe knew it too. Out of his mind, he had been, off his head and ready, *determined* to batter his way up to the Mounsey farm and with his own bare hands slowly squeeze the life from Bert Garnett's body. No, he would not be satisfied even with that, he had snarled, for it was too quick, too merciful. He would beat him to death, methodically, slowly, until Bert lay dead and bloody at his feet. His hard fist on Bert's hard bone, shattering, breaking, blood flowing, Bert screaming, his own mind empty of all but the satisfying need to have revenge, *justice* for what Bert Garnett had done to his love, the darling of his heart and not only to her, but to Phoebe. Charlie Lucas, mild mannered, good-natured, easy going had lost control, his violence exploding in a great shellburst of savagery which had the three dogs cowering away from him before slinking off into the parlour where the old man lay.

Charlie had brought him down from the fell after Annie's wounds had been seen to but it had taken all her strength of mind to make him do it since he was in such a hurry to get to Upfell.

"You will leave him to lie there until it is convenient then, will you, Charlie? Until you have attended to more important matters such as the flogging you mean to give Bert Garnett?"

"There will be no flogging, Annie. There will be a killing. I mean to . . . Dear Christ . . . I mean to make him pay dearly for . . ."

"Very well, Charlie, do what you have to do but before you go to Upfell collect your belongings and take them with you for you will never come back into my house."

"*Annie!*" Charlie's voice was anguished and the crazed dementia which had him by the throat and which was threatening to topple him over the brink of sanity, lessened a fraction.

"I mean it, Charlie. Go and get Natty, for if you don't, Phoebe and I will."

"I won't let that bastard . . ."

"I know. I shouldn't have told you about him. I could have blamed it on a tinker or a passing drover but I was not . . . in my right mind . . . after what he'd . . . after . . . then to find Natty . . . Oh, Jesus Christ, when is it to end? First Cat . . . my fault, and now . . . again . . . my pride and stubbornness . . . he said it would happen if I continued to roam the fells alone but I took no notice."

"He . . . ?"

"Yes . . . and now, because of me . . . Natty is dead . . ."

Her weeping sorrow had been inconsolable and as Phoebe rocked her in the only arms Annie would have about her, Charlie had been half-way across the yard to Upfell and would have got there had she not leaped up, throwing Phoebe to one side and gone after him, hanging on to his arm like a limpet, even when he dragged her from her feet. It was only then, when her flesh was scraped raw on the cobblestone and her voice screamed his name, did Charlie's derangement lessen, at least enough to help Phoebe get her to her feet and back in the kitchen. And to go up on the fell to bring Natty home.

The constable looked at them, waiting to see if one of the three had anything further to say on the matter. There was no doubt in his mind that the woman had taken some sort of a beating. There were bruises on her throat and a nasty cut on her lip where she had evidently been struck by a hard fist, but she was so bloody calm, so *uncaring*, just as though what had happened to her, whatever it was, was something to which she was not unaccustomed. And perhaps that was the case. This chap who lived with her, so it was said, was like a caged beast snarling about the kitchen, smacking one fist into the palm of the other, looking violent enough to flatten anyone so perhaps it was *him* who had set on her. Women were funny creatures where their men were concerned. And no one knew anything about him. Just came out of the blue, he did, a year or two back, and had stayed. There was talk of her and Mr Reed Macauley up at Long Beck, and of a certain amount of animosity between him and this chap here, and who was to say they had not fought over her? Perhaps she'd stepped between them and got caught in the crossfire, so to speak, though why she should pick on poor Bert Garnett to blame for it, who'd never caused a minute's bother in the district since he'd married the Mounsey girl, was a mystery.

"Ah'll put it before my superiors," he said pompously, opening the door on the cold, blustery wind which was sweeping across the fells and ruffling the water of the lake. The weather had taken a turn for the worse overnight, the hazed autumn sunshine of the day before hidden behind racing clouds of torn grey in every shade from pale grey to pewter.

No one answered him. At the parlour door which stood partly open, for somehow it had seemed to Phoebe that it was callous to leave poor old Natty all alone, Blackie and Bonnie pushed enquiring noses sensing a diminishing of the oppression which had so alarmed them. Natty's dog could be seen, his muzzle on his paws, his old eyes never leaving the still figure of his master on the table.

For a moment the constable wavered. It was all so . . . so quiet . . . so resigned and helpless, so *law-abiding*, so *normal*. Apart from the man, who appeared to be helpless in the grip of some awful pain, some tamped down, stamped upon emotion he was forced – for some reason – to control. The room was filled with peace, warmth, comfort even. An ordinary farmhouse kitchen where the only catastrophe to mar the day would be the failure of the farmwife's bread to rise. The woman still gazed sadly into the fire, her beautiful, tragic face – and the constable admitted it was both of these – pale as alabaster, her eyes, which he knew to be of a strange transparent brown, shadowed by her long, drooping lashes. Her hair was brushed back from her brow and braided high at the back of her head, the braid wound into an enormous coil. The other one, the little, plain one, held her hand between her own, her expression one of agonising remorse, and what he thought might be shame at her own inability to protect her mistress, if that was what she was, to speak up for her, to stand up and speak for her in this dreadful affair. Women like her were afraid of such things, afraid to make a fuss. It was believed in male circles that a female should remain in her home where she would be safe from harm and temptation and that any woman foolish enough to be out alone deserved to be molested. That the local constabulary should not be troubled with such sorry episodes. That incidents such as this were best left to settle themselves. Male violence in such cases was well known but it would not become a case if women, decent women, that is, stayed where they belonged. As this woman had not!

"Ah'll be off then," he told them briskly.

"And that's the end of it then, is it?" the man said bitterly, turning to glare at the constable. The dogs, catching his menace, turned and faced him too since he was the intruder, their hackles rising.

"Mr Lucas, ah've 'eard what Miss Abbott 'ad ter say an' ah've listened ter what Mr Garnett 'ad ter say an' both say different. 'Tis 'er word against 'is and . . ."

"And of course you would be bound to take the word

of a fine, upstanding chap like that bastard who regularly
beats his own wife and . . ."

"That's nothin' ter do wi' me, sir an' wi'out a witness
ter this supposed attack there's nowt' ah can do."

"SUPPOSED . . . !"

"There's no evidence ter support . . ."

"There's the evidence of the scars on Miss
Abbott's . . ."

"Charlie! For God's sake leave it. What would you have
me do? Strip myself naked so that the constable may see
for himself what's been done to me?"

Charlie was appalled. "Darling, of course not
but . . ."

"Then that's an end to it."

"Is it? Is it really? Do you imagine I'm going to let
Bert Garnett put his evil hands on you . . . and other
things . . ." His face worked in agony as the frightful, filthy
images of what Bert Garnett had done to her crowded
into his fertile and imaginative mind and he turned away,
his hand covering his eyes as though to block them out.
"I can't allow it, Annie. I won't allow it. What sort of a
man would I be if I simply went on as though it had not
happened?"

Still he kept his back to the room and the constable
shifted uncomfortably, not at all used to seeing such painful
emotions in a man. But then perhaps *he'd* be the same
if it was *his* wife or *his* girl who'd been . . . Dear God,
what was he thinking of? The anguished atmosphere in the
room was beginning to influence him into making judgements and convicting Bert Garnett of a crime for which
there was absolutely no evidence against him. He'd
best be off before his impartial concern in the matter
was impaired, though of course what he thought – what
did he think? – made no difference one way or the other.
But she was so *sad*, there was no other word to describe
Annie Abbott, the one they called the woman from
Browhead.

But it seemed Mr Lucas had not yet finished.

"I only held back yesterday because you made me,

Annie. Fetch Natty, you said, and I did. Go and thrash Bert Garnett and I won't allow you back in my house, you said, so I stayed. The law is on our side, you said. He will be punished by the due course of the law and though I didn't believe it since I have seen the way the ordinary man is treated by the law on my marches to the . . . well, you will know what I mean. I realise now that all you said was merely a . . . a stratagem to prevent me taking the law into my own hands, but as you can see for yourself the law of this land . . ." turning to look contemptuously at the constable, ". . . does not concern itself with . . ."

"Now look 'ere . . ."

"No, you look here, constable. If you will do nothing to punish Bert Garnett for the horrors . . . for his brutal attacks on these two women . . ."

"TWO . . . !"

"Oh yes, not so long ago he beat Phoebe here senseless . . ."

"It was not reported."

"No, she . . . denied it was him . . ."

"Why is that then?"

"She had her reasons." Charlie turned away wearily. "Oh, what's the use? The man must be punished and it seems there is no one but myself willing to do it so if you will excuse me . . ."

"*Charlie . . . no . . . !*"

"Now look 'ere, sir, you can't tek law inter yer own 'ands. There's nowt ter prove that Bert Garnett attacked your . . . your . . . Miss Abbott an' if . . . well, sir, should 'e be found injured in any way it would naturally be assumed that you were t' culprit an' ah would . . ."

The screams could be heard only faintly at first and the constable did not appear to have heard them, his calm voice, for surely this chap needed calming, continuing to flow from him in what he hoped were soothing waves. The dogs pricked their ears and both Annie and Phoebe turned their heads towards the open door where the constable still leaned. Leaves had been tossed in by the wind, scurrying about the flags like small animals and a billow of smoke spluttered from the chimney caused by the draught the open door allowed in.

The screams grew louder and the constable turned in alarm, his face plainly showing his bewilderment. What in tarnation was up now, his expression said, on this bedevilled day? The screams were that of a woman, perhaps attacked by the same chap who had brutalised Miss Abbott, he remembered thinking, and when Mrs Garnett, whom he had seen no more than two hours ago in the rather unsavoury comfort of her own kitchen, lumbered into view, her children in a long, wailing line behind her, his face gaped in consternation.

She could not speak as she clutched at his arm. Her hair was about her like that of a mad woman's and through it her eyes peered in terror. She still had her baby under one arm, its fists flailing, its cries piteous and for several minutes it was bedlam in the kitchen as the constable endeavoured to extract some sense from the heavily pregnant woman. The two other women were calm though, putting Mrs Garnett on the settle, soothing the crying children with biscuits, brewing tea and even Mr Lucas who, it appeared to him, loathed the very sound of the name Garnett, took one child on his knee before the fire.

"What is it, Sally?" Miss Abbott was saying compassionately and the constable began to believe at that moment that . . . well, that there might be some truth in her story. "Is it . . . has he . . . ?" She could not, it appeared, quite bring herself to say his name.

"Bert, aye, it's Bert . . ."

"Has he . . . hit you . . . ?"

"No . . . oh, no . . ."

"Then what . . . ?"

The constable shut the door behind him and moved forward since it seemed to him this might be a matter in which the law could be involved. Mrs Garnett kept turning to him as though she thought so too, ignoring Miss Abbott's kindness.

" 'Tis Bert, constable . . ." Her face was as white as bleached bone and her eyes looked haunted.

"What about Bert, Mrs Garnett? Has he had an accident?"

"Oh, no . . . at least . . ."

"Yes?"

"Three men come . . ."

"Yes?"

"They took 'im away. Jesus, 'e were screamin' it weren't 'im. That she'd made it up . . ."

"What? She'd made what up? Who did 'e mean?"

Sally turned her gaze on Annie but in her eyes there was nothing but a kind of sad regret.

They found Bert Garnett the next day, high on the highest point of Skiddaw where he had lain all night. A note pushed under his wife's kitchen door told her where he could be found. One of his legs was broken, and his right wrist, and when he was brought down Sally was hard pressed to recognise him. No more than a crumple of bleeding bones, his cheeks gashed, his teeth gone, his ribs broken. The painful scrape of his breath testified to damage in his lungs, the strange look in his eyes to the damage in his head.

They helped her, all the women of the parish, rallying round her as she and her mother had always rallied round them in times of trouble. But not one would stay, they told her, if she allowed the woman from Browhead across her threshwood. This was *her* fault, they said venomously, flaunting herself all over the fells and in the village causing men to . . . well, of course they were not saying it *had* been Bert who had assaulted her, that is if she had been assaulted, which they doubted, and if the constable had not been at her farm and that man of hers under the constable's nose when Bert was taken, he would certainly have been arrested for the crime. Dear Lord, there'd been nothing but trouble ever since she'd come back to Bassenthwaite and if they had any say in it, which, being women, they hadn't, she'd have been tarred and feathered and flogged out of town like they used to do in the old days.

He came that night, Reed Macauley, knocking quietly

at her door and when Charlie opened it, tipping his hat curtly before pushing past him into her kitchen. His eyes went straight to her as she stood up and in them was the deep and abiding truth of his love for her, his compassion, his fear.

"Are you all right?" he asked. The other two in the room were of no concern nor interest to him.

"Yes."

"He did not . . . ?" His voice faltered for a moment, ". . . rape you?"

"No, only . . ."

"He was telling the truth then. I thought so."

"It was . . . you?"

"Yes. Some men I know brought him to me. It was a fair fight. Just myself and Bert Garnett. I won. He couldn't be allowed to get away with it. I wouldn't allow him to."

He turned to Charlie then and though his voice was flat and quite without expression, it was very evident that the remark was aimed at him.

"You're still here then." It was not a question. His eyes were a flat, cold blue and around one of them was a deep purple bruise where Bert Garnett's fist had found its mark and his bottom lip was split. "Don't you think it's time you moved on? I can supply Annie with all the hired help she needs."

"You bastard." Charlie's voice was no more than a whisper and at once Annie went to stand beside him, putting her hand through his arm.

"Charlie wanted to thrash Bert but I wouldn't let him."

"Really." Reed smiled.

"There is no need for you to defend me to this man, my darling. I know what I should have done and wanted to do, and his opinion is of no concern to me . . ."

It seemed Reed Macauley's attention had gone no further than the endearment.

"*My darling!* My darling . . ." he snarled, his arrogant presence suddenly immensely dangerous in the small room. "She is not your darling, you insolent bastard, nor ever will be and I'd be obliged if you'd take your filthy hands off her before I give you a taste of what I gave Bert Garnett since you were too much of a coward to do it yourself. *Move away from her . . . !*"

"I have more right to her than you, you swine. Tell me, is it not true that you already have a wife?"

"Not for long. I am waiting to hear from my lawyer . . ."

"So you said several months ago."

"My wife has left me and . . ."

"Oh, please . . . stop it . . . stop it . . . Phoebe, can't you make them stop it . . ."

"Annie, come with me to Long Beck. You will be safe there from the kind of abuse you were subjected to yesterday. Let *me* protect you . . ."

"Reed, please . . ."

"Leave her alone, you bastard . . ."

"Come with me, Annie . . ."

"Reed, please . . . if you don't leave my home I will . . ."

"Yes, Annie, what *will* you do?"

"Oh, God, I don't know . . ." and before the appalled gaze of the three who loved her most in the world she slid bonelessly to the floor, putting her face in her hands and beginning to weep with the inconsolable intensity of a child. "I cannot stand another moment of this . . . can't you see . . . both of you . . . you are destroying me . . . I want peace . . . peace, not this . . . Oh, God, not this."

At once they were both bending over her but with a curt word of dismissal Phoebe was there, helping her up, holding her close, moving with her towards the twisting staircase.

"Yer like two dogs fightin' over a bone," she said through clenched teeth, ". . . an' should be ashamed o' thissen. An' what about that poor old man in there, tell me that? 'Appen if tha' was ter see about 'is coffin an' gettin' 'im along corpse way to 'is funeral it'd give 'er more comfort than thy brawlin' over 'er. That's what she needs. Comfort an' a bit o' peace."

Natty Varty was laid to rest by Charlie Lucas and Reed Macauley two days later, causing consternation in the community, for what was the hussy up to now? they wondered. They carried the coffin between them without a word, standing silently by the open grave, the two women beside them and when it was over, parting the same way.

33

The winter was hard and cold, long weeks of blizzards which locked them in the farmhouse as though they were prisoners in jail. Long weeks of freezing after that, during which Annie's main concern was for her pregnant ewes. They were quiet months in which the three of them saw no one but each other. Months of calm and peace and the slow fading away of the horrors of the previous year. Not Cat of course, she would never be forgotten, nor would the grieving and sense of loss be totally absent, but an acceptance was painfully gained day by slow day, until it was possible to live in some content and blessing.

The great white bowl of the valley glistened under a sky so deep and intense a blue it was almost the colour of the bluebells which carpeted the woods in May. The sheep had been brought down, a long dark ribbon etched thinly against the whiteness as they came in single file, each following the tail of the one in front directed by Blackie and Bonnie, though not Natty's dog, who kept close to the fire now, and at the bottom Charlie and Annie threw out great flaps of hay for the hungry sheep to feed on. The goodness of summer was in the hay and the sheep consumed it at great speed, keeping a wary eye on the dogs whilst Annie and Charlie watched in smiling silence. When he put his arm about her shoulder she moved away, pretending a concern for a ewe but he knew it was really an excuse to avoid his touch and he sighed, anguished, his hopes of last year when she had seemed to him to be ready for his love, dashed away.

He would never know who had caused it, Bert Garnett or Reed Macauley. Neither had been seen since that day in October when Bert had tried to rape Annie and Natty

had died. Of course Reed Macauley was a businessman
as well as a farmer, with concerns that took him to Carlisle,
to London and even, it was rumoured, abroad to foreign
parts, and those who had been his guests before his wife
left him and who speculated on his whereabouts were in
no doubt that wherever it was and whatever he was doing,
he would be doing it in style. A man who enjoyed the
pleasures of the flesh was Reed Macauley, a fastidious
man accustomed to luxury, good living, every comfort his
considerable wealth could achieve for him. It was said he
had been a time or two to Long Beck checking on his
assets there, making sure those he left in charge were
doing their duty but he had certainly not gone near the
woman from Browhead, whose name had been linked, on
several occasions, with his. Speculation abounded, mouths
pressed to ears that were pricked for any gossip which
was fed by the interest Reed Macauley had always aroused
in them. Did he see his lovely young wife? Was he trying
to effect a reconciliation? Or was he, as it had been whispered last year, still pursuing that elusive something called
'a divorce' which it was said he had been seeking in
London? Not one of them knew anyone who had been
divorced or even how one went about obtaining such a
thing, and it was certain that if one did, one would instantly
become a social outcast. Divorces were granted of course,
but only by a special Act of Parliament and then only after
the Ecclesiastical Court granted a decree similar to that
of judicial separation, which still did not dissolve a marriage, and was granted only on the grounds of adultery or
cruelty and how could the lovely Mrs Reed Macauley be
accused of either of these? It had been known for a man
of the nobility to free himself from an adulterous wife, the
law taking the view that a man such as he must be free
to re-marry and get himself an heir but Reed Macauley
did not fall into that category.

The winter drew to its end and in April spring flowers
began to appear. There were morning mists which rolled
away to reveal purple mountain saxifrage among the damp
mountain rocks and the exquisite beauty of the early purple

orchids which shyly raised their heads among the trees. Blue moor-grass studded the dry limestone rocks. Hellebore and bitter vetch poked their heads through last year's vegetation and in the hedgerows, purple bush-vetch, sweet woodruff, red lungwort and water-avens suddenly burgeoned, all the life-giving plants from which Aggie Mounsey had once prepared potions to ease the living and comfort the dying.

At Upfell Bert Garnett shuffled about the yard on the makeshift crutch someone had fashioned for him, his face quite blank, his eyes slow moving, his mind indifferent to the gradual disintegration of his farm. His flock, most of which had survived the winter, thanks to his brother-in-law Ben Postlethwaite, had been brought down from the high fell, and at the right time, Ben had put the tup he owned to the ewes. Upfell's inland pastures were lush and fertile, the Mounsey ewes thrived but when their lambs were dropped Bert was unaware of it.

Annie was alone in the front pasture when Sally came. Charlie was planting the oats and bigg and in the cow barn Phoebe was fondly contemplating the new addition to Annie's livestock, the calf born to Clover a fortnight ago. Clover was Phoebe's pride and joy, a handsome black-and-white Friesian, serviced by Reed Macauley's bull last year when it was walked over by Jake Singleton, and when put to the task, had obliged right willingly. It had been a part of the unspoken support Reed had ordered his men to give Annie after Cat had died, and about which Annie had been unaware. From March until the end of May when Charlie returned, and with him Annie's senses, small services had been performed by Jake and Maggie, and the calf, a heifer and, in Phoebe's loving opinion, as pretty as a picture, was the result of one of them. Of course, the calf drank all her mother's milk, that with which Phoebe had made her cheese and butter, but when she was weaned, which Phoebe meant to do when the calf was five weeks old, she told Annie importantly, for she was a strong little devil, Phoebe's butter- and cheese-making would resume. Flaked maize and bruised oats mixed with

her own mother's skimmed milk was what Phoebe meant
to give the calf, clean water and good hay and next month
when the weather turned warmer she could be turned out
in the field with her mother.

The lambing was done with, timed to coincide with the
new growth of grass, and they had all three worked for a
solid month from six in the morning until after dark, lambs
coming in an ever-increasing number, those born in the
first week marked up and ready for the fell. Taking them
up there no more than a score at a time and aided by the
two dogs, Annie had found the task immensely satisfying
as she watched her growing flock, past the first dangers
of infancy, leap enthusiastically towards the new grass and
bracken of their first summer. This was her fourth spring
since she and Charlie had brought her ewes from Rosley
and now, from that dozen, she had over a hundred, a
sturdy flock of Herdwicks which, this year, God willing,
would yield almost twice that number.

Sally's voice was hesitant at her back, and she started,
for she had been deep in contemplation of her growing
success. Blackie and Bonnie were down the field, gently
urging some recalcitrant mothers and babies towards the
gate which led to the open fell, and Annie had been sitting
on the wall, watching as they worked. She scarcely needed
to give the dogs commands now as they moved instinctively and in complete unison at their work.

"Hello, Annie," Sally said, and when Annie turned
sharply, Sally stepped back as though she would not have
been surprised had Annie struck her.

"Sally! I was . . . day-dreaming and did not hear you."
Annie threw her legs over the wall and jumped down as
light and free in her neat breeches and knitted jerkin as a
lad of twelve. Her hair was severely braided away from
her face and she looked very different from the golden,
graceful woman, her hair in a magnificent tawny tumble
down her straight back, who had captured Reed
Macauley's wilful heart almost five years ago. Still as
beautiful but in a neutral way, cool, detached, tempered.
Gone was the vital spark burning within her, the radiance

which had shimmered in her golden eyes. Remaining was a sculptured perfection of lovely bone and flesh, unwarmed by emotion. She was slender, almost but not quite thin and the wary caution with which she now viewed the world was very apparent in the way she turned to Sally.

"Sorry, Annie, I didn't mean to disturb thee."

"Not at all Sally, I'm pleased to see you."

"Really," Sally was clearly amazed and Annie smiled.

"Really. Come inside and have a cup of tea, Phoebe and Charlie are not about so you and I can have a chat."

"Eeh Annie tha's a good lass. I thought . . . well, after what 'appened last year that . . . well . . ."

Annie stopped and turned again to Sally, taking her chapped, none too clean hands in hers. Her face was serious but gentle.

"Look Sal, you mustn't blame yourself for what . . . what *he* did to me. I don't blame you and neither does Phoebe. We know what sort of a . . . well, he's your husband and . . . whatever he has done I suppose you would stick by him but . . ."

"Nay, lass, if he were in his right mind my life'd be hell but he's different now and I can't help but be sorry for him."

"Well, I'm afraid I don't feel the same, Sally." Annie's voice was cold, hard and she dropped Sally's hand, turning away, but Sally put it on her arm again, forcing her to stop.

"I know that, lass, God, don't I know it. I were never wi'out a black eye and a bairn under me pinny but that beatin' he got changed all that. Senseless he is now and crippled and if it weren't for what Mr Macauley sends down . . ."

Annie became utterly still. They had entered the kitchen. The fire blazed, the flames reflecting on all the dozens of polished surfaces Phoebe vigorously burnished each day, dancing in golden shadows on the white walls. There were bowls and jugs of spring flowers on every window bottom and in front of the fire on the rag-rug Phoebe had made especially for him, Natty's dog raised his head and thumped his tail a couple of times before resuming the doze in which he spent his old days. Dandy, the marmalade cat, was curled companionably at his back, sharing his rug, and a couple of kittens from her last litter chased a feather which had somehow got into Phoebe's clean kitchen. The kettle spluttered pleasingly, the kail pot bubbled with a tasty stew and on the 'bakstone' oatcakes, baked that morning, were kept warm for their meal. There was a feeling of comfortable plenty, of ease and modest prosperity and Sally looked about her, not with envy, though it did remind her of how her mother's kitchen had been, years ago, but with admiration. She had always known Annie Abbott was a girl of forbearance and iron resolve. Well, she'd had to be with a faither like Joshua Abbott but she'd gone further than Sally had ever thought she could.

". . . looks a treat in here, Annie, an' it's clear tha's worked 'ard and done well for thissen . . ." she was saying.

"What did you say?" Annie's hand had been reaching for the teapot on the ledge above the fire but it fell limply to her side as she turned to look at Sally.

"I said it were a treat in 'ere, lass, especially as tha' . . ."

"No, before that."

Sally looked puzzled. "Before what?"

"About . . . Reed Macauley."

"What about him?"

"You said he was sending . . ."

"Oh, aye, 'tis true. That yardman of 'is comes down every week wi' summat in a basket. Enough to feed us all on account o' Bert not being right yet. 'Tis a mystery, really it is, for the Macauleys weren't right well known for their charity. Old Mrs Macauley wouldn't spit on yer if you was on fire. Cut a currant in 'alf, her cook used ter say an' now there's her lad sendin' great baskets o' grub down to Upfell. Don't like ter think o' the children wi'out a bite to eat, I suppose, an' often enough there's a few bob screwed in a bit of paper. Just until Bert gets on 'is feet, that Jake Singleton said, that's what Mr Macauley told him ter tell me . . ."

So he was at it again. Dispensing largesse to those in need and who more deserving of it than poor Sally Garnett whose husband Reed Macauley had crippled and from what Sally said, scrambled his brains to the extent he could no longer function as a farmer, as a man. His leg and arm broken, it was said, and his face smashed to pulp but those would mend, Annie had thought, but it seemed no part of Bert Garnett was mending, especially his mind. And so Reed . . . Reed . . .

Her heart moved painfully in her breast and a great longing to see him swept over her in such terrifying waves she had to turn away from Sally, only preventing herself from swaying dangerously close to the fire by leaning on the shelf. All these months she had shut him out, her mind closing like a trap every time a vagrant thought had eluded the tight rein she had on herself, and tried to enter it. All these months when she and Charlie might have . . . what? . . . perhaps become lovers? . . . married? . . . given comfort and love and true friendship to one another . . . to have known a certain pleasure in one another's arms . . . *he* had been there . . . always . . . lurking just out of sight and sound . . . hidden behind a rippling curtain of mist . . . unseen but *there*, preventing it, preventing her from becoming a real woman again. At first it had been Bert Garnett, a spectre of male violence, of male dominance, of the cruel, degrading, disgusting things he had done to her which had made her shrink away from Charlie's masculinity, but later, she had admitted it to herself, that had become the excuse she used to keep Charlie at arm's length. She loved Charlie so much, his hurt had been hers. He was the dearest man in the world to her, but he was not Reed. She loved Reed as a man. She wanted Reed as a woman wants her man and the simple, unvarnished truth was that her body could not contemplate the merging of itself with any but Reed Macauley's. She did not even know where he was. Presumably he came back to Long Beck to give orders to his servants and, it seemed, to dispense charity to Sally and her family. Perhaps he lived elsewhere with his wife, how was she to know, and more to the point, did it really matter? He *had* a wife whether he lived with her or not . . . Oh, sweet, sweet Jesus, but she loved him, longed to see him, to see that ironic smile . . . aah, don't . . . she could not bear to remember . . . the shape of his lips . . . on hers . . . his hands brown, hard . . . gentle on her body . . . it was killing her, this agony of feeling she didn't want, this love she didn't want. She was afraid of it, afraid of loving, not just Reed but *anyone*. It was so much easier to be detached, to be unaroused by anything more exciting than a healthy lamb, a fine crop of early potatoes, a warm fire to drowse by. Friendship, such as she and Phoebe had, demanding nothing, but not love, not *love* for when love went, when *loss* came, the pain was unendurable. She could not endure it, not any more . . . she must stop before Sally . . .

". . . so 'tis like havin' seven bairns with Bert as he is, you knew I'd another lass, didn't you? . . . *No!* . . . oh, aye, just after Bert fell ill. Kitty she's called but she'll be the last, thank God, what with Bert shamblin' about the place half-witted. Don't want me anymore, poor sod, or *can't*, an' I've to think of the bairns, haven't I? 'Tis a snug little cottage up by Binsey an' I'll be near our Mim and 'er two. Ben's mother died last backend so it all worked out right well. Ben wanted the farm hisself but it's too far for 'im ter come over an' work it, what with 'is own and he can't afford to pay anyone, an' then o' course wi' Mim to 'elp me, well, we can 'elp each other, bein' so close . . . anyway, I said to Bert . . . well, I still talk to him, Annie, even if he don't answer . . . I said ter Bert, Annie's doin' that well, 'appen she'll be interested, so I come over ter give thi' first refusal."

Sally was sitting at her ease in the chair which had been Joshua Abbott's and for a moment Annie could feel his presence in this kitchen, on this farm where he had struggled and laboured for almost fifty years as a boy and as a man and had never in all that time known true success. Blight and murrain had swept through his crops and his sheep with devastating regularity, and yet each time he had patiently, often with great bitterness, heaved himself upright and carried on. Now, or so it seemed to her stunned brain, Sally was asking her, *her*, Joshua Abbott's daughter, if she cared to buy Upfell Farm. Upfell and its splendid acres of rich inland pastures, its intakes and woodland, its snug farmhouse, all lying neatly beside her own land, twice the size of hers and if . . . dear God in Heaven . . . if she could do it . . . perhaps a loan . . . the bank . . . Mr . . . what was his name? . . . the lawyer in Lancaster . . . she would have a farm, not as big as Reed's, but bigger than most . . . a flock of hundreds . . . cattle . . . it was just too much to take in . . .

"Shall I mek tea?" Sally said sympathetically as Annie fell back on the settle.

"How much money have you got?" were Charlie's first words when she told him, and her fine and ecstatic rapture ebbed away. She felt a surge of resentment, a distinct need to stand up and stamp about in high dudgeon for how dare he spoil her lovely dream, the rainbow-coloured, star-dazzled, brilliantly glowing dream she had dwelled in ever since Sally had ambled off up the path towards Upfell. But of course the question must be answered, considered first, and answered. She certainly did not have enough to buy a farm, let alone the livestock on it but if she could get a loan . . . perhaps using Browhead as . . . what was the word? . . . collateral . . . ?

"How much, Annie?" Charlie asked again, his eyes grave, his expression withdrawn. "You know you have to examine . . ."

"I could borrow against Browhead, Charlie." Her eager face was flushed, lovely again, alive with an animation she had not known, or shown for months. It was as though she had been given a new lease on life itself, the chance to begin again, to seize hold of something worthwhile, something wonderful which she had thought would never come again.

"Who from?"

"Well . . . there's the bank in Keswick or . . ."

"Or Reed Macauley."

The silence which followed was deep and painful and in her quiet corner, Phoebe's hands stilled on the bit of work she had in them. She never sat down without something, knitting, a sock to be darned, a tear mended, a button to be sewn on Charlie's shirt, since it went against all she had been taught from the time she had been considered old enough to ply a needle, that idle hands meant mischief. That is what they had said to her, though what mischief a frightened, blank-eyed four-year-old foundling could get up to in her hard, fourteen-hour day, had never been explained to her. She looked from one awkward face to the other, seeing the confirmation she looked for in Annie Abbott's eyes, though Annie of course denied it.

"I said nothing about Reed Macauley, Charlie."

"You don't have to, Annie."

"And what does that mean?"

"It means that . . . you . . . still think of him . . ."

"Don't be ridiculous."

". . . and that you . . . because you want Upfell so badly, you would go to him for the money. He is the only man of real wealth in these parts. He lends money to . . . to those who need a loan and feeling about you as he does, a fact he made very clear when he almost killed Bert Garnett, which I should have done and didn't, he would not hesitate to further his claim, indeed he would give you the money *and you know it.*"

"That's not true . . ."

"Which part is not true, Annie?"

"Any of it."

"Do you deny he loves you?"

"Charlie . . . please . . . don't . . ."

"And by your tone I would say you still feel the same about him."

"Charlie, I beg of you, don't do this . . ."

"What, speak the truth or make you face it?"

"He is nothing to do with me, Charlie. He has a wife . . ."

"And if he had not, would I still be here?"

"Charlie, you know what I feel for you."

"Indeed I do, Annie, that is what is so sad about it. I keep hanging about like some faithful old dog hoping for a kind word, a glance, a pat on the head but really it is not enough. I am making a pathetic figure of myself and . . ."

"No, that's not true Charlie, I . . ."

"Don't! don't say you love me, Annie, truly I could not bear it if you did. I don't want what you have to give me, which is what you would give to another woman, what you give to Phoebe. I'm a man with needs of my own which have been sadly neglected over the past years as I've waited patiently for you to . . . Jesus . . . *to notice me*. I'm not a bloody machine, I want you . . . I love you . . . for Christ's sake, can't you . . . ?"

His face moved in a great spasm of self-loathing and he turned away, looking towards the corner in which Phoebe sat. She shrank from his glance, longing with all her heart to leave this room in which emotions flared and grew out of control but Charlie did not even see her there.

"I hate myself for being like this, Annie. I want to beg, to plead with you to let me . . . to let me love you . . . to love me . . ."

"I do . . . Charlie, I do."

He turned on her savagely.

"No, you don't, *you don't*. You love *him* and really, I cannot take much more of watching you do it."

"Charlie . . ."

"No . . . no . . . don't . . ."

In his headlong haste to get away from her, from the possessive love she aroused in him, from the suffering she caused him, from his hatred of Reed Macauley, from the compassion, the fascination, the tenderness, the enchantment of Annie Abbott, he almost knocked her over as she stood up. Fumbling for the door catch, he jerked open the door, crashing his head on the low frame, disappearing into the dark night. They could hear him as he vaulted the wall and the distressed bleating of the sheep as they divided before him, then it was silent.

The dogs, who had sprung to their feet, alarmed by the commotion, settled down again slowly, watching anxiously as Annie moved wearily across the room to close the door.

"He'll be back, Phoebe, he's upset."

"Aye, an' reason to be, I'd say."

"Oh, Phoebe, please don't you start on me now, I can't take much more, really I can't."

"An' neither can Charlie. For God's sake wed him or let him go."

Annie turned to stare in amazement at Phoebe who had resumed her patient stitching.

"*Let him go?*"

"Aye, or he'll never be right again. I know nowt about men but I do know what it's doin' to Charlie watchin' you fret after a chap what . . ."

"I'm not fretting over any chap, Phoebe. I have had . . . sadness."

"I'm not sayin' tha 'asnt, lass, more than most. But face the truth like Charlie said. Give Mr Macauley up. Let him make his peace with his wife 'cos he would if tha' was married to another man."

Annie bent her head and her breath left her on a shuddering sigh. She put her face in her cupped hands and her pain was an appalling menace in the room. It threatened to strike her to her knees from where she would never rise again, to bend her proud, strong back, to break it, to crush her. Blackie stood up hesitantly and moved across to her, pushing his muzzle against her knee and, when her hand dropped to his head, staring up at her with patient, loving eyes.

At last she spoke again.

"I know, Phoebe, what you say is true but . . . but I cannot marry Charlie just to keep him here, which is what I would be doing, and as for Reed . . . and his wife, that is their affair, not mine. They . . . both of them will do what they think fit, which is what I will do. Charlie . . . must make his own choices, Phoebe. I cannot say how I will feel in . . . say, six months. Last year, after Cat died, I was very close to . . . giving in . . ."

"Aye, I noticed."

"You don't miss much do you?"

"No, an' neither did Natty. We both thought that . . ."

"You and he discussed it?"

"Why not then? We're family . . ."

"Of course you are, Phoebe. You and Natty . . ."

"And Charlie?"

"Yes, I love Charlie, but not as he would want." She sighed deeply. "Well, I'd best go and look for him and make my peace."

"Don't do that, Annie. It's not peace he wants. You go ter tha' bed for if I'm any judge, tha'll be off t' bank in Keswick first thing."

She was.

The bank manager in Keswick knew her, as everyone in the parish of Bassenthwaite knew her by now. Who had not heard of her wild ways, her outlandish manner of dressing, her unconventional, outspoken behaviour, her notoriety with regard to Mr Reed Macauley, her capricious flouting of all the laws of decency and morality? Certainly not the bank manager in Keswick and would those who trusted their money and their investments in his honest and trustworthy hands, thank him for lending it to a woman such as her? She had certainly proved herself resourceful, turning her father's farm from failure to a small measure of success, but would it continue? And if it did not, how, he begged her to tell him, averting his eyes from her long trousered legs, the fine turn of her ankle in their highly polished boots, would she repay her debt?

She tried to tell him but he would not be moved. She was a woman, infamous and, more to the point, a risky one.

It was the same with Mr Hancock in Lancaster to where she took the train. Yes, he remembered her, he said kindly, looking not at what she had on for this time in desperation she wore the black mourning dress Reed's women had put on her when Cat died, but at her frail loveliness, for surely this brittle woman who looked as though she would snap like a dried twig, was not capable of running *two* farms, and certainly not of repaying a substantial loan on one of them.

A week later Upfell Farm was sold to a farmer from Lancashire. It was rumoured he had bought it for his younger son, who, having no expectations of inheriting any part of the family farm, wished to strike out on his own.

34

She had been shearing her sheep, her mind dazed with how she was to get through when the shearers from Long Beck came down.

"We've come ter do tha' 'boon clip'," one said dourly, his short pipe clenched between his teeth.

"But . . ."

"Mr Macauley says if tha' was ter give us an argument to tell thi' tha' can coom and give us a hand next week."

She could not help but smile though Charlie did not, at the idea that Annie Abbott would make the smallest difference in the shearing of Reed Macauley's 2,000 ewes and gimmers, his yearlings and twinters and the fine rams he owned to keep his flock pure and strong. She could just imagine him, his eyes gleaming with sardonic humour, giving the message to this man, knowing her and her stubbornness against taking what she would see as charity. He had been at Long Beck for several weeks now, so they were told, the news brought by Maggie Singleton who could not resist her natural pride in the fine son she had borne Jake Singleton, when she came down to Browhead to show him off to Phoebe.

Annie and Phoebe, thankfully, both of them, left the yard to the men who had brought their own shears and shearing stools, and with Charlie and a boy to heave the sheep in their direction and a couple of others to salve those shorn, the two women contented themselves with the women's age-old task of feeding the workers.

It was Charlie, not the presence of the Long Beck men, who had inclined Annie to move indoors. She and Charlie were not easy in one another's company these days and she knew she would have to come to some decision, make a commitment, one way or the other, either to Charlie, or to a life of loneliness, spinsterhood even, without him. He had said he would wait for ever, positive he meant it at the time, certain in his male heart and masculine pride that Annie would turn to him eventually. He may not have thought it consciously, for Charlie was not given to arrogance, but his logical mind would reason that she had no choice. She loved him, more than a friend, if less than a lover and it was pretty reasonable to assume that Reed Macauley would never be free of his pretty wife. So what other option was open to Annie Abbott? She was not fashioned for celibacy, for barrenness, for the arid life of a woman alone. She needed warmth, love, emotionally and physically, children, a woman's life in which her capacity for all these things would be fulfilled. So surely everything was tilted in Charlie's favour and soon, when her mind was at peace and the anguish of losing Cat had lessened, when her equilibrium was restored and the even tenor of their life together resumed, Charlie and Annie would be man and wife, and very well they would do together.

But he *and* Annie had not bargained on her body's stubborn refusal to consider any but Reed Macauley's, nor on her wayward female heart which, now that it was released from the icy paralysis it had known for over a year, bucked and plunged and leapt with gladness at the very mention of Reed Macauley's name.

Annie fidgeted fretfully about the kitchen that day, getting in Phoebe's way, until Phoebe began to tut-tut irritably. She had her own way of doing things, devised over the four years she had been at Browhead. This was *her* kitchen, her parlour, her dairy and cow shed and vegetable garden, and in them she worked tirelessly, methodically, contentedly, with no other woman to say her 'yea' or 'nay'. She knew very well that had the men not come down from Long Beck, a circumstance not at all to the liking of Charlie, who even now from the side door which stood open, she could see had a face on him like thunder, she and Annie and himself would have blundered on, day after day, in an attempt to get the flock clipped. An impossible task for one woman since Charlie, though he had tried to shear, hadn't the knack for it. The ewe he had started on had nearly bled to death from the numerous slashes in her skin and Charlie himself, at the end of a long struggling hour, had a cut so deep in his forearm Phoebe had threatened to stitch it up for him with her own needle and thread. He and the ewe looked as though they had just come from a slaughterhouse, slicked in the blood of both of them, Charlie grim faced, the sheep the same, the atmosphere of tension so deep and dreadful Phoebe had feared he and Annie might come to blows. He felt useless, she knew, less than a man as he was forced yet again to let Annie do the work he should have been able to do, and no matter how Annie assured him it really was of no consequence and she would manage, and though it was no fault of hers, Charlie was tight-mouthed with frustration at his unhandy ways. In the old days, of course, before this awkwardness had come upon them, he would have grinned engagingly, made a joke, laughed at himself, but not today.

Where was that lovely lilting harmony they had known a year ago, she asked herself despairingly? That lively joy and anticipation of each day they had dwelled in. Annie, Charlie, Phoebe, Cat, and later Natty, living in peaceful understanding beside one another, the future shimmering ahead of them like a silver ribbon. Natty's, short certainly, but filled with the warmth of friendship, the satisfaction and fulfilment of knowing, even at his age, that he was a trusted, *needed* member of the household. Cat had been at school and ahead of her were the days and years her splendid education would bring her, her clever young mind nourished and complete, her lovely young body giving promise of the same. Herself, here, as she had wished to be until the day she died, serving those she loved not in self-sacrifice but in joy for it was in doing so that *she* was complete. And Charlie and Annie growing closer, growing softer, growing together until their children came to complete the natural circle of love which filled this house.

Now there was nothing but strain, awkwardness, politeness, Charlie's face sad and empty, Annie's always turned in the direction of Dash Beck, or so it seemed to Phoebe who watched her. Gone were the laughter, the songs, the impish endearing humour with which Charlie had entertained them. Charlie, honest, sincere, candid and true-hearted, was becoming truculent, inward-looking, *bitter*, waiting for Annie. And how long would it be, as he waited, before he was spoiled, his love and need and sweet gentleness soured within him?

"See, get out o' me way, Annie, ah've put that milk to set and if tha' keeps movin' it it'll tek three days instead o' three meals for t'cream ter come."

"Well, let me help you with the churning."

"There's no need lass. Ah've managed it these months gone an' . . ."

"I could make the clapbread."

"An' how long is it since tha' made clapbread?"

"I've been making it since I was tall enough to stand at that table, Phoebe, which is longer than you."

"'Appen it is, but ah've got me own way o' doin' it and I can't abide havin' it messed about."

"Messed about! This is my kitchen, you know."

"No, it's not, it's mine, so go an' . . ."

"Go an' what? What do you suggest?"

"Isn't there summat in t' fields tha' can be checkin'?"

"No. The hay isn't ready to be cut yet."

"Well . . ." Phoebe tutted again, looking vexedly round her clean and shining kitchen which she could not abide having 'messed about'.

"Tek this tea out to t'chaps . . ."

"No, Phoebe . . . I don't want to do that." Annie's eyes turned to look out of the side door to where Charlie had a firm grip on a bawling sheep. They were both determined to have their own way, Charlie and the ewe, the ewe to get back to its frantic lamb, Charlie to heave it on to the shearer's stool. Charlie was soaked in sweat, his brown face grim, the muscles straining in his strong neck. With an enormous effort, he landed the ewe in its proper place, stepping back to grin in triumph and as he turned to get another, his eyes caught Annie's. Both looked away hurriedly, not in embarrassment but in an effort not to have a confrontation of any kind, even one as simple as a sympathetic smile.

"Lord's sake then, why don't tha' take Royal up to t' . . ."

"No . . ." for Charlie would see her and wonder where . . .

"Well, I don't know, but just stop gettin' under me feet."

"I'll go and cut some peat then, if that's the case."

"Aye, tha' do that." Phoebe was obviously relieved. "Sledge's at back and Charlie left the flay spade with it . . ."

"Really, it's coming to something when I have to be sent from my own kitchen so that . . ."

"Oh, get on wi' thi'! Tha' knows tha'll enjoy a walk up to t' peat moss."

She simply stepped through the back door whilst Charlie was bending over a salved sheep and before he straightened she was up behind the farmhouse dragging the loyal sledge behind her, moving through the deep tunnel of bracken towards a stand of trees and the peat moss which was beyond it.

The wood was in full summer bloom. The air beneath the canopy of trees was cool and damp-smelling, the energy of the hot sunshine soaked up by the leaves which spread above her head. The leafy crowns were so thick, barely any light got through, forming a solid mass which seemed to float above the tall, straight trunks of the graceful trees. Beech trees and oak, and growing freely beneath them were rhododendrons, their natural purple blossom gone now with the month of May. There was an open glade in the wood's centre where the sun reached, thick now with bilberry bushes, nettles, the bright yellow of celandine, the white of wood anemone, the delicate pale green fungus growing on fallen oak branches.

The silence was broken only by the droning song of a heavily laden bee and the sudden broken laugh of a jay as it was startled up from the tangle of a fallen tree when she approached. She continued upwards, moving again

through bracken and gorse, following a sheep trod beside
the rushing noisy waters of the beck, skirting the deep fern
garlanded tarn into which the beck emptied. The sound the
water made was deafening after the peace and calm of the
woods but beyond it, as Annie reached the flatter area of
the peat moss, the silence fell again.

It was sultry now, the sun scowling from behind the
frown of a cloud. She dug for an hour, her thin cambric
shirt clinging wetly to her back and breasts as she stacked
the cut peat neatly on the sledge. Sweat trickled unpleas-
antly down her body and she thought longingly of a bath
and of the jugs of cool water Phoebe would pour over her.
Her hair, which had started the day braided tightly about
her head, had fallen in its usual vigorous tangle across her
back and shoulders and she thrust it impatiently from her
face with both hands.

The man who studied her felt the hot glow begin and
he shifted uncomfortably in his saddle. He was above her,
hidden from her by a natural buttress of boulders which
formed a screen from all eyes but that of the hawk. His
face was quite inscrutable, dark and brooding, brows
scowling over his darkened blue eyes and he slouched on
the mare's back, one arm resting on the pommel of his
saddle, both feet hanging loose from the stirrups.

He continued to watch her for several more minutes,
then with a deep sigh, one of resignation to a fate which
seemed greater than his own will, he threw one leg over
the mare and jumped to the ground. Several sheep cropping close by twitched nervously, moving away with their
heads held high and the collie dog who dozed by the mare's
hooves, eyed her master in anticipation. Throwing the
mare's reins over a jagged piece of rock from which she
could not stray, Reed Macauley spoke quietly to both animals and then began the slow descent towards Annie. He
could see her small figure in the distance all the way down
the sprawling slope, but as he gazed at her, only taking
his eyes from her to keep a sharp watch on the rough rock
strewn track he walked, she straightened up, threw her
spade on to the peat-laden sledge and began to manoeuvre

it across the peat moss towards the wooded ravine a hundred feet below where she worked. There was a rocky gutter to which she kept as she went down, moving behind the sledge, clinging to the rope to prevent it from going too quickly. It was heavy, too heavy really and it took all her strength to hold it. Had the path been less rocky, it would have careered away from her. Now and again it became stuck and she was forced to go to the front and pull it free.

When she reached the tarn she was so hot and uncomfortable, she felt as though she had been plunged into a warm bath, her clothes sticking to her body like a second skin. Trickles of perspiration ran down from her hair, slipping across her eyebrows to her eyelashes. One drop kept catching at the end of her nose, and others ran into her mouth, salty and unpleasant. She paused to get her breath, bending down with both hands on her knees, gasping in the warm air, and beside the rocky path the water of the small tarn glistened deep and black. Above her the cloud had moved on, not a wisp remaining and the sun scorched down from the blazing blue of the sky. She could feel it on her back and when she straightened, pushing her heavy hair from her face, a heat haze danced, with the midges, across the surface of the pool. Dragonflies clung to the stalks of the reeds, and two delicate yellow butterflies waltzed madly in the heat. There were birch trees on the water's edge, leaning over gracefully towards it as though they would like nothing better than to dip their heads into its icy depth and beside them, crowding in great sheltering profusion were fern, flowering rush, water violets and crowfoot, green and lush and fragrant. The water ran into the tarn from the beck which careered down the ravine. It quietened when it reached the still pool, sliding sinuously round and across the satin smooth grey rocks, then moved on to the rushing drop of the waterfall and down again to follow the course of its rocky bed. A tiny breeze had stolen through the gorge to the pool. The dripping mountain plants which clung to the glistening vertical walls surrounding it moved and the dancing, tossing spray drifted across it, a million crystals shimmering where the sun touched them. The churning waters of a thousand years had carved this smooth basin from the solid rock and its peaceful beauty enchanted the mind and stole reason and good sense.

Annie hesitated for no longer than ten seconds. She looked about her, first up the path from where she had come, and then down to the wood through which she must go to reach Browhead, but there was no sign of another living human being. Kicking off her old clogs, she unbuttoned her shirt and tossed it on to a nearby clump of fern, stepped out of her trousers and the short drawers she wore beneath them and moved, trance-like, to the water's edge. Her body gleamed, white in the sunshine, clean-limbed, straight and slender, her breasts high and pink-tipped, her waist fine as gossamer, her hips curving slimly away from it. The triangle of darkness at her thighs' division had a glint of russet in it as did the fluff in her armpits and all about her flew her vibrant hair. She was glorious, glowing, polished as a russet apple and the man who watched her, drew in his breath in rapt wonder.

"Shall I jump?" he heard her say to herself, and his heart moved in him smilingly, but caution prevailed as she warily put a toe in the water.

"Dear heaven," she gasped out loud, "it's cold," and again the man felt his mouth curve in a smile. She stepped down the shallow bank, gasping with the shock of it, but at the same time her mouth widened in a delighted grin. The dark inviting depth of the water which had never known the sun's touch drew her on and beneath her white feet as she stepped on them, was the tinkle of sliding pebbles. The sound of the waters splashing and gurgling among the boulders, the roaring of the falls further on masked the sound of the approach of the man and when he reached the pool he stood between a tall clump of fern for several bewitched minutes to watch her.

"Ye gods, but it's cold," she gasped again and he could see the skin of her back prickle into a million goose-pimples. Suddenly, taking a deep breath, she plunged under the water and there was nothing to see but the ripples she left behind her.

Annie dived down and down and down between the dank walls, getting nowhere near the bottomless depths, and above her as she turned, she could see the sunlight, the green of the trees as they rushed to meet her and the tall wavering figure of a man. She broke the surface, gasping, her heart plunging in sudden terror. It was Reed, Reed Macauley. He was standing quietly by the edge of the water, his legs apart, his hands resting low on his hips. Their eyes met and clung, and could not look away, a clinging which was strong and vibrant with their suppressed emotions, suppressed these five years, but unwilling, they seemed to say, to accept it any longer. It had a sweetness about it, that exchange, a sweetness which was mixed with a sensual need so great, it was like an explosion and this time she knew she could not escape him, and did she want to? He was unsmiling, he did not speak and neither did she, though the shock of seeing him there had been severe. They had no need to speak, not now, for they had become fast in the drifting dream world of the moment, the moment towards which they had been moving ever since they had met again, as adults on the road from Penrith. He had known how it was, how it would be even then, though she had not, for she was, despite her experiences, no more than a girl, and ever since they had felt their desire grow, a desire in him which was not romantic, but was the fierce need of a man to put the mark of love on the woman who belonged to him; in her, the female need of submission to that mark.

She continued to look at him, understanding in those last few seconds what he had in his mind, and knowing that at last the time had come. Almost, but not quite, it had happened before, but now, out here where it was wild and free, uninhabited by anyone but Annabelle Abbott and Reed Macauley, was the place, the time, the appropriate place and time *for them*.

Her body gleamed white beneath the clear waters. She

moved her legs slowly to keep herself afloat and just below
the surface of the water her breasts lifted gently to reveal
the rock-hard peaks of her nipples. Her face was white
and calm but in her eyes was the narrowed glow of sensuality. For a moment, the tick of a clock, no more, as his
hands went to the belt of his breeches, her lips parted in
denial and a cool clear voice inside her told her how insane
this was, but when at last he stood before her, his beautiful
male body, brown and hard, stripped of the packaging of
civilisation, the words died within her.

"I love you, Annie," he said, almost idly, knowing full
well that there would be no going back this time, but
wanting her to realise all the same that this was no idle
thing. He lifted his arms and dived into the water. He was
gone for five seconds, no more, then he rose until they
were face to face. He did not gasp with the cold as she
had done, but pulled her at once against his body, his arms
tight about her, his mouth on hers, her breasts against his
chest, his penis questing between her thighs. There was
no gentleness in him, nor in her. They almost fought one
another in their hunger, and when she wrapped her legs
about his waist, he penetrated her at once, the water
surging and threshing about them as he moved ferociously,
deeply inside her, immersed in her, loving her, the strokes
of him, long, hard, insistent. She threw back her head,
her arms clinging about his neck, her legs about his body
and when the white-hot, ice-cold joy raced through her,
she cried out loud, the sound rising and echoing about the
ravine.

"Dear God . . . aah . . . my dearest, dearest love . . ."
His own full-throated roar was triumphant, magnificent,
silencing the sounds of the small creatures in the undergrowth, even the thunderous cascade of the waterfall
dying into insignificance beside it.

For a full five minutes they remained fast together, not
speaking, her face buried in his neck and shoulder, his
against her wet hair. It floated about them like a rippling
curtain of tawny seaweed and beneath them his legs moved
keeping them both afloat.

He sighed, replete for the moment, five years of longing satisfied.

"We had best get to the bank my darling, or we shall both sink without a trace." He smiled down at her, murmuring into her dazed face, kissing it tenderly, then lifted a hand to brush back a wet, shining strand of copper hair which had wrapped itself about them both. Gently he towed her back to the bank, then lifting her into his arms, carried her to a sun-warmed patch of tufty grass and laid her down on it.

She sighed and stretched, lifting her arms above her head, deliberately displaying her proud breasts for his hands to cup, bending one knee so that the most secret part of her body was revealed to him. Her eyes were narrowed and hazy, the eyelashes tangled with drops of water, but when she smiled, the sun put a hot golden glow in their depths. He stood over her, male triumphant, his manhood a proud and flaunting thing, then, kneeling across her once again, he plunged into her until she wept with the rapture and glory of what he did to her.

The sun was setting across Bassenthwaite Lake when they kissed a lingering farewell. He had examined her body, with his hands, with his lips, his tongue exploring every inch of her, gently probing, his teeth nipping, his hands smooth and caressing, light as a butterfly until her skin shivered in delight, then hard, cruel even, making her arch her back in an ecstasy which could easily have been mistaken for pain. He devoured her, took her again and again, groaning as though he himself was in agony, and when he lay back she covered him with her own slippery wet body, moving her mouth gently on his then sliding down and down, brushing her lips across his flesh until he was roused again.

They had played in the water, two children again, young and carefree again, the years of pain tumbling joyously away, jumping and splashing one another, swimming hand in hand beneath the surface of the clear water, their bodies in lovely unison, diving down into the icy grey depths then up, moving through grey to clearest amber to a pale golden glow as the sunlight shone through the water. They were oblivious of time, of those who might wonder where they were, of everything but this great and shining happiness which had at last become theirs. They did not talk much. The word 'love' was scarcely needed to be spoken. It was everywhere, bathing their smooth skins, singing through their veins, beating in their hearts and illuminating their eyes to the glory which had come to them. They kissed and touched and marvelled, but of course, it had to end.

"You are mine now, you know that, don't you, Annie?" His voice was very serious. "There is no going back. I don't know what is to happen. That is for you to decide. You know that too. I have no intention of forcing you – that's if I was able to – my darling, none at all. I've loved you for so long now, with all my heart, feeling it grow stronger inside me all these years. Have you the least idea how much pain you have caused me . . . ?"

"Yes . . . and me."

"I know, I've wanted you for so long . . . taken other women . . . oh yes . . . I'm a man with a man's needs and my wife . . . well . . . I will not speak of her since she is no more than a child and cannot be blamed . . . but you . . . you are my companion, Annie, in the true sense of the word, and I need you beside me . . . with me . . . you understand what I'm saying . . ."

"Yes, my love."

"A lover to delight me, a friend to support me . . . that is what I want in my woman . . . laughter, love . . . what we have shared this day . . . I cannot let it go . . . nor you, for you are that woman."

"I love you, Reed, I always have."

"And you will come to me . . . ?"

"There is so much to consider."

"I know, and we will consider it, at *your* pace, but we will consider it, Annie. I'm getting nowhere . . . with the divorce. She has done nothing to . . . given me no cause . . . she, or her father, says she will come back whenever I . . . wish it but that I must . . . well, you must no longer be part of my life . . ." He swallowed painfully, his face anguished for he wanted her to be the woman, he wanted himself to be the man, who would be the two halves of the Macauleys of Long Beck. It was a gift he needed to give her, and amongst all those he *meant* to give her, this would not be amongst them.

"May I come down to visit you at Browhead?" The shock of the words took her breath away. So quiet, so . . . so reasonable, the aggression, the arrogance, the overbearing challenge with which he dealt with anything which stood in his way, gone with the strength and steadiness of his love for Annie Abbott. For several moments she could not answer. He spoke for her.

"It's him, isn't it?"

"Yes." Her head bowed in pain, for how was she to tell Charlie? Tell him what? her clear mind asked and her dazed and drugged heart answered the question. Tell him that you love Reed and are to . . . to . . . *live with him* somewhere? Is that it? Has it been decided then? Have you decided, her mind asked her heart? and she supposed, somehow, that she had. That she had finally come to the realisation that she could fight it no longer. That what she had jibbed at time and time again, the submission of her will to Reed Macauley's, the acceptance of that stylish villa in Penrith or Ambleside or Carlisle, must be undertaken. She could not exist apart from him, not now, not after this enchanted afternoon but . . . there was Charlie.

"There is . . . something." He lifted her chin, forcing her to meet his gaze, smiling a little, for Charlie Lucas no longer frightened him.

"Yes?"

"The farm at Upfell."

"Yes?" Her voice rose questioningly.

"I am giving it to you. It is my first gift to you as my . . . love."

Her mouth opened and then shut again. He put a hand to her chin, beginning to laugh, ready to swing her round in a great circle of joy for at last, *at last* he could do something for her, satisfy that need in him to shower her with all the things he thought she should have, all the many and expensive things he thought she *needed* to have.

"You own Upfell?" Her voice did not warn him as it should and he continued to grin down at her.

"I do. Do you think I would let anyone have it when I knew you had set your heart on it? Oh yes, I heard of your efforts to raise a loan."

"Is there anything in this parish that you don't know about, Reed?"

"If there is, it's not worth knowing." His wide smile was like that of a child who has just been given a glimpse of fairyland, "and if I hadn't been away when you approached that fool of a bank manager in Keswick, I would have had a quiet word in his ear. Fortunately, I returned in time to get my hands on the property and now I am giving it to you. I was just waiting for the right moment and this seems to me to be *exactly* the right moment. You have enriched me with the greatest gift a woman can give today and in return . . ."

"I don't need paying for my . . . favours, Reed."

He recoiled as though she had struck him, then acting instinctively, he dragged her into his arms and held her by brute force.

"No! . . . no! . . . I will not let you do it again. *Damn* your bloody pride, your stubborn *obsessive* pride. Yes, that's what it is, obsessive. I love you, dammit, I love you and I wanted to . . . *give* . . . but, God's teeth, if it means that much, buy the bloody place from me . . ."

"Reed . . ." She was overwhelmed by the intensity of his anguish, and her own outraged pride and resentment drained away from her. She relaxed against him and he sighed thankfully.

"Annie, it's hard for me. I am a man who has, for all of my adult life, done, and been exactly what I wanted to do and be. If I had been denied in the past I have simply ridden roughshod over that denial because quite simply I did not care enough about what the other man was feeling. I've taken what I wanted and it has not been easy for me to . . . accept that with you . . . oh, Jesus . . . help me . . ."

She looked up into his face and it was haggard with the truth of what he said. His mouth was hard and tense, his shoulders slumped and weary, telling her he really could not stand it if he was to lose her again. The fatigue, the pain in him stirred her compassion and she put a gentle hand on his cheek.

"Annie . . ." he could not hide his eagerness, ". . . could we not try, start afresh, give ourselves another chance? I would dearly like to attempt it. One step at a time. The farm, the farms, for I'm sure you and I can come to some amicable agreement over Upfell." He grinned his weary grin. "They will need to be put in good hands . . . so many things . . . arrangements . . . but with care . . ."

"You mean me to live in some fine house you will build me, is that it?" Her voice was sad but resigned.

He looked astonished, then lifting his head he began to laugh, the sound again alarming the denizens of the undergrowth. He pulled her fiercely to him, tucking her head into his shoulder, his hand in her hair.

"Oh no, my darling, I am to do nothing of the sort. You are to come and live at Long Beck. You will be my wife, not legally at the moment but when Esmé, or her damned father agrees to it and I have my divorce, then we will be married. Browhead and Upfell will be yours to run as you like with no interference from me and if the folk of Bassenthwaite don't care for it, then they can go to the devil."

35

Day after day went by and still she had not told Charlie, nor Phoebe. Reed would be patient for a while, but not for ever, she was well aware of that, for no matter what he had said to her in the rapture of that afternoon by the pool, he was still Reed Macauley whose temper was short, whose forbearance was the same, whose patience was infinitesimal, whose need of her was enormous. He had told her 'at *your* pace' but she knew that meant at her pace as long as it went at a speed he thought suitable.

She had diverted him from his intention of calling on her at Browhead as he had wished to do, somewhat in the manner of a suitor paying court to his intended betrothed, for the result of that would not only have been disastrous but would have been a cruelty to Charlie she could not bear to make him suffer. Instead she saw him almost every day on the fell, slipping out of the farmhouse when Phoebe was in the dairy and Charlie up in the coppice wood, telling neither of them where she was going, or even that she was to go. The weather was warm and the days golden with sunshine and for an hour or two they would be together in the secluded gorge in which they had first made love, not speaking much, for as far as Reed was concerned everything was settled and needed no discussion. Their future together at Long Beck was a fact now, known only to themselves at the moment, and though he found it hard, he was doing his best to bend to her wishes, to let her settle her concerns and the question of how to run her two farms in her own time. Not with the best of humour since he wanted her in his bed and at his dining table this very night, he said, but allowing it just the same.

There was so much she wanted to do and one day, towards the end of July, when they had made love to Reed's exact requirements, which meant unhurriedly, imaginatively, erotically, until every one of his five senses was completely satisfied, and her own cries of joy had erupted from her again and again, as they drowsed in one another's arms in the aftermath of it, she began, hesitatingly, to tell him of it. She was uncertain of his reaction, knowing his need to dominate, to be the innovator, the giver, the protector, but this was a test, a gamble she must take for on this their whole life together, if they were to have one, might rely.

"Did you mean what you said about running my own farms . . . and business, Reed?"

"I did." He was satiated, replete, drained, empty and yet full of her and his voice was no more than a languorous murmur.

"No matter what I decide?"

"Mmmm."

"I will have complete control and the right to make any decision I care to, even if it does not agree with what you think it should?"

"What have you in mind?" and beneath her cheek which rested on his chest, she felt the faint tension in him. She sat up and her breasts fell forward, soft and heavy in his hand. He cupped them, smiling, his fingers smoothing her peaked nipples, his mind which had been about to become guarded, distracted from the matter of farms and 'business concerns', whatever they may be, as his male body prepared itself for another delightful onslaught on Annie's.

"You will not try to . . . take over?"

"My darling, even if I wanted to I couldn't 'take over' as you put it. Until you are my wife everything you own belongs to you. Even though we are to live at Long Beck as husband and wife . . . Dear God, Annie . . . when? . . . when? . . . it's four weeks since we decided and still you're under the same roof as . . . well, you know who I mean and I can't say I like it. Why don't you come over

to Long Beck and take a look round? Perhaps you would
like to . . . well, I don't know . . . move things around,
re-decorate the bedroom where . . . or even choose
another and make it as you want it? Anything you want to
do, I don't care my darling, just as long as you are there.
You must be introduced to the servants and they must
accept you as their mistress and if they don't then they
can find other employment. There is so much to be
arranged . . . your clothes and . . . listen, why don't you
and I take a trip up to Carlisle? There is a woman there,
a dress maker, who is a marvel, a skilled seamstress and
embroideress, a genius of design and if I pay her well she
could design and make you a complete wardrobe within
the week . . ."

"Reed . . ."

". . . her velvets and brocades are . . ."

Restraining her instant jealous need to know how Reed
Macauley was so well acquainted with velvets and
brocades and the marvellous dress maker in Carlisle, she
put an imperious hand across his mouth.

"Stop it, Reed. You are doing it already, arranging me
and what I should wear in the way you think I should
be . . ."

"Confound it! Annie, you don't mean to wear those
bloody trousers forever, do you?"

"No, but I mean to change them when Annie Abbott is
ready, not Reed Macauley. In the meanwhile I want to
. . . to talk to you, ask your advice . . ."

"Of course, my darling." He was at once gratified, she
could see, by her female, or so he thought, dependence
on him.

"I mean to . . . put in a man to run Upfell, under my
supervision, naturally. No one knows it's mine yet, and of
course it isn't until I have paid you what I owe. Two
hundred guineas will take a lot of finding . . ."

"Annie, I don't want it."

"Reed . . . !" Her voice was forbidding.

"I'm sorry, Annie."

". . . but I should make a fair profit out of the combined

flocks of Upfell and Browhead which brings me to the question of my swills . . ."

"Swills?" Sitting up, he pressed his lips to her shoulder, his hands still at her breasts, tweaking her nipples between his thumb and forefinger. He hitched himself behind her, his legs splayed one on either side of her body and she could feel the thrust of him between her buttocks. His hands ran down her belly as his mouth moved on her shoulders and at the nape of her neck. His fingers found the sweet, moist parting of her and involuntarily she opened herself wider to allow them to slip inside. The hot fire ran from them, down the inside of her thighs, up into her belly and thrusting breasts and she arched her back . . .

With a cry of rage she dragged herself away from him, turning on her haunches like a wild cat, her eyes flaring, her teeth bared, her nails ready to claw him and he fell back.

"Jesus Christ, what have I done now?" he gasped, his face still slack with his desire, his body at the full peak of his arousal.

"Nothing, except what all men do with women."

"And you did not *want* it?" His eyes had become dangerous. He did not like to have his love flung in his face, nor did he care for the crass foolishness of his own male rejected body, which *she* had caused.

"Of course I did, but would you deal with a man in the same contemptuous way as you have . . ."

"Don't be so bloody ridiculous! It is not the same at all." He began to laugh at the very idea, ready to take her in his arms, to smooth the outrage from her naked, female body, but she would not have it. Instead she reached for her clothes and with stiff and trembling fingers, fumbled her way into them.

"Annie . . ." He was still ready to be amused, to laugh, to forgive, to continue, but she turned on him again, her wild temper beautiful and unrestrained.

"Treat me seriously, Reed," she spat at him.

"I do! By God, I do. Am I not demonstrating it by begging you to come and live with me at . . ."

"Not that." Her voice was scornful "Not that, not *us*, but me, *me*, Annie Abbott. I am to be . . . in business as a man is in business and I want respect for it. A serious consideration of how I am to go about it and I am asking you to help me. As a man who has many business connections I wish you to advise another on how to go about . . . well, all the things that will need to be done . . ."

"Could we not wait until a more appropriate time . . ."

"You mean when I am sitting prettily in your drawing room, the certainty of my life with you firmly established and the chains you have put on me, locked and secured so that I may be more easily kept at your side with nothing of my own, no one but you, dependent on . . ."

"Chains, *chains*! Christ Almighty, would that I could. If you'd let me keep you, comfortably, of course, in a room where no one, no *man*, could lay eyes on you and where . . . Annie . . . don't do this . . . *don't* let me do this to you . . . I'm sorry . . . sorry . . ." He groaned, bending his head and she was made terribly aware of how much this strong man loved her.

"Christ . . . oh, sweet Jesus . . ." and she could hear plainly in his voice the cry that meant 'I can't bear it' and she winced, for despite his strength he was very frail, weakened by his love for her.

She knelt down and took him in her arms, rocking him as a mother would a hurting child.

"Tell me," he mumbled into her shoulder, "but first let me get dressed."

She meant to go into the business of producing swill baskets, she told him, when they were both calm. She leaned in the curve of his arm as they rested their backs against a rough grey stone which grew out of the grass.

"Not just a dozen swills at a time, but a hundred, a thousand even. I have the coppicing at Browhead and now at Upfell, and could purchase more. There is a coppice wood for sale by auction in November, at Wood Top near Stepthwaite. Mostly oak of fourteen years' growth so it is almost ready for harvesting, but of course . . . well, when I have the money, that is the kind of land I will be looking for. And I will need a . . . a . . . place to work. I have the building, the barn, which could be turned into a small workshop, but I will need more, and then there are the men to make them. They are used in so many industries, the need is enormous. Coal mines, the shipping lines, farming, they could even be sent abroad. I have served my apprenticeship, Reed, so I know what I'm talking about. I could train boys, men, to be swillers, or take on men who are fully trained themselves. All it needs is someone to find the market for the swills and supply it."

"And that would be?"

"Perhaps myself . . . or . . ."

"I thought so. You would tramp about the country treating with men of business?"

"I already have a contact in Whitehaven. A sea captain who said, for a small commission, of course, that he would take my swills to Liverpool and sell them for me."

"I see."

Dear God, it was hard and would get harder, she agonised, feeling the struggle of him as he did his best not to turn and shake her into obedience and submission. He didn't like it. He was doing his best to allow her to be the woman she wanted to be, to do what she longed to do, but it went against every instinct in his masculine world which told him that she should be in his life, in his home, in his bed, safe and loved, at least by him; an instinct that detested the very idea of her being independent, free and at liberty to do as she pleased.

"Will you help me, Reed? Tell me where to start? Where you would start?"

He was silent for so long she sat up, turning to gaze anxiously into his face. He was looking out over the pool, his attention centred on the still depths of it, his face set, his eyes flat and expressionless.

"Reed?"

"I shall lose you if I don't, won't I?"

"Oh no, my darling, I love you . . ."

"I know you do, and I also know that if I let you struggle

on, unaided, you will do your damnedest to succeed, but you will resent me. Resent my unconcern, though of course, I *shall* be concerned. I have no choice, have I?"

"Of course you have."

"No, I knew it long ago. To keep you I must set you free so . . ." turning to smile sadly into her eager face, ". . . let us begin. Your first lesson in sharp business dealings . . ."

"*Honest* business dealings, Reed."

"Indeed, but you must learn that the two can run together."

She was vaulting the wall at the back of Browhead when Charlie rose up at her feet. Her heart was light, her face vibrant with it, her eyes dreaming, her senses enthralled with the marvel that was to be her future. With Reed, with her love, with her satisfying attack on the world of business where only men went. For that moment her farm, her sheep, her expansion into Upfell, the life she had lived with Charlie and Phoebe, and before that with Cat and Natty, had evaporated as easily as the mist at the top of Skiddaw when the sun touched it.

"Where in hell have you been?" he snarled, catching her wrist with a cruel, savage hand, one which meant to hurt.

"Charlie, you scared me, jumping up out of nowhere like that. What were you doing behind the wall . . . ?"

"Never mind what I was doing, tell me what *you* were doing, and who with, and not just today but every day for the past few weeks? I've seen you go up there to the peat moss and come back with an empty sledge. You thought I was in the coppice working, as I am supposed to, as I have been doing for the past four years, without wages mind, whilst you crept up there on the fell, and by God, the temptation to see for myself what you were up to has been almost too much to bear, and only the . . . the horror of knowing, of actually *knowing*, what I only suspect, has kept me from it. I could not stand it you see, having the images which torment my over active imagination, actually

come to life so I stayed away, but I knew, of course I did
. . . oh God, Annie . . . tell me I am imagining it, that you
have . . . have been . . . elsewhere . . . *anywhere* .. but
not with him . . ."

"Charlie . . ."

"Don't . . . don't try to . . . to comfort me, Annie. Don't
lie." His face was haunted. "I have never known anyone
as honest and brave and beautiful as you, my dearest love,
and I couldn't bear it if you lied to me now. I've watched
you taking on the whole of Bassenthwaite parish, all by
yourself, fighting them and their prejudices, hurting I
know, but always getting up again when they knocked you
down. You have been my pride and delight and glory and
. . . even now . . . I cannot help but love you. I have
not been celibate, Annie. It is possible to enjoy a sexual
relationship without love in it you know, but nothing, none
of them, drove you from my heart."

They stood on the high ground at the back of Browhead,
the land sloping away to the farmhouse and the patchwork
of fields beyond it, each one divided from its neighbour by
a grey ribbon of drystone wall. There was a sudden flicker
of wind straight from the fell, bringing the summer
fragrance of heather and bracken. Nothing moved, only
her painful heart as it beat for Charlie's anguish.

"Charlie, please listen." She put a warm, steadying hand
on his arm, affectionate, reassuring, but he threw it off
with a violence she had not known was in him.

"Listen to what?"

She shook her head for really all she had to tell him,
everything she had to tell him would hurt him beyond
endurance, so what was she to say? Only the truth, surely.

"Charlie . . ."

"Annie, I don't think I can bear to hear this, really I
can't."

"Charlie, you must know . . ."

"Must I? must I?"

"Yes," and she could see him freeze, become suspended
in the ice of his pain, his vitality an inanimate thing as he
did his best to find mercy. He was fighting to remain calm,

to keep a hold on hope, but his eyes told her he knew she
was going to leave him. The raw pain in them burned her
but she could not look away. She had kept this man here,
perhaps against his will, giving him reason to believe that
one day, when she was mended from all the many hurts
she had sustained in her passage through life, she would
turn to him in love. She had smiled on him, leaned on him,
laughed and cried with him, relied on his strength, taken
his strength, all the while hiding from him the honest truth
which was that she could never love, or give herself to
any man but Reed Macauley. He had believed the promise
she had, perhaps unintentionally, held out to him, and had
remained. He had tried to go away once, but *her* need had
brought him back and she had used him as a crutch to get
her through. Would he ever forgive her? Could she ever
forgive herself?

"Charlie . . . I am so sorry. This is my fault. You made
no secret of how you felt about me and I have not been
honest . . ."

"Christ . . . don't . . . don't tell me . . ."

"I must . . ."

"No . . ."

"I'm not . . ."

"Don't say it, please, my darling. Don't say you're not
the right woman for me, when what you mean is that I
am not the right man for you. I have been mistaken in
believing that you . . . that one day you would . . . forget
him, but it seems . . . well, I had best pack my . . ." His
voice petered away and he turned from her, stumbling on
awkward legs towards the farmhouse, blinded it seemed,
and her heart broke for him but she knew she must not
go after him. Not now. Not this time. He must be allowed
to make his own decision without the truth of her need of
him to cloud his brain. She did need him. She could not
imagine life without Charlie in it, as she could not imagine
her life without Phoebe in it. They were her two true
friends, both of whom she loved and for whom she would
give her life. She wanted him to stay but she also wanted
him to be happy and he could not do both. He was a decent

man who deserved a decent life. A wife, children, a home, the satisfaction of a day's work well done and perhaps she could give him the latter if he would accept it.

But not now. Not at this moment when there was nothing but hatred and despair in his heart. He might, as she stood here, held fast by her sorrow for him, be stuffing his few possessions into his bag, taking his leave of a bewildered Phoebe, striding off down the track to Keswick. She might lose him for ever if he went, but she must leave him alone, for now.

He was not in the farmhouse, nor anywhere in the vicinity of it when she finally went down there. His things were still in his room. The books he had read to them years ago, those which Cat had loved so much, his woollen jerkin, his scarf and worn overcoat were all where he had left them.

"Tha'd best give Mr Lucas a shout, Annie," Phoebe advised. "His supper's on t' table, tell him, an' I've baked 'im an apple pie. I've saved 'im a drop of cream an' all. Got over two gallons of milk today from Clover, I did, which is right good, or so Maggie told me when she came by with young Jonty. He's a fine lad, that un. Six months old he be an' already tryin' to pull 'isself up. Crawl, he's like a little monkey an' into everything. I 'ad to put all me things away . . ."

"I am to buy Upfell, Phoebe."

The words cut off Phoebe's pleasant ramblings on the happenings of her contented day just as though someone had clamped a gag in her mouth. Her hands which had been busy with pans and ladling spoons, with the proper arrangement of knife and fork and plate, became still. She turned slowly her plain country face, rosy now with good health, as astonished as if Annie had said she had purchased a tiara of diamonds.

"What?"

"I am to buy Upfell Farm and almost everything in it, and on it. The farmhouse and what furniture Sally didn't want. The gimmers, wethers, ewes, the cows and a couple of pigs Sally couldn't take with her to Binsey. All the dairy utensils. What was stored in the cow barn. Wood and hay coops, the cart, horse, coppice land . . . everything. It will cost me two hundred guineas . . ."

"Two hundred . . . !" Phoebe's mouth fell open and the spoon she held dropped from her hand to the floor. Dandy drifted over to it, her sinuous body gracefully twining about Phoebe's skirts before she began to lap delicately at the cream which had splashed on to Phoebe's immaculate flagstones.

"Wheer d'yer get the money? Not the bank, nor that lawyer from Lancaster. Tha' told me that." Phoebe's words were flat and suspicious, disapproving, for hadn't she known for weeks now what Annie Abbott got up to almost every day on the fell and where else would she get the money but from the man whom she met up there?

"I haven't got it from anywhere yet. I have some put by and I shall use that as a down payment and pay the rest whenever I can. With interest, of course," she added hastily as though she knew full well what Phoebe was thinking and was determined to let her know this was a bona fide business transaction.

"I see, an' would I be wrong in thinkin' tha' intends borrowin' from him up at Long Beck?"

"No, you wouldn't be wrong, Phoebe. In fact I am to buy the farm from him up at Long Beck. It was Reed who got it from the . . ."

"Tha' knows tha'll be in his debt don't tha'? An' that he's not a man who'll be shy of collectin' it."

"What is that supposed to mean?"

"If tha' falls behind he'll mek tha' pay in other ways, lass."

At once Annie's face became brightly flushed and she felt a great need to avoid Phoebe's steady, penetrating eyes as the images of herself and Reed as they had been this very afternoon and on the many afternoons of the past four weeks, flooded her mind.

"An' what about Mr Lucas?" Phoebe went on, knowing exactly why Annie's face had flooded with colour. "He's not goin' to like it, you borrowin' money from Mr Macauley. It wouldn't surprise me if he refused ter work for thi'. It'd be like workin' for *him*, that's 'ow Mr Lucas'd see it."

"Nonsense!" Annie tossed her head in an effort to appear offended, and then suddenly letting out her breath in a resigned sigh, she moved away to gaze out of the window and down the slope to the lake below.

"What's the use, Phoebe? I cannot hide the truth from you. I have just . . . spoken to Charlie. Not about Upfell but about me . . . and Reed Macauley."

"Oh, aye, an' what's there to tell?"

"Well . . ." Somehow it was very difficult to say the words. To say to Phoebe, "I'm taking up residence at Long Beck and I shall be running both farms from there. I shall be putting in men, here and at Upfell to farm, and herd my sheep. You, of course, will come with me to Long Beck since you are my friend. You will have a comfortable life as my companion. A decent wage, pretty clothes and . . . and . . ."

Her mind tried to form a picture of Phoebe at Long Beck, sitting perhaps in a cosy chair in a cosy room, sewing, reading, or in the garden which she herself knew as a child as being extremely grand. She would ride in a carriage beside herself when they went to Keswick on business, naturally, and then . . . ?

She just could not imagine it. It just would not happen in her mind's eye and she sighed deeply for she knew it would not happen at all. Phoebe could not be made to fit into that pretty picture Annie tried to imagine her in. *This* was Phoebe, hardworking, cheerful, content to bake and darn, to scrub and scour and polish, to milk her cow and churn her butter and do all the practical, everyday jobs she had performed all her life. She would be uncomfortable in silk, in a carriage, in a formal garden, and the idea of Phoebe sitting down to read a book when there were so many more interesting things to do in the kitchen, was ludicrous.

Phoebe, if she agreed to come, and there was no guarantee that she would, could only be miserable in such a setting. But how could she leave her? her anguished mind begged to know. She had lost Cat, she had lost Natty, and there was every probability she would lose Charlie . . . if what she hoped for came to nothing. So could she bear to lose Phoebe as well? And if Phoebe stayed here, how was she to fit in with the man – who would probably have a wife – who would come to run Browhead?

"What is it Annie?"

"Charlie . . ."

"Aye, what about him?"

"Reed Macauley and I are . . ."

Phoebe shook her head testily, her patience with the vague ramblings of the woman who was usually sharp and decisive, coming to an end. Something was up, something pretty drastic if Annie's behaviour was anything to go by and the sooner it was said and done with, the better. It involved him up at Long Beck, that was very evident, for when had he not been involved with every drama which had been played out at Browhead ever since Phoebe had come to live here?

"Ah know tha's bin seein' him, Annie, so that's no surprise. Nay, lass, tha' face gives thi' away, an' if I knew, so did Mr Lucas . . ."

"Yes . . ."

"Yes, what does that mean?"

"He knew. He saw me coming down . . . just now and . . . I had to admit it . . ."

"Wheer is he?" Phoebe pushed Annie aside brusquely, peering down the field for a sight of Charlie. Royal cropped the grass contentedly on its far side, deep in the shadows cast by the tree and at the gate which led into the field, the three dogs, eyes glistening, tongues quivering, sprawled panting in the shade of the wall. It was all so normal, so as it should be, as it HAD been for the past weeks of the heatwave. Phoebe felt her heart quieten for a moment, but as though her instinct, that sixth sense which recognises danger when there is none to be seen, could sense it, little ripples of fear ran through her body.

"Wheer is he, Annie?"

"I don't know, Phoebe. He ran off down the track towards . . ."

"Wheer, for God's sake?"

"I don't know . . ."

"Tha' don't know after all that man's done for thi' . . ."

"Do you think I don't know that, but I couldn't lie to him, Phoebe. I love Reed Macauley. I had to tell him the truth . . ."

"And what else?"

"What d'you mean?"

"There's summat in tha' face that ses there's more. That tha's plannin' summat an' if I can see it, so would Mr Lucas. What is it, Annie, tell me?"

She couldn't. She couldn't tell Phoebe and she couldn't *do it*. She wanted Reed but she was afraid of him. Afraid of what a life with him at Long Beck would do to her. Was she capable of being the woman he wanted her to be? Did she *want* to be the woman he wanted her to be? If she sacrificed her independence would she, little by little, be completely possessed by Reed for he believed, quite sincerely, that the only right way was Reed Macauley's way. He would own her. She would be his completely and, though she longed for it joyfully, longed to spend each night moaning and sighing in his bed, was she able to submerge herself totally to HIS will, or was it all a dream? Had she been dreaming, living in a dream world where she and Reed would be together, sharing their lives, existing side by side in a house where his wife should be? Probably sleeping in a bed he had shared with her, giving orders to his wife's servants, taking his wife's life, the one Reed had promised to give her when he married her, and was it in Annie's power to do it? She loved him and she would always continue to give everything of herself she could offer. Gladly, rapturously, but NOT THERE, not at Long Beck, not in another woman's place. Not in his wife's place. She did not know how he would take it. Perhaps her dream would be stamped on and destroyed, for they were all in his hands. The farm at Upfell, not yet legally hers. Her plans for her basket industry which included

Charlie, if he would let her . . . Dear God in Heaven . . . so much . . . and all depending on Reed Macauley . . .

Suddenly her mind cleared and her heart became steadied. No, it didn't all depend on Reed Macauley. Upfell farm did and her intention to form a business, a swill basket industry on a scale not known before in the district, but not everything. Not everything. She still had Browhead.

Phoebe's light touch on her arm startled her and she turned abruptly.

"Annie . . ." There was a quiver of fear in Phoebe's voice but Annie smiled reassuringly.

"It's all right, Phoebe. There is nothing else. And we can do nothing about Charlie. He had to know. You told me that long ago. He had to know I could give him nothing more than my loving friendship. We cannot force him back, dearest Phoebe. He will come if he needs us and in the meanwhile everything will go on just as it always has. Nothing has changed."

"There is summat, lass." Phoebe's face was troubled.

"What is it?"

"I was keepin' it fer . . . well, when it was needed the most."

"What?"

"I know it were none of my business but I thought . . ."

"What Phoebe?"

"Tha'd best come wi' me, 'tis in the . . . well, come wi me an' I'll show thi'."

36

She was convinced for several minutes that he was going
to kill her, or beat her senseless, or both. She was afraid,
but she had been expecting it, and, knowing his strength,
his ruthless determination to have what he wanted, and
her own frailty against it, she did her best to let his bitter
fury blow over her, bending to it, swaying with it so that
it should not break her. He had been so certain of her. So
convinced that finally she was to be his, not just up on the
wild fell where no one could see, but here in his home,
his life, where no one could fail to miss it. He wanted it
acknowledged that Annie Abbott, who would one day be
Annie Macauley, was Reed Macauley's woman, his wife
in fact, if not in name.

"You bitch," he said, his face quite blank and holding
her with one hand so that she could not escape him, he
hit her twice across the face, his aim so hard and so true
she felt the muscles in her neck pull in agony. When he
let her go she reeled backwards, striking the wall behind
her and out in the kitchen where the servants gathered in
avid, breathless anticipation, the blows were clearly heard.

"Dear Mother of God . . ." Mrs Lewis, who was a
staunch Catholic, sketched a hasty cross on the bib of her
starched white apron. "What's he doing to her?"

"No more than she deserves," Mrs Stone said tartly.
Mrs Stone had answered the door when Annie Abbott
knocked on it, the elegant butler employed by Mrs
Macauley long gone, and she had been so thunder-struck
she had allowed the hussy, trousers an' all, over the
threshwood and into the hallway before she could collect
her senses and shut the door in her face.

Annie straightened up slowly, deliberately not putting

her hands to her face though she could feel the swelling coming up about her eye and taste the blood in her mouth.

"It's him, isn't it?" he said, just as Charlie had done and for a despairing moment she wished the pair of them to the devil, for how much easier her life would have been without men in it.

"No, he's gone."

"Gone? Gone where?" Still there was that terrible blankness in his eyes and she was appalled by it but she had come here for a reason and she must keep true to it.

"I don't know. I told him about you and me, and he . . ."

"You and me! You have just informed me there is to be no 'you and me', that you have changed your mind again and can no longer face the prospect of living here as my wife . . ."

"Not your wife, Reed."

"Please! For the love of God don't let's have that again. It becomes tedious after a while and I find it no longer interests me. If you will ring the bell, my housekeeper will show you out."

His manner was insulting. She was no more than an unwelcome caller, it said, not only one who was unwelcome but who had already stayed too long. He could scarcely contain his black, menacing anger and she was terribly aware for her own female frailty. He wanted to hurt her badly and was afraid himself that he might do it, so to prevent it he must get rid of her quickly, his taut, perilous expression told her.

He brought the flat of his hand down hard on the desk, setting everything on it to jumping, warning her of her danger.

"Go, Annie, get out. I don't want to see you again, and no, I don't want the money you are offering me for Upfell. It's no longer for sale . . ."

"Reed . . ."

"Don't, Annie, I'm warning you . . ."

"Reed . . . despite this . . . I love you. Can you not find it in you to understand? I don't give a damn about anybody but you. I don't care what *they* say . . ." indicating with a toss of her head those in the kitchen and even beyond to encompass the whole of the parish of Bassenthwaite. "It's me, me, don't you see? I can't live *her* life . . ."

He pushed back his chair and strode to the window then back to the fireplace where he took a cigar from a box on the mantelpiece. He lit it with a taper from the fire, then moved again to the window presenting his back to her, keeping his distance, holding in his lethal temper, barely in control of himself.

"So you have said before."

"Then may I not . . . will you not come to Browhead . . . ?"

"Now that *he* has gone I'm welcome, is that it?"

"No . . . yes . . . Reed . . . please . . ."

"Don't beg, Annie, it doesn't suit you, nor me."

"Listen to me, Reed."

"I've done nothing but listen to you for five years and I've had enough. Either you come here and live with me as my wife, *be* my wife to all intents and purposes, make a commitment, as I am willing to do, or . . ."

"Yes?" Her voice was a whisper.

"Don't expect to see me again, Annie."

She bowed her head, then lifted it, the savage marks of his hand clearly visible on her white skin. She looked at his back, his stiff lethal jealous back, then turning on her heel, left the room and the house. When she had gone he sat down heavily and stared with empty eyes into the space in front of him where she had stood.

Phoebe had found the box at the back of a loose stone in the dairy, a box so heavy she could barely lift it. She had been whitewashing the wall, 'going at it' with her usual intransigence, her unyielding determination to stand for no muck or muddle and when her brush would keep spattering her and her floor as it met a resistance of some kind in the smooth pattern of the stones, she put it in the pail and leaned forward to investigate more fully.

It had taken her no more than a second or two to discover the stone was loose, sticking out a half inch beyond

its neighbours, but when she set about it, as she was wont
to do with anything which was perverse enough to defy
her, it would not be 'set about' but continued to shift whenever she touched it. In fact it was so loose she could pull
it out and when she did she found the box.

Annie looked at it, standing away somewhat as though
it contained a deadly snake which might strike her with its
venom when she opened it.

"'Tis full o'money, Annie." Phoebe's voice was filled
with awe. "Ah've never seen such a lot o'money."

"Did you . . . count it?"

Phoebe reared back. "Nay, tis not mine ter count, lass.
Wheer d'yer think it come from?"

"I can't imagine."

"Are tha' goin' to open it?"

"I suppose I better had."

It was filled to its very brim with coins. Pennies and
halfpennies and farthings, no higher value than that, but
hundreds and hundreds, thousands of them which when
laboriously counted out into neat piles, came to not quite
three hundred pounds. There were coins with the head of
their own Queen Victoria on them, coins depicting George
III, George II and George I, the dates on these last, 1725.
At the top of the box was a note. It was written by Lizzie
Abbott and dated 1843, two weeks after Annie had fled
to Keswick and the arms of Anthony Graham.

'To my daughter Annie,' it said. 'I found this when I
came to Browhead. For all these generations, a hundred
years and more, it seems Abbott women have saved their
few pence. It weren't mine, but I added a bit when I could,
as they did. It's yours now, God bless you, Annie.'

"Dear God . . . oh, dear Lord . . . Sally said my mother
was trying to tell them something just before she died . . .
Dear God in Heaven . . ."

She could imagine them, probably five or six generations
of them, a chain, each link a thrifty woman putting by for
a rainy day which, when it came was got through somehow
without touching that precious hoard. A trust, a continu-
ation, carrying on from mother to mother, to the wives of

their sons, to the daughters of their sons, year in and year out, each one with a man to take care of them, to work for them, to work *for*. A picture of her mother on her knees at Sarah Macauley's scrub bucket struck her a blow which left her gasping and she began to weep, to weep for her mother and all those faithful women who had 'put by', who had been comforted by the knowledge that in the tin box at the back of the stone in the dairy was a 'bit put by' just in case. If things got too bad, each one had thought, then it was there so that her family would not starve or go clogless. 'Just in case' and not one of them had used it, nor counted it, nor even realised its value. Pennies, farthings, but which, when added up would begin a new life for Annie Abbott.

"Oh, Phoebe, women are such brave creatures. Strong and brave, faithful and yet foolish. They stay true to what they have been put to. A man, a child, a life, an idea, never wavering and yet man is supposed to be superior. The women who saved this have gone to bed hungry but not their men, not their children and they were content for they knew it was here in case of desperate need. Dear God, how desperate did my mother have to be before she dipped into this . . . Christ, she worked like a slave and yet this was here to . . ."

And what would have happened had Joshua Abbott got his hands on it, her mind, her practical woman's mind asked, as the practical minds of all the women who had gone before her, must have asked, eyeing their husbands who, perhaps, would have purchased what *they* thought was needed without a by-your-leave to the women who had saved it.

Aah . . . and now it had fallen into the hands of the only one who could, and would, if allowed, act as a man, but with a woman's careful, watchful, brave heart. It was here, in her hand, the means to do all the things she had wanted to do ever since she had come back to Browhead and the irony of it was, though she had the means now, the black, intransigent savagery of Reed Macauley's jealous will would not allow her to achieve her goal. Upfell Farm and

all its livestock, to run beside her own was what she
wanted but it was going to waste, its animals carelessly
attended to, since they knew of his lack of interest in it,
by Reed Macauley's men. The cows milked and the hens
fed, the pigs seen to. The ewes were grazing with Reed
Macauley's flock and had been serviced last backend by
his tup, the lambs born, the clipping done, the flock
expanding, but there was profit there going to waste for
want of a man, or woman, to market it, for want of a
man or woman who CARED about it. The land was lying
untended, going to seed with no crops planted. A whole
year since Bert Garnett had lost his wits in the beating he
received at Reed Macauley's hands and now, in the twisted
way life had of laughing behind its hand at human endeavour, it was all to be squandered to a man's pride. There
were other farms for sale, she was sure of it, but not in
such good heart as Upfell and certainly not as easily and
conveniently run.

"What are thi' ter do, Annie?" Phoebe asked hesitantly,
recovering somewhat from the shock of realising that – in
her eyes at least – Annie Abbott was rich beyond their
wildest dreams. She was not at all sure she liked the idea
of having all that money lying about the place but as it had
been behind the loose stone in the dairy for 125 years, or
so Annie reckoned, and nobody had disturbed it, nor even
discovered the hiding place, Phoebe supposed it was safe
enough if they put it back there and she said so to Annie.

But Annie had different ideas for it.

"No, I'm taking it into Keswick."

"Keswick? what on earth for?" Phoebe was flabbergasted.

"Do you know how much this might have earned if it
had been properly invested, Phoebe?"

Phoebe didn't, nor even what Annie meant.

"You can't just leave money lying about, Phoebe, it
should be made to earn."

Earn! What next? Really, Phoebe didn't know where
Annie got her knowledge from, nor her ideas, though she
supposed Mr Lucas, who had been an educated man and

who had talked to Annie by the hour, might have given some of it to her.

"No, this is going to the bank, Phoebe, and if that bank manager there can't suggest something, then I'll find someone who can and then, when the time is right, at least I will have a decent capital to start off my Swills Industry."

The farming year was almost at its end. The hay was in, the reaping and binding done, her stock sold and new ewes bought, the salving and marking of the sheep over with, and Clover and her growing calf housed in the byre for the winter to be fed on hay and straw. The tup was up on the fells with Annie's flock doing his joyful duty by them and the casual Irish labourers she had hired to settle her in for the winter, paid off and gone on their way. Without Charlie, she and Phoebe had managed but it had been a cheerless time of hard work, stoically borne. Her money, which Royal had dragged to Keswick in its tin box, hedged about on the sledge with trussed chickens and eggs, swills and besom brushes had been deposited with the speechless bank manager in Keswick. Yes, he could invest it safely for her, he had managed to stammer, his eyes unable to look away from the mountain of coins on his desk, astounded by her casual reference to her 'savings', and when she and Phoebe had purchased the provisions they needed for the winter, amongst which were several dress lengths of soft woollen fabric, cambric and lace, they had settled in at Browhead at the end of November to wait for spring and lambing time and what she intended would be the start of her new business. There were enough quartered logs in the barn, ready to be rived into strips to keep her and Phoebe busy making swill baskets during the winter months.

She had grieved badly for Reed during the two months since she had last seen him. He was still at Long Beck, or so Maggie Singleton innocently told them when she came down to visit Phoebe and proudly display her sturdy son and, equally innocently, to share the hope that she and Jake might be allowed to take over the farm at Upfell.

It was going to waste since the Garnetts left, she said, and Jake, who had never actually run a farm, was nevertheless a good all-round man outside and could turn his hand to anything, sheep, cattle or crops, and as for herself, she couldn't wait to get her hands on some real dairy work again. Jonty was thriving and she and Jake were no strangers to hard work. Nobody could have been more surprised than them, she confided over a cup of tea, to Phoebe, when it was discovered that it was Mr Macauley who had bought it and not some farmer from Lancashire as had, at first, been believed. Why he had kept it to himself for so long, no one could imagine, but then she supposed they should have guessed when he left instructions for Dobby Hawkins to go down to milk the cows and feed the pigs and hens, but then they had thought at the time he had been doing it as a favour to the farmer from Lancashire who must be an acquaintance of his. But no, Upfell was his, though why he had bought it and then done nothing with it was still a mystery. Anyway, somebody had to run it and why not her and Jake? She herself had a fair head for business and with her and Jake's farming knowledge she reckoned they'd do right well.

Annie had listened when Phoebe told her, saying nothing, for what was there to say? Although she went about her days with the same thoroughness and diligence to her farm's welfare that she had always applied, she felt as though there was no heart in her. As though she was a machine which functioned with the precision and power for which it has been fashioned, but a machine, though it works faultlessly, has no life of its own, no vital spark, no joy nor hope for the future. Her life had reduced itself to the level of what must be done each day to keep her farm and her animals alive, each one to be endured and got through until the time came, which she hoped to God would be soon, when she would know, if not rapture, then peace, if not love, then friendship. She had drawn away from Phoebe and Maggie with their simple and contented capacity to enjoy life, glad of the tasks which must be attended to before the long winter set in. Her eyes burned with unshed tears, her bones ached and her body felt hollow, her female body which had, for a few short weeks, been so rapturously filled with Reed Macauley's. She was haunted by the hatred she had seen in his eyes, dreaming of them, dreaming of him, existing from one dragging day which did not have him in it, to the next. She lay on her bed at night, sleepless, longing to fall into an oblivion which did not have Reed's deep blue eyes smiling in it, the reluctant but humorous quirk of his mouth, the steady strength of his arms about her for when she woke and they were gone, her heart broke again and again as it had done on the day they had last confronted one another. Was this all there was to be for her, her wounded heart pleaded? Am I to be no more than a woman who has loved and become lost because of it? Sad-eyed, sad-faced, empty-hearted, with no meaning in my days but that which can be achieved through hard work to be followed by empty nights without love.

It was Jake Singleton who brought Charlie back to them. December the first it was and her twenty-fourth birthday although no one knew of it. She and Phoebe were in the barn sorting the coppice timber into suitable lengths for splitting when they heard the dogs barking.

"Now what?" Phoebe said, clicking her tongue with every sign of the utmost annoyance, though with things the way they were at the moment any visitor was welcome if perhaps it would cheer Annie up. God knows she'd suffered these last eighteen months but without Charlie's cheerful humour to support them, Phoebe was having a hard time of it trying to keep Annie from plunging deeper into the melancholy that devil up at Long Beck had flung her in. Nearly two months now and Phoebe was worried out of her mind, really she was, watching Annie get thinner and more grim-faced with every passing day.

"Who is it, Phoebe?" Annie asked without much interest, carefully stacking the quartered logs into piles of the same size.

"Tis Jake Singleton. He's comin' up track on't cart. Now

what's he want d'you think, an' why's he fetched cart?"

"I really couldn't say, Phoebe. Perhaps you'd best go and find out," for does it really matter, her attitude asked. She continued to sort and stack the wood, her mind working methodically, despite her total lack of concern with what it was doing.

Phoebe's voice dragged her from the grey gloom, the world of shadows which still allowed her to do what was necessary but at the same time, mercifully dulled the pain her grieving brought.

"Annie, come quick . . ." Phoebe's shriek exhorted her and she turned, the shriek slicing through her apathy and quickening her step as she moved to the door of the barn.

"What is it?"

"For God's sake, Annie . . . come quick . . ."

The man was lying in the bottom of the cart, some rough sacking tucked about him, his head supported on several others folded beneath it. He was asleep, or so it seemed, for his eyes were closed in the sunken greyness of his face and his mouth was partly open as he snored, if that was what he was doing. His breath whistled in his throat and rasped hoarsely in his chest and across his unshaven face, a slick of sweat was filmed. His hair was dusty and uncombed, snarled about his head, long and uncut, and from him came the unsavoury smell of unwashed flesh.

Charlie? It *was* Charlie, wasn't it? . . . no, it couldn't be Charlie, not this crumple of old bones and foetid clothing, this stinking, gin-raddled heap of rotting human skin and sinew. Not *their* Charlie, whom they had loved and laughed with, shared their lives with, who had brought them through storm and trouble and sorrow, who . . .

"Ah' found 'im in Penrith, Miss Abbott. Ah'd tekken some stuff for Mr Macauley an' ah' were just ready ter set off 'ome when he fell down right in front o't cart. Good job I were only goin' slow on account o' t' traffic. Ah don't know why Jed didn't step on him but he's a good sensible animal an' . . ."

"Yes, yes Jake, but how . . ?" Annie was eager to get Jake off his rambling description of how the horse had avoided trampling on Charlie.

". . . well, ah' climbed down, thinking Jed 'd stamped on 'im, but he seemed all right, though ah' can't say ah' fancied touchin' 'im, ter tell truth, not the state 'e's in. Course, I didn't know it were Charlie Lucas, not then. Well, you wouldn't, would you?" eyeing the appalling condition of the man in the bottom of his clean cart. "Drunk as a bloody lord an' swearin' like a trooper 'e was. Ah don't know 'ow I recognised him really."

No, and neither did Annie and Phoebe who stared at Charlie in appalled, frozen silence.

"Well," Jake said, fidgeting about at the cart tail, "wheer d'yer want 'im put?" for the two women seemed incapable of thought and he had to get back to Long Beck before dark. He'd come out of his way to bring Charlie Lucas back to Browhead since, being a decent sort of a chap himself, he couldn't just leave a man he knew lying in the gutter could he?

It was Phoebe who took charge.

"In t' kitchen Jake, lay 'im on t' floor," which Jake did, and really, Charlie Lucas being no heavier than a half-grown lad, he could have been managed by the women themselves. Not that he minded helping, of course, for it was fair flummoxing to see what had become of the fine fellow who had once been Annie Abbott's . . . well, no one quite knew *what* his role was in her life but you couldn't deny he'd been anything else but well set up and likeable.

They stripped him down to the filth-ingrained, hollow-textured, bony, six-foot skeleton that was beneath his stinking clothing, which they tossed outside the door ready for burning. He muttered feverishly, fretfully, shrugging their hands away, his breath appalling as he wheezed into their faces. The smell of cheap gin clung to his skin as though it oozed from his pores and when, struggling with him, since it seemed he did not care to be heaved into the tub of hot water Phoebe had placed before the fire, he fell into a state of insensibility which frightened them, at least it meant he was easier to handle.

They emptied and re-filled the tub several times before he was clean. There were many things skulking in his hair and hiding on his body which, when disturbed, jumped and scurried and floated in the thick scum of the first dousings, and both women began to scratch vigorously at themselves before they finally hauled him naked up the stairs and tumbled him into the warmed bed which had been his since Cat died. They wrapped him about in half a dozen blankets for he had begun to sweat again, shivering and mumbling about being cold, his limbs trembling, his teeth chattering, the sweat turning icy on his body, a ferocious shaking which moved the bed beneath him. They could get him to take neither a sip of the broth Phoebe had simmering on the fire, nor of the milk which had come only that morning from the placid Clover.

"Oh, God, what are we to do, Phoebe? I don't like the sound of his chest. I wish Mrs Mounsey was still at Upfell for she'd know what to give him for a fever. He's not just drunk, you know."

"Ah can see that, lass, but don't thee fret, us'll get 'im right. He needs to sleep now and then when he wakes an' he's sober, a good feed."

"What's he been doin', d'you think, since he left here?" Annie agonised.

"Drownin' in gin by t'smell of 'im, an' starvin' whilst he's bin at it. Nowt but skin an' bone an' all I can say is thank God it weren't winter for he'd not 'ave survived."

Annie knelt beside the bed, smoothing back Charlie's long wet hair from his forehead. His face was bony, the flesh sunk into the skull, his eyes set in deep black circles of bruised skin, the dark straggle of his beard hiding his chin. His eyelashes, long and fine, were like those of a child and his eyebrows still quirked, one slightly higher than the other as though in humour. His mouth in the depth of his beard was vulnerable in his insensibility and on an impulse she bent down and laid her own gently against it.

"Oh, Charlie, dear Charlie, what have I done to you,"

she whispered, kneeling at his side, her arm cradling his head to her breast.

"Don't, Annie . . ." Phoebe's voice was sharp, "unless tha' means it. Unless tha' really means to give 'im what he's always wanted from thi', don't do this to 'im."

"But he's asleep, Phoebe, or dead drunk, he doesn't know . . ."

"It mekks no difference. Don't let 'im think there's 'ope, if there isn't. Even the state he's in he might know what tha's . . ."

"I'm only comforting a friend . . ."

"No, tha's not. Tha's comfortin' thissen because tha' feels guilty. Nurse 'im by all means, mek him better, or do thi' best, as I will, but don't go . . . puttin' tha' arms about 'im. Treat 'im as I do, fer if tha' break his heart all over again, ah'll not forgive thi'."

"Phoebe!"

"Tha's jittered about for the past four years between this lad an 'im up at Long Beck, leadin' them both on a bit o'string, not able to mek tha' mind up which one tha' wants, hurtin' them both an' thissen. Ah don't know what 'appened between you an' Reed Macauley at backend, and ah don't want ter know. Tha' let 'im go, so let this one go an all, or tek him for thy . . . well . . . but leave 'im alone ter . . . ter recover as best he can."

Annie stood up slowly, looking down into the thin face on the pillow, the thin face of the frail and defenceless man who was in this state because of her. What Phoebe said was true. Her own guilt at what she had done to him, her own compassion which wanted to do anything, *anything* to heal him, to make up to him for all that he had suffered at her hands, must not influence her, nor encourage Charlie, when he was himself again, to think that there could ever be a relationship between them that was anything other than that of friends. She had almost destroyed him in her weakness. Now she must do her best to rebuild his fragile strength, his endearing humour, his engaging, warm-hearted understanding, his clever, nimble mind, his peace, his life.

"You're right, Phoebe. But . . . I love him you see and I only want to give him . . . a reason to . . . go on . . ."

"Tha' can do that wi'out . . ."

"Building up his hope that one day I might . . . ?"

"Aye, love, unless tha' mean ter . . . settle wi' 'im . . ." Phoebe let the sentence delicately trail away.

"No . . . there will never be anyone but . . ."

"Right, then." Phoebe was all bustle and briskness. "I'll stay wi' 'im for a couple of hours whilst tha' sleep an' then tha' can tek tha turn. He'll need some lookin' after, will Mr Lucas. So go thi' an' tidy up downstairs first an' if ah give thi' a shout, come runnin' cos when 'e comes to himself he'll be a bit of a 'andful."

37

It was a week before Charlie 'came to himself' and in that time Annie and Phoebe took it in turns to nurse him, one of them constantly at his bedside. For six days he tossed and muttered and sweated in fever, knowing neither of them in his delirium, hallucinating about his childhood, calling Phoebe 'Mama' and urging all men to speak up for their rights. 'One man, one vote,' he ranted, fixing a stern eye on Phoebe, who patiently covered his naked body, not at all embarrassed by the tasks she must perform for him, only disconcerted when he whispered far into the night of his love for Annie, and what he would do to her in his bed. He burned in the sweat which poured from him, then was consumed in a fierce dry flame which stripped his skeleton of every ounce of fat upon it, layer after layer. Dying, Phoebe was convinced of it, parched, but unable to drink without vomiting, his body so weakened by the cheap gin he had drunk for the past eight weeks, and by the slow starvation he had subjected himself to, that she despaired of his recovery. She said nothing of this to Annie. They cleaned him again and again, scrubbing his fouled sheets, dribbling patient teaspoon after teaspoon of fresh milk or water into his mouth, exulting when he kept it down, agonising when he vomited it up again. He looked like a corpse ready for burial, his unique individuality burned away from him so that he might have been any sixty-year-old stranger they had taken in. The carefree, easy-going young man who had not yet reached his thirtieth year was gone and in his place was a human being without identity.

Annie was snatching an hour's sleep in the room next to his when he opened his eyes, eyes which had awareness in them for the first time since he had been brought back to them. Phoebe did not see it at first. The room was soft with rushlight, the curtains drawn against the keen December wind and the squally rain which lashed across the lake. They had brought the rocker upstairs and she moved it rhythmically, her feet flat on the floor her head resting on its tall back. He had been quiet for a couple of hours, seeming to sleep, and she had relaxed, almost asleep herself. His voice brought her to instant wakefulness.

"Phoebe . . ." No more than a whispered croak, but she was out of the chair and kneeling beside him, her hand on his brow, smoothing back his lank hair, her pale blue eyes shining into his with all the love she had successfully hidden, even from herself, flowing over him, ready to nurture and sustain him with every breath she drew, with her own steadfast heart, her own life if necessary.

"Aye, 'tis me, Mr Lucas." Her breath fanned his gaunt cheek as she leaned closer, afraid if she did not keep a tight hold on his return to lucidity, he might slip from her grasp again.

"When are . . . you going . . . to call me Charlie?" he asked in a faint semblance of the wry humour which was the essence of him.

"Eeh never mind that, tha' silly beggar. Tell me how tha' feel? Are tha' hungry? Can ah get thi' a drink? Ah've fresh milk keepin' cool in t' kitchen, or 'appen tha'd fancy a sip o'broth?" For whilst he was in his right mind she meant to stuff something in him before he drifted away again. He was nothing but bones, his flesh loose and empty of the strong sinew and muscle which once filled his frame. "Are tha' warm enough lad or do tha' . . . ?" She had been about to ask him if he needed to perform one of the bodily functions she herself had cleaned lovingly and without offence from him over the past week but now that he was himself again, she found the subject awkward.

"Nothing, Phoebe . . . only . . ."

"What?" Her eyes were soft, the expression in them as revealing to Charlie Lucas, even now in his weakened state, as though she had told him in so many words of her

feelings. "What does tha' want? Tha've only t' say." He
had wanted to ask for Annie, but with Phoebe's face so
close to his, its plain intensity deepening almost to beauty
in her love, he could not, at that moment, bring himself
to speak her name.

"How . . . ?"

"How did tha' get here?"

He nodded, his store of strength too meagre for much
more.

"Jake Singleton found thi' in Penrith. Tha' was . . ."

"Drunk?"

"Aye." Phoebe looked stern for a moment for she did
not hold with strong drink, at least not with those who
imbibed too freely, then her expression returned to the
innocent, unrecognised love she was ready to devote to
him. Not in the way a woman in love devotes herself to
the man she loves for Phoebe would not have the presump-
tion to consider herself as such a woman. She would nurse
him, care for his damaged mind and body, work herself to
a standstill in bringing him back to health, but it would not
occur to her to even consider the hope of having her love
returned. She had made up her mind long ago that she
would remain as she was, nourishing those she loved,
creating tranquillity and order in which to do it, devoting
her life and strength and health so that those she cherished
might know happiness. In this way *she* was made whole,
fulfilled, satisfied. Mr Lucas had loved Annie for years.
That was a fact, a truth, and to consider anything else was
foolhardy, or would have been if it had occurred to her to
consider it.

"But tha' was ill with a fever an' all. 'Tis bin a week
now an' tha's had nowt to eat." Her anxious face begged
him to consider, "so won't tha' try an take a drop of
summat? Tha' always liked my broth, Mr Lucas, an it'll
tek no more than a minute to fetch thi' some."

"Wait . . ."

"Yes, what is it?"

"Are you . . . alone?"

Phoebe looked astonished. What sort of a question was

that? Then comprehension dawned and she smiled, putting
a work-roughened hand to his bearded cheek. It seemed
somehow to find its way there all on its own, but it didn't
matter, did it, since she was only checking to see if any
vestige of his fever remained, wasn't she? Her hand was
gentle as she smoothed the silky texture of his beard which
she herself had washed only that evening. Of course, her
mind reasoned, eight weeks ago he had thought Annie was
. . . well, that she and him from up Long Beck were . . .
well, honestly, she didn't know herself what Reed
Macauley and Annie had had in their minds eight weeks
ago, but whatever it was, it had come to nothing, but not
before sending Mr Lucas off, half out of his mind, she
supposed, driving him to the state he now was in. And
naturally, him being in Penrith and drunk for most of the
time, no doubt, he had no idea of the state of affairs here
at Browhead.

"Annie's asleep in her bed. We've taken turn an' turn
about lookin' after thi'." She sighed rapturously into his
face, her breath sweet, evidently well pleased with the
way things had turned out.

"Annie's . . . nursed me?"

"Aye, but see, won't tha' let me fetch tha' broth?"

Charlie Lucas sighed painfully and turned his head on
the pillow, looking towards the childish paintings which
still adorned the walls of what had been Cat's room. Nothing had changed. Phoebe was the same. Plumper now than
the scrawny child she had been when Annie brought her
home from Keswick, nearly five years ago, so he supposed
she would be eighteen or nineteen years old. Her cheeks
had become almost rosy but she was still plain and wholesome, like fresh new bread and as she had always been,
ready to give her life in great bounteous plenty to those
she loved.

And Annie. What was *her* condition? Was she still in
that state of indecision into which her love for Reed
Macauley had plunged her? She had been Reed Macauley's
mistress in the weeks before Charlie had fled from her,
he had been agonisingly aware of it. He had fled from his

love for her, his passion, his urgent need of her, from the tumult of loving her so uselessly. It had been destroying him. He had been positive that she was about to tell him something of great importance regarding her relationship with Macauley, some development which Charlie had known quite definitely he could not bear to hear about, and yet she was still here at Browhead. Everything was, apparently, just as it had been then, so what had happened? Strangely, he found he could not really care a great deal. It was probably due to his weakened state, brought about by the past eight weeks of which he could remember very little. It was as though it had all happened a long, long time ago. He had suffered for love, he supposed in those weeks, pouring the cheap raw gin down his throat to alleviate his suffering, labouring at the most menial of tasks to earn the few pence to pay for it. He had not eaten a great deal, nor cared much about his condition.

And now what was to happen? These two women, both of whom loved him, would return him, he supposed, to his normal good health and then . . . ? Well, what did it matter? He was empty of all but a great need for peace, stillness, quiet, pared down to the bone, not only by the last weeks and the fever which had consumed him, but by the passion of life which he really did not think he cared to suffer again. He found that even the thought of the woman in the bed on the other side of the wall caused him no emotion beyond a flicker of surprise at the absence of it.

There was a flurry of white flannel wrapped about by a hodden-grey shawl, a swirl of tumbled hair, a drift of the lavender she kept in the chest beside the bed and there she was, Annie Abbott. He watched her come towards him, warm, beautiful, her skin as smooth and unlined as white alabaster, the weight of her hair drawing her head into that proud and haughty defiance which had incensed the outraged community of Bassenthwaite parish, its colour glowing in the light from the rush like the rich pelt of a fox, her eyes deepening to a warm chocolate brown in the soft shadows.

How lovely she is and how afflicted, he thought, amazed at his own lack of feeling, then she bent over him, her cool hands at his face, her smile radiant, her fragrance all around him. He waited for a tense moment for his own affliction to begin. For his heart to leap, his pulse to race, his breath to become ragged, but nothing happened. He was happy to see her, as he had been happy to see Phoebe, but her nearness did not unduly distress his male susceptibilities, as Phoebe's hadn't.

"The bad penny . . ." he smiled ruefully ". . . always turns up . . ." He could barely speak, he was so weary.

"Charlie . . . dear, dear Charlie."

"In . . . the . . . flesh . . ." and his eyes drooped.

"What about that broth . . ." he heard Phoebe say in an aggrieved voice, then the mist of healing sleep drifted over him as sweetly and gently as a spring shower.

He spent three weeks in Cat's narrow bed before Phoebe would allow him to set a foot out of it, lying under the warm blankets she piled on him, drowsing against the nest of pillows she arranged at his back, eating the food she shovelled into his mouth. First there were eggs beaten up in milk. Bread soaked in hot milk to put a lining on his sadly malfunctioning stomach, then egg custards until she was satisfied he could keep it down and was ready to progress to thick vegetable soup, to 'crowdy' and neaps and taties, to rich mutton stew and all the good and nourishing meals she was determined to get inside him. Apple cake and clapbread, 'poddish' with cream, oatcake with butter, cheese, minced mutton pies and all produced by her own clever hands.

"See, open tha' mouth," she would command him, "or I'll hold thy nose until tha does," and when he obeyed, resignedly, she would feed him as though he was a finicky child who knew no better.

"Here's some broth for thi'," she would say, clumping into his room, disturbing the peace and quiet he dwelled in. "Ah got some shin of beef when I was in Keswick yesterday an' it's bin simmerin' for six hours so get it in thi'."

"Phoebe, it's no more than an hour since you poured that egg and milk down me," he would protest, but it made no difference, she would stand over him until it was all gone, then off she would go, telling him to have a good rest as though he was capable of doing anything else.

But the day came when, with Annie on one side and Phoebe on the other, he was able to swing his legs out of the bed, thin white sticks, the sight of which made him snort with laughter much to Phoebe's annoyance, since she had seen them a lot thinner than that, she said, and had it not been for her good food, they still would be!

"No doubt, Phoebe, but you must admit they are foolish things and the question is, will they be able to get me downstairs?"

"You're not going to attempt the stairs are you Charlie?" Annie asked anxiously. She had his right arm across her shoulders and her left was at his back. She had not been involved as much as Phoebe with his nursing, making the excuse that she had tasks to do about the farm, which was true. The real reason, of course, was her reluctance to undermine in any way, his slow recovery by placing herself too much in his company. Might not his love for her stand in the way of his progress? she had reasoned; wound his already wounded heart and body, chafe and rankle so that his healing would be slow? Phoebe was patient and cheerful, a good cook, an uncomplaining nurse, tireless and untroubled by the complexity of emotion which gnawed at Annie Abbott and Charlie Lucas. Annie had done her share of the washing of bed linen and the nightshirts Phoebe had 'run up' from the length of flannel she purchased in Keswick market. She had done many of the manual tasks in the dairy whilst Phoebe tended to Charlie but with the best will in the world Phoebe could not be expected to get Charlie up on his feet without some help from herself.

"Why not? I feel almost myself again now and a sight of something other than these four walls will do me good."

Annie was not so sure. She had noticed Charlie's tendency to gaze into the far distance across Bassenthwaite Lake, his eyes unfocused and . . . well, not blank, exactly but . . . not the same as they once had been. Calm, cool, his smile was now, not the warm and wonderful thing which had invited all about him to share his laughter. He had an air of weary acceptance, no, it was not even that, it was . . . an emptiness which, though she supposed it stopped all pain, was not really the essence of the merry and audacious man she had loved so well. But then he had been ill, she comforted herself, and really did she want back again, that urgent, vitally alive desire Charlie had once felt for her? He had wanted to love her and be loved by her. He had seen no one but her and had needed her to look at no one but him, but now he was smiling down at Phoebe with affectionate regard and could she be anything but glad that he seemed . . . content?

He grew stronger each day, getting out of his bed, sitting by the window, creeping downstairs where he was greeted ecstatically by the dogs when they were not out on the fell with Annie. The snows came on the last day of the year and for five weeks they were shut up together, going no further than the cow byre, the dairy, the barn, only Annie moving heavily through the drifts, up to the inlands where her flock, which numbered nearly 150 now and would, in the spring, be doubled, were gathered. There was plenty of hay in the barn, and with Royal to pull the sledge up the track she had laboriously cleared, she was able to get it to the flock. The thought of what she would do in April when the lambs were dropped was a constant worry to her, but by then perhaps Charlie would be himself again and able to help her in the checking of them and their dams. That is if he was still here. She had no idea what he meant to do when he was completely recovered and not wishing to appear as though she was prying into his affairs, or giving him the idea that perhaps it was time he moved on, she had not pressed him. Dear God, it was hard, not for her alone, since she was frozen for ever in her gnawing love for Reed Macauley, but for her and Charlie since she did not want to drag up the past by referring in any way to how it had once been.

Have you come to terms with it now Charlie? Have you

accepted that I don't love you as you wanted me to? Do you in fact love me at all, or has it all been burned out of you by its own fierce heat? Are you content? Can we live side by side in friendly companionship, you and I? Work together as once we did, or are you merely gathering your strength in readiness to move on? Am I to hire a man to help me? Not just with the lambing as I know I must do, but a shepherd to watch my flock?

She could not ask such questions of him.

The thaw set in at the end of February and the sound of the icy streams which carried the melting snow down to the lake was loud and musical. No sooner did it seem spring was on its way than winter returned, not snow this time, but a hard, cruel frost. Bright sunshine which had no warmth it in but cast itself over the sparkling hoar-frost until it hurt the eyes to look at it. It crackled beneath the feet, every ridge in the track, every furrow in the fields, every blade of grass stiff and white and crackling. The tussocks of heather up on the fell sparked and winked. The sky was blue and gold, flecked with dusty grey clouds which looked like gunbursts. The sunshine glinted on Phoebe's clean windows, burnishing them to gold, and whooper swans sailed low over the fields. At night there was a fine half-moon in the cold blue sky with a single star beside it shining on a crisp, white, silent world.

Maggie Singleton came over the fell from Long Beck in March, the first time she had been able to manage the walk since the snows first came. She had her boy on her hip, eighteen-month-old Jonty, and another one on the way, she confided smilingly to Phoebe who had willingly put aside her spring cleaning to gossip with this woman who, surprisingly, wanted to be her friend. No, Maggie went on disconsolately, Mr Macauley had not put her and Jake in to run Upfell farm, and what a sad waste it was to see that snug little farmhouse going to rack and ruin. All the livestock had been fetched up to Long Beck, the flock put with Mr Macauley's, since it seemed Mr Macauley could not spare Dobby Hawkins to run up and down the fell to see to them, he had said before he went away.

"Is he not here then?" Phoebe asked. They were alone, she and Maggie, Annie up on the inlands checking on her flock, Mr Lucas in the barn trying his hand at the swills, just making sure he could still make one, he had said. He was nearly himself again now, tall and lean and sinewy, handsome too, with his eyes so pale and cool, and his thin face regaining its amber hue. Quieter than Phoebe remembered, but content enough, she thought, and seemingly well settled back at Browhead. He and Annie were at peace with one another, none of the tension remaining which had once strained the very walls of the farmhouse.

"No, he went off with himself as soon as the snow began. I'm off to Keswick he says to Will, who is head shepherd, so mind tha' looks after the flock. My bank manager knows where I am if anything is needed. Will tha' be stayin' in Keswick, Maister, Will ses. No, ses Mr Macauley, I'm to go further than that, an' he got that funny look on his face, sort of far away as though, despite still being there, he'd gone some distance from where he started and didn't quite know where he was."

"An' what's the news of . . . Mrs Macauley? Is she to come home then?" Phoebe's voice was diffident since she did not really care for prying into other folks affairs but this concerned Annie who was her friend, at least it might do, and it was best to be prepared for any eventuality.

Just outside the door where she had bent down to remove her stout boots, Annie froze to stillness. It was not that she wanted to eavesdrop, or even wanted to know what Reed was doing, and certainly she did not want the sound of Esmé Macauley's name in her ears, it was simply that the paralysis which had gripped her at the mention of his name would not allow her to move.

"Nay, I couldn't say, Phoebe. Poor soul, what is she to do? But then she should never have left him, should she, no matter what . . . well . . ." Maggie stopped speaking, suddenly aware that she was treading on thin ice, for had not the cause, or so it had seemed at the time, of Mrs Macauley's departure, been Annie Abbott in whose home she now sat?

The boy who had been playing quietly with two pewter mugs and some smooth pebbles from the beck, putting them solemnly from one to the other, suddenly began to bang them on the stone floor, his childish delight with the noise he made bringing both women to their feet.

"I'd best be off, Phoebe," Maggie said, swooping him in her loving arms and kissing his cheek soundly; in the ensuing farewells it seemed quite natural for Annie to step inside, smiling as she did now, no sign of the pain which, though it nagged her constantly like a bad tooth, had flared in raw agony at the sound of Reed Macauley's name.

"Eeh Miss Abbott, tha's lookin' grand," Maggie said kindly, though Annie looked nothing of the sort.

"And so do you, Maggie. Your son has grown tall and handsome, and will you not call me Annie, please?"

Maggie bobbed her head in pleasure, wondering for the umpteenth time why folk in the parish of Bassenthwaite hated this woman so much.

"Well, thank you, Annie, ah will. Ah hope tha' don't mind me comin' to see Phoebe."

"This is Phoebe's home, Maggie. She may invite whoever she pleases. And I'm glad to see you. I will not forget your kindness when . . ." She put out a tentative hand to the boy, her face working, and when he beamed at her, she smiled, then turning, moved up the stairs.

"Goodbye, Maggie," she called over her shoulder, "come again soon," and they could both hear the painful tears in her voice.

The letter was delivered in May. The lambing was over and on Annie Abbott's inlands, her intakes and further up the fell where the first-born had been shepherded, her flock of almost three hundred hoggs, gimmers and wethers and their dams drifted contentedly across the new tufted grass. The ploughing had been done, the plough pulled by the patient strength of Royal and guided by the equally patient and quiet strength of Charlie Lucas. Clover and Daisy, her calf, had been put out to pasture and in her fields Annie watched the tiny new start of her crops, oats and rye and barley, which had been sown a month ago.

She had even bought a cart from the blacksmith whose forge lay just outside Hause. She had taken Royal to be shoed and had seen it, somewhat knocked about, but when she and the blacksmith had agreed a price and he had made a few repairs, Royal had pulled it up the track with herself at the reins, feeling as proud as Her Majesty Queen Victoria, she had said, grinning at the admiring Phoebe.

During the winter months, from the materials she had bought at 'backend', she had cut out and made a gown for herself, and Phoebe had done the same, sewing side by side in the light of the sieves and when Charlie had gone to his bed, trying them on, fitting one another with a pleasure which was the deeper because of the uniqueness of it. It was the first brand new dress either of them had ever owned. Phoebe's was a deep lavender blue which enhanced the colour of her eyes and contrasted becomingly with the dark brown sheen of her hair.

"Leave off that silly cap, Phoebe," Annie had told her, and surprisingly Phoebe had not argued "You're . . . pretty, Phoebe," she added, meaning it, though it was not strictly true for Phoebe would never be other than plain, fresh and sound, with the bloom of good health about her, but never pretty.

Her own gown was of wool in a tawny shade somewhere between russet and gold. It was almost the same colour as her hair, full-skirted with a well-fitted bodice down which a long line of pearl buttons ran from neck to waist. She had tied a sash of tawny velvet about her waist, an indulgence she had allowed herself, another being the pair of high-heeled, high-sided black kid boots, wondering at the time whether she would ever wear them. She had made a deep fringed shawl from the same material as her gown and with her hair twisted into an enormous shining knot at the back of her head, the height and weight of which lengthened her white neck, she looked quite, quite superb.

The letter was addressed to Miss Annie Abbott and asked her in the most courteous tones if it would be convenient for her to call in at the bank in Market Place in Keswick, where the manager had something of importance to discuss with her. He could not reveal what it was in the letter he said, since it was a matter of the utmost delicacy. She had only to call in at *any* time and he would be honoured to receive her, *any* time.

She put on her new gown.

"I think it would be appropriate if you accompanied me, Phoebe."

"Me?" Phoebe was flabbergasted. "But ah've the butter ter churn an' them potatoes . . ."

"Never mind the potatoes. They can be done tomorrow."

"But cannot tha' go on tha' own? Tha' always do."

"Not this time, Phoebe. Put on your new dress and Charlie will drive us in the cart. It's market day after all."

"But . . ."

"Don't argue, Phoebe, it's time."

"Time for what?"

"For wearing dresses," and with this mysterious answer, it seemed Phoebe must be content.

38

They caused a minor sensation in Keswick. It was the day of the Hiring Fair and the market place was packed from building to building with all the men and women who had been there on that day, five years ago, when she had come looking for work at the inn. They all knew her and her notorious past. They had become accustomed to the indecent way she dressed, to the sight of her long heavy hair rippling carelessly down her back, to the way she strode out with her trousered, unwomanly legs, and to her complete lack of concern with the niceties which even the poorest woman in the district regarded. They didn't like it, but they had become used to it, and to her. Her name had been sullied many years ago when she had run off with that strolling player and when she had returned she had deliberately, or so it seemed to them, flaunted convention by taking in, presumably as her lover, that well-spoken but flippant fellow from God-only-knew-where. Her name had been linked with that of Reed Macauley, so much so it had driven his young wife out of her own home, and now, *he* was gone for good, some said, and it could only be the fault of the woman from Browhead.

The cart moved slowly along the market place, Charlie speaking soothingly to Royal who was not awfully sure he cared for the press of people about him, towards the Moot Hall in its centre, the lower floor of which housed the covered market, its upper the council chamber where the Lords of the manor held court. Their passage was slow since those who had come to the twice-yearly hiring fair, placing themselves where they might be studied by those who were looking for maidservants, labourers, shepherds, yardmen, stable lads, stood in long meandering lines down the street. There was little interest in the cart at first for everyone in the market place was hurrying and scurrying here and there, intent on their own business or standing behind their stalls, arranging and re-arranging their wares more attractively, haggling with customers and generally engaged in the business of making a profit. There were other vehicles, a carriage or two, farm carts, passing along the street and the one carrying Annie, Phoebe and Charlie was almost at the Moot Hall before a farmwife from up Orthwaite way recognised the elegant young woman who swayed gracefully with the movement of the cart as it passed her stall. The woman in the cart was not only elegant, she was beautiful in her tawny gown and slipping shawl, her russet hair catching fire in a gleam of sunlight. Her back was straight and her head tipped imperiously with the weight of her hair and when she turned to speak to her companion, her long golden eyes narrowing in a smile, the woman from Orthwaite could only stand and gawp, her hand still held out to receive the few coppers a customer was putting in it. The customer, herself a regular visitor to the market, turned to look where the stallholder stared and her own mouth fell open. The live chicken she had just purchased squawked indignantly, and she was so startled she let go of it, allowing it to flutter awkwardly under the feet of a passing farmer. He cursed, ready to give her 'what for' but he, in his turn, followed her gaze, his eyes popping as he watched the progress of Annie Abbott along the market place.

It spread like wildfire, men nudging other men, women whispering to a neighbour, and though those who had come to hire themselves out did not know her, for many had tramped from places as far away as Penrith or Windermere, they stared nevertheless, for Annie Abbott was a woman worth staring at. The cart continued on to the left of the Moot Hall into Station Street. By now the word that some stupendous sight might be seen had reached the Royal Oak Hotel on the corner of the street, and men crowded at every window.

"It seems we are giving the good folk of Keswick

something to talk about, Annie," Charlie's voice was laconic.

"That's nothing new, is it?"

"I suppose not. But they have not seen you dressed so superbly before."

"No, they will be speculating on where, or how, I got the money to buy such finery. It would not, of course, occur to them that I earned it honestly, and with hard work."

"Annie, don't you realise by now how much you liven up their drab lives? They would be quite devastated if you turned respectable."

"I *am* respectable, Charlie."

"I know that, Annie, but they don't."

Charlie, whose clothing, that which he had worn when he first came to Browhead, had been burned when he was ill, was dressed in the casual manner of a man of the land. A pair of well-made hodden-grey breeches, contrived by Phoebe and Annie who swore they could easily make a living in the tailoring trade, they were becoming so proficient, with knee-length military-style boots. A shooting jacket like that of a gamekeeper with many pockets beneath which he wore a hand-knitted woollen jerkin. A 'wide-awake' hat with a low crown and a wide brim was set at a jaunty angle over his eyes. These had been purchased at one of the second-hand clothes stalls which abounded in the market, but by now Annie was paying Charlie a wage and he meant to have a decent suit of clothing made when he had saved enough money, he told her.

He handed them down from the cart with such a flourish it might have been a carriage drawn by four matched greys, and the crowd of onlookers had the strangest inclination to applaud for really, could you help but admire her, the woman from Browhead? She had turned to smile at them like visiting royalty, the smile somewhat sardonic, before she entered the bank which stood in Station Street and what, they asked one another, was she doing there? By God, she looked well, the men told one another, remembering perhaps, those who had been served their ale by her at The Packhorse many years ago, the shabbiness of her dress then. The women were inclined to pull their faces since it seemed to them the wages of sin must be very high indeed.

The manager sat them down with much ceremony, wringing his hands and bowing, overcome by the honour of having them in his office, and the three of them exchanged amused glances for it seemed the possession of a little money had a magical charm for Mr Burton. By now, of course, Charlie was aware of the finding of the tin box, the contents of which generations of Abbott women had accumulated, but surely it was not enough to cause Mr Burton to bow and scrape as he was doing? Three hundred pounds was more than the majority of men in the parish saw in a lifetime but there were many wealthy farmers, industrialists and the like in Cumberland, owners of mines, and those who held shares in the new railways which brought them in more in a twelve month than the whole of Annie's savings, and which they deposited in Mr Burton's bank. So why was he so fulsome, lavish even, with his bowing and scraping?

"Now then, Miss Abbott, to the purpose of this meeting if I may," having enquired of her health, the state of her farm, the weather and everything else connected with her which came to his mind. He had before him some documents, one of which he took up, studying it for a moment before laying it carefully on his desk again. "I have here the deeds to Upfell Farm. They are in your name and have been for the past twelve months almost, but . . . well . . . I was asked not to present you with them until . . . until now. They were purchased by a certain person who wishes to remain anonymous and . . ."

"Reed Macauley." The name was spat out as though it was made of bitter fruit and Mr Burton looked up sharply.

"I am not at liberty to . . ."

"Don't be ridiculous, Mr Burton. Everyone in the parish knows the farm was bought by him and . . ."

Mr Burton held up his hand. He did not think he cared to be called ridiculous, not in his own office, and certainly not by this woman who, until today, or at least the last time he had seen Mr Macauley, had, in his opinion, been a fast hussy who was no better than she should be. His expression said so.

"Miss Abbott, that may be so but the deeds were inscribed directly from the name of Garnett to that of Abbott. The name of Macauley was never . . ."

"Where is he?" She could feel the anger, an anger so weighty and hard to control she knew she was in danger of it getting away from her. If it did, Mr Burton might be the one to carry the burden of it and it was really nothing to do with him. He was not at fault, poor man, he was merely the messenger who carried the news and could not be blamed for Reed Macauley's madness.

"Where is he?" she repeated, oblivious of Phoebe, who, feeling uncomfortable from the first in this splendid room, was now ready to stand up and get back to Browhead as soon as possible. Even her own transformed appearance had lost its wonder. She hadn't the slightest notion of what was going on, only that it was making Annie so murderously angry, she seemed about to hit Mr Burton. Charlie was saying nothing, and nothing showed in his face beyond a mild interest and a cool contempt for Mr Burton and, or so it seemed to Phoebe, all he stood for.

"Miss Abbott, I cannot divulge the whereabouts of my client. I am merely doing what he asked me to do which is to give you these deeds and to tell you that you may take up the care of your livestock . . ."

"*My* livestock? None of it is mine."

"Your name is on this document, Miss Abbott, therefore it belongs to you."

"No." She wanted to scream and strike out at him. Of course she really wanted to strike out at Reed Macauley. To strike him hard and fatally, but since he was not here, anyone would do. The heavy outraged stone in her chest which was pressed high against her lungs, making it difficult for her to breathe, would not shift and she could feel herself fighting for air. But into her mind had come a tiny probing question which asked her why she felt so angry,

so overwhelmed by the need to lash out, if only he had
been here, at Reed Macauley for doing what he had always
done. He had given her what he knew she wanted. Ever
since he had bundled that hamper of food down the track
from Long Beck to Browhead it had been the same. In
any way he could, whether she agreed or not, he had
provided for her, protected her, watched out for her interests, and she *did* want Upfell, she had let him know it,
and here it was ready to fall into her lap. She had been
prepared to buy it from him but he had struck her and told
her to leave his house and his life and since then she had
not seen him, nor heard about him except Maggie's words
telling Phoebe that he had gone. Where was he? Dear
God, was she never to have peace? . . . Dear God, Reed
. . . would she ever know the peace of not loving him?
. . . Reed . . . Reed . . .

"I cannot accept it." Her voice was harsh. "I will not
accept it."

"Then what am I to do with it, Miss Abbott? Mr
Macauley was quite adamant in his instructions and I
cannot just leave a valuable property lying idle with no
one to care for it. I have sent instructions up to Long
Beck only this morning, as Mr Macauley told me, to return
the livestock to . . ."

"That is nothing to do with me."

"It is your farm, Miss Abbott, and they are your animals,
therefore it seems to me that it *has* something to do with
you. It is your responsibility."

"NO!"

"Miss Abbott . . ."

"Inform Mr Macauley that he must return at once and
see to them for I will not . . ."

"I cannot do that. He has gone abroad and I cannot say
when he will be back."

Mr Burton closed his mouth in a white line of anger,
aware that he had said more than he intended, but really
this splendid woman with her great dazzling eyes and heaving bosom was too much for any man to withstand. She
had not deliberately gone about wheedling information out

of him, as many women would, but she had got it just the same.

The silence was deep and long and into it Charlie's voice fell quite casually.

"There is an answer, of course."

Annie turned to him like a drowning sailor clutching at a piece of driftwood floating by and he wondered at the intensity of this love she had for Reed Macauley. It made her, a woman normally so practical, level-headed and thoughtful, act in a way that was none of these things. There was nothing she wanted more, he happened to know, than to run Upfell next to her own farm and yet her stubborn, illogical, proud and female mind would not allow her to accept it from a man who, it was very evident, loved her more than his own life. Reed Macauley was willing to go away, leave the life he had known since he was a boy so that she might live in peace. Or was it that *he* needed it, needed to get away from her, as he himself had needed to do six months ago? She was a flame, warm, bright, lovely but very lethal, a dangerous flame in which an unwary man could be consumed, as *he* had been, and the heat of her had burned him out, as perhaps it was burning out the essence of Reed Macauley, leaving no more than an empty husk.

"What is it, Charlie?" Annie's voice was eager and Mr Burton found he too was on the edge of his seat.

"You have some three hundred pounds deposited with Mr Burton's bank, have you not?"

"Yes, I intend to start a business . . ."

"Why do you not buy the farm instead? The business could come later."

"Mr . . . er . . . Lucas, Miss Abbott cannot purchase what she already owns."

"I presume Mr Macauley has an account with you, Mr Burton?"

"Really, that is Mr Macauley's business, but . . ."

"Surely it would be a simple matter to transfer the money from Miss Abbott's holdings to Mr Macauley's? You can put money *in*, I presume?"

"Well . . . yes . . ."

"Then what is there to stop you? Miss Abbott will then, in effect, have bought the farm. At least she will have paid Mr Macauley three hundred pounds which . . ."

"Oh, Charlie, that is a splendid idea but I believe the price was two hundred guineas. I want Upfell Farm, of course I do, but I don't want it given to me by . . . Well, I want to feel that I have . . . Charlie, really you will know what I mean . . ."

"I know exactly what you mean, Annie," and in his cool grey eyes there was a faint memory of the passionate love she had evoked in him once. He could no longer be stirred by that kind of emotion, he knew it now. It had been scourged out of him in the eight weeks he had hated her, been obsessed by her, suffered for her and had returned a different man; one remoulded and emptied of the masculine hungers he had once known. But in that moment as she turned to him in passionate relief he remembered how it had felt and he was very aware that Annie Abbott still suffered it.

As they drove jubilantly back to Browhead – at least Annie was jubilant, for Phoebe kept repeating she couldn't make head nor tail of it and therefore, as yet, could see no reason for jubilation – Reed Macauley stood beside his wife, his arm supporting her weeping, fainting figure as the coffin which contained the body of her father was lowered into the ground.

He had been about to board ship for America since he had heard there were many business opportunities to be found there and now seemed as good a time as any to go and see what they were. His affairs were all in order with men of integrity to keep them that way and his farm, efficiently run as he had designed it to be, would continue to flourish under the supervision of the factor he had employed.

The news of his father-in-law's death could not be ignored. His wife's inheritance which, by the laws of the land, now belonged entirely to him, must be put in order, the estate settled, his father-in-law's mills organised, along with his home, his servants, his wife and his daughter. His married daughter who had spent the last two years living the life of a 'daughter at home' or that of a widow, but was, in law, the wife of Reed Macauley.

Those who stood about the grave exchanged furtive glances as Esmé Macauley clung to her husband in much the same way she had clung to Edmund Hamilton-Brown, whose widow was quite overlooked. Mrs Hamilton-Brown was composed, tearless, standing somewhat apart, as though the man who had been her husband had really been nothing to do with her, the right to grieve his death belonging solely to his daughter.

The last mourner had left, the carriages following one another in an orderly line down the long gravelled driveway of Edmund's splendid house in Bradford. Reed stood, as was correct in a bereaved son-in-law, between his wife and his mother-in-law, shaking each hand which was held out to him, speaking the right words, knowing exactly what was in the curious minds of those who had come to pay their last respects to the hard-headed and ruthless businessman who had been Edmund Hamilton-Brown. There was a lot of money and how was his empty-headed daughter and his self-effacing wife to manage it without him? So was this husband of Esmé's to do it in his place? Run his mills and his home, his womenfolk, and if so were Mr and Mrs Macauley to live together again as man and wife, as, shockingly, they had not done for the past two years?

It was in Esmé's eyes as she sat down in the chair opposite the man she had married four years ago, the look of pleading, the desperate look of an animal at bay, one that knows its fate, its very life hangs in the balance and will be decided in the next few moments.

"I think I will go and rest, my dear," Esmé's mother murmured, smiling in a vague way at Reed as he opened the door for her, but in her eyes was an awareness of the importance of the next hour, not only to Esmé and her husband, but to herself since her own future lay in the hands of Reed Macauley.

"May I ring for tea, Reed, or would you prefer . . . perhaps a brandy?"

"I think brandy, Esmé, but don't trouble the servants. I will help myself."

A silence fell and still Esmé's eyes held that imploring expression. He smiled, gently, for she was so young.

"Don't worry, my dear," he said in the softest way he knew how. "I am not about to drag you back to Long Beck, nor make you do anything you don't wish to do. You are my wife and I know the law gives into my hands everything you have inherited from your father but I don't intend to use it to enforce my will on yours. Your father protected you and now I will continue to . . ."

"No, Reed, you don't understand." Her head rose proudly and her eyes were steady. What he had thought to be the entreaty of a frightened child to be told that all was well, was in fact that of a woman who is afraid that she is about to be made to do what the man who owned her, demanded that she do. "I am your wife," she went on, "and as such I must obey you, but you made it very clear two years ago that you . . . did not care for me. My father was incensed and was determined to punish you. I was . . . hurt . . . offended. I was a discarded wife and my pride was wounded. My father had made a pet of me and I had grown up believing, as he taught me to believe, that I had only to ask for something and it would be mine. Papa was a . . . ruthless man, I know that now, one who did not like to be crossed, something like yourself, and when you . . . directed your affections elsewhere he took it personally and wanted to hurt you. I . . . dissuaded him. I loved him very much and shall miss him. His death was hard for me and I shall grieve." Her eyes brimmed with tears and she dashed her hand across them in the way small children do and for the first time Reed Macauley felt a warmth towards her which he had never known before.

"I'm sorry, Esmé."

"Let me finish, Reed."

"Of course."

"I . . . do not want to be your wife, Reed, and I am

afraid that if I . . ." She took a deep breath which lifted
her magnificent bosom, ". . . my mother and I are used
to a certain standard of living . . ." She smiled a little,
". . . luxury I suppose you might call it, and now if you
are . . . if you . . ."

"It is up to me how you, indeed IF you are to continue
to live in it? Is that what you are saying?"

"Yes. It is not unknown for a man to force his wife to
live in penury whilst he spends her fortune on his
mistress." Her expression was defiant and Reed was
made very aware that his child-bride was no longer a child
but a woman of strength and maturity and he wondered
on how it had come about.

"I have no mistress, Esmé." He said it mildly.

"But . . . the woman . . . ?"

"From Browhead?"

"Yes, I thought . . . that is . . ."

"No, it is all over. She loves . . . elsewhere. There is
a man . . ." The look of pain in his eyes was fleeting but
Esmé saw it.

"I'm sorry, Reed. I know how you must feel."

"*You*, Esmé?" He shook his head wonderingly for what
did Esmé Hamilton-Brown know of love?

"You still love her?"

"Oh, yes."

"Then we are a sorry pair, Reed." She rose from her
chair and crossed the rich comfort of the deep-piled carpet
Edmund Hamilton-Brown had thought appropriate for himself and his family to walk on. Reed was staring sightlessly
at the manicured expanse of Edmund's spring garden, *his*
spring garden now, he supposed indifferently, but he
turned at her words. She was almost twenty-two, a beautiful young woman, composed, elegant in her fashionable
and beautifully made black mourning gown. Her skin was
smooth, flawless, her mouth full and rosy and in her cornflower blue eyes was a serenity, a look of . . . of something
he did not at first recognise but when he did his expression
of amazement made her smile.

"Yes, you are right." Her voice was soft, marvelling.

"You . . . ?"

"I am in love, Reed, and more importantly, I am loved."
She put a hand on his arm, hesitant, not awfully sure what
his reaction would be since a man does not often hear his
wife confess to loving another man. Though she knew he
did not love her, might he not take it amiss to know that
she did not love him either and might he not show his
displeasure with the violence he was certainly entitled to
feel?

"Esmé, I am speechless," but nevertheless he had
begun to smile and she relaxed, ready to lean against him
in the way she had leaned on her father. But he was not
her father, he was her husband and what was to become
of them? That was what she wanted him to tell her.

She said so.

"What do you want, Esmé?"

"I would like to marry him but of course, that is
impossible. As you well know."

"I do indeed." His smile was weary and Esmé Macauley
was saddened by the change which had taken place in
this compellingly vigorous husband of hers. He was still
handsome, tall, lean, hard, but the whimsical humour
which he had allowed the world to see now and again was
gone entirely. The brilliant blue of his eyes seemed
dimmed as they gazed beyond her, beyond the room to
something a great way off, remote, aloof, far removed
from anything which had once concerned him. His dark
hair had a dusting of grey above his ears and there were
deep lines scored from his nostrils to the corners of his
mouth. His eyebrows dipped in a scowl, fierce and chal-
lenging, but it seemed to her the challenge had gone leaving only the habit it had formed over the years.

"What do you want, Esmé?" he asked again.

"I want to be . . . with him but I cannot do it without
your consent."

"*My* consent!" He turned to smile in amazement.

"You . . . hold the purse strings, Reed. As your wife I
know I would be kept in comfort for the rest of my life
even if we did not live together, but if I was to go away

with . . . my lover . . . Oh, yes, he is my lover in the true sense of the word, though how I kept it from Papa I shall never know. We were discreet and I suppose lovers always find a way, and we did. He has no money, you see . . ." Her face was radiant, eager, hopeful, a quality of stillness and awe about her as though she had discovered something not revealed to other women, those who were not loved by the man who loved her. "He is the third son, you see," she went on. "There is nothing for him. He is a soldier but he intends to leave the army and then, if you agree and will . . . it *is* my father's money, Reed, and *my* inheritance, after all, but . . ." She pulled herself together, aware that her future lay in this man's hands.

"He would be content to . . . I can think of no other way to put it, Esmé, he will live on *your* money? What I *allow* you to have?"

"*You* will not refuse it, Reed, despite it being my father's, and now mine. Is there a difference? And if I was free he would marry me for it."

"And you don't mind that?"

"He loves me, but he has been brought up knowing that second and third sons of . . . his class, must marry where there is money."

"And you?"

"I love him. He loves me. We want to . . . we intend to . . ."

"What, Esmé? If I allow it, what will you do?"

"Live abroad. In Italy. We can be man and wife there where no one knows us."

"And your mother?"

"She will remain here quite happily. She and I were never close. She will scarcely know I am gone."

"I am quite overwhelmed," he said slowly, sadly, so that Esmé Macauley was left in no doubt that this quiet man who was her husband was very hurt indeed, but not by her. Damaged, weary, burdened with something he could barely lift, let alone carry. He was not at all put out that his wife not only wished to run off to Italy with her lover but that he was being asked to finance it.

Reed should have been outraged but all he felt was a small tremor of amusement. Once he would have been overjoyed for now he had the means to sue Esmé for divorce. Desertion and adultery, which were the two causes needed for a man to take his case to the courts but now, now it was too late. The woman he loved was a liar and a cheat. A woman of easy virtue who had betrayed his love. A breaker of hearts who had shared her favours between himself and the man who had moved back into her bed six months ago.

It was all too late.

39

Charlie Lucas moved in to Upfell Farm in August, and Phoebe, Phoebe Lucas as she was by then, went with him.

Charlie had come to Annie at the end of June, quiet and steady as he had been ever since he was brought back from Penrith. There was still a certain endearing sweetness about him, a twinkling sense of humour that shone occasionally in his pale, cat-like, grey eyes, but the lively wit, the jaunty, devil-may-care impudence which had drawn her to him at Rosley had been purged out of him and she was sorry for it. She must take the blame for it, she knew that and if there was anything she could do to atone for it, she would, and when he asked her for Phoebe, though she could not have been more astonished, she could do nothing else but agree.

"You did not know, Annie?" he asked her quietly.

"That you and Phoebe were . . . ? No, I'm ashamed to say I didn't. I have been somewhat involved in the running of two farms, Charlie, which is really no excuse since you are both my dearest friends and I should have seen it," but even as she said it she wondered why she should apologise, for nothing in Phoebe's manner, or in the way she spoke to Charlie, still calling him 'Mr Lucas', had indicated that there was anything between them other than the affectionate regard they had always known.

"She loves me, Annie."

"And you?"

"I seem to have lost my talent for grand passion, my dear, but I am left with a great capacity for friendship. Affection, if you like which is very soothing with none of the wounding effects of what is known as 'being in love'.

I think Phoebe understands this. I *know* she does. She is
. . . pregnant, Annie. I did not mean it to happen but you
have been busy elsewhere, and Phoebe and I have been
thrown into one another's company a great deal. She is a
lovely young woman, oh, not in the sense most men mean
when they use those words though I find her most pleasing
to look at. She is fresh and wholesome, strong but at the
same time gentle and wise. She . . . steadies me, Annie,
and when I made love to her . . ."

"Please, Charlie, that is something between you and
Phoebe."

"No, I want you to realise that . . . she is not second
best. You know how I felt about you but that only happens
once in a lifetime, to a man, or a woman I suppose. She was
reluctant at first, believing in some way that I belonged to
you, but when I showed her that I didn't and that I was
not merely giving in to a male fancy, that I meant her no
offence, and wanted to marry her, she . . . she allowed
me . . . *no*, she shared with me the greatest sweetness
a man and a woman can share. We both felt . . . much
joy. She is very honourable, Annie, and will go no further
unless she has your permission, despite the child, and
really, I don't know what I have done to deserve such
bounty, such a rich content as she gives me. So, we want
to be married as soon as possible. The child is due in
October . . ."

"October!"

He grinned, something of the old Charlie in him, impish,
even a little wicked, as though he knew quite well that
what he had done would not be considered gentlemanly.
Almost as though the man of the house had made free
with the housemaid whilst the mistress looked the other
way, but that had not been it at all, and Annie should know
it. He was a man, of course, and Phoebe, though he did
not, naturally, say so to Annie, was soft and pliant and
rounded beneath her prim apron and cap, and it had been
no hardship to make love to her.

Annie, who had been sitting at the table beneath the
window making up the wages for the men she had

employed to help with the clipping of her sheep, and who, now that it was finished, were moving on to a farm further north, stood up and moved to the open door. Phoebe was in the dairy and Annie could hear the regular 'thump, thump' of the butter churn. Phoebe was singing, some song the four of them had sung before Cat died and which Charlie had taught them. She was happy. It was in her voice, Annie could hear it. She was loved and wanted, *needed*, and inside her was a child. The child of the man she loved. For four months she and Charlie had been . . . Dear God, what word could she use . . . courting?, right here under Browhead's roof, it appeared, and not one whisper of it had reached her own ears. Had they slept together on the other side of the wall, making love . . . ?

For an appalling moment she could hardly believe her own . . . what was it? envy . . . outrage . . . jealousy? Was that it, a bitterness that Phoebe had what Annie Abbott would never know again? A part of her had closed down when Reed left. She had shut it away, set it in ice whilst she busied herself with her ambitious, endless plans, overburdening herself since it was the only way she could put out of her mind the totally consuming obsession of her love for Reed Macauley. She had directed an absolute concentration of will and energy into the exhausting organisation of running two farms, two efficient farms, at the same time doing her best to make a decent profit from both. She had Charlie, of course, and had he not been there, going at her command wherever he was needed, she could not have done it, and yet, behind her back . . . no, *no*! How could she say it like that, as though they had been underhand and deceitful, as though they should have asked her permission. Had she asked what *they* thought when she had gone up to the tarn on the fell to make love to Reed? Had she cared? Had she given them a thought as she had indulged in the rapture which, it seemed, was now theirs?

"Annie?" Charlie's voice broke into her reverie and she swung back to him. "We'll do very well together, you know, Phoebe and I, really we will. We . . . both need

. . . someone and . . . I hope you will agree to it but we felt . . . Lord, this is difficult, but we felt that perhaps we might take over the farmhouse at Upfell. Phoebe wouldn't hear of it at first. She couldn't leave you, she said, not on your own but . . . well . . . I cannot help but think that it would be . . . inappropriate for the three of us, four soon, to remain under one roof, can you? Not after . . ."

Annie smiled ruefully, then held out her hands to him. He jumped up and took them, smiling too, then pulled her into his arms, hugging her as a friend would, and she was made very aware that Charlie Lucas's affections and loyalty lay elsewhere now.

There was a step behind them and when Annie turned there was Phoebe, flushed, a little dishevelled, a shining tendril of dark hair wisping over each ear. She was stiff, even shy, inclined to drop her eyes since it was very evident that Annie knew. She placed the crock of butter she carried on the table and one hand fell to rest protectively on her rounded stomach as she waited.

"Phoebe, oh, Phoebe, do you know how happy I am for you? For you both?" Annie held out her arms and her tears fell, for her own sad state and for Phoebe's happy one. Phoebe moved into them and the two friends clung together lovingly.

The parish rocked with it! The banns were read in the Church of St Bridget by the lake, the woman from Browhead and her two companions there to hear them and the gasp which sighed round the church and up into its high rafters drowned the parson's voice for a full five seconds. The congregation had wondered, mouths agape, eyes wide, why the three of them should have chosen to come to church on this particular Sunday, since they had never done so before. The man was in a decent suit of good grey broadcloth, his shirt-front and stock a snowy white, his hair neatly brushed, his boots with a high polish on them. The woman who held his arm, the *other* one, was dressed in blue, a lovely lavender blue with a tiny white lace cap on her dark and gleaming hair. It was noticed that the man was most solicitous of her, placing her gently in

a pew as though she was made of spun glass. Had she
been ill then? they asked one another, though she didn't
look ill. Far from it. She was rosy and rounded but even
then they did not guess for all eyes went to her, the one
who had fascinated them ever since she had come home.
The woman from Browhead.

It had been – again – the talk of the parish when it was
learned that *she*, the hussy, actually *owned* Upfell. That
somehow or other she had got together the money to
purchase the farm from Reed Macauley, or had she paid
for it in a coinage of a different kind? But if so, where was
Mr Macauley? Why was he not here collecting what was
owed him? Dear Lord, the questions were endless, and the
answers very hard to come by, and now the congregation
watched her with avid speculation, as though some of them
might be written on her composed face.

She wore the tawny gown which had been new on the
day the deeds to Upfell Farm had been put in her hands.
Her hair was tied back with a length of tawny ribbon and
allowed to hang down her back in that defiant tumble to
which they were well accustomed. No bonnet for her but
a spray of creamy roses pushed carelessly behind her ear.
No shawl, nor gloves, nor hymn book but a posy of the
same roses picked from a hedgerow somewhere and
which, later, she was seen to place on her child's grave.

The reverend gentleman's voice tried to rise above the
sibilant hiss which moved about the congregation. It took
them several minutes to convince themselves that the
names he announced, Charles Edward Lucas and Phoebe
Abbott, were correct! Surely he meant *Annie* Abbott? He
was known to be somewhat absent-minded, but even he
would not make such a dreadful error! Then it was seen
that Charlie Lucas held the hand of the maidservant, smiling at her with every evidence of affection and the congregation fell silent, stunned by the realisation that Annie
Abbott's lover was to marry her maidservant – and what
were they to make of that? they asked one another the
moment they got out of the church.

The wedding in August was attended by very few, but

those who came were Annie Abbott's good friends. She had not many in the parish but the tiny congregation which gathered for the ceremony smiled and nodded as Phoebe and Charlie exchanged their vows, the child they were to have kicking quite visibly beneath the stretched lavender blue of its mother's gown.

Sally Garnett was there, a changed woman now that she had charge of her life and the ordering of her simple-minded, harmless husband. She was clean, decent, her rosy face wearing that scrubbed and shiny look her own mother had once scoured into it, her plain brown dress tidy, her bonnet joyful with a bobbing spray of roses from about the door of her own spruce cottage. Her six children, the last born two years ago, were being 'minded' by her sister Mim who, it turned out, was a living replica of her mother, Aggie. Sally had 'pulled herself together' now, she said cheerfully to Annie, without Bert's nightly embrace and the steady stream of children which had resulted from it. She had a few sheep on her brother-in-law's intakes and a bit of land on which to grow her oats and bigg and vegetables, and with Bert, who did as he was told without a murmur, and a chap who worked for Mim's husband, to help, they did very well. What with the cash they had got for Upfell which Mr Macauley had . . . now what was the word? . . . oh yes, invested for them, and which brought in a decent little sum each month, they were doing right nicely. He'd been that good to them, Mr Macauley, sorting out all that there legal stuff and making sure that she and the children wanted for nothing and were well and comfortable in their cottage at Binsey. She seemed to bear him no ill-will for the 'heft' he had given to Bert . . . oh, aye, she and the rest of the community were well aware who it was who had beaten Bert, the community blaming Annie for the whole thing, naturally, Bert's part in it not proved, it seemed to them, but Sally knew, oh, yes, indeed! Hadn't she lived with Bert for eight or so years and who knew better than she his nasty disposition? She could well believe he had set upon Annie and he had got what was his due, the bugger. No, it had all turned out for the best, and, following Annie's example, Sally was making a fair go of it in her little cottage up Binsey way. She'd always admired Annie's gumption in running her farm and she could see no reason why she herself could not do the same.

Maggie and Jake Singleton were there, walking over from Long Beck in their best 'setting-off' clothes. They had another boy whom they had called Thomas, Tom for short, and he and Jonty crowed and laughed throughout the service to no one's annoyance, not even the parson's, for he was well aware that this was not your ordinary sort of wedding. Will Twentyman and his Eliza, in their own finery, came down from Gillthrop, defying the disapproval of their 'regulars', or at least their regulars' wives, for Annie was beginning to find favour with the men of the community for her sheer bloody-minded determination to succed in the face of all she had endured, which they were inclined to admire.

A few curious women servants from Long Beck crept into the back of the church, among them Lily Gill and Nell Tyson, the two who had wrapped Annie about in their compassion when Cat was killed. There was Willy North, and Dobby Hawkins with his fiddle and not one refused to walk over to the farmhouse at Upfell after the simple service and sample the thin, currant 'bridecake' Phoebe herself had made the day before. There was no attempt to 'throw the stocking' for it was very evident that the new Mrs Lucas was no virgin going to her marriage bed, indeed, though there was plenty of ale and a sip of port for the ladies and everyone was flushed and mellow when they bid the newly married couple a long life and a happy one before they took their leave, they could sense the strange melancholy which was in the air despite the bride's obvious happiness.

At the last moment Phoebe clung to Annie as though she really could not bear to see her go. About them was the shining wonder of Phoebe's new home and it was hard to picture the state it had once been in when poor Sally Garnett had it in her care.

"It looks like when me Mam 'ad it," Sally had remarked simply, sighing for her Mam who had once reigned in the kitchen which was now Phoebe's. Charlie and Phoebe had scrubbed and polished and whitewashed the farmhouse, returning it to the warm and comfortable home it had been years ago. A kitchen, a scullery, a tiny parlour and above them a couple of bedrooms. Phoebe had arranged the few pieces of old country furniture Sally had left behind, since they would not fit into the cottage at Binsey, burnishing them to a mirror gleam. The square fireplace in the parlour was set with logs in readiness for her 'callers' and at the window were the newly washed and ironed curtains which would keep out the vicious draughts which were a constant plague on the fells of Lakeland. The dresser in the kitchen was crowded with her brand new crockery and the glowing fire, lit even in August, had a couple of chairs placed before it in which Mr and Mrs Lucas would take their ease of an evening. Of course, 'at ease' to Phoebe would mean rush-light making, knitting, weaving, spinning, darning, for she had never in all her life sat with her hands folded in her lap. There was a basket of kittens purring like a hive of bees, their careless mother still in residence at Browhead, and beside them lay Natty's ancient dog.

"Eeh lass, ah can't bear ter think o' thi' goin' back ter that empty 'ouse. Will tha' not stay an' . . ."

"Phoebe darling, you are a married woman now with a husband to consider," laughing over Phoebe's shoulder at Charlie. "I shall be perfectly all right. Browhead is my home, you know that, and this is yours now. We are only a mile apart and no doubt you will be heartily sick of seeing me come up the hill to visit you."

"No, eeh no, Annie, tha' must come whenever tha' like, mustn't she, Charlie? Every day if tha' wants to an' ah shall be down first thing ter mek sure that . . ."

"Phoebe, you will do no such thing. You have a farm to run now, and besides, you musn't exert yourself, not with . . ."

"Oh, don't talk daft, Annie Abbott. Ah'm as right as a trivet an' if ah want ter run up an' down ter Browhead,

ah will. Ah know thee, lass. Tha'll be eating bread an'
cheese or owt else what's 'andy instead o' cookin' summat
nourishin' . . ." meaning, of course, that without Phoebe
to put a dish of crowdy, or neaps and taties or a decent
plate of mutton and vegetable stew in front of her, and
with no one but herself to be concerned about, Annie
would fade away to nothing before the week was out.
Annie was left in no doubt that even from as far as a mile
away, Phoebe would still be in complete control of the
kitchen at Browhead and whilst Phoebe was on her feet
Annie Abbott would want for nothing.

"Keep her from doing too much, Charlie," she said, as
he walked her down towards the gate which led on to the
track to Browhead. "It will take her a while to realise that
I *can* manage without her. She has been in charge of me
for so long now she cannot help but believe that the
moment she takes her eyes off me I will fall apart."

"And how will you *really* be, Annie?" He put a hand on
her arm, drawing her round to face him and his face was
filled with his concern. Yes, it said, I am married to
Phoebe. She carries my child and I will love and care for
them both with all the power that is in me, but you, you
Annie Abbott, brave, honest, humorous, loyal Annie
Abbott will always have that special place in my heart. He
rested his hands on her shoulders, looking down into her
face and she lifted one hand to rest it on his.

"I shall do very well, Charlie. Now that I know you are
settled, I shall do very well. Will it be enough for you,
Charlie?"

"Oh yes, and you?"

"I will . . . make it enough."

"I was meaning . . ."

"I know who you were meaning, but he is married. He
is committed elsewhere and I have a commitment of my
own. To this farm. To you and Phoebe at Upfell. To *us*.
The three of us will make . . ."

"I am not speaking of farms, Annie."

"I know, but I am."

There was nothing more to be said. Bending his tall

frame he placed his lips against hers. A brief kiss, soft and sweet, which said goodbye, at last, to the two people who had been Charlie Lucas and the woman he had loved.

Reed Macauley spent the last hours of 1853 in his bed with a beautiful woman whose very rich husband, twenty or so years older than herself, and no longer able to satisfy her in the ways of the flesh, if indeed he ever had, she confided to Reed, slept the sleep of the very drunk in the suite next door. There had been a ball at the splendid hotel in New York where Reed had kept rooms since he had come to America six months ago. He had danced with the beautiful woman and, briefly attracted to her sleek good looks, her smoothly chignoned black hair, the slumbrous depths of her black eyes and the half-exposed sensuality of her full white breasts, he had been drawn into the net of her undoubted charms, allowing himself to be tempted away from the dancing; out of his clothing; invited to take hers from her and spend himself in the plunging of his man's body into hers, which he had obligingly done.

She had fallen asleep and, easing his exhausted body from between her twined legs and clinging arms, he moved towards the window, slowly, wearily. As he did so he thought with wry amusement of those days, long gone now, when he could have made love to this . . . this strumpet from dusk to dawn, then, shouting for his boots gone striding out on the fell to examine his flock from dawn to dusk.

He took a cigar from the box on the table next to the window, lit it, then drew the smoke deeply into his lungs, blowing it out to wisp upwards in the dark stillness of the luxurious room. Lifting the heavy velvet curtain he looked out across the wide and handsome thoroughfare which divided Manhattan Island and which was lined with fine buildings consisting of business houses, public offices and hotels such as this one. Many had façades of white marble, testifying to the prosperity of this young and bustling nation, and it was here in this teeming city, and in others, that Reed had conducted much of his business, to do with his wool, his mills in Bradford and the many miles of woollen cloth which they produced. He had been a wealthy man when he sailed for America six months ago, even after the generous sum he had settled on his wife and her lover, but he had doubled his fortune since he left England's shores. To get money one needed money, he had often heard his own father say, and it was true for with Edmund Hamilton-Brown's hard-earned brass behind him it seemed he could do no wrong. He had lived the life of an Arabian prince, fêted and showered with invitations from America's finest society and in all that time there had not been a moment when he had not longed to go home. Home, of course, did not mean England, or Cumberland, nor even Long Beck but the particular square of earth where Annie Abbott stood.

His gaze was sombre, his face set in brooding lines as he looked back on the memories he knew full well were best forgotten, for they could only hurt him and had he not suffered enough that he should inflict pain deliberately on himself? He could see his own naked reflection in the dark glass of the window and the glowing end of the cigar as he drew on it. There were vague shadows behind him and the woman on the bed grunted as she threw herself on her back. He turned to look at her, her long white body draped bonelessly across the tumbled sheets, her hair spilling over its side like a dark and shining waterfall. She was very lovely and so had been the dozens of others with whom he had shared his nights, and many an illicit afternoon, for it seemed the cities of America were filled with wives whose husbands, busy at their desks making another million or so dollars, had not the time to love them. What was *this* one's name, he mused? studying without the least interest the slender line of her leg, bent at the knee, and the mysterious dark triangle between her thighs. He *had* known, surely, for she must at some time during the evening have been introduced to him, but he could not for the life of him remember what it was.

He turned back to the window, considerably startled

when another face took shape beside his own. A composed and serious face, exquisite in its oval flawlessness, the mouth long and tender, the nose strong and straight, the jaw set at a determined angle, the dark eyebrows finely etched above the eyes. Eyes that were a deep and tawny brown with specks of gold in them; eyes that suddenly narrowed in laughter, the soft mouth stretching over white teeth, the head thrown back with such infectious merriment he felt his own lips begin to tug into a smile and his own laughter to bubble in his chest. The image lifted a hand, pushing back the thick tangle of curls which fell over its brow and with the movement it vanished, becoming what it had always been, the misted reflection of a lamp which stood at the back of the room and which his imagination had transformed into *her*. She was gone and for a moment the pain was more than he could bear.

Where was she? he sorrowed, grieving as he had done for so long now, the death of his love. Not *his* love for her, but for the love she gave to another man. He held it at bay successfully for the most part, for he knew it would seriously embarrass those with whom he did business, those women with whom he danced and laughed and flirted, those he made love to, if they knew of the despair that festered within him. When he was completely alone he gave in to it, putting his face in his hands, holding in the flood of tears which surely were unmanly and which threatened to burst forth and drown him. He would rock back and forth, his mind bursting with all the lovely pictures he had of her, and with those of his future which was empty and stagnant without her in it.

"Annie," he whispered, his eyes on his own reflection, "Annie . . ."

"Reed . . ."

It was so real he turned about to stare into the dark shadows which, apart from that one lamp by the door, filled the room. His heart thudded, first one great leap which hurt his chest and then raced away so quickly he could hardly breathe.

"Annie . . . ?"

"Reed . . ." Dear God, what was happening to him? Was he going mad now? losing his sanity along with his hope and his capacity to take much interest in anything his life had to offer him? He made business deals with half his mind, the other half wondering on how to get through the tedious evening ahead, the long empty night, despite the woman he knew would no doubt share his bed, the next day, week, month. He managed it somehow but if he was to start imagining he could hear her voice speaking his name how could he cope with? . . . perhaps it was *her*, what's her name on the bed. Perhaps she had spoken to him but when he jerked himself across the room to look down at her she was sleeping with her mouth open emitting tiny snores.

Then? . . . He swung about, striding back to the window and, quite distinctly, as his gaze followed the slowly moving line of carriages which took the merrymakers away from the ball, though he knew without a shadow of doubt that, apart from the snoring woman on the bed he was completely alone, he felt a hand touch his shoulder, gently, *her* hand, of course, for who else could reach him over the thousands of miles which separated them?

"Dear God, Annie . . ." he groaned, the agony inside him absolutely more than he could bear and really, why did he not open the bloody window and . . . ?

"Reed . . . please . . ."

He lifted his bowed head and blindly placed his hands one on either side of the window. He glared madly at his own reflection, ready to drive his fist through the pane of glass but slowly, amazingly, he felt a great sense of peace come over him, dissolving his limbs and releasing his aching body and mind to stillness, a stillness and a resolve which astounded him.

"All right, Annie." He heard the words, the impossible words come from between his lips but they did not seem at all unusual. "All right, my beloved, I'm coming."

Sitting down in the armchair beside the window he fell at once into a deep and dreamless sleep and by her fire at Browhead, where she sat with Dandy in her lap, the dogs at her feet, her face still wet with tears, Annie did the same.

The next day Reed Macauley booked his passage on the 1100-ton Packet ship *Rainbow*, commanding a private state room. He sailed two days later, arriving in Liverpool on the eighteenth of January. It was raining so heavily the water was several inches deep on the roadway up to Lime Street Railway Station but he did not notice it in his tranced state.

He had two hours to wait before his train left and, unable to content himself with pacing the platform, he went across the road to the hotel which had been built to serve the constant stream of travellers who moved through the great seaport, by train and by ship. A brandy would settle him whilst he waited for . . . for whatever was to happen in the next days. A few brandies, in fact, for it would take more than one to calm the emotions which churned so fiercely inside him.

"Reed Macauley, where in the hell have you been keeping yourself?" a man's voice asked and somehow, in the strange, confusing, euphoric state he had been in for the past eighteen days he was not at all surprised to find himself in the company of Ezra Hodgson, the man with whom he had done business in the past and who had dined at his table on more than one occasion.

"I've just arrived from America," he answered, prepared to be polite.

"I heard you'd gone abroad, Macauley. A business trip, or is your pretty wife with you?" glancing about him conspicuously, though a lady such as Mrs Reed Macauley would hardly be seen in a bar like this. The whole parish of Bassenthwaite had held its collective breath when the news of the death of Reed Macauley's father-in-law had exploded amongst them, and speculation on whether Mrs Macauley would return to Long Beck was rife.

"No, oh no, she is . . . living in Italy."

"Her . . . health, perhaps?"

"No, her lover." Reed grinned wickedly, amazingly, or so Ezra would have said, for it was not something which

would make a man smile, surely? Ezra did not quite know
how to continue but he chatted on manfully, drinking the
brandy Reed offered him, casting about in his mind for
some topic which might stifle the embarrassment he at
least felt. There was one, of course, and he grasped it
thankfully.

"Of course, you will not have heard of *our* particular
infamous tidings, will you? Really, you would scarcely
credit it. After all the gossip and downright scandal that
has been caused you will find it hard to believe, but that
fellow, the one who took up with her from Browhead, you
know the one I mean? Of course you do. Who doesn't?
Well, if he hasn't gone and married . . . no, not Annie
Abbott, but her bloody maid. Could you conceive it?" he
begged Reed to tell him, "because those in the parish
couldn't, though it serves her right, of course, the
trollop . . ."

"I knew it, I *knew it!*" He was amazed to hear Reed
shout in an exultant tone. "She was telling me . . . all
those miles . . . Jesus Christ . . ."

Ezra was even more amazed when Reed Macauley drew
back his clenched fist and knocked him to the floor.

"And don't you let me hear you call my future wife a
trollop again or the next time I'll kill you."

40

The snow had been exceptionally heavy that winter, even by the standards of the Cumberland fells, falling silently, steadily, menacingly for days and nights on end until farms were buried up to their eaves, and flocks disappeared completely. A white curtain behind which the mountains hid as they were swept with great, tumultuous eddies of snow moving blindingly across perilous white slopes and crags, throwing deep drifts to lean against walls and gates and filling every gully and gill, levelling the 'slacks', the slight depression between hillocks so that they appeared to be compeletly flat and featureless.

For two days Annie could not get even beyond the frame of her back doorway. She made a slight hollow in the solid wall of snow which stood outside it, just big enough to allow Blackie and Bonnie to creep on to the step to relieve themselves, both bewildered by the quite alarming strangeness of it, but her main concern was for her farm animals, Clover and Daisy, who were safe enough in their byre but who would be badly in need of milking, and for Royal who was stabled in the barn. Her sheep, brought down to the intakes by her and Charlie at the first sign of the dangerous-looking snow clouds at the beginning of January would have to take their chances for there was nothing she could do about them. They had been bred for generations to winter on this inhospitable high land of the north, fending for themselves as best they could and, providing Annie could get to them with the hay in her barn before too long, they would survive. Once the blizzard stopped she would dig herself out, as she knew Charlie would be doing at Upfell and they would get through somehow.

She had plenty of provisions and a great pile of peat and logs stacked inside her kitchen door to feed the fire and so she settled herself as best her restless nature would allow to sit out the storm, taking up her knitting, doing some spinning, reading the newspapers Charlie had brought from his last trip to Keswick and, when he had read them, passed on to her.

For what reason she did not know, it seemed there was to be a war in some far-flung corner of the world she had not even heard of before. The Russian Fleet had attacked and destroyed a Turkish Squadron at a place called Sinope, all the seamen massacred, the newspapers reported and war fever was being stirred up in London and Paris. The British and French had entered the Black Sea to protect the Turkish coasts, though why it should concern *them* was a mystery to Annie, she decided, before she got up from her chair by the fire to roam restlessly again, to the bedroom to peer out from the window at the wall of snow in which she was imprisoned. The trouble was she could not even see if it had stopped falling. She knew it was night time because the quality of the light which shone through the impacted snowflakes during the day was different to the way it looked now, but beyond that she could tell nothing of what was happening beyond her own front door.

God, she wished it would let up and allow her to go about her daily round of tasks before she went mad with it. With nothing else to do she could not get Reed out of her mind. Whatever she concerned herself with, the newspapers, a frantic flurry of baking she indulged in, a positive mania of cleaning, even if it was not yet spring, she could not rid herself of the strange and yet surprisingly comforted state into which she had fallen on the day the old year had ended and the new begun.

It had been early morning, still dark and she had not slept, nor even gone to her bed despite her own tiredness. The snow had not then begun, and she and Charlie had gone up the fell to check on the sheep, looking for signs of lameness, blindness, weakness of any sort which might have been brought on her pregnant ewes by the hardness of the winter.

On the way back to Browhead, at Charlie's insistence, she had called in at Upfell to have a cup of tea with Phoebe and to admire the infant sweetness of Phoebe and Charlie's two-month-old daughter. Elizabeth, Beth for short, Phoebe had called her after asking Annie's permission, in memory of Lizzie Abbott who had, in her own way, made Phoebe's happiness possible. If it had not been for the tin box which Lizzie had guarded none of this would have happened, for Phoebe was in no doubt that without Upfell to go to she and Charlie would have been forced to move away from Browhead and the district. Could they have lived at the farm side by side in the uneasy acquiescence left by the knowledge that Charlie had once loved Annie? and deep down in the secret depths of him, hidden away from himself, still did. He cared for her, Phoebe knew it, and their baby daughter, in their life together, and was content, but the passionate love which had burned in him for so long was not easily quenched. It would smoulder for ever, unseen, like embers which burn deep beneath grey, smoking ash. Phoebe was not jealous, nor did she resent it. She was a practical woman and made the best of what she had, and in their bed at night she gave everything of herself that she had, satisfying her husband, holding him in strong, soothing arms if he should need her in his dream-filled sleep.

The baby was a plain, no-nonsense baby, like her mother, who knew right from the start what her place in her mother's scheme of things was to be. Loved, she was, and right proudly, well cared for, none better, strong and sturdy-limbed but there was to be none of the folly such as the 'grizzling' which Sally Garnett's babies had indulged in, and certainly no misconception that her mother's full breast was immediately available to her whenever Beth Lucas felt the need of it. Meals were to be taken at meal times when her hard-working mother herself had a moment to spare from her kitchen, her vegetable plot, her dairy and pasture, and if Beth soiled her napkin then, unless it was unpleasant enough to offend the senses, it remained where it was. Charlie it was who – as Phoebe tartly put it – spoiled her, lifting her up whenever she had the temerity to whimper, cradling her, kissing her rosy satin cheek, gazing into her unwinking baby eyes which were the only thing of him in her, a pure silvery grey, until Phoebe declared the placid child would be ruined. But there was a certain soft gleam in her own eyes as she said it and she made no protest, watching fondly as father and daughter forged the bond which she knew was so essential to Charlie Lucas.

Annie had nursed Beth and admired her progress on that last day of 1853, sitting before Phoebe's immaculate hearth on which an enormous log fire crackled, drinking a cup of Phoebe's tea and munching a hot, buttered oatcake, a dozen of which were wrapped in a snow-white square of linen 'fer thi' supper', Phoebe said scoldingly. It was as though she was convinced that, but for her own efforts in that direction, Annie would starve herself slowly to death and so, whenever Annie called, which was most days, either on her way up to the fell or on her way back, there would always be something in a pot, or wrapped in a neat bundle, 'to be warmed up' or 'put in th'oven fer later'.

"Phoebe, you can't keep on feeding me as well as yourself and Charlie. After all I don't pay Charlie a fortune and at this rate you'll be paupers. You should be saving . . ."

"Stuff an' nonsense! The amount *you* eat wouldn't feed a sparrow an' if ah can't give thi' a bite to eat now an' then 'tis a poor do. See, tek that custard tart wi' thi' . . ."

"Phoebe, please, I *can* bake a custard tart."

"When was the last time, tell me that?"

"Well . . ."

"Ah thought as much, so stop tha' bletherin' an' get another cup o' tea inside thi'. 'Tis a cold walk down ter Browhead."

She missed her. She missed them both as she brooded before her own fire at night with only her dogs for company. The room seemed to hold the images and echoes of the people with whom she had spent the last years, those she had loved and who had left her. Cat, sweet Cat, her bright face screwed into lines of fierce concentration as she bent over the long words in the Bible, and those in the stories of Miss Jane Austen and Mr Charles Dickens. Cat, laughing in delight as she mimicked Charlie's chanted pronunciation of French verbs. Cat, lovely, flushed with merriment as she bellowed forth the 'Cocking Song' into the lop-sided and amazed faces of her three animals. Cat, her bright face and bright smile quenched as she lay peacefully beside Natty in the lovely little churchyard by the lake.

Natty himself, brusque, exacting, testy, stubborn, his good heart shattered in Annie's defence on that last day, but his blunt presence still here in the shepherd's crook he had carved for her, in the chairs he had methodically repaired and the samplers he had wordlessly re-framed after Bert Garnett's destruction.

Phoebe and Charlie . . . Dear God, they were everywhere, smiling at her from the chimney corner as Charlie had done, winking and ready to share a joke, Phoebe standing with her arms up to the elbows in flour, labouring in everyone's service but her own, begging Annie to eat that there poddish, change her wet clothes, keep her mucky feet off the clean floor, get to her bed, sit herself down by the fire . . .

She was lonely and she didn't know what to do to ease it. She had what she had always wanted, what she had set out to get for herself, but what a price she had been forced to pay for it. She had the rest of her life . . . Dear God, she was only twenty-five . . . to get through and it frightened her for she really didn't know how she was to get through this *night*, never mind the rest of her life, this night which was supposed to be the end of something, and the start of . . . of what? . . . a new beginning? But the beginning of . . . of what? She must go on, and of course she would, but to walk a path alone was hard and dangerous, and though Annie Abbott was brave and strong for had she not been told so by more than one man, her heart quailed at the thought of doing it alone.

She sat on by her fire, not going upstairs to her bed, and it was cock-crow when she came to herself, her face wet with tears, her heart drowning in sadness, her body aching to be held by the arms she needed more than any others in the world.

"Reed . . ." she whispered.

"Annie . . . ?" The answering voice had a question in it but it was so real she turned her head, looking quickly towards the door, the yearning etched in her fire-glowed face, but of course he wasn't there. The dogs had not even stirred and yet . . . somehow . . . somehow it was as though his presence, the warm memory of his loving eyes, his smiling, whimsical mouth, his infuriating arrogance, his long-limbed powerfully masculine body, had entered the room, enfolding her in a comforting embrace, and she fell at once into sleep, her head resting on the chair back, the tears drying on her tranquil face.

Two weeks later the first snows began.

"Dammit man, you don't mean to tell me that the bloody train can go no further than this? The line is clear as far as I can see so why should the service be stopped? I have a most important engagement in Gillthrop." For a moment an expression of such blinding joy lit up the face of the speaker the harrassed station-master to whom the words were addressed was quite taken aback. He was a very tall and high-handed gentleman and he had the station-master backed up against his own office wall in the most disconcerting way. There was water on the line beyond Clifton and the track to Penrith was closed, he had already told him. Indeed it was a miracle the Lancaster to Carlisle had got as far as this, the rain they'd had recently. And, of course, the further north you got, the colder it became and there had been blizzards of such gigantic proportions, the fells of Westmorland and Cumberland had been closed to all traffic for weeks. There was no way anyone could get through.

"Is that so? Well, we'll see about that. Where's the nearest livery?" The arrogant gentleman's face was set in lines of stubborn challenge and he seemed ready to square his truculent jaw and stick his clenched fists into the handiest face he could find and the stationmaster did not care for it to be his.

"Down't street towards end o' t' village. But I doubt tha'll get Fred Strong ter allow one of his nags out in such weather," for the rain had fallen in a dense and straight curtain from the leaden skies, one that could be scarcely seen through, for days on end.

"Don't bank on it," the gentleman said, setting his jaw and narrowing his eyes before stepping out from the shelter of the station platform into the street where he instantly disappeared in the deluge which, even in these parts at the edge of the great Lakeland fells where wet days were more frequent than dry, they were beginning to talk of records and when had anyone, even old Arthur Blamire who was nearly ninety, seen weather like it?

Almost overnight the temperature rose from below freezing to a mildness which was so amazing, even the dogs seemed bewildered by it, sniffing the spring-like air and pricking their ears as though waiting for the command to go and fetch the flock down for lambing.

"No, lads," Annie laughed, watching the steady flow of melting snow cascade from about her windows in pretty, glittering bursts, followed by heavier, thundering falls as it slid down the roof and hit the ground. It was still a couple of feet deep, almost up to the window-sills but melting so rapidly it looked as though it would be gone by morning, thank God. She would be able to get up to see Phoebe and Charlie before the next lot set in for there was nothing more sure in this land of bitter winter than the certainty that there would be more blizzards before spring finally came. She and Charlie might even be able to get up to the intakes and check on the flock, perhaps fetch them down to the inlands about the farms. Four hundred sheep she had now, with those that had come with Upfell, and all the ewes were pregnant.

She had got to the distressed cows, both of them

yielding a great deal of milk and they, and Royal, were fed and mucked out. By the time she had finished, the earth about the barn and byre could be seen through the rapidly thawing snow, but it was so soggy she sank almost to her knees as the liquid mud sucked at her boots, nearly dragging them from her feet. She could hear the sound of water thundering down the beck as the melting snows aggravated its usual blithe undersong to a deep throated roar, accompanied by the steady drip, drip of water coming from every tree and every building about her. From somewhere up the fell there was a sharp crack and she shaded her eyes to peer upwards but there was nothing to be seen.

But the sheep must be inspected now that her farm animals were seen to, and whistling to Blackie and Bonnie she began the trudge up the track to Upfell.

Charlie had gone on, Phoebe told her, and would see her on the intakes, he had said. He'd been up since daybreak, thankful for the early thaw, surprised by it too, for it was not like a Lakeland winter to finish so soon. Yes, they were all well and so were the animals though, like Annie's Clover and Daisy, their cows had been much afflicted by their lack of milking. And Charlie had been fretting about her up at Browhead on her own, Phoebe admitted, smiling without resentment at Annie. Now would she have a hot drink before she went . . . no? . . . oh, and by the way, Charlie had met an old friend of his the other day when he was in Keswick, just before the snow began and wanted to talk to her about the possibility of him, this old friend, taking on the job of . . . well, Phoebe supposed you would call him a travelling salesman, in the selling of Annie's swills when she got round to it. A man from Charlie's days as a Chartist, Charlie had said, very reliable and accustomed to travelling. They'd gone to school together in Yorkshire, meaning, though she did not say so, that he was a well educated gentleman and would, because of it, have the knack of talking to and presumably selling to, the men with whom Annie hoped to do business. Of course, it was up to Annie but Charlie said . . . what? . . . oh, aye . . . she'd best get up to Middle Fell because those clouds above the lake looked like rain to her.

It began an hour later and by the end of the morning they were both wet through to the skin, rain dripping from noses and hat brims, heavy persistent rain, the water and melting snow combining to form a deluge which cascaded down the fellside in an ever-increasing torrent. They had found dozens of ewes, for the rapidly thawing snow had revealed them almost at once, most sheltering wherever there was a rock or two, a dip in the ground, even a bit of taller vegetation. They were all alive, miserable, drowned-looking creatures, their swamped fleeces crusted with melting snow, but alive.

They continued up Barkbethdale, coming to White Horse where a scatter of boulders afforded good protection and where again they found some of their flock and not only theirs but half a hundred bearing the smit mark of Reed Macauley. They were bedraggled and forlorn, all of them, but so far none seemed to have suffered any harm.

They leaned for a moment or two to catch their breath in the shelter of the rocks, some of them as big and as tall as a farmhouse. Their faces were raw and stinging and they were both shivering violently. The dogs, their coats plastered to their lean bodies, quivered at their feet, their eyes sharp and intelligent, their noses questing for the rank odour of a buried sheep for up here patches of snow still remained.

"It's getting colder again." Charlie had to put his mouth close to her ear to make himself heard. A squally wind had begun to blow, dashing the heavy rain at them with headlong speed, howling directly into their faces and no matter where they stood, moving round the tall stones, it seemed to seek them out. A racing slick of water was flowing across the squelchy grass and over their booted feet and on the slippery slope it was becoming increasingly difficult to keep from going with it.

Annie could barely see Charlie though he was standing shoulder to shoulder with her, and she felt for the first time a deepening twinge of alarm. She knew this country

like her own farm kitchen and would have sworn no matter
what the weather she could have found her way home.
She had been out from being a small child with her father,
in all weathers since Joshua Abbott would stand for no
foolishness such as considering her age, her size, her gender or the state of the fells outside his farmhouse door.
If he believed it was suitable to go up, up they went.

"We'd best get back, Annie. We're doing no good
huddling here," Charlie shouted. "There's no way we're
going to find any more ewes in this. Those we *have* found
seem to be in good shape so let's hope the rest will be
the same."

As he spoke the rain became even more violent, the
raindrops – if the hurtling precipitation which flung itself
down on them could be described as drops – had
thickened, turning to hailstones. Hailstones so big and
vicious they were ready to slice at any unprotected flesh.

"Jesus . . . !" Charlie turned into her, doing his best to
lend his body in the protection of hers, the hailstones
lashing at his back. He wore an oilskin, strong and suppos-
edly weatherproof though the fierceness of the rain had
found a way beneath it, and the hailstones hit it with a
sound like gravel thrown on a pane of glass. His face had
a streak of blood on it.

It took them over two hours to get down, hanging on
to one another, Charlie's arm strong and supportive, clinging to any rock they could get a grip on, any tussock of
grass which was not already drowned by the headlong race
of water which was going in the same direction as they
were. They came across another huddle of sheep, though
when Blackie and Bonnie, at her command, tried to get
them on the move for they would surely drown or be
swept down the fell if they stayed where they were, they
refused absolutely, in their senseless terror, to get to their
feet. The dogs nipped and threatened but the ewes would
not be moved. Annie could hear, even above the stinging
slap of the hailstones against Charlie's oilskin and the
drumming of it on rock and earth, the thunderous uproar
of the unchained water exploding down Chapel Beck,

Sandbeds Gill, Southerndale Beck and Barkbeth Gill, all of them emptying in storm-tossed fury into the lake at the bottom of Skiddaw.

"I wish you would come to Upfell, Annie," Charlie managed to gasp when they reached the safety and comparative quiet of the Browhead kitchen. They could barely speak, either of them, bending forward, hands on their thighs as they gulped air into their tortured lungs. "I don't like to think of you here alone in this."

"In what, Charlie? This will soon let up. It's a bit unusual for the snows to thaw so early . . ."

"I know that, but this rain after the thaw is going to make it much more . . ." He had been about to say 'dangerous' but she was smiling as though to reassure him that this Lakeland where she had spent most of her life could not frighten Annie Abbott. She was concerned for her flock, naturally, but when the rain stopped there would be vegetation for them to crop and they were knowing enough to come down and gather on the inlands above the farm where she would feed them the hay from her barn. Royal would drag the loaded sledge up the slope and, before it snowed again, as she knew it would, her flock would have a nourishing, life-saving meal to see them through the next few weeks.

"I'll have to go, Annie. Phoebe will be worried."

"I know, Charlie, and don't concern yourself about me. I have plenty to eat and enough peat and wood to last a month, though I don't expect it will be that long. And these two will keep me company," pointing to the dogs who steamed before the fire.

"I'll come back as soon as I've let Phoebe know we're all right."

"You'll do no such thing. You can't divide yourself between two farms, and you must put your wife and child first, Charlie. Besides, this farmhouse has stood here for hundreds of years and will continue to do so for a long time to come. Now go on, off you go, and tell Phoebe I'll be up as soon as this lot stops."

*   *   *

Reed Macauley urged on the weary mount he had persuaded the owner of the livery stable in Clifton to sell him. He would let no animal of his out in this weather, the man had told him churlishly, and only when Reed had offered to buy the beast – a somewhat ancient grey – which would then, Reed explained, keeping his sharp temper in check, belong to himself and would therefore no longer be the livery owner's responsibility, had the man parted with the sorry-looking nag.

He had moved in an almost straight line from the village of Clifton, across low, rolling hills through the villages of Tirril, Dacre, Hutton and Wallthwaite until he hit the Penrith to Keswick road at Burns. He crossed the River Eamont, the waters almost reaching the arch of the bridge, thundering down its course in full spate, carrying on its surging torrent the flotsam and jetsam it had picked up on its mad journey. Broken branches, great swathes of torn-out vegetation, birds, small animals, boxes and chairs and planks of wood which were becoming jammed against the structure of the bridge. It was the same at the Glenaeramackin river and at Trout Beck, the water beginning to overflow and flood the surrounding fields. When he reached Keswick it was a foot deep, the Market Place filled with frightened horses, bogged-down carriages and carts, shop owners, their clothing plastered to their bodies as they tried unsuccessfully to stem the inundation as it crept over their doorsteps. Moot Hall stood like an island in the middle of it. The Derwent and the Greta were both in flood, pouring not only their swirling, swollen waters into the town but all the rubbish they had collected on their race down the high fell.

And still the rain poured out of a low and surly sky, sweeping in a great impermeable curtain across Little Man as Reed rode out of Keswick, blotting out the high peaks of Skiddaw Forest until it seemed to Reed he was riding into the skies themselves. He had exchanged his exhausted grey for a fresh mount in Keswick, paying over more money, for though the livery owner knew him, he was reluctant to part with a good beast, especially to hazard it, a roan mare this time, in the elements which shrieked their furious spite on the fells.

"Nay, Mr Macauley, tha' don't mean ter ride over ter Long Beck in this, do tha'?" for you are a fool if you do, his thunderstruck expression said.

"I do, Archie Wilson, and what is it to you?"

"'Tis nowt ter me, sir. What yer do is yer own business but this animal is mine." The feel of good solid cash in his hand quietened any misgivings he might have had!

The hailstones began to hurl themselves down on him and the roan just as he reached Dodd Wood. He had decided against going up and over the top of Skiddaw when he came out of Keswick and saw the water pouring down the slopes on to the road as he inched his way beyond Mallen Dodd. If the road here was already a debris-filled swirl of water, what would it be like higher up from where it came? he asked himself. The roan was badly frightened, shying nervously at everything which brushed against her legs, flinching and rolling her eyes, difficult to handle. There was muck and mud, ripped-out heather and gorse bushes, loose scree, timber, and the bodies of many small, fellside animals bobbing madly about her and she did not like it.

When the hailstorm began Reed was forced to dismount, moving to the roan's head, holding her with both hands, soothing her terror. She was slippery with the rain, her coat giving the appearance of having been oiled, and from her mouth great lines of spittle drooped and were whipped away in the wind. The hailstones, as big as pigeons' eggs, sliced into her flesh and with a pain-filled scream of terror she broke free of Reed's restraining hands, rearing up above him, her hooves flailing, one catching him a glancing blow on the temple.

"Steady . . . steady, girl . . ." he tried to shout, the blood beginning to pour across his forehead and into his eye. He hung on grimly to the reins but even as he did so she turned towards the lake, escaping, as she thought, the tumult which crashed about them from the fell. He could not hold her and she went, vanishing in a moment as though the earth, or the lake as was more likely, had swallowed her up and Reed's last thought as he sank to his knees and then on to his face was that Archie Wilson had been right after all.

Though it was no more than three o'clock in the afternoon it was so dark it might have been midnight as the cloudburst emptied over the giant of Skiddaw. The wind had risen to a howling gale and both dogs cowered at Annie's feet. Moving to the window which rattled with every beat of her frightened heart, the dogs clinging to her heels, Annie peered out at her own reflection. There was nothing to be seen, absolutely nothing and she might have been buried in a great black hole. There was nothing from which she might get a bearing. No building, no tree, not a star in the sky, nor a shape on the ground, and the feeling of disorientation was appalling. Not in all her years in Lakeland had she seen such black nothingness and she wished now she had gone with Charlie. At least she would have had the comforting, comfortable good sense of Phoebe to sustain her and the baby's sweetness to cheer her. She had hoped she would be able to make her way over to the barn where Royal was stabled for he must be hungry by now, and probably terrified out of his wits. The cows would be easier to get to for the byre was attached to the house and she had only to feel her way along the wall to reach it but she would have left the animals to fend for themselves, really she would, if she could have crawled up the track to Upfell and the company of Charlie and Phoebe.

She was badly alarmed by a sudden thump at the back of the farmhouse, then another, the second one so violent she could feel the tremor of it in the soles of her feet as it shook the sturdy building. What was it? Had something fallen, a tree perhaps or . . . ? The thought had not had time to formulate itself in her mind when she felt the icy cold surge of water bite into her bare feet. She looked down and to her horror, seeping under the door was a dark slick which stained the floor with the sediment it contained. It moved inexorably about her feet and across the stone flags, rising, even as she watched in stupefied amazement, to lap at her ankle bone.

"Oh, dear God . . ." she moaned, shaking her head in denial, ready to wrench open the door and escape it, to run screaming up the track for Charlie and Phoebe, for *anybody* since she did not want to drown here all by herself. Not here in this dark and empty space where she existed alone. Alone because of her love for one man. A self-chosen loneliness but terrifying nevertheless and she could not bear it. Reed . . . I need you, Reed . . . I am so afraid in this cold and alien place . . . Reed . . . Oh, dear Lord . . . where? . . . where should she run to? . . . the dogs . . . Dandy, they were beginning to panic . . . to howl in fear, catching it from her and if she did not get a tight grip on herself . . . help me . . . someone . . . Reed . . .

She looked about her, fighting her panic and as suddenly as it had come, and for no apparent reason, it left her. It was as though his strong and vital presence was standing beside her filling her with a calming peace, and she was calm. As though his mind had reached into hers, giving her comfort, touching something in her, steadying her, soothing her pounding heart, and she was renewed by it.

"Come on, lads, stop that noise, Dandy," she said firmly to the animals, "it's upstairs for us. There's nothing to be done here until the rain stops. Now, let's see . . . food . . . water, rushlights, flint and striker . . . and there's the milk. Up you go, Blackie . . . aye, it's all right, boy, up you go," for even in his terror he was not sure he should move up the stairs where he was never allowed. "Good boy, up you go."

It took her ten minutes to collect as much food as she could, the hot 'tatie-pot' which had been bubbling on the fire, the last to go, and even as she moved to the bottom stair the water was already there before her and on the hearth the fire was doused for only the second time since she had returned to Browhead, its acrid smoke billowing up the howling chimney.

41

It was the water flooding into his mouth which brought him to his senses, choking him to consciousness, coughing and spluttering, though at first he was so confused he had no idea how he had got where he was, or even who he was.

He sat up, held fast in a violent bout of shivering, the pain at once beginning to bang agonisingly inside his skull. Dear God in Heaven, where? . . . what? . . . he was soaked through, his clothing plastered to his body like wet cement and just as heavy, but he could not seem to be able to collect his wits sufficiently to tell him how he had got into such a state. He could hear nothing but the thunder of water and the howling of the demonic wind accompanied by an occasional thud which he could not recognise though it sounded dangerous. What in hell's name? . . . where was he going? . . . how? Jesus Christ, but his head hurt, and it was as he put his hands to it, unable to bear the pain of it a moment longer that a dead sheep came to rest against his back, almost thrusting him from the flooded road and into the lake where . . . yes . . . *where his horse had gone!* He remembered that . . . his horse galloping away into that impenetrable curtain of hailstones . . . He had been on his way to Browhead . . . to Annie, when the ice particles had sliced at him and the roan he had purchased in Keswick, but how had he come to be hurt? There was blood coursing down his face, mixing with the pelting rain. He could taste the saltiness of it in his mouth, but he really could no longer sit in the rising water, pondering on how he had come to be here when he needed – with all his heart he needed – to get to Annie. She would need *him*. She would be alone now that chap had married her maidservant and presumably taken her off to a life of their own, and Annie would be in need of him. He knew that with a certainty which had first come to him in New York and had grown with every mile he had travelled to get to her. At last, *at last*, Annie Abbott needed Reed Macauley.

He rose unsteadily to his feet and the dead animal behind him thudded into the backs of his legs almost knocking him over again. It *was* a dead sheep as he had thought but the force of its journey down the rocky fell had shorn it of its fleece as neatly and cleanly as if it had just come from a 'boon' clipping. He watched it in absolute horror as it hurtled away from him towards the turmoil of the lake. He knew the terrifying elements of the Lakeland weather, but he could scarcely believe the forces which had been capable of such a thing. What power had been called up that was so fierce it could strip a fleece from a sheep and what damage was it causing up on the mountains, and more importantly, between here and Browhead? He must get on. He had almost five miles of road to cover and already he was up to his ankles in a rushing, foaming torrent of water. His head was bursting in a pain which almost blinded him, and the rain continued to drown him in its vicious clutch. The wind whipped about him, lashing the downpour into a frenzy and as he straightened himself, turning his sightless gaze towards the head of Bassenthwaite Lake the trees in Dodd Wood, their tops whipping and soughing like demented souls in hell, began to move towards the lake.

"Jesus God!" he moaned. "Oh, Jesus . . ." for before his horrified eyes a whole line of them, enormous oaks which had stood for hundreds of years, slid slowly from their birthplace and on to the road, the earth in which they had stood torn cleanly away by the force of the water which carried them. They remained upright for a moment then slowly, painfully, lifted by the boiling, brown fury which had convulsed down the mountain, they toppled over.

It was terrifying, unbelievable. They were a fortress,

those trees, unassailable, invincible, and though he had seen it happen with his own eyes, Reed could not believe it. He had ridden past their enormous trunks, in the shadow of their grandeur, beneath the magnificence of their summer foliage since he was a boy on his first pony, taking them for granted, not really seeing them, or their beauty and now they were gone, humbled by a strength greater than their own, torn from their roots as though they were no more than young saplings. He felt he wanted to weep for their destruction and yet he had no time for it. He must get by them, or over them or through the jagged root system which barred his way, standing twenty feet or more in the air, tangled and clogged with earth, for beyond them was his love and there was nothing more sure in this terrifyingly unsure world than the certainty that she needed him.

Annie stood at the top of the stairs looking down them to where the pale gleam of the rushlight she held aloft showed the flood water. It gave the appearance of lying still but in reality it was creeping inch by slow inch towards her. It had reached half-way up the stairwell, black and silky and in it floated minute particles of debris which had been forced under the door by its strength. There were other things, familiar things, pots and pans and cups, the stool on which she had rested her feet to the fire several hours ago. The box in which she kept her rushlights, the rushlight holder, the one Phoebe had used, and the snuffer. They turned idly in the water where the light reached, bumping against the stairs and each other as though trying to be the first to get up to her. Which they would soon if the water continued to rise.

She had no idea of the time, nor even of how long she had been up here but she knew if the water came any higher, reaching the upper floor she would have to get out. As soon as it was as high as the top of the bedroom windows her escape route through them would be cut off. She would be trapped. She would drown and so would the animals.

She moved back into her bedroom and closed the door behind her, an instinctive action which came from her need to shut it out, to bar its entrance, that which lay behind her, though her commonsense told her there was no shutting it out. The menace was behind her, beneath her, all around her. And if she got out, when she got out, what would she do? Where would she go? The wind howled viciously beyond the window and there were constant thuds at the back of the farmhouse as, she supposed, debris was brought down from Middle Fell, from Ullock Pike, Great Calva and Skiddaw on the seething discharge of floodwater. If only she could see out into the vortex of madness which she could only imagine and which was crashing and thudding about the building, but apart from the window-sill which was revealed when she placed the rushlight up to the glass, it was as black and dense as it had been for the . . . for the? . . . how long? . . . what time of day was it? . . . or night? . . . She really couldn't seem to assemble any sensible thought into her brain for it had lost its bearings in this strange and displaced world into which the storm had thrust her. She must think . . . *think* . . . decide . . . make a plan, some action which, if it came to it, would get herself and her animals to a place of safety, if such a thing existed in this mad confusion, this violence and destruction which was threatening her. If only she had someone to talk to, to discuss the predicament she was in. Someone to whom she could say, 'what d'you think? Shall we hang on and hope the water goes down, that the deluge stops and the tempest ceases to rage, or shall we get out now, climb up on to the roof, perhaps . . . ?' She had no one, only her dogs who were whimpering at her feet, and Dandy, the straining unease showing plainly in three pairs of eyes as they looked up at her.

She sat down on the bed, the dogs huddling against her legs, the cat at once crawling into her lap. She was cold, so cold she could feel the violence of her shivering shake the bed. It was January, the coldest month of the year up here on the fells. She had no heat, only the blankets on her bed and the clothing she wore, to warm her. She was tempted to get into the bed but if she should fall asleep what would she find when she awoke? Her bed floating on the water, her nose to the ceiling . . . ?

A short, nervous laugh erupted from her. God, this was no time to be laughing, she thought, but it had the effect of steadying her. She must eat something. The tatie-pot was cold now but if she was to . . . Oh, Lord Jesus, but the thought terrified her . . . if she was to climb out of the window into the unknown terror beyond it, then she must be strong, fortified at least by a nourishing meal for the struggle ahead of her.

She stood up, moving again to the window and suddenly, as though a giant match had put a light to a rush, the moon appeared from behind a scudding cloud, shining against a backdrop of deep and silvery blue across which tattered and wind-tossed clouds raced, ragged, uneasy and dark. The light of the moon, intermittent as the clouds whipped by it, revealed the full horror of the flood and even as Annie stared at it, appalled, there was an angry roar as an avalanche of rocks, tons and tons of them leaping and tossing as though they were no heavier than a handful of pebbles flung by a child, hurtled by the end of the farm-house and in their path was the barn.

"NO! . . . Oh, dear Lord! . . . No! . . . Royal . . ." She strained against the window, screaming out the name of the good-natured, loyal animal who had been her friend for almost three years as though in warning but even as she did so her practical mind told her that Royal was, in all probability, already dead. The waters of the flood had reached the upper level of the barn just where its sloping roof began and above which she stored her hay. Below it, and below the water line Royal had been stabled. She could imagine his terror as the water crept up his legs, up the sides of his rough flank until it reached . . . He would have kicked and kicked, doing his best to free himself . . . she could not bear it . . . the thought of his desperate, lonely struggle to escape.

Tears rolled down her cheeks and her shoulders heaved

as she wept and she turned away from the window, trying
to shut out the images which flashed across her vision.
Her eyes caught the movement by the door and her heart
bucked in terror as the slick black waters, silent and
menacing as a snake, rippled across the floor towards her.
It was here . . . Reed . . . it was here . . .

The moon came out as Reed reached High Side, just where
the road branched off to Hause. He had struggled through
the fast flowing floodwater, at first to his ankles, then,
as the level of the lake rose on his left, to his knees, the
wind threatening to tear his clothes from his body, the very
hair from his head, the rain pouring across his ice-cold flesh
with the force and persistence of the ice-cold overflow of
the waterfall where he had made love to Annie. The deluge
coming at him from the fell to his right, bringing down
dead cows, sheep, horses, chickens, pigs, gates, rocks,
whole trees, spinning wheels, sledges and smashed carts,
must be constantly watched for if anything heavy caught
him he could be carried on down across the low-lying fertile
pastures and into the lake. The dark had a hidden menace
in it, though it was possible to see the raging shapes of
the trees of Dodd Wood and the meandering flatness of
the water-logged road ahead. He kept his head bent and
his shoulders bowed, his eyes searching for his way, his
weary legs moving slowly – too slowly – through the surging water. It deepened steadily, moving up to his thighs
so that his progress became even more sluggish. He would
have to swim soon if the flood continued to rise, he
thought, almost idly, as if the idea of not getting there at
all had not even crossed his mind. Annie was waiting for
him. She was in a danger so menacing it could scarcely be
contemplated and he must reach her. It was as simple as
that. He could not even stop to rest, exhausted as he was,
for he had waded through four miles of raging floodwater.
She needed him. Annie needed him, and it was the certainty of that which kept him moving, dragging one heavy
leg after the other through the thick, impenetrable water.
It was like trying to walk through syrup, but no matter,

syrup it was, and if it needed wading through then wade
through it he would. He would not despair, *he would not*,
and as he lifted his head for a moment to get his bearings
the rain stopped and the moon raced out from behind a
cloud. Just like that. As though a barrier had been flung
across the sky, it stopped and he wanted to shout out his
relief. He had been disorientated but now he could see.
He had been lost but now he was found, and he was
exultant for it would be easier now. He tried to remember
when he had last slept, last eaten but he honestly could
not bring to mind when that might have been. On the ship,
perhaps? The Packet ship *Rainbow* which had brought him
from New York . . . when? . . . yesterday? . . . the day
before that? . . . Jesus . . . when?

God, but he was tired, and as the rebel thought whispered into his mind he glared about him, just as though
someone had spoken the words out loud. His blazing eyes
fell on rocks and tumbled trees, on more dead, skinned
sheep, on still bundles of clothing which he did not care
to investigate, and the flame in them was hot and hating
for *nothing* would keep him from her this time. He thought
he could be losing his mind. Many would say so, to love
a woman as he loved Annie Abbott, and perhaps he was,
but whatever it was she had lit in him over six years ago
it would not let him rest, would keep him on his feet until
she was here, held safe in his arms where she belonged,
damn her.

"Give up?" he snarled into the teeth of the biting wind,
as if some ghostly voice had suggested it. "Give up?
Never!" and his voice was whipped back over his shoulder
as he began to crawl on all fours up the slope from the
road and on to the walled inlands which led to Browhead
Farm.

"We'll have to go, lads. It's no use, but we'll have to go
before it's too late." Her own voice startled her, it seemed
so loud, and all three animals looked up at her, the dogs'
heads cocked, their ears pricked. Three pairs of eyes were
bright with intelligence, but all three animals cast uneasy

glances at the water which was creeping across the floor towards them. Annie bent to them, fondling their ears in turn, her heart heavy with sadness. She had lost Royal tonight, she was sure of that, and was she to lose these three as well? She could not leave them here. She could only coax them, or fling them out of the window and into the water, praying to some God, or gods in which she found she could really not believe, that they would make their way to safety. She herself meant to climb up on to the roof and tie herself to one of the chimney stacks, she had the sheet torn up in readiness, and perhaps they would come with her if their fear did not panic them into swimming off into the storm water.

She was just agonising over the advisability of wearing her warmest clothing, or virtually none at all, since she would get cold and wet anyway, and perhaps clothing would drag her down, when something struck the farmhouse such a colossal blow she distinctly heard the stonework shatter and the building move. Both dogs began to bark frantically. They milled about her in terror and Dandy leaped up the curtain to crouch on the window pole, her tail lashing, and Annie felt a distinct urge to do the same. Her mind was an ice-cold, blank and senseless thing, incapable of making a decision, and she turned frantically, first to the door, then back to the window. The farmhouse was breaking up, shifting, sliding down the fields to the lake where it would come to rest in the deep waters and her with it. She had no time . . . she must *hurry*. . . the window . . . oh, please . . . someone . . . Reed . . . "Reed . . . Reed . . ." She was screaming out loud, her own voice striking at the strangely tilting walls of her bedroom . . . but she needed him . . . *she wanted him*. . . Reed . . .

She could not remember making any conscious decision but somehow she was at the deep, recessed window, dragging at the tiny half-opening, pushing it out into the teeth of the wind which still howled across the front of the farmhouse. It whipped right into her face, the spray it carried lashing against her and wetting her through before she had even climbed out on to the ledge. The floodwater was about six inches below the sill and she knew she had but minutes to spare. She could feel it behind her creeping up over her feet and clawing at her ankles and the two dogs moaned in terror, but, sensing with the natural instinct of her kind that escape was to be found only now, only here, Dandy went first, twisting her boneless body through and *up*, clawing her way on to the roof.

"Good girl . . . oh, good girl . . . now Blackie, come on, boy . . . Bonnie . . . come here to me . . ." She shrieked their names, hardly able to hear her own voice above the roar of the wind and the water it churned, but they did not move.

"Come to me, Blackie . . . come on, Bonnie . . . good boys . . . come here, come here . . ." but neither would obey her.

"I can't leave you . . . I just can't leave you . . . please . . ." She began to weep . . . "come here . . . come . . ."

Inspiration came as the water reached her knees. Both animals had leaped on to the bed, their eyes mad with fear. She knew she *must* go, *now*, for the water was nearly up to the sill. A minute, no more and it would pour into the bedroom, not only through the door, but the window, a great surge through which she would be unable to struggle.

"Come by, Blackie . . . Away to me, Bonnie." Her voice was steady and firm and at the familiar words both dogs instinctively moved, one to the right, the other to the left, swimming towards her round the walls of the room until they reached the window.

"Good boys, out you go," and without hesitation, trusting her, they jumped cleanly into the racing torrent beyond it.

"Wait for me, lads," she called. She took a deep breath and followed them, at once sinking down into the black, clogged depths of the water.

*   *   *

He sobbed in agony as he hung on to the gatepost from which the gate had long gone. He could see the farmhouse. It was there no more than a hundred yards away, a light flickering in one of the bedroom windows, but no matter how hard he fought he just could not get beyond this point. Three times he had crawled on his hands and knees through the boiling, mud-filled fury of the waters which howled down the fell and across the inlands, clutching at any handhold which would bear his weight, and three times he had been swept down again to the road. His clothing, but for his undergarments, had been torn from his body and he knew his flesh was bleeding from many places. His skin was scraped raw and he felt as though his hair had been wrenched from his scalp. Three times he had done it, that tiny light which he knew Annie had lit beckoning him on, and each time he had been flung down the slope again, his limbs dragged about like that of a rag doll, his head crashing and banging against shattered drystone walls, and the thousands of tons of stone which had been gouged out of the mountain by the force of the water.

He did not know how he survived it, for surely the body cannot take the punishment his was suffering, but each time he had crept to his knees and through his bitten tongue and lips, howled her name to the broken skies. All along the valley and in every farmhouse on the fells, his own included, men and women would be fighting for their lives as the deluge tore down walls, carved out new ravines, destroyed bridges, spewed out landslides which would bury farms and outbuildings for ever. Huge sections of the fellside would be laid bare as every beck and tarn, stream and river overflowed in a wild and headlong turmoil of water. He had seen bodies go by him, swept down to the lake which was at a level never before known, drowning trees at its edges which had once been tall and proud. He had seen it, suffered it, drowned in it almost, but still he would not let it stop him. Not until he was dead. Not until the last flicker of life in him, that last flame of his love for Annie was quenched, and even then his spirit would wing its way up this bloody hill to strengthen her.

He could feel the gatepost lean towards him, the strong deep roots of it which some farmer had secured for eternity, beginning to tear from the ground and he looked wildly about him for something, some anchor to which he might cling, and from there to another, and another, fighting his way until he got up to her. Dear sweet Christ . . . let me . . . please . . . she is so near, so near . . . the farmhouse, the tree beside it . . . both there, strong and safe and her within it . . . the light . . . the light . . . oh, Jesus . . . *the light. . . the light had gone*. . . No! . . . No! It couldn't be . . . not Annie . . . not his Annie . . . his love . . . perhaps she had blown it out . . . but why? . . . perhaps . . . ?

"ANNIE . . ." he roared, furious with her, ready, the moment he had her standing beside him where she belonged to let her see that he would not, absolutely *would not* be treated with this bare-faced defiance . . . why? . . . *why* would she not do as he wanted her to . . . *why*? Savage he was in his anger . . . at *her*, at Annie who had left him . . . Annie, dear God, Annie, why has the light gone out . . . why? . . . Had she climbed into her bed and carelessly snuffed the rushlight whilst he was killing himself? struggling to get up to her . . . Jesus, oh Jesus, let her be peacefully asleep in her bed . . . *why had the bloody light gone out*? He could not bear the not knowing, nor the images that darkened glow had conjured up. The possibility that . . . he could not face it . . . Annie, fighting the water . . . the creeping water . . . her lovely face contorted . . . gasping . . . drowning . . .

"ANNIE . . . ANNIE . . ." he roared again, throwing back his head in torment, feeling the gatepost drive its thick splinters deep into the palms of his clinging hands. The grief and agony in his voice seemed to stifle even the hateful roar of the waters for a moment, echoing about the devastated fells. "Annie . . ." His voice sank to a whisper and he bent his head, ducking it under the water since he no longer wanted to live . . . not without . . .

"Reed . . ." He did not hear his name on the wind.

For ten seconds he held his head beneath the raging

torrent but the instinct bred in all living creatures, to survive, no matter how the will denies it, brought him threshing to the surface, choking, demented, cursing. Well, if he could not do away with himself here where she had died, then all he had to do was let go of the bloody gatepost and let the floodwaters take him . . .

"Reed . . ."

He thought for a bewildering moment that he had actually been successful. That he had drowned and so had she, waiting for him on the other side so that they could go together to wherever it was . . .

"Reed . . ." and that was no heavenly voice calling to him to hold her hand as they met St Peter at the bloody pearly gates. It was her . . . *her*. . . *Annie* and she was coming full tilt towards him, her mouth wide and screaming, borne on a wave of scum coated water, clinging to what looked like an oak chest, its lid still tightly closed – they knew how to make a decent chest in the old days, he remembered thinking, marvelling on the ways of the human mind and its capacity to be distracted by trivia at times of great danger – then he had her in his arms, the well-built chest beneath them both, going as though it was a sledge on runners, down the long slope towards the road at the bottom.

"Hold on to me," he yelled, ready to laugh with the sheer magical joy of it, not caring really if they were both smashed to pieces or drowned in Bassenthwaite Lake since they were together, *together*. She was in his arms, clinging to him, needing him, *needing* his strength, which was suddenly prodigious, to save them both. God knew where they would end up, but by the look of it it might be in the little churchyard of St Bridget's, which was appropriate if you thought about it. If they drowned it would be side by side, and side by side they would be buried there, and if not he would take her into the church, no matter what its flooded state and extract from her her promise, give her his, force the damned words from her somehow until their wedding vows could be exchanged properly and in full view of the community of Bassenthwaite. She was here in his arms, still, both of them, in the direst of danger, but by God, she'd never get away from him again.

They came to rest by the church porch. The water still poured into the lake a hundred yards or so further on but it was slackening as the fury of the elements died away. There was debris lying all about them right down to the water, grotesque shapes only half-seen in the lightening gloom of the new day. Timber beams and walls of stone, old joists and chicken coops, stiff-legged bodies of animals wedged against one another, trees and a solid mass of mud in which a cradle was jammed testifying to the tragedies which had taken place this night.

They stood up slowly, stiffly, neither of them recognisable except to each other. They were both almost naked but for a shred or two of clothing which had not been ripped from them in the maelstrom of their flight down the fell and they shivered violently.

Annie looked steadily into Reed's eyes, penetrating with her own the goodness of the love she saw there. They had known passion, a fierce enchantment which had been indescribable, and would again, but this was stronger, sweeter, *good*. He watched her, waiting, but not for long, his expression said. He had waited too long as it was. Seven years and in that time she had achieved all that she had set out to achieve. Seven years and in a few nightmare hours it had all been lost again. Browhead. Did it still stand? Her flock. How many survived? Her farm, her pride, her satisfaction in what she had carved out for herself in this hostile land, among these hostile people. It was all gone and amazingly, did it matter? Her life was here, with this man. Reed Macauley.

He held out his hand to her and she took it submissively. He smiled, knowing it would not last, her submissiveness, his teeth a white slash in his heavily bruised face. He led her into the church and up the aisle, moving through ankle deep water in which prayer books and footstools floated, until they reached the altar steps.

"Kneel," he commanded her and when she did, knowing what was to come, he knelt beside her. They made a strange sight, Annie Abbott and Reed Macauley and yet the beauty in them, in their eyes and softly smiling faces was very real.

"Now say after me," he began.

They were hand in hand, looking, Phoebe screeched at them, like two lovers wandering in the sunshine beside a summer lake. Had they no thought for anyone but themselves, for God's sake? Her voice became even more frenzied as she scrambled over tumbling rocks and great fallen trees, ready to knock their two silly heads together in her wild fear. She and Charlie had thought Annie had drowned and really, she might have come up and told them she was still alive. She had the baby under one arm, bouncing her about like a half-filled flour sack which Beth submitted to amiably enough, and behind her was Charlie, his strained face breaking out at the sight of them into that wide, endearing grin they knew so well. Neither seemed surprised to see Reed and why should they, for did not the most amazing things occur in Annie Abbott's turbulent life?

Yes, yes, Upfell had been saved by some fluke which had sent the main torrent racing to Chapel Beck and not in the direction of their farm. Of course it was flooded and there was some damage . . . Long Beck? They didn't know but as it was higher up the valley perhaps, but for God's sake, did it matter? Jesus Christ, did it matter? They were alive. They were all alive and unhurt . . . when they had seen Browhead, not that there was much left of it. Dear God in Heaven, did Annie know? They had thought. . . .

Here Phoebe began to cry inconsolably, a great precipitation as immense as the one they had just survived, burying her face in the soft neck of the startled baby.

"Phoebe . . . Phoebe, darling. . . ."

"Give over, Annie Abbott, don't tha' say 'owt or I'll land thi' one. I were right worried. . . ." she wailed, her normal guarded reserve breaking down in the face of her vast relief.

Wordlessly Annie put her arms about her friend, the

only one she had had before Charlie came, and they stood clasped together, the baby between them, watched by Charlie and Reed, themselves inclined to blink rapidly and clear their throats a time or two.

They wept in one another's arms, Phoebe and Annie, in sorrow for what had gone and would never be replaced, for Cat and Natty and perhaps Browhead; in thankfulness for what was left and in sudden joy when two bedraggled forms crept hesitantly over the gouged out enormity of what had once been an ancient oak tree. They hesitated for a moment, Blackie and Bonnie, then raced ecstatically across the sodden ground towards the two women.

"Now then, don't tha' go puttin' tha' great muddy paws on my skirt," Phoebe remonstrated tartly to the two animals, "oh, an' that cat's sittin' skrikin' on top o't'wall back at Browhead. 'Appen tha'd best go an' see to it, Annie Abbott."

AUDREY HOWARD

ALL THE DEAR FACES

Edwardian Liverpool – the greatest port in the Empire, a sprawling, brawling city of poverty and wealth, slum tenements and civic pride, vice and hard-won respectability.

Mara O'Shaughnessy, eighth of thirteen children, longs to escape from the crowded tumult of her family, while her sister Caitlin, quiet but determined, is already, to her mother's horror, involved with the Suffragettes.

Woodall Park, 2,000 acre estate home of Elizabeth and her parents, Sir Charles and Lady Woodall, could have been a million miles away. With their neighbours, the Osbornes of Beechwood Hall, life is lived in servanted ease, country pursuits and suitable marriages.

Yet in the golden years before World War I, Liverpool Irish and English gentry are to become fatefully, passionately entangled . . .

HODDER AND STOUGHTON PAPERBACKS

AUDREY HOWARD

A DAY WILL COME

When Miles Thornley rides into her life, everything begins to change for Daisy Brindle. For the first time she catches a glimpse of a very different life to the one she has always known.

Daisy is a field girl, tramping the roads of Lancashire in a gang of women and children, hired out by a brutal master for stone picking, harvesting, winter work down the pits.

But Miles, heir to a great estate, arrogant and spoilt, who teaches her to love, seduces her and casually casts her aside. He teaches her to hate.

Driven onto the streets of Liverpool, Daisy is rescued by a man of honesty and restless energy, sea captain Sam Lassiter.

First as his mistress and then as his wife and business partner, Daisy comes to enjoy the better things in life. But her unrelenting drive for revenge on the dissolute Miles begins to threaten the destruction of everything she has worked for and achieved. Begins finally to threaten her relationship with Sam Lassiter himself . . .

HODDER AND STOUGHTON PAPERBACKS

AUDREY HOWARD

SHINING THREADS

The sequel to *The Mallow Years*

When beautiful Tessa Harrison and her twin cousins take over the lucrative Lancashire mill from their parents, they are plunged into responsibilities for which their luxurious upbringing has ill-prepared them.

For Tessa, there is an added but forbidden attraction at the mill. The foreman, Will Broadbent, with his genuine understanding of the business and its workers could not be more different from the dashing cousins. Yet, like the twins, he is hopelessly in love with this untameable girl. Their love for Tessa will lead one to death, one to the arms of another woman, a third too faint-hearted to take up his rightful inheritance.

And Tessa, the girl who could choose any man she wanted, is forced into more commitments than she could have imagined, before she can be united with the one man she truly needs.

HODDER AND STOUGHTON PAPERBACKS

AUDREY HOWARD

ECHO OF ANOTHER TIME

Celie Marlow first begins working in the Latimers' kitchen when she is only ten, learning her art from kindly Mrs Harper. By the age of eighteen, she has become a talented cook.

Celie knows her place, and longs only to run a kitchen as skilfully as her mentor. Until she falls in love with the wrong man: Richard Latimer, eldest son of the house. And all their lives change with frightening swiftness.

Driven from her home, Celie finds unexpected success in a new venture with Mrs Harper – then loses everything once more. Thrown on to the streets of Liverpool, penniless and desperate, she will have to find her own way.

HODDER AND STOUGHTON PAPERBACKS